BEYOND

THE

PALE

BEYOND
THE
PALE

BOOK ONE OF
THE LAST RUNE

MARK ANTHONY

EARTHLIGHT

LONDON · SYDNEY · NEW YORK · TOKYO · SINGAPORE · TORONTO

First published in Great Britain by Earthlight, 1998
An imprint of Simon & Schuster UK Ltd
A Viacom Company

Simon & Schuster UK Ltd
Africa House
64-78 Kingsway
London
WC2B 6AH

Simon & Schuster Australia
Sydney

A CIP catalogue record for this book is available from the British Library.

ISBN 0-684-85167-9

1 3 5 7 9 10 8 6 4 2

Printed and bound in Great Britain by The Bath Press, Bath, Somerset

For Carla Montgomery—
who has the Touch.

For Christopher Brown
a true Knight Protector.

And for Sean A. Moore—
who understood the magic
of Circles.

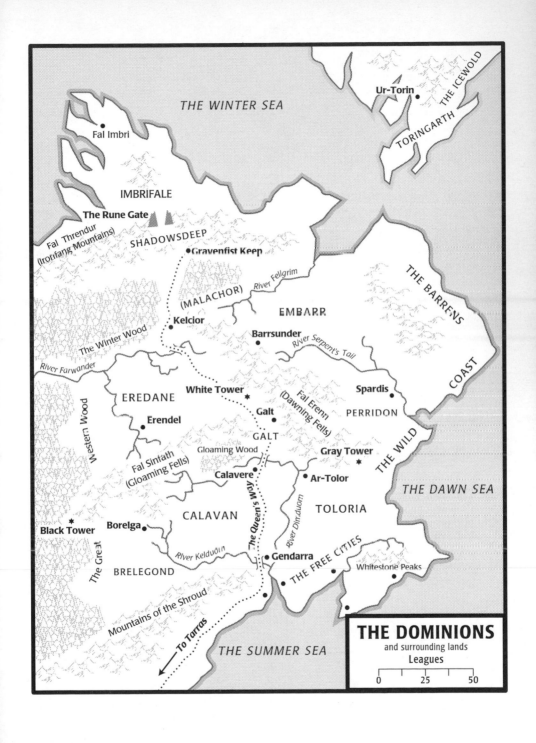

THE WINTER SEA

Ur-Torin

THE ICEWOLD

TORINGARTH

Fal Imbri

IMBRIFALE

The Rune Gate

Fal Threndur
(Ironfang Mountains)

SHADOWSDEEP

Gravenfist Keep

THE BARRENS

(MALACHOR)

River Fellgrim

EMBARR

Kelcior

The Winter Wood

Barrsunder

River Serpent's Tail

River Furwander

White Tower

Spardis

COAST

EREDANE

Galt

Fal Erenn
(Dawning Fells)

PERRIDON

Western Wood

Erendel

GALT

THE WILD

Gloaming Wood

Gray Tower

THE DAWN SEA

Fal Sinfath
(Gloaming Fells)

Calavere

Ar-Tolor

TOLORIA

The Queen's Way

River Dimduorn

Black Tower

Borelga

CALAVAN

The Great

BRELEGOND

River Kelduorn

Gendarra

THE FREE CITIES

Whitestone Peaks

Mountains of the Shroud

To Tarras

THE SUMMER SEA

THE DOMINIONS
and surrounding lands
Leagues

0   25   50

For a thousand years the Pale King lay mantled in dark, enchanted slumber, imprisoned in his desolate dominion of Imbrifale.

And then . . .

Two worlds draw near.

The spell is broken.

PROLOGUE

BROTHER CY'S APOCALYPTIC TRAVELING SALVATION SHOW

The derelict school bus blew into town with the last midnight gale of October.

Weary brakes whined in complaint as the vehicle pulled off a stretch of Colorado mountain two-lane and into an open field. Beneath a patina of highway grime that spoke of countless days and countless miles, the bus's slapdash jacket of white paint—a shade called Pearly Gates, just five-ninety-nine a gallon at the Ace Hardware in downtown Leavenworth, Kansas—glowed like bones in the phantasmal light of the setting horned moon. The bus's folding door squeaked open, and two painted-over stop signs flopped out from the vehicle's sides like stunted angel wings. One sign admonished *Repent Your Sins Now*, while the other advertised *Two for the Price of One*.

A figure stepped from the bus. Wind hissed through dry grass around his ankles and plucked with cold fingers at his black mortician's suit. He reached up a quick, long hand to keep his broad-brimmed pastor's hat planted on his head, then gazed into the darkness with dark eyes.

"Yes, this will do fine," he whispered in his steel-rasp and Southern-honey-pecan voice. "This will do just fine."

Then the man—who had been called many names in the past, but who these days went by the moniker of Brother Cy—leaned his scarecrow frame toward the bus, like a lodgepole pine bending before the storm, and called through the open door.

"We have arrived!"

A chorus of excited voices answered him. Someone flicked on the bus's high beams, and two cones of light cut through the night. The rear emergency door swung open, hinges creaking, and a dozen shadowy forms leaped out. They dragged a heavy bundle into the field and unrolled it with deft movements. More dim figures scurried from the back of the bus, wrangling poles and rope, and hurried to join the others. Brother Cy stalked to the center of the field and paced a wide circle, digging the heel of his worn black boot into the turf at measured intervals. When the circle was complete, he stood back and looked on in satisfaction. Here would stand his fortress.

Canvas snapped like a sail.

"Blast and damnation, watch that pole!" Brother Cy shouted as his workers strained to stand a length of wood as tall and thick as a tree on end. A billowing shape rose up before him, like an elephant lumbering to its feet. Brother Cy prowled around it: the hungry lion.

"Stake down that wall!" he roared. "Untangle those lines. Get a rope through that tackle. Now pull! Pull, or you'll think the Dark One's domain a sweet paradise compared to the hell I'll show you!" Brother Cy thrust his lanky arms above his head. *"Pull!"*

A score of dim forms strained. The mound heaved itself higher into the air, and higher yet, like a mountain being birthed. At last its pointed peak reached the top of the high pole. Ropes were lashed around wooden posts and tied off, stray edges of canvas were skewered to the ground, lengths of cord were tucked away. Where minutes before there had been empty moonlight there now stood a tent. It was an old-fashioned circus tent, what in days gone by had been called a big top, torn and patched in so many places it looked as if it had been sewn from the trousers of a hundred penniless clowns.

Brother Cy clapped his big hands together and laughed like thunder.

"Now, let the show begin!"

Like wraiths in the half-light, the shadowy roustabouts bustled in and out of the tent. Parti-colored banners were unfurled. Collapsible bleachers were pulled from the back of the bus. Fire sprang to life in dozens of punched-tin lanterns, carried inside in a glowing procession until the tent shone gold in the night. Last of all a sign was planted in the earth before the tent's entrance. It proclaimed in bold, Gothic letters:

BROTHER CY'S APOCALYPTIC TRAVELING SALVATION SHOW
Ailments Cured—Faith Restored—Souls Redeemed

And below that, scrawled in crude script like an afterthought:

Come on in—we want to save you!

Brother Cy stepped back, crossed his arms, and surveyed his domain.

"Does all go well?" a clear voice asked behind him.

He whirled around, and a cadaverous grin split his gaunt face.

"Indeed it does, Sister Mirrim." He reached out to help a woman down the steps of the bus. "Do you see? Our citadel stands once more."

Sister Mirrim gazed at the tent. Her visage was smooth, even beautiful, but her old-fashioned garb was severe. She wore a tight-bodiced dress of funereal black, as well as high-buttoned shoes, the kind that could still be found to this day in the downtown five-and-dime of any number of dusty Oklahoma towns—the kind that bespoke the unforgiving hardness of another century. Yet, even in the pale light of the crescent moon, Sister Mirrim's long hair shone flame red and flew about her on the wind.

A child followed Sister Mirrim down the steps, a small girl clad in a black dress that was the older woman's in perfect miniature. Her hair, however, was the color of the night, and she regarded Brother Cy with wise purple eyes. He lifted her into his arms. She coiled a small, cool hand around his neck and pressed her soft rosebud mouth against his cheek.

"I love you, too, Child Samanda," Brother Cy said in bemusement.

"But of course you do," she murmured.

He set her down, and hand in hand the trio approached the tent. The wind whistled through the ropes and lines, conjuring a sorrowful hymn.

"Will they come, Brother Cy?" Sister Mirrim asked, her voice like the call of a dove. "I have been looking, but I cannot see them yet."

He looked past the tent, down into the valley below, to a haphazard collection of sparks that twinkled in the high-country night. Castle City. There they huddled in the warm light of their little houses, unknowing of the darkness that approached. But it was so distant, this darkness, so strange, and so terribly far away. How could they know? How could they realize that their very souls hung in the balance? Yet somehow they must. That was why the three had journeyed here.

"They have to come," Brother Cy said at last. "There are so many who have a part to play."

Sister Mirrim shook her head, her question unanswered. "But *will* they?"

It was Child Samanda who spoke this time.

"Oh, yes," she whispered. "They will come." She slipped her tiny doll hands from the larger grips that enclosed them and took a step nearer the lights below. "But there are two whose tasks will be far harder than those of the others. We cannot know if they will have the strength to bear their burdens."

Brother Cy gave a solemn nod. "Then we can pray, my little bird."

A chill gust rushed down from the high peaks, and the three looked up to see the tent shake under the blast. Shadows played crazily across the canvas walls, cast from within by lanterns dancing on their wires, as the roustabouts scrambled to brace the tent against the gale. Some of the silhouettes were squat as stumps, while others were oddly tall, with fingers as slender as twigs. Some of them bore what seemed antlers, branching like young saplings from their heads, while others looked as if they walked on crooked legs, tails swishing in agitation behind them. However, rippling canvas could be a twister of shadows, and a player of tricks. The wind blew itself into nothing, the tent grew still, the shadows slipped away from the walls.

"Come, let us go inside," Brother Cy murmured.

"To wait for them?" Sister Mirrim asked.

Child Samanda nodded in conviction. "Yes, to wait."

Hand in hand once more, they turned their backs on the night, stepped into the tent, and left the small mountain town to sleep alone in the night below.

PART ONE

A
COMING
DARKNESS

1.

Sometimes the wind blowing down from the mountains made Travis Wilder feel like anything could happen.

He could always hear it coming, long before the first telltale wisps of snow-clean air touched his face. It would begin as a distant roar far up the canyon, nearly and yet not at all like the ancient voice of a stormswept ocean. Before long he could see it, rushing in wave after wave through the forest that mantled the granite-boned ranges that encircled the valley. Lodgepole pines swayed in graceful rhythm, while cloudlike aspen shivered green, then silver, then green again. Moments later, in abandoned fields just outside of town, he could hear the witchgrass rattle a final portent as it whirled around in wild pagan circles.

Then the wind would strike.

It would race down Elk Street—Castle City's broad main avenue—like an invisible ghost-herd of Indian ponies. Past McKay's General Store. Past the Mosquito Café. Past the abandoned assay office, the Mine Shaft Saloon, the Blue Summit Earth Shop, and the faded Victorian opera house. Dogs would bark and snap at passing newspaper tumbleweeds. Strolling tourists would turn their backs and shut their eyes to dust devils that glittered with gum wrappers and cigarette-pack cellophane. Dude-ranch cowboys would hold on to black hats with turquoise-ringed hands while their dusters flew out behind them like rawhide wings.

Maybe he was the only one in town crazy enough, but Travis loved the wind. He always had. He would step outside the buckshot-speckled door of the Mine Shaft Saloon, which he had the dubious distinction of owning these days, and lean over the boardwalk rail to face the gale full-on. There was no way to know from where the wind had journeyed, he reasoned, or just what it might blow his way. He would breathe the quickening air, sharp with the scents of cold mountain stone and sun-warmed pine, and wonder whose lungs it had filled last—where they lived, what language they spoke, what gods they courted, if they courted any at all, and what dreams they dared dream behind eyes of a hundred different shapes and hues.

It was a feeling that had first struck him the day he stepped off a mud-spattered bus—a flatland kid raised between the straight and hazy horizons of Illinois—and drank in his virgin sight of Castle City. In the seven years since, the sensation had come to him with surprising and comforting regularity, never lessening in potency with time. Facing into the wind always left him with an ache of wordless longing in his chest, and a feeling that he didn't have to choose between anything, because everything was possible.

Still, despite his many musings, there was no way Travis could have imagined, on a chill evening caught in the gray time between the gold-and-azure days of fall and the frozen purple of winter night, just exactly what the wind would blow into Castle City, and into his life. Later, looking back with the empty clarity of hindsight, he would sift through all the strange and unexpected events to pinpoint the precise moment when things began to change. It had been a small happening, so small that he might not have remembered it had it not been for the fact that afterward things would never—could never—be the same again.

It was when he heard bells.

2.

Afternoon sunlight fell as heavy as gold into the mountain valley as Travis Wilder piloted his battered pickup truck toward town. Faint music crackled on the AM radio in time to the squawking dashboard. A paper air freshener shaped like a pine tree bobbed on a string beneath the rearview mirror, all the fake pine smell long since baked out of it by years of the high-altitude sun. The engine growled as he down-shifted and swung around a curve at precisely twice the speed recommended by a nearby road sign: a yellow diamond so full of shotgun holes it looked like a chunk of Swiss cheese.

"You're late, Travis," he said to himself.

He had spent most of the afternoon on the roof of the ramshackle hunting lodge he called home, nailing on tar paper and replacing shingles torn off by last night's windstorm. It was past time to be getting ready for the snow that the fat, red-furred marmots foreshadowed. When he finally thought to look up, the sun had been sinking toward the wall of mountains that ringed the valley. Travis never had been good with time. But then, he never had been good with a lot of things. That was why he had come here, to Castle City.

The regulars would start straggling into the Mine Shaft Saloon by sundown, and there were usually a few hapless tourists who had taken a wrong turn off the highway and had ended up in Castle City by accident. Legions of them cruised the twisting two-lanes this time of year, to ogle the gold splendor of the mountain autumn from the heated comfort of their rental cars. To make matters worse, Moira Larson's book club was meeting in the back room of the saloon that evening. The topic: Nineteenth-Century French Novels of Adultery. Travis shuddered at the thought of facing a dozen book lovers thwarted in their hell-bent desire to discuss implications of class structure in Flaubert's *Madame Bovary*.

A nervous whistle escaped his lips. "You are really, *really* late."

Of course, Max would be at the saloon.

Max Bayfield was Travis's one and only employee. Max was supposed to be working the day shift today, although more likely he was poring over the saloon's books, trying to find money between the lines. Travis supposed that was what he got for hiring a refugee accountant from New York, but at least there would be someone there to pour a drink if a customer asked. Then again, it wasn't really a great idea to let Max wrangle the bar on his own during busy hours. Travis could only hope Max wasn't hovering around the jukebox again, telling customers that while listening to classical music temporarily raised one's IQ, country-western songs—with their simplistic melodic structure and repetitive rhythmic schemes—did just the opposite.

His sense of urgency redoubled, Travis punched the accelerator, and the truck flew out of the curve like a rock out of a slingshot.

He was about a mile from town when a dilapidated shape flashed past the truck's cracked windshield. Hulking beside the road were the remains of a house. Although he had passed it countless times, like always, Travis found his gaze drawn toward the ruin. The old place had burned years ago, long before he had come to Castle City, yet somehow he knew that even before it caught fire, this had been an ugly building. It was squat and sprawling, with rows of small windows that stared like hateful eyes at the beauty of the mountains. Now the structure was nothing more than a shell, the husk of some gigantic beetle that had died next to the road.

According to the stories Travis had heard, the house had been an orphanage once. Built during the days of the Great Depression, the Beckett-Strange Home for Children had endured for decades as one of the largest orphanages in central Colorado, but about twenty years ago the place had burned. By then orphanages were well out of fashion, and the Home was never rebuilt. Travis couldn't say he was sorry. There was something . . . *wrong* about the ruin. He wasn't sure what it was, but often when he passed it he found himself thinking dark thoughts. Thoughts about fear, or suffering, or mayhem. Maybe it was just that he knew people had died in that fire. Not any of the children—they had all escaped—but several of the Home's workers had been trapped in their rooms, and they had all been burned alive. At least, that was what the rumors told. Travis didn't know if the stories were true, but if there was ever a place for ghosts, it was the remains of the Beckett-Strange Home for Children.

The old orphanage slipped out of view, and Travis fixed his gaze on the road ahead. This was the time of day when deer were inexplicably compelled to leap out and fling their bodies in front of moving cars. He kept his eyes peeled. Except a moment later something caught his attention, and it wasn't a deer. He downshifted, his hurry forgotten. Gears rattling in protest, the pickup slowed to a crawl.

It was a billboard.

Tires ground on gravel, and the truck rolled to a halt on the shoulder of the road. Travis peered out the driver's side window. Like so many wooden artifacts in the high country, the billboard was bleached and splintering but curiously intact. The thing had to have seen a good sixty or seventy mountain winters in its existence, and even the most recent advertisement plastered across its face was long faded. However, he could still make out the ghostly shapes of people wearing clothes that had been fashionable two decades ago, laughing as they sucked smooth, delicious smoke out of white sticks propped between long fingers.

Hinges groaned, and the truck's heavy door swung open. Travis climbed out. Cold air sighed through clumps of dry weeds, and he was glad for his thick sheepskin coat. Beneath this he wore faded blue jeans and a tan work shirt. Travis was a tall man, just on the lean side of big, but he had an unconscious tendency to hunch his broad shoulders. At thirty-three years his face was boyish, and when he smiled, his crooked grin suggested a mischievousness that was not altogether misleading. His hair was the exact color of dull yellow sandstone, but his beard, which he sometimes let grow against the winter cold, or simply out of sheer laziness, had sparks of copper and gold in it.

Travis adjusted the wire-rimmed spectacles that perched in front of his pale eyes. Jack Graystone had given him the spectacles a few years back. Jack owned the Magician's Attic, an antique store on the west side of town, and he was one of Travis's oldest friends, maybe even his best. The spectacles were over a hundred years old, and once they had belonged to a young gunslinger named Tyler Caine. Jack always said the best way to understand the here and now was to gaze at it through the eyes of a distant time and place. Sometimes Travis thought Jack was the wisest man he knew.

Travis approached the billboard, his scuffed boots crunching against the hard ground. There—that was what had caught his eye. Last night's gale had ripped away a piece of the old cigarette ad. He drew in a cold lungful of air. Through the hole in the advertisement he could see what appeared to be a painting of a rugged landscape. Only it didn't quite look like a painting. It was too *real*, more like a photograph, breathtaking in its perfect clarity. He could just see the edge of a snow-covered peak, and beneath that the hint of an evergreen forest. Without even thinking, Travis reached a hand toward the billboard, to peel off more of the ad's colored paper.

That was when he heard them.

The bells were faint and distant, yet clear all the same, and crystalline. The sound made him think of sleigh bells on a winter's night. His hand fell to his side, and he cocked his head to listen. Now all he heard was the low moan of wind over granite. He shivered and remembered he needed to get to the saloon. Whatever the sound had been, it was gone now, if he had ever really heard it in the first place. He started back for the truck.

The wind shifted and brought with it, fleeting but clear, the chime of music.

Travis spun back around. Once more the bells faded into silence, but this time he could tell from which direction the sound had come. His gaze traveled across a sere expanse of grass until it reached a dark hulk a few hundred yards away. *You don't have time for this, Travis.* But he was already walking across the field, hands jammed into the pockets of his coat.

A minute later the orphanage loomed above him, taking a bite out of the blue-quartz sky. He had never been this close to the ruin before. Now the windows seemed more gaping mouths than staring eyes. Lichen clung to scorched clapboards like some sort of disease. Even after all these years a faint burnt smell emanated from the place, acrid and vaguely menacing. Travis held his breath: the eerie voice of the wind, and silence, that was all.

He pushed his way through a patch of dried thistles and walked around the side of the house. Behind the place was a pair of outbuildings. They were far enough away from the main house that the fire had not gotten them. Dull paint peeled from their walls, and their doors were sealed shut with rusted padlocks. Storage sheds of some sort. Between the buildings was a narrow run, almost like an alley. Had something moved there in the dimness?

He took a step into the space between the sheds, and in the murk he glimpsed a pile of scrap metal and an old rain barrel. That was all. He was about to turn away when he noticed a glint of light by his feet. He squatted down and saw tracks in the ground. Water had seeped from the earth to pool in the tracks and reflect the waning daylight. The prints had been made by small, cloven hooves, probably a mule deer. They wandered all over the valley. With a shrug, Travis stood and turned to head back to the truck.

This time the bells were closer. Much closer.

Travis whirled around. There. Something *had* moved—a dim form by the rain barrel.

"Who's there?" he called out. No answer. He took another step, deeper in. Shadows closed behind him, and a new sound drifted on the air, a sound almost like . . . laughter. It was high and trilling, the mirth of a child, or that of an ancient woman. The rain barrel rocked back and forth, then toppled. Water gushed onto the ground, dark as blood.

Travis's heart shriveled in his chest. He started to back out of the alley. The mocking laughter rang out again. He bit his lip to stifle a cry of fear, turned, tripped over his boots, and broke into a run.

He was brought up short by a tall, stiff object, and this time he did cry out. He stumbled backward and looked up.

"Can I help you with something, son?"

The man standing before Travis looked like he was eighty years too late for a funeral. His black suit of moth-eaten wool was archaic and oddly cut, with a long hem and a high collar. The suit hung loosely on the man's spare frame, while the shirt beneath had turned the yellow of old bones, its neck bound with a limp string tie that flapped on the air. The man snatched a hand up to keep his broad-brimmed hat from taking off on a gust of wind.

"I said, can I help you, son? I mean, are you in need of some aid? Forgive my saying, but you look as white as Lot after he slipped on out of Sodom."

The man's voice was dry, like the rasp of a snake's belly against sand, but coated with a sticky Southern sweetness. This was a voice to invoke dread and devotion in one fell swoop. A grin split the man's face. His teeth were the same dull yellow as his shirt, and his eyes glinted like black marbles.

"You aren't simple, now are you, son? You can talk, can't you?"

Travis managed a nod. "I'm fine, really. It was nothing, just an animal by the sheds."

Instinct told him to get out of here. The man gave Travis the creeps, him and his papery skin and that skeletal smile. He had to be some sort of vagrant, what with those thrift-store clothes. And there was something foreboding about him. Not violent, but perilous all the same.

Travis swallowed hard. "Listen, I need to get going. I have . . . I have something I need to do."

The man watched him with those black eyes, then gave a solemn nod.

"So you do, son. So you do."

Travis did not reply. He hurried past the other, kept his eyes fixed on the ground, and hoofed it as fast as he could across the field without looking like he was out and out running. To his great relief, he made it back to the truck. He climbed inside, then cast one last glance over his shoulder. The man in black had not moved. He still stood in front of the ruined orphanage and clutched his hat while waves of grass surged around him. He gazed at the horizon, like those dark marble eyes of his could see something coming, something other eyes could not.

Travis shivered, shut the truck's door, and cranked the key in the ignition. With a spray of gravel the pickup launched itself down the road.

Travis laughed as the oddness of his encounter at the orphanage evaporated in the mundane task of piloting the truck. Now that he thought about what had happened, it no longer seemed so strange. There had been some sort of animal between the sheds, and the man in black was just a drifter, peculiar but harmless. As for the sounds—he could chalk those up to wind and imagination. Either that or he was going insane, and there was nothing at all special about *that*. He hummed along with the radio as he drove.

A pointed shape came into view up ahead. As he drew closer, Travis saw it was a big circus tent pitched in a field next to the road. Its canvas roof was patched in countless places, and parked to the side was an old school bus covered with a blotchy coat of white paint. He slowed down as he passed the tent. In front was planted a crude sign.

As always, it took a moment of concentration to stop the words from roaming, then he reined them in. The sign read:

BROTHER CY'S APOCALYPTIC TRAVELING SALVATION SHOW
Ailments Cured—Faith Restored—Souls Redeemed
Come on in—we want to save you!

It was an old-fashioned revival. Travis hadn't thought these sorts of things still existed. He shifted into fourth, and the tent vanished behind him. At least now he knew where the strange man had come from, and he had been right on one count. The old guy was a nut, although not the kind he had thought.

The battered pickup cruised down the road, and he turned his attention to everyday matters—how many kegs of beer he needed to order for the bar, who he had to call to get rid of that skunk holed up under the saloon, and when he was going to find time to patch the leak in the storeroom's roof.

Yet all the way into town, Travis couldn't quite forget the far-off music of bells.

3.

Twilight was drifting from the sky like silver snow by the time Travis turned onto Elk Street and brought the pickup to a halt in front of the Mine Shaft Saloon. Only the summit of Castle Peak rose high enough above the valley to be gilded by the last of the sunlight. He stepped out and shut the vehicle's door without bothering to lock it. Small-town living had its own little luxuries.

Elk Street hadn't changed much in the last hundred years. If cars could be traded for wagons and potholed pavement for red mud, Castle City's main drag wouldn't look much different than it had at the height of the mining days. It ran broad and straight through the heart of town—unlike the narrow, convoluted roads of Eastern cities, constructed by people who were still accustomed to the cramped burgs of the Old World, before they came to realize just how much elbow room this new continent truly had to offer. Weather-corroded false fronts rose sharp and square against the sky, and hitching rails stood in front of most buildings, although these days they usually kept mountain bikes from wandering off instead of horses.

Lights were coming on all along Elk Street against the deepening night. People strolled the boardwalks, heading to the Mosquito Café for the best cup of cappuccino in Castle County, or chatting in front of McKay's General Store, or stopping to look at the smoky quartz crystals, obsidian bolo ties, and hand-drawn tarot cards in the window of the Blue Summit Earth Shop. At the end of the street, graceful as a ghost, hovered Castle City's old opera house, with its Greek Revival columns and baroque marble facade.

Travis hopped onto the boardwalk in front of the saloon just as the neon sign above sizzled to red-and-blue life. He reached out to turn the brass doorknob, then paused. He frowned and leaned toward the door to peer at the upper left corner. There. It was so small and inconspicuous he had nearly missed it. Something had been scratched into the door's faded gray paint, an oval shape formed of two curved lines:

What it signified Travis couldn't say. Most likely it was just some piece of graffiti. Castle City didn't have much of a vandalism problem, but it did happen on occasion. Whatever it was, he was certain it hadn't been there yesterday: The scratch marks looked fresh. Travis let out a sigh. Well, he needed to repaint the door anyway. He added that job to his growing list, then headed into the saloon. The comforting rumble of conversation and the clink of beer glasses told him that Max hadn't driven away all of the customers. At least not yet.

Max stood behind the bar and pored over a mass of papers spread out before him on the expanse of old wood. His long hair was tied back in a ponytail, and a yellow pencil perched behind one ear. He stroked the drooping black mustache he had copied a few months back from the local ranch hands and slid a bowl of pretzels across the bar to a customer. All at once he grabbed the pencil and scribbled on one of the pages, then he leaned back, chewed on the eraser, and smiled the smug smile of a kid who had just traded two *Green Lanterns* and a *Superboy* for a *Batman Giant Special*. Travis had been right. Max was going over the saloon's books again.

Like the street outside, the Mine Shaft Saloon hadn't changed much in the last century. These days electric bulbs shone in the wrought-iron chandeliers that hung from the pressed-tin ceiling, and neon beer signs glowed above the beveled bar mirror, but that was about it. Mummified heads of elk, deer, and mountain lion stared down glass-eyed from the walls, draped in funeral shrouds of cobweb and dust. Time-darkened Wanted posters plastered the posts that supported junk-filled rafters. An antique player piano stood against one wall, still capable of plunking out its tinny music with nail-studded hammers.

The regular customers greeted Travis with hellos and raised mugs as he wound his way through the haphazard scatter of tables and chairs. He smiled and waved back. Maybe he didn't have a family anymore, but these people came close. Some of the hands from the dude ranch down the highway sat around a table where they played cribbage and drank single-malt scotch. A pair of red-cheeked German college students in wool sweaters and Birkenstocks had stowed their big backpacks in a corner, and now the two young men were trying to go shot for shot against a blue-haired contingent from the local chapter of the Daughters of the Frontier. They were losing. A pair of cowboys in Wranglers and bright geometric shirts two-stepped together to a country song in the warm glow of the jukebox. And in a corner, Molly Nakamura patiently taught several others how to fold origami animals out of stiff sheets of paper, although none of their crumpled-looking creations quite looked like Molly's graceful cranes and prowling tigers.

Local legend held that no one came to Castle City by accident. Travis didn't know much about legends. All he knew was that people who passed through Castle City on their way to someplace else had a tendency never to leave. Each of them always said the same thing—that the first time they laid eyes on Castle City it felt like they had found something they didn't even know they were looking for. Maybe it was the beauty of the place, maybe it was that they felt like they *belonged* here, or maybe, as some people believed, it was that the valley had called to them, and somehow they had listened. Travis couldn't say which explanation was right. Perhaps they all were.

Travis himself hadn't decided to come here. Like everything in his life, it had just happened to him. He never had been good at making choices. At eighteen he had left the faded Illinois farmhouse where he had grown up to attend junior college in Champaign. He never saw his parents or that house again. Travis couldn't remember exactly what he had studied in school. He had simply drifted from one subject to the next, until one day he had found himself with a paper in his hand standing at a bus stop. He had stepped on the first bus that had come by, figuring it was as good as any. It had been headed west, and after that inertia had kept him moving in the same direction. For a time he would stop in some city, work awhile, maybe make a friend or two. Then he would find himself on another bus heading west again. Until the day he ended up in Castle City, and he felt that first breath of clean mountain wind against his face.

Andy Connell had owned the Mine Shaft then. He had hired Travis to help out behind the bar, and Travis had rented the beat-up cabin outside of town. He hadn't decided to stay here any more than he did anywhere else. One day he just woke up and realized he had been here for years, and that he didn't have any plans for leaving. And that was about as close to making a choice as Travis ever got. When Andy died two years ago, Travis had scraped together enough cash to buy the saloon, though whether he was going to keep it was a point he and the bank disagreed on monthly.

He made his way to the bar, and Max looked up from his pile of papers and grinned.

"Didn't think I could handle the place on my own, did you, Travis?"

Travis lifted a hinged section of wood and stepped through. "What makes you say that, Max?"

"Nothing really. Just little things, I suppose. Like the fact that you're always muttering under your breath that you don't think I can handle the place on my own."

Travis winced. "Oh." He pulled a brown bottle of homemade root beer from the chiller and twisted the top. "Let me guess. I have a tendency to think aloud sometimes, don't I?"

"Don't worry, Travis. It's just one of your endearing little quirks."

Travis wondered what the others might be but opted not to ask. He wasn't altogether certain he would like the answer. Instead, he checked the kegs to see if any needed changing, then started washing dirty mugs in the bar sink. Max tapped his pencil against the papers in front of him. He might have fled the anxiety of his Wall Street job for the peace of the mountains, but number crunching was in his blood.

"You know, I think we're going to owe some back sales tax for last year." He fixed Travis with a speculative look. "This may just be a wild guess, but . . . you haven't ever actually considered using a calculator, have you?"

"I've always found that doing the books is a much more creative experience without one," Travis said. The fact was, Travis was about as good a mathematician as he was a brain surgeon. He had been more than relieved to surrender the books to Max, but he wasn't about to let his employee know that.

Max shut the ledger and groaned in despair. "Why don't you just stick a pencil in my heart and get it over with, Travis? It would be simpler for both of us."

"Oh, I don't know," Travis said. "This way isn't nearly so messy."

Defeated for the moment, Max tromped back to the storeroom to hunt for more paper napkins. Travis grabbed a rag to wipe down the bar and enjoyed his victory. As an employer it was his duty to torment Max. That he enjoyed it so much was simply an added bonus.

It was just after eight o'clock when Castle County sheriff's deputy Jacine Windom stepped through the door of the saloon. For a moment Travis thought she had come by for a beer, then he noticed the gun at her belt. She was on duty. Jace tipped her hat toward Travis from across the room, then marched through the maze of mismatched tables toward the bar.

"Evening, Travis," Jace said, her brassy voice tinged with a melodic Western twang. She thrust out a hand.

Travis smiled and took the proffered hand. "Nice to see you, Deputy Windom." His expression edged into a grimace when she returned his grip with one of crushing strength. After she let go he had to resist the urge to rub his fingers. Deputy Windom was a small woman in her late twenties, but she carried herself with an air of authority that made her seem taller and older. She had short brown hair and wore a khaki uniform with creases sharp enough to cut a well-done steak.

Jace set her Smokey-the-Bear hat on the bar and perched on a stool, then scanned the saloon with cool eyes. "Looks like business is good tonight."

Travis filled a mug with hot black coffee and pushed it toward her. "It's not bad. Max hasn't scared too many customers away."

Jace took a swig of the scalding coffee and fixed him with a stern look. "If you don't mind my saying, Travis, you're too hard on Maximilian. It isn't his fault that living in a big city makes a man soft and nervous. Your employee has a lot to overcome. But I think he's starting to fit in nice."

Their gazes traveled across the saloon. Now Max laughed and shook his head while the Daughters of the Frontier, with their blue cotton-candy hair and red-fringed denim jumpsuits, tried to get him to country line dance with them. Max looked up, saw Travis and Jace, and shot them a goofy hound-dog grin.

"Real nice," Jace said and gripped her coffee mug. "In fact, get that boy a haircut and a pair of Wranglers, and he'd make a fine little cowboy."

Travis's eyes bulged. He stared at the deputy as she gazed in Max's direction, and for the first time he noticed that a gold earring gleamed against each of her small, pretty ears. There was a resolute cast to her square jaw and a fierce gleam in her eyes. Something told him Max was in for a bit of a surprise.

He cleared his throat and changed the subject. "So, what was it I can help you with, Deputy Windom?"

Jace snapped around on her stool, all business once more. She pulled a small notebook from the pocket of her jacket and flipped several pages.

"We received an unusual report at the sheriff's office earlier."

A chill skittered along Travis's spine. "An unusual report?"

"That's correct. Waunita Lost Owl phoned the station at about four P.M. You know her, Travis. She works behind the counter at McKay's General Store, lives in a double-wide just north of town. Mrs. Lost Owl was quite agitated at the time of her report. It seems she saw a . . ." Jace glanced down at her notebook. ". . . it seems she saw a *delgeth* in her backyard."

Travis took a pull on his ever-present bottle of root beer. "Should I know what that is?"

Jace slipped the notebook back into a pocket of her brown leather jacket. "Not unless you happen to have a degree in Native-American folklore. I had to look it up at the library. It's a Plains Indian myth. As far as I can tell, a *delgeth* is a kind of antelope spirit."

Travis gripped the edge of the bar. He remembered the shadow he had seen that afternoon behind the old orphanage and the hoofprint pressed into the mud—a print which, now that he thought about it, could have belonged to a pronghorn antelope as easily as to a deer. He licked lips gone dry. "You don't think Waunita really saw one of these *delgeths*, do you?"

Jace let out a chuckle. "I don't think Sheriff Dominguez is worried about creatures creeping out of old myths to prowl Castle City. But he *is* concerned that a mountain lion might have come down from the hills. Mrs. Lost Owl did see something. I checked in at McKay's and the Mosquito Café to ask if anyone else had seen it. I just thought I'd do the same here."

For a moment Travis considered telling Jace about what he had seen. But if he told her about the shadow, then he would also have to tell her about the bells and the eerie laughter, and he didn't want to do that. The day had turned strange enough as it was.

"I'm sorry, Deputy Windom, but if anyone has seen anything out of the ordinary, they haven't told me about it."

Jace scraped her barstool back, then stood and rested a casual hand on the gun at her hip. "Looks like I had better move on then. Thanks for the cup of java, Travis." She donned her hat, tipped it toward him, then headed for the door. She cast one last piercing look in Max's direction, then with a puff of night air the deputy was gone. Travis grabbed a tray, collected empty beer glasses, and did his best not to think about the deputy's words.

Half an hour later, the phone rang.

Max answered, then with a resigned look held the phone out across the bar toward Travis. That Max never got any calls had been a slight point of contention lately. Max was of the opinion that at least some of the calls to the saloon should be for him, and he seemed to think it some sort of conspiracy that this wasn't the case. The fact that Travis was the owner of the Mine Shaft and not he didn't seem to play a significant role in Max's logic. Travis set down a tray of mugs and took the phone.

"Travis," the voice on the other end said in hoarse relief. "Travis, I am so thankful to have reached you."

"Jack?" Travis cupped a hand around the phone and tried to block out some of the clamor of the saloon. He recognized the voice of his old friend Jack Graystone. "Jack, is that you?"

"Listen to me, Travis." Jack's faint words buzzed in his ear. "I am afraid I haven't time to explain properly, so I can only hope that, as your friend, you will see fit to trust me." There was a potent silence. Then, "You must come to the Magician's Attic at once."

Travis was taken aback. He had never heard Jack sound like this. Jack's voice was shaking, almost as if he were alarmed. No, Travis realized with a chill—almost as if he were *afraid*.

"Jack, I can't just leave the saloon." Travis tried to keep his voice down. All the same, Max shot him a curious look. "This is our busiest night of the week."

"But you must, Travis." As if through great force of will, Jack's voice calmed and slipped into the smooth, indeterminate European accent with which Travis was so familiar. "I wish I could explain over the phone what has transpired. However, I dare not."

"Explain what?" Travis said.

"I am afraid that must wait until you come to the antique shop. I cannot trust anyone who might be listening to our conversation. Now, you mustn't repeat to anyone what I have said." Jack's voice dropped to a whisper. "But you have to believe me when I tell you that my life is in grave—"

There was a *click*, then a hissing noise filled Travis's ear as the phone went dead.

4.

The saloon's door shut behind him, and Travis stepped into the night. He hunched broad shoulders inside his sheepskin coat. The crescent moon hovered over the parapets of Castle Peak, and its light rimed dark ridges like frost. The warmth and glow shut behind the buckshot-dented door of the Mine Shaft seemed suddenly far away.

He had left without much explanation, but Jack Graystone was his best friend and, however odd they seemed, Travis couldn't go against Jack's wishes. Besides, Max had been only too happy to have a chance to run things himself for a while. Yet what *had* Jack been talking about? Travis couldn't imagine what anyone might gain by threatening the grandfatherly proprietor of a small-town antique store. There had to be a more mundane explanation for the phone call.

Travis headed to his pickup. He reached for the handle, noticed something wedged into the door crack, and plucked it out. It was a tuft of fur, silver-brown in the moonlight. He frowned. Now how had this gotten stuck in the door? A chill breath of wind snatched the tuft from his fingers, and it danced away on the wind. That most likely answered his question. He climbed into the truck, mashed down the clutch, and cranked the ignition. The engine turned over three times, then wound down with a feeble whine. He tried again. This time he was rewarded with a metallic death-knell buzz that signaled yet another battery had succumbed to the high-country climate. He smacked his forehead against the steering wheel in frustration, then climbed out.

Common sense said he should head back to the saloon and ask someone for a jump start, but if he did, people were bound to ask where he was going, and he had promised Jack. With a sigh he began hoofing it down the street. The Magician's Attic was only a mile away: He could manage the walk. It was just nine o'clock, but the town's lone traffic light already winked like an amber cat's-eye in the dark. He tried not to think about Deputy Windom's *delgeth* story. Once already that day he had let his imagination run away with him, and that had been enough.

Travis moved up onto the boardwalk. He passed by the door of the darkened hardware store, then paused and pushed his wire-rimmed spectacles up his nose. There it was again—the same odd symbol that had been scratched on the saloon's door. He continued down Elk Street and saw other doors marked in similar fashion. Travis shivered and quickened his pace.

To his relief, fifteen minutes later, he found himself in front of the Magician's Attic. The antique shop occupied the ground floor of a rambling Victorian on the west edge of Castle City, and Jack reserved the upper stories for his living space. The house was lightless and quiet, from the tower that reminded Travis of a castle's turret to the velvet-curtained parlor windows that stared outward like heavy-lidded eyes. Was Jack even still here? Travis ascended the steps of the front porch and reached out to knock, but the door flew open before his hand touched it.

"Wotan's Beard! It's about time you arrived, Travis."

Travis lurched through the doorway into the cluttered foyer beyond and barely managed to keep from falling. Jack shut the door. He carried a tin hurricane lamp, its speckled golden light the only illumination in the place.

Jack Graystone appeared to be about sixty years old, although Travis couldn't remember him ever looking any different in the seven years they had been friends. He was a striking man, with a Roman nose and eyes of sky blue. His iron-gray beard was neatly trimmed, in contrast to his thinning hair of the same color, which had a tendency to fly rather madly about his head. He was dressed in an old-fashioned but elegant suit of English wool over a starched white shirt and a flannel waistcoat of hunter's green. Travis had never seen him wear anything else.

"I'm sorry I took so long, Jack." Travis tried to catch his breath. "My truck wouldn't start, so I had to walk here."

"You *walked* here?" Jack fixed him with a grave look. "That wasn't a terribly good idea, you know, not on a night like this."

Travis ran a hand through his sand-colored hair. "Jack, what is going on? I didn't know what to think after the phone went dead."

"Oh, that. Do forgive me, Travis, I'm afraid that was all my fault. You see, I thought I heard a noise in the parlor while we were talking. I turned around and accidentally cut the phone cord with a sword I was holding."

Travis gaped at him. "A sword?"

"Yes, a sword. It's like a large knife often used by knights in—"

"I *know* what a sword is."

Jack gave him a sharp look. "Then why did you ask?"

Travis drew in an exasperated breath. As much as he liked Jack, talking with him could be a challenge. "Jack, would you please tell me why you asked me to come here?"

Jack regarded Travis with perfect seriousness. "A darkness is coming."

With that he turned and disappeared into the dim labyrinth of the antique shop. There was nothing for Travis to do but follow. The gloom all around was filled with the flotsam and jetsam of history— chests of drawers with porcelain knobs, lead-backed mirrors, lion-clawed andirons, velvet chaises, and weather-faded circus posters. Jack never rested in his hunt for curious and wonderful antiques. That was how he and Travis had become friends.

One day, not long after Travis started working at the Mine Shaft, Jack Graystone had stepped through the door of the saloon, incongruous in his old-fashioned attire, yet not uncomfortably so. He had asked if he might be allowed to cull the saloon's storeroom for any "artifacts of historical interest." Andy Connell had been out of town, but one of

Travis's assignments while Andy was away had been to clear a century's worth of junk out of the back storeroom. Travis had been more than happy to let Jack do some of the work for him.

Yet before long—and afterward he was never quite certain just how it happened—Travis found himself on the storeroom floor, covered with grime and cobwebs, sorting through tangled piles of hundred-year-old clutter, while Jack, neatly ensconced on a barstool, politely offered direction. In the end, the saloon's storeroom got cleaned, Travis hauled a pickup truck full of copper lanterns, bent-willow chairs, and thick-glassed purple bottles to the Magician's Attic, and somewhere along the way Jack had apparently decided he and Travis were the best of friends. Travis had never bothered to disagree.

Still, nothing in their long friendship had prepared Travis for Jack's behavior tonight. With Travis following on his heels, Jack wended his way to the back of the shop, his tin lantern casting off shards of gold light. He stepped over a heap of broken Grecian urns and edged past a wooden sarcophagus that leaned against the wall and stared with knowing eyes of lapis lazuli. They started up a narrow staircase that Travis, in all his visits to the Magician's Attic, had somehow never noticed before.

Old photographs in antique gilt frames lined either wall of the stairwell. One caught Travis's eye. He paused and peered more closely at the photo. It showed a group of grim-faced men and women clad in somber attire. Some gripped shovels or pickaxes, and a hole had been torn open in the earth before them. A caption was written at the bottom of the photo in spidery ink. Travis strained to make it out: *The Beckett-Strange Home for Children, 1933.* It was the ground-breaking ceremony for the old orphanage. However, it was something else that had caught Travis's attention. A rectangular shape floated in the picture's background, blurry and half-obscured by a woman's hat, but he recognized it all the same. The old billboard by the highway—only in this photo it was not covered by the cigarette advertisement. Although dim and murky, he could just discern the wild landscape. So the painting had been there back in 1933. Yet what was it advertising? There seemed to be flowing words written at the bottom of the billboard, but Travis could not read them.

A perturbed voice broke his concentration. "Travis, do stop dawdling. There simply isn't time."

Travis tore his eyes away from the old photo and hurried up the steps after Jack. The odd staircase ended in a blank wall. Jack pressed against a mahogany panel to his right, and an opening appeared. Travis ducked his head and followed his friend through the small door. Bronze light flared to life as Jack used the candle from his hurricane lantern to light an oil lamp atop a wrought-iron stand. Travis adjusted his gunslinger's spectacles in amazement.

"Jack, what is this place?"

"Minerva's Thread! You can't stifle your questions for five seconds, can you, Travis?"

Travis hardly heard him. The windowless room was circular, and by that he knew it to be somewhere within the house's tower. He was familiar with the rooms above and below. Why had he never considered what might lie between? Now he stared in wonder.

The walls were covered with artifacts. Flat-bladed swords gleamed in the light of the oil lamp, their blades etched with flowing designs and incomprehensible symbols. Beside them hung half-moon axes hafted with bone and leather, and massive hammers that obviously had been designed for pounding in skulls, not nails. There were wooden shields inlaid with silver, and neck-rings of fiery copper, and helmets crowned with goat horns and yellow horsehair. It was like a collection from a museum, but not quite. For what startled Travis most of all was the way the objects shone in the warm light. Most of them were worn and well used, but none seemed to display the signs of decay and corrosion that came with centuries of burial. Well-oiled leather still looked supple, and steel glowed without a speck of rust.

This was too much for Travis. "Jack, I have a request, and I really don't think it's all that unreasonable." He advanced on his friend. *"Tell me what is going on."*

Jack gave him a sour look. "Do spare the dramatics, Travis. And sit down."

As usual, Travis found himself obeying. He sank into a chair beside a table that occupied the room's center. Jack filled a glass from a decanter of brandy and handed it to Travis.

"I don't want it," Travis said in a sulky tone.

"You will."

Something in Jack's voice made Travis hold on to the glass. "Jack, what are all these things?" He gestured to the artifacts that decorated the walls of the room. "Where did you get them? And how come you've never offered any of them for sale?"

Jack waved the questions aside with a dignified flick of his hand. Jack could do things like that. He paced around the table, lips pursed in thought. At last he spoke. "I'm dreadfully sorry to have to involve you in all this, Travis. However, I'm afraid I don't have any choice. There simply isn't anyone else I dare trust. And these matters are far too crucial for me to take unnecessary chances." He sighed, a sound of profound weariness. "I am going to be leaving."

Travis stared at his old friend in shock. "Leaving? You mean Castle City?"

The older man nodded in sad affirmation.

"But why?"

Jack sat down, folded his hands neatly before him, and met Travis's eyes.

"I am being hunted," he said.

5.

Travis gripped the empty brandy glass and listened numbly while Jack explained in a tone of infuriating calmness that certain individuals had been searching for him for a long time. Now they were on the verge of discovering him at last, and Jack was obliged to leave Castle City, at least for the time being. Travis started to wonder if Jack was dealing in black-market artifacts. Maybe the swords, axes, and helmets that adorned the walls of the hidden room had been smuggled into the country, and others who wanted them were after Jack. Hard as it was to believe, it seemed the only logical explanation.

Travis realized Jack had asked him a question. Dazed, he shook his head. "I'm sorry, Jack. What did you say?"

"Pay attention, Travis," Jack said with a disapproving frown. "This is important. I said I was hoping you could keep something for me while I am gone. It is a small object—of no market worth whatsoever—but of great personal value to me. I would rest far better if I knew it was in good hands while I am away." He unlocked an oak cabinet and pulled out a box, black and small enough to fit in the palm of his hand. He set it on the table before Travis. "Will you keep it for me?"

"Of course I will, Jack, if you want me to." Travis picked up the box. It was heavy, and he realized it must be fashioned of iron. Its surface was decorated with angular symbols he did not recognize, and a simple hasp held the lid shut. Travis started to undo it.

"By the Lost Fraction of Osiris, don't open it!" Jack clamped his hand down on the lid of the box and glared at Travis. Then, with a chagrined look, he leaned back in his chair and smoothed his waistcoat. "Forgive me, Travis. It really would be best if you left the box closed."

"So I gathered," Travis said.

"There's no need to be flippant. Just promise me you'll keep the box safe and secret."

Travis sighed in defeat. "All right. I promise."

"Thank you."

However, Travis was not finished. "Jack, what's really going on? Who are these people who are after you? Where are you going? And when will you be coming back?"

Jack's tone was reproving, if not unkind. "You know better than to ask such questions, Travis. I have already told you more than I should." With that Jack stood, giving clear indication that the conversation was over. Travis knew there was nothing else he could do, although that didn't keep a heaviness from weighing on his heart.

Travis picked up the iron box and slipped it into the breast pocket of his sheepskin coat, then followed Jack downstairs. The two paused before the antique shop's front door. Travis chewed his lip. Was this the last time he would ever see his old friend? "I'm going to miss you, Jack."

Now a wistful expression touched Jack's mien. "And I you, Travis. You are a true friend. Thank you for understanding."

Travis didn't bother to say he didn't understand any of this. It would be no use. "Good-bye, Jack." He couldn't believe he was speaking these words. "Wherever you're going, take care of yourself."

A spark flashed in Jack's blue eyes. "Oh, you can be assured of that." Without further ado, he opened the shop's door and ushered Travis outside.

Travis started through, then halted in mid-step. A chill coursed through him. "There it is again," he said.

Jack's bushy eyebrows knit themselves together. "What is it, Travis?"

Travis reached a hand toward the upper left corner of the door, and his fingers brushed over a design scratched into the paint. It was the same symbol he had seen on the front door of the saloon and the other doors around town. Except this one was different in that an X had been scrawled beneath:

Jack peered at the scratch marks, and at once his blue eyes went wide. "Oh, dear," he whispered. "This isn't good. This isn't good at all."

Travis looked at his friend in astonishment. "You know what this symbol means, don't you?"

Jack brushed the scratch marks with trembling fingers. "It is the mark of their servants. I had not guessed they were this close, not yet. But if their minions have been here, they cannot be far behind."

Travis shook his head in confusion, but before he could speak a beam of blue-white light tore apart the fabric of the night. Travis raised a hand to shield his eyes. It was like the searchlight of a police helicopter, except it was too low to the ground, and there was no sound accompanying it, only the murmur of the wind. Whatever the source of the light, it was coming toward the antique shop. And coming fast.

"Go inside, Travis." Jack's voice resonated with low urgency.

"What is it, Jack?" Travis squinted against the light. He thought he saw something moving within—tall silhouettes backlit by the glare.

Jack's voice became a stern command. "Now, Travis!"

This time Travis didn't argue. He stumbled backward into the shop. Jack hurried after him, slammed the door shut, and slid the dead bolt into place. He shut the drapes that covered the shop's iron-grilled front window, and the room was plunged into gloom. Only a razor-thin plane of hot white light found its way through a gap in the curtains: It sliced the dusky air like a glowing knife.

Alarm surged in Travis's chest. "It's them, isn't it? The people who are after you." Jack did not disagree. That was all the confirmation Travis needed. Alarm crested into outright panic.

"Calm yourself, Travis," Jack warned with a stern look.

"I don't want to be calm," he whispered. "Now is definitely not the time for calmness."

"On the contrary, there is no better time to remain calm than when one is in danger."

Travis groaned. Jack had to go and say the word, didn't he? *Danger.*

Jack moved to an old-fashioned typesetter's desk, opened a drawer, and drew out an object wrapped in black silk. He unfolded the cloth to reveal a slender, murderous stiletto. A bloodred stone glistened in its steel hilt. He handed the knife to Travis.

"Take this, just in case."

Travis fumbled with the weapon as though he had just been handed a live snake instead. However, a scowl from Jack kept him from dropping the knife. Travis had never owned a weapon of any sort in his life. It felt cool and disturbingly smooth in his hand. He slipped it through his belt. At least that way he wouldn't have to hold it.

"Just in case what?" he asked in a croak.

Jack ignored the question. "Follow me," he whispered and moved through the chaotic clutter of the shop.

Travis started to stumble after him, then froze. An electric humming pierced the silence, and a line of brilliant light flared beneath the front door. With menacing slowness, the doorknob turned right, then left, then right again. Travis felt a warmth against his hip and glanced down. The gem embedded in the stiletto's hilt now shone bright crimson.

"Travis, get over here!"

Jack stood beside an open doorway that led down to the shop's cellar, but Travis could not move his feet. His eyes locked on the antique shop's front door. A sharp beam of frosty light shot through the keyhole. The doorknob twisted faster, until it rattled in its socket, then the rattling ceased. A moment later the entire door shook with a *thud*. There was a long pause, followed by a second strike.

"Travis!"

The roar of Jack's voice shattered his paralysis. Travis lurched toward his friend and bit his tongue as he barked his shin on a cedar trunk. Just as Travis reached Jack, one last blow resounded behind him. Hinges shrieked, old wood exploded in a spray of splinters, and searing light flooded the shop.

Jack pulled Travis through the cellar doorway onto the top step. As one, they turned to shut the door at the head of the staircase. For a fleeting second, through the closing gap, Travis glimpsed a figure silhouetted against the blazing light. The outline of the intruder was tall and slender, and moved toward them with swift, sinister grace. Then the door slammed shut and blocked out the sight. Hands shaking, Jack slid a stout wooden bar across the doorway. Together, the two men half ran, half fell down the staircase into the cellar below. Sheet-draped furniture clustered around them like a spectral chorus, and the cellar air was as cold as a tomb. Above, the first violent blow struck the cellar door. Ethereal light poured through the crack beneath and drifted down the steps like livid mist.

Jack's thin gray hair flew about his head. "That bar will only hold them for a few moments. You must go, Travis. Quickly." He hurried to the far wall and opened a small wooden door. Beyond was a dark passage. "This tunnel leads to the garden shed out back."

"What about you, Jack?"

A second blow struck the cellar door.

"Don't argue with me, Travis. There simply isn't time."

"But why aren't you coming?" Every instinct told Travis to flee, to scramble through the tunnel, to run as fast as he could into the late-October night. Yet he couldn't just leave Jack like this.

"I have my reasons for staying."

Jack's voice was flint, his expression steel. Travis had never seen him like this before.

"Then let me help you."

"You don't know what you're dealing with, Travis."

Travis shook his spinning head. "I can't just leave you, Jack!"

At this Jack's expression softened a fraction. "Don't be afraid, Travis. I had not planned this, but I see now it is the only way. If I am fortunate, I can give you time to escape. However, you must use it." A sad light shone in his blue eyes. "You are our hope now."

He reached out and took Travis's right hand between his own two and gripped it firmly.

"Forgive me, my friend."

Agony raced up Travis's arm. For a fractured moment it felt as if his entire body was on fire. White-hot radiance washed over him, pierced flesh, blood, and bone—streamed through the very substance of his body as if he were as transparent and brittle as glass. Travis tried to scream, but his voice was lost in the roar of the wildfire that engulfed him. In another heartbeat it would burn him into nothing.

The moment shattered. Travis reeled away from his friend. The blazing fire had vanished, and now chill sweat trickled down his sides. Although he dreaded what he would see—crisped flesh and blackened bones—he looked down at his throbbing hand. The skin was smooth and undamaged. However, all that was left of the hair on the backs of his knuckles was a fine gray ash.

He looked up at Jack with a mixture of fear and wonder.

"Go, my friend," Jack said. "May the gods walk with you."

Travis shook his head in dull incomprehension. Another impact shook the cellar door. The thick wooden bar cracked with a sound like breaking bones.

"Go, Travis!" Gone now was the kind and slightly absentminded old man Travis had known for seven years. In his place was an imposing stranger: face sharp, voice commanding, eyes vivid as lightning.

This time Travis did as he was told.

He dived into the cramped tunnel. Cobwebs clung to his hands and face. With a cry he tore them to shreds. From behind came a crash as the cellar door shattered. A high-pitched sound crackled on the air, like dry ice on metal. Travis ran hunched through the tunnel, propelled by terror. Seconds later the passage dead-ended. For a panicked moment he thought he was trapped, then his groping fingers found the wooden rungs in the blackness. He clambered up the ladder, threw open a trapdoor, and found himself in the cluttered garden shed. He stumbled out the shed's door and into the frigid night.

The antique shop loomed thirty feet away. Light—hot and brilliant as a burning strip of magnesium—flickered behind the windows.

Travis took a staggering step toward the antique shop. At that moment every one of the shop's windows exploded outward in a spray of glittering glass. The shock wave struck Travis like a clap of thunder, threw him to the ground, and knocked the breath from his lungs in a grunt of pain.

He gritted his teeth and struggled to his feet. Now the flames that poured out of the antique shop's windows were red and orange. Fire, real fire. The place was going to burn.

Travis whispered a single word. "Jack. . . ."

Then he turned and ran into the night.

6.

Just north of town, the billboard faced blindly into the moonlight.

The highway was empty, a silent river of blacktop cutting across the high-country plain. The night was still. Stars glittered in the purple-black sky, and added their glow to that of the crescent moon. Somewhere a coyote warbled a mournful song that would have spoken of cold rushing water, of old splintered bones, of lonely mountains stretching to the end of the world, had anyone been there to listen to it.

The moon brushed the sharp horizon. That was when it began. Like a drop of water on a hot iron skillet, a spark of blue light skittered across the face of the old billboard. The spark burned itself into a cinder of darkness and was gone. Another pinprick danced across the billboard. Before this one dimmed another spark joined it, and another, and another. In moments the entire face of the billboard sparkled with blue incandescence.

A faint hum buzzed on the air. As the sound grew louder, a strip of the faded cigarette advertisement peeled itself off the surface of the billboard and fell to the ground. Sparks clustered like blue fireflies around the edges of the hole left by the chunk of old paper. Bathed in their sapphire glow, a patch of the picture beneath showed through—a jewellike fragment of a wild landscape.

Winking like tiny eyes, the sparks spread outward. More strips of paper curled themselves into tight coils and dropped to the ground, then still more, to reveal the long-hidden image beneath.

7.

People in the Emergency Department always told Grace Beckett she had a good grip on reality.

If they meant she could pull hot chunks of car shrapnel from the chest of a screaming motorcyclist without blinking . . . if they meant she could perform a caesarean on a seventeen-year-old mother killed in the crossfire of a drive-by shooting and somehow still smile at the perfect smallness of a premature baby's toes . . . if they meant she could get called away from the other residents in the TV lounge to resuscitate the elderly victim of a hit-and-run and still make it back before the commercial was over . . . if that's what people meant, then Grace supposed they were right. She was good, she knew she was, and she knew it without any sense of hauteur or self-importance. It was simply a fact. Everyone had a talent, a gift—something they did better the first time they tried than most people could do after years of practice—and this was hers. Grace could put broken people back together.

She always knew when a rush was coming.

Of course, there were all the usual signs even a first-year intern knew—a full moon, a rising barometer, a hot Friday night in June. But even when there were no signs, when the city drowsed, and there hadn't been anything more serious than a sprained thumb all day, somehow she could feel it about to happen, like a prickling on her skin. Even as the others played broom hockey in a slick-tiled hallway—a game they resorted to in those rare ebbs—Grace would slip on a pair of latex gloves and stand, expectant, before the automatic doors.

With a hiss the doors slid open. Then they were there, streaming into the Emergency Department of Denver Memorial Hospital, pulled from an overturned bus, or a burning hotel, or a twenty-car freeway pileup. While the others scrambled to grab gowns and stethoscopes, Grace already weaved her way among the wounded, the frightened, the dead, soothing hurts and fears with precise hands. Some in the ED mistook this cool and focused efficiency for aloofness, but Grace never bothered to correct them. She had not come to this place to make friends.

Yet, sometimes, in the quiet hour that always came at four in the morning, when everything in the world seemed to sleep and the Emergency Department grew still and tomblike, Grace would sit in a vacant wheelchair, holding a foam cup of dull beige coffee drizzled from a dull beige vending machine, and she would think that people were wrong—awfully, utterly, hilariously wrong—and that it was really just the opposite. Grace didn't have a good grip on reality.

Reality had a good grip on her.

Bullet wounds, mangled bodies, burnt children . . . despite her effort to keep each instance distinct and sharp and tragic, all inevitably blurred into one endless tapestry of suffering. For every hole she patched, for every shattered limb she straightened, for every heart she shocked and battered and cajoled into beating again, there would be another to take its place.

Still, in all her wheelchair reveries, there was no prescience that could have warned Grace of, or even hinted at, the queer happenings that would weave themselves around her on that purple autumn night. Not that it mattered. For in the end, whether she gripped it, or whether it gripped her, the result would have been exactly the same.

Grace Beckett's reality was about to unravel.

8.

Grace watched as two interns pushed the gurney down the institutional green hallway. One of the thing's wheels was askew and rattled like an old grocery cart as it hurtled along. Neither of the fresh-faced young men seemed to notice. Elevator doors lurched open, and a moment later interns, gurney, and patient—victim of an apartment building fire—were gone. Grace leaned against the wall and pressed her cheek to the cool tiles. The doors of Trauma One flapped behind her like the palsied wings of an old bird. She let her eyes droop shut for a delicious moment, then forced them open again. She shucked off her papery sterile gown, crumpled it into a ball, and tossed it into a receptacle where it could await the cleansing fire of the incinerator. With a deep breath she started toward Admitting to get her next injury. The day wasn't over yet, not by a long shot.

She navigated her way through an antiseptic labyrinth of corridors, past color-coded examination rooms and dim alcoves where emergency medical equipment lurked like alien creatures, waiting to suck vital fluids from human bodies held in their metallic grips. Spare wheelchairs and gurneys littered the hallways, along with a haphazard collection of patients. Most were bored refugees from the recuperative wards—those able to walk, hobble, or wheel their way out of their rooms, exploring in curiosity, maybe looking for a place to smoke a cigarette in secret, oxygen tanks and clattering IV stands dragged in tow.

Grace detoured for a moment and pushed through the door of the ladies' rest room. She bent over the chipped sink, splashed water on her face and neck in an attempt to wash away weariness and the smell of blood, then used damp fingers to comb short, ash-blond hair. With a snap she straightened the white coat she wore over a blouse and chinos, then surveyed her appearance in the mirror—not to see if she looked attractive, but rather to determine if she looked capable, professional. Beauty was no concern of Grace's, though in fact she was beautiful. She was a tall woman of thirty, lean and angular, almost stiff in bearing, yet possessed of a subtle elegance. Had her voice had substance, it might have been smoke, or butterscotch, or fine cognac. She never wore cosmetics, and although she thought her features sharp, others described them as *chiseled* or even *regal*. She had absolutely no idea that her green-gold eyes had the power to mesmerize.

"It'll work," she murmured to the reflection.

True, her skin was too pale, but there was nothing she could do about that. She spent far too much time in the fluorescent glare of the ED, far too little under the Colorado sun. She promised herself next summer she would try to get outside more, even as she knew she would not. Why should she, when all she needed was here?

TEEN STUDIES MEDICINE, the headline had read, RECALLS PARENTS SHE NEVER KNEW.

Newspapers adored that sort of stuff. Human interest, they called it. Grace still had the clipping, crisp and yellow, folded between the pages of a high school scrapbook she was too cynical to take out of storage and too sentimental to throw away. The photo showed a gangly sixteen-year-old wearing a too-big lab coat, her shorn hair looking like it had been hacked off with a scalpel. She held a human skull and stared at the camera with an earnest expression that couldn't quite conceal the spark of grisly mirth in her eyes. But the pretty reporter had been squeamish of the skull, and it was a weakness that, even as a child, Grace had found funny and—more importantly—contemptible.

"So, honey," Colleen Adara of the *Denver Post* had snapped around an apparently delicious piece of gum, "you never knew your parents, is that right?"

"No, I didn't," Grace had said. "That's because, when I was a baby, they both . . . *died*."

With that last word, she had thrust the skull at the reporter for dramatic effect. A look of horror had spread across Ms. Adara's perfectly made-up face like a webwork of cracks on a sun-baked mud pan. It was a minor victory, but one Grace had relished all the same. That had been in the foster home days—the five years she had referred to at the time as one long game of Pass the Orphan—and she had needed all the small triumphs she could get.

In the end, of course, Ms. Adara's article had been hopelessly wrong. It wasn't the regretful ghosts of her parents that propelled Grace onward. No, if Grace was haunted by anything at all, it was something very much alive.

She had studied premed at the University of Colorado with fierce abandon and was accepted to the prestigious medical school at Duke University. Packing everything she owned into her primer-gray Mustang, she had traded the bright dryness of Colorado for the damp and shadowed green of North Carolina. It was her first time in the South, and, as a semiarid Western child, she had not been prepared for the rank lushness of it all. Everything here was alive. Not just the rhododendron and dogwood and moss-speckled pine, but the rocks, the soil, the rivers—all were choked with life. Even her shabby Georgian apartment, with its high ceilings and sloping wood floors, seemed to breathe and grow, and it wasn't just because of the cockroaches, or because of the mold in the bathroom, which she had renamed the Terrarium. For on steamy August nights, when she lay awake and naked beneath a rattling metal fan, the walls would sweat and groan as if they too felt the heat.

During her four years of medical school, Grace displayed a hunger for knowledge that disturbed her professors as often as it impressed them. While other students dissected human cadavers with delicate disgust, she dug into hers with such intensity, determined to discover how every bit of bone and tissue and nerve was strung together, that one of the anatomy professors dubbed her Michelangela. She merely gave him a tight-lipped smile and kept cutting. When she graduated, it was eleventh in her class, not first. To rank higher required someone more personable, someone less intelligent and more disarming. Of course, not all specialties required bedside manner, and her advisor, Dr. Jason Briggs, had expected her to place well. Then she informed him she had turned down an internship in radiology, the dream specialty of every medical student with country club aspirations, and had accepted one in emergency medicine instead, at a public hospital to make it worse. Furious, he had told her she was making a foolish mistake. Grace had nodded, then had returned to her apartment, packed her belongings—everything still fit neatly inside her old Mustang—and had headed back to Colorado. Saying good-bye had been easy enough. She had made no true friends, and she would not miss the roaches.

Now she was in the third year of her residency at Denver Memorial Hospital, and the occasional letters from Dr. Briggs had dwindled and, finally, stopped. Of course, Briggs had been as dead wrong about Grace as Ms. Adara of the *Denver Post*. Not that she cared. This was where she had to be, and that was all anybody needed to know. Healing was a strange and bittersweet revenge.

Grace left the rest room and headed down the hallway to the ED's admitting area. It was nearly deserted. A few people attempted to doze on plastic chairs while they waited to hear news of a friend or relative. A heavyset nurse floated by, silent in her angel-white crepe-soled shoes. Grace checked, but there were no charts—no more patients to see. She moved through the door near the ambulance entrance, taking a shortcut to the lounge, then she saw a crumpled form on a gurney. There was one more who needed her after all. She took a step forward.

A hand closed on her shoulder to stop her.

"That one is mine, Grace."

Startled, she turned and found herself looking into quiet brown eyes. They belonged to a lean black man with a salt-and-pepper beard.

If Grace had anything resembling a friend at Denver Memorial, then it was Leon Arlington. Leon was the swing shift manager of the hospital's morgue. He had been working with dead people so long that, over the years, he had picked up a number of their habits, from his slow calm to his placid and slightly disconnected gaze. These days few of Grace's patients made the final elevator ride down to see Leon. She was shooting for none.

Leon nodded toward the gurney in the corner, and Grace glanced over her shoulder to see a nurse pull a sheet over the still shape. She let out a shuddering breath. The adrenaline rush that always propelled her without thought from patient to patient evaporated and left her weak and empty.

"Come on," Leon said in his husky voice. "Let's get some coffee."

"I remember her now," Grace said a few minutes later. The two sat in a bank of green vinyl chairs. She took a sip from her foam cup: The coffee was hot and bitter. "I examined her myself. She was one of the apartment fire victims. One look, and I knew her lungs were gone. She knew it, too." Grace shook her head in wonder, then looked at Leon. "How is it people always know when they're about to die? We spend years trying to learn how to read the signs, but they just seem to know. I could see it in her eyes. And you know what I did? I smiled at her, and then I turned away and moved on to someone I had a chance of saving. Any of the other residents would have done the same."

For a moment she remembered the woman's eyes, so blue, like two jewels in the fire-darkened ruin of her face.

She shook her head. "Whatever happened to our hearts, Leon?"

Leon just shrugged. "You did what you were supposed to, Grace."

"I know that." She searched his lean brown face, hoping to find a bit of that easy calm she could keep for her own. "But did I do what I *should* have?" She took another swig of her coffee, winced as it burned her tongue, and swallowed it all the same. "Sometimes I wonder if all I'm doing is prolonging the pain. I let that woman suffer so I could keep alive a man who will have to undergo at least a half-dozen skin grafts, and who will spend the rest of his life horribly scarred. Pain for pain. Is that a fair bargain?"

Her voice trailed off. For a long time Leon's face was expressionless, and when he finally did react it was not as she had expected.

He bared his white teeth in a grin. "I don't know, Grace, but you might be surprised at the number of folks who, if you gave them a choice, would stick with good old suffering. What do you think that man you just sent upstairs would choose? To suffer the pain of staying alive? Or to sleep in one of my drawers downstairs?" Leon let out a hoot of laughter. "I sure know what I'd choose."

Grace wondered if she could be so certain. She glanced at a wall clock. Five P.M. Her shift had ended an hour ago, not that official starting and ending times meant much around here. She stood and rubbed the back of her neck with a hand.

"I'm going to get out of here while I can. Have a good night, Leon."

"Oh, I always do," the morgue manager said and tipped an imaginary hat toward her.

On her way out, Grace stopped by the office she shared with some of the other residents to shrug off her white coat and pick up her briefcase and beeper, then she headed down a hallway toward a back exit. If she really wanted to escape this place it was best not to be seen. An automatic door slid open, and she stepped outside into the late-autumn evening. The light of the westering sun warmed her cheeks, and she breathed in cool air. Traffic buzzed past, like a line of shiny army ants cutting down all that stood in their path. Grace was on foot. She headed down the tree-lined tunnel of a side street and for the next twelve blocks tried not to wonder if she had made the world better or worse that day.

9.

Twenty minutes later, Grace walked up the steps to her second-floor studio apartment and unlocked the peeling door. Inside, she groped in the dimness until her hand found a light switch, then flicked it on.

The electric glare of the overhead lamp was not kind to the space it found. What had been fresh and modern in 1923 when the San Tropez was first constructed had become dingy and ugly in the intervening years. The white paint slapped on the plaster walls had turned the yellow of an old wedding dress, and the green shag carpet was so worn in places that the original linoleum tiles—probably made of compressed asbestos—showed through. Grace's meager possessions did little to brighten the place. She saw that the last of her houseplants was withered and brown. At least she wouldn't have to worry about watering it anymore.

She headed to the apartment's afterthought of a kitchen, rummaged in the rusty refrigerator, and came out with a carton of Chinese takeout. She sat cross-legged on a futon on the floor—it was the one piece of furniture she owned—and ate cold rice while she watched the evening news on a blurry television set almost as old as she was.

But she wasn't hungry, and the news was the same parade of disasters and violence it was every night, and suddenly she did not want to be there, in that dim little apartment, alone and brooding and trapped. She stood and looked around, as if seeing the place for the first time. It didn't seem real. Was this where she lived? She knew it was, and yet it couldn't be. How could it, when she felt so disconnected from it all? This place—none of this—was hers. It was an irrational feeling, and yet so strong and certain she could only believe it was true.

Grace did not belong here.

She left the greasy carton of food on top of the TV set, stood, and grabbed a jacket. The door shut behind her, and only as she started down the steps did she realize she had not locked it. She almost halted, almost turned to head back up the stairs. This was not the best of neighborhoods. Until that moment she had always been obsessive about locking the door. Now giddiness rose in her chest, and along with it an odd sense of premonition. Somehow she knew, if she left this place now, she would not come back again, and if that was true, whether she locked the door or not mattered nothing.

Grace hesitated only á heartbeat, then descended the steps. She shoved her hands in the pockets of her jacket and walked into the gathering twilight.

After a few blocks she found herself on the edge of an expanse of green-brown grass speckled here and there with trees. City Park. She started down one of the park's asphalt trails. Soon she found herself humming. It was a half-remembered song, from her childhood perhaps. The melody came easily to her lips, although she did not know its name, and she could recall only a few snatches of murmured lyrics:

*"And farewell words too often part
All their small and paling hearts. . . ."*

The words made little sense—she supposed they had been trans-muted in her mind with time—but they were comforting all the same. As she often did when she walked, Grace reached up and drew out a silver necklace that hung around her throat. On the end was a pendant, a wedge-shaped piece of metal incised with an angular design. Like the song, the necklace was a thing of her childhood. She had been wearing it when the people from the orphanage had found her, although she had been too young to remember. Still, it was a link to the parents and the life she had never known, and although it was a sad reminder, it was precious as well.

Grace walked on. It felt good to distance herself from the oppression of the city's buildings. The air was lighter in the park, pearl instead of gray, and she could feel a hint of the vastness of the world that lay beyond. The mountains stood in silhouette on the horizon, as sharp and flat and black as if a child had cut them from construction paper for an art project. The first stars glimmered in the sky. She drifted on through the park.

It was the girl's eyes that caught her.

Grace nearly did not see her at all, for the child's old-fashioned dress was the exact shade of twilight, and her hair was a shadow floating about the pale-moon oval of her face. However, her purple eyes glowed in the dimness, and when Grace saw them she froze in mid-step. The girl appeared to be no more than eight or nine years old. She stood quietly beneath the slender ghost of an aspen tree to one side of the path, small hands folded neatly before her, fingers soft and pink as the petals of an unfurled rose. *Come to me,* Grace thought she heard the child whisper, although that would have been impossible. All the same she moved toward the girl, responding to that instinctual power children some-times have over adults. In moments she stood before the child.

"I am not lost," the girl said in a clear voice.

Grace snapped her mouth shut, for that was the question she had been about to ask. She stared down at the girl in wonder, then shiv-ered. There was something extraordinary about the child, something sorrowful, and knowing, and even ancient. All at once Grace felt that *she* was the one who was lost. The bare limbs of the aspen tree made a forlorn music in the breeze.

"Who are you?" Grace asked. It was all she could think to say.

A pretty frown creased the girl's forehead. "Who are *you?* That is a better question, I think."

Grace shook her head, unsure how to answer. The world had fallen silent. She could hear no traffic, no sirens, no circling airplanes waiting to land. It was as if the city had vanished into the night. A crescent moon hung in the sky, although she could not remember seeing it earlier. The wind held its breath.

The girl's eyes reflected the moonlight. "A darkness is coming," she whispered.

Grace stared at the girl in incomprehension, then a shrill chime pierced the silence. After a confused second Grace realized what it was. Her beeper. She fumbled for the small device clipped to her belt, grabbed it in numb hands, and glanced at the glowing liquid crystal display.

"Damn it," she said. "They want me back at the hospital." She looked up. "I have to—"

Her words trailed off. The girl was gone. She spun around and scanned the deepening night, but she had no real hope of seeing the child, nor did she.

10.

Fifteen minutes later, Grace dashed through the door of Denver Memorial's Emergency Department. For a moment she leaned against a wall, eyes squeezed shut, mouth open, and panted for breath. She had half walked, half run the ten blocks from City Park, and now her lungs felt as if she had been the one caught in the smoke of the apartment fire earlier that day. The long hours of a resident left little time for exercise, and although she was thin enough—maybe even too thin—Grace wasn't in top physical shape. She took one last breath, then opened her eyes.

The ED was a madhouse.

In front of the receiving counter, a man argued with his wife even as he gripped the carving fork she had stuck in his side. Down one hall, a couple of gang members hurled expletives and death threats at each other while a frightened intern tried to bandage their knife wounds. A gray-faced man stumbled through the door, asked to see a doctor, then vomited in the middle of the floor. Every chair in the waiting room was occupied by someone clutching a broken limb, or sweating with fever, or wheezing for breath. Above it all, like a dissonant chorus of sick angels, rose the crying of children.

Grace gathered her will, pushed her way through the throng of injured toward one of the nurses' stations, grabbed a pair of gloves, and put them on with an expert *snap*.

"Grace, where the hell have you been? I page you three times and it still takes you thirty minutes to show up?"

"Fifteen," she murmured. She turned around and found herself gazing at the young, angry face of Chief Resident Morty Underwood. Grace disliked Underwood, but she never displayed her feelings. She refused to give him the satisfaction of knowing he had gotten to her. "It took me fifteen minutes, Morty. I came as soon as you paged me."

This latter statement was not entirely true. For several minutes, after her beeper had first gone off, she had stood in the park and gazed into the gloom, looking for the child, but the girl in the old-fashioned dress had vanished like a ghost. Maybe, in a way, that was what she had been. Just before Grace had noticed the girl she had been thinking about the orphanage, and there were ghosts enough in those memories to haunt a hundred walks. Yet Grace didn't quite believe that. The girl had seemed so real. Almost *too* real. As if everything else Grace had seen that day—the hospital, the city, her own apartment—had been the apparitions, and among them all only the girl in the archaic clothes had been solid and true. Besides, if the child had been a phantasm of memories, why had she spoken of what was to come?

Underwood lifted a hand to check the comb-over plastered with large quantities of pomade to his prematurely balding head. "Take this long to show up again, and I'll be reporting it, Grace."

Just wanting to get away from Underwood and get to work, Grace feigned contrition. "Which one is mine?" she asked.

The doors of the ambulance entrance *whooshed* open. A stretcher hurtled through, propelled by a pair of emergency medical technicians in crisp white uniforms. One of the EMTs shouted for help. Behind them came two Denver police officers, hands on the guns at their hips. On the stretcher, torso smeared with blood, a man writhed in agony.

"I think that's your ticket now, Grace," Underwood said with a noxious smile. "Looks like a nice sucking chest wound. Enjoy."

"Thanks," was all Grace said. She turned her back on Underwood and moved to help with the stretcher.

"What have we got?" she asked one of the EMTs.

"Penetrating trauma from gunshot," he said. "Two entrance wounds, no exits."

Grace grabbed a passing intern. "Get me two units of O-negative and a portable X-ray, and meet me in Trauma Three." The intern sprinted away, and she commandeered another resident and a pair of nurses.

"How did it happen?" Grace asked as they raced down the corridor. One of the police officers, a woman with gray-flecked hair, answered. "The suspect was caught breaking and entering at an antique store on South Broadway. We arrived on scene to see the suspect assailing a woman, the owner. When the suspect wouldn't desist, I brought him down with two shots."

Grace looked up at the officer. "And the owner? Where is she?"

"There," the other officer answered, his boyish face grim. Grace followed his gaze. Across the ED, she saw Leon Arlington push a gurney into an elevator. On it lay a sheet-draped form. Leon nodded in her direction as the elevator doors slid shut.

"The store owner was dead on the scene," the young officer went on. "Her neck was broken, the suspect did it with his bare hands. He's a strong bastard, I'll give him that much. Although why he was breaking into an antique shop, I don't know. There was less cash on the premises than in a convenience store."

"Maybe he's a collector," Grace said. She shook her head. "All right. We'll take it from here."

Moments later, wearing sterile gowns, Grace, resident, and nurses wheeled the stretcher into the trauma room. On her count they lifted the patient onto the table. Within seconds the nurses had taped electrical leads to his chest, started an IV drip, and had a catheter in him.

Grace took her first good look at the patient. He was a white male, late twenties, curiously groomed and affluent-looking for a typical break-in suspect. However, she didn't care who he was. He was wounded, that was all that mattered now. With instinctual speed she assessed his condition. He was cyanotic, his flesh tinged blue. Pink froth bubbled from the holes in his chest. Probable pneumothorax. The intern rushed into the trauma room. Grace took the two units of blood from him, hung them, then glanced at the other resident. "Intubate him."

He nodded and guided a plastic breathing tube down the patient's trachea. Grace made an incision beneath the armpit, inserted a chest tube, and attached it to a vacuum bottle. Blood and fluid bubbled into the bottle. Grace and the others stepped back as the intern positioned the X-ray arm over the table, then moved in again after he swung the unit aside and continued their work to stabilize the patient.

"I've got the film," one of the nurses said minutes later.

Grace straightened, and the nurse held up the X-ray for her. Grace's own gloved hands were now smeared with blood. She glanced at the image on the film, then frowned. "What is *this*?"

The two slugs showed up on the X-ray as white dots. One was lodged next to the right lung. The other was situated dangerously close to the descending aorta, had perhaps nicked it. However, Grace noticed these only in passing. For just left of center in the patient's chest was another white blot, except this one was huge, as big as a fist, and rough-edged. It lay directly in front of his heart.

"Your guess is as good as mine," the nurse said. "But something tells me this isn't his first chest wound."

Grace pushed aside the X-ray and glanced back at the patient. The other nurse had cleaned away most of the blood. Now the two gunshot wounds stared upward like angry red eyes. In between them, down the center of his chest, ran a jagged line of pink scar tissue. The scar looked barely healed. Grace studied again the white blotch on the X-ray. Only metal would show up that clearly.

"It's almost like he's got some huge chunk of shrapnel in his thoracic cavity," she said. She had seen a lot of strange things in the ED—an attempted suicide who drove himself to the hospital with a bullet lodged in his cerebral cortex, a woman complaining of heartburn who gave birth to twins, a girl with a piece of grass growing from a seed that had taken root in her eyeball—but this had to be the strangest. How could a man live with a piece of metal that big in his chest? And how did it get there in the first place?

A monitor beeped. "Pressure is fifty and dropping," the other nurse called out. "I think we're losing him."

Grace called for a syringe of epinephrine and injected it into the IV tubing. A second later the patient's eyes flew open. He screamed and arched his back off the table, hands clenched into claws.

"Get him down!" Grace shouted. "Get him down *now*!"

It took all of them to hold the man on the table. Convulsion after convulsion wracked his body, and he mumbled something in a ragged voice.

". . . sin . . . have to find . . . *Sinfath* . . ."

"What's he saying?" the intern asked.

"I've lost his pulse!" a nurse shouted.

The patient stiffened, then his eyes fluttered shut, and he fell limp. The intern grabbed defibrillator paddles from the crash cart and handed them to Grace. She rubbed them together to spread the conductive gel, then placed them on the man's chest. The defibrillator whined as the charge built up.

"Everyone clear!"

The patient's body jerked as the electric charge surged through him, then went still. Grace glanced at the monitor. Only a few erratic spikes broke the flat green line. She shocked him again, and again. No response.

"All right, let's crack him," she ordered. "I'm going to massage his heart."

Grace grabbed a scalpel and made a deep incision in the left side of the man's chest. She took a stainless steel rib-spreader from the intern and in one deft motion opened him up. Without being told, a nurse positioned a suction tube and cleared away excess blood so Grace could see. Grace reminded herself to compliment her coworkers. They were top-notch and deserved to know it. She reached into the thoracic cavity, deftly moved aside the left lung, then plunged her hand deeper, toward the sac that contained the man's heart.

Her fingers closed around something hard, rough, and bitterly cold. With a hiss of pain she snatched her hand back. It felt as if she had just touched a lump of dry ice.

"What is it?" the other resident asked.

Grace shook her head and cradled her hand. "I don't . . . I don't know."

She shook her hand, then picked up a retractor and pulled back the left lung. The suction tube gurgled and drained away the blood in the patient's chest so that all could see what lay within.

Grace stared in perfect shock.

"Oh, God . . ." one of the nurses breathed, while the other clamped a hand to her mouth to stifle a scream.

"Jesus, what is *that*?" the intern said, his eyes wide.

Grace worked her jaw, unable to form words. She could only gaze at the fist-shaped lump of metal that lay in the center of the man's chest, exactly where his heart should have been. The monitor beeped frantically, then let out a piercing whine.

The suspect was dead.

11.

It was getting late.

About an hour ago the tide in the ED had finally turned, and after that more patients were wheeled out the doors than were wheeled in. The throng of wounded dwindled to a scattering of people waiting to be seen for minor injuries, and the roar of anger and pain faded to a patient murmur. Somewhere, far down a corridor, an infant cried. It was a weak and forlorn sound, and along with it drifted the weary music of a woman's lullaby.

We are born to this. To life, and to hurt. Grace sighed and gripped a chipped mug with both hands. Ripples shivered across the brown surface of the coffee within. Circles spreading to nowhere, containing nothing, vanishing when they struck the boundary that imprisoned them. Maybe that was all they were, ripples on a pond. Maybe she was foolish to try to fight.

"Dr. Beckett . . . ?"

Grace jerked her head up. A police officer sat in the chair opposite her, a concerned expression on his face. "I was asking you a question about the suspect, Dr. Beckett."

She blinked. "Yes, of course, I'm so sorry. Please go on."

"Did the suspect say anything that might help us in learning his identity? Did he mention a name? Or a place he might have come from?"

Grace concentrated, thought back to the urgent chaos in the trauma room, then shook her head. "I'm afraid not. For a minute he did mumble something, but I couldn't understand what it was. I'm not even certain it was English. It might have been something about *sin* or *sinning*."

The officer nodded and scribbled on a notepad. "We'll run his fingerprints through the system, but any additional information could help narrow down the search. Did he say anything else you could make out? Anything at all?"

Grace shook her head again. She watched as he jotted down a few more notes. Officer John Erwin, read the tag on his blue shirt. He was middle-aged, with kind brown eyes. He and several other police officers had arrived at the hospital not long after the happenings in Trauma Three, called in by the original two officers. Erwin had explained it was standard procedure to file a report on how the suspect had died, and—he had paused here—to describe any unusual circumstances associated with that death. At first Grace had been nervous, but Erwin had sat her down, pushed a mug of coffee into her hands, and with his considerate manner had put her at ease.

Earlier, Morty Underwood had done just the opposite.

Not long after she had sewn up the body of the John Doe and had sent it down to the morgue, she had rounded a corner to find herself face-to-face with the Chief Resident. His comb-over flew above his head, and his expression was one of panic. He had just gotten out of a meeting with the chief of the ED. The hospital's management had decided it was necessary to keep the *incident* with the police suspect quiet. Everyone remembered the *incident* at another hospital a few years back, when toxic fumes emitted by a woman's blood had nearly asphyxiated a half-dozen hospital workers. Some people had gone so far as to suggest she had been an extraterrestrial alien. Denver Memorial Hospital did not want that kind of publicity. Things like that happened in tabloids, not here. A detailed autopsy would certainly reveal a more mundane explanation for the patient's condition. Until then, no one—including Grace—was to say anything about the *incident* to any-one.

Incident. Grace was rapidly getting sick of that word. This hadn't been just an *incident. Incidents* were things to be written up, filed away, and forgotten. But this had been *real*. She had seen inside the man's chest. There had been no living, beating human heart there. Instead there had been only a metallic lump—she had touched it with her own hand. Yet somehow that thing had worked to pump blood through the man's body. They had detected the pulse. If the story did make the tabloids, then the headlines would be exactly and terribly right. The man had a heart of iron.

She had run a hand through her hair, her words scathing. "What do you want me to do when the police ask me why their suspect died, Morty? Lie to them?"

Morty had said nothing, and had fidgeted with the collar of his shirt instead. It was clear from his expression this was exactly what he wanted.

She had stared at him in genuine amazement. "Do you actually enjoy being a worm, Morty?"

He had assumed a self-important air. "Whether I enjoy it or not isn't important. It's my job."

Grace had taken that opportunity to accidentally step on his toes. While he clutched his foot she had made her escape. And she had told Officer Erwin everything, just as it had happened. It seemed impossible, even absurd, but she knew what she had seen. While some people could deny the truth in order to protect their small minds from any-thing that might expand them beyond the comfortable and ordinary, Grace was not one of those people.

Nor, she suspected, was Officer Erwin. He asked her several more questions, and while he raised his eyebrows more than once at her answers, he did not express any doubt that she was telling the truth. He shut his notepad and slipped the pen into a pocket.

"Thanks for your help, Dr. Beckett." He fell silent and gazed into space. Finally he turned his eyes back toward her, his words quiet. "We think we have it all figured out. But we don't, do we? We're not even close."

A shiver coursed up Grace's spine. She had no answer for that.

Erwin stood. "I'm going to talk to the nurses who assisted you, Dr. Beckett. If you don't mind, that is."

Grace thought of Morty Underwood's puffy, anxious face. "Be my guest." She lifted the mug. "And thanks for the coffee."

"I bet it's cold by now."

"I don't mind."

Officer Erwin grinned, then moved away across the ED's admitting area. Grace sipped the cold coffee, and though she wouldn't have thought it possible then, she found herself smiling. Then her smile faltered, the small hairs of her neck prickled, and she looked up.

After a moment she saw him. He stood some distance down one of the hallways that led from Admitting, watching her. Dark suit, dark hair. He leaned against a wall in a casual, elegant posture. How long had he been there? For a moment his deep-set eyes locked on hers. His gaze was searching, as if he wanted something of her.

Curious—or was it compelled?—Grace started to rise from her chair. Just then a gurney rattled by and blocked her view. A moment later the gurney passed through a doorway. Grace looked back down the hall. It was empty. The dark-haired man was gone. She sank back into her chair and clutched the coffee mug. Maybe the man hadn't been watching her after all, maybe he had been waiting for someone else.

Maybe, but she doubted it.

12.

Leon Arlington liked his job.

In fact, he liked it a lot. Leon always had been a night person, so he didn't mind the late hours. And with its thick cement walls, the place was nice and quiet, which made it good for thinking. Leon liked thinking, too. He thought about lots of things while he worked down in the cool silence of the morgue. Things like, how long it would take to walk to the moon, if you really could walk there? And what was the best kind of tree? And if he could drink just one drink for the rest of his life, would it be water or Mello Yello? Hoo boy, that was a good one. He still hadn't figured that out yet.

But the biggest reason Leon liked his job was simple: Dead folk gave him no trouble. No trouble at all. He had worked plenty of other jobs where he had had to deal with living people. They were always wanting something different from what he gave them, or telling him how to do things he already knew, or acting like he was stupid just because he was slow and quiet and didn't easily get mad. Too often in this world people mistook fast for smart, loud for important, and angry for righteous. But Leon knew the difference. Beside, the customers here didn't care what pace he did things at.

Whistling a tuneless song, Leon adjusted the plastic sheet that covered a cadaver lying in an open body drawer. He had to make certain there were no gaps in the wrapping. The morticians hated it when the corpses dried out. Leon wasn't sure why. Maybe it made it harder to paint the makeup on them for the funeral. That was something else to think about. He paused to regard the old woman in the stainless-steel drawer. With her blue-gray skin and white hair it looked almost like she was frozen in a piece of ice rather than wrapped in clear plastic. It made him think of a story he had read as a child, a story about the queen of Snow. Only the queen had been cruel, and she had imprisoned a little kid in her palace of ice.

Leon slid the drawer shut and shivered. That was the one real problem with this job—it was too damn cold down here sometimes. The chill radiated from the bank of drawers and soaked into the floor and walls, where it lingered like permafrost. The cold had never bothered Leon in the past, but this last year he had noticed it creeping deeper into his joints and bones, like something hungry and alive. Maybe one of these days he would have to get a different job. Something warmer.

He rubbed his lean hands together for heat and turned to see to his next customer. The naked corpse lay on its back on a stainless steel table—white male, late twenties, in good physical shape. Leon picked up a clipboard and checked his notes. That's right. This was the John Doe the police had shot before bringing in. They had cracked this one's chest open, but the wound was neatly closed up now. Leon recognized the precise stitches that bound together the two raw edges of flesh. Even when they were dead, she always took care in what she did to them. This had been Grace Beckett's patient.

Leon grabbed a pen and made notes concerning the corpse's condition: height, weight, appearance, the locations of the two bullet entry wounds. He turned the body over, then noticed a small tattoo on the underside of the John Doe's forearm. He bent closer. No, it wasn't a tattoo, but a brand. The puckered scar tissue formed a symbol:

It wasn't anything Leon recognized, although it did make him think of some sort of religious sign. If it *was* from a religion, then it had to be a crazy one to brand its disciples like cattle. Leon shook his head at the sorry state of the world, then turned the corpse back over and scribbled some more on his clipboard. A moment later he halted and frowned.

"Now, I thought I already shut your peepers."

The cadaver only gazed upward with unseeing eyes. Leon snapped on a fresh pair of latex gloves and closed the corpse's eyelids. Staring was one impertinence he did not tolerate of dead people. He made a few last notes, then prepared the cadaver for storage. Leon had it down to a system these days. Toe tag, plastic bag, then into the deep freeze.

"You were a healthy boy, now weren't you?" he grunted as he wrangled the heavy corpse from table to drawer. Sometimes the bodies seemed to fight him in this, as if they did not want to be shut away in the dark, as if they wanted to hold on to the lighted world for a little while longer. Mostly, though, it was just rigor mortis and the slippery plastic that made it so hard. At last Leon succeeded. He leaned on the open drawer to catch his breath. Maybe he really was getting too old for this job. He supposed he could go work at his cousin Benny's upholstery shop. It sure would be warmer, and he wouldn't have to talk to customers if he didn't want to, not if he stuck to the shop's back room. Besides, Benny owed him a favor. He resolved to call his cousin in the morning, then started to slide the drawer shut.

The cadaver stared up at him through the clear plastic sheet.

Leon halted. "What the hell . . . ?" he whispered. He was sure he had closed them this time. But the corpse's dull eyes were wide-open. Leon shuddered, the damn chill again. He leaned over the drawer and bent down for a closer look, to be sure he wasn't mistaken. His breath fogged on the plastic as he gazed into the dead man's eyes.

A hand punched through the clear sheet, reached up from the drawer, and closed around Leon's throat. Leon tried to struggle, tried to scream, but the grip on his throat was far too tight: He could not break it. Even as his mind fought to understand what was happening, his lungs started to burn for want of air. Bright pinpricks exploded in his brain like fireworks. Somehow he managed to look down at the cadaver. His gaze locked with that of the dead man in the drawer, and in those dull eyes he saw . . . evil. It was a malevolence so vast, so deep, that suddenly he knew it was ancient beyond all reckoning. In that second, Leon Arlington understood everything. A darkness was coming. His very last thought was of how cold he felt, how awfully cold. Then, with terrible strength, the dead fingers tightened around his throat.

The sound of snapping bones echoed off the hard tiles.

13.

Grace drained the last of the coffee, then stared at the bottom of her empty mug. Despite the sense of disconnection she had felt earlier that day, she thought maybe she could return to her apartment after all. Maybe she could curl up with a blanket on her futon and fall asleep to the drone of late-night TV, and when she woke in the morning, things wouldn't seem so strange, so alien, and so like she didn't belong.

Grace rose and headed for the break room to rinse out the coffee mug. Along the way she nodded to Officer Erwin. He stood at one of the nurses' stations and talked with the intern who had assisted Grace earlier. Erwin nodded in reply. Nearby, Morty Underwood looked on with a sour expression and fumbled as he tried to unwrap a roll of antacid tablets. Grace did not resist the small wave of satisfaction she felt as she continued past.

She was halfway across the admitting area when the elevator let out a chime. Afterward, she was never quite certain what made her pause and turn to stare as the elevator doors slid open. Maybe it was that, in the back of her mind, the chime sounded almost like a death knell. She watched transfixed as the doors rolled to either side, like an opening eye turned on its side. A figure stood inside the elevator, silhouetted by fluorescent light. Grace blinked against the sterile glare. The sounds of the ED receded into the distance, yet her pulse throbbed in her ears, mixed with the thrum of a hundred other heartbeats, as if the very air had become a stethoscope transmitting the life and sudden fear of all those around her. The figure stepped out of the elevator.

It was him. The man she had pronounced dead three hours ago. He was naked, his skin mushroom pale. Black blood oozed between the stitches that bound the wound in his chest. His eyes stared forward with dead intensity. Then, with mindless deliberation, the man with the iron heart walked forward, his bare feet slapping against the tile floor.

Sound rushed back into the ED. Screams sliced the air in all directions as people scrambled to get out of the dead man's way. One EMT was too slow. The dead man thrust out a hand, and the EMT was hurled to one side. He slid a dozen feet along the floor before he struck a bank of chairs. He twitched but did not get up. Morty Underwood stood only a few feet from the crumpled form of the EMT, but the Chief Resident did not even glance at the fallen man. Fear twisted his mealy face. He tossed aside a handful of papers in a multicolored flurry and turned to flee the admitting area. The dead man walked on, headed for the main entrance of the ED. Grace backed up against a wall. She knew she should run, but it was a dull knowledge, and could not connect with the nerves and muscles of her limbs. The coffee mug slipped from numb fingers and shattered against the floor with a sound like breaking bones.

A dark blue blur moved past her. Erwin. The police officer approached the dead man, one hand held out before him while the other reached for the gun at his hip.

"Just stop right there—" Erwin began.

He never got any further. The corpse shot out a hand, contacted Erwin's forehead, and thrust the officer backward with brutal force. Erwin's skull struck the wall an arm's length away from Grace. There was a sharp noise, like a firecracker exploding. Then, as if all his bones had turned to jelly, Erwin slid to the floor. His head left a trail of gore on the green paint.

The walking corpse did not pause. Staring forward with hideous calm, he continued toward the automatic doors and passed within five steps of Grace. A paralyzing odor rose from his body: the foul reek of congealed blood and the sweet taint of decay.

It was the smell of death.

The admitting area was virtually empty now. Most had fled, although a few people peered out of side corridors in dread fascination. The EMT had crawled away. Only Grace and the fallen officer did not move. Then, along with the damp *flop-flop* of the dead man's feet, another sound drifted on the stifling air: a metallic creak accompanied by a fearful muttering. Grace cast her gaze over the room in search of the sound's source.

In front of the ED's automatic doors, a white-haired woman in a bathrobe struggled with her wheelchair. One of the wheels was stuck and would not turn. With arthritic fingers she tugged at the brake, then tried again. The wheelchair spun in a slow circle but did not move forward. Confused by its proximity, the automatic doors slid open, then shut, then open again, as if wracked by silent, spastic laughter. The woman looked up, and fear touched her faded eyes. Her wheelchair stood directly between the dead man and the doors.

He was going to kill her. The dead man would not move to one side, would not go around her. Instead, he would destroy anything that lay in his path. That was the nature of this . . . creation. Grace knew it—knew it with strange and perfect certainty. But then, this was not the first time she had come face-to-face with evil.

In that fractured moment, Grace made a decision. She could not allow this thing to do whatever it was it had been made to do. The naked man bore down on the wheelchair. The woman had stopped struggling and now simply gazed at the approaching corpse. Like all the very old, she knew the Angel of Death when she saw It coming.

With dreamlike calm, Grace knelt beside Erwin, unbuckled the leather holster at the dead officer's hip, and pulled out the revolver. She stood, turned, and pointed. The gun seemed an extension of her arm.

The dead man reached for the old woman. Grace did not hesitate. She squeezed the trigger and called down the thunder. The dead man jerked and arched his back, as if struck a blow by an unseen enemy. A wet blossom appeared on his right temple. He took a staggering step forward. Grace pulled the trigger again. Light and sound shattered the air like crystal. The corpse's arms flew out to either side, the wings of a weird bird trying to take flight. Again she fired, and again. With the last shot the entire right side of the man's skull exploded. Dark fluid stained the old woman's face, and she watched in dull amazement as Death died before her.

The man with the iron heart toppled to the floor. For a minute he convulsed violently, legs jerking, hands scrabbling at the tiles. Then he went still. One last trickle of blood oozed from his chest before the flow ceased. Even this thing needed a brain to function. It was over.

Her back against the wall, Grace slid to the floor and crouched beside the dead police officer. No, that wasn't right. It wasn't over. Somehow she sensed it was just the opposite. She leaned her cheek against the wall, cradled the gun against her chest, and gazed into Erwin's peaceful, empty eyes. The words whispered by the purple-eyed girl in the park drifted once more in her mind, and with them came a strangely exultant sensation.

Yes, a darkness was coming.

Excited voices sounded around her. People rushed into the admitting area now. Two police officers knelt by Erwin and swore as they examined him. Grace did not look their way. Instead, her gaze was drawn to the floor before her, to the shards of the broken coffee mug. A faint smile of wonder touched her lips. So sometimes the containing circle could be broken after all, and the ripples sent free.

14.

It wasn't until he saw the revival tent glowing in the distance that Travis realized where he was going.

How long he stumbled through the night after fleeing the destruction at the Magician's Attic he didn't know. Perhaps it was minutes, perhaps hours. For a time the keening of sirens echoed in the distance. Then the blocky shapes of Castle City shrank behind him, and his boots scuffed against weathered asphalt. After that there was only darkness and the hiss of the wind.

As he walked, he rubbed his right hand—the hand Jack had clasped just before everything had gone mad. It still throbbed, but now the pain had dwindled to a swarm of pinpricks, like the aftereffects of an electrical shock. Travis remembered the fierce light that had blazed in

Jack's usually kind blue eyes. *You are our hope now*, he had said, and even more mysteriously, *Forgive me, my friend*. Travis didn't know what to make of those words. None of this made any sense. All he knew was that his best friend in the world was quite possibly dead.

Through his sheepskin coat he felt the small, heavy lump of the iron box. What did it contain? Whatever it was, it couldn't possibly be worth all that had happened. Or could it? After all, Jack had told him to keep the box safe—no doubt from the people who were after him, the people who had broken into the antique shop and had set it ablaze. Except, now that he thought about it, Travis wasn't so certain it *had* been people who had attacked the Magician's Attic. At least not any sort of people he knew. He saw again the silhouette he had glimpsed for a fleeting second. So tall, so thin, moving with eerie grace. It might all have been a trick of the light, but even the light itself had seemed *wrong*. Too bright, too piercing. Travis shook his head. He had so many questions and no place to go for answers.

His boots ground against the pavement as he slowed to a halt. For a moment he considered returning to the light and warmth of the Mine Shaft. But that wasn't possible, was it? Maybe they were following him, the beings in the light. What would happen if he led them back to the crowded saloon?

Travis shivered inside his coat. He supposed it was midnight by now. Far below, the lights of Castle City gleamed in the mountain dark, beautiful as stars, and as utterly unreachable. His eyes traveled up the desolate stretch of highway, and for a moment he wondered if maybe he had been following the road back to his cabin, with its drafty log walls and leaking roof—if maybe he had been going home. Yet even as the thought occurred to him, he knew it was not so. He did not belong there any more than he belonged amid the lights shining in the valley below. Somehow, during the course of that night, Travis had stepped outside the boundaries of his usual world—he had gone beyond the pale—and he did not know how he would ever return. It was the loneliest feeling he had ever known.

"I'm afraid, Jack," he whispered, but the words turned to fog on the cold air and melted away.

He turned to continue on, and that was when he saw it, beside the highway not far ahead. The old-fashioned circus tent. Golden light spilled from the half-open entrance flap and through rents in the canvas to give the big top the aspect of a great, grinning jack-o'-lantern. Travis stared for a long moment. Then, before he even knew what he was doing, he started walking toward the tent. But the man in black had gazed into the darkness gathering on the horizon with knowing eyes, and Travis had nowhere else to go.

As he drew closer to the tent, he passed the blotchy white school bus he had seen earlier. Parked beside it was a motley collection of vehicles, ranging from pickups and rusted-out station wagons to suburban minivans and gleaming sports cars. Travis hesitated a moment before the entrance. Did he really think he would find answers here?

There was only one way to find out. He took a deep breath, then plunged into the golden light beyond.

15.

Despite the lateness of the hour, *Brother Cy's Apocalyptic Traveling Salvation Show* was in full swing.

The first thing Travis noticed was that the tarnished light came, not from electric bulbs, but from punched-tin lanterns suspended below the canvas ceiling. A haze of smoke hung on the air like an atmosphere of mystery. To either side of the entrance hulked a bank of wooden bleachers. A scattering of people sat upon the splintery planks, perhaps two dozen in all. It was an unlikely mélange. A walleyed trucker in faded flannel kicked up his battered boots, smoking a cigarette. Nearby, a woman in a smart blue business suit perched on her bench like a stiff bird. Beyond her, an old blind man in thrift-store garb leaned forward on his rattan cane, head bowed, listening. Sitting in the front row was a young woman—barely more than a girl—clad in a nylon coat of dirty sky blue with matted fake fur around the neck, a small child clutched on her lap. The young woman's thin face was tightly drawn—in weariness, and perhaps in trepidation—but the child stared around him with wide eyes, a look of wonder on his grubby cherub's face.

Feeling conspicuous, Travis found a vacant place and sat down. He lifted his head, and that was when he saw him.

The man in black.

Or Brother Cy, for that was certainly his name, and this was most certainly his traveling revival show. The preacher prowled on a stage opposite the bleachers, clad in that same black coffin suit, and paused now and then to thump a bony fist on a podium that looked as though farm animals had drunk out of it in its last incarnation. He had taken off his broad-brimmed pastor's hat to expose a phrenologist's dream of a cranium. With a start, Travis realized the rich music he had heard rising and falling on the smoky air was in fact Brother Cy's magnificent, terrible, honeyed-rasp voice, preaching up a storm.

". . . and you, my friends, you who lurk in your comfortable tract houses," Brother Cy thundered with as much spit as volume, "believing yourselves protected from all harm, wallowing in your reclining chairs, drinking your six-packs of beer, and prostrating yourselves before the altar of television. You are in for a surprise, my friends." The podium shuddered under his fist, and his eyebrows bristled like black caterpillars. "For whether you live in a hilltop mansion or a river bottom shack, it will find you just as easy and knock upon your door. For I say to you again—there is a darkness coming!"

"Amen!" a smattering of voices said, and there was even one faint "Hallelujah!" Brother Cy grinned, fire lighting the pits of his eyes, as if it had been an affirmation a thousand voices strong. But he was not finished yet.

"It creeps nearer every day, this darkness—every hour, every minute. But have any of you seen its coming? Have you felt it, like a shadow falling across your soul?" He shook his head, perhaps in sorrow, perhaps disgust. "No, you have not! You have turned your eyes inward, you have shut your ears, and you have drowned yourself in the petty comforts of your material possessions." He thrust his arms out to either side, and his voice vaulted to a crescendo. "I say, is there not even one among you who has dared to gaze into the heart of the approaching dark?"

Two dozen faces stared at Brother Cy, fearful, entranced. Then one tremulous voice rose on the smoky air.

"I . . . I have."

It was the young woman who held the child.

Brother Cy gazed down at her for a protracted moment, like he was judging her with those black-marble eyes. Then he stepped off the stage and moved to her with his scarecrow gait. He cupped a long hand beneath her fragile chin and lifted it until her look was lost in his.

"So you have, child," he said in a secret voice. "So you have." They remained that way for a long moment, as if some unheard conversation passed between them. Then he leaped back onto the stage and pounded the podium until its sides bowed.

"Are you not ashamed?" Brother Cy said. "Here before you sits one with a tiny child, who is little more than a child herself, pitiable and full of fear. Yet she has found the strength to do what the rest of you have not, to lift up her eyes and stare into the very heart of shadow!"

The spectators shifted on the hard bleachers.

"Yes, I see the truth now," Brother Cy said. "There are disbelievers among us tonight, aren't there? You know who you are." He thrust out a skeletal finger and swept it over the audience. When the accusing appendage pointed toward Travis, it seemed to pause. Travis squirmed in his seat, and he felt naked. Then Brother Cy's finger moved on past him.

"It seems I lack the power to convince all of you disbelievers," the preacher said. "However, you are fortunate, for there is another here tonight who sees this darkness more clearly than anyone else. And with her is one who understands its nature far better than I." Brother Cy thrust a hand toward a side curtain of moth-eaten velvet and bowed like a macabre facsimile of a game-show host. "May I introduce to you Sister Mirrim and Child Samanda!"

The curtain parted, and onto the stage stepped a woman and a girl. They approached Brother Cy hand in hand, and Travis had the sense that it was not the woman who led the girl but rather the reverse. Both wore heavy dresses of black wool that contrasted with their moon-pale skin. However, there the similarity ended, for the woman's hair was wild and fiery, and she gazed forward with distant green eyes, a stricken cast to her otherwise impassive visage, as if she looked upon some far-off place, while the girl's hair was raven dark, and her purple eyes seemed far too knowing for the angelic cameo of her face.

Brother Cy stood behind woman and girl, and encompassed but did not touch them with the half circle of his arms. "Sister Mirrim is possessed of great and unusual sight," he said in a stage whisper. "Would you have her see for you now?" He held up a silencing hand. "Wait! Before you answer, know that what Sister Mirrim sees may be good or ill, and in these times I say of the two it is far more likely to be ill she will glimpse. But then, from knowledge of evil can come great good, for those who dare to listen. Do any of you so dare?"

A chorus of affirmation rose from the bleachers.

"So be it." Brother Cy bent close to Sister Mirrim. "See for us, Sister," he murmured, then retreated. Sister Mirrim stood at the fore of the stage, her hands resting like frail doves on the small shoulders of Child Samanda, who stood quietly before her. At last Sister Mirrim spoke, and as she did her eyes grew more distant yet, gazing on things no other within the tent could glimpse.

"It comes from a place far distant," she began in a chantlike voice. "Yet in that distance lies no protection. For I can see it growing now, sending forth dark shoots, and digging down dark roots, drinking a world to make it strong. And when it has drunk that world dry, and all that is left is ash and bone, it shall lift its gaze in this direction, and it shall slake its thirst upon this unwary world." Her voice rose, shrill now. "Can you not see it? The birds of night have taken wing. Their pale master wakes, and his heart is colder than winter. Where are the Stonebreaker and the Blademender? I cannot see them yet. But there is something more, something darker still, a shadow behind the shadow." She shook her head. "I cannot . . . I cannot quite . . ." Her voice was galvanized by panic, and the stricken look in her eyes became one of terror. "Alas! Alas! The eye that was blinded sees once more, and all is blackened and withered beneath its fiery gaze!"

Sister Mirrim swayed and would have fallen save for Child Samanda, who grasped her arm. In two long strides Brother Cy was beside them to add his own steadying grip to the fire-haired woman's shoulders.

A cracked voice rose from the audience.

"I've seen them, too."

It was the blind man. He lifted his wrinkled sockets toward the stage.

Although his voice was low, Brother Cy's words pierced the stillness of the tent. "What have you seen?"

"The dark birds." The old man gripped his cane. "I ain't seen a thing since I was a boy, but I seen them of late, flying before my eyes, like blacker patches of black on the black I always see. And . . ." His voice dropped to whisper. ". . . and I seen him as well."

Brother Cy watched him with interest, and the old man shifted in discomfort, as if he could feel the force of the preacher's gaze.

"Who have you seen?" Brother Cy asked.

"Him," the blind man said, and his knuckles went white around the cane. "The pale one. I saw him once, with the night birds whirling round him, and he was white as snow—or so I'm guessing, as I ain't seen snow in 'most a lifetime—and he shone against the blackness, tall and fierce and wearing a crown of ice, it seemed to me. And he was laughing. Laughing at me." The old man shook his head. "He was something terrible, he was."

The middle-aged woman in the skirt suit stood on the heels of the old man's words. "Is it too late?" She wrung her hands. "Is it already too late for us to do something about the darkness?"

"No," Brother Cy said. "It is never too late, not until the end—and even then, who's to say if all is really over? The darkness approaches, but it is not yet fully here, and if we all do our part, it may never be."

"But what is it?" a voice called out in frustration. "What is this darkness that everyone keeps saying is coming?"

Travis was shocked to realize the voice had been his own. He was standing now. Somehow all this hysteria about doom and darkness had gotten to him.

"That is the question I have been waiting for."

It was not Brother Cy who spoke, but the girl. Her voice was soft, and it lisped slightly, yet there was power in it. The girl stepped forward, and her black-buttoned shoes tapped against the wooden stage like tiny deer hooves. Although her voice addressed the entire gathering, Travis was convinced that her too-knowing gaze was for him only.

"The nature of the darkness is both singular and multifidous," the girl said, and heads nodded, as if the onlookers understood her cryptic words perfectly. "Singular, in that it stems from one deep well. Multifidous, in that each of us must face it in our own way." With a tiny hand she pointed to the audience. "Each of you has a battle to fight. That is why you came here tonight—although there are many, many more such as yourselves. Most of your battles will be small ones, yet that does not mean they are not important. For that is how this war will be won or lost, by a thousand little battles, each fought by one person standing alone against the darkness—or surrendering to it."

"But how will we know our battle when it comes?" the trucker asked.

A secret smile touched Child Samanda's rosebud lips. "You will know," was all she said.

With that, the revival was over.

"Thank you all for coming," Brother Cy said with a dismissing sweep of his arms. "Do not forget the seeings of Sister Mirrim or the words of Child Samanda. And do not forget to consider a small donation—a pittance that will allow us to bring our message to others like yourselves—as you depart."

Brother Cy leaped from the stage and stood beside the tent's entrance. Seemingly from nowhere, his broad-brimmed pastor's hat appeared in his bony hand, and he thrust it out before him. A few people tossed in a handful of change or a crumpled bill as they shuffled past. Onstage, Child Samanda led Sister Mirrim toward the curtain. As they stepped through a slit in the ratty velvet, Travis caught a fleeting glimpse of a dim space beyond. He blinked, for it seemed to him that a number of figures gathered behind the curtain, tangled in a queer knot of crooked legs, sinuous arms, and curved swan necks. One of them, a young man—or was he old?—peered back at Travis with nut-brown eyes. Something sprouted from his forehead, something that looked almost like . . . antlers? Then the gap in the curtain closed. Sister Mirrim and Child Samanda were gone. Travis supposed it was all simply a trick of smoke and shadows, yet he found himself thinking of Waunita Lost Owl's *delgeth* all the same.

He realized then he was the only one left inside the tent except for Brother Cy. He hurried to the exit. Avoiding the preacher's piercing gaze, he dug into the pocket of his jeans, found a creased five-dollar bill, and dropped it in the hat.

"Thank you, son."

Travis said nothing. Head down, he reached for the canvas flap covering the exit.

"Your battle will be harder than most, son, if you choose to fight it."

Travis turned around and laughed. It was a hollow sound. He rubbed his right hand. "You mean I have a choice?"

A knife-edged grin cut across the craggy landscape of Brother Cy's face. "Why, we all have a choice, son. Haven't you heard one word I've been saying? That's what this is all about."

Travis shook his head. "But what if I choose the wrong thing?"

"What if you choose the *right* thing?"

"How will I know?" Travis said. "Sometimes I don't even know right from left. How can I possibly choose?"

Lamplight gleamed off Brother Cy's eyes. "Ah, but you have to, son. Light or dark. Sanity or madness. Life or death. Those are our choices, those are the battles we must fight."

Travis tried to absorb these words. Was there more to Brother Cy than he had guessed? Without really thinking, he reached into the breast pocket of his coat and drew out the iron box Jack had given him. He held it toward the preacher.

"You know, I think the man who gave this to me saw the same darkness you do. Maybe . . . maybe it would be better if you took it."

Brother Cy laughed, a great booming sound. Then his laughter fell short, and his stony face went grim. He took a step backward, as if loath to so much as touch the box. "No, son. That which you carry is not for the likes of me. It is your burden to bear now, and no other's."

Travis sighed. He had been afraid the preacher would say something like that. There was nothing more for him here. He slipped the box back into his coat pocket and opened the tent flap.

"Wait, son!" Brother Cy said. "You need a token, something to bolster your faith, something to remember when all seems too dark, and home seems too far away." He reached into his hat, pulled out a small and shiny object, and pressed it into Travis's hand. It felt cool against his hot skin.

"Thanks," Travis said, unsure what else to say. "And I hope you stop your darkness, whatever it is."

"It's not my darkness, son. It belongs to all of us."

In a disconcerting instant, the smoky world of the tent was replaced by one of empty gloom. Travis gasped. He stood outside the revival tent now, although he did not remember stepping through the door. He lifted his hand and uncurled his fingers. On his palm lay a silvery half circle. It was a coin, or rather a piece of one, for it was broken along a rough edge. There was a picture on each side of the coin, and he tried to make them out in the cast-off radiance of the revival tent, but could not.

All at once, like a lightbulb switching off, the tent went black and left Travis alone in the cold night.

16.

Travis slipped the half-coin into the pocket of his jeans and started walking, although he had no idea where he was walking to. The crescent moon had gone behind a cloud, and the road seemed to lead only from darkness into darkness. His boots beat a lonely rhythm on the pavement.

He had gone only a short distance when, without warning, the fabric of night was riven by brilliant light.

Travis spun around, held a hand before his eyes, and squinted against the white hot glare. The world had fallen silent except for an electric hum that vibrated on the air. It raised the hairs on his arms and neck, like a harbinger of lightning. How had they found him? But it was not so hard to understand. If they had not found what they were seeking at the Magician's Attic, they would have kept searching. And there was only one road out of Castle City. This road.

For a moment he stood frozen, an animal caught in a fatal headlight snare. He caught a glint of crimson and glanced down. The stiletto Jack had given him was still tucked into his belt, and the gem in its hilt glowed bloodred. He jerked his head back up. The brilliant light floated down the highway. At last fear broke through his paralysis. Travis turned and ran headlong into the night. His lungs caught fire. He ignored the pain, leaned his head down, and ran faster yet.

A rectangle loomed in the dark before him and brought him up short. He skidded to a halt and barely managed to avoid colliding with the thing. It was the old billboard. He stared at the back side now, for he had come upon it from the opposite direction than before. The webwork of posts that supported the flat plane looked like bones in the gloom. Urged by a compulsion he could not name, he moved around the billboard to gaze upon the front. Just then, in the sky above, wind tore a cloud to tatters, and the horned moon broke free. Its light drifted down to illuminate the face of the billboard. Travis gasped.

The cigarette advertisement was gone. In its place, fully revealed now, was the picture of the wild landscape. Before, when Travis had glimpsed a fraction of the picture through the overlying ad, it had seemed to depict a daylit scene, yet it was a night land that covered the billboard now. Mountains rose into a star-sprinkled sky, like a crown perched above the endless forest, and everything was dusted with a pearly sheen, as if the light of the moon above fell somehow too upon it. There was a beauty about the landscape that was both fresh and ancient, as though it had stood unspoiled for countless eons, waiting to be seen.

In all, the billboard looked just as it had in the 1933 photograph he had seen at the Magician's Attic. Only as he realized this did Travis drop his gaze to the words written at the bottom in flowing script. He concentrated, and after a moment they sorted themselves out:

Find Paradise

And below that, in smaller type:

Brother Cy's Revival, 1 mi. N. of C. City

Laughter rose in Travis's chest. So Brother Cy had been here back in 1933. That knowledge should have shocked him, should have sent him reeling off-balance. Yet, somehow, after all that had happened, it did not. In fact, it all made an absurd sort of sense.

He looked up as something on the billboard caught his eye. No, it wasn't on the billboard, but *in* it—something wispy, like a puff of cotton. Something that was . . . moving.

It was a cloud. It drifted above the brooding mountains, floated from right to left, and passed off the edge of the billboard and vanished. Fascinated, Travis took a step closer. It wasn't just the cloud, he saw now. Everything in the picture was moving. Tiny trees swayed in the wake of an unseen wind, and the silver thread of a waterfall glinted as, from its base, clouds of mist billowed upward. Even the stars were alive, twinkling like real stars, now bright, now dim, now bright again as they wheeled in the sky.

It wasn't a picture on the billboard at all. Somehow it had become a window looking into another—what? Another place? Another time? He thought of Sister Mirrim's words. Another . . . world?

His thoughts were drowned out as sound sizzled on the air, growing louder every second. He turned and saw, over a rise in the road, a white glow. Even as he watched, the glow crested the hill like some terrible dawn. Then he saw them in the center of the light, coming toward him: sinister, spidery figures. Had they seen him yet? Had they recognized him from the Magician's Attic? Travis didn't know, but he couldn't run anymore, he was too tired. Whatever the things in the light were, in seconds they would have him. He wondered if it would take long, and whether it would be very painful.

"I'm sorry, Jack," he said. He clutched the iron box through the thick fabric of his coat. "I'm sorry I let you down. But there's nowhere left to . . ."

His words trailed off. He turned and stared at the face of the billboard. Maybe that wasn't true, maybe there was somewhere after all. It was impossible, but so had been a dozen other things he had witnessed that night. Maybe it made sense to try something impossible himself.

There was no more time to think—the willowy figures moved toward him with malevolent speed. Travis clenched his jaw. He hesitated only a heartbeat, then he threw himself forward . . .

. . . and fell into the billboard.

17.

"All right, Dr. Beckett, I have just a few more questions for you," the police detective said in a weary voice. He flipped a page of the legal tablet that rested on the cluttered desk before him.

Grace shifted on the hard wooden chair. For the last hour she had sat while the detective took her statement and prompted her for details concerning the deaths at Denver Memorial. Back at the hospital, when a pair of officers had told her they would have to take her to the Denver police station for questioning, Grace had offered no resistance. She had let them pry the gun from her fingers, and was grateful they did not handcuff her as they led her to the patrol car. But the two young officers had been sympathetic, and even admiring, as they bantered in the front seat.

"Bastard didn't have the sense to know he was dead the first time around," one of them had said with a low whistle. "Must have been high on something pretty damn amazing."

"Takes a licking and keeps on ticking," the other had joked.

The first officer had laughed at that. "Not after the doc here took care of him, he wasn't."

The second officer was angry now. "Yeah, she took care of that copkiller real good." He turned around to look at Grace through the intervening grill. "You did the right thing, Doc, taking him out like that. You did the exact right thing."

Grace had only squeezed her eyes shut and saw again the man with the iron heart, the way his head exploded outward in a spray of white, and gray, and brilliant red. She had said nothing. Yes, it had been the right thing to do, but these thick-necked boys playing cops and robbers had no idea of the true and terrible reason why. And she would never tell them. How could she? *I'm sorry, Your Honor, I shot him because he was a creature of perfect evil.* She had a feeling it would not provide much of a defense in a murder trial.

The detective droned on, and Grace listened as best she could. As she often did when nervous, she had drawn her necklace from beneath her blouse and now fidgeted with the pendant. The touch of the cool metal calmed her. It was hard to breathe in the detective's cramped office. The overhead light seemed to leak its dirty illumination only grudgingly, and thick smoke curled from a lit cigarette he had left in an ashtray. She noticed a plastic nameplate amid the litter of his desk. Det. Douglas L. Janson. Something told her people usually called him *Doug.* She could almost imagine a young, handsome, high school year-book version of Detective Janson. But with twenty-five years had come twice that many extra pounds, along with thinning hair and circles beneath his small eyes. A crooked mustache framed his thin mouth, and stubble speckled his jowls like grains of sand.

He gripped a pencil in thick fingers and checked off items on his list with bored efficiency. In measured words Grace responded. No, she had never seen the suspect in the ED before that night. Yes, she had believed the life of the old woman in the wheelchair to be in danger. No, she had not called out to the suspect to halt before she had shot him. Yes, she had shot him exactly four times. Yes, she would do it again if she had to.

At last Detective Janson set down his tablet. "Thank you, Dr. Beckett. I think that's enough." He stood, took his holster from the back of his chair, and slung it over his shoulder. "I've got to confer with my superior for a minute on this, but I doubt we'll be making an arrest, at least for the time being."

Grace gave a jerky nod in reply and felt a jolt of relief. Maybe this night was finally almost over.

Janson promised to return in a few minutes. The detective shut the door behind him. There was a *click* as the lock turned, then the receding sound of his heavy footsteps. Grace glanced at the wall clock. Almost midnight. It had been just six hours. Six short hours since she had encountered the strange girl in the park. Six small notches on the face of the clock, that was all. When the police did release her, she wondered where she would go. Not back to the ED. Knowing what she did now—awakened to the awareness of what things walked the world—she could never again sink into the safe preoccupation that had been her life. Knowledge was perilous, and it changed everything.

The lock on the door rattled. Grace glanced up. She had not expected Janson to return so quickly, nor had she heard his footsteps approaching. The lock continued to rattle, as if the detective was having difficulty getting the key to work, then the dead bolt turned. The door opened and shut again as a man stepped into the office. It was not Detective Douglas L. Janson.

With a start, Grace recognized the dark-haired man. He was the one who had watched her from a distance at the hospital, not long after the man with the iron heart had died. Had died for the first time, that was. Grace started to rise from her chair in alarm, but the man held up a hand to halt her. She was not certain how, but some instinct told her that while this man might be dangerous, he was not her enemy. She sank back down into her chair.

"Who are you?" she asked, surprised at her own calm.

"A friend," he answered.

The man moved away from the door and slipped a thin piece of wire into a pocket. He was tall, middle thirties perhaps. His tailored suit was of European cut, and his visage made her think of a bust of a Roman general: curly hair, proud nose, full and sensual lips. When he spoke, it was in a cultured voice from which an expensive education had purged all but the faintest traces of an indeterminate accent.

"You are in danger here," the man said in a grave voice.

Grace sighed and thought of the girl in the park. She had had enough mysterious admonitions for one day. "I'm afraid I don't take cryptic warnings from strangers anymore," she said.

The hint of a smile played across his lips. "I apologize, Dr. Beckett. In my urgency to warn you, I have neglected to introduce myself. A regrettable oversight. I hope it has not predisposed you toward suspicion." He held out a hand. "My name is Farr. Hadrian Farr."

Grace did not accept the proffered hand. Rather than expressing embarrassment at this snub, Farr deftly altered his gesture and reached into the breast pocket of his suit coat to draw out a gold cigarette case, as though that was what he had intended to do all along. He begged her permission with a raised eyebrow, and when she did not protest took out an unfiltered cigarette, then touched the end to a flame that sprang from the side of the case. Rich tobacco smoke curled upward and blended with the haze that already hung on the air. The man called Farr sat on a corner of the desk to regard Grace. What could he possibly want of her?

"I don't want anything of you," he said. "But in a moment, after you hear what I have to say, you may want something of me. That is why I followed you here."

Grace crossed her arms and treated him to a skeptical look. The man was peculiar, but he did not seem particularly menacing. Despite his air of education—which, she was beginning to suspect, was an affectation—she guessed he was a reporter for some tabloid newspaper, hot after the story of the man with the iron heart. The detective was going to return any minute, so she supposed there was little risk in indulging Farr. Grace indicated for him to continue speaking.

"I belong to an international organization," Farr went on after a drag on his cigarette. "The name is not important right now, but know that this is an organization that studies—how shall I say it?—*unusual* things."

"Things like people with hearts made of iron?"

"Yes, things like that. And more. We take an interest in many sorts of curious items and occurrences, all of which, you might say, have a preternatural character to them. That is, they lie beyond the world of the usual and mundane. It is the purpose of my organization to seek out, investigate, and catalog such instances." He took another pull on his cigarette. "We are scholars, you see."

"And the connection between all this and me is . . . ?"

"Oh, there's the obvious connection," Farr said. "We often attempt to interview those who have had encounters with the unusual. But there is a more immediate concern here." He snuffed out the cigarette among the butts in the cheap ceramic ashtray and leaned forward. "I have already said it once, but allow me to reiterate. You are in peril here, Dr. Beckett."

A chill danced along Grace's skin. Grim intensity shone in Farr's eyes, and it was suddenly hard not to believe his words.

"How?" It was all she could manage.

"The man you shot at the hospital was not the only one of his kind, Dr. Beckett," he said in a hushed voice. "My organization has been aware of them for some time, and we have been studying them—though as of yet we have been unable to make direct contact, so we know little of their origin or purpose. But I imagine you will be interested to know your detective friend here is one of them."

"One of them?"

"Yes. Janson is an ironheart, Dr. Beckett."

Grace shook her head in mute disbelief. It was impossible. It *had* to be. Janson seemed so drab, so uninteresting, so . . . normal. How could he be another one of *them*?

Farr did not give her a chance to reply. "There is more you should know. It might have been chance that brought you in contact with the ironheart at the hospital. Then again, I might be inclined to question that. Regardless, there is no blind luck in Detective Janson's present interest in you. It is your necklace, you see."

Grace reached up to grip the pendant at her throat. "My necklace? What does my necklace have to do with any of this?"

"Perhaps a great deal." Farr reached out and uncoiled Grace's hand from around the pendant. He brushed a fingertip over the designs incised upon it. "As I said, we know little of the purpose of the ironhearts. But we do know they have, in the past, expressed an interest in runes—that is, symbols such as these engraved on your necklace."

"Runes?" Grace thought she had heard the word before, but she wasn't exactly certain what they were. "Aren't those some sort of things New Age types use when their tarot cards wear out?"

Farr gave a soft laugh. "Yes and no," he said. "Yes, in that the runes used for entertainment today are descended from symbols of power that were used centuries ago by various Norse and Germanic peoples." He paused a heartbeat. "No, in that the type of runes the ironhearts are interested in—the sort that are on your own necklace—are extremely rare, and of unknown origin."

Grace tucked a loose lock of ash-blond hair behind one of her small ears. Farr's words were ludicrous, yet for some reason they frightened her. "What am I supposed to do?"

"First you must get away from Detective Janson," Farr said. "Get out of the police station as quickly as you—"

He was interrupted as, faint but approaching, the sound of heavy footfalls drifted through the open transom over the door.

Grace stared at Farr with wide eyes. "But how can I know what you're saying is true?"

Outside, she could hear the echo of Janson's voice. He had paused to speak to someone. Farr stood, reached into a pocket, and drew out an object. He thrust it into Grace's fumbling hands.

"Use this. See the truth for yourself. Then—and I entreat you—*get out of here as fast as you can.*"

The footsteps approached once more. Farr moved to the door, then turned to regard her for a fleeting moment. "Good luck, Dr. Beckett." The door opened and shut, the lock turned, and Hadrian Farr was gone.

Grace glanced down at the object in her hand. It was a plastic compass, the kind Boy and Girl Scouts used on hiking trips. The needle wavered back and forth, disturbed by her shaking hand, but never veered more than a few degrees away from magnetic north. The door opened. Grace jumped to her feet and thrust the compass into the pocket of her chinos. Detective Janson stepped in, a folder of papers in his hand, his expression just as bored as ever. Apparently he had not seen Farr's departure.

"You're all cleared, Dr. Beckett." The detective tossed the folder onto the desk. "We just need you to sign a few things, then you can be on your way. I'm going to have some coffee. Would you like some?"

"Sure," Grace managed to say. Now that Janson had returned, it seemed harder to believe Farr's outlandish words. She did not doubt there were others walking the world with lumps of cold iron lodged in their thoracic cavities instead of warm, living hearts. But Janson was just another overweight, overworked, disinterested police detective. Still, she would sleep better if she was absolutely certain. . . .

Janson turned his back to her, picked up a pot from a hot plate, and filled two paper cups. She drew the compass from her pocket and stepped toward him. She glanced down. The needle pointed straight toward magnetic north. Nothing had altered its direction. Relief coursed through her. Just to prove the point, she stretched out her arms and brought the compass within a foot of Janson.

The needle spun in circles.

Grace stared in horror. Even as she watched, the needle steadied until it was aimed once more in a single direction. Only this time it was not pointing toward magnetic north. It was pointing directly at the center of Detective Janson's back.

"Now, let's get you signing those papers so you can go home," Janson said in an amiable tone. He picked up the coffee cups and turned around.

Grace stepped back and thrust the hand with the compass into her pocket. Janson held out one of the steaming cups, and she gripped it in her free hand, certain he had to see the way she trembled. However, the detective seemed not to notice anything was amiss. Grace clenched her jaw, terrified she was going to scream.

"So, Dr. Beckett," Janson said, and a spark of interest ignited in his small eyes, "tell me where you got that interesting necklace of yours. . . ."

18.

In every progression, in every series of changes great or small, there comes a single moment—one thin sliver of a second—in which all that lies behind, and all that lies before, stands in perfect symmetry, like a beam balanced on a fulcrum. Step back from the point of the fulcrum, and the balance shifts to the side that was trod before, back toward the familiar and the usual. But step over the fulcrum, and the beam tilts forward, and one who stands upon it careens down the slope, carried beyond all control into possibilities unknown. And once the fragile balance of the progression has been altered, in either direction, it can never be restored. Step back, and the chance to step forward will never come again. Go beyond, and lose all hope of ever returning to what once was.

Detective Janson's question trailed off, the echo of his words oozed false nonchalance, and his once-bored eyes were now alive with hungry light.

In that moment, Grace stood upon the fulcrum. She clutched the hot cup of coffee, and a vision passed before her, such as that glimpsed by people during near-death experiences. She was at the hospital, caught up once more in the breathless chaos that gave her—thankfully—no time to think. Morty Underwood laughed, and a stream of injured poured through the automatic doors. Grace bent over each patient, to quiet fear, soothe pain, and mend hurts with deft fingers. Treating the wounds of others left her no time to notice her own.

It was still possible to go back—back to the hospital, back to her carefully constructed life. All she had to do was give Janson the necklace. It was the necklace he was interested in, not herself. If she gave it to him, he would certainly let her go, would almost certainly forget her. And the hospital's board of directors wanted to keep the incident with the ironheart quiet. She would never have to think of him, or of the cold lump of metal in his chest, again. She saw herself striding through the corridors of Denver Memorial once more: confident, in control, a queen in her own dominion. Even Leon Arlington was there. He leaned against a counter and gazed at her with his sleepy brown eyes. . . .

Leon!

But Leon Arlington couldn't be there. Poor Leon, who was now himself lying in one of the metal drawers in the hospital's morgue. Dear Leon, who had worked so long with dead people he had become like them, then had become one of them. Yet now he was there, and he fixed her with his placid gaze.

The vision slowed, and each moment, each movement, was protracted into agonizing slowness. Everything around her seemed flat and distorted, like a wide-angle film compressed onto a square television screen. Leon opened his mouth, as if to tell her something, but only a rumble issued forth. Her mind reeled. *Leon Arlington could not be there.*

That was what he was trying to tell her. The low rumbling phased into watery, understandable words.

This ain't real no more, Grace. . . .

As if someone had thrown a switch, the image vanished. Detective Janson still stood before her. Grace panicked. How long had she been frozen, lost in the haze of possibilities? Had Janson grown suspicious at her silence? But his eyes still rested on the pendant at her throat. No more than a second or two had passed. Grace took a deep breath and gathered her will. Then she stepped beyond the fulcrum.

Grace affected a pretty smile and performed her finest imitation of a North Carolina belle. "This old thing, Detective?" she said with a winning laugh and touched the necklace.

A grin spread across his face. "Those symbols on it—they're quite . . . unusual." He bent toward her to take a closer look at the pendant.

Grace did not hesitate. She thrust the paper cup toward Janson. Boiling coffee splashed across his face. A strangled scream escaped his throat as he lurched backward, eyes clenched, and stumbled into a filing cabinet. He clutched at his face with shaking hands and hissed in pain. The skin was already turning an angry red. Grace did not waste the moment. She stepped forward, grabbed the pistol from the holster slung over his shoulder, and leaped back. Janson groped for her, tried to grab her arm, but his fingers closed on empty space. He started to lunge for her, then froze at the click of a gun's safety being switched off. Grace allowed herself a sharp smile and tightened her fingers around the smooth grip of the pistol. She was getting pretty damn handy with these things.

"What the hell do you think you're doing?" Janson squinted at her through swelling eyelids. "This is a goddamn police station!"

"I know what you are," she said through clenched teeth.

For a moment Janson stood utterly still, then came a transformation so sudden and complete Grace nearly dropped the gun in shock. As if he had cast off a mask, the detective's confused expression was traded for one of utter malevolence. Evil light shone in his beady eyes.

"How?" Janson hissed. "How can you possibly know?"

With one hand Grace reached into her pocket and pulled out the plastic compass. She tossed it at him, and he flinched as it landed on the floor at his feet. The needle spun in spastic circles. With a grunt of disgust, he stepped on the compass and ground it into plastic shards with the heel of his shoe.

"You can't escape us." He spat the words like venom. "I don't know who you are, or where you got that necklace, but I guarantee you my master will want it for his own. Once he hears about it, he won't stop until he gets it, even if it means taking it from around your dead neck."

"Then maybe he'll never hear about it," Grace said.

Janson let out a strangled snarl and tensed as if to spring at her. Grace leveled the gun at his head.

"I know how to kill your kind," she said without emotion. "I've done it once, and I can do it again. A bullet in your chest won't stop you, but a few in your brain will do just fine."

Janson glared at her in hate. "I'm a detective, this is a police station. Kill me and you'll rot in jail—if they don't give you the chair first."

"I'm willing to risk that."

A sneer twisted his puffy face, but he did not move. "What are you going to do with me?"

A glint of metal caught the corner of Grace's eye. She reached behind her toward the desk, and her hand came back with a pair of handcuffs.

"Take a guess."

Keeping the pistol trained on Janson's head, Grace instructed him to sit and handcuff himself to the desk chair. She was surprised at the steel in her own voice. It was as if she were born to giving orders like this. Janson did as he was told. In moments he sat at the desk, wrists securely cuffed to the arms of the heavy chair.

He shook with rage. "You'll never get out of here."

"Care to place a bet?"

Janson's eyes were nearly swollen shut now, yet she still caught a glint of such inhuman fury in them that her breath caught in her lungs.

His voice dropped to a whisper. "Run, Beckett. Run as fast as you can. It won't make any difference. In the end, he'll find you. I know." A shudder surged through his body. "In the end, he finds everybody."

Dread trickled down Grace's throat and filled her chest. She could not possibly imagine the evils this man had witnessed, or what temptation had compelled him to sacrifice his own living heart in trade. For a moment she almost felt pity for him. Almost. For whatever had once resided in him that might have been sad and pitiable, it had been cut out and replaced by a lump of iron. Detective Douglas L. Janson was already dead, and upon the dead, as Grace well knew, pity was a wasted thing.

She held the gun with one hand and used the other to grab a handful of paper towels from a stack by the coffeepot. She crumpled them into a ball, then ordered Janson to open his mouth and rested the gun against his left temple for incentive. He complied. She shoved the wad of paper into his mouth. His muffled shout of protest verified the gag was functional. It was time.

She bent forward to whisper in his ear. "Tell your precious master, whoever he is, that he had better think twice before he picks on me."

Grace moved to the door and slipped the hand with the gun into the deep pocket of her chinos. She opened the door and glanced in both directions. The hallway was empty. She stepped outside and shut the door behind her. Heart thumping, she started down the corridor. She walked quickly, but not so quickly as to arouse suspicion. If she was lucky, it would be several minutes before anyone discovered Janson, and Janson's superior had approved her release. People would be expecting her to leave the station. She just had to stay calm.

She rounded a corner and collided into a young woman officer. Grace stuttered an apology, certain the officer must have noticed the gun Grace gripped in her pocket. But the young woman only smiled, told her not to worry about it, and continued on. Grace passed several other officers, and she imagined that some of them looked at her with more than passing interest. A terrifying thought occurred to her. Perhaps Janson was not the only ironheart at the police station, perhaps there were others as well. The more she thought about it, the more it seemed unlikely he was the only one. She forced her face to remain expressionless and kept walking.

The corridor opened onto the station's main office. At first the noise and chaos startled Grace. A dozen harried officers sat at paper-clogged desks, where they took phone calls, talked with belligerent suspects, or tried to reassure frightened victims. Other officers milled about in an attempt to keep the flood of accused moving. After a moment Grace realized the confusion gave her the distraction she needed. She wended her way through the throng, and no one gave her so much as a second glance. She pushed through the police station's front doors and stepped into the night. The bracing air cleared her head. She descended the steps and walked down the street. She was going to make it.

An engine roared behind her. Grace turned in renewed alarm to see a car speed toward her. Tires squealed as it came to a halt scant feet away. It wasn't a police car, but a sleek, black sedan. Before she could consider running, the driver's door opened, and a man stepped out. In the moonlight she recognized the elegant form of Hadrian Farr. He gestured to the open door.

"Get in, Dr. Beckett," he said.

She gaped in openmouthed astonishment, and once again Farr answered her unspoken question.

"Detective Janson has been discovered. Even now he is informing his fellow officers of what you did, and that you have escaped. They'll be pursuing you in moments."

Bewildered, she shook her head. "But how do you know that he—?"

Farr raised a hand. "Please, Dr. Beckett, there isn't time." His cultured voice was as polite as ever, but there was an edge of authority to it that shocked her and forced her to listen. "You must take my car.

Drive it out of the city, it doesn't matter where you go. They won't be able to follow you."

"But what about Janson?" she said.

A hard gleam touched his eyes. "Do not worry about Janson. I will take care of the detective myself."

With that, she found herself gently but forcefully helped into the driver's seat of the sedan. The engine was still purring. Farr leaned through the open door.

"Please take this." He handed her a small, thin object. "Contact me as soon as you can."

With that he shut the door and sealed Grace inside the soft interior of the sedan. She looked down at the object Farr had pressed into her hand. It was a white business card. It read simply:

The Seekers
1-800-555-8294

Grace stared at the card. Then Farr's voice jerked her out of her stupor. "Drive, Dr. Beckett," he said. "Now!"

Instinct took over and she punched the accelerator. The car lunged forward with surprising speed and pressed her back into the leather seat. Grace tightened her grip on the steering wheel and gained control of the vehicle as it sped into the night. She glanced at the rearview mirror and tried to glimpse the world she was leaving behind. However, the sedan's glass was too heavily tinted. All she could see was darkness and her own pale reflection staring back at her with haunted eyes.

19.

"Thank you, come again," the dull-eyed clerk behind the counter mumbled. He handed Grace her change without looking at her, then turned to wipe the soda machine with a grimy rag.

Not much worry of having my face recognized here, Grace thought with slightly manic mirth. Never again would she complain about apathetic service. She glanced around the fluorescent-lit convenience store where she had stopped to purchase gas for Farr's sedan. A cryptic pictograph caught her eye. The women's rest room, she assumed, and pushed through the stainless-steel door. She slipped her necklace beneath her blouse, then splashed water on her face and finger-combed her hair in an effort to make herself look somewhat less like a fugitive from the law. A thought occurred to her. She locked the rest room's door, then pulled Janson's pistol from her pocket and wiped it with a paper towel. She wrapped more towels around it and shoved it deep into a trash receptacle, then she unlocked the door, walked through the store, and out into the night. A glance through the plate-glass window confirmed her expectations. The clerk still wiped the soda machine with mindless diligence.

Grace hurried back to the car and climbed in. She was still on the outskirts of Denver. It was time to put some distance between herself and the city. She turned the key and noticed a white shape on the dashboard. The business card Hadrian Farr had given her. She picked it up and glanced at it again. *The Seekers.* That must be the name of the organization to which he belonged. The society of scholars, as he had called them. But who were they really, and why would they go to such great lengths, and at such great risk, to help someone such as she? The only reason that made any sense was the one Farr himself had given her: that the Seekers were observers of the unusual, that to study strange happenings was their purpose, and that she had unwittingly found herself in the midst of one of their investigations.

Grace slipped the business card into her pocket, then piloted the car out of the parking lot. As soon as she was someplace safe, someplace where the police could not find her, she resolved to call the telephone number on the business card. She wanted to thank the Seekers for helping her escape. However, there was more to her desire than merely gratitude. Certainly the Seekers possessed more knowledge of the men with the hearts of iron than Farr had revealed to her. Now that she was aware of their existence, Grace could not simply forget them and their evil. She wanted to learn more about them—where they came from, what they wanted, how the seemingly impossible organs of cold metal functioned to keep them alive. Perhaps she could even help the Seekers in their study of the ironhearts. After all, she was a doctor. She could perform dissections on any deceased specimens they might acquire, to examine their anatomy in hopes of discovering what it was that made them tick. A warm spark of excitement flared to life in her chest. Perhaps, in time, she might even become a Seeker herself. . . .

The sedan sped down a deserted road and left the glowing lights of the city behind. A smile spread across Grace's lips. Buoyed by a sudden exhilaration, she pressed the accelerator and sped deeper into the folds of night.

Time slipped by, like the shadowed world outside the tinted windows of the car. Grace had not noticed when the hulking shapes first rose around her. Now they loomed in all directions, sharp against the star-strewn sky. The car's headlights cut a swath through the dark as it wound its way up the twisting two-lane road. She had not decided to head into the mountains, yet it made sense to stay off the main inter-state highways. Besides, once she did see them, the rugged silhouettes of the mountains beckoned to her and drew her deeper in.

She wasn't exactly certain where she was now. Not that it mattered anyway. It wasn't important where she went, as long as it was some-where far away from where she had been before. Like water in the wake of a ship, the night closed behind the car as it glided down the road.

Grace nearly did not see it in time.

She slammed on the brakes, and the car skidded to a violent stop. The seat belt locked, and that was all that kept her body from striking the steering wheel. She peered through the windshield. White light glinted off pointed antlers and silver-brown fur. A shadow darted across the road and vanished into the gloom of the night. Grace let out a breath of relief. That had been close. The last thing she needed to do now was hit a deer.

She pressed the accelerator and drove on. A minute later it struck her. She had seen the antlers, but something about the shadow had been wrong. Then she had it. How many deer walked on two legs?

She shook her head. Her eyes were playing tricks on her, that was all. Sleep-deprived interns in the ED were known to hallucinate.

"You're tired, Grace," she said. "You're way too tired. You're going to get yourself killed."

She glanced at the dashboard clock. Almost three in the morning. She was far away from Denver now. It would be safe enough for her to pull over to sleep, just for an hour or two. At least, she had to believe it was.

Just ahead, in the dimness, she glimpsed an abandoned building next to the road. In front was a flat area. It would do. She slowed down, pulled off the highway, and brought the car to a halt before the blocky hulk. With a yawn she shut off the ignition and reached to flick the switch for the headlights.

Something made her hesitate. She gazed through the window at the abandoned structure. It was impossible, but this place seemed familiar to her. She felt a tingling against her chest, lifted a hand, and touched the pendant through the fabric of her blouse. Compelled by a force she could not name, she opened the car door and stepped out.

She shivered as the wind tangled cold, substanceless fingers through her hair. Silence ruled the night. Before her, half-revealed by the head-light beams, the old building glowered against the sky. A dozen empty windows stared out like hooded eyes. Of all the places where she might have driven that night, of all the roads she might have traveled, what trick of fate or long-submerged memory had led her here? She knew this place. This was where it had all begun. This was where she had first learned about the existence of evil.

The Beckett-Strange Home for Children.

Grace approached the ruin. It was difficult to believe she had spent ten years of her childhood here. But it was just miles from this place, on a mountainside, that she had been found as a child: no more than three years old, alone, abandoned. It was here she had been given her Christian name, Grace. It was from this place her legal name, Beckett, had come. And it was within these walls she had first learned to treat the wounds of others.

Much of the Home's roof had collapsed inward, and only a few shards of glass clung to the window frames to glint like broken teeth in the last of the moonlight. The board nailed over the entrance had fallen to one side, and through the gap, brooding in shadows, she glimpsed the front door. Its surface still bore the blistered scars of old fire. The building was just a husk now, like the cast-off skin of a snake—an empty reminder of the evil that had once dwelled within. Even after all these years, a burnt smell hung on the air. But the fire had come last of all, and long before the fire there had been the cries of owls, and the hands reaching out of the dark.

A voice spoke behind her and jerked her back to the present.

"Can I help you, child?"

Grace gasped for breath, like a swimmer who had just surfaced after long submersion. She turned around and blinked against the glare of the car headlights. He stood before her, although she had not heard him approach, an unusually tall man clad in a shabby black suit that hung loosely on crooked scarecrow limbs. Eyes glinted like chips of obsidian in the cratered moonscape of his face.

"Who are you?" she whispered, but even as she asked the halting question she thought she already had an inkling of the answer. For there was something about him—in his old-fashioned clothes and in his ancient, knowing gaze—that reminded her of the purple-eyed girl she had encountered in the park.

With long fingers, the man in black touched the edge of his broad-brimmed pastor's hat and affected a mock bow. "The name is Cy," he drawled in a voice smooth and gritty as new-oiled rust. He reached out, as if to hand her a calling card. "That's Brother Cy. Purveyor of faith, peddler of salvation, and prophet of the Apocalypse. At your service."

"I see," she said breathlessly, for it was an introduction difficult to fathom in just one hearing. She glanced down and saw that instead of a calling card, her cupped hand held only a faint glow of starlight, and as she watched even this ran through her fingers and was gone. To conceal her startlement, she blurted out her own name. "I'm Grace. Grace Beckett."

Brother Cy gave an absent nod, as if he already knew this fact, or did not care. His eyes flickered past her to take in the brittle shell of the orphanage. "The past lies dark and heavy on this place. Can you feel it?"

"Yes," she said after a moment, for she could.

He brushed bony fingers against scorched clapboards. "Even fire and time cannot make the wood forget. Not entirely. The memory of evil lingers in the grain."

Grace crossed her arms over her chest. How could they know so much? Both of them—this weird caricature of a preacher, and the ethereal, porcelain-doll girl.

She whispered it again, desperate now. "Who *are* you?"

A grin, both terrible and impish, split Brother Cy's visage. "We are what we are and have always been. We go where the winds of chance blow us, and do what our natures require. But then, who is anyone, child?"

It was testament to Grace's odd frame of mind, and the disconnection she felt from all that she had once thought of as real, that his words almost made sense. She turned her back to him and gazed once more upon the orphanage. "Can we never be free of the past then?"

"No, child," Brother Cy said from behind her. "We cannot shape the past, for it is the past that shapes us, and without it we would be as dim shadows, lacking form or substance." There was a long pause. Then, "You cannot shape the past, and the future is beyond our reach, but remember this, child: You do possess the power to shape your present."

Grace searched the blistered slab of the orphanage's door. What would she glimpse if she were to open it? Would she see clumps of dry thistles nestled among burnt timbers, scattering downy seeds like fine ash? Or would she see a small girl, shivering in a torn nightgown in a corner? Present or past? She didn't know.

"Then find out," came Brother Cy's raspy whisper. "Open the door, and see what lies beyond. Only then will you know."

"I can't," she said in dread, even as a queer compulsion blossomed in her chest. Yes. Why had she come to this place if not to open the door?

She felt something small and cool being pressed into her hand. Her fingers closed around the object.

"It is merely a token," Brother Cy said. "Yet in it there may reside some small reservoir of strength. And by it, perhaps, you will better remember my words." The preacher's whisper grew faint, as if he receded into a far distance. "Open the door, child. What you see beyond is up to you. . . ."

The preacher's words melded into the night wind, and Grace knew she was alone. Step by step she approached the door of the orphanage. Her heart fluttered at this strange homecoming she had never imagined. The scarred door stood before her. She reached out and closed her hand around the tarnished knob, almost surprised to find it cold against her skin rather than molten with fire. For a second she held her breath. Then she turned the knob. With a creak, the door swung open before her.

At first she saw only darkness, and she was afraid maybe that was all there was left for her. Then something cold and damp touched her face. A moment later another chill, feathery caress brushed against her cheek, followed by another, and another. Then she saw them in the glow of the headlights. Tiny flecks of white danced on the air and settled on her arms, her hands, her hair. It was snow. Pure, white, beautiful snow. It swirled out of the door in a glittering cloud to surround her.

After all the day's happenings it was, at last, too much. She reeled. The snow cast a veil before her eyes, and a rushing noise filled her ears. Past was forgotten. Present was forgotten as well. There was no light, nor was there darkness. There was only snow. A soft sigh escaped her lips and fogged on the icy air. Only dully did she hear a sound like a door shutting behind her.

Then Grace fell forward and sank into cold and perfect whiteness.

20.

Hadrian Farr turned away from the burned-out building and raised a hand to shield his face against gritty wind. The black helicopter lifted off the stretch of two-lane highway and rose over the abandoned structure, into the hard blue sky. From inside the plastic bubble the pilot saluted in farewell. Then, like an onyx insect, the helicopter sped away and disappeared behind the mountains that bounded the valley. The morning air fell still.

Hadrian lowered his hand and walked back to the sedan parked before the ruin—once an orphanage, according to the remnants of a sign he had stumbled upon. He had traded his suit of last night for wool pants and a fisherman's sweater. He reached through the car window, opened the glove compartment, and switched off the transmitter inside. They had picked up the signal just after dawn, but the moment they landed Hadrian had known they were already too late. Although obscured by the cloven hooves of a wandering deer, he had been able to follow Dr. Beckett's footprints to the door of the structure. There her trail had ended. He had searched within the orphanage and found nothing but thistles and charred timber. It was as if she had vanished. However, Hadrian knew well people did not simply vanish. They always went . . . somewhere.

He pulled a small cellular phone from his pocket, pushed a button, and held the phone to his ear. A polite voice answered.

"I've located the car," Hadrian said without preamble.

The voice asked a dispassionate question.

He shook his head. "No, there's no sign of the subject. Nor do I expect to find any." He drew in a deep breath before speaking the words. "I believe we have a Class One on our hands."

The voice on the other end paused, then spoke again in careful tones.

"Yes, you heard me correctly." An edge of annoyance crept into Hadrian's voice. "That's a Class One encounter. Extraworldly translocation."

There was a long moment of silence. When the voice resumed, a note of excitement had broken through the formal veneer.

Hadrian nodded. "Yes. And send an observation team out here immediately. There may be residual signs—energy signatures or compound residues—I can't detect on my own."

The voice acknowledged his words. Hadrian pressed a button and slipped the phone back into his pocket. He gazed around. Dry grass danced under the lonely mountain sky. It was beautiful. He almost wished he could stay here, but there was work to do. He was to return to the charterhouse in London at once, to make a full report. Efforts to locate the ironheart known as Detective Janson had failed. However, last night, his operatives had managed to acquire the corpse of the ironheart from the morgue at Denver Memorial Hospital, and he had the photos he had taken of Grace Beckett's necklace. Together, it would be enough to make his case for Class One determination. It would mean a great victory for him, perhaps even advancement. Class Three encounters—rumors of extraworldly beings—were common. And while rare, Class Two encounters—meetings with those who had interacted with extraworldly forces—were well documented. But in the entire five-hundred-year history of the Seekers, there had been no more than a dozen Class One encounters: direct contact with an extraworldly traveler.

Hadrian sighed on the cool air. A mixture of emotions filled him. Excitement at having made so great a discovery. Concern for Grace Beckett, who was now far beyond his reach. And strange envy as well, to think she was almost certainly now experiencing that which he had always dreamed of. A Class Zero encounter—translocation to another world oneself.

He laughed at himself and shook his head. Hadn't he found what most Seekers spent their entire lives searching for? Evidence of worlds other than this Earth? He climbed into the car and turned the key.

He pulled the sedan around, then paused by the highway to let a splotchy white school bus pass. Inside, the shadowy figure of the bus's driver waved in thanks. Hadrian waved back, and the dilapidated vehicle roared by. He pulled onto the highway, then piloted the sedan in the opposite direction. A few moments later something caught his eye. Beside the road was a billboard. Its blank surface was covered with a fresh coat of primer-gray paint, ready for a new picture. Empty paint cans lay scattered in the grass before it. For a moment Hadrian imagined his life like that billboard: fresh, clean, ready to be worked anew. Maybe that was what it felt like to journey to another world.

A smile touched his lips. "Good luck, Dr. Beckett," he whispered.

Engine purring, the sedan sped down the highway and left the blank billboard behind.

PART TWO

ELDH

21.

Travis blinked.

The first thing he noticed was that he stood in a forest. The second thing he noticed was that misty light filtered its way between the pale trees all around. He adjusted his wire-rimmed spectacles before wide gray eyes. A moment ago the world had been cloaked in the dark of night. Now it was nearly dawn, and snow dusted the frozen ground. But how?

It was hard to think. He drew in a deep breath and tried to clear the buzzing from his head. The forest air was cold and moist, redolent with the tastes of ice and pine. He could not remember a time when he had breathed air this good. For a moment he almost believed these were the woods north of town. Almost. Except, now that he looked at them more closely, the trees he had taken for aspens didn't seem quite right. They looked like aspen trees should—but they were all a little too tall, their branches spread a little too wide, and their papery bark was a little too silver. And while the occasional conifer scattered among them was as tall and straight as a lodgepole pine, he didn't remember that lodgepoles had that purplish tinge to their needles. Where was this place? Then the fog in his mind cleared and he remembered everything. The revival, the words of Brother Cy, the beings in the light, and last of all the . . .

He spun around and expected to see it hovering there, like a window looking out over the moonlit highway that meandered north of Castle City. The billboard. However, there was no floating window behind him, no crisscrossed timbers of a billboard's back side, nor was there a highway anywhere in sight. He stumbled forward and searched desperately to either side. His walk became a jog, then a headlong run through the forest. Branches whipped at his face, he batted them aside. It *had* to be here. Yet all he saw were unfamiliar trees that stretched bare limbs toward the sky.

Wherever this place was, it was not Colorado.

At last Travis halted and gasped for breath. His head spun. The air was too sharp, too thin, like that on a high mountain summit. He gripped the trunk of an aspen—or whatever sort of tree it was—to keep from reeling.

"Well now, I had not expected to have company for breakfast," said a deep voice behind him. "But then, company is the best sort of surprise, isn't it? Especially in a place as lonely as this. Won't you join me?"

Travis turned around in astonishment.

The speaker sat on the ground a half-dozen paces away, cross-legged before a campfire. He was a man of indeterminate years, although he was more likely older than younger, for his dark, shoulder-length hair was shot with gray, and lines accentuated a strong mouth and eyes the exact faded blue of the wintry sky above. The man was dressed in curious fashion. He wore a long shirt of heather-gray wool, belted at the waist with a broad strip of leather, and a kind of tight, fawn-colored trousers. Leather boots shod the man's feet, and gathered around his shoulders to ward off the chill was a cloak the color of deep water. The cloak was fastened at his throat with an ornate silver brooch.

In all, the man reminded Travis of the actors from the local medieval festival that was held each summer a few miles down the highway from Castle City. The festival workers often wandered into the Mine Shaft after the fair closed for the night, to have a drink at the bar or shoot some pool, still clad in their anachronistic costumes, posing as noblemen, ladies, knights, and thieves. However, there was something about the man's clothes that made Travis think they were not part of a costume. They seemed too well worn, too travel-stained, too . . . *real.*

Travis's dizziness was replaced by alarm. If the billboard really had taken him somewhere else—somewhere far enough away to have strange trees—then there was no telling who he might meet. He eyed the man in suspicion. He could be a criminal, a fugitive, maybe even a murderer.

The stranger grinned, as if he read Travis's thoughts. His voice was like the sound of a horn. "You need not worry, friend. I am almost certainly the *least* dangerous thing you will encounter in these woods." He gestured to the fire. "You're cold. You should sit and warm yourself awhile. What could be the harm in that?"

After everything that had happened, Travis could think of plenty of possibilities. However, despite his sheepskin coat, he *was* cold. His hands ached, and his feet were blocks of ice in his boots. He decided it was better to fall in with an outlaw than freeze to death, so he approached the fire and sat on a cushion of pine needles. He held his hands over the flames and soaked in the warmth. Without further words, the stranger picked up a wooden spoon and stirred the contents of a pot balanced over the fire on a tripod of green sticks. The man filled two wooden bowls with thick stew and handed one to Travis along with another spoon.

"Thank you," Travis managed to stammer.

The stranger simply nodded and began to eat. Travis hesitated, then tentatively tasted the stew. A moment later he was wolfing down the food, heedless of the way it scorched his tongue. It was delicious— seasoned with an herb he had never tasted before—and after the first bite his stomach had reminded him he had not eaten since lunch the day before.

At last he sighed and set down the bowl. Warmth crept through his body. After a moment he realized the stranger was watching him. No, *studying* him. Travis shifted on the ground. There was something peculiar about the man's keen blue eyes. They seemed too old for the rest of his face.

The stranger winked, and his gaze was no longer so piercing. "Do not fear, friend. My eyes are not as sharp as some, and if I have seen anything at all in you, then it is neither shadowed nor wicked. Friend I call you, and so you will be considered, at least by me."

He gathered up the bowls and spoons, wiped them clean with a handful of pine needles, and placed them inside the pot. He stowed the cooking gear in a small pack, then turned his attention back to Travis. "Well then, it is against all laws of hospitality to ply a guest with questions when his stomach is empty. Yet now we have had our breakfast, and I think the time has come for introductions."

Travis started to speak, but the stranger held up a hand to silence him.

"Hold, friend," he said. "One cannot make proper introductions without a hot cup of *maddok*. This may not be a civilized land these days, but that does not mean we have to act as barbarians."

Travis bit his tongue. Something told him the stranger was not accustomed to contradiction. The man pulled a tin kettle out of the coals and poured dark liquid into two clay cups. As he did this, Travis noticed he wore a black leather glove on his right hand, while his left hand was bare. It seemed a curious affectation, but there was much about the stranger Travis found curious.

Travis accepted one of the cups and gazed into it. He had never heard of *maddok*, but it looked suspiciously like coffee to him. He raised the cup and took a sip. Instantly he knew *maddok* was *not* coffee. It was more bitter, although not unpleasantly so, and richer as well, with a nutty flavor. Almost immediately Travis detected a tingling in his stomach. He shook his head, wide-awake as if he had just had a full night's sleep. He stared at the cup, then downed the rest of the hot liquid.

The stranger laughed, raised his own cup, and drank deeply. Then he spoke in a formal tone. "My name is Falken. Falken of Malachor. I am a bard, by right and by trade."

Travis took a breath, it was his turn. "My name is Travis Wilder." Somehow it didn't sound quite as interesting as the stranger's introduction. He searched for something to add. "I don't know that I'm anything by right, but I'm a saloon owner by purchase."

"A saloon?" Falken asked with a frown.

Travis nodded. "That's right—a saloon. You know, it's like a bar." By his expression, Falken evidently did *not* know. Travis kept on trying. "A pub? A tavern?"

Understanding flickered across Falken's face. "Of course, you are a tavern keeper. An old and honorable profession, at least in this land."

Travis just shrugged, although inwardly he felt a note of pride. He had never thought about anything he did as being *honorable* before.

Falken set down his cup. "Then again, something tells me you are not from these parts."

Travis scratched his chin. "I'm not quite sure." A question rose to his lips. It was utterly mad, but he had to ask it. "Just where *are* these parts exactly?"

To his surprise, Falken did not laugh. Instead, the bard regarded Travis with grave eyes, then spoke in measured words. "At the moment we are deep in the Winter Wood, a vast and ancient forest which lies many leagues north of the Dominion of Eredane."

Travis shivered at the sound of the strange names. "The Dominion of Eredane?"

Falken leaned forward, his expression suddenly one of sharp interest. "That is correct. Eredane is one of the seven Dominions which lie in the north of the continent of Falengarth."

Travis gave a jerky nod, as if this made sense, when it made nothing of the sort. "I see." He searched for a way to phrase his next question that would not sound utterly absurd. It was no use. He asked it anyway, doing his best to sound nonchalant. "And the world we're talking about here is . . . ?" His question trailed off on the cold air. He was suddenly freezing again.

Falken raised a dark eyebrow. "Why, the world Eldh, of course."

The words struck Travis like a clap of thunder. He had not stepped through the billboard to another place, but to another *world*. The world Sister Mirrim had spoken of at the revival. There was no other explanation. The strange trees, the unfamiliar air, Falken's odd clothes. As impossible as it seemed, it was the only answer that made sense.

This was not his Earth.

With this knowledge came a new, terrible thought, and a wave of panic crashed through him. There was no sign of the billboard on this side, no window that looked out over Castle City.

How was he going to get back?

22.

Travis felt something being pushed into his hands. It was a clay cup of *maddok*. He raised the cup and gulped the warm liquid. After a moment his mind started to clear, and his panic receded a bit, although it did not vanish. Falken was beside him now, concern written across his wolfish features.

"Are you well, Travis Wilder?"

Travis shook his head in a daze. Was he well? In the last day he had lost his best friend, his home, his entire world. He was anything but *well*.

"I don't think I'm going to faint, if that's what you mean," he said.

Apparently satisfied with this, Falken leaned back on his haunches and rubbed his jaw in thought. He spoke in quiet wonder, almost more to himself than Travis. "So you come from a world other than this. I have heard of such things, although I never expected to come face-to-face with the proof myself. Yet I must confess, the moment I saw you I knew there was something unusual about you. And it was not simply your queer garb and manner of speaking. There is an otherworldly air about you, friend."

The *maddok* had done its work to steady his mind, and Travis actually managed a weak laugh. "An otherworldly air? Funny, but I would have said the same thing about you, Falken. Except I suppose this is *your* world, not mine." His hand shook as he set down the empty cup. "But if this truly is a different world, then I have just one question. What am I doing here?"

Falken clasped his hands together. "A good question, and one I would like to know the answer to. The morning is wearing on, and I had hoped to get an early start today, for I have a long way to travel, but it might be the time it would take to hear your tale would be well spent. If you would care to share it, that is."

As peculiar as he was, there was something about Falken that put Travis at ease. Besides, right now Travis didn't have another friend in the world. This world, anyway. A lump of loneliness welled up in his throat, but he did his best to swallow it.

He nodded. "All right, Falken. Maybe you can make more sense out of what's happened to me than I can."

As the sunlight brightened from silver to gold among the trees, Travis recounted everything that had happened to him since yesterday evening. It was almost a relief to share all the strange events with another. There was only one thing Travis left out of his story, although he wasn't quite certain why. Maybe it was simply too personal, and too disturbing, to think about. Regardless of the reason, Travis did not speak of the moment when Jack had gripped his hand, and how it felt as if lightning had struck him.

Throughout Travis's tale, Falken listened intently, and interrupted only now and then to ask about a word that was unfamiliar to him, things like *truck* or *telephone*. Travis reached the end of his story, and for a time the bard was silent, his expression thoughtful. The only sounds were the hiss of the dying fire and the music of the wind in the trees.

At last Falken spoke. "I imagine your friend Jack Graystone was a wizard of some sort."

Travis gaped at the bard. "A wizard?"

Falken nodded. "Clearly there is magic at work in your tale, and it seems to center around your friend. Wizards often have an interest in ancient objects, just as you've described Graystone. While there is no way to be certain, it seems the likely explanation."

Travis started to protest that this was impossible, then stopped. Was it really? The more he thought about it, the more magic seemed a better explanation for everything that had happened. He wasn't sure he believed in magic, but then he wasn't sure he *didn't* believe in it either. As with so many things in his life, he had simply never decided one way or the other.

"It might help us to know what is in the box," Falken said.

Travis reached inside his coat and closed his hand around the iron box. Jack had warned him not to open it, but that had been when Jack had feared his pursuers nearby. For all Travis knew, the beings in the light were an entire world away now. Besides, he was suddenly filled with a burning curiosity to know what was inside. He drew it out and set it on the ground between Falken and himself. It looked dark and ordinary in the morning light, the symbols carved on its sides and lid barely visible. He hesitated a moment, then in one quick motion undid the box's latch and raised the lid.

It was a stone.

The stone was small enough to fit easily in the palm of one's hand and perfectly round, like an oversize marble. It was a mottled gray-green in color.

Travis groaned in amazement. "A rock? I went through all of this for a *rock*?"

He reached out and picked up the stone. Instantly he sensed there was something more to it than he had guessed. It was slick, almost oily, although it left no residue on his skin. He turned it around and noticed a fleeting iridescence to its otherwise dull surface as it caught the morning light. The longer he looked at the stone, the more he realized how beautiful it was. He held the stone out toward Falken.

"Here, take a look at it."

The bard shook his head and thrust his hands behind his back, as if to avoid temptation. "No, I do not think I will, Travis Wilder. Your friend Graystone gave it to you and you alone. I do not believe it is meant for other hands, at least not hands such as mine."

Travis didn't quite know what to make of Falken's words. He gazed at the stone a moment more, then placed it back in its box. With reluctance he shut the lid. Now that he had seen the stone and how beautiful it was, it seemed a shame to hide it away again. Already he missed the smoothness of it against his skin, the weight of it in his hand. He started to open the box once more, but Falken's movement halted him. The bard scattered a handful of dirt over the remains of the fire to extinguish it, then he placed the clay cups and the kettle in his pack, tied it shut, and stood.

"Well, I think we have wasted quite enough of this day." Falken squinted up through the treetops at the hard blue sky. "It is best to get moving while the weather is fair, for storms can blow out of the Ironfang Mountains without warning this time of year." He lowered his gaze toward Travis. "At present I am journeying southward, to the petty kingdom of Kelcior, where I hope to meet an acquaintance or two of mine. It is a trek of some days on foot, but you are welcome to join me as I travel. In fact, I would rather recommend it, for there is not another fortress or village to be found in many leagues of this place. At least, not one in which folk have dwelled in a thousand years." He slung his pack over his shoulders.

Travis grabbed the box and leaped to his feet in renewed panic. It was one thing to sit in this strange forest and have coffee—or whatever the stuff was—with Falken. It had been almost pleasant. But to go tramping after the bard, farther and deeper into this . . . this world . . . was something else altogether. This place was where the billboard had brought him. If he left it behind, he didn't see how he could ever hope to find it again.

"Wait a minute, Falken," he said. "You still haven't answered my question. What am I doing here? And how am I supposed to get back home?"

The bard shook his head. "I am afraid I have answers to neither of your questions, Travis. Though as we journey, it is my hope we might discover some. At any rate, I am beginning to think it was not chance I met you here."

Some of Travis's panic was replaced by puzzlement. "What do you mean?"

Falken's faded eyes grew distant. "Fate is an efficient spinster. She wastes no thread needlessly, and it is fair to say she will weave as many destinies into one happening as possible." Now a mysterious smile played across the bard's lips. "So we will just have to keep our eyes open for those answers of yours, friend."

With that, Falken turned and marched off through the leafless trees. Travis stared after him. What should he do? But even as he wondered, he knew he didn't really have a choice. Once again in his life he had simply drifted with the tides of circumstance, and this was where they had stranded him. With a heavy sigh, Travis stuffed his hands into his coat pockets and trudged after the bard.

23.

All that day, Travis followed Falken through the frozen silence of the Winter Wood.

As they went, Travis was filled with questions—How far away *was* this Kelcior place? Who exactly *were* these people Falken was meeting? Would any of *them* be able to help him find a way home?—but he was forced to forgo asking them in favor of gasping for breath. The bard set a stiff pace over the uneven forest floor, up steep slopes, and down snow-dusted ravines. Despite his long legs, Travis was hard-pressed to keep up. The forest changed little during that first day, and consisted mostly of pale *not-aspens* dotted here and there by stands of purplish *not-pines*. Before long Travis noticed a third sort of tree, or rather shrub. This was a bluish evergreen, its feathery boughs speckled with pearlescent berries. Striving for consistency, Travis decided to call it *not-juniper*.

Soon the sun rose above the bare trees into the cobalt dome of the sky. Like everything else here, there was something peculiar about the sun. It loomed a little too large in the sky, and it cast a glowing yet dusky patina over everything, like the shellac on a Renaissance painting. Finally Travis remembered when he had seen daylight such as this before. It had been a few years ago in Castle City, during a partial solar eclipse. For a short time, the moon had taken a small bite out of the circle of the sun, and a gloom had descended over the valley, dim yet somehow rich, like tarnish on copper. The half-light had made everything look curiously old, and so it did in this world as well.

From time to time, when they crested a low hill, Travis caught a glimpse through the trees of mountains that thrust upward from the horizon like a dark wall. Although the rest of the sky was clear, clouds brooded behind the knife-edged line of peaks. He wasn't certain why, but gazing at them filled Travis with a nameless foreboding, and he was glad they were heading away from the mountains rather than toward them.

It was late afternoon when he lost Falken.

With a grunt, Travis pulled himself up a rocky slope. At the top he bent over, hands on knees, to catch his breath. His stomach rumbled in complaint—the stew eaten beside Falken's campfire seemed woefully long ago now—and he wondered how long it would be before they stopped to rest and, he hoped, have a bite to eat. He lifted his head to see how far ahead the bard had gotten.

Falken was nowhere in sight. Travis looked around, but all he saw was empty forest. Dread rose in his chest, and he cupped his hands to his mouth.

"Falken! Where are—?"

"Don't shout, you fool!" a voice hissed in his ear.

Travis clamped his mouth shut and nearly shed his skin in fright. He whirled around, then terror gave way to relief when he saw Falken before him. The bard wore a disapproving frown on his face. The echo of Travis's cry died on the air, as if suffocated by the preternatural quiet.

"I'm sorry, Falken." Travis whispered the words, loath to break the oppressive silence of the forest again, for it reminded him of another silence, one that had hung over the Illinois farmhouse where he had grown up.

He had been thirteen. Day after day his father had lurched around the house, like some robot from a late-night space movie, while his mother had faded as steadily as the gingham curtains that drooped over the kitchen window. The air in the house was so brittle Travis had hardly dared say anything, let alone the one word that meant something, anything. *Alice.* As if now that she was gone, lowered in her small coffin into the ground, they had to pretend she had never existed.

"Travis?"

He shook his head. Falken still glared at him.

"I thought I had lost you," Travis said.

"And lost me you had," the bard said. "Though I certainly had not lost you." His expression softened. "It is my fault, of course. I should have warned you earlier. So let me warn you now—it is not a good idea to shout or even raise your voice in a place such as this. This is not an evil land, and yet it is not so far from evil, either. It is best not to draw attention to one's self when there is no telling who might be listening."

As if to punctuate Falken's admonition, a shadow flew overhead and let out a harsh croak that rang out through the forest. The two men looked up in time to see a raven wing swiftly over the treetops and vanish into the distance.

Falken shook his head. "It appears my warning comes too late. Yet I suppose we can hope it was simply an ordinary raven, disturbed from its roost by the sound of your call. If it was something else, then it is too late to trouble ourselves about it now."

Travis wondered what the *something else* might possibly have been, but he was unsettled enough as it was, and he did not ask. Yet he could not help noticing that the raven had flown in the direction of the jagged peaks.

"It would be best to be as far from the mountains as possible by sundown," Falken said.

With that, the bard hefted his pack and started off again through the forest. Despite his weariness, Travis found he had no desire to linger in this place. He mustered his strength and hurried after Falken.

They made camp that evening beneath the shelter of a stand of *not-pines*, and soon twilight mantled the forest. Falken started a small fire with flint and tinder and heated the remainder of the morning's stew. They ate in silence, hungry after the day's long march. However, when the dinner things were stowed once again in Falken's pack, they sat close to the warmth of the fire and talked in low voices.

Travis would have asked questions, but he had no idea where to start. Fortunately, Falken seemed in a mood to talk, and for a time he spoke of things he thought a stranger to this world might be interested to know. He started with the names of the trees around them. The purplish pines were called *sintaren*, which meant duskneedle. The juniperlike shrubs were *melindis*, or moonberry. And the ghostly trees that reminded Travis of aspens had the most beautiful name: *valsindar*, which meant king's silver. But, as Falken explained, they were more commonly called quicksilver trees for the manner in which they quickened, or trembled, under the slightest breath of wind.

Later Falken discussed something of Eldh's geography, so Travis might know where in this world he was. At present they walked the far north of the continent of Falengarth. Kelcior, to which they journeyed, lay to the south, and beyond that were the seven Dominions, where many folk dwelled.

Travis gazed into the forest, and a question struck him. "What about this place, Falken? Doesn't anyone live here?"

A shadow that might have been sorrow flickered over Falken's visage. "Long ago, they did. We tread now in lands that once lay within the boundaries of the kingdom of Malachor. Then, all the north of Falengarth lay under the crown of that realm. But Malachor fell seven centuries ago and is no more."

Travis frowned at this. Hadn't the bard introduced himself that morning as Falken of Malachor? Of course, it was possible that Falken traced his ancestry to the ancient kingdom. That might explain what the bard was doing tramping around this desolate forest.

Falken went on. "I would hazard that knife of yours is of Malachorian make."

Travis looked down in surprise at the stiletto tucked into his belt. Until that moment he had forgotten about the knife. At the Magician's Attic—and again on the highway north of Castle City—it had shone crimson, but now the ruby embedded in the hilt was cool and dark. Travis looked up at Falken. "My friend Jack Graystone gave this to me. But what would Jack be doing with a knife from this world?" Even as he voiced the question he knew the answer. His eyes widened in shock.

Falken gave a sober nod. "Yes, Travis, I believe your friend Graystone came from Eldh. Though they are rare enough here, it seems wizards are more common in my world than yours. So you see, it is not chance at all that brought you to this place, though what the real reason might be I still cannot begin to guess." He gestured to the stiletto. "At least your friend gave you a precious gift in parting. A Malachorian blade is a treasure few kings possess. Finer smiths have never worked metal in this world, unless one counts the dwarfs in their mountain forges—but the dark elfs are only a legend, and one barely remembered, like all the Little People."

Travis traced a finger over the knife, as if he could feel the long years that lay upon it. Another question occurred to him, but even as he voiced it he wished he had not, for the fire seemed to dim, and the cold pressed in hungrily.

"Is there a country beyond the dark mountains?" he whispered.

Falken gave him a piercing look. "It is best not to speak in the dark of what lies beyond the Fal Threndur."

With that, their conversation was finished. Falken banked the coals of the fire in the ashes, it was time for sleep. A half-moon had risen into the sky. Like the sun, it was larger than the moon Travis was accustomed to, only far more so. It seemed to hang only just beyond the treetops. And, as if to erase any doubt that might have lingered in Travis's mind that this was truly another world, even the stars were too near and too brilliant and traced unfamiliar constellations against the heavens.

His shivering did not go unnoticed.

"Here, take this." Falken pulled a bundle from his pack and handed it to Travis. "It is old, and a bit frayed around the edges, but the weave is still warm."

Travis unfolded the bundle. It was a cloak. The pearl-gray cloth was thick and soft, and it seemed to absorb the moonlight.

"There are no finer garments than the mistcloaks woven in Perridon," Falken said. "It will keep you warm, even in the deepest, dampest chill."

Travis regarded his curious traveling companion, amazed at his kindness, but grateful for it all the same. "Thank you, Falken," he said. "Thank you for everything."

When at last the bard spoke, his eyes glittered in the gloom. "You may not wish to thank me yet, Travis Wilder." But what those words meant, he did not say.

Travis lay down on a bed of pine needles and moss near the remains of the fire, then wrapped himself in the cloak. Soon his shivering stopped. He thought of all the strange and incredible things that had happened to him in the last two days, and was certain sleep would be impossible. However, exhaustion from the day's labor soon won out over worries, and before long, slumber stole over Travis.

Afterward he was never quite certain, but as Travis drifted down into sleep, it seemed to him Falken still sat by the glowing coals, and that he drew an instrument, like some sort of lute, from his pack. The bard strummed a soft melody, and after a time, as the strange stars glowed in the sky above, he began to sing in a low voice. The bard sang about memory, and loss, and most of all about beauty. And whether it was a dream or not, the words lingered in Travis's mind for the rest of his life:

The shining tower has fallen,
The high walls stand no more—
Yet I have been
On wings of dream
Again to Malachor.

How silent dwelled the garden,
Beneath that shadowed keep—
Still one rose bloomed
Amid the gloom
And dew its petals wept.

Before a throne of silver,
Stood columns two by two—
But did the hall
In ruin fall
Where valsindar now grew.

Alone there I did wander,
And yet when I did halt—
Still voices rang
And mem'ries sang
Within that forest vault.

At last the gloaming deepened,
And then I dreamed no more—
But sweet I own
That I have known
The light of Malachor.

24.

Either the going was not as rough as the day before, or Travis was already getting used to the thinner air of this new world. All day he tramped after Falken through the still reaches of the Winter Wood, and he kept pace so that never once did he lose sight of the bard.

As the ghostly *valsindar* slipped by, Travis's thoughts turned to Castle City. He supposed he had been missed by now. No doubt Sheriff Dominguez had put out a missing person bulletin, and Deputy Windom would be questioning everyone in town concerning his whereabouts. At least Max was there to keep the saloon running. A longing filled Travis then—for the smoky warmth of the Mine Shaft and the familiar sound of Jack's voice. A sharp pang of loss pierced his heart, and he rubbed his right hand.

After a time Travis shook his head. These were melancholy thoughts, but then the Winter Wood was a melancholy place. A shadow lay upon it, yet the shadow was not *of* it, and it was almost a sweet sadness that lingered there among the trees, like a memory of beauty. He sighed as he trudged after Falken. Sometimes it was all right to be sad.

It was late afternoon, and the sun had just dipped behind the sentinel trees, when Travis and Falken came upon a clearing. The silence of the wood weighed on this place, and the two men slowed to a halt. The clearing was roughly circular and about thirty paces across. Nothing grew on the frozen ground, not even moss or witchgrass.

In the center of the glade was a standing stone. The stone was as tall as a man and about half that much wide, hewn of some dark volcanic rock. Its surface was weathered and pockmarked with time. Propelled by curiosity—or perhaps some other force—Travis approached the stone. He now saw it was covered with carvings, but they were faint and illegible, all but worn away by centuries of wind and rain and ice. As he neared the standing stone, the air dimmed and grew colder, as if he had stepped into a shadow. In answer to a wordless compulsion, he lifted his arm and reached toward the rough surface of the stone.

"No, Travis, do not touch it," a voice beside him whispered, gentle but insistent.

Travis stood frozen. The stone seemed to fill his mind and blotted out everything else. Then, with great effort, he shuddered and withdrew his hand. He tried to swallow, but his mouth was dry as dust.

"What is this place, Falken?" The unnatural hush stifled his words.

"It is evil," the bard said, the line of his mouth grim. He paced around the stone, careful to keep his distance. "It is a relic of an ancient war, a war fought in this land long ago. A *pylon*, I believe such things were called then. I had thought all such traces of the Pale King were cast down in ages past. It seems I was wrong."

Travis stared at the standing stone. The bard's words thrummed in his mind, and he thought he saw a thousand sparks of crimson, like fire glinting off raised spears as a shining army marched toward a vast, shadowed host. Faint but clear, the sound of horns rang out as the army of light pressed onward, until it seemed like a tiny white ship lost in an undulating sea of darkness.

"Let us go," Falken said. "We will find nothing good in this place.

Even after all these centuries, the land has not forgotten the evil that dwelled here."

Travis shook his head, and the vision melted away on the cold air. He stepped away from the standing stone, and the day brightened once more. He cast one last troubled glance at the stone, then hurried after Falken. While the bard had set a brisk pace before, now Travis almost had to jog to keep up with him. However, he did not complain, and soon the two left the glade and the pylon far behind.

For three more days they traveled south. As they marched, Travis found he had little extra energy to worry about how he was going to return home. Each day they rose with the frigid dawn and pushed on until twilight mantled the Winter Wood. They subsisted mostly on *maddok* and a thin soup Falken concocted of bitter herbs and hermit's root—a kind of white root which the bard always seemed to know where to find. Once or twice a day Falken would pause in their trek to kneel and pry several of the roots from the frozen soil with his knife. Travis would not have ventured so far as to term the soup filling, but it did keep the worst of his hunger at bay. Then, late on the fifth day of their journey, the trees thinned, and the two found themselves on the edge of a gold-brown plain. At once the oppressive silence that had hung over the forest lifted, and the air, although it remained crisp, grew a trifle warmer.

"We have journeyed beyond the shadow of the Fal Threndur," Falken said in answer to Travis's unspoken question. "Winter comes early to this part of the world and lingers late, but in the Dominions autumn still wanes. We should find the climate a bit kinder as we travel on."

Travis glanced back over his shoulder. True to Falken's words, he could no longer glimpse the brooding line of mountains through the barren trees. However, to the south and east, the land rose up to meet a new range of mountains—a lower yet still rugged jumble of peaks. These Falken named the Fal Erenn, or the Dawning Fells.

"That way lies Kelcior," the bard said.

Together they set out across the plains, leaving the sadness of the Winter Wood and the *valsindar* behind.

25.

Two days later they came upon the ancient road.

"This is the Queen's Way," Falken said as they scrambled over a grassy bank and onto the broad swath of the road. "Folk still call it by that name, though few know the true reason why they do."

Travis plopped down on the side of the steep road bank to catch his breath, and Falken sat beside him. As far as they could see in either direction, the surface of the road was covered with flat stones. The paving stones were cracked and worn with centuries of wind and rain, and the passage of countless feet. Wind rattled through dry grass that had pushed up between them. However, the road was still passable, and it cut across the rolling landscape—straying from its course for neither hill nor valley.

They rested beside the road for a time and sipped water from a flask Falken pulled from his pack. The sun was bright, but the wind was sharp, and Travis was grateful for his new garb. In place of his jeans, work shirt, and jacket, he now wore a forest-green tunic and fox-colored breeches along with the gray mistcloak. The breeches fit him well enough, and while the tunic was on the baggy side, he had cinched it with a wide leather belt, into which he had tucked the Malachorian dagger. He had slipped the iron box and the half-coin Brother Cy had given him into a pocket sewn inside the tunic.

Falken had pilfered the clothes the day before from a ramshackle farm—the first sign of human habitation they had come upon.

"I cannot say I enjoy resorting to thievery," the bard had said as he handed Travis the clothes. A mischievous light had twinkled in his faded blue eyes. "Nor can I say it is the first time. Regardless, now that we have reached the edge of settled lands, it is important you look less outlandish. Times were troubled when I left the Dominions, and they may have grown more troubled yet in my absence. It is best if we do not draw undue attention to ourselves."

Travis had bathed in the frigid stream next to which they had made camp, and had donned the new attire. When he had returned to the campfire he had discovered, much to his chagrin, that Falken had burned his old clothes while he wasn't looking. He had belatedly realized his wallet had still been in the back pocket of his jeans. Now his cowboy boots and his gunslinger's spectacles were his only connections to Earth.

Travis scratched the red-brown stubble on his chin, then reached into his pocket and drew out the silver half-coin. He had all but forgotten about Brother Cy's gift until last night. Now he studied the broken coin. There was something engraved on each side, but he couldn't make out what the carvings were. It would take the other half to determine what the pictures represented.

Falken leaned over and peered at Travis's hand. "What have you got there?"

Travis explained how the strange preacher had given him the coin after the revival.

Falken gave him a peculiar look. "May I see it?"

With a shrug, Travis handed the half-coin to him. The bard examined it closely, then shook his head.

"*Kethar ul-morag kai ennal,*" Falken said. "*Sil falath im donnemir.*"

The words that tumbled from the bard's lips were flowing and beautiful but completely incomprehensible.

Travis gaped at Falken in confusion. "What did you say?"

This time it was Falken who looked confused. "*Min uroth, kethar ul-morag kai ennal.*" He handed the half-coin back to Travis. "As I mentioned, you'll probably want to hold on to it. Whatever land this is from, it is very ancient. And do try not to mumble, Travis. I couldn't understand a word you just said."

Travis stared at the broken coin that glinted on the palm of his hand. "You weren't the only one," he said. Then, quickly, he explained what had occurred.

A few more experiments confirmed Travis's suspicions. If he held the half-coin, or if it was anywhere about his person, he could understand Falken's speech perfectly, and the bard could understand his. However, if Travis was not in contact with the coin, neither could understand a word the other said. There was only one answer. The language Falken spoke was not English—a fact that made perfect sense once Travis considered it. After all, this *was* an entirely different world. However, the half-coin Brother Cy had given him functioned as some sort of translator and allowed Travis to speak and understand Falken's tongue, even though it seemed to him he still spoke English.

Falken's expression was thoughtful. "It seems your friend Graystone was not the only wizard in this Castle City of yours. Tell me, are there any more surprises you have yet to spring on me?"

Travis gave a weak smile. "Only ones that will be surprises to me, too."

The bard shot him a speculative look, then stood. "Come," he said. "The day is wasting. If we press on, we may reach Kelcior before nightfall." He shouldered his pack and started southward down the road, and Travis followed after.

"So just why *is* it called the Queen's Way?" Travis asked after they had been walking for a time.

"It's an old story," Falken said. "This road was built a thousand years ago, in the years after the army of the Pale King was defeated by King Ulther of Toringarth. It is for Elsara, Empress of Tarras far to the south, that folk call it the Queen's Way, although they do not remember it. It was she who commanded a road be forged, running from the city of Tarras on the shore of the Summer Sea, all the way to the then-new kingdom of Malachor in the north, where her son sat upon the throne side by side with Ulther's daughter. But all those names are forgotten now."

"Why were they forgotten?"

Falken paused to scoop up a handful of dirt in his gloved hand. "Malachor fell to ruin, and the Tarrasian Empire dwindled. Its borders moved ever southward, and left only barbarian lands in its wake, until the Dominions were forged centuries later. Of them all, only Toringarth endures to this day, although little is heard from the icy land beyond the sea. Kingdoms rise and kingdoms fall, Travis." The dirt slipped through the bard's fingers and was gone. "It is simply the ebb and flow of history."

With that Falken started once more down the ancient highway. He began to sing in a clear voice, and Travis felt his blood stir, as if he could see the great battle conjured by the bard's song:

"With Fellring sword of Elfin art,
Ulther smote the Pale King's heart—
The magic blade was riven twain,
But Berash did not stand again.

Then came the Runelords to the vale,
To bind the gates of Imbrifale—
And witches too with their fey art,
Wove passes high with perils dark.

Lord Ulther knelt before the Queen,
And a pact they forged between—
They set the guard of Malachor,
That shadows gather nevermore."

It was late afternoon, and the sunlight had turned to gold, when they came to the crossroads. The old road had plunged into a dense copse. There, within the leafless stand of trees, a narrower road intersected the Queen's Way at right angles.

"We turn east from the Queen's Way here," Falken said. "It is not far now." With that he started toward the left-hand road. Travis followed after.

The road left the copse behind, then began to wind its way up a series of ridges that rose ever higher, like gigantic stone steps. Not only was this road narrower than the Queen's Way, it was in far worse repair. The paving stones were crumbling and treacherous, and in places they were gone altogether, leaving patches of hard ground where little grew besides stinging nettles, though these did so in great profusion. Soon Travis's shins were burning with nettle stings, for the barbs seemed to prick right through his breeches.

Just when Travis's lungs were starting to burn, the two men crested the shoulder of a ridge and came to a halt. Below them the land fell away into a bowl-shaped valley. In the center of the valley was a lake, its waters molten with the light of the westering sun. A rough finger of rock protruded into the lake, and atop the craggy peninsula stood a fortress of stone. Even from here Travis could see that at least half of the fortress had fallen into ruin. Broken columns loomed like rotten stumps over jumbles of stone that might once have been walls. Even the part of the fortress that still stood sagged under its own weight as if, with one final sigh, it might collapse inward at any moment.

"There it is," Falken said. "Kelcior."

Travis eyed the weathered keep, his expression dubious. "I hope you won't be insulted, but it really doesn't look like much."

Falken laughed. "These days, it *isn't* much. Though once, long ago, this was the northernmost garrison of the Tarrasian Empire, and after that it was a keep of Malachor. However, these days the fortress—or at least what's left of it—is occupied by a scoundrel named Kel. Barbarian though he is, Kel fancies himself a king, and it's a good idea not to disagree with him, at least not in his own great hall."

A gloomy thought occurred to Travis as he gazed at the keep. He let out a troubled breath.

"What is wrong, Travis?"

He shook his head. "I don't know. It's just that you're going to be meeting your friends here, Falken. That means your journey is over. But I still have no idea where I'm supposed to go to find a way back to my world."

Falken studied Travis for a moment, then reached out to grip his shoulder. "I never said my journey ended at Kelcior, Travis." He chuckled softly. "Given the nature of Kel's court, it would be ill luck indeed if that were the case." His visage grew solemn once more. "To speak the truth, I'm not certain either where best you should journey. But there is some hope one of my acquaintances will have a better idea of that than I. And do not forget the weavings of Fate. Who knows? It may be our paths lie together for a while yet, friend."

Travis gave the bard a grateful smile. He was far from the world he had known all his life, but at least he wasn't alone. Together the two started down the road toward the ancient fortress below.

26.

Grace clung to the knight's broad back as his horse galloped toward the castle that loomed in the distance.

Castle?

The word skittered off the surface of her frosty mind. She tried to grasp at its meaning, but it was no use. Like a fish beneath the surface of a frozen lake, it flashed brightly and was gone.

She was cold, so terribly cold. A rolling landscape slipped by in blurs of gray and white. Yet a moment ago there had been something else, hadn't there? She remembered branches against a pale sky, sharp and black as lines of ink on paper, forming angular words she could not read. *Trees?* Then there had been an expanse of silver, and the drumbeat of hooves on stone. However, the names for these things could not break the icy plane of understanding in her brain. After that the trees had fallen behind, and on a distant hill before them she had glimpsed towers and high walls muted by swirling shards of ice, just like a scene inside a child's snow globe. Yes, it almost certainly had to be a . . .

She was too cold to grasp the word again. Perilously cold. She huddled inside the woolen blanket the knight had wrapped around her. It smelled of sweat and horses. Her half-frozen blouse and chinos clung to her skin, yet she was not shivering. Wasn't she supposed to be shivering?

You're hypothermic, Grace, spoke a dispassionate voice deep in her turgid brain. Even now, while the rest of her was numb with cold, the doctor in her evaluated the situation and offered its precise diagnosis. *Your heart rate is depressed, your blood pressure is dangerously low, and you are clearly experiencing an altered mental state. You know these symptoms, they're the first signs of a patient going into shock. You have to get warm, Grace. If you don't, you will die.*

It was so hard to move: Her muscles were lead. Yet somehow, ever so slowly, she tightened her arms around the knight's chest, and pressed her body against the heaving back of the horse beneath her. This action drained the last remnants of her strength. Paralysis stiffened her limbs, the landscape around her faded away. Darkness pressed from all sides. It was neither cold nor warm, nor was there fear in its soft folds. There was only sweet and endless emptiness. Though a tiny presence seemed to whisper something to her—*you can't sleep,*

Grace, not now—she could not quite comprehend its words. She slipped deeper into the gently suffocating darkness.

It appeared as a tiny but brilliant spark against the black backdrop of her consciousness. It flashed and was gone. Grace ignored it and continued her descent into the abyss. Just a little farther now and she would never be cold again.

Another bright pinpoint flared in the dark, and another. Then there were thousands of them, small and sharp and white-hot as stars. At last she realized what the specks were. Pain. Countless pinpricks of pain crept along the surface of her skin. The sparks tore apart the darkness that surrounded her. She felt a twinge deep inside, followed a moment later by a noticeable twitch. Then, all at once, a violent shiver wracked her body.

She opened her mouth, drew in a shuddering breath, and only then did she realize she must have stopped breathing. Pain sparkled up and down her limbs as warmth from the horse and the knight crept into them. Again a shiver coursed through her, and again. After that she could not stop shivering.

This is a good sign, Grace, the doctor's voice said without emotion. *The reflexive action of your muscles will generate chemical heat and restore blood circulation to your extremities. The pain indicates you don't have frostbite. You're going to make it.*

Shiver-warmth continued to seep through Grace's body as the horse pounded onward through the wintry day. The dullness in her mind began to melt, and she grew more aware of her surroundings. For the first time she saw the knight as something more than a dim blur before her. She sensed that if he stood, he would not be a tall man, but he was powerfully and compactly built. He gripped the horse's reins with mesh-gloved hands, and he wore a kind of long, smoke-gray shirt, slit on the sides, beneath which Grace felt numberless small, hard, interlocking rings of metal. A black cloak hung from his shoulders, and on his head he wore a flat-topped helmet of beaten steel.

The man glanced to one side, and Grace caught a glimpse of his profile. Pockmarks dinted his skin here and there, the legacy of some childhood disease. Ice clung to his drooping black mustaches, and his breath fogged on the air. His nose was hawkish beneath brown eyes, and creases framed the grim line of his mouth. She guessed the knight to be in his forties.

Knight?

Where had she gotten that word? Perhaps in her fog she had heard him use it. Or perhaps the term had been dredged out of her unconsciousness in response to the sword sheathed at his hip and the metal rings beneath his long shirt. Either way, the term suited the man. Noble, solemn, slightly dangerous. He looked like a knight should look.

She wondered then if she had been rescued by some sort of anachronist, a mountain recluse who styled himself as a kind of medieval warrior. The more she thought about the possibility, the more it began to make sense. Although it was difficult, she forced her brittle mind to search back and remember what had happened before she had found herself on the horse, riding with the knight through the frozen forest. She could almost recall a place, a door, a voice. Then, like dark water bubbling up through a hole in an icy lake, memories welled forth.

She remembered the orphanage. Yes, that was it. She had driven to the mountains in Hadrian Farr's sedan, fleeing Denver, and the police, and the men with the hearts made of iron. Then she had been too weary to go on, and somehow, by chance or fate, she had ended up before the burned-out husk of the Beckett-Strange Home for Children. Now darker memories threatened to gush through the hole in the ice, but Grace forced them back. She did not want to remember those things. Not here, not now. It was already too bitterly cold.

What next?

An image flashed before her, of obsidian-chip eyes and a cadaverous grin. The man in black. Yes, that was right. She had spoken with the weird preacher in the old-fashioned suit, the preacher who was certainly akin to the porcelain doll girl in the park. What had the man in black told her?

Open the door, child. What you see beyond is up to you. . . .

That was just what she had done. She had opened the charred door of the old orphanage, and beyond the door had been . . . *snow*. The last thing she remembered was the sound of a door shutting behind her. Everything had turned white as she fell, and then—

—then she had been here, gripping the knight as the horse galloped on.

No, that wasn't quite right. There had been something before that. The memory was as pale and fragile as the drifting snowflakes, but she recalled a moment when she had opened her eyes. Trees had woven their dark fingers against a white sky above her, and a shadowy form had bent over her as a deep voice spoke in wonder.

Why, 'tis a lady!

Piece by piece, her analytical mind began to patch together the puzzle. Of course—it all made sense. She had seen snow when she opened the orphanage's door, but that was only because it had been snowing outside. It was hardly unusual for the mountains in late October. No doubt the flakes had drifted down through holes in the building's ceiling. At that moment she had collapsed, an inevitable physiological reaction to stress and exhaustion. It was luck plain and simple that the knight had found her before she died of exposure.

Grace turned her thoughts to her rescuer. She supposed he was some sort of historical re-creationist. No doubt he lived in a remote valley, rode his horse, wore his costume, and pretended he dwelled in a time long past. Certainly it would have been better if someone passing by on the highway had seen her prone form, but Grace would not complain. She was grateful to have been rescued before hypothermia stopped her breathing for good. She supposed the knight was taking her to his hut or fort or whatever structure it was he had built for his home. Once she was warm enough, and when the weather permitted, she could walk back to the highway. And then? She wasn't sure, but she could worry about that when the time came. She remembered the card the mysterious man, Hadrian Farr, had given her. It was still in the pocket of her now-thawed and wet chinos. Perhaps she would call the number on the card. The Seekers might be able to help her decide what to do next.

Carefully, for she was still dangerously cold, Grace parted the blanket in which she huddled, then peered around the knight's broad back. She was curious to see if she could recognize any landmarks in the direction in which they rode. After all, this area had been her home once. Certainly she would recognize something.

Through the gap in the blanket, she watched fields bordered by low stone walls slip by, all dusted by the snow that fell from the colorless sky. None of it looked remotely familiar. Only after a long moment did Grace realize she could see no mountains. Instead, they rode across an undulating plain. But that couldn't be right. Maybe the falling snow had obscured her vision. She leaned to one side, in order to get a view of what lay directly ahead of them.

She had forgotten about the castle.

It was closer now, standing atop a low hill that rose above the horizon. Turreted towers reached toward the sky, surrounded by a wall of gray stone. With sudden certainty she knew there was not now and never had been a place like this in Colorado. And the knight was riding directly for it.

Grace's carefully crafted explanation shattered like so much ice.

27.

"Where . . . ?"

The word was barely a whisper and was snatched away by the frigid wind. Grace drew in a gulping breath and pressed her lips together in an attempt to warm them. She tried again.

"Where are we?"

This time it was something between a whisper and a croak. The knight craned his neck and glanced back at her over his shoulder. For a fleeting moment he smiled, displaying whiter and straighter teeth than Grace would have guessed. Then his expression grew solemn once more.

"So, my snow lady is awake," he said in a grave voice that was rich with a lilting accent Grace did not recognize.

It seemed he had not understood her faint words. With great effort, she spoke the question one more time.

The knight frowned, as if this were a peculiar thing to ask. "Why, we are in Calavan, of course." He let out a forlorn sigh and his shoulders slumped. "But that was greatly discourteous of me, was it not? I will ask your forgiveness, though I doubt you can possibly grant it. You must feel distressed after your ordeal. Indeed, it is a wonder your mind was not completely addled by the cold, and that you can speak at all. So allow me to answer you again. We have been in the Dominion of Calavan proper ever since we crossed the old Tarrasian bridge over the Dimduorn, the River Darkwine." He pointed toward the rapidly growing castle. "Yonder is Calavere, the seat of King Boreas."

Grace did her best to digest this information. She could not fathom precisely what it meant—there were far too many intriguing but unrecognizable words. However, it all seemed to confirm her suspicion this was somewhere very far from Colorado. She tried to swallow and found she could.

"Why did you call me your snow lady?" Her voice was stronger this time.

The knight glanced back at her again, his brown eyes somber. "Because, my lady, when I came upon you in the forest, you were as white as the drift of snow in which you lay." He shook his head. "I feared you were dead when I found you. In truth, I half fancied you had never been a living creature at all, for your skin was as white as ivory, and when I lifted you out of the snowbank your flesh was as hard and cold as stone. But when I laid my ear against your chest, I heard the faintest sound of a heart beating. 'Durge,' I said to myself, 'somehow your snow lady is alive. But if you don't get her to the castle, and as quick as lightning, she'll be as cold as the snow indeed. No doubt you are too late, and there is no hope, but you ought to try all the same.'"

Grace's forehead furrowed. The knight, whose name was apparently Durge, seemed a gloomy fellow. "But you *did* save me," she said.

The knight looked startled at this. "We'll see," he said. "It isn't much farther now, but I imagine you cannot endure the cold any longer. I suppose it would be all the more ironic if you expired a mere furlong from the castle gate."

She shook her head. "I'll make it." A thought occurred to her. "You said you found me in the snow?"

"That is so, my lady. There has been an early snow—a queer storm for a land so far south as this. I rode into a clearing, and there you were, lying in a drift as peacefully as a princess on her feather bed. Nor were there footprints in the snow around you. It was as if you had drifted down from the sky."

Here the knight paused and cast a look at her out of the corner of his brown eyes. However, if he wondered how it was she had come to be in the woods, he did not ask her. But how *had* she gotten from the old orphanage by the highway to a snowy forest here in . . . wherever this was? At the moment she had no idea, but she intended to find out.

"It is a wonder anyone found you at all, my lady," Durge said. "It is spoken that Gloaming Wood is a fey and ancient place. Few of the common folk will venture within its shadowed eaves. I suppose they fear the Little People. Though it is the mundane dangers—boar and bear and poison mushrooms—rather than old myths that are likely to harm them."

"Why . . . why were you in the woods?" Grace asked. The words came easier now.

"I am making haste to Calavere, my lady," the knight said. "A Council of Kings has been called for the first time in long years, and the rulers of all seven Dominions ride to Calavan. I have journeyed south from my homeland ahead of my liege, King Sorrin of Embarr, to make certain things stand ready for him when he arrives at the castle. At dawn I decided to cut through the fringes of Gloaming Wood, for the way is faster, and I had hoped to find a fat stag to offer for King Boreas's table. But winter comes early this year, and game is already scarce. I found no trace of stag in the woods. Thus King Boreas will have to make do with your company instead."

Grace thought the stern knight had made a joke, then she reconsidered. Something told her Durge was not one for making merriment. Whoever this Boreas person was, she would almost certainly need his help to learn where she was, and it would not aid her cause if it seemed she was the reason there was no meat for his board.

Grace lifted her eyes to the dark shape that rose before them and studied it. She had seen castles before in pictures, and had been inside replicas of them at amusement parks. However, the fortress that loomed before her was neither a crumbling relic of a bygone age nor an anachronistic re-creation constructed to amuse and elicit money from tourists. Somehow Grace knew this castle was *real*.

Counting, she saw the castle—*Calavere*, the knight had called it— possessed nine towers. None of them were alike. Some of the towers were tall and spindly with pointed roofs, while others were stout and square. Most were set into the many-sided wall that ringed the hilltop, while the largest dominated the center of the fortress. This last tower was a great, blocky structure as wide as it was tall, with narrow windows and high crenellated parapets. The haphazard towers gave the impression the castle had been built in many stages over several centuries with no common design. The result was a kind of stark and craggy majesty that seemed as natural and unplanned as the beauty of mountains.

Durge nudged the flanks of his soot-colored mount. "Come now, Blackalock. This is no time to dally." The horse stretched its legs to gallop faster, yet the stallion's gait remained smooth, even careful, and he rolled his eyes back to glance at the passenger who rode behind the knight.

In minutes they reached the base of the hill on which the castle perched. Durge guided Blackalock onto a broad path that wound in a spiral up to the summit. For the first time they encountered others on the road, and the higher they went the more people they passed. These were all on foot, dressed in drab but warm-looking clothes cut of rough cloth. Some pushed wooden carts filled with peat or firewood, while others carried bundles on their stooped backs or prodded flocks of goats with willow switches. To Grace they all looked curiously old: their limbs crooked, their faces weathered. All except for their eyes, which seemed too young for the rest of them.

A memory crept into her mind, of old men in patched overalls sitting on a rickety front porch. Only they hadn't been old, had they? She had seen people like this once before, while on a vacation in the Blue Ridge Mountains of North Carolina. In Appalachia there were places where people still lived under the same primitive conditions their ancestors had three centuries before, in ramshackle cabins that lacked refrigerators, running water, and electricity. Most of them had looked years older than their twentieth-century counterparts—wrinkled, gnarled, toothless. Something told Grace these people here were a similar case.

Peasants, the word drifted from her subconscious. With great effort, she dredged up dusty recollections from her undergraduate world history course. Didn't every castle have peasants who paid tithes of goods and labor to the lord in exchange for protection? Except, according to the course professor, the feudal system had vanished over six hundred years ago. *At least on Earth*, a disconnected voice in her mind added. However, she was still too cold to consider the implications of that. She tightened the blanket around herself and tried not to stare at the people who trudged along the road.

They came to the castle gate. This was a high arch in the wall flanked by a pair of square towers. Massive doors of iron-reinforced wood stood open to either side. The knight slowed his horse to a walk and followed the stream of people into the opening. Beyond was a dim corridor. The sounds of people and animals echoed off the stone walls. At the far end of the passage was a raised iron grill. Grace craned her neck and saw dozens of holes in the ceiling. Their purpose was clear. Intruders who broke through the first gate would be stopped by the second and caught within the tunnel while defenders rained down arrows or boiling lead from the murder holes above. Whatever this place was, it certainly was not unfamiliar with the concept of war.

Two men stood at the far end of the tunnel, clad in mail shirts, swords belted at their hips. Like the peasants, they were small but powerful-looking, with weathered faces and young eyes. The men-at-arms collected a copper coin from each of the peasants who passed through the far archway. The knight nudged his mount forward. One of the men-at-arms looked up, then saluted, fist against chest.

"Where will I find King Boreas's seneschal?" Durge asked.

"In the king's stable, in the upper bailey, my lord," the guard said and gestured through the archway.

Durge nodded and guided Blackalock toward the opening. As they passed, the guard's eyes widened. The man elbowed his companion, who affected a similar expression. Durge kept his gaze fixed ahead. Grace cast one last glance back and saw the two men-at-arms make some strange sign with their hands. Then the horse passed through the archway and into the space beyond.

It was a courtyard. High walls enclosed an area as large as a city block. The courtyard—or bailey, to use the guard's word—was ringed all around by stone buildings of myriad shapes and sizes, each built with its back against the castle's outer wall. Smaller buildings of wood were scattered throughout the courtyard. It looked as if some sort of market or fair were in progress, for the entire bailey bustled with peasants and various castle folk. The hooves of livestock and the wheels of carts had churned the ground into a mire. There was as much to smell as see, and Grace's nostrils were assailed by the odors of smoke, manure, and roasting meat. Any last doubts this place was anything but real were erased from her mind.

Knight, horse, and passenger moved through the crowded courtyard.

"What was that all about?" Grace gestured back toward the castle's gate. "The guards acted so strangely when they saw me."

The knight cleared his throat. "It was nothing that should concern you, my lady. They wonder who you are, that is all. You must forgive them. They are simple men."

Grace accepted this, but she thought there was something more Durge was not telling her. A flash of silver caught her eye, and she glanced down at the ground. It was a puddle of water, a mirror to the sky above. A ghostly face gazed up at her: thin, ethereally pale, green-gold eyes like summer gems above sharp cheekbones. It was her own reflection in the puddle. No wonder the guards had stared at her so. The horse continued on, and the reflection was gone.

At the far end of the bailey was a wall that was darker and older-looking than the others. There was a second gate in this wall, and it was toward this that Durge steered his horse.

"We are going to see Lord Alerain, my lady," the knight said. "He is the king's seneschal, and so is concerned with visitors to the castle. I must announce myself to him, and he will be able to see to your needs."

Grace gave a jerky nod. It was not as if she had any other suggestions.

They passed through the gate and entered a smaller courtyard. The upper bailey was quieter than the lower bailey. This was the oldest part of the castle, Grace decided, for here the stonework looked heavier and more weathered. Against the far wall rose the high, square tower she had glimpsed before. It must have been the hill fort's original keep, although its layers of different-colored stone indicated that the tower had been expanded many times in its history. Stone wings stretched from either side of the main keep and turned the corners to encircle the courtyard on all sides.

In the center of the upper bailey was a thick and tangled garden that looked like a tiny forest. Even in this wintry weather, Grace caught the faint perfume of flowers on the air, and from somewhere in the garden drifted the music of water. She sighed. It was a peaceful and private refuge. Even the thick stone walls were comforting rather than confining.

There were fewer people about the inner courtyard—men-at-arms and others Grace took for servants. Durge asked a grizzled guard to direct them to the king's stable, and the fellow pointed toward a long wooden building. As they approached the structure, Grace caught the rich scent of horses.

The knight brought his horse to a halt and dismounted, then reached up to help Grace. She was stiff and clumsy and nearly fell, but Durge caught her in strong arms and set her on the ground.

A sharp voice emanated from the stable. "And the next time I catch you sleeping, boy, you can clean all the stalls yourself—and without the benefit of a rake, mind you!"

"Yes, Lord Alerain," answered a youthful and contrite voice.

A figure stepped from the shadows of the stable. He was a lean, precise man of later years. His white hair was closely cropped, and a neatly trimmed beard adorned his pointed chin. His garb was fine but understated, all in shades of maroon and black, and a cloak was clasped at his neck by a simple but large gold brooch. He cut an imposing figure, yet there was something grandfatherly about him all the same. Perhaps it was the preoccupied look in his watery blue eyes. He started toward the keep, an intent cast to his face.

"Pardon me, Lord Alerain," Durge said.

The seneschal looked up, searched for the source of the voice, saw them, and approached. He studied the knight, then seemed to make a decision. "The earl of Stonebreak, I presume?" he asked in a formal tone.

"You presume correctly," Durge said.

A smile broke through Alerain's stern expression. "Then I have not lost all my skill. Well met, my lord. You have the look of your father, Vathris keep him." He reached out and gripped the knight's hand. "It seems Embarr is the first to arrive for the council. Is King Sorrin far behind you?"

"At least a fortnight, my lord. Though it would surprise me little if his traveling party were delayed by bandits, or lamed horses, or a fallen bridge."

Alerain scowled at this. However, his eyebrows were too bushy for the expression to be genuinely fierce. "You Embarrans! Such a gloomy folk—always expecting the worst of things. I'm certain King Sorrin will arrive in good order."

Durge shrugged. "If it pleases you to say so, my lord."

The seneschal rolled his eyes but let it pass. He glanced at Grace, who was still wrapped head to toe in the blanket. "Tell me, my lord, who is this who accompanies you?"

"I cannot truly say, Lord Alerain." Durge gazed at her with his solemn eyes. "I came upon her half-frozen in the snow, in the eaves of Gloaming Wood."

Alerain gave the knight a sharp look. "You ventured into Gloaming Wood?" The seneschal shook his head. "You are a brave man, Sir Knight. Or, if you'll forgive me, a foolish one. You might have become as lost as this poor lass." He took a step toward her. "Now, what have we here?"

Grace opened her mouth, but Alerain clucked his tongue to silence her. "Do not fear, my child. We'll get you out of that damp blanket and into something dry at once. There will be plenty of time to tell us your name after you've warmed yourself by a fire." He reached a hand toward her.

Grace hesitated. Yet it couldn't hurt to wait until she was warm and dry to start asking questions about where she was. She reached out to take the seneschal's hand. As she let go of the blanket, it slipped back around her shoulders, away from her face.

Alerain sucked in a hissing breath. "My lord!" he said to Durge. "Why did you not tell me who your companion was?"

The seneschal dropped to one knee right there on the muddy ground in front of the stable. Grace cast a startled look at Durge. The knight gave a nod, as if something he had suspected had just been confirmed. Then he too bent to one knee before her.

Grace watched the men in confusion. What was going on? As if to answer her question, Alerain bowed his head and spoke in a ritual tone.

"Welcome to Calavere, Your Highness. How may we serve thee?"

28.

The door shut behind Grace and she was alone inside the drafty bedchamber. Outside, footsteps faded away as the two maidens who had led her through the castle's labyrinthian corridors retreated. She let out a deep breath.

"What would a princess do in this situation, Grace?"

She grimaced. It had been absolutely no use trying to convince Lord Alerain she was nobody special. In the courtyard, after the flustered seneschal had managed to recover his composure, she had attempted to explain he had made a mistake. Her name was Grace Beckett. She was not royalty, and there was absolutely no need to keep bowing his head or calling her *Highness.*

Despite her repeated protests, Alerain had given her a conspiratorial wink. "As you wish, Your Highness," he had said. "It is not my place to question why a lady of high station might desire to travel in disguise. It is a curious happening, to be sure, but these are curious times. Though I confess, I cannot fathom from whence you hail. The line of your jaw speaks of the noble houses of northeast Eredane, but your cheekbones could belong to a duchess of southernmost Toloria. And your eyes are like those of no royal family I can think of." He had stroked his short beard. "It is part of my office to know every noble in the Dominions on sight, whether we have met before or no. But I know you not. This Beckett must be a dominion far distant from Calavan."

"Very far," Grace had replied.

After that she had given up. It was simpler that way. Besides, she was too numb really to protest. Alerain had summoned a half-dozen servants, and with crisp commands gave orders for a room to be prepared for her. Most of the servants had dashed off at breakneck speed, but two pretty women—barely more than girls—clad in dove gray dresses had remained behind. Each took one of Grace's elbows and had led her at a more careful pace toward one of the wings of the keep. She would have shaken off their hands and told them she could walk on her own, but she wasn't entirely certain that was true. Her knees shook, and she felt light and hollow.

She had wondered then what had become of Durge in all of the chaos, and had glanced over her shoulder. Gloomy as he was, she rather liked the knight, and though she seldom made friends, she thought she could use one in this unfamiliar place. However, the brown-eyed knight had been nowhere in view, and before she could ask about him the maidens had led her through a door into the keep.

Now Grace let her gaze wander over the room. It was perhaps five paces across and nearly twice as long. One end of the room was dominated by a gigantic four-posted bed. The top of the bed was so high off the floor that a stepping stool placed before the footboard was the only practical means of climbing up. At the other end of the room was a fireplace in which a cheerful blaze crackled, and on the far wall was a narrow window glazed with thick glass. All around the room colored tapestries hung against the walls and depicted flowering trees, lushly tangled vines, and clear fountains. So vivid were the images in the weavings that if she half closed her eyes, Grace could almost believe she stood in an idyllic spring glade. Almost. For despite the fire and the tapestries, and a worn carpet beneath her feet, a chill radiated from the stone walls and floor. By this, and the musty odor that lingered on the air, she suspected this room had not been used in some time.

Grace decided to look out the window in an effort to get her bearings—she had lost all sense of direction in the castle's mazelike corridors—and moved toward the far wall. Halfway there she halted—something she had not noticed before caught her eye. In a corner near the fireplace was a large wooden tub filled with water. Even as she watched, a crisp curl of steam rose from the water's surface. On a stool next to the tub lay a neatly folded cloth towel, a brown lump she took for soap, and a porcelain bowl filled with dried herbs and flower petals.

Grace cast another look at the window. She wanted to learn more about where she was. However, the window wasn't going anywhere, and right now her chilled body ached to feel itself immersed in hot water. She debated the issue—window or bath?—for a second more.

Bath won out.

She stood before the fire, kicked off her cold shoes, and started to unbutton her blouse. It was only then she noticed her left hand was clenched shut in a tight fist. She thought about it and realized it had been so all along. With her right hand she had clutched the blanket around her while on the knight's horse, and it was also with the right she had reached toward Alerain. Her left hand had remained closed throughout all of it, so numb with the cold she had not noticed. Now, with her right hand, she unclenched the left.

Something small and silver shone on the palm of her hand.

Grace peered at the object she had clutched so tightly. It looked like half of a coin. There was a design on each side, but she could not make them out, for the half-coin was too worn. It must have been very ancient. Yet where had it come from?

A raspy voice seemed to speak again in her mind. *It is merely a token. Yet in it there may reside some small reservoir of strength.*

Of course. *He* had given it to her. The weird preacher man in black. Brother Cy. She remembered something small and cool being pressed into her hand, just before she had opened the door of the orphanage. Just before everything had gone white and she had awakened to find herself here, in this . . .

". . . world?" she whispered aloud.

Yes. That was the word that had been hovering on the edge of her understanding, waiting for her to voice it. This was not present-day Earth. Nor was this even Earth as it had been in some past century. She wasn't certain how she knew this, only that she did. Perhaps it was some deep and primeval human instinct, embedded in her chromosomes over the course of millions of years of evolution—sensitive to slight discrepancies in the color of the light, or the force of gravity, or the chemical composition of the atmosphere—that told her *this was not her world.*

Yet that did not seem entirely right. If that were truly the case, then the knowledge she was no longer on Earth—that she had somehow stumbled through an impossible doorway into another, alien world—should have flooded her veins with fear and adrenaline. Wasn't that how instincts worked? However, for all its strangeness, there was something about this place that felt oddly . . . comfortable.

None of this served to answer her primary question. How had she gotten here? Had *he* sent her to this world? But the preacher had told her what lay beyond the door of the orphanage was up to her. Perhaps something deep inside of her had wished to find a way to another world.

She dug into the pocket of her chinos and pulled something out. It was damp and rumpled but still legible: the business card Hadrian Farr had given her. Farr had told her it was the mission of the Seekers to search for and study strange occurrences.

A jolt of grim humor hit her. "You should have stuck with me, Farr. It doesn't get any stranger than this."

A shiver reminded Grace of the steaming tub of water. She set the card and the half-coin on the mantel above the fireplace, then took off her necklace and placed it beside them. When she got back to Earth—*if* she got back, she amended, then suppressed the thought—she would call the number on the card and talk to the Seekers. However, right now there were other matters to concern her, the most immediate of which was survival.

As quickly as she could with her stiff fingers, she shucked off her wet clothes and piled them in a heap before the fireplace. Then, without even testing the water, she climbed into the tub.

She let out a gasp. The water was shockingly, painfully, and deliciously hot. A series of violent shivers surged through her body, and needles of pain danced across her skin. She forced herself to stay submerged. Her shuddering eased, and the bright pinpricks faded to a pleasant tingling. Finally the heat seeped into her chilled core, and her shivering ceased. She let out a luxuriant sigh and sank deeper into the tub as her stiff muscles melted.

She decided it was time to scrub and reached for the lump of soap. It was soft and fatty, and its smell was faintly rancid. However, it was soothing as salve when she rubbed it on her skin. She sprinkled the dried herbs and flowers into the water, and a sweet fragrance rose upward, effectively masking the unpleasant odor of the soap, as was clearly their purpose.

After this, Grace leaned back, soaked, and drowsed for a time. At last the water started to cool. With a sigh, she climbed from the tub and toweled off in the glow of the fire. Soon she was dry and warm. And, she realized, quite naked. She eyed the clothes piled on the hearth. They were steaming now, but still sopping.

She gazed around the room, and her eyes fell on a tall cabinet in a corner. She threw open the cabinet's doors, and this action confirmed her initial suspicion. It was a wardrobe. Inside were several gowns, each a different color, but all fashioned of soft wool. Folded on a shelf above were some sort of undergarments, made from undyed linen. All looked to be about her size. No doubt these things had been brought here ahead of her, along with the tub of water. Grace gave the odd clothes a dubious look. None of them were exactly her style—chinos and a blouse were about as dressy as she ever got—but she supposed necessity superseded fashion.

The undergarments were easy enough to comprehend. They were soft and not unlike a pair of long underwear. She slipped them on, then started to reach for one of the gowns, but at that moment a wave of weariness washed over her. Between her ordeal in the woods and the warmth of the bath, she was exhausted. Her gaze drifted toward the massive bed, and immediately her only thoughts were of sleep. She clambered up the stepping stool, flopped onto the bed, and sighed as she sank down into expansive softness. *Goose down.*

Then, for a time, she did not think of all that had happened to her. She did not think of the man with the heart of iron, or of Hadrian Farr, or of Brother Cy. She did not think of this strange world, or of how far away from Earth she might be. She did not even think of the hospital, or of the endless stream of broken people that streamed through the Emergency Department's door.

Grace's last conscious effort was to burrow under the heavy bedcovers. Then she shut her eyes and drifted into a deep and peaceful sleep in which she thought of nothing at all.

29.

Travis and Falken reached the ancient keep just as the sun sank behind the rim of the valley and the lake turned from copper to slate.

"Shall we see if anyone is home?" the bard said. His black-gloved hand slipped to the knife belted at his hip, and belied his light tone. Travis didn't need a magical translator for *that* message. He swallowed hard and gripped the hilt of his stiletto. Falken made a fist of his left hand and pounded on the door—a huge slab of scarred wood—three times.

There was a grating sound. Then, with a groan, the door opened a crack—just enough to reveal a single, bulbous eye. The bloodshot orb rolled back and forth, then focused on the two men.

"Who goes there?" a chalky voice said.

Falken answered in a formal tone. "Two travelers seeking shelter against the coming night."

"Well, then you had better find another keep," the voice said in a croak. "We've already taken in our share of vagrants. We couldn't possibly squeeze in another, let alone two. Good-bye!"

The door started to shut, but Falken wedged the toe of his boot in the crack to keep it open.

"In case you hadn't noticed, there *are* no other keeps," the bard said. "We might be on the far frontier of the Dominions, but even here the laws of hospitality hold sway. Or have you forgotten?"

This resulted in a burst of cackling. "I have forgotten nothing. Yet I'm afraid King Kel doesn't go in much for laws—except for ones he makes up himself, of course. Still, I doubt you'll find a lord more hospitable to those he favors—or more harsh to those he does not." The eye squinted to a slit. "Which be you, Falken of the Blackhand? Friend or foe?"

Another burst of laughter answered Falken's surprised expression.

"Yes, I know who you be, wanderer. Of little worth would be the doorkeeper who did not know the sight of the Grim Bard coming!" The eye rolled in Travis's direction. "But what is this delicious morsel you've brought with you?"

Travis squirmed under the orb's scrutiny, uncomfortable for a reason he couldn't quite name.

Falken glowered at the eye. "Just answer my question. Are you going to let us in or not?"

"Oh, very well," the voice said. "If you absolutely must, you may pass. But you would be wise to answer *my* question, at least to yourself. Be you friend or foe? As I recall, King Kel was not altogether pleased with the name Falken Blackhand when last you left here." With that the eye vanished.

"What was that supposed to mean?" Travis whispered.

"I'm not entirely certain."

Travis didn't like the sound of that, but before he could question the bard further the door swung inward with a creak. Torchlight spilled out. The doorkeeper was nowhere in sight. Travis took a deep breath and followed Falken into the passageway beyond. There was a great booming as the door slammed shut behind them. The two men spun around.

It took Travis a moment to realize that what he had at first mistaken for a pile of rags in the dim light was in fact an old woman. She slid a wooden bar across the door, then scuttled toward them. Bony arms and legs stuck out of the tatters that wrapped her shapeless body, like the limbs of a spider. She stared at the two with her one bulging eye.

"Welcome to Kelcior!" she said in a facetious croak.

Falken was obviously unimpressed. "So King Kel has been reduced to this? A single hag to guard his door? What happened to those famed warriors of his?"

"Bah!" the old woman said. "Warriors." With a gnarled hand she gestured toward an alcove. Two men clad in greasy leather slumped within, snoring. "These ones drank themselves into a stupor by sundown—as usual."

Falken's eyes narrowed. "And I suppose they didn't have any help in this matter from you, witch?"

A snaggle-toothed grin split her face. " 'Tis not my fault if they don't look at what's floating in their ale before they quaff it!"

Falken shot Travis a look. "So are you going to take us to Kel or not?" the bard asked.

"Ah! Too important to hang about with the likes of Grisla, are we?" The witch affected a mocking bow. "Very well, Lord High-and-Mighty. Grisla will do as you bid, and with quivering pleasure. Come this way, come this way!"

The hag Grisla grabbed a smoking torch from the wall and led them down a murky corridor to a set of doors. A dull roar emanated from the other side.

The hag gestured to the doors. "Beyond is the great hall. The king is holding a feast tonight."

"When *isn't* Kel holding a feast?" Falken asked.

Grisla scratched at her matted hair. "I think there was a Melinsday morning two years ago when everyone decided to go on a picnic instead."

Falken let out a groan. "Enough, witch! Back to the door with you."

Venom perfused her words. "As you wish, Lord Irritability."

Before she left them, the crone plucked at Travis's sleeve with knobby fingers. "I have an eye for you, my lad!" She cackled and pressed something into his hand.

Travis looked down, then gagged. On his palm was a glistening eyeball. It lolled damply back and forth, staring up at him. With a yelp he dropped the eye, and it rolled away down the hall.

With a shriek, Grisla chased after the orb and groped for it with blind hands. At last her fingers closed on the loose eye. The witch stuck it back in its socket, grunted in satisfaction, then scuttled down the hallway.

Travis wiped his hand on his tunic. He felt vaguely ill. "How did she do that?"

Falken shook his head. "Believe me, you don't want to know." He motioned to the doors. "Shall we?"

Together the two pushed through into the space beyond.

Travis's senses reeled, overwhelmed as they tried to take in the dizzying scene that greeted them. The great hall of Kelcior was a cavern of a room. High walls of stone rose to a ceiling crisscrossed by soot-blackened beams. Two lines of trestle tables ran the length of the room, perpendicular to the high table, which stood upon a dais at the head of the hall. Torches lined the walls, but their light barely cut through the haze of smoke that hung on the air. Travis took a breath and nearly choked on a powerful reek—a mélange of burnt meat, spilt beer, sweat, and vomit.

King Kel's feast was no formal affair. As many people stood on the tables as actually sat at them. Brawny men used swords to hack apart huge joints of roasted meat, while others drank out of rusted helmets. Serving wenches swaggered as they plunked down platters of food and deftly evaded large, groping hands. One warrior managed to grab a smudge-faced maiden and got a dagger through his hand as a reward. Children in patched tunics ran shrieking back and forth in some rule-less game, while wildmen—clad in rancid animal skins, their hair caked with blue mud—fought and snarled with mangy dogs for scraps under the tables.

Travis gave his companion a dubious look. "Are all your friends like this, Falken?"

The bard treated Travis to a withering glance, then wended his way through the throng. Travis followed close on his heels. They reached the steps below the high table.

A great bellow thundered over the roar of the feast. "Bring me another haunch of aurochs! Hold on there—better make that two. I'm feeling a bit peckish!"

Travis craned his neck and stared upward in awe. The largest man he had ever seen sat at the center of the high table. The man had the shoulders and chest of a grizzly bear, and his huge head was crowned by a shock of red hair that was surpassed in wildness only by the tangled bush of his beard. Eyebrows bristled like living things over the blue sparks of his eyes. A sizzling hunk of some dead beast was plunked before him. Kel displayed pointed teeth in a barbaric grin, then tore into the joint of meat with hands like paws.

As befit a king—even a petty king—sitting with Kel at the high table were the most important members of his court. That is, the burliest warriors, the most buxom wenches, and the wildest-looking wildmen. Once, years ago, while in an unfamiliar city, Travis had accidentally stepped into a rough and seedy biker bar. Harrowing as that experience had been, that bar had had nothing on this place. If he turned and left now, would he have a chance of getting to the door before getting a sword in the gut?

"Don't even think of running," Falken said under his breath. "They can sense fear." With that, the bard ascended the first step of the dais.

"Greetings, Kel, King of Kelcior!" Falken spoke in a resounding voice.

The king looked up, and his blue eyes widened into circles. The joint of meat slipped from his hand and fell to the table. As if that were a cue, the entire great hall went silent. Warriors froze in mid-brawl, wenches gripped serving trays with white-knuckled hands, and wildmen cowered beneath tables, where they whimpered along with the frightened hounds.

30.

"Falken Blackhand!" King Kel's voice was a growl. "I had not expected to see your bleak face in my hall again. At least, not so soon after the last time. Have you come to bring me another disaster? We've only barely finished burying the bodies after the last one, you know."

Falken raised a hand to his heart in a gesture of feigned surprise. "So the north guard tower did fall, then?"

King Kel shoved back his chair and stomped around the high table to tower over Falken. "Aye, it fell! Just as you said it would, and mere hours after you disappeared without begging proper leave from my kingdom, you scoundrel. Killed my best hunting dog when it went." Kel wiped a tear from the corner of his eye. "Oh, and a few dozen members of my court as well."

"I warned you the tower's foundation was weak."

Kel grunted in suspicion. "Aye, you did at that, Falken Blackhand. It seems you're always warning of disaster, and it seems you're always right." He glowered at the bard. "A man might start to wonder if dark happenings follow you, or if, just maybe, you have a hand in making your warnings come to pass."

At this accusation a hiss ran around the great hall. Kel wasn't the only one with this idea.

Falken held out his arms, begged for silence, and somehow received it. "It is true I have often warned you against impending trouble, Your Majesty. And if you heeded my warnings, it might be little ill would come of them. Be that as it may, I am saddened you have forgotten all the other admonitions of Falken Blackhand—the ones that have brought good rather than ill."

Falken paced on the dais. His voice rose, as if this were a performance of some sort. Travis held his breath. Perhaps it was at that, a performance which, if not compelling enough, could cost them their heads.

"Who told you where in the lake to search for lost treasures of Tarras?" Falken asked. "Who told where to mine salt, when you had no salt for your table? And who sang to you the entire *Lay of Boradis* for three days without pause or rest, just so you could hear over and over the verse in which the dragon eats the army?"

The king's eyes sparkled. "I love that part!"

Falken fixed Kel with a sharp look. "Who did these things?"

The king heaved his massive chest in a sigh. "You did, Falken."

Falken crossed his arms and nodded.

Kel scratched his furry chin in thought, then snapped his thick fingers. "I know! I'll ask my advisor what I should do."

Falken's brow furrowed. "Your advisor?"

The king's bellow rang out over the great hall. "Where's my witch? Somebody bring me my witch!"

"I'm right here, Your Boisterousness." A spidery form scurried onto the dais.

Falken raised a single eyebrow at the hag. "You're his advisor, too? If you don't mind my saying, you seem to get around."

Grisla shrugged her bony shoulders. "A witch's work is never done."

King Kel looked to the hag. "What should we do with them, witch?"

She reached into the mass of rags that covered her body and drew out a handful of thin, yellow objects. Only when she cast them upon the steps did Travis realize they were bones. Grisla hunkered down to study the pattern made by the fallen bones.

"Humph!" she said. Then, "Hmm." At last she concluded with a harsh "Hah!"

Kel clasped a big hand to his chest. "What is it, witch?"

Grisla looked up and fixed Falken and Travis with her one bulging eye. Travis's heart fluttered.

"The oracle bones speak clearly," Grisla said. "These two come on dark business."

The king let out a snort. "I hardly need your charms to tell me that, hag."

"I'm not finished! Dark as their business is, it does not concern us." Grisla gazed again at the bones, and her face pursed into a frown. "Yet it does not *not* concern us."

"That's conveniently vague," Falken said.

Grisla snorted. "I don't make the oracles, I just read what they say." The hag gathered up the bones and tucked them away among her rags.

King Kel mulled over this new information. He scratched his head and made his wild red hair even wilder. Then he nodded. "I have made my decision." He towered over Falken and Travis. "I will not grant you the hospitality of my hall, Falken Blackhand."

Travis shot Falken a look of open alarm. The bard started to protest but was silenced as Kel raised a meaty hand.

"However," the king went on, "I *will* allow you to earn it."

At this Falken's grim expression was replaced by a broad smile, and Travis let out a breath of relief.

"I will be only too happy to earn my keep with my lute, Your Majesty," the bard said. "And, if it would please the court, I might even sing the *Lay of Boradis* a time or two."

A toothy grin split Kel's face. "By Jorus, I never could stay mad at you, Falken!" He grabbed the bard and crushed him in a bear hug. The great hall erupted into merriment once again.

"I can't play if you break me," the bard said in a muffled voice.

Kel dropped Falken to the dais. The bard staggered and might have fallen save for Travis's steadying arm. The king returned to the high table and called to his servants. Two stools were set upon the steps before the high table, one each for Falken and Travis. The only chair in the entire great hall belonged to the king—everyone else sat on benches. A wench thrust a foaming tankard into Travis's hand. Thirsty, he took a deep draught and immediately started choking. The gritty liquid in the tankard was neither Budweiser nor oatmeal but something in between.

"Don't just sit there sputtering, Travis," Falken said. "Unwrap my lute and hand it to me."

Travis managed to catch his breath. "But the pack's right by you. Can't you get it yourself?"

"I could," Falken said. "But it's an apprentice's job to serve his bard. Unless, of course, you don't wish to pose as my apprentice, and would prefer to find your own way to earn King Kel's hospitality. I'm sure the drunken warriors over there could use someone to hold up their knife-throwing target."

Travis hurriedly reached into the pack and retrieved the bard's lute.

The feast resumed, and Falken strummed his lute and sang of ancient battles, proud kings, and fey treasures. Travis was content to sit quietly on his stool and sip his beer. It wasn't so bad once he learned to filter it through his teeth. He listened to the bard's songs and let his gaze drift over the great hall. In one corner of the hall he noticed two people—a man and a woman—who did not seem to fit in with the rest of the barbaric revelers. The woman was beautiful, her hair black, her skin coppery, her amber eyes striking. She wore a midnight-blue kirtle trimmed with silver. Her companion was a big, rangy, fair-haired man. He appeared to be a knight of some sort, for he wore a heavy-looking shirt of chain mail, and a helm rested on the table before him. The knight watched the merriment in the hall with an expression of amusement, while the woman's gaze was turned inward, as if she gazed upon some secret place.

Falken handed Travis the lute, and his attention was turned away from the two strangers. It was time for a break. Kel called out in his thundering voice for food to be brought for the bard and his apprentice. Each was handed a hunk of meat on a slice of hard bread, which Falken called a *trencher*. Travis was ravenous. Not caring what animal it might have come from, he took a bite of the meat and chewed. And chewed. And chewed. It was more gristle than flesh. He managed to swallow, although just barely.

He snapped his head up at a low growl. A hunting dog stood before him, muzzle pulled back in a snarl. Travis decided it wasn't worth losing a hand over and tossed the rest of the unidentifiable meat to the dog. He settled for gnawing on the trencher, which, while stale, was somewhat edible.

Another call went out from the high table and was quickly picked up by others.

"Bring on the play! Where is Trifkin Mossberry? Bring on the play!"

"We had better get out of the way," Falken said to Travis.

They grabbed their stools and retreated to one side of the dais. A curtain behind the high table parted, and a diminutive figure popped out. The small man leaped onto the table, performed a capering dance in which several tankards and bowls were upset, then launched himself into a handspring and landed nimbly on the steps of the dais. A great whoop went up from the crowd at this entertainment.

The little man was clearly full grown, though he was no more than half Travis's height. He had a broad face and nut-brown eyes, and his pointed chin was beardless. His clothes were of green and yellow, and a red-feathered cap perched on his tousled brown hair. He doffed his cap, bowed deeply, then rose to address the crowd in a piping voice:

"My name is Moss, and Berry, too,
But your names I'll not ask you.
For I have come to wonders show,
Not to drink, nor mischief sow.
Behold, my friends—turn not away—
As Trifkin's troupe performs the play."

At that cue the curtain behind the table parted again, and a dozen forms dashed out to stand upon the dais with Trifkin. The actors were clad in elaborate and outlandish costumes. A man in white robes with a long white beard tossed dried petals like snow into the air. Tree-women clad in bark-brown dresses shook long arms that ended in branching twigs. Bare-chested goat-men with horns tied to their heads scampered about in fuzzy trousers. In the center of the troupe stood a radiant maiden in a green dress, her long hair tangled with leaves and flowers. Trifkin raised his arms, and the noise of the crowd died down as all leaned forward to watch the actors at their craft.

Though he tried his best to follow the action, Travis didn't quite understand the play. As far as he could tell, it had to do with Winter and Spring. The old man in white was obviously Winter. He walked around what seemed a forest and tossed his snowy petals on the ground while the tree-women shivered their twiggy arms. Then Winter came upon the beautiful maiden in green—who was clearly Spring—and, affecting a salacious grin, snatched her up and ran off, an action which caused the audience to let out a reaction that was equal parts hisses and cheers.

After this, the scene changed, and the goat-men bounded onto the dais. Travis wasn't entirely sure what this part of the play was about, but it seemed to involve a fair amount of capering and trouser-dropping. The scene shifted again. Now Spring languished in Winter's chill grip. However, the goat-men soon came to her rescue. They grabbed Winter, heaved him off the stage, and thus freed young Spring, who showed her gratitude by letting the goat-men cavort around her. At last the goat-men surrounded Spring and concealed her from view. When they dashed away again, Spring had a large bulge in her dress.

At this point, Trifkin Mossberry himself bounded into the scene with an energetic series of flips and tumbles. He came to a stop before Spring and reached up her dress, then snatched out the bundle and held it aloft. It was a crude doll dressed all in yellow with a yellow crown. Travis decided he had just witnessed the birth of Summer. The play concluded in a dance that made the rest of the drama seem sedate by comparison, then the actors dropped to the steps in exhaustion as the audience roared its approval. The tree-women and goat-men sprang up to take their bows, followed by Winter and Spring. Last of all Trifkin himself rose and bowed, then spoke once more in his piping voice:

"I hope you liked our merry play,
Yet if not, then hear me, pray.
For we are like to shadows see,
Treading soft on memory.
And now let fall your weary heads,
As off you journey to your beds."

The curious troupe of actors dashed off the dais and disappeared through a door on one side of the great hall. The audience blinked and yawned, and, as if Trifkin's words had been some sort of enchantment, the revel wound down to an end. The trestle tables were folded and pushed against the walls, and people spread sleeping mats of woven rushes on the floor. King Kel disappeared into the room behind the frayed curtain, and the mysterious woman and her knightly compan ion were nowhere to be seen—they must have departed to a private chamber during the play. Even Falken looked weary as he strummed his lute, then slipped it into its case. It seemed Travis was the only one who was not ready for sleep. He gazed at the side door through which Trifkin's troupe had vanished. He could not stop thinking about the little man and his actors. There had been something *extraordinary* about them and their peculiar play, though he wasn't certain just what.

Torches were doused, and soon only the ruddy light of the fire filled the great hall as the folk of Kelcior readied themselves for sleep. Falken found a spot in a corner, and he and Travis lay down and curled up in their cloaks. Sounds drifted around them in the dimness: snoring, murmured talk, the soft noises of lovemaking. Travis tried to close his eyes, but he wasn't tired.

"Do you think he really would have thrown us out?" he whispered after a while. "King Kel, I mean. He seems a bit on the barbaric side."

"No, we were in no real danger," Falken said in a sleepy voice. "At least, I don't *think* we were. Kel likes to act terrible, but I suspect a large heart resides in that burly chest of his." He gave a weary sigh. "Now go to sleep, Travis Wilder."

Despite his exhaustion, Travis stared into the dusky air long after Falken's breathing had grown deep and slow.

31.

Travis opened his eyes. The fire had dwindled to a heap of coals, and the great hall was quiet except for the soft sounds of breathing. It was the deep of the night. He sat up, cocked his head, and listened. What was it that had awakened him? He wasn't certain, but it had sounded almost like . . . bells.

Now Travis was wide-awake. He glanced at Falken, who lay beside him in the murk. The bard's eyes were shut, and he snored gently.

"You should go back to sleep, Travis," he whispered to himself even as he quietly stood up. He cast one more look at Falken, then picked his way among the bodies that littered the floor of the great hall. He should not be doing this. At the very least it was foolish to go wandering around a strange castle at night, and at the very worst it could be perilous. Yet the last time he had heard bells—on the highway outside Castle City—was when everything had started to change. Maybe there was a connection here that could help him find a way back home.

His boot trod on something soft, and there was a sleepy grumble of protest. Travis froze and bit his lip to stifle a cry. He peered down in the gloom and saw he had stepped on the foot of a wildman. Travis's heart raced. Then the wildman let out a sigh, rolled over, snuggled against a slumbering hunting hound, and after that was quiet. Travis let out a silent breath of relief and continued on.

He came to a side door—the same door Trifkin Mossberry's troupe of actors had vanished through earlier. He pushed open the door, thankful that it did not creak, then stepped through and shut it behind him. He found himself in a narrow corridor. While the great hall had been warm with the heat of fire and dogs and people, here the stones radiated a wintry chill. At one end of the corridor lay an alcove which, his nose told him, contained the privy. At the other end was a small arch that opened on a spiral staircase. Travis headed for the stairs. The steps were steep and narrow, and he grew dizzy as he wound his way upward. At the end of the staircase was another archway. This opened onto a hallway similar to the one below. Doors lined one wall, leading to rooms that must lie above the great hall. The corridor was dark except for a single line of golden light that glowed beneath the farthest door.

This time there was no mistaking the sound. As he drew near the door, the music of bells shimmered on the air, followed by laughter as clear as creek water. Only when he stopped before the door did Travis realize he was trembling. A single beam of light poured through a keyhole. Before he even thought about what he was doing, he knelt and peered through the aperture into the chamber beyond.

The first thing he noticed was that the room was bathed in a radiance the color of sunlight in a forest. The second thing he noticed was that there was no visible source for this light: no candles in sconces, no torches on the wall, no oil lamps hanging on chains from the ceiling. The light simply *was*. It filled the chamber with its golden radiance.

Trifkin Mossberry's troupe gathered inside the room. At first glance nothing seemed out of the ordinary. This was merely a band of actors relaxing after a performance. Yet the more Travis stared, the more things seemed peculiar. For one thing, none of the actors had removed their costumes. A few of the goat-men reclined on the floor and balanced wine goblets on their naked chests. Another goat-man played a melody on a reed pipe while three tree-women danced in a circle around him and laughed as they shook their branch arms. The young actress who had played Spring leaned back on a lounge and hummed to the music, while a tree-woman combed her green hair with twig fingers. Old man Winter spun around and threw handfuls of his white petals in the air. Above it all, on a high shelf like a red-cheeked cherub, sat Trifkin Mossberry. The little man swung his short legs in time to the dance below. He gripped a silver cup and beamed beatifically, as one who was joyfully drunk.

Travis blinked. Suddenly he was no longer certain the actors *were* still in costume. The more he looked, the more he was certain the goat-men's crooked legs were not merely clad in shaggy trousers, but in shaggy *hair*. The tree-women did not simply grip bundles of twigs in their hands. Their hands and fingers *were* twigs, thin and lithe as willow-wands. The white flecks Winter tossed into the air melted into diamond droplets of water as they touched the floor. And Travis was now sure that the flowering vines had not simply been braided into Spring's hair. Instead, they were part of it, and grew from her scalp with the rest. Of them all, only Trifkin Mossberry seemed no different than he had earlier in the great hall. He still wore the same yellow breeches and green jacket, and the same red-feathered cap was perched on his curly brown hair.

As if he sensed eyes upon him, the little man turned his head toward the chamber's door. There was an odd look in his nut-brown gaze: curious, knowing, and slightly mocking. Travis's heart ceased to beat. Somehow Trifkin knew he was there!

Travis stifled a cry, scrambled backward, and ran for the stairwell.

The sound of high laughter pursued him. He did not look back. At breakneck speed he careened down the steps, ran to the side door, and hurried across the great hall. This time his clumsy steps left a string of grumbles and muttered curses in his wake. He reached Falken, knelt, and shook the bard's shoulder.

Falken groaned, and his eyes fluttered open. "What is it, Travis?"

"I saw them, Falken," he whispered. "They weren't costumes. They were . . . they were *real*."

"What on Eldh are you talking about?"

In quick words Travis described how he had heard the sound of bells and had followed, and what he had seen through the keyhole. However, even as he described the experience, it seemed more and more absurd. His words trailed off. Falken wore a disapproving look.

"You were dreaming, Travis," the bard said with no small amount of annoyance. "I'll grant you, the play was peculiar enough to give one nightmares. These days actors seem to think they can perform any bit of tomfoolery and label it art. What's more, dim-witted nobles are too prideful to say they don't understand it, and so lavish gold upon the actors to hide their ignorance. It *is* a trick, but hardly magic. Now go back to sleep."

Without waiting for a reply, the bard rolled over, shut his eyes, and soon snored again. Travis lay down and tried to do the same. Falken was probably right. The play *had* been peculiarly vivid, and it was little wonder it had encroached on his dreams. Yet when he closed his eyes, he saw again the goat-men and the tree-women dancing, and he remembered that he had glimpsed similar creatures before. The moment had been so fleeting that, at the time, he had decided he had seen nothing at all. Now he was not so certain what to believe.

It had been at Brother Cy's revival in Castle City, and he had seen them behind the curtain.

32.

This time it was Falken who woke Travis. The bard shook him—a bit more roughly than was strictly necessary—and grinned when Travis sat up.

"So, any more strange visitations last night?"

Travis worked his dry tongue. "Just this taste in my mouth."

"Feasts have a way of doing that." He gave Travis a hand up. "Let's go find something to wash away the remnants of last night's revel."

Though the hour was early, the keep's folk were already up and about, and the great hall was nearly empty. An ashwife stirred the coals in the fireplace, and a pair of girls scattered fresh rushes on the floor. Travis followed Falken down a set of stairs and through a door outside. Here, behind the keep, was a courtyard bounded by crumbling walls. The sun had just risen over the lake, and had set aglow the mist and the smoke of cookfires.

Despite what Falken had intimated last night, apparently there wasn't *always* a feast in progress in the petty kingdom of Kelcior. Last night's revelers were now engaged in a variety of tasks. Old women boiled mash for beer in a great iron cauldron. Boys cleaned the stalls in a thatched stable full of horses. Several men worked to bolster a sagging wall, and others sharpened swords, repaired harnesses, or hammered horseshoes over a hot fire. One of the shaggy wildmen led a flock of sheep out a gate in the courtyard's wall while a hound barked happily at his heels.

Travis and Falken made their way to the cooking shed, which leaned against one wall of the courtyard. The bard charmed the red-faced kitchenwife into giving them a pot of beer and a loaf of yesterday's bread, and they made their breakfast atop a pile of stones. Beer would not have been Travis's first choice to wash the taste of last night's feast from his mouth, but the stuff in the alepot turned out to be more yeast than fire, and it did the job. The black bread was hard, but it was flavorful and filling.

As they ate, Travis watched the men repair the courtyard wall. According to Falken, there were barbarian chiefs and bands of outlaws in this land who would be more than happy to take over the ancient keep if Kel gave them the chance. Here on the edges of the Dominions life was rough and only barely civilized, and a petty king ruled by the might of his warriors, not by the right of inheritance. However, Kel had held the keep for some years. He had forged alliances with several of the chiefs, and, in exchange for tithes of grain and meat, his warriors protected the villages scattered along the Queen's Way to the west. It was not a perfect system, yet it worked.

Falken stood up. "All right, let's get moving."

"Where are we going?" Travis asked around his last mouthful of bread.

"You will see."

Travis knew he would get no further explanation from the bard. He swilled down the last of the beer and followed. They returned the empty alepot to the kitchen, then left the courtyard through a gate. To their left lay a ruined portion of the fortress, and it was in this direction the bard turned. They picked their way among heaps of broken stone, and soon Travis realized they were making for the broken stump of a tower that stood on the end of the peninsula. Sweating despite the morning chill, they reached the tower and stepped through an open archway. Inside, the tower was roofless, its circular floor covered with dry grass. Sunlight spilled through a gap in the east wall. Only after a moment did Travis realize he and Falken were not the only ones in the tower. An amber-eyed woman in a midnight-blue kirtle sat upon a large stone, while a tall, fair-haired knight stood behind her, hand on the hilt of his sword—the same pair he had seen at the feast the night before.

"Well, it's about time you got here, Falken Blackhand," the woman said.

Travis shot the bard a nervous look. "These are the friends you talked about, aren't they?"

"However did you guess?" Falken said. The bard approached the duo. "I'm sorry it took me so long to get here, but I ran into a few . . . *complications* along the way."

The woman turned her startling gaze on Travis. "So I see."

He squirmed under her attention. Something about the way she looked at him made him feel transparent. He sighed in relief when she turned her attention back toward Falken.

"We were about to give up on you. It has been nearly a month since we were supposed to meet here, and I must tell you King Kel's hospitality, although graciously given, grows a trifle wearisome by the sixth or seventh feast."

"Oh, I don't know," the knight said in a cheerful tenor. He scratched the scruffy blond beard that clung to his cheeks. "I rather like Kel's court. One doesn't have to think about what to do every night. The social activities are all sort of planned out."

The woman stood. "So, are you going to introduce us to your companion, Falken? Or have you decided to dispense with all semblance of manners in order to better blend in with King Kel's courtiers? I must confess, it appears to be a role quite within your reach."

Falken winced, then turned toward Travis. "Travis Wilder, I would like you to meet my friends." He shot the others a dark look. "Though sometimes I wonder if that's really the proper word. At any rate, the big blond oaf in the metal suit is Beltan. And the lovely woman with the tongue of steel is the Lady Melia."

Melia shot Falken a warning look. "I might be happy to see you, Falken. Then again, it would be wise not to press the point." She approached Travis with a swish of wool, held out a hand, and affected a disarming smile. "I am pleased to make your acquaintance."

Unsure exactly what he was supposed to do, Travis took her hand in his and kissed it.

"Well, at least somebody here has manners," Melia said, and her eyes glinted.

"You might want to find a place to sit, Travis," Falken said. "Lady Melia and I have a bit of catching up to do, and it might take some time."

Falken sat on a stone near Melia, but Beltan continued to stand behind the dark-haired lady. Travis found a place in the sun not far away from the others. He sat cross-legged on the ground and let the morning light warm his face as he listened.

It was Melia who began. "A great deal has happened in the year since we parted ways and set off on our separate journeys, Falken. Beltan and I have traveled to all of the seven Dominions, and we have seen and heard much that is troubling. But let me begin by giving you what might be the most pressing news. A Council of Kings has been called at Calavere. Even at this moment, the rulers of the other six Dominions journey toward Calavan."

Falken let out a low whistle. "Things must be bad indeed. I'm afraid where I journeyed in the last year, I heard little news of the rest of Falengarth. Tell me more."

As sunlight crept across the grassy floor, Falken and Melia continued their exchange, with occasional additions from Beltan. Travis watched them with keen interest. After all, these were the people who might be able to help him get back to Colorado. There was little in their conversation he truly understood, yet during the course of their talk he managed to glean a bit of information about the two strangers. Apparently the big knight, Beltan, came from the Dominion of Calavan, where this *Council of Kings* was to be held. No one mentioned from what land Melia hailed, though Travis got the impression she came from the far south, and that she was a lady of some importance there. At least she acted like one.

At one point as he watched the three, Travis adjusted his wire-rimmed spectacles, and he almost thought he glimpsed a faint aura shining around each of them. Beltan's aura was bright gold, though there was a dark streak in it, almost like tarnish. Falken, too, had an aura Travis had not seen before—as pale as silver, and as sad as *valsindar* in winter. Brightest by far shone the corona around the Lady Melia. It was the same rich amber as her eyes, yet it shimmered with azure as well.

Melia turned to fix Travis with a piercing look. Startled, he fumbled with his glasses, and the auras were gone—if he had ever really seen them. Melia turned her gaze back toward Falken.

From what Travis could understand of their talk, Melia and Beltan had parted ways with Falken in the Dominion of Calavan last autumn, and had agreed to meet again in Kelcior in one year's time. The purpose of their travels had been to search for the source of an evil that had begun to stir in Falengarth. As Melia and Beltan told their tale, it became clear that, during the intervening year, things had gone from dark to darker.

Everywhere in the Dominions the summer had been short and blighted. Crops perished in the fields, while plague swept village after village. Now winter came early, and by the looks of things it meant to stay long. A hard winter meant that bands of barbarians and outlaws, who usually prowled the marches on the fringes of the Dominions, were likely to strike deeper into the heart of civilized lands in search of food and warmth. Fear and unrest already grew among the peasantry, and that made the nobles more than a little nervous. Yet raiders were not the only things of which the peasants were afraid. In some of the villages Melia and Beltan had passed through, the common folk had been worked up about rumors of strange creatures prowling about and causing mischief.

Travis's ears pricked up at this. He thought of Trifkin Mossberry's troupe of actors, and the queer figures he had glimpsed behind the curtain at Brother Cy's.

"Strange creatures?" Falken asked, his eyebrows drawn together.

It was Beltan who answered. "That's right. It's always in the most remote villages—those on the edges of deep forests or high mountains. Time and again, folk claim to have seen creatures right out of old stories and legends. Things like goblins, and greenmen, and even fairies." He let out a skeptical snort. "Of course, even I'm not stupid enough to believe those tales. I would guess they're just rumors told by village drunkards and gossipy goodwives."

"And most likely your guess is right," Melia said. "However, I'm not entirely surprised such rumors are on the rise. People grow more fearful and superstitious in troubled times. They do not know the real causes of disasters like plagues and famines, and so turn to old legends as a source of explanation." A grim light shone in her eyes. "Either that, or they turn to new religions."

Falken cocked his head.

"There's a new mystery cult on the rise in the Dominions," Melia said.

The bard ran a hand through his hair. "But that doesn't make any sense. The mystery cults are ancient. All the ones practiced in the Dominions came north across the Summer Sea centuries ago. How can there suddenly be a new cult?"

Melia smoothed her gown. "That's a good question, and one whose answer I would give much to know. From what I can gather, disciples of the Raven Cult must renounce their spirit into the keeping of their god. What's more, they hold that life itself is unimportant, for in death they will become one with the Raven god and know eternal ecstasy."

"That's awfully convenient," Falken said in a caustic voice. "You're saying the cult's priests don't have to try to explain any of the current strife and trouble. In fact, they can actually exploit it to win new converts."

Anger colored Melia's cheeks. "Exactly. And it all leads to a horrid kind of apathy. Disciples of the cult don't try to do anything to counter suffering in this world because, according to their priests, there's no point. If life becomes too hard, it simply makes them yearn for the bliss of death all the more. To the followers of the Raven Cult, life has no meaning. Only death does." She clenched a small hand into a fist. "It's utterly perverse," she said with a vehemence that seemed some-how personal.

Falken rubbed his chin with his gloved hand, his expression sad and weary. "Yes, it is. Unfortunately, it's also just another sign of dark times." He took a deep breath. "Well, I think our course from here is clear. We have to journey south as fast as possible, to the Council of Kings at Calavere, to report what we've learned."

"Wait a minute, Falken," Beltan said. "You have yet to tell us where you journeyed and what you found there. Have you forgotten?"

The bard's faded blue eyes grew distant. "No, I haven't forgotten. The truth is, I'm not yet entirely certain what I learned, and I don't want to say more until I'm sure. But I will tell you this: My journey was dark and long, and it took me to the Fal Threndur, and after that into Shadowsdeep, and all the way to the Rune Gate itself, beyond which lie the shadows of Imbrifale."

Melia and Beltan stared at Falken. A chill danced up Travis's spine. So that was why the bard had been traveling south through the Winter Wood, away from the Ironfang Mountains.

Falken's gaze snapped back into focus. "More of my journey I won't say at present. Yet I suppose now is as good a time as any to show you this, Melia. I wouldn't mind a second opinion." He pulled a cloth bundle from his pack. "I found it in Shadowsdeep."

The bard set the bundle atop a flat rock. Drawn by curiosity, Travis rose and approached. Falken unwrapped the cloth and revealed the object within. It was a disk of some sort of white stone, about as large as Travis's splayed hand. Embedded in its surface was a silver symbol:

$$\downarrow\!\!\!\diagup$$

A jagged break ran down the center of the disk and separated it into two halves.

Melia peered at the artifact and pursed her lips in interest. "It looks to me like some sort of bound rune. In which case, it's quite ancient. The Runebinders' art has not been known in Falengarth in centuries."

Falken nodded. "A bound rune—that's what I thought, but I'm glad to hear the same answer from the lips of another. I know only a little of runes, yet I think . . ."

The bard's words dwindled to a drone in Travis's ears. He gazed at the broken rune. The stone looked as smooth as cream, and his fingers itched. What would it feel like against his skin? Before he knew what he was doing, he reached out his right hand and touched the broken rune.

The stone disk flared with blue incandescence, and the silver symbol glowed bright white. At the same moment a voice spoke an unfamiliar word in Travis's mind.

Krond.

But that was not the strangest thing, for he knew the voice. It sounded exactly like Jack Graystone's.

Travis let out a cry of alarm, and the others gaped at him. He snatched his hand back, and at once the azure radiance vanished. The symbol on the disk dulled, and the voice in his mind faded and was gone.

Travis rubbed his hand—it tingled fiercely—then Falken reached out, grabbed his wrist, and turned it over.

A wave of disbelief crashed through Travis. The others looked at him as if he had just grown a second head. All except for Melia, whose expression was sharp and calculating.

It marked the palm of Travis's right hand—the hand Jack had grasped that night at the Magician's Attic—glowing silver-blue like some impossible brand. A symbol, but not the same as the one which marked the broken rune. A low moan of fear escaped his lips.

"Oh, Jack," he whispered. "What did you do to me?"

33.

"I believe, Falken," Melia said as she paced across the grassy circle inside the abandoned tower, "that it is time you told us more about this *complication* of yours." She fixed her amber gaze upon Travis.

Travis slouched on a rock, head hung low, and gripped the wrist of his right hand. The symbol on his palm had already faded away, but he could still feel it there, like a prickling beneath his skin. The glowing image had burned itself into his brain, so that every time he blinked he saw the symbol again, three crossed marks:

Questions whirled in Travis's mind. How had Jack placed the marks on his hand? And what did the symbol mean?

No, it wasn't a symbol. Though it was different from the mark on the broken disk Falken had brought from Shadowsdeep, certainly it was of the same ilk. What had the bard called the stone? A rune? Yet that still did not answer his question. *What had Jack done to him?*

Beltan shifted from foot to foot but said nothing. The rawboned knight clearly deferred to Falken and Melia on the topic of magic. Yes—*magic*. There was nothing else it could be. Except that, in the stories Travis had read as a child, magic had always been a wondrous and exciting thing. Instead, this was dark, and frightening, and isolating. Even now the others watched him with wary expressions.

Falken crossed his arms over his gray tunic. "I had thought we were done with these little surprises of yours, Travis."

"So did I." Travis looked up at the bard. "I need to tell Lady Melia and Beltan, don't I? About everything that's happened to me."

"I think that's probably a good idea."

Travis took a deep breath, then spoke in a quiet voice, recounting all that had happened to him starting with that last, fateful night in Castle City. Throughout it all Melia watched him with a calm and even intensity, as if nothing he might say could possibly have worked to surprise her, but Beltan's eyes grew wide.

Travis's words trailed into silence. Melia rose and approached him with a rustle of blue wool.

"May I see the box?"

He jumped to his feet. "Of course." He pulled out the small iron box and held it toward Melia.

She shook her head. "You open it. Please."

Polite as they were, Melia's words seemed less a request than they did a command. Travis undid the latch and opened the lid. Inside, the gray-green stone shone in the morning light. Melia peered into the box and examined the stone, though she was careful not to touch it. Then she indicated he could shut the lid.

"What do you think it is?" Travis asked.

She cupped an elbow in one hand and rested the other beneath her chin. "I don't think anything. At least, not yet. However, I suspect you would be wise to keep the box well hidden, Travis. Do not open it again unless for some reason it is absolutely necessary."

Travis tucked the box back into his pocket. Falken treated Melia to a speculative look. Obviously the lady had some suspicions regarding the stone's nature but was unwilling to say what these were. Travis, for one, was not about to ask her. He had had more than enough surprises for one day.

Falken rewrapped the broken stone disk in its cloth and tucked it away. "Let's get going, then. I think it's time to beg our leave from good King Kel. It's a long way to Calavan."

Melia made a subtle gesture toward Travis. "And what are we going to do about our little problem?"

"Well, unless you have any ideas, we still have no way of getting him back to his own world."

Melia tapped her cheek with a finger. "I think we had better take him with us to Calavere. After that little incident with the bound rune, I imagine it's best if we keep an eye on him."

"My thoughts exactly."

"Excuse me," Travis said, annoyed at being spoken about as if he wasn't standing right there, "don't I get a say in this?"

Evidently he did not. Melia and Falken exited the tower, then started back toward the keep, discussing plans for the journey south along the way.

Travis stared after them, feeling more than a little sorry for himself. "No one ever tells me what's really going on."

Beltan clapped a big hand on Travis's shoulder. "You might as well get used to it," the knight said with a grin. "Those two aren't much into explaining things." He started off after the bard and the lady.

Travis stood alone in the empty tower. Then he took a deep breath and followed the others through the ruins.

34.

Grace awoke to a soft sound, like the movements of a mouse.

She opened her eyes and blinked. Honey-colored light filled the bed-chamber. She turned her head on the pillow and saw golden sunbeams slant through the room's narrow window. It had been both morning and snowing when Durge brought her to the castle. Now the clouds must have broken, and the day had turned to late afternoon. She had been asleep for hours.

Her forehead creased in a frown. There it was again, the sound that had awakened her: a rustle followed by a faint *pad-pad*, as of quiet footsteps. Grace pushed aside the bedcovers and sat up.

Like young does caught in the beam of a hunter's flashlight, two servingwomen in gray dresses froze and stared at Grace in round-mouthed surprise. One stood beside a table that had not been there earlier and was in the act of setting down a tray laden with dishes. The other was just picking up Grace's clothes from the hearth.

Grace cleared her throat. "Hello."

She might have screamed the word in her loudest voice rather than murmured it, for the reaction it caused. As one, the serving maidens let out a cry. The one dropped the tray on the table in a bright clatter of crockery. The other snatched up the damp garments and crumpled them into a ball. Both scurried toward the chamber's door.

Grace reached out a hand in alarm. "Wait! Those are my clothes!"

It was too late. The serving maidens both shot her one last look of terror, then fled the room and shut the door behind them.

Grace chewed her lip. What had that been all about? Certainly she didn't look as frightening as she had earlier—although belatedly she realized she had not combed her hair, and a probing hand confirmed that it was wild and tangled from sleep. Yet that didn't really explain why the maidens had seemed so afraid of her. And why had they taken her clothes?

Grace climbed down from the bed and moved to the hulking wardrobe. There was nothing to do but try one of the gowns. She examined each of the garments in growing despair, then finally chose the one that seemed the least complicated. This was a voluminous affair that consisted of more yards of blue wool than Grace could count. She shrugged the gown over her head and almost went down under its weight, but she gritted her teeth and managed to keep her feet. After this ensued a great deal of tugging, pulling, and adjusting in which she tried to figure out the gown's myriad and inexplicable straps and fastenings.

It was futile.

Grace considered herself an intelligent woman, but the logic of the gown was beyond her. No matter what she tried, the gown bunched up or gapped open, and generally made her look like an overstuffed chair. Huffing with exertion, she untangled herself from the dress and heaved it back into the wardrobe with a few choice exclamations.

She was about to shut the door of the wardrobe—she did not want to even *look* at the gowns again—when she noticed something balled up in a corner. She drew out the bundle and unfolded it. There was a long shirt of brown wool as well as thick green leggings, along with a leather belt. Now these were more to her liking. Grace shrugged on the clothes over her undergarments. Both the tunic and hose were baggy, and she suspected they belonged to a servingman who had forgotten them here. However, the garb was warm and comfortable, and—most importantly—comprehensible. She cinched the tunic around her waist and noticed, attached to the belt, a leather pouch. She moved to the mantel, slipped her necklace over her head, and tucked the pendant beneath her tunic. Then she took the Seekers' card and the half-coin, placed them inside the pouch, and tied it.

"There," Grace said in satisfaction.

She turned from the wardrobe, and a savory smell reached her nostrils. Her gaze moved to the tray on the table. A chair had been placed nearby. Her stomach let out a loud growl of protest to let her know it had been ignored far too long, and it was high time she paid it some attention. Grace considered the tray for a moment, then moved to the table and sat. After all, hunger impaired the thinking process. It simply made more sense to come up with a plan on a full stomach.

Grace lifted various lids and covers and explored the contents of the crocks. The fare was peculiar: slices of cold meat accompanied by a green jellied sauce, tiny poached eggs that floated atop a thick beige soup, a bread pudding freckled with mysterious herbs, and a kind of dried fruit she did not recognize swimming in thick cream. She eyed the food for a moment, then hunger won out over caution.

She sampled the contents of one of the crocks. Seconds later she was shoveling food into her mouth. The meat was rich and delicious as long as she avoided the green stuff, and while the eggs had a strong, unpleasant flavor, the yellow soup tasted of leeks and potatoes and was quite acceptable. The bread pudding had a note of anise, which she had always liked, and the dried fruits were edible, if leathery. In all, Grace had partaken of far worse meals, though given her hunger she supposed she would have made do with dog kibble.

Serious eating had given way to pleasant nibbling when she noticed something near the hearth where her clothes had been. It was a pair of boots. She set down her spoon, rose, and retrieved them. They were fashioned from creamy deerskin. She sat on the chair and tried them on. They slid over her feet and calves like butter, and she could not help letting out a soft gasp of delight. The boots fit perfectly. So perfectly she suspected they had been made especially for her while she slept, using her old hospital shoes for a model. She stood and walked around the chamber to test her new footwear. They hugged her feet, yet flexed with every step, like a pair of boots she had owned for years. She suspected she could walk twenty miles in them and not get a single blister.

Her path brought her near one of the room's narrow windows, and she realized then she had yet to look outside. She halted and peered through the window. It was glazed with rippled glass dotted with bubbles, inclusions of sand, and other imperfections. These sparkled in the sunlight, and the effect was beautiful rather than distracting.

She saw that she was on an upper floor of one of the wings attached at right angles to the main keep. To her left she could see the king's tower. To her right was the gate through which she and the knight Durge had entered the upper bailey. Across the way was the other wing of the keep, and in the center of the courtyard lay the tangled garden. Bare-limbed trees obscured her view of the garden's center, but she could just make out meandering footpaths as well as the evergreen labyrinth of a hedge maze. The sun sank behind the castle's spires and turrets, and gilded them with molten gold, while dozens of banners snapped in a stiff wind, bright against the darkling sky.

Grace still stared out the window when a soft knock sounded on the chamber's door.

35.

Grace turned and stared at the door. The knock came again, gentle yet insistent. She froze in panic. What was she to do? She could face any gruesome injury, could treat any hideous disease, could manipulate the wounded like broken puppets. So why did whole people terrify her so?

She cleared her throat. "Come in," she called out and winced at the wavering of her voice.

There was a pause, then the latch turned, and the door swung open. A young woman stepped into the chamber, and Grace knew at once that this was no serving girl.

So that's what those gowns are supposed to look like.

The dress hung elegantly on the slender young woman, and its sweeping lines enhanced her willowy shape rather than bound or concealed it. A pleated fold of cloth gracefully draped her right shoulder. The gown's sapphire color perfectly matched the young woman's large eyes and contrasted with her dark hair and ivory skin. Her features were fine, but they were strong and gentle rather than merely delicate. Though at present she was pretty, she would, with age, become beautiful.

The young woman curtsied deeply. How could she possibly manage the action in that heavy gown? But she made the motion appear effortless.

At last the young woman straightened. "Am I disturbing you, Your Highness?" she asked in a clear voice.

Grace's surprise gave way to exasperation. She let out a groan. "Not you, too."

A look of alarm crossed the young woman's visage. "Has Her Highness been disturbed previously in her rest?" Alarm turned to quiet outrage. "Be certain I will find the perpetrators of this terrible act and have them suitably drubbed, Your Highness!"

Grace thought of the two frightened servants and shook her head. "Oh, no—no drubbing. Please. Really, no one disturbed me. It's just . . ." She took a step toward the young woman. "It's just everyone keeps calling me *Your Highness*, and I really wish they wouldn't." There, she had said it.

The other nodded, and a knowing smile touched the corners of her mouth. "Lord Alerain warned me you would maintain this, Your High—that is, *my lady*. Of course, I will respect your wishes. However, you must let me know how I am to address you."

Manic laughter tickled Grace's throat. "How about if you just call me Grace? It even happens to be my name."

"Well, that would seem to be the logical choice then, wouldn't it?" the young woman said.

Either she had entirely missed the wryness of Grace's comment, or she was responding with an even subtler humor. Grace could not decide which. Curiosity began to replace her trepidation.

"And you are . . . ?"

A chagrined look crossed the other's face. "Well, it seems I left my manners in my other gown today."

Grace breathed in relief. Definitely humor.

"I am the Lady Aryn, Baroness of Elsandry." The young woman said this in a slightly pained voice, as if she found the title somewhat trying. "However, if I am to call you Grace, then you must call me Aryn, and were you the queen of lost Malachor, I would still not accept a refusal in this regard."

Never in her life had Grace been comfortable around other people. Yet she felt almost at ease in the company of the young noblewoman, as if there were some connection between them she could sense but not quite name. She made her own clumsy attempt at a curtsy.

"I wouldn't dream of refusing your request, Aryn." Feeling positively brave, she fixed the baroness with a sharp look. "Now, do you plan to come in and shut that door, or is it your particular intention to let in that icy draft? I've already been half-frozen once today, and that really was enough."

"I'm so sorry, my lady!" Aryn hurried into the room and shut the door behind her. The playful mirth had fled her expression, and concern clouded her eyes.

Grace groaned inwardly. *Well, you've certainly done a good job of botching the mood. I suppose that will teach you to try being funny.*

She spoke in earnest then. "Please don't worry, Aryn. I was only being foolish."

She did not want the baroness to leave in fear as the servants had. Rarely in her life had Grace sought out companionship, but at that moment she realized just how profoundly *lonely* she was. But what could she say to convince the baroness to stay?

"I'm afraid I have a tendency to be a bit too wry for my own good sometimes. Please, you have to forgive me."

A radiant smile lit Aryn's face. "You needn't apologize, Grace. Certainly not after all you've endured today."

They gazed at each other, then the baroness rushed forward and reached out to squeeze Grace's left hand with her own.

"Oh, I'm so glad you're not dreadful!" she said, then she snatched her hand back and bowed her head.

Grace was unnerved in the wake of the baroness's gesture. "What made you think I would be dreadful?"

Aryn glanced up. "Usually noble ladies who visit Calavere are troubled only with asserting their status over the highest-ranking woman in the castle." She let out a despondent sigh. "Which, I'm afraid, at the moment happens to be me. I'm King Boreas's ward, and ever since Queen Narena passed away, it has been my duty to greet and entertain all visiting ladies of importance. This typically consists of listening politely while I am told in no small amount of detail how much grander and more luxurious their households are compared to mine, how much finer and more expensive their clothes, and how much faster and more fearful their servants."

"Sounds delightful," Grace said. Aryn's description reminded her more than a little of the power plays in Denver Memorial's Emergency Department. There, the residents had constantly jockeyed against each other to win the favor of the attending physicians. It was a game Grace had not cared to play. "However, as I told Lord Alerain, I'm not royalty, so there's certainly no need to be afraid of *me*."

"Of course, Grace," the baroness said. "As you wish."

It was clear the baroness believed Grace's denials of nobility as little as had the king's seneschal. However, Grace did not press the point.

Aryn continued with increased enthusiasm. "Regardless of your station, or your reason for traveling to Calavere, I'm glad you're here, Grace. You see, there are so few women of manners in the castle who are even remotely near my age. I must confess, I had secretly hoped you would be absolutely wonderful, and that you would wish to spend time talking together, and taking walks in the garden, and . . ." Her cheeks flushed. "But I'm being horribly presumptuous, aren't I?"

"Yes, you are," Grace said. "However, you're also lucky in that you've happened to presume correctly."

There was a moment's silence, then Aryn laughed. To her surprise, Grace found herself joining in. Apparently she was much better at humor when she wasn't actually trying to be funny. She would have to remember that.

After this, Aryn gestured to a stone bench set into the wall before the window. The two sat together in the honeyed light of late afternoon. Grace shifted on the bench and searched for something to say. She had never excelled at the art of conversation, though it might have been for lack of practice.

"So, do I have the king to thank for the kind hospitality I've been shown?" She tried to make the question sound as if it weren't completely forced.

Aryn shook her head, and a fleeting smile played about her lips. "Oh, no. I'm afraid that King Boreas is usually far too preoccupied to see to the needs of his guests. Ruling a Dominion is a rather distracting job. At least, so I would imagine. The king rarely so much as exchanges pleasantries with visitors to Calavere, unless they are of the greatest importance. Taking care of guests is my job."

"Then I would like to thank you," Grace said. "For everything. And especially for these." She gestured to the deerskin boots she now wore. "They're absolutely wonderful."

"I'm so glad you like them, Grace." A shadow of concern touched Aryn's forehead. "Alas, I see none of the gowns I left for you were similarly suitable. I was afraid that might be the case. However, you're quite a bit taller than I, so I had few choices. Those are Queen Narena's gowns—she was almost exactly your size. I had dared hope they would do temporarily, but they *are* rather out of fashion. However, if I could impose on you terribly to wait, by tomorrow I could have the king's tailor alter one of my own gowns for—"

Grace shook her head and interrupted. "No, it wasn't the gowns, Aryn. I'm afraid it was me. I just couldn't figure out where all the straps and hoops were supposed to go. I've never worn anything like it before."

Aryn raised an eyebrow. However, if she thought Grace's statement odd, she was too well mannered to say so. "Well, then, I will simply have to show you." The baroness moved to the wardrobe.

After a moment Grace decided to ask the question that had been growing on her mind ever since coming to the castle. "Why are people here afraid of me?"

Aryn turned around. "What on Eldh would make you say a thing like that?"

Eldh? Was that the name of this world? Grace filed that question away for later. Now, before she lost her nerve, she explained the way in which the guards had looked at her, and how the two serving maidens had reacted when she woke. When Grace finished, Aryn pressed her lips together in worry.

"You know the reason, don't you?" Grace said.

Aryn sat down beside her, her expression concerned. "You really mustn't worry about it, Grace. They're common people, after all— predisposed toward superstition. And toward gossip as well. I fear you hadn't been here an hour before the story of how the earl of Stonebreak found you in Gloaming Wood had run thrice around the castle. Of course, the tale grew more fantastic and further removed from the truth with every telling, until soon the servants had convinced themselves that you are in fact a . . ."

"That I am what?"

Aryn drew in a deep breath. "That you are in fact a fairy queen." She shook her head. "I know, it is a great fancy, but there *are* many strange stories about Gloaming Wood. Of course, these are nothing more than tales to frighten children by firelight. Still, you were perfectly white when the earl brought you into the castle, and you are certainly beautiful enough to be one of the fey folk. I've never seen eyes the color of yours. They're remarkable, like a forest in summer. So I hope you won't be *too* upset that the servants mistook you for a queen of the Little People."

The baroness laughed at this, then her mirth faltered. "They *are* mistaken, aren't they?"

This was the first time Grace had ever been accused of being a fairy queen. She did her best to sound reassuring. "I'm sorry to disappoint you, but I'm afraid I'm completely mundane."

Aryn's smile gathered strength once more. "I rather doubt that. There's nothing mundane about you, Grace of Beckett." The baroness leaned forward, threw her left arm around Grace's shoulders, and pressed a cheek to hers. "We're going to be friends, aren't we, Grace?"

Grace stiffened, alarmed by this sudden display. This was exactly the sort of intimacy she had guarded herself against all her life. She didn't dare get this close to another, not now, not yet. It was far too dangerous. However, gradually, the baroness's warmth melted through her fears, and Grace tentatively returned the embrace.

"No, Aryn," she said to her own amazement. "I think we already are."

It was then Grace realized what had been bothering her. The second the baroness of Elsandry had entered the chamber, her doctor's instincts had pricked up in alert, had sensed something was *wrong*. Until that moment those instincts had been content to remain in the back of Grace's mind, patiently and dispassionately observing. Now they rushed to the fore. Before she even considered what she was doing, she gently pushed the baroness away and regarded the young woman with probing eyes.

"May I look at your right arm, Aryn?"

The baroness's face paled, and a shadow stole into her eyes. "My arm? Why should you want to look at my arm?"

"I'm a doctor," Grace said in a solemn voice. "I might be able to help you."

"A doctor?"

"I heal people, Aryn."

At last the baroness nodded. "I see. You mean you are a chirurgeon."

"You're surprised," Grace said. "Are there no women doctors in this . . . in Calavan?"

Aryn gave her a puzzled look. "All healers are women, of course. Men consider it beneath them, though in truth I think they are simply squeamish. Besides, they lack the patience for so subtle a craft. But I might have known you were a chirurgeon. You have the look of a woman of wisdom about you." The baroness braced her shoulders. "Of course you may examine me, Grace, but I doubt there is anything you can do to help me."

With the same precision she always used when examining a new patient in the ED, Grace lifted the fold of cloth that draped Aryn's shoulder. Beneath, the baroness's withered right arm rested in a sling fashioned from a linen kerchief.

Aryn sat perfectly still and stared impassively out the window while Grace examined her and systematically formulated a diagnosis. Unlike the left arm, which was normally developed, the right was malformed and profoundly atrophied, being perhaps two-thirds the length of its companion. Bones were visible beneath the wax-pale skin, twisted and fragile, like the braided tendrils of a wisteria vine. Wisp-thin muscles clung to these, displaying that perfect liquid smoothness that comes only with persistent disuse. The hand was folded in on itself and held in a perpetually flexed and pronated position—wrist and palm downward, digits curled in. The last three fingers, only partially developed, were syndactylous, contained within a single sheath of skin. The result was disturbing and alien, yet beautiful, like the white, contorted arm of a *kabuki* dancer, frozen in a gesture of quiet sadness: the fall of a wounded dove, the stillness of a yew branch in winter.

"Can you squeeze my fingers?" Grace asked in her crisp doctor's voice.

Aryn frowned, concentration written across her forehead. The curled digits closed softly around Grace's hand. Then, with a gasp, the baroness pulled her arm back and held the withered limb close against her side. With her left hand she deftly replaced the fold of her gown and concealed the arm once more.

Grace took a deep breath. "You're right, Aryn. It's a congenital defect. There's nothing I can do."

Aryn nodded in reply. "You mustn't worry, Grace. I don't mind. Truly, I'm quite used to it." With this, the baroness smiled. It was a brave and brilliant expression.

Grace did her best to smile in turn. "I could show you some simple exercises. They would help increase your strength and range of motion. Nothing drastic, but you might be able to use your arm a little more than you can now."

"That's kind of you," Aryn said.

A distant look crept into her eyes, and she gazed out the window. Her voice became a murmur.

"In a way we have something in common, Grace. When I was born, my mother died in childbed, and when the midwife saw my . . . my arm, she told my father, the baron, that I was a changeling—a child spirited into my mother's womb by the Little People. I was born in winter, and the old midwife would have set me out in the snow to perish. However, I was my father's only child, and he was not a superstitious man. He cast the midwife out instead." Her eyes returned from the window to focus on Grace, and her lips smiled once again. "So now both of us have been mistaken for the kin of fairies. I suppose that makes us sisters of a sort."

Grace could only stare in sorrow. How many times had she tried to resuscitate a baby pulled from a cold metal Dumpster? Maybe this world was not so far from Earth after all.

A sharp knock sounded at the chamber's door. Grace and Aryn exchanged looks, then the baroness rose to answer the knock. The door opened to reveal a stocky man clad in a mail shirt and a black cloak. Grace rose to her feet.

The man-at-arms bowed, then cleared his throat and spoke in a loud voice. "I bring a summons from His Majesty, King Boreas of Calavere. The king respectfully requests the presence of the Lady Grace of Beckett in his chamber. Immediately."

Grace shot Aryn a look of terror. The baroness's mouth dropped open.

"I thought you said the king was too busy to greet his guests," Grace said, breathless.

"He is." Aryn fixed Grace with an awed expression. "Unless . . . unless, as I said, those guests happen to be of unusual importance."

Grace lifted a hand to her chest and tried to breathe.

36.

Grace hurried after Aryn down the torchlit corridor while the man-at-arms marched behind them.

In the bedchamber, the baroness had clucked over the drab serv-ingman's clothes Grace had donned. However, the guard had contin-ued to stand in the doorway in wait for them, and there had been neither time nor opportunity for a change of costume. Aryn had taken a moment to pull an ivory comb from a pocket and subdue Grace's ash-blond hair. Then the two had rushed out the door to half walk, half run through the castle's maze of passages and hallways. Grace gath-ered one did not keep the king of Calavan waiting.

"Whatever you may think when you first meet him, King Boreas really isn't so terrible," Aryn said. "Well, *most* of the time, that is."

Grace winced. "That really isn't all that reassuring, you know."

Aryn gave her a tight smile. "Sorry. I guess I left my wits in my other gown as well. I'll try harder."

They rounded a corner, and the corridor widened into a long hall.

"Boreas is a rather simple man," Aryn said so only Grace could hear. "Though do not take this to mean he lacks intelligence, for he most certainly does not. However, the king tends to see things in absolutes, and he greatly favors action over debate. So if he asks you a question or wants your opinion on something, cut to the heart of the matter in as few words as you possibly can. And be warned: He may say things to deliberately startle or frighten you. It's his way of testing people. The best reaction is to react as little as possible—don't flinch or gasp. If he thinks you weak or flighty, he'll dismiss you immediately. Although in his favor I will say he is no more biased toward women than men in this regard."

Aryn tapped her chin. "Oh, and one more thing. The king thinks he's a good deal funnier than he actually is. So do try to pay attention to what he's saying, and if it sounds at all like a joke, laugh. The louder the better."

Grace clenched her jaw. How was she possibly going to remember any of this? Facing Aryn for the first time had terrified her nearly to the point of paralysis, and she couldn't imagine a person milder than the baroness. How was she going to face a loud and demanding king? If he was bleeding and unconscious on a gurney in the ED, she wouldn't even blink. But whole and talking, asking her questions? That was a far different matter.

"You'll do just fine, Grace," Aryn said, as if she sensed Grace's thoughts.

Grace made an attempt at a courageous smile. "I'll try my best."

They rounded a corner and were brought up short by an unexpected obstacle in their path. Grace's jaw went slack, and Aryn let out a gasp.

"Well, if it isn't our dearest Lady Aryn."

The lady—for certainly she was a noblewoman—was older than Aryn, more of an age with Grace. Though, next to her, Grace felt like a gawky and boyish teenager. The lady's beauty was lush and sensual, mature without the faintest trace of decline. *Ripe.* That was the word. She was perfectly, lustrously ripe. Her hair was dark blond, her complexion smooth ivory, her eyes the same bold green as her gown. It seemed she favored the color, for a large emerald pendant rested in the deep cleft of her bosom, which was barely contained within the confines of the gown's bodice. Instinct prickled the small hairs on the back of Grace's neck.

Aryn's forehead crinkled. She gave the other a curt nod. "Good eventide, Lady Kyrene," she said in a tight voice.

Kyrene lifted a hand to the arch of her throat. "Sweet Aryn, you hardly seem pleased to see me. And here I was only just thinking how lovely it would be to talk with you."

Aryn chewed the words. "Forgive me, Kyrene. We're in a bit of a hurry right now."

The emerald-gowned lady affected an ingenuous expression. "But whatever for, love?"

The baroness groaned. "We don't have time for this, Kyrene. You know exactly what we're about. Hardly a mouse shakes its whiskers in this castle that you don't know of it. I doubt you simply happened to be wandering in this particular corridor at this moment by chance alone."

Kyrene's full lips parted in a smile. A kitten-pink tongue ran across tiny, milk-white teeth. "My, you are a clever girl, aren't you?" It was not in any way a compliment. The lady's green gaze moved to drink in Grace, cool with a glint of curiosity. "And who is this accompanying you on your weighty errand?"

"Please don't expect me to believe you don't already know," Aryn said.

A delicate expression of annoyance touched Kyrene's visage. "What a wild thing you are, Lady Aryn. Haven't you manners enough to introduce me properly to a new guest of the court?" She shook her head and sighed. "But I am cruel to scold you. It's hardly your fault, raised as you were by that crude bull of a king, and without the benefit of a woman's tempering influence. You must forgive me, love."

Aryn gritted her teeth. "Oh, think nothing of it." She drew in a deep breath. "Kyrene, this is the Lady Grace of Beckett. Grace, allow me to introduce you to the Lady Kyrene. Kyrene is the countess of Selesia, in southern Calavan."

Grace had absolutely no idea what to say. She settled for, "Pleased to meet you."

"Of course you are, love," the countess said. Interest flickered in her languid gaze. "It is rather unusual for a traveling lady to be summoned by the king so soon upon arriving, is it not? Do you know what he might wish of you?"

Grace shook her head. "I'm afraid I don't have an answer for you."

Kyrene's eyes narrowed. "I see the courtly game is played as skillfully in this Beckett of yours as it is here in Calavere. I will have to remember that."

What did *that* mean? Grace wasn't trying to play a game, she was simply being honest. Yet now the countess regarded her in—what? Fascination? Contempt? Suspicion?

Kyrene turned toward Aryn. "I must be on my way, love." She inclined her head toward Grace. "I wish you well in your audience with the king, my lady. But I won't say good-bye. After all, I am quite certain we will see each other again."

Whether that was a threat or a promise, Grace wasn't sure. The Countess Kyrene brushed past them with a rustle of fabric, swept down the corridor, and was gone.

Aryn's expression was part shock and part wonder. "She has absolutely no shame."

"There's no room for it in that dress," Grace said.

Aryn bit her lip. "I'm a baroness and she's only a countess, but somehow she always manages to make me feel like I'm a serving maid and she's a queen." She shook her head, lost in thought, then she let out a small cry. "King Boreas!" She clutched Grace's elbow in panic. "We have to hurry!"

"What will the king do if we're late?"

"You truly don't wish to know."

Grace needed no further inducement. With the guard in tow, they hastened down the corridor into the heart of Calavere.

They turned down a side passage and came to a stop before a broad door. An ornate crest had been carved into the surface of the door and inlaid with silver: two swords crossed beneath a crown with nine points.

The man-at-arms who had accompanied them cleared his throat and addressed Grace. "The king is expecting you, my lady. You may enter at once." The guard rapped on the door, then pushed it open and held it for Grace. Beyond she glimpsed flickering red light.

Aryn gave Grace's hand a warm squeeze. "Good luck. And try to remember what I told you."

Horror flooded Grace. "But aren't you coming in with me?"

The baroness shook her head. "The summons was for you, Grace, not for me. But I know you'll do wonderfully." The light in her sapphire eyes wasn't quite as confident as it had been before. "May Yrsaia's strength be with you." With that, Aryn withdrew her hand and stepped away.

Grace had to think of some way to get out of this, some excuse why she couldn't see the king. But her mind was frozen, and it was already too late. The guard took her arm and gently but irresistibly propelled her through the portal. Grace caught her toe on a crack in the floor. She stumbled forward, gasped, and heard the door shut behind her with a *boom*.

"Come in, my lady," said a deep voice.

Grace lifted her head. The walls and floors of the chamber were strewn with rugs, and a claw-foot table of dark wood dominated the room's center. A fire roared in an open fireplace, and what she at first took for a lumpy fur rug before the hearth was in fact a pile of sleeping black mastiffs. Each hound's head was bigger than her own. She might have been afraid of the dogs, but another feral figure caught and trapped her attention.

King Boreas of Calavan was at once compelling and terrifying. He was not so much huge as he was *solid*. His presence weighed so heavily on the air that she thought she might start orbiting around him, caught like a piece of flotsam in his gravity well. His visage was fiercely handsome, and his keen eyes sparked like flint on steel. A few flecks of gray in his trimmed beard and dark, slicked-back hair—along with a series of fine lines around his eyes and nose—were the only hint of his advancing middle years.

Belatedly, she decided some obeisance was expected of her. After all, this *was* a king before her. She started a curtsy, then realized she had absolutely no idea how to complete the action, and turned it into a clumsy sort of bow halfway through. She straightened and expected to see anger or derision in the king's eyes. There was neither. Instead he regarded her with an intensity that was far more alarming. It felt as if he were trying to look inside her.

"Allow me to welcome you to Calavere, my lady." His voice thrummed in her chest.

A jerky nod was all the reply she could manage. She could not breathe, and a cold hand constricted her throat.

The king crossed his arms. "I suppose it is proper etiquette for us to exchange long salutations and overwrought soliloquies concerning our overwhelming joy at meeting before we discuss anything remotely resembling business. However, I'm not certain I have the time or patience for such niceties." His voice deepened to a growl. "Does that trouble you, my lady?"

He flung the question at her like a knife. Grace remembered Aryn's admonitions and somehow managed to keep herself from flinching. She cleared her throat.

"No, Your Majesty. It does not."

The king eyed her for a moment, then grinned. It did not seem an expression of mirth. There were far too many teeth involved, and they were all far too pointed. Boreas scratched his beard, then nodded.

"Excellent, my lady. Consider yourself well met, for I am glad indeed you have come to Calavere. Now, I will bandy words no more, but will get right to the point." He approached her with fluid strength. "I require your help, my lady."

Was this one of the king's poor attempts at humor Aryn had warned her about? However, something in the king's frank expression told Grace this was no joke. She swallowed her forced laughter.

"My help?"

"That's right." Boreas pointed a finger directly toward her heart. "You, my lady, are going to help me save Calavan."

37.

King Boreas paced before the fireplace like a caged animal. The crimson light flickered across his handsome face and made his features sharper yet. The king snorted as he gathered his thoughts.

Grace watched in silent awe. *He is indeed like a bull, a great, dark, restless bull.*

She clutched the goblet of wine he had thrust into her hands moments before. The king had downed his wine in a single gulp, then tossed the cup aside. Grace might have liked to do the same, but she was not certain she could trust her shaking arms to bring the goblet to her lips without spilling. She was an overworked resident in the emergency department of a city hospital. What could she possibly do to help the ruler of a medieval kingdom?

Boreas halted and turned to impale her with steely eyes. She braced her shoulders.

"Have you ever heard of a Council of Kings, my lady?"

Grace shook her head. "No, Your Majesty. I haven't. Other than to hear it mentioned by the earl of Stonebreak after he . . . after he came upon me in the forest."

She expected the king to give her a look of suspicion, like the Countess Kyrene, who had seemed to take nothing Grace said at face value. However, Boreas nodded, as if he had not considered for a moment that she might be telling him anything other than the truth.

"I am little surprised," he said. "There has not been a Council of Kings in over a century, not since the horde of barbarian Thanadain marched out of the west to threaten the Dominions. I had to have Lord Alerain dig through all of Calavere's records just to find the proper protocol for calling a council."

"Then it was you who called the council, Your Majesty?" Grace asked, apprehensive at her boldness after the fact. Her impulse to drink her wine overpowered her fear of spilling it. She raised the goblet and actually managed to get some of the liquid into her mouth. She swallowed. The wine was cool, rich, and smoky. She gulped some more and set the goblet down.

The king gave her a curious look. "Yes, I did call the council. Somebody had to do it." He clenched a big hand into an even bigger fist. "By Vathris, I wasn't going to sit here on my throne waiting for one of those other fool monarchs to get around to it while the Dominions fall apart around my ears!"

Grace jumped back, as if Boreas's wrath might scorch her like fire. That should teach her to ask questions of a king. It was time to stop this charade right now. There was nothing she could do to help King Boreas. She summoned her will and told herself it would be no worse than informing one of the ED's attending physicians that his diagnosis was completely wrong. After all, she had done that often enough.

"I understand your urgency, Your Majesty." She tried to keep the quaver from her voice. "However, I really don't know anything about kings or councils, so I think it's best if I don't—"

Boreas dismissed her words with an impatient wave of his hand. "Unimportant. In fact, the less you know concerning the machinations of courtly politics, the better. An outsider always has a clearer view of a quagmire than those mucking about within. Besides, my lady, it means I might actually be able to trust you. And that's a rare enough virtue these days." He reached down to stroke the head of one of the mastiffs.

Grace shook her head. Well, *that* certainly hadn't had the intended effect. She would have to try again. In an effort to be brave she took a step forward. "But, Your Majesty, you don't know who I am. Or even where I come from."

He snapped his fingers. "Exactly!"

Grace groaned. She should just stop before she inadvertently managed to convince Boreas he should give her the crown of the kingdom, while he became her court jester.

The king started pacing once more and slapped the palm of one hand with the back of the other, shaggy eyebrows knitted in concentration. "If you must know, my lady, I don't care one whit what land you hail from. The fact is, it suits my purposes far better if no one—including myself—knows the truth of your origin or station, or why you have chosen to travel in disguise. Your bearing marks you as a woman of noble birth, and a mysterious foreign lady with power and purposes unknown is exactly what I need."

He bore down on Grace, his mien grim. "These are dark times in the Dominions, my lady. It is imperative the council act swiftly, instead of bogging itself down in petty argument and meaningless debate. I need to divine the intentions of the other rulers, to shape their opinions, and to convince the council to take action. And you, my lady, are going to help me do just that."

Grace's trepidation gave way to confusion. "But I don't understand. What help could a stranger possibly be to you? I'm sure no one will even bother to talk to me."

Boreas let out a grunt. "You truly don't understand the workings of court politics, do you, my lady? Things must be different in this Beckett of yours."

"Very different." Grace didn't know whether to laugh or cry. She settled for a wry sort of grimace.

"Then you must trust me in this," Boreas said. "The task I require of you is really quite simple. I have called the council to convene on the first day of Valdath. Nobles from the royal courts of the other Dominions will arrive soon to prepare things in advance of their kings and queens. You've already met Durge of Embarr. All you have to do is observe, speak to the other nobles when you have opportunity, and report to me all of interest you learn." He regarded her, his eyes solemn. "Will you deign to accept this task, my lady?"

Grace decided to give reason one more chance to prevail. "Forgive me, Your Majesty, but I just don't think I can be of any help to you."

Boreas glowered at her. "That was not my question, my lady." He drew close, until his face was mere inches from hers. She could almost see intensity radiating from him like waves of heat distortion. "I will only ask you once more." His voice dropped to a thrum. "Will you help this king, Grace of Beckett?"

Exasperation gave way to awe. She knew nothing of politics, and she was hardly the right candidate for a job mingling with nobles. However, it no longer seemed her place to protest. This was, after all, the *king*. In disbelief, Grace found herself murmuring in reply.

"Of course, Your Majesty. I would be honored to help you."

Boreas nodded. "I am gladdened at your answer, my lady. You see, I find I rather like you, and I would have been quite distressed to have had to toss you in the dungeon. The rats start to get hungry this time of year, what with winter coming and all."

Grace's eyes bulged.

The shadow vanished from King Boreas's face, and sparks of mirth danced in his eyes. He grinned again, but this time the expression was only slightly fearsome. He had been making a joke. Aryn had warned her, all right. The king really did think he was funnier than he actually was.

"I got you, didn't I?" Boreas said in triumph.

Grace let out a deep breath of relief. "Oh, yes. You certainly did."

The king clapped his hands together at his victory. "Now," he said, "to find what's become of the Lady Aryn. I have a task for her as well."

"Would you like me to go look for the baroness, Your Majesty?" Grace tried not to sound too eager to take her leave of the king.

A sly light crept into Boreas's eyes, and his voice dropped to a whisper. "No, my lady, I don't think that will be necessary." He stalked to the chamber's door, his boots making no sound against the thick carpets. "I think I know exactly where to find my ward."

The king paused beside the door, then in one swift motion jerked it open. Something blue tumbled into the chamber with a gasp of surprise.

"Greetings, Aryn." Boreas folded his arms and gazed down at his ward.

The baroness straightened and smoothed her sapphire gown, her face pale. "I wasn't listening at the door, Your Majesty," she said. "I swear!"

"Yes, you were."

Aryn's look was stricken. "All right, I *was* listening at the door, but

I didn't hear a thing about the Lady Grace helping you at the coun—" She bit her tongue.

Boreas shook his head in reproach. "I'm beginning to think I failed somewhere in the course of your upbringing, Aryn. Who taught you to lie like that?"

The baroness hung her head. "You did, Your Majesty."

"Yes," he said. "But it's apparent you weren't listening very closely. You won't survive a minute at court if you don't learn to lie more believably than that." The king held a hand beside his mouth to give Grace a half-whispered aside. "I'm afraid the poor thing has an incurable streak of honesty in her, though I have no idea where it comes from. There must be common blood in the House of Elsandry somewhere."

Grace did not even attempt a reply to *that*.

Aryn let out a forlorn sigh, and the king's expression softened. He laid an affectionate hand on the young woman's shoulder. "There, there, child. It isn't your fault. You tried your best. And I really do think you're improving."

Aryn looked up, her face shining with hope. "You do?"

"No," he said. "I was lying. But see how natural it can sound?"

Aryn sighed again, this time in exasperation. "Does His Majesty have a task for me?"

"As a matter of fact, he does."

Boreas treated Grace to a critical look, as if noticing her attire for the first time. Clearly he was not pleased by what he saw. She willed herself to vanish, but unfortunately it didn't work.

"The Lady Grace of Beckett is going to be attending the coming Council of Kings," Boreas said. "I would be most grateful, Lady Aryn, if you could help her to become slightly less . . ." Here he fought for the proper word. ". . . slightly less *irregular* in terms of dress and manner."

Aryn's brilliant expression returned. She nodded in excitement. "Of course, Your Majesty. I'll show her everything a lady needs to know." The baroness winked at Grace and whispered, "Don't worry. This is going to be fun."

Grace swallowed hard. *Fun* wasn't exactly the word she would have chosen. She cast a nervous glance at the king. What in the world— what in *this* world—had she just gotten herself into?

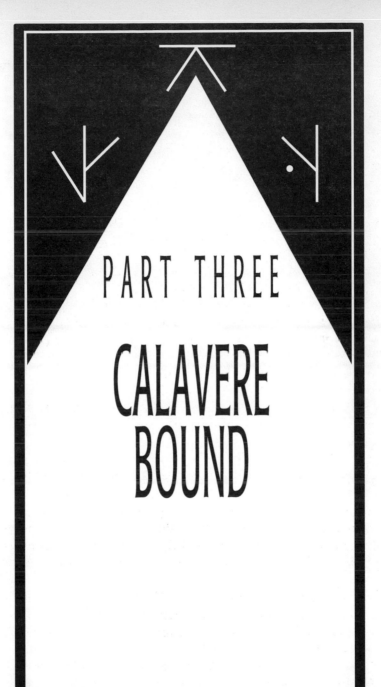

PART THREE

CALAVERE BOUND

38.

The four travelers set out from Kelcior in the brilliant late-autumn sunlight to begin the long journey south to Calavere and the Council of Kings.

In the muddy courtyard behind the old Tarrasian keep, Travis and Falken mounted the horses that had been King Kel's farewell gift. The bard's steed was a jet stallion with a white streak in its forelock. Travis, in turn, sat astride a shaggy brown gelding with intelligent eyes and a star in the center of its forehead. Melia and Beltan mounted their own horses, which they had ridden to Kelcior. The blond knight's horse was a bony roan charger, while Melia, her blue kirtle artfully arranged, perched upon a mare as pale as mist, with delicate legs and a graceful neck.

Earlier that afternoon, they had gone to find King Kel and beg his permission to leave Kelcior. As Beltan had explained to Travis, under the laws of hospitality, a guest could not depart—be it from castle or hovel—without first being granted leave by the master of the house.

"What?" Kel had said with a glower after Falken had made the formal request to depart the keep. "Leaving so soon?"

They had met with the shaggy king in his solar. This was a cozy, if cramped, chamber located behind the curtain which crossed the end of the great hall.

"Some of us have been indulging your hospitality for nearly a month, Your Majesty," Melia had said. "Surely any longer and we will overstay our welcome."

Kel's voice had rattled the very stones of the fortress. "Impossible!"

Then he had snapped his fingers. "Would you stay, my lady, if I were to command a feast in your honor?"

Melia had refrained from answering, although by her expression the effort cost her. Falken had expressed their need for urgency, and at last Kel had acquiesced—though not without some grumbling when he learned a Council of Kings had been called and he had not been invited.

"Just because I have a few wildmen in my court, they think they're so much better than me." He had let out a disgusted snort. "Why, I have half a mind to march down to Calavere and show King Boreas how a *real* kingdom is run."

"Now that is something I would pay good gold to see," Beltan had whispered to Travis with a grin.

The travelers had spoken their good-byes, then had made their way from the keep. As they passed through the great hall, Travis had looked around, for he had hoped he might catch one last glimpse of Trifkin Mossberry. However, there had been no sign of the little man or his troupe of actors. They had vanished, like a strange dream, with the night.

Now, astride his horse in the courtyard, Travis cast a sidelong glance at Falken and Melia. He was still wounded by the way they had decided his fate that morning in the ruined tower. For the tenth time that day, the two were engaged in some discussion which they did not seem compelled to share. Travis sighed and turned his attention to adjusting the gear strapped to the saddle behind him.

Each of the horses bore a pair of saddlebags that bulged with provisions from Kel's kitchen. The king had not been given the chance to hold a farewell feast in their honor, so he had apparently decided to send one with them instead. Tucked away in the saddlebags were smoked meats, hard-crusted breads, cheeses contained in protective rinds of mold, and clay pots of wild honey. Kel had also provided the travelers with extra clothes and blankets.

After he tightened the straps, Travis stared at the saddlebags. He was starting to feel like just another piece of baggage himself.

Falken shaded his brow with his one gloved hand and eyed the sun overhead. "Are we ready yet? It's a long way to Calavere, and we're not getting any closer just standing here in the courtyard."

Melia adjusted her slate-blue cloak. She was seated on her gray mount sidesaddle—a feat she somehow made appear graceful and natural. Travis suspected that, if he tried the same, he would promptly slide into the muck below.

"I am ready," Melia pronounced, as if this were the only factor constraining their departure.

Apparently it was. The others nudged their horses into motion, toward a gate in the ramshackle wall, and Travis followed suit. A brisk wind picked up, and the smoke of the castle's cookfires scudded across the courtyard like blue mist. They had just reached the gate when a drab figure scuttled out of a swirl of smoke and brought the horses to a sudden halt.

"What?" Grisla the witch said in her chalky voice. "Leaving without so much as a simple fare-thee-well?"

Falken glared at her, annoyance written across his wolfish face. "The laws of hospitality require a guest to ask leave of a castle's lord before departing. I'm afraid I don't recall a line in there about hags."

"It's in the fine script." The tatters that served as the ancient woman's clothes fluttered on the wind along with her scraggly hair.

Melia guided her mount forward a few steps. "Do you know you delay our departure on a crucial errand?"

The hag clasped a gnarled hand to her cheek and affected a look of mock mortification. "Oh, forgive me, Lady High-as-the-Moon! How foolish of me to stand in your all-important path. Please don't punish me for being drawn to your grandness. I am like a lowly fly, you see, compelled by nature to alight upon all great heaps of dung."

Melia's coppery skin blanched, then her eyes narrowed to slits. "What do you want of us, Daughter of Sia?"

The hag spat on the ground. "I want nothing of you, Lady Vitriol." She turned her lone eye on Falken. "Nor you, Lord Calamity." She bared her snaggled teeth in a sly grin. "I wish to have a word with the tasty young lad, here."

The witch scampered on stick legs to stand before Travis's horse, then pointed a clawlike finger at his chest. "I believe you have a bone to pick with me, lad."

"What?" he said in confusion.

"A bone, boy!"

His expression of puzzlement only deepened.

Grisla gave her head a rueful shake. "Why does Fate always shine upon such dimwits?" She thrust out a greasy leather bag. "Go on, lad. Pick one!"

Travis eyed the lumpy sack, wary of its contents. However, there was only one way out of this situation. He clenched his jaw and slipped a hand into the bag. He half expected to touch something wet and slimy. Instead, his fingers brushed several hard, smooth objects. He drew one out and gazed at it. It was a yellowed knucklebone, three lines scratched into its surface.

"Humph!" Grisla said. "I wouldn't have thought you would draw that one. One line for Birth, one line for Breath, and one more for

Death, which comes to us all." Her eye rolled toward Falken for a moment. "Though for some of us later than sooner."

Travis shook his head. "But what does it mean?"

"What do you think it means?" Grisla said.

Travis chewed his lip and stared at the bone. He was reminded of Trifkin Mossberry's play about Spring and Winter and the birth of Summer. "It seems like it's about endings. Or maybe beginnings." He shook his head. "But which is it?"

"Perhaps it's both, lad. Perhaps there's no difference between the two." Grisla shrugged her knobby shoulders. "Or perhaps the oracle bones can lie after all."

The witch snatched the bone from his hand and spirited the bag into the depths of her swaddling rags.

"Are you finished with your amusement yet, hag?" Falken said.

"As a matter of fact, Lord Impatience, I am." The witch brushed Travis's hand with her gnarled fingers. "You know, you've taken a little piece of my heart, lad." She cackled, scuttled into a cloud of smoke, and was gone.

Travis felt something warm and damp against his skin. He looked down to see a piece of raw meat on his palm. With a yelp he shook his hand and flung it into the mud. He wiped his hand on his tunic. "I really wish she would quit doing that!"

With the way clear once more, the four urged their horses through the gate and picked their way across the causeway that led from fortress to shore. The air was cold, but the autumn sunlight was warm, and it gilded the lake like gold filigree on blue enamel. It was a fine day for traveling.

"What do you suppose that was all about?" Melia asked Falken after they had ridden for a time.

"You mean the hag Grisla?" The bard shrugged. "I doubt it was about anything other than spectacle. As far as I can tell, witches derive their chief entertainment from baffling people. But I suppose there was little harm in allowing the old crone to indulge herself for a minute or two."

Melia nodded at his words, but whether the regal woman agreed with them or not, she did not say.

A question occurred to Travis. He nudged his gelding toward the others. "Who is Sia?"

Falken gave him a piercing look. "*What* is Sia, might be a better question. But I suppose you could say she is a goddess of sorts."

Travis thought about this. "Like one of the gods of those mystery cults you were talking about before?"

"No," Melia said with a sharpness that startled Travis. "Sia has nothing to do with the gods of the mystery cults, nor they with her."

This did little to answer Travis's question. However, given Melia's reaction, he decided not to press the point. The horses clambered up the steep trail to the summit of the ridge that ringed the valley. Wind tangled Travis's sandy hair—a wind like the one that sometimes rushed down from the mountains around Castle City, that carried with it an ache of longing, and a sense of infinite possibility.

Beltan cast one last wistful glance over his shoulder at the old keep below. "So much for feasts," he said. "And I was really getting rather used to them."

Then the horses started down the other side of the ridge, back toward the crossroads and the Queen's Way, and the ancient Tarrasian fortress was lost from sight.

39.

All the rest of that day they journeyed south along the grassy swath of the Queen's Way.

The four travelers soon fell into a pattern. Beltan periodically spurred his rangy charger and galloped down the ancient highway to scout for danger. Falken and Melia rode side by side, their heads often bent together to exchange some murmured bit of conversation. Travis kept a short distance behind them and tried not to look as if he were leaning forward in an attempt to catch what they were saying. However, the wind was behind him, and any interesting items of information the bard and the lady might have uttered were blown in the wrong direction, although once, in the wake of a swirling gust, Travis did catch a snatch of one of Falken's quietly spoken sentences.

". . . that we shouldn't dismiss the stone in the White Tower even if it is . . ."

The wind changed again and took the bard's words with it. Travis's frustration at not being paid any attention became unbearable. He urged his horse forward.

"So, how long will it take us to get to Calavere?" he asked Falken and Melia.

Falken looked up in surprise, as if he had forgotten Travis was even there. "The Queen's Way will take us all the way, but it is a long and arduous road. Once we cross the headwaters of the River Farwander, we will be in the Dominion of Eredane proper. However, we must traverse all of Eredane and cross the highlands of Galt before we reach the northern marches of Calavan. In all, it is a journey of nearly a hundred leagues. It will take us well over a fortnight, if the weather holds." He cast a glance at Melia. "Of course, there is also the matter of a small detour I intend to make along the way."

"If we have time," Melia said. "The Council of Kings is to convene in less than a month. We're going to be slicing it rather finely as it is."

Falken ran a hand through his gray-shot hair. "It's not as if I'm proposing this for the sheer fun of it, you know. It's really rather important."

Melia's amber eyes flashed. "So is getting to the council before it's over."

"Where is it you want to go, Falken?" Travis said. "Is it a white tower?" Instantly he regretted the question, for both Falken and Melia fixed him with penetrating looks.

"Someone has sharp ears," Melia said.

"So it seems." Falken considered Travis for a moment. "It's not *a* white tower, Travis. It's *the* White Tower."

Travis didn't understand, but the bard offered no further explanation. Instead, he and Melia urged their mounts ahead, and thus signified this was all the information Travis was going to get. Feeling terribly sorry for himself, Travis let out a sigh. However, nobody seemed to notice, so he turned his attention to not falling out of the saddle.

The ancient Tarrasians had been engineers of great skill, for the Queen's Way continued to cut across the rolling landscape. At times it sliced through the tops of hills and at others leaped over deep ravines, supported by stone arches that, while crumbled at the edges, still bore the weight of centuries with ease. As the travelers progressed south, the hills to their left grew into rugged mountains: the Fal Erenn. Westward, to their right, the land swept away in a sea of dun-colored waves. It was all vast and beautiful, but achingly empty as well, and only served to remind Travis that this was not his world.

The sun had sunk into a bank of bronze clouds when Beltan rode back to report he had found a place to make camp for the night. This turned out to be a flat knoll a few hundred paces east of the road. The knoll was ringed by scrub oak, which offered some protection, and a spring trickled from beneath a rock near the hill's top. Travis climbed down from his gelding and groaned. The last time he had ridden a horse had been at a county fair, and he had been eleven years old. It felt like someone had rearranged all his muscles while he rode and wedged them into places they did not belong.

They made camp as twilight mantled the knoll. Though Melia

seemed to feel no compunction in ordering the others around, she did not shirk her own share of the labor. The dinner fashioned from Kel's provisions was her work, and she seemed pleased by the compliment the other three paid her efforts by eating ravenously. Then again, she might have preferred it had Beltan not been *quite* so vigorous in his praise.

"And what will you be eating for the rest of the journey, Beltan?" she asked in a pleasant voice as he took his third helping of stew and bread.

Beltan swallowed hard and set the food back down. "You know, I'm really not as hungry as I thought I was."

"I didn't think you were, dear," Melia said.

Travis finished his own food quietly and did not even consider asking for more.

Night deepened around them, and they spread their blankets by the fire. Beltan moved a short distance off, mail shirt jingling, to take the first watch. Travis shivered with the chill, then wrapped himself in his mistcloak and shut his eyes.

He awoke to strange stars.

They blazed against the jet sky, shards of diamond and sapphire. He thought he could see pictures in the stars, shapes far clearer than the sketchy, half-imagined constellations of Earth: feral beasts, winged maidens, warriors wielding swords of cool starlight. The murmur of conversation drifted on the air—it was this that had awakened him. His mind was turgid with sleep, but it seemed to him Melia and Falken spoke in soft voices by the embers of the fire.

The bard's quiet words drifted on the night air. "But surely you should be able to tell if Travis comes from the same place."

Travis struggled to sit up. *If I come from the same place as what!*

He didn't think he even managed to ask the question aloud. However, Melia turned her amber gaze upon him. Her expression was stern, though not unkind.

Go to sleep, Travis.

Her lips did not move, yet her voice spoke clearly in his mind. Travis tried to protest, but a wave of drowsiness crashed over him. Unable to resist the pull, he shut his eyes and sank once more into deep and starless sleep.

40.

By the time the crimson orb of the sun rose above the horizon, it found them already riding hard down the Queen's Way. It was midmorning, and the autumn day had turned crisp but fine when they reached a moss-covered stone bridge that arched over a narrow defile. At the bottom of the gorge rushed a small, frothy river. According to Falken, these were the headwaters of the River Farwander.

The bard spoke over the roar of the water. "It isn't much to look at here, but this is the start of a river that stretches three hundred leagues from source to mouth. By the time it reaches the Sunfire Sea, the Farwander is over a league wide. Or so the stories say, for I know of no one alive in the Dominions who has traveled to the farthest western coast of Falengarth."

Melia arched a single dark eyebrow. "No one? Not even a great wanderer like yourself, Falken?"

He shook his head, gazed into the distance, then spoke in a low voice that was nearly lost in the rushing of the river. "There was but one road to Eversea, to the Far West, and its beginning was in Malachor. Yet that road lay in one direction only, for those who took it never returned, and the way is lost to all of us now."

The bard smiled, and though there was sadness in the expression, there was genuine mirth as well. "Yet that is all old history. We have our own road to journey, and to less melancholy lands."

He spurred his mount and, hooves clattering, the dark stallion crossed the Tarrasian bridge. The others followed after.

They rode all that day with only a few short breaks to chew some bread and allow the horses to drink. Finally, as the sun dipped toward the far horizon, Beltan once again rode back to tell the others he had found a place to make camp. He seemed particularly pleased with his find.

It turned out to be a small depression no more than twenty paces from the road, ringed by a circle of gnarled trees. In the center of the circle was a spring, and around this grew a thick patch of herbs, still green and fragrant even this late in the year. As they drew near, Falken explained this place was a *talathrin*, or a Way Circle. The Way Circles had been made by the Tarrasians when they built the road, and were intended as safe places for travelers to spend the night. They picketed the horses outside and entered the *talathrin* through an archway formed of branches that had centuries ago melded together into living, braided columns.

Falken's breath fogged on the cool air as he spoke. "Some say there is an enchantment in the trees that ring these circles, a magic that protects those who sleep here. However, I cannot speak to the truth of that, for I know little of Tarrasian magic."

"That's because there is little enough to know," Melia said. She allowed Beltan to help her step over a twisted root. "The Tarrasians were always far better engineers than sorcerers. And while there is no magic in the *talathrain*, it is equally true there is a goodness that abides yet in these places. The trees are *ithaya*, or sunleaf, which grow along high cliffs above the Summer Sea, and their bark, when brewed in a tea, is good for aches and fevers. And the plants by the spring are *alasai*, or green scepter, and can be used to flavor food, as well as to remove the taint from spoilt meat. Both are of great use to travelers."

Melia approached the spring, drew up the hem of her gown, and knelt to part the thatch of sweet-smelling herbs with her hands. This action revealed a figurine carved of rain-worn ivory beside the spring.

"You see?" she said with a smile. "Naimi, Goddess of Travelers, keeps watch over this place, though her name has not been worshiped in this land in long centuries—not since the people of Tarras dwelled here." Melia dipped her fingers into the spring and sprinkled a few droplets of clear water before the figurine. "I hope you don't mind us using your Way Circle, dear one," she murmured.

Travis couldn't help thinking this seemed a little informal for a prayer to a goddess. However, Melia knew far more about such matters than he. Holding her dark hair behind her neck with one hand, Melia bent over the spring and used the other to bring cool water to her lips. She drank, then rose.

"We may make camp now."

They ate their supper as night fell around the Way Circle, then readied themselves for sleep. Melia seemed to feel there was absolutely no need for one of them to keep watch, but Beltan did so all the same. He stood by the *talathrin*'s gate and gazed into the night. Falken promised to relieve him later.

Travis sat on his bedroll and used a leaf of *alasai* to clean his teeth. It wasn't exactly a toothbrush, but Falken had shown him the trick, and it worked fairly well. He would not have minded a shave as well. The red-brown stubble on his chin and cheeks itched to become a full-fledged beard. However, the only blade he had was the Malachorian stiletto Jack had given him, and that was likely to shave him a little closer than he wished. He settled for scratching. Then he rolled up in his mistcloak and lay down.

The hard ground did nothing to ease his cramped and complaining muscles after the long day's ride. All the same, exhaustion won out over pain, and Travis fell asleep.

41.

On their third day out of Kelcior the clear autumn weather gave way to dreary clouds and cold drizzle. Rain slicked the road's paving stones and made them treacherous for the horses, which in turn made the going slower. The landscape was lost in a shroud of fog, and there was little to occupy Travis's attention. He had given up even trying to eavesdrop on Falken and Melia's conversations—it was impossible to make out anything over the clatter of hooves and the constant patter of rain. Sometimes as they rode he spoke with Beltan, for the knight was more amenable to answering questions, but most of the time he sat in silence on the back of his horse.

More than once Travis wished it would just get cold enough to snow. Beltan and Melia had said that winter had come early to the Dominions, but that didn't seem to be quite the case here. When he asked Melia about it, the lady only shook her head.

"It's almost as if winter has been moved from where it should be to where it should not."

She spoke these words to Falken rather than Travis. The bard nodded as if he understood them, but Travis didn't, although he knew better than to ask for more explanation. He huddled in his mistcloak and stared into the drizzle.

It was late one particularly foggy afternoon when Beltan came cantering back to the group on his roan charger. The knight wore a grave expression on his face, but there was a gleam of excitement in his eyes as well.

"I've got some bad news," he said. "About half a league ahead, the road passes through a narrow gap between two hills. There's a band of outlaws camped on top of one of them. It's a convenient location if you plan to ambush people traveling on the road below."

Falken swore. "So how many of them are there?"

"Oh, only a half dozen or so." The blond knight grinned and gripped the hilt of his sword. "I should have no trouble handling them."

Melia folded her arms across her chest. "Really, Beltan?"

He squirmed in his saddle, chain mail squeaking. "All right. So there might be a *little* trouble. But I still say I can handle them."

Melia reached out to pat his hand. "Of course you could, dear. But why don't we try it my way first?"

Beltan heaved a breath of disappointment, then nodded.

"Now," Melia said, "did the brigands notice you approaching?"

The knight shook his head. "I'm fairly sure they didn't. I could hear them as clearly as if they were an arm's length away, but I don't think they could hear me at all. Sounds carry strangely in the fog."

Melia nodded. "We'll just have to hope they don't already know we're coming." She gazed around at the foggy air, then let out a resigned sigh. "I'm much better with shadows than with mist, but I suppose this will simply have to do." Her tone became crisp and commanding. "All right, everybody gather around me. And do stay close. I'm going to have to concentrate, and I won't be able to pay attention to make certain none of you are wandering off."

Travis nudged his shaggy gelding near Beltan's charger. "What's she going to do?"

"You'll see."

Melia shut her eyes, and a furrow of concentration marked her forehead. At the same time she held her hands close to her body and made small movements with her fingers which reminded Travis of someone knitting. The fog closed in around them. It grew thicker and more opaque, as soft and gray as Travis's cloak. Melia opened her eyes.

"Is this really going to be enough?" Falken said. The fog seemed to absorb his words even as he spoke them.

Melia urged her horse into a slow walk. "There's only one way to know for certain."

The four moved down the road, their horses huddled in a close knot. They proceeded by sound rather than sight, for the fog remained thick as they went. Except, after a while, Travis started to think they weren't moving *through* the fog at all. Rather, the dense cloud of mist seemed to be moving *with* them. On impulse, he leaned forward in his saddle and blew against the fog with all the breath he could muster.

"Please don't do that, Travis," Melia said.

Travis jumped in his saddle, then glanced at Melia. She was not looking at him, but instead continued to frown into the fog. He hunched down in his saddle and after that did not attempt any more experiments.

They rode in near-perfect silence. The footfalls of the horses, the creak of the saddles, the jingle of Beltan's mail shirt—all were muffled by the preternatural fog.

A voice cut through the gloom. Travis clenched his jaw to stifle a cry of alarm. It sounded as if the speaker were no more than ten paces away.

"Sulath's Balls, it's cold today!"

Another rough voice answered the first. "You think you're cold now? Go back to camp and tell Guerneg you're too chilly to keep a lookout for travelers to rob. Then you'll be cold all right. Stone cold, and with his sword stuck in your stinking guts."

The first outlaw spat in disgust. "There's nothing on the road today except this blasted fog. Look, there goes a whole cloud of it, just floating by. It's not normal, this mist. It has the feel of the Little People about it. We're probably being cursed just breathing it."

"Better cursed by fog than skewered by steel," the second outlaw said.

The first grunted but did not argue with this bit of wisdom.

The voices of the outlaws fell behind and faded away. Only when he let out a tight lungful of air did Travis realize he had been holding his breath. The group came to a halt. With a weary sigh, Melia waved a hand. The cloud of fog that surrounded them broke into ragged tatters and melted away on the late-afternoon air. To the north, two shapes rose dimly in the haze. Those must have been the hills where the highwaymen had waited to ambush unwary travelers. Somehow the four had passed by the outlaw encampment unseen.

Travis looked at Melia in wonderment, but he did not even consider asking her how their safe passage had been accomplished. Sometimes answers could be far more disturbing than their questions.

"It looks as if the fog is lifting," Melia said in a bright voice.

"What a coincidence," Falken said.

With that they continued on their way and cantered down the ancient road.

42.

Two days later they came to a town.

The morning after their near encounter with the outlaws, the fog gave way to sunshine that gilded the rolling landscape between plains and mountains, and changed browns to russets and tans to bright golds. Despite the sunlight, the weather turned cold and sharp. Winter had not forgotten this land after all. Beltan's mail shirt jingled on the crisp air, and the breath of the horses was white and frosty. Travis kept warm inside his mistcloak, but his hands seemed to freeze around the reins of his gelding, so that by day's end it was almost impossible to unclench his stiff fingers.

They encountered more and more signs of human habitation the farther south they traveled. From the swaying back of his mount, Travis saw thatch-roofed farms, muddy villages, and stone signal towers atop which bonfires could be lit in troubled times to warn of danger or invasion. They were deep in Eredane—although, according to Falken, the Dominion's most populous lands lay many leagues to the west, along the banks of the River Silverflood. The eastern marches of Eredane, where they journeyed now, were considered rough and provincial lands these days.

The sun was high overhead when Beltan spurred his charger back toward the others. As usual he had ridden ahead to scout the way. Now he bore the good news.

"There's a town just over the next rise in the road."

Falken shot him a speculative look. "And just why are you grinning like that?"

Mischief sparked in Beltan's green eyes. "Where there's a town, there's got to be ale."

Melia clucked her tongue. "You know, contrary to popular Calavaner belief, one actually *can* survive for considerable lengths of time without ale."

Beltan gave her a puzzled look. "Yes, but what would be the point?"

After a small amount of discussion, Falken and Melia concurred that, despite their need for haste, they should spare an hour or two to enter the town. Though generous, the foodstuffs King Kel had given them were beginning to dwindle, and Melia wanted to replenish their supplies. Also, Falken hoped to hear more news of affairs in the Dominions. The matter settled, they urged the horses into a canter. Minutes later they crested a low swell and came to a halt.

"I don't remember Glennen's Stand being a walled town," Falken said with a frown.

Beltan shrugged. "Maybe they've had problems with outlaws or barbarians coming down from the mountains."

"Maybe." The bard sounded less convinced. "Regardless, I don't think Glennen would be pleased to see what has become of his namesake."

Travis lifted a hand to shade his eyes and studied the town below. Glennen's Stand was situated in a hollow beside a small river, no more than three furlongs from the Queen's Way. He guessed there to be about a hundred buildings in all. Those upstream were of stone with dull slate roofs, while those downstream were little more than shacks thatched with dirty straw. A wall surrounded the entire town, and while a dark patina of age hung over Glennen's Stand, the wall was pale and rough-edged, a testament to its recent construction.

Following Melia's lead, they nudged their horses into motion and made for the town. As they rode, Travis guided his horse toward Falken's.

"Who was he?" he asked the bard. "Glennen, I mean."

The bard gave him a thoughtful look. "You remember the war I told you about, the one that took place long ago against the Pale King?"

Travis nodded.

"Glennen was one of King Ulther's earls. When things looked darkest for Ulther's army, Glennen rode south to tell Empress Elsara to make haste to Shadowsdeep. However, in this very dell Glennen was assailed by minions of the Pale King. He defeated them, and he reached Elsara to give her Ulther's warning. Except after he spoke his message he died at her feet, for he had been mortally wounded."

Travis sighed.

"Given its history, this town has always been welcoming to travelers." Falken gazed at the walled town, his eyes sober. "Or at least it used to be."

When the travelers reached the town's gate they found it guarded by a pair of men-at-arms in greasy leather jerkins, hands on the stubby swords at their hips. Travis wasn't entirely certain what a town on Eldh should be like, but he expected to see more people entering Glennen's Stand: farmers with a late harvest of grain, merchants bearing goods to trade, herders bringing flocks of sheep to shear for wool. Instead, only a handful of peasants in ragged clothes trudged through the archway, faces grim and dirty, small bundles of rags or firewood on their stooped backs.

The men-at-arms halted the peasants as they passed and questioned each about his or her business. Alarm surged in Travis's chest. What would he say if the guards stopped him? However, the men-at-arms seemed not to notice as the travelers approached. Melia rode through the gate, regal aback her pale mare, and the others followed. The guards did not even glance in their direction.

Travis leaned toward Beltan. "I don't understand. Why didn't the guards stop and question us like the others?"

Beltan snorted. "Commoners don't question nobles."

Travis glanced at Melia but said nothing more. Together the four passed through a rough tunnel and into the town beyond.

Outside the wall things had looked bleak. Inside they were worse. Gray buildings leaned together overhead, all but closing out the sky. A haphazard scattering of people picked their way through the narrow tracts of muck and sewage that passed for streets. All of them wore the same grim, furtive faces as had the peasants at the gate, and none looked in the direction of the travelers. As quickly as they appeared, the townsfolk vanished again into shadowed openings or peeling doorways.

"Cheerful place," Beltan said under his breath.

Melia's nose wrinkled. "Fragrant as well."

They rode on through the town. Soot streaked walls and roofs like a taint of disease, and windows stared out of abandoned houses like blind eyes. They were near the town's center when they came upon the remains of a small wooden structure, smashed to bits. Melia brought her mount to a halt, her expression one of outrage. Travis saw the fragments of a statue half-trampled into the mud: a slender arm, a white foot, the corner of a serene, smiling mouth.

"What is this place?" he whispered to Falken.

The bard shook his head, his eyes sad. "This was a shrine of one of the mystery cults. It's hard to be certain from what's left, but I would guess it was sacred to Yrsaia the Huntress, as well as those who follow her mysteries."

"Yes," Melia said. "It was." A dangerous light glinted in her amber eyes. "And I would give much to know who it was that committed this act of sacrilege."

Falken clenched his black-gloved hand into a fist. "This doesn't make sense. Granted, it's been some years, but last I knew, Glennen's Stand was one of the busiest towns in eastern Eredane."

"Things change," Beltan said. "And not always for the better."

They were silent. Then Melia said, "Let us not linger in this place any longer than we must."

Falken nodded. "If I remember right, the town market is this way."

They came to a halt on the edge of a barren square. The ground was a mire of churned mud, and in the center of the square steamed an open cesspool. Travis covered his nose with the hem of his cloak. Had Falken misremembered? Then he noticed a handful of disheveled stalls set up on the farside of the square.

Beltan let out a melancholy whistle. "I suppose it's too much to hope there's any ale in this place."

"If there were, I wouldn't suggest drinking it," Falken said. "Unless you happen to think a few floating rats impart a pleasant tang to one's beer." He turned toward Melia. "I'm going to wander off for a while and try to learn something about what's happened to this place. Why don't you see if there's anything worth buying here in the market?"

"That shouldn't take long."

Falken guided his stallion down a narrow street and disappeared from sight. Melia, Beltan, and Travis rode toward the scant collection of merchant stalls, then climbed down from their horses. Cold mud squelched up around their ankles.

Melia sighed. "I'm really not going to enjoy this, am I?"

Travis held his tongue. It was one of those questions that did not require an answer.

Melia lifted the hem of her gown out of the muck and picked her way toward one of the stalls to examine the pitiful collection of moldy turnips and worm-eaten apples.

A quarter hour later, Travis helped Beltan pack the few things Melia had bought into their saddlebags, and they mounted their horses. Just then Falken returned, a scowl on his wolfish face.

"Did you learn anything interesting?" Melia asked.

Falken grimaced. "I didn't even learn anything *un*interesting. Nobody in this town would speak to me. They're all afraid of something—so afraid they won't talk about it. But what it might be, I can't say."

Melia swept her blue-black hair over her shoulder and adjusted her cloak. "We might as well be leaving, then. I don't think there's anything else for us here."

The others did not disagree, and they started off through the grimy streets. They were nearly to the town gate when they turned a corner and came upon a group of men and women clad in black robes. The robed ones had just stepped from a doorway some distance off, and they turned to walk down the street in the direction of the four riders. As they did, Travis saw that each one's forehead had been marked with a symbol drawn in ashes. His heart caught in his chest, and with terrible certainty he knew he and the others were in danger.

Beltan noticed his expression, and the knight's brow furrowed in concern. "What's wrong, Travis?"

The robed men and women continued to walk down the street. It was only a matter of seconds until one of them looked up and noticed the riders.

"Please!" Travis said, his voice hoarse. "We can't let them see us!"

His companions hesitated, but the urgency of his expression spurred them to action.

"This way," Beltan said.

They ducked down an alley, then waited in tense silence as the dark procession passed by. Travis clenched his jaw and resisted the urge to scream. When they were certain the robed ones were gone, the four emerged into the relative light of the street.

Falken fixed Travis with a sharp look. "And now you're going to tell us what that was all about."

Travis took a deep breath. "Did you see that symbol, the one drawn in ashes on their foreheads? The curved lines that looked almost like some sort of eye?" He licked his lips. "I've seen that symbol before."

In quick words, Travis explained how he had seen the same symbol scratched onto doors all over Castle City the night when everything had changed.

When Travis finished, Falken shook his head, a grim light in his faded eyes. "I'm not sure what this means, but it can't be good."

"Indeed," Melia said. "Especially given the fact those people were members of the Raven Cult."

Falken stared at her. "What?"

The lady nodded, her jaw set in a hard line. "That symbol is the mark of the new mystery cult of which I told you in Kelcior." Her gaze moved to Travis. "Only it's not meant to be an eye. From what I've gathered, it symbolizes the wing of a raven."

"I'm liking this less and less by the moment," Falken said. "But I still don't understand Travis's story. What does it mean?"

"It means," Melia said in measured words, "the connection between his world and ours runs in two directions."

Travis tried to grasp the implications of her words, but he couldn't, not fully. Still, one thing he knew now beyond all doubt: He was not the only one who had traveled between worlds.

"Come on," Falken said in a gruff voice. "Let's get out of this blasted town."

43.

The next day dawned gray and sullen. So dim was the sunrise that when Beltan shook his shoulder to wake him, Travis blinked in confusion, thinking it still the middle of the night. He nearly crawled back inside his mistcloak, dawn or no dawn, but the big Calavaner pushed a steaming clay cup into his hands. By reflex, Travis inhaled. A rich, bitter scent filled his nose. *Maddok.* He gulped the hot liquid down as fast as he could and found, if not the desire, at least the energy to get up.

They rode south all that morning—although before long Travis wasn't certain *morning* was the right word, for as the hours passed, the day seemed to grow darker rather than lighter. Droplets of moisture clung to everything—grass, stones, trees—and beaded like tiny pearls on Travis's cloak. Before long the sound of thunder rumbled across the landscape, distant but drawing nearer. Black clouds, lit from within by flashes of green lightning, rolled out of the north to mantle the sky.

Beltan slicked wet, pale hair away from his brow and glanced up at the sky. "Isn't it a little late in the year for thunderstorms?"

"Yes," Melia replied in a guarded voice. "It is."

Her words sent a shiver up Travis's spine.

As if to punctuate the knight's comment, a flash of lightning rent the clouds overhead, and the first big, cold drops of rain began to fall upon the paving stones of the Queen's Way.

"We'd better find shelter, and soon," Falken said.

Before the bard finished speaking, Beltan had spurred his charger ahead and vanished into the murk. The others rode on. A frigid wind rushed out of the north, snatched at their cloaks, and drove the rain in horizontal sheets across the land. In moments Travis was soaked to the skin. The mistcloak did little good, no matter how tight its weave, if he could not keep it wrapped around himself.

Another flash of lightning revealed the silhouette of Beltan riding toward them. The knight brought his horse to a skidding halt and shouted over the roar of the storm. "There's a house not far ahead. I think it must be the manor of some local lord."

Falken wiped at the stream of water that poured down his brow. "Then I believe we should prevail upon the lord's hospitality."

They were nearly upon the manor before Travis saw it—a blocky shape backlit by a flash of lightning. They dismounted, and Beltan grabbed the reins of their steeds.

"There's a stable over there." He pointed to a black rectangle. "I'll take care of the horses." The knight led the fearful animals into gloom and was gone.

Holding on to each other, Travis, Melia, and Falken stumbled toward the manor's door. The bard pounded against the wooden surface.

"Open up!" he shouted. "Travelers seek shelter from the storm!"

There was no answer. Falken pounded again, but still the door did not open. Was the place abandoned? It was hard for Travis to tell through the rain, yet an atmosphere of decay seemed to hang over the manor. Falken exchanged grim looks with Melia, then struck the door one more time, so hard it rattled under the blow. His voice rang with authority.

"If this is still a civilized land, then by all the laws of hospitality, let us in!"

His words must have had an effect, for there came the sound of a bar being drawn, and the door swung inward. At the same moment Beltan returned from the stable. Together the four stepped inside.

The door shut and sealed them in a cramped entryway little brighter than the gloom outside. Travis's eyes adjusted to the dimness, and he saw the one who had let them in. She was barely more than a girl, clad in a mouse-brown dress. Dirt smudged her plain face but did not mask the fear in her expression. A grimy kerchief was knotted around her forehead, and a dark stain had seeped through the center of the cloth.

"Thank you for opening your door to us," Falken said. "It is a dark day out there."

The serving girl stared mutely and did not meet his gaze.

Falken tried again. "Can you take us to your lord, so that we may beg his hospitality?"

The girl gave a jerky nod. Without a word, she led them down a corridor and through a doorway. They found themselves in a drafty hall. Mold clung to stone walls, and a sullen fire sputtered in a gigantic fireplace, giving off much smoke, little light, and seemingly no heat. Beams—blackened with soot and time—arched overhead, and they made Travis think of the ribs of some huge beast that had just swallowed them alive.

A rattling voice spoke. "You must forgive my serving maid for not allowing you to enter at once. Kirtha is stupid, but I have no one else, and so I must tolerate her."

Travis searched for the source of the voice, and only after a moment did he realize someone sat at a rickety table near the fireplace. The man was thin to the point of wasting. Pockmarks pitted his sallow face, and his lank hair clung to his skull and forehead. His purple robe might once have been fine, but was now soiled and threadbare.

With a bony hand, the lord gestured toward benches beside the table. Though his voice was haggard, it was not unpleasant. "Come, sit beside the fire and warm yourselves. I cannot offer you the greeting I once would have, but you are welcome to all that I have. Things change, yet let it not be said that Sebaris of Thale has forgotten the laws of hospitality."

Melia made a graceful curtsy. "Thank you, my lord."

With trembling hands, Kirtha took their wet cloaks from them and hung the garments near the fire. The travelers sat on the splintery benches, and the lord himself poured them cups of mulled wine. Travis took a sip. The wine tasted of vinegar and was cut heavily with water, but at least it was warming. The lord did not ask their own names, but for all Travis knew this was part of the laws of hospitality that seemed so important in this world. Or perhaps the lord was simply mad. Now that they were closer, Travis noticed a feverish light in his eyes.

Kirtha, who had left the hall while they drank their wine, now entered again with a tray she set upon the table. There was little enough for her to carry: some stale bread, a few cooked turnips, and some bits of gristly meat. Lord Sebaris gestured for the travelers to serve themselves, and they did so without relish.

"You wonder why there is so little for my board, yes?" Sebaris said. "I can see it in your faces. It is shameful, you think, that a lord should live thusly."

"Not at all, my lord," Melia said. "We are grateful for your generosity."

Sebaris laughed: a forlorn sound. "You are well mannered, my lady. A few years ago, I would have offered you a feast suited for a queen." His eyes grew distant. "But there is so little left now. They take it, you see. They take it all." He gripped the arms of his chair with hands like claws. "Yet that is well, is it not? Better they take the silver, the wine, the food. Better they take those things than your—"

His words descended into a fit of coughing. Spasms wracked his emaciated body. At last the lord's coughing subsided. He wiped his lips with a napkin, and the cloth came away dark with blood.

Melia regarded Sebaris, her expression solemn. "Who are *they*, my lord?"

He waved a thin hand to dismiss her words. His gaze was *present* once again. "Forgive me, my lady. I was babbling, that's all. I've had a fever of late. Yet it's nothing with which you need concern yourself."

After that they ate in silence.

When they had finished, the lord cleared his throat. "I see there is a minstrel in your company."

Falken had drawn out his lute and now wiped the instrument's polished wood with a cloth.

"May I beg a song from you?" the lord said. "It has been long since this hall was graced by music."

Falken lifted his lute and tested the strings. "This is an old song. Yet it is fitting for a day like this, I think." The bard strummed the lute, then sang in a clear voice:

"With twilight to the dell they came:
Glennen brave and swift Frostmane.
A hundred leagues behind them lay,
Ahead long dark ere break of day.
Though weariness his heart did press,
He fain would die in place of rest.
On raced the earl and noble steed,
To warn the Queen and bid her speed.
When did the gloam asunder break,
And to his steed thus Glennen spake:

'Run, fair Frostmane, fleet as night,
'The Pale Ones come, and fey their—' "

A blood-chilling shriek interrupted the bard's song.

"Stop, you fool!" Sebaris cried. "They will hear you—they hear everything!" The lord was standing now, his eyes wild and filled with fear. "Don't you know that song is forbidden?"

The travelers could only gape.

Several heartbeats passed, and Sebaris seemed to regain his senses. He slumped and let out a deep sigh. Falken helped the lord into his chair, and Melia poured him a cup of wine, which he gulped down.

Falken regarded the emaciated man. "If my song has given you offense, then I beg your apology, my lord."

Sebaris shook his head. "No, do not apologize, good minstrel. It is clear you have traveled from distant lands—you could not know. And let us talk no more about the song. Kirtha will show you to a chamber now, where you can rest."

Melia bowed her head. "You are most kind, my lord."

"Not kind enough, I fear."

He murmured these words, as if he spoke more to himself than the others, and it seemed to Travis the light of madness shone in the lord's eyes once more. But perhaps it was only the glow of the dying fire. They took their leave of Sebaris, gathered up their still-damp cloaks, and followed Kirtha from the hall. The serving maid led them down a murky corridor. She paused before a door and gestured for them to enter.

Melia gazed at the stained kerchief that bound the serving maid's forehead. "I have some skill with healing, child," she said in a gentle voice. "May I see your hurt?"

Melia started to reach for the bandage, but the girl shrank away from her touch like a frightened animal. She shook her head, her eyes filled with mute terror.

Melia withdrew her hand. "As you wish, dear." Only the glittering of her amber eyes expressed her interest at this strange response.

Without asking for leave, Kirtha scurried down the corridor and was gone.

Falken shot Melia an inquisitive look. "I guess she didn't appreciate your offer for help."

"Indeed. But why, I wonder?"

Beltan let out a surly snort. "Well, you two can stay out here and talk about the motivations of serving girls all you'd like, but I'm going to go inside and get out of this mail shirt before it rusts solid. Riding all day in the rain is not good for armor."

"Or for temperaments," Melia observed.

They found the chamber as dank and chilly as the rest of the manor. The walls were cracked, the fireplace empty, and cobwebs dangled from the ceiling. There were a few benches for furniture, but these were so rickety the travelers spread their cloaks on the floor and sat there instead.

Melia smoothed invisible wrinkles from her midnight-blue garment. "Well," she said in an exasperated tone, "what on Eldh was *that* all about?"

"You mean Sebaris, back in the hall?" Falken said. "That's a good question. I would just like to know when it became forbidden to sing the *Lay of Glennen* in Eredane. It doesn't make a great deal of sense." He strummed the strings of his lute with a thumb, then shook his head. "In fact, none of this makes sense. A lone serving girl is hardly enough to make up even a provincial lord's household. There should be a dozen servants and retainers here. What's going on in Eredane? First the town, now this place. Something is not right."

"So it seems," Melia said. "Regardless, I don't think we should overstay our lord's welcome."

Falken nodded. "The storm should blow over soon. We can set out at dawn. I'm sure Sebaris will be more than happy to see us go."

They turned their attention to readying things for the journey tomorrow. Beltan sharpened the edge of his sword with a stone, while Falken polished the rich wood of his lute with a cloth, and Melia hummed a faint song while she sorted through the remaining foodstuffs in their packs. Only Travis was without a task.

"Is there anything I can do to help?" he asked Falken.

"Just stay out of the way, Travis," the bard muttered.

Travis slouched in a corner. He sat for a time and fidgeted with the Malachorian dagger Jack had given him, but only succeeded in nicking his finger. At that moment he felt utterly and irrevocably useless. He stood up.

"I'm going to go for a walk," he said.

Melia spoke without looking up from her work. "Just don't wander too far, Travis."

Melia's quiet comment was too much. Being in this strange world was hard enough without everyone always telling him what to do. Anger blossomed in Travis's chest. He clenched his hands into fists.

"I'm not stupid, you know." His voice was more hurtful than he intended, but he didn't care.

Melia looked up from her work. Her expression was neither shocked nor outraged, but merely thoughtful. "I never said you were, dear."

Travis hardly heard her words. He turned and pushed through the doorway. Another voice murmured something behind him. Falken, most likely. Melia's voice countered. Then the door shut, and he was alone.

His anger cooled on the dank air. He peered into the dimness all around, and he wasn't certain if this was the lord's manor in Eredane, or if it was the farmhouse in Illinois where he had grown up. Maybe it didn't make a difference. He would have felt the same, whichever place it was.

Just stay out of the way, Travis. He had heard those words before. Only it was his father's voice that had spoken them years ago, not the bard's. *That's the only job morons are good at. Leave the real work to people who can tell left from right.*

Travis shook his head. The memories of Illinois melted like shadows on the dim air. He was in Eredane once more.

"Wherever that is," he said with a bitter laugh.

Travis knew he should go back into the chamber, but he was restless, and he wandered down the corridor instead, past closed doors and clumps of cobweb. After a few dozen paces, the corridor ended. A shuttered window was set into the stone wall. He pushed against the shutters, but they were stuck tight. He gritted his teeth and pushed harder. There was a groan of straining wood, then all at once the shutters flew outward.

Travis leaned through the window and breathed in rain-sweet air. He found himself gazing at what must have once been a garden behind the manor house. Now it was a profusion of nettles and witchgrass. Falken was right. The storm had blown over. Night had fallen, and only a few tatters of cloud drifted against the sky. They glowed in the light of the moon.

The night air was frosty, but Travis did not mind. The cold cleared his head. For a time he was content to stare into the moonlit garden. Sometimes life was as tangled as the nettles, and just as stinging.

His breath clouded on the air. It was past time to be getting back to the others. He reached out to draw the shutters closed.

Movement caught his eye. Travis froze. Deep in the garden, a patch of shadow stirred. It flowed toward the far wing of the manor, opposite Travis's window, and there it joined with another, thinner shadow that had clung close to the wall of the manor. A sound drifted on the air, like the moan of the wind. Or like the whisper of voices.

The moon passed behind a cloud, and the garden was plunged into darkness. Travis held his breath, afraid to move. He counted a dozen heartbeats. The cloud drifted on, and the light of the moon spilled into the neglected garden once more.

The shadows were gone.

Travis breathed out. He scanned the garden but saw nothing. Most likely the shadows had been tricks of the moonlight. A jaw-cracking yawn escaped him, and only then did he realize how tired he was. He pulled the shutters closed and turned back down the hallway.

He paused when he reached the door to their chamber. No sounds came from the other side. The others would be asleep by now. Travis did not want to wake them—he had caused enough trouble with his outburst. There was a small alcove set into the wall a few paces away. It was not exactly a proper bed, but at least it would protect him from the worst drafts, so he wrapped himself in his mistcloak and curled up inside. Travis would have thought sleep difficult, but weariness stole over him, and he sank into dreamless slumber.

44.

A sizzling sound woke him. With it came an uncomfortable heat against his face. Travis opened his eyes. At once he sat up in terror, his back against the wall of the alcove. He could not tear his eyes away from the glowing iron brand that hovered before him, inches from his forehead.

Lord Sebaris clucked his tongue. His glassy eyes reflected the red-hot glow of the brand. "Better you had not awakened, my friend," he said in a whisper. "The pain is worse when you know it is coming." The brand moved an inch closer.

Travis tried to speak through the fear that constricted his throat. The stench of hot metal was sharp in his lungs. "Why?" he said. "Why are you doing this?"

Now the look in the lord's eyes was one of regret. "I must mark you. I must mark all of you. It is the only way to be safe." He licked thin lips. "Don't you see? They will not kill you if they think you are one of them!"

Sweat rolled down Travis's forehead and stung his eyes. He tried to back away but could retreat no farther. He gasped the words. "Who are they?"

"Who else?" Sebaris said. "The dark ones! The followers of the Raven!"

The lord hesitated, then lifted his free hand to push the lank hair away from his forehead. Two puckered lines marked the flesh of his brow. The ragged scars formed a symbol—a symbol Travis knew well. It could almost be an eye, but it wasn't. Instead it was meant to be the wing of a raven. Only at that moment did Travis realize the end of the brand had been wrought into the mirror image of that shape. He stared, his horror renewed.

"Ah, you understand!" Sebaris's voice was a croak of triumph. "You have seen the dark ones before. You know I must do this." He tightened his thin fingers around the grip of the iron brand. The end glowed like a coal. "If you do not struggle, the pain will be a little less."

Travis knew he should cry out, that he should resist, but fear paralyzed him. With a mad grin, Sebaris tensed, ready to press the brand against Travis's flesh. Just then the muffled sound of shouts came from behind the door where the others were. Travis heard the dull ring of a sword being drawn. There was a low thump, and a bubbling cry of pain.

Sebaris glanced toward the door.

Travis knew this was his only chance. The paralysis of fear shattered. He grabbed Sebaris's arm, thrust the glowing brand aside, and knocked the lord backward. The two rolled into the corridor, and the brand clattered against the stone floor. Travis tried to disengage from his foe, but Sebaris fought back with a shocking strength Travis had not expected, given his emaciated body. With a grunt of pain, Travis found himself on his back. Sebaris dug sharp knees into his chest and wrapped clammy hands around his throat. Travis choked for breath. Sebaris grinned and tightened his cruel grip. Now stars exploded before Travis's eyes. That was when the voice spoke.

The word, Travis. Remember the word I spoke to you.

Travis supposed the voice was a figment of his oxygen-starved brain. Yet it sounded so much like Jack's—just like the voice that had spoken when he touched the broken rune in Kelcior. The world spun around him. It would be so easy to sink down into darkness. All he had to do was close his eyes, then peace would come.

No, Travis! Don't close your eyes!

He fought to remain conscious. Sebaris frothed at the mouth now. The sounds of fighting behind the closed door had ended.

You must speak it, Travis. Speak the word!

Travis was tired, so terribly tired. But he couldn't let Jack down. He lifted a hand and rested it against the lord's sunken chest. The sound that issued from his lips was a barely audible croak.

"Krond."

Flame burst into being around Travis's hand. Crimson tongues licked at Sebaris's robe, and the threadbare cloth ignited like tinder. With a shriek, Sebaris threw himself back, away from Travis. He beat at the flames with gnarled hands, but the effort was futile. In moments the lord blazed like a torch. He raised bony arms above his head in a gesture of exultation.

"I come to you, my dark king!"

He stumbled backward, into a tapestry that hung upon the wall. Flames raced up the rotten weaving to lick the wooden beams above. Sebaris pitched forward. By the time the lord struck the floor, there was nothing left of him besides a charred husk.

Travis gagged, clutched his bruised throat, and pulled himself to his knees. He looked up to see Falken in the open doorway. Melia and Beltan were just behind him. The big knight gripped his sword, the blade dark with blood. All of them wore looks of astonishment.

"How, Travis?" Falken asked softly. "How did you do that?"

Travis looked at his hand, but the skin was smooth and undamaged. The flames that had incinerated Sebaris had not so much as touched him. He opened his mouth but could not speak.

"There's no time for that now," Melia said.

Flames raced along the wooden beams of the ceiling. Falken gave Travis one last hard look, then nodded. Beltan pulled Travis to his feet. Together the four stumbled down the corridor. Thick smoke filled their lungs, and blazing beams crashed down on their heels. Travis wondered what had become of the serving girl, Kirtha. Then he remembered the bandage that had covered her forehead and knew that, wherever she was, it was already too late to save her.

Gasping for air, the four burst into the night outside. They did not stop running until they reached the stable. Then they turned just in time to see the entire roof of the manor house collapse. The stone walls cracked with a sound like thunder and sank inward. Sparks rose into the onyx sky, winking like crimson eyes.

Travis drew a cooling breath into his seared lungs. It was painful to speak, but the words were audible. "What happened in the chamber?"

"Two men slipped through the window," Falken said. "They were Raven cultists. I think they would have slain us had Beltan not been keeping watch."

"No." Travis shook his head. "They didn't come to kill."

Melia gave him a sharp look, but his throat hurt too much to explain any further. Later he would tell them about the iron brand and Sebaris's terrible words.

Beltan wiped his sword against the grass and thrust it back into the scabbard at his hip. "Whatever the cultists wanted, they weren't easy to kill. I ran one through the gut, and he still kept coming. He didn't stop until I lopped his head off. But that was nothing compared to what you did to old Sebaris, Travis. How by Vathris did you—"

Melia laid a gentle but firm hand upon the knight's arm. "Enough, Beltan. Such things can wait."

Travis shivered. He wondered the same thing as Beltan. He closed his eyes and saw Sebaris again, writhing as the flames consumed him, cackling in mad glee.

"There's enough moonlight to ride by," Falken said. "Let's get the horses."

45.

The Lady Grace of Beckett's education in courtly manners and feudal politics began promptly at dawn the day after her conversation with King Boreas.

She woke to a chiming sound. On instinct her hand went to her hip and fumbled in search of her beeper. The hospital was calling her. Probably Morty Underwood, damn the little worm. She groped, but her blind fingers found only soft cloth. Then the chiming came again, and it was not the electronic whine emitted by a silicon chip, but the bright sound of metal on metal. She threw back the bedcovers and sat bolt upright. Memory of the previous day flooded back to her. Denver Memorial Hospital was a world away now. The thought should have caused her alarm. Instead a feeling like relief washed through her.

Aryn stood at the foot of the high, four-poster bed, a cheerful expression on her pretty face. Her gown today was a lighter shade of blue, the color of the wintry dawn sky outside the chamber's window. In her left hand she held a silver bell.

"I'm glad you're finally awake, Grace." The baroness set the bell on a sideboard. "I was afraid I had chosen far too small a tool for the task, and that I was going to have to call for the king's trumpeters instead."

"Mrumph," Grace said. It was far too early in the morning for humor.

With stiff motions she climbed down from the bed, still clad in yesterday's rumpled tunic and hose. Though a great deal had happened to her in the meantime, it still had been only a day since the knight Durge had found her lying in a snowdrift. Her bones ached, and she was shivering again.

Now the mirth in Aryn's large eyes was replaced by concern. "Are you well, Grace?"

Was she well? Grace bit her tongue to stifle a mad laugh. She had left her apartment, her job, her life, had fled men with hearts made of metal, and had found herself in an entirely different world. Was she *well*?

"I'm fine," she said.

Aryn smiled.

Grace forced her teeth to stop chattering. "Now, this is my first morning in Calavere, and I have absolutely no idea what I'm supposed to do. What's first?"

"Bath," Aryn said, and the word was music to Grace's ears.

Grace had always thought, in medieval periods, people bathed once a year whether they needed it or not. Two baths in two days seemed to disprove that theory. On Aryn's order, a pair of serving maids—the same two young women in dove-gray dresses whom Grace had glimpsed yesterday—brought in a wooden tub and pitchers of steaming water. She noted the serving maids seemed less fearful than the day before. But then, yesterday she had been half-frozen, found on the borders of a mysterious forest, and dressed in what were—for here, at least—outlandish clothes. She supposed it was a little harder to mistake a bony woman shivering in a tunic for a fairy queen.

Aryn and the serving maids retreated from the room, and Grace soaked in the marvelously hot water until, one by one, her muscles unclenched. However, at last the water grew cool, and she knew there was no more putting it off.

It was time to try the gowns again.

She dried off, shrugged on the simple linen shift Aryn had left for her, then eyed the dusky purple gown the baroness had selected. Aryn had said the color would contrast nicely with Grace's green-gold eyes and ash-blond hair. Grace could only take her word for it. They hadn't taught fashion design in medical school.

Grace shrugged the gown over her head, staggered under its weight, recovered, then arranged it as best she could. To the gown's sash she attached the small leather pouch that contained the silver half-coin and the business card Hadrian Farr had given her. After a moment's thought she added her necklace to the pouch, for the metal pendant seemed too large and heavy given the low cut of the gown's bodice. At least, that was what she told herself, but she remembered the way Detective Janson had leaned toward her to peer at her necklace, interest shining in his small, evil eyes.

With a gentle knock Aryn entered once more. Her blue eyes flew wide, but it was a hallmark of her nobility that she did not burst out laughing. "It's a good start," the baroness said, "but let's work with it a bit."

There was some struggling at first, but once Aryn asked Grace to stand still and quit resisting, things went more rapidly. Aryn adjusted the gown with deft fingers, and Grace found that, once properly arranged, it was neither so heavy nor binding as she had thought. There was a definite trick to walking in the thing, and sitting was a feat in itself, but after a few pointers from Aryn, Grace found she was not at all hopeless. In fact, it was almost fun to feel the soft material swishing around her.

"You're doing wonderfully, Grace," Aryn said.

Grace smiled in reply and spun in a circle. Her smile became a grimace as she tripped over a fold of cloth and flopped down into a chair.

The baroness winced. "But don't get overconfident."

"Thanks for the advice."

Aryn helped her out of the chair, and they proceeded next to a breakfast of brown bread, soft cheese, and dried fruit. The baroness used the meal as an opportunity for a lesson. Here in Calavan—as in all the Dominions, Aryn explained—common folk paid tithes of food and other goods to their liege lord in exchange for protection and justice. In addition to being king, Boreas was a baron and held several duchies as well, and thus possessed fiefdoms of his own from which came the food, the wool, the iron, and other materials that were required for the keeping of Calavere.

Grace picked up a piece of bread. "It all seems like an awfully complicated way just to get your breakfast."

"And how does one procure food and protection in your homeland?"

Grace chewed the bread and thought. "I'm not entirely certain. We buy food in a store. And I suppose we pay police officers to protect us."

Aryn's words were polite, but it was clear from her expression she thought this arrangement inferior. "I see. Markets and mercenaries. I have heard things are so in the Free Cities to the south. Perhaps you hail from one of them?"

Grace looked away. How could she tell Aryn the truth about where she came from? People here had been afraid enough when they thought she might be a fairy queen. What would they think if they knew she came from another world?

Now Aryn's voice quavered with worry. "I'm so sorry, Grace. It's none of my concern where you come from. Can you forgive me?"

Grace turned back, forced herself to smile, and found it was not so difficult. "There's nothing to forgive."

All the rest of that day, and for several days after that, Grace's education continued. In a way, it was like being in school again. Although even medical school—despite Grace's love for dissection and examination—had not been so interesting as this. Most of her time was spent in her chamber, and she sat by the fire and gazed into the flames as Aryn lectured. The baroness would sip spiced wine while Grace favored steaming cups of *maddok*. She had discovered the remarkable substance one morning when a clay pot of it was left on her breakfast tray by mistake. Apparently *maddok* was considered a vulgar drink, suitable for commoners only, while nobles preferred wine. However, after her first cup, Grace did not care what anyone thought of her for drinking it. In multiple ways *maddok* reminded her of the coffee in the Residents' Lounge back at Denver Memorial—thick, black, and energizing—only without that battery acid aftertaste and the accompanying shakes. It was good stuff.

Each day, Grace looked forward to Aryn's visits more and more. Before long, by the time the baroness arrived at the chamber door, she would discover Grace already risen and dressed. What was more, Aryn was forced to rearrange Grace's hopelessly tangled gown only on the first two or three occasions. After that, Grace found she could manage by herself, albeit with some minor lifting on the part of one of the serving maids. The first time she was able to properly don one of the gowns alone she beamed in triumph. It was amazing what a feeling of independence it gave one to be able to dress oneself.

Aryn, it turned out, was a good teacher.

The baroness was knowledgeable and explained things in a clear manner, and, while patient, she was also demanding of her pupil. Though far from perfect, a picture of this world—at least the part of it in which she had found herself—began to form in Grace's mind. She listened as Aryn spoke of the history of the Dominions, and of kingdoms and empires far older. And she learned something of geography as well, when one afternoon the baroness used bits of charcoal stolen from the hearth to draw maps on pieces of stretched sheepskin vellum. It was fascinating, yet—just as Grace had expected in a world without automobiles and satellites—Aryn's knowledge of the land grew more vague with increasing distance from Calavan.

Of all Aryn's lessons, politics was Grace's least favorite, and the one upon which they spent the most time. If Grace was to be at all effective in observing the upcoming Council of Kings, Aryn explained, it was crucial she possess a thorough understanding of all the players involved.

"And the ruler of Brelegond is?"

The baroness paced before the fire, her left hand on her slender hip, and her expression serious. She had taken to quizzing Grace, who sat on a stool, to test how well her pupil had paid attention.

Grace thought a minute. "King Lysandir."

Aryn nodded. "Good. Now, tell me the seat of Queen Ivalaine of Toloria."

That was an easy one. The names were so similar. "Ar-Tolor," Grace said without pause.

The baroness did not give Grace a chance to rest. "And the primary export of Galt is?"

Grace wracked her brain but could not recall the answer. This was worse than the gross anatomy final her first year in medical school. "Rocks?" she said with a hopeful look.

Aryn sighed. "Close. The primary export of Galt is goat's wool."

Grace's lips twisted in a wry expression. "I should have guessed. What with all those rocks, there are bound to be lots of goats." She looked up at Aryn. "So, I didn't pass, did I?"

The young baroness hesitated, then shook her head. "But you were wonderfully close, Grace."

Only Aryn could make failure sound like an accomplishment. "I don't know how you keep track of everything, Aryn," Grace said. "You're amazing."

The baroness turned away and hunched her slender shoulders. "It's nothing, really. It's a noble's job to know such things, that's all. It behooves us to be familiar with our allies and rivals. Still, my knowledge is only a poor fraction of what Lord Alerain knows. It is said the king's seneschal can recognize every noble in the Dominions, down to the least earl, on sight."

"He didn't recognize me," Grace said softly.

Her own words startled her, she hadn't meant to utter them aloud. Aryn turned around, her expression thoughtful, although what she was thinking Grace did not know.

"I believe it is past time for a rest," was all the baroness said.

46.

Not all of Grace's hours were spent in study in the small stone chamber, for Aryn had other duties to attend to besides Grace's education. As King Boreas's ward, and as the highest-ranking lady in Calavere, it fell to her to make the household ready for the nobles that would soon arrive. Rooms that had not been used in a decade needed to be reopened and aired. The stores in the cellar had to be inventoried. And there were countless other details to oversee, from making certain there were linens enough for all the guests, to examining every spoon in the scullery to be certain each had been polished. Just listening to all Aryn's activities was enough to make Grace tired. She decided she would rather work double shifts in the ED on a full moon Friday than be the lady of a castle for a day.

To keep Grace occupied in the times she was away, Aryn brought an armful of books from the castle library to Grace's chamber.

"Oh!" Aryn gasped as she set the stack of books on the sideboard.

Concern touched her forehead. "You do read, don't you, Grace? I simply assumed . . . a lady of your station, that is . . . but if you haven't learned, that's perfectly. . ."

Grace held up a hand. "It's all right, Aryn. Yes, I do read. Almost everybody reads where I come from. Well, they *can* read, that is. I'm not certain they always *do*."

Aryn looked shocked. "Only a fool would squander such a precious gift."

"I won't argue with you on that one."

The books were like nothing Grace had ever seen. Each was lettered painstakingly by hand and bound in leather gilded with gold and silver leaf. She opened one of them and turned the pages of stiff vellum with growing delight, for the margins of every page were decorated with intricate drawings of moons, stars, and intertwining leaves. These were not so much books as they were works of readable art. Grace eagerly gathered them up in her arms.

For several afternoons in a row, while Aryn saw to her various duties about the castle, Grace curled atop the massive bed and read. The books Aryn had brought were largely histories that described the founding of Calavan and, in lesser detail, the other Dominions. Most of what she read was difficult to follow, and consisted of long lists that recounted the names of which knights and nobles had fallen in this skirmish with barbarians or that battle with a neighboring fiefdom. Still, it was enough to make Grace realize that, however kindly people had been to her, these were harsh lands, carved not all that long ago out of wilderness by sword and fire.

It was while reading one of the books that Grace discovered the secret of the silver half-coin the strange preacher man had given her, at the ruins of the Beckett-Strange Home for Children back on Earth.

One night she shucked off her gown and, clad only in her linen shift, climbed into bed. She took one of the books with her, to read by the light of a tallow candle. Except when she opened the book the words on the page were gibberish, as if written in some ancient, alien language. Yet she had been reading this same volume no more than an hour ago.

Wait a minute, Grace. You're a scientist, be rational about this. What's different now that wasn't a little while ago?

Perhaps it was intuition. Perhaps it was a leap of logic based on some clues or evidence she had unconsciously noted earlier. Either way, a thrill ran up Grace's spine. She moved to her cast-off gown, reached into the leather pouch fastened to the sash, and drew out the half-coin.

After a little experimenting her initial hunch was confirmed. If she held the coin, or if it was anywhere about her person, she could read the books as if they were written in English, albeit a somewhat archaic dialect. However, if she was not in contact with the coin, the words were meaningless scribbles. When a serving maid entered Grace made another discovery. The coin affected not only written words, but spoken words as well. At first the serving maid seemed to speak in a lilting foreign tongue. Then Grace gripped the coin, and the girl's words phased into meaning.

"Forgive me, my lady, but I asked if you required anything?"

"No. No, I'm fine."

The serving maid curtsied and left.

It made sense, of course. Why would the people of another world speak English? It should have occurred to her sooner. But somehow the coin had worked to translate the language of this land, and she had not noticed. Grace opened her hand and gazed down at the broken coin on her palm. The partial symbols engraved on each surface glinted in the candlelight, but she could not guess what they might be. Whatever they were, one thing was for certain. Whoever he was, wherever he had come from, Brother Cy had some sort of connection with this world, with Eldh.

Knowing that left just one question. *Why?* Why had he come to her at the orphanage? *Or did I come to him?* Grace sensed that if she knew the answer to that question, she would understand much. She tucked the half-coin back into her pouch.

It was not a feeling she was accustomed to, but the next morning a strange sense of loneliness crept into Grace's chest. She wished Aryn was there, but the baroness was off seeing to one of her myriad tasks. She moved to the window and watched the people below through rippled glass: squires, nobles, servants, all with names and purposes unknown.

Grace drew in a deep breath. She knew this place was a world away from Denver. Yet it was not so different from the hospital, was it? At Denver Memorial she had never spoken much with the other residents and doctors, had never taken part in their impromptu hallway games or lounge chat sessions. She had felt there just as she did now, watching the bailey—distant, disconnected, observing but not taking part.

Grace clutched the stone sill. There was nothing for her beyond the window. She started to turn away—

—then halted. There, in the upper bailey, a figure walked toward the stable. He was clad all in black and gray, and his mail shirt seemed to weigh down his shoulders. Even from here she could see the way his long black mustaches drooped, and by that she knew him for certain. It was Durge, the knight who had found her in the forest.

Over the last several days, Grace had often wondered what had become of her rescuer. Despite his gloomy demeanor—or perhaps even because of it—she had liked the Embarran knight. Though she had never been one to make friends easily, she had been oddly disappointed the knight had not come to visit her, if only to see how she fared. Durge was the representative of King Sorrin of Embarr. No doubt the knight was busy making certain things were ready for the arrival of his liege. Still, it would be good to at least say hello.

Grace fumbled with the latch and threw open the window. A blast of frigid air struck her. She leaned out, raised her arm, and opened her mouth to call out to the knight below. As she did, a dread came over her. It was that same overwhelming fear she always felt when dealing with other people. Whole people. She froze. *This is ridiculous, Grace. There's no reason to be so afraid. He's just a man, that's all.* She steeled her will and tried again to call out, but by then it was too late. Durge had stepped into the shadow of the stable and was lost from sight. She lowered her arm, her hand aching with cold.

Grace stared at the empty bailey below. Why was she always so afraid of others? She thought of the man she had shot at the hospital, the man who had killed Leon Arlington, who would have killed the old woman in the wheelchair if Grace had not stopped him—the man with the lump of iron in his chest. She lifted her hand to the bodice of her gown, but her fingers were so cold she could feel nothing. Maybe she was missing her own heart. Maybe they had taken it from her at the orphanage all those years ago, just like Detective Janson's had been taken from him. Maybe that was why she couldn't feel.

Finally the cold was too great to bear, and she closed the window once more.

47.

The next morning, Grace's fifth in Calavere, Aryn did not knock on the chamber door. The night before, the baroness had explained she was to be in audience with King Boreas for most of the day, working out details in preparation for the council. Grace was on her own.

For a time she sat by the fire and read. She was determined to teach herself the language of this place. The half-coin was a remarkable artifact, and certainly it had saved her life by allowing her to communicate with the people of this world, but she dared not count on it. What if she were to lose the coin?

It was painstaking work. First she would read a passage of the book with the coin in hand, then she would set it down and study the strange words once she knew their meaning. Already she could read a few phrases without the coin's help.

At last she blinked, eyes bleary. *No amount of* maddok *is enough to cure brain-death, Grace. Put it up.*

She rose, set the book on the sideboard with the others, then began to pace, restless. It dawned on her that she had not left this chamber since her conversation with King Boreas four days ago. True, before there had been little need. She had been content with Aryn's company, and the books, and rest. Food was brought to her at regular intervals, and in the corner there was a covered chamber pot, which the serving maids replaced twice daily. However, it was more than that. Beyond the door lay an entire world she did not understand, but within these four walls was a small space she could control and command, like the ED at Denver Memorial. Except now the chamber was starting to seem more like her old apartment. Grace felt bored and trapped, her legs ached to be stretched. It was time to leave her room.

And go where?

She thought this over, then an idea occurred to her. She could go speak with King Boreas. Certainly he would have some task for her. Perhaps there were some in the castle who were ill or injured. While she could not say she missed the Emergency Department or Denver Memorial Hospital, she did miss the healing—finding the places where others were wounded or hurting, and taking that pain away.

Quickly, so as not to lose her resolve, she braced her shoulders, opened the chamber door, and stepped into the hallway beyond. If she had thought there would be someone there to stop her from leaving, then she was wrong. The corridor was empty, save for a young page who was walking past on some errand.

"Your Radiance!" he said, then bowed and hastened on.

Grace winced. Even though they did not know her rank or from where she hailed, somewhere along the way King Boreas and Aryn had decided Grace was at least a duchess. And, Aryn had explained, the proper term for a duchess was *Your Radiance*. It wasn't much of an improvement over *Your Highness*, but Grace supposed beggars couldn't be choosers.

She gazed down the corridor in either direction. One way looked much like another. She tried to remember something of the route by which Aryn had taken her to see King Boreas but could not, so she made her best guess as to which way the main keep lay and started down the corridor.

After an hour she knew she was lost. By then she had made her way through a labyrinth of passageways, stairwells, and high-ceilinged halls. Each time she came upon a window, she would look out to find herself gazing on an unexpected part of the castle. She passed numerous people as she wandered—servants, men-at-arms, and, by their fine clothes, nobles of various ranks. All bowed or nodded their heads as she passed, depending on their station. While she might have liked to ask some of them for directions, none paused to speak to her or question where she was going. Apparently duchesses were supposed to know what they were doing.

Eventually she found herself in a part of the castle that appeared little used. Not even the occasional servant or guard walked these dim corridors. A dusty scent hung on the air, and cobwebs dangled from the ceiling. She was beginning to wonder if she would ever find her way back to more traveled ways when she rounded a corner and, to her relief, found herself gazing at a familiar face.

"Your Radiance!"

This time the words were uttered by Lord Alerain, the king's seneschal. Alerain was dressed much as he had been the day Grace had first met him by the stables, all in black and maroon, with a long vest overlying all. For a fraction of a heartbeat Alerain seemed surprised. Then the moment passed, and everything about him was as sharp and precise as his close-cropped gray hair. He placed a beringed hand against his chest and bowed toward Grace. She made her best attempt at a curtsy and did not worry too much whether she had gotten it right. One advantage of a gown was that it was awfully hard for others to see exactly what you were doing inside of it.

"Pardon me for just a moment, my lady," Alerain said. He turned toward a man who stood a few paces away. The man looked to be a servant of some sort, dressed in a nondescript tunic and a leather cap. He would have been completely ordinary except his eyes were of different colors: one brown, one blue.

"You may go now and see to your task," Alerain said in a low but commanding voice.

The man nodded—the gesture seemed a trifle curt—then started down the corridor. As he passed Grace, he glanced at her with his peculiar eyes, and for a moment a grin split his unshaven face. This struck Grace as strange—none of the other servants in the castle would so much as meet her eyes. Then the man was gone, and her attention was turned toward Alerain as the seneschal spoke.

"I would not have expected to find you in this part of the castle, Your Radiance."

"You're not the only one." Grace lifted her hands in sheepish gesture. "I think I'm lost."

"Well, we shall have to correct that." Alerain extended his arm, and after a moment's hesitation Grace accepted it. The seneschal guided her down the corridor. For a time they were silent as they walked. At last Grace found the courage to speak.

"I was hoping to find King Boreas." She meant to explain further, but that was all she could get out for the moment.

Alerain shook his head. "I'm afraid the king won't be able to see you today, my lady. He's quite occupied with preparations for the coming council. Do you have a request I might relay to him?"

Alerain's kindly demeanor bolstered her courage. "I was hoping to ask the king if there was anything I could do for him." She was about to explain she was a doctor, but Alerain spoke first.

"Are you learning about the Dominions and their various rulers and histories?"

Grace nodded. "Yes. The Lady Aryn has taught me a great deal already."

"Good. That is all the king requires of you for now, my lady. He will be pleased to know of your progress. And when he wishes for you to do something else, I'm certain he will summon you."

These words caught Grace off-balance. She opened her mouth to reply, but nothing came out. No matter what world she was in, conversation was not one of her strengths. They had reached a well-traveled hall now, and Alerain disengaged her arm.

"I fear I must see to other, less pleasant duties than escorting you, my lady. Can you find your way from here?"

Grace peered around. The hall looked vaguely familiar. If she remembered her wanderings rightly, her chamber was not far off. "I think I can manage." She tried to sound more confident than she felt.

Alerain smiled and made a precise bow. He bade her farewell, then turned and strode away. Grace sighed, then moved down a corridor. She was disappointed when she found herself before the door to her chamber. *So much for adventures.* But there was nothing else to do, so she opened the door and stepped inside.

48.

The next day a young page came to Grace's chamber with a message from King Boreas. A feast was to be held at Calavere that night, and the presence of the Lady Grace of Beckett was required. At this news, Aryn laughed in excitement. Grace, in turn, panicked.

"A feast?" She slumped into a chair by the fireplace. "I don't think I'm ready for this."

"Nonsense," Aryn said. "Feasts are easy. You just have to eat a lot."

"Something tells me King Boreas isn't inviting me just for the food. After all, I'm supposed to be his spy." Grace looked up at the youthful baroness. "So who else is going to be there?"

Aryn scanned the remainder of the king's missive. "The feast is being held to honor the various representatives of the kings and queens of the other Dominions. They've all arrived now, to make the necessary preparations for the Council of Kings before the rulers themselves get here."

"You mean everyone at the feast is going to be a noble?" Grace asked in growing dread.

Aryn nodded. "But it won't be so bad, really. You've already met one. Remember? Durge of Embarr. And he's certainly the most dour of the lot."

Grace thought about the stern but kind knight. "Actually, I rather liked that about him."

Aryn shrugged. "Well, he *did* rescue you from Gloaming Wood, so I suppose you're predisposed to be forgiving." The baroness brightened then and knelt beside Grace's chair. "I know this all seems frightening, Grace. But it's not every day one gets invited to a feast by the king of Calavan. It's going to be fun. You'll see."

Fun. Aryn seemed to have a fundamental misunderstanding of the meaning of that word.

A knock sounded on the chamber door. Startled, the two women leaped to their feet.

"Come in," Grace called after a moment. The door opened, and danger glided through in an emerald-green gown.

Aryn nodded, a stiff gesture. Her sapphire eyes were wary. "Lady Kyrene."

The Countess Kyrene displayed her small teeth in a smile. Her dark gold hair fell in ringlets about her shoulders. "Lady Aryn. It is a delight you are so eager to greet me that your manners have fled you, but may I gently remind you this is the Lady Grace's chamber, and so it is her right to offer first greetings?"

Aryn's cheeks flushed. Grace hurriedly stepped forward.

"Good morrow, Lady Kyrene." She hoped the trembling in her voice was not entirely obvious. "It's nice to see you again."

The countess moved farther into the room, and the scent of ripe apricots followed. "I'm so glad to see you've had time to indulge yourself with more courtly attire, Lady Grace. I know the urgency and need of your travel here did not allow it. And your choice of dress is so charming. My mother always loved that style of gown."

"I'll take that as a compliment," Grace said, though it clearly was not one.

Kyrene smiled again, but the expression did not quite conceal the shadow of dissatisfaction at the corners of her mouth. "Are you looking forward to tonight's feast?"

Grace chose her words with care. "I've only just heard about it. King Boreas sent a missive a short while ago."

"Ah, yes, the king."

Kyrene's voice was a purr, as if Grace had unwittingly revealed some great secret. It seemed no matter what she said the countess would read some ulterior meaning into it.

Kyrene approached the window and gazed out. "I am certain you wish to express your gratitude to King Boreas for the kindness he has shown you. But then, you are a lady of noble blood. It speaks well of you to show such concern for your host." She turned her gaze on Grace. "Yet, as I am also a visitor to this court, and thus we are sisters of a sort, I feel it is my place—nay, my duty—to warn you about the king."

Aryn stepped forward, her left hand clenched into a fist. Her face was pale with anger. "Warn her? Warn her of what, Kyrene?"

The countess laughed. "Gentle Aryn, you are so guileless, and that is only as it should be in one so fresh and young. But do try to understand, love. The Lady Grace and I are women grown, and dare not pretend such innocence."

Aryn opened her mouth to retort, but Grace shook her head, and the baroness held her tongue, though she looked wounded. Grace was sorry if she had hurt Aryn, but she sensed it was important to hear what Kyrene had come to say. Not that she felt any kinship with the countess. She eyed the full outlines of Kyrene's pearled bodice. *I doubt anyone would ever mistake us for sisters.* However, Boreas had told her to talk with the other nobles at the council, to learn what they were thinking. She might as well start with Kyrene.

Grace stepped forward. "What do you mean, Kyrene? What do you want to warn me about?"

A triumphant smile touched Kyrene's full lips. "Do not misunderstand me. No one would ever say that Boreas is not a fine and good king."

They just think it a lot, Grace added the unspoken implication.

"However," Kyrene said, "it is true Boreas follows the Mysteries of Vathris. And the Cult of the Bullslayer is a cult of warriors. One cannot fault them for being predisposed toward conflict and violence. It is in their blood."

Grace bit her lip. The Cult of Vathris? Was that a religion of some sort? Knowing would certainly help her in grasping Kyrene's motives, but she couldn't ask the countess about it—to do so would show her ignorance.

"Are you saying you think King Boreas is a warmonger?" Grace asked instead.

Kyrene clucked her tongue. "Words are such tricky things, love."

And so are you, Grace said to herself. *Love*.

Aloud she said, "I can't claim to care much for war, but sometimes it's necessary in times of trouble."

"There are other methods for averting trouble. Subtler methods, but just as powerful—perhaps even more so. Men are such obvious creatures. They have difficulty seeing these things. But there are those who do."

Grace did not like guessing games. "And they are?"

The glint in Kyrene's eyes matched that within the large emerald in the cleft of her bosom. "For now I believe it is enough to say there will be those at the Council of Kings with interests different from those of Boreas. You may not wish to sell your allegiance just yet, my lady."

"I wasn't aware that I had."

Kyrene drew near. Now the scent of apricots was cloying. It filled Grace's head, made her mind dull and torpid. The countess spoke in a low voice.

"Boreas is a strong king. But do not be mistaken by that strength. He is a man, and like all men he can be controlled. A few herbs, the proper words—I can show you the way. Why should you serve him, my lady, when it can be the other way?"

Grace could not look away from Kyrene's eyes. They filled her vision, as if she were falling into deep emerald seas. Then she felt it—a presence reached for her, groped, searched for secret places. A spark of rage flared in Grace's brain. No. She had vowed. No one would ever touch her like that again.

Leave me alone!

Grace did not speak the words, but Kyrene stumbled back as if struck a blow. A look of shock was written across her lovely face. Then something else crept into her expression. It might almost have been . . . admiration.

Aryn stepped forward, and her slight form trembled inside her blue gown. "King Boreas is not a warmonger! He's simply concerned about the Dominions. As everybody should be in these times!"

By the time Aryn finished, Kyrene had already regained her composure. Her nod was curt. "As you wish, Lady Aryn." She paused for a moment beside the chamber door. "Consider my words, Lady Grace.

Come to me if you wish to know more." Then with a flash of green the countess was gone.

Aryn let out a frustrated groan. "What on Eldh was that all about?"

Grace shook her head. "I'm not sure." Her mind was still vague and dizzy. It had felt as if Kyrene had come close—too close—and she had pushed the countess away. But how?

"She thinks she's so important." Aryn glared at the door. "I don't recall anyone crowning *her* queen."

Grace hardly heard the baroness. A terrible weariness seized her, and she sank into a chair. "I don't think I can do this, Aryn."

Aryn turned around at these quiet words.

"I don't think I can go to the feast." Grace hugged her knees to her chest. "Or be King Boreas's spy. It's too much."

"Of course you can do it."

"No, I can't. I'm not who you think I am."

The baroness sighed. "Is that what troubles you, Grace? But it doesn't matter what kingdom you hail from, or what your rank really is. King Boreas doesn't care, and neither do I. You're a noble lady, and you're here to help us, and that's all that matters."

"No, you don't understand, Aryn. I'm not royalty. And I'm not from any kingdom. I'm not even from this . . ."

It rushed out of her before she could stop it.

". . . I'm not even from this world."

Aryn gazed at her, confusion apparent on her face.

Now, Grace. You have to tell her. You have to end this game before it's too late, before it starts getting dangerous. If it hasn't already.

Still curled in the chair, Grace gazed at the coals on the hearth, and the words tumbled out of her. She spoke about the hospital, and the man with the iron heart, and the weird preacher who had shown her the door at the old orphanage. She spoke about everything—everything except her true connection with the Beckett-Strange Home for Children. Because if she talked about the orphanage, then she would have to talk about the hands that had reached out of the dark, and the fire that had consumed them, and she could never talk about them. Never.

"Grace . . . ?"

The word startled her, and only then did she realize she had fallen silent. She looked up and expected to see disbelief—or mocking, or even disgust—on the oval of Aryn's face. Instead she saw tears. They traced shining trails down the baroness's cheeks.

"You . . . you believe me?" Grace whispered.

Despite her tears, Aryn smiled. "How could I not believe you, Grace? You're my friend." She let out a deep breath. "No, I don't pretend to understand everything you've told me. Yet, from the moment I saw you, I knew there was something different about you, an other-worldly air—if not from the Twilight Realm of the Little People, then from this *Earth* of which you speak. While I find great wonder at your story, I confess I am not altogether surprised by it."

Grace opened her mouth to reply, but she could manage no words. She had never expected to find this kind of trust, this kind of acceptance. Certainly not here, a world away from the life she had always known.

"Now," Aryn said, her tone brisk, "we still have a feast to get ready for. No matter who you are or where you're from, tonight, here in Calavere, you're the Duchess of Beckett, and the king is expecting you." She opened the wardrobe and drew out a pair of gowns. "Tell me, does Her Radiance prefer green or violet?"

Grace laughed as sunlight poured through the window.

49.

That afternoon, Aryn was called away to help Lord Alerain with preparations for the feast, and Grace began to contemplate escape. She stared out the lone window of her chamber at the cobblestones two dozen feet below and finally decided facing a room of strange lords and ladies was in fact preferable to plummeting to her death, although only just barely. She donned the violet wool gown Aryn had chosen for her, fastened the leather pouch containing the silver half-coin and her necklace around her waist, and sat down by the fire with a book to study. At sundown a young page whose haircut spoke volumes about the bowl which had inspired it came to her door, and she nodded wordlessly when he asked her to follow him.

They paused before a set of double doors. Low sounds emanated from the other side. *Just don't faint, Grace. It would be very un-duchesslike.*

The doors swung open and created such a draft that Grace was whisked into the great hall of Calavere before she even thought to take a step. A trumpet to either side let out a piercing note, and she cringed as if a gun had gone off by her ear.

"Her Radiance, the Duchess of Beckett!" announced a booming voice.

The dull roar of conversation that had filled the hall dropped to a murmur. A hundred pairs of eyes turned in Grace's direction. She froze like a deer in the headlights of a car. What was she supposed to do? She searched the hall in panic for a face she recognized—someone, anyone she could pretend she was glad to see, move toward, and in the process extricate herself from the scrutiny of the crowd.

There was no one. Every face in the great hall—knight and noble, servant and attendant alike—was a stranger's. Grace could not remember the last time she had felt so utterly alone.

"Come with me," a deep voice growled in her ear.

Grace was too relieved to be startled. A strong hand gripped her elbow and steered her toward a nearby alcove. She blinked and found herself gazing at the handsome face of King Boreas.

"Your Majesty!" She began a flustered curtsy.

He scowled. "Didn't I order you not to do that?"

"I don't think so, Your Majesty."

"Well, I am now. I hate the way everyone is constantly bowing and curtsying around me. It makes me seasick."

Grace snapped up straight. She had forgotten just how imposing the king was. He was clad all in black and silver, and his black hair and beard shone in the torchlight.

"As you wish, Your Majesty."

This elicited a bullish snort. "If only people *would* do as I wished. Then I wouldn't have had to call this damnable council in the first place. So, have you found out where the nobles of the other Dominions stand?"

"I only just arrived at the feast."

The king grunted, as if he found this a poor excuse.

Grace hurriedly continued. "You asked if I had found out where the other nobles stand. Where they stand on what, may I ask?"

He clenched a big hand into a fist. "On war. What else? I need to know which of the Dominions are ready and willing for war, and which are not."

"War against who, Your Majesty?"

His steel-blue eyes narrowed. "Who do you think, my lady?" he asked in a perilous voice. "Against those who would threaten the Dominions, of course."

She took an instinctive step back. "Of course, Your Majesty." Even as she said this, she could not help thinking about Kyrene's words. Why was the king so interested in war? While Aryn had spoken of an early winter, and disease, and outlaws roaming the highway, Grace had heard nothing of an organized threat such as one might fight with an army.

"I'll leave you to your task," Boreas said. "I have guests I must attend to before Lord Alerain starts scolding me like a mother hen."

The king stalked away and left Grace to catch her breath. Aryn appeared a moment later. Clearly she had been watching from a short distance. The baroness was wearing the same gown she had the day Grace had first met her—a sapphire blue that matched her large eyes—and her dark hair was braided and coiled beneath a net of fine cloth studded with small gems.

"Isn't this exciting, Grace?"

Grace raised an eyebrow. "That's a word for it—though probably not the one I would have chosen."

The baroness sighed. "I wish I could be like you, Grace."

"Why would you wish for a thing like that?"

"You're so noble, so regal. Even that first day, in a servant's tunic, Alerain and Kyrene and King Boreas took you for royalty. And now . . ." She shook her head and halted Grace's protest. "Yes, I know what you told me earlier. I know on . . . on your world, on Earth you're a doctor, but that doesn't change what you look like, the way when you entered the hall just now you commanded everyone's attention."

The words left Grace dumbfounded.

Aryn whispered in amazement. "You really don't know, do you?"

She took Grace's hand and led her toward a corner. A mirror of polished silver had been hung upon the wall, so that courtiers might check and adjust their attire during the course of the feast. Grace did not recognize the woman in the mirror. She was tall, clad in a trailing gown the color of winter violets, with a slender neck and high cheekbones. Her hair was short but elegant, swept back to reveal small ears, and her eyes shone like sun on leaves. *She looks like a queen.* Only then, with a start, did Grace realize the image was herself.

Was that why everyone had stared at her? Not out of mockery, but out of . . . ? It was too absurd. She was an overworked resident from an underfunded city hospital. That was all. Grace turned away from the mirror. She opened her mouth to speak, but at that moment a voice rose over the noise of conversation.

"Aryn of Elsandry!"

The baroness winced.

Grace gave her a wry smile. "It sounds like the king wants you."

"However did you guess?" Aryn started to move away, then hesitated.

"Go," Grace said. "I'll be fine. Really." She tried to sound as if she meant it.

Aryn gave her a small wave. "I'll come find you again when I can."

For the first time since she had entered the hall, Grace was both alone and out of the glare of attention. She took the opportunity to look around and get her bearings.

The great hall of Calavere had been decorated to resemble a winter forest. Boughs of evergreen and holly hung from the soot-blackened beams high above, and more had been heaped along the base of the walls. Their icy scent mingled with the smoke of torches. Leafless saplings stood in the corners of the hall, to suggest the edges of a sylvan glade, and even the tapestries on the walls added to the illusion with their scenes of stag hunts and forest revels, woven in colors made dim and rich with time.

Only one object countered the forest illusion and seemed out of place. It stood against one wall, not far from the doors, a hulking thing of dark stone. Grace drew near. It was a massive ring as wide across as she was tall. It hung over a wooden base, parallel to the floor, balanced between two thick posts. Now that she studied it, Grace was not certain if the artifact was hewn of stone or metal. Unable to guess what purpose it could serve, she moved on.

The floor of the great hall was strewn with fresh rushes, and a dozen long trestle tables stood at right angles to the king's table, which rested on a dais at the far end of the hall. A score of servants still scurried about. The feast proper had not yet begun, and the gathered nobles wandered the hall, goblets of spiced wine in their hands, and paused here and there to make conversation. Grace was oddly reassured. Except for the archaic costumes and the stone walls, it didn't look much different from the annual Christmas party at Denver Memorial, and she had survived enough of those. Besides, medieval nobles couldn't possibly be more arrogant and scheming than hospital management.

She was right. The moment she started wandering the great hall she knew that, given a tunic and a feathered hat, Morty Underwood would have fit right in. What she had forgotten was, at Denver Memorial Hospital, she had been a lowly resident. Here she was Grace, the duchess of Beckett. In moments they had her cornered.

"Good eventide, Your Radiance." This was from a severe woman in a red gown. A thick coating of powder could not disguise the pockmarks that scarred her cheeks. A countess most likely. "I see you prefer to make your entrance last, so all others will witness your arrival. An interesting choice."

Grace shook her head. "It wasn't a choice, my lady. The page must have come for me late."

Her eyes glinted like hard stones. "Is that so?"

"Pardon me, Your Radiance," said a young lord.

An earl, Grace guessed by his fine but relatively uncomplicated clothes.

"Can I have one of the servants get you something to drink? I imagine your journey to Calavere was a long one." A sly light crept into his eyes. "Or was it not so very long at all? Let me see, the road you would have taken from Beckett is . . . ?"

"I'm afraid I didn't come by any road," she said.

The young lord acted as if she had slapped him, and he skulked away. Apparently he had forgotten about her drink. Grace was sorry. She could have used it.

Several other nobles pressed forward to take his place. Boreas had been right. Simply being here was enough to make the lords and ladies talk. Their questions all seemed polite and innocuous enough, but it was obvious all of them wanted to find out who she was, where she was from, and what her agenda was.

A short man in a gaudy tunic of crimson and gold approached, and by the way the other nobles parted he was of a higher rank. He sketched a half bow in Grace's direction. It was doubtful the significant girth of his waist would have allowed anything more.

"I am Lord Olstin."

He pronounced this as if Grace should know immediately who he was, and after some thought she found she did. Aryn had told her the names and ranks of the various representatives of the kings and queens who would be coming to the council. Olstin was seneschal to King Lysandir of Brelegond.

"My lord," Grace said.

Olstin fidgeted with the empty goblet in his hand. His plump hand was cluttered with rings. "King Boreas did not tell us he would be hosting other noble guests at Calavere during the council." His voice rose, so that all around might hear. "What else, I wonder, has he failed to tell us?"

The other nobles looked on with interest.

"I'm sure I wouldn't know," Grace said.

Olstin's beady eyes glinted. With his free hand he stroked the short beard that speckled his jowls. "Is that your stance on the matter, my lady?"

"It isn't a stance, my lord. It's simply the truth."

A murmur rose all around, as if she had just uttered some biting insult. Grace resisted the urge to groan aloud. Couldn't she say *anything*?

Olstin opened his mouth to make some reply, but Grace beat him to it. "My lord, I will take my leave now. I don't wish to keep you from your pressing appointment with another goblet of wine."

Olstin's jaw dropped, and the onlookers gawked. Grace did not wait for further reaction. She turned and moved away, feigning great purpose. Only when she stopped did she realize she was trembling.

"A drink, my lady?"

Grace looked up. The speaker was a tall, elegant man clad in a pearl-gray doublet. He looked to be forty, by the silver at his temples and the chiseled lines around his mouth. A thin scar ran along the length of his right cheekbone, but the effect was striking rather than detracting. He steadied her with a strong hand. She accepted the goblet of wine and drank. Her encounter with the nobles of Boreas's court and with Lord Olstin had been more of an ordeal than she had thought.

"Thank you," she said at last.

He smiled and took the empty goblet. "That was skillfully done, my lady. How did you know Olstin is a drunkard? There are some few of us who do, yet it is something he goes to great lengths to keep a secret, even from his liege."

"His eyes," Grace said. "The whites were yellow. That told me his liver isn't functioning well. The broken blood vessels on his nose are another sign. It was enough to tip me off, along with the bad teeth—wine is acidic, and that's how I guessed it was his preferred habit."

"You have great knowledge, my lady."

"Not really. I just see it all the time in the . . ." She caught herself. ". . . that is, I've seen it before."

The man gave a deep bow of appreciation. Warmth flushed Grace's cheeks—the wine must be stronger than she thought. The stranger offered her his arm, and they walked through the hall.

"Lord Olstin is an ostentatious fool," her companion said. "Of course, he's a Brelegonder, so that's very nearly a requirement on his part. Yet he does voice some concerns that others of us share."

"Concerns?" Grace tried to make the question sound natural.

"I would not wish to place you in an awkward position with your host, my lady."

"He's your host at the moment as well, my lord," Grace pointed out.

He laughed, a rich sound that thrummed in Grace's own chest.

"Truly spoken, my lady. Very well, then. It is simply that no one is certain of Boreas's motives in calling the Council of Kings. The missive he sent to the other Dominions was far from forthcoming. My queen was quite . . . *distressed* by this."

Grace suspected this was a milder word than he might have chosen. "Couldn't she—your queen, that is—couldn't she simply refuse to come?"

"No, my lady. There is much custom and history bound up in the calling of a council. Even Boreas, quick to anger and action as he is, would not call the council lightly. And for a Dominion to refuse to come would be an act of war."

Grace thought about his words. They seemed important somehow, but she wasn't certain exactly why.

With a deft motion he slipped her arm from his. "I must take my leave, my lady. There are others I must speak with this night. Though none, I fear, as charming as yourself. I trust we will meet again."

Grace opened her mouth to reply, but nothing came out, which was probably just as well. He gave an elegant bow, then started away.

Panic gripped her. "Wait! I forgot to ask you your name."

A flash of white teeth. "Logren of Eredane." Then he was lost in the throng.

Perhaps it was the wine, or perhaps it was her little victory over Lord Olstin, but after that Grace started to feel positively brave.

Once she had a moment to think, she knew who Logren was. Aryn had mentioned his name, along with those of the other representatives. Logren was high counselor to Eminda, Queen of Eredane. It was a fortunate encounter. Or had it been chance at all? Grace wandered on, and soon she had spoken with nearly all the representatives of the other six Dominions. There was no need to seek them out. They seemed to find her first. And each, to one degree or another, echoed Olstin of Brelegond's concerns: They all wondered at Boreas's true motive for calling the Council of Kings.

Still, despite all her encounters, there was one noble Grace did not see, though she looked for him more than once.

A trumpet fanfare sounded, signaling that the feast proper was to begin. At once people took their places at the trestle tables. Uncertain exactly what she was supposed to do, Grace sat on the nearest bench.

It was a strategy she might have thought through a little more thoroughly.

"You can butter my trencher anytime, my lady, if you know what I mean," said the lord seated to her left with a leering wink. He was a grizzled man with lank hair and fewer teeth than fingers, of which he had something less than ten. His tunic was stained with grease, and a fetid atmosphere hovered around him.

Earlier that day, in preparation for the feast, Aryn had given Grace a crash course in table manners. Two people customarily shared a single wine goblet. One did not use the tablecloth to blow one's nose. And it was expected of a lady to sprinkle salt from the bowl for the gentleman on her left. However, there had been nothing in the lesson about buttering trenchers, or putting up with lewd suggestions.

She reached for the wine goblet. "You know," she suggested a moment later, "we might find drinking more convenient if we tried it one at a time."

"Ah, but it wouldn't be nearly so fun." He tightened his three-fingered hand around hers, so that she could not let go of the goblet.

A note of alarm rose in her chest. For the first time that night she felt she was truly in danger. He started to lift the goblet.

"Come, my lady, let us drink together and—"

His eyes bulged in their sockets and went dull, then he slipped beneath the table.

"He must have dropped something down there," spoke a gloomy voice.

Grace looked up and felt a surge of relief. "Durge!"

The Embarran knight had traded his chain-mail shirt for a smoke-gray tunic, but she would have recognized his drooping black mustaches and melancholy brown eyes regardless of what he was wearing.

Durge made a solemn bow. "I believe you are wanted at the king's table, my lady."

He offered her a hand, and she gratefully accepted it. She wasn't certain just what the knight had done to her dinner companion, but she was happy to leave Lord Seven Fingers to sleep it off under the table.

"That's twice now you've rescued me," Grace said.

"I'm afraid I hadn't been counting."

They made their way to the long table that rested on the dais at the end of the great hall. Logren, Olstin, and the other visiting seneschals and counselors were all seated there, as were Aryn and Alerain. Grace might have liked to sit with the baroness, but the seats to both sides of her were occupied. Olstin leaned over to speak something in Aryn's ear, and she gazed forward with a pained expression. Grace felt a pang of sympathy, but there was nothing she could do.

Durge guided her to the two remaining chairs at the far end of the table. "I'm certain you would prefer better company than me at table, but I'm afraid these are the only seats left."

"On the contrary," she said, and took one of the chairs. "There's nowhere else I'd rather sit."

Durge raised an eyebrow in a bemused expression, but there was nothing for the knight to do save sit. Pages brought platters of meat to the table, and the scent elicited a growl from Grace's stomach. As Aryn had instructed her to do, she split the trencher of hard bread that rested between her and Durge, placed a few slices of meat on her half, and placed a good number more on the knight's.

Durge nodded to her in thanks. "I trust you have been enjoying your stay in Calavere, my lady?"

"Yes, very much," she said, and was startled to realize it was the truth. Despite the strangeness of it all, despite her fear at meeting so many new people and not knowing what she was supposed to do, she felt more alive than she could ever remember.

She took a sip of wine from a goblet, then used a napkin to wipe the rim so Durge might drink. He did.

"I never had the chance to thank you, Durge, for finding me in the forest and bringing me to Calavere. You never came to see me after that."

"I asked Alerain daily how you fared, my lady. There was no need to disturb you with my presence. I am certain the Lady Aryn was far brighter company."

So Durge *hadn't* forgotten her. This made Grace smile. "Your presence would never disturb me, Durge."

His look was skeptical, but he was plainly too polite to disagree.

Pages approached the table with more platters of food: whole swans cooked with their feathers still on, lampreys floating in thick sauces, steamed puddings of blood and raisins. And those were just the things Grace recognized.

Once the food was served, two men—one gray and stern, one broad-faced and smiling—moved down the length of the high table. They paused before each platter, raised their hands, and spoke a single, peculiar word: *Krith*.

"Who were those men?" Grace asked after the two had departed.

"They are the castle's Runespeakers," Durge said. "I had heard Boreas kept some men of the Gray Tower at Calavere. It's good to see he pays attention to the old ways."

"But what were they doing?"

"I believe they spoke a rune of wholesomeness over the food," Durge said. "It is a small magic, to be sure, but a useful one. One is more likely to die from a bit of rotten meat than a robber's sword."

Runes. Grace thought of Hadrian Farr's words back in the police station in Denver. Hadn't Farr said the ironhearts were interested in runes? Yes, but they were a world away . . . weren't they? She touched the pouch that contained her necklace and could not suppress a shiver.

As the feast progressed the entertainments began. Jugglers, fools, and minstrels all plied their trade before the king's table, then wandered around the hall. Desserts were served, including a kind of paste that had been sculpted into all sorts of fantastical forms. Durge called them subtleties. As far as Grace could tell, subtleties consisted mainly of sugar and lard, and were surprisingly reminiscent of the stuff in the middle of an Oreo cookie. She ate two unicorns and half of a castle.

After that, she let her gaze wander across the hall. She halted when she caught two glints of emerald. Kyrene. The countess sat at a nearby table. She raised her goblet, as if in toast, and treated Grace to a knowing look. Grace felt a prickling on her neck. She turned in time to see King Boreas scowl at Kyrene. The countess's smile merely deepened as she returned her attention to the handsome lord seated beside her. Grace could feel Boreas's scowl turn on her, but she did not meet his eyes. There was some contention between the king and Kyrene, and Grace had managed to land herself in the middle of it. She had grown bold during the course of the evening, but now she realized how dangerously little she understood about the politics of this place. She let out a troubled breath.

"Is something amiss, my lady?" Durge said.

Grace made a decision. "I'm supposed to find out where everyone stands on the Council of Kings, but I'm afraid I'm not very good at being a spy."

"I see."

She went on before she lost her nerve. "I've spoken with the counselors and seneschals and advisors here, and they've all told me what they think about the council, but it still doesn't seem like I've learned anything."

"Truly?"

"No. Yes. I mean, everyone seems to think King Boreas has some hidden reason for calling the council. I suppose that's something. But it doesn't really tell me where anyone stands. After all, they had no choice but to come to the council. Logren said that to refuse would be an act of—"

Then it hit her. She looked at Durge.

"—an act of war," he said.

She nodded. The thought was so disturbing she almost didn't want to think it. What if Boreas had hoped one of the other Dominions *wouldn't* come to the council?

Durge stroked his drooping mustaches. "I can't say I know much about being a spy. However, I suppose the first rule is to be suspicious of everyone. That includes me, of course." Now he frowned. "Which means, I suppose, that you really shouldn't listen to my advice."

Grace shook her head. "No, it's good. Your advice, I mean. You're right—if I've learned one thing tonight, it's that I can't trust anybody." *Even King Boreas*, she added to herself.

"You mean I was a help to you, my lady?"

She touched his hand. "Yes, you were."

After this the feast began to wind down, and Grace found herself yawning. The sounds of conversation turned to a low drone in her ears, and the smell of smoke made her mind dull and hazy. She sipped her wine and stared absently at a heap of evergreen boughs in a corner.

The heap of evergreen boughs stared back.

Grace sat up straight in her chair. There, among the tangled branches—a pair of nut-brown eyes gazed straight at her. Something moved and shook the branches. She caught a glimpse of a round, bearded face and small hands. However, that was not the strangest thing. For face, hands, and beard alike had all been as green as the boughs of fir themselves.

Grace turned and grabbed Durge's arm. "Look!" she whispered. "Over in the corner!"

But even as she turned back she knew it was gone. The heap of branches was still.

"I see nothing, my lady."

She shook her head. "I'm certain it was there. A small man, with brown eyes and green skin. . . ."

Even as she said it she realized how absurd it must sound.

"Perhaps it was simply the wine," Durge said.

Grace sighed and gripped her stomach. "Maybe it was the subtleties."

Either way she decided to call it a night. She bade Durge good-bye, gave her farewells to the king, and found a page who was willing to take her back to her chamber.

And all that night she dreamt of subtleties shaped like small green men.

50.

The day after the fire at the mad lord's house, Travis received his first lesson in runecraft.

They left the glow of the burning manor far behind and rode all the remainder of that night. Shortly after dawn, weary from the night's ordeal, Falken decided they should stop to rest, but then Beltan rode back from scouting ahead. The big knight had seen a robed procession of men and women approaching on the Queen's Way. The others exchanged frightened looks. Perhaps the Raven cultists were on the road by chance. But perhaps not—for Travis had told the others of the hot brand Sebaris had tried to use to mark his forehead. The four travelers hid in a tangled thicket beside the road and watched the cultists pass. Some carried staves decorated with black feathers, and all wore the sign of the Raven traced in ashes on their foreheads.

When the way was clear they emerged from cover, then rode south all the rest of that morning and well into the afternoon. At last they came upon a *talathrin* hidden in a hollow beside the road. The cool scent of *alasai* was a balm to their fire-scorched lungs.

"The Raven priests will not trouble us here," Melia said.

Travis was not sure if she meant this was because of the innate goodness of the Way Circle, or because of something the amber-eyed lady had arranged herself. Either way, when they dismounted and entered the tangled circle of trees, his fear receded.

They made camp and ate a small meal in silence. They had just finished stowing away the cooking gear when Falken spoke the words Travis had been dreading all day.

"I think it's time we had a talk, Travis."

Travis didn't need to look up to know Melia's gaze was turned in his direction. Beltan sat a short way off. The knight sharpened his sword with a stone, a task that appeared to absorb him, but from the way his head was cocked it was clear he was listening.

"You want to know how I did it, don't you?" Travis knew his tone was defensive, but he couldn't help it. "You want to know how I set him on . . . how I started that fire."

Falken nodded. "As a matter of fact, I do."

Travis shut his eyes and saw the mad lord again, his hands curling like the claws of a black bird as he writhed in the flames. He opened his eyes and shook his head. "I don't know, Falken. I don't know how I did it."

"I do."

They turned toward Melia. She had been plaiting the blue-black wave of her hair. Now she gave it a final twist to bind it neatly at the nape of her neck. When she spoke again it was to Falken, not Travis.

"Just as we opened the door to our chamber, at Sebaris's manor, I heard him speak it."

"Speak what?"

"The rune of fire."

Falken let out a low oath. "He *spoke* a rune? But how could that be? It takes apprentices in the Gray Tower a year before they can invoke the simplest of runes."

Melia's eyes glittered. "Unless one is a wild talent."

"A wild talent? They've never been anything more than a legend—stories to make apprentices feel inadequate and study harder."

"You saw the flames as well as I."

The bard only grunted.

"Then there was the incident in Kelcior with the bound rune," Melia said. "What else might explain both occurrences?"

Falken looked unhappy, but he did not disagree. "So what are we going to do with him?"

"I'm not entirely certain. But I think you had better teach him something about runes before he incinerates himself and the rest of us."

Travis winced. Once again the bard and the lady were speaking about him as if he wasn't even there. He let out an exasperated sound, and they turned their gazes toward him. He opened his mouth to protest, but one look at the set of their faces and he knew there was no use. He slumped his broad shoulders inside his baggy green tunic.

"So, when do I start my lessons?"

Falken's expression edged into a wolfish grin. "Now seems as good a time as any."

Despite the lateness of the year, the tall sunleaf trees that ringed the *talathrin* still bore the radial, yellow-green leaves for which they were named. Travis and Falken sat together beneath one of the ancient trees. The bard's faded blue eyes bore into Travis.

"Before we can begin, there is one thing I must know, Travis. How did you learn the name of the rune of fire?"

"I didn't learn it. At least, I didn't know I had." He took a deep breath, then in a rush explained how the voice had spoken the word in his mind when he touched the broken rune Falken had found in Shadowsdeep. What he didn't say was that it was the same voice that told him to speak the rune at the manor, and that both times the voice had sounded exactly like Jack Graystone's.

Falken rubbed his stubbled chin. "I am no expert on the craft of runes. My knowledge is not a tenth that of the master of the Gray Tower, and his not a tenth of what the Runelords mastered long ago. What the nature of the voice that spoke to you is, I don't know. But over the years I've learned some small amount concerning runes, and I think I know enough to teach you how not to harm yourself or others should the voice speak again."

The bard smoothed the dirt between them with his black-gloved hand. He drew a symbol with a finger:

"This is the rune of fire. Its name is *Krond*."

Travis bent closer to peer at the three lines in the dirt. The symbol was the same as the one on the broken rune disk he had touched.

"When the name of a rune is spoken, its power is invoked," Falken said. "By speaking *Krond* you called upon the power of fire. I believe you saw the result."

Travis shuddered, then looked up as a thought struck him. "Wait a minute. How can you speak it now, Falken? The rune of fire, I mean. Why didn't you invoke it when you said it just a second ago?"

"Good, Travis. You're paying attention. Now shut up and listen."

Travis did not interrupt the bard's lesson again.

"If all it took to invoke a rune's power was to mumble it," Falken said, "there would be little need for the Gray Tower, and every peasant in the Dominions would be a runespeaker. But that is not the case, and even were the Runespeakers not out of fashion these days, they still would be rare enough. To call upon a rune's power, one must will it to be invoked as it is spoken, and learning to focus one's will properly takes years of practice." He gave Travis an appraising look. "For most people, that is."

Travis squirmed under the bard's scrutiny but held his tongue.

"I have heard tales of apprentice runespeakers invoking runes beyond their reach under great duress," the bard went on. "My guess is your fear last night was enough to invoke the rune *Krond*. That means it's crucial you learn to control your will, Travis. The next time it might be yourself you set on fire, or Melia, or Beltan, or me."

Travis hung his head. He had not thought of that. A cold knot tied itself in his stomach. *I don't want this power. I don't want any power.* But what he wanted seemed to matter as little in this world as it had in the last.

"Then teach me, Falken," he said. "Teach me so I don't ever hurt anyone again."

Falken gave Travis a questioning look. Travis only stared forward. There was no point in explaining. Only one person would have understood. *Alice.* And she was much, much more than a world away.

The bard nodded. "Very well, Travis. I'll teach you."

The lesson continued for a time, until Melia called to them. Supper was ready.

"Where did they come from, Falken?" Travis said as they stood. "The runes, I mean."

The two approached the campfire and sat beside Melia and Beltan, and Falken answered Travis's question.

"Legend tells that the god Olrig One-Hand stole the secret of runes from the dragons long ago," the bard said, "and he gave them as a gift to mankind."

"Olrig? Is he a god of one of the mystery cults?"

"No," Falken said, "there were gods long before those of the mystery cults."

Melia dropped the spoon with which she had been stirring a pot. She shot Falken an annoyed look.

"Well, it's true," he said.

She sighed. "I know. It's just not one of my favorite topics."

After that Travis said nothing, except to tell Melia that the stew was delicious.

Over the next several days, as they journeyed south through Eredane, they came upon a dozen more towns and villages. All of them showed the same signs of decay and malaise as had Glennen's Stand. And all showed evidence of the Raven Cult as well. Here and there the symbol of the raven's wing was scratched on a stone wall, or carved into a wooden beam, or—once—painted in rust-red blood on the door of a darkened building.

It was a gray afternoon, two days after their flight from Sebaris's manor, when they came upon the pikes.

Tall wooden poles had been driven into the ground along either side of the road, stretching like bony fingers toward the sky. But it was not the poles themselves that had made the four riders stop—that made them choke and clasp their hands to their mouths. It was what had been lashed to each.

Falken broke the terrible silence. "There must . . . there must be a score of them."

"More," Beltan said.

"By all the Seven, who would do such a thing?"

Sorrow shone in Melia's eyes. "It is not by any of the seven mysteries that this act was done."

Against his will, Travis gazed up at the nearest pole. It was little more than a skeleton that dangled there, held together with dried sinew, bound to the wooden shaft by the hands and feet. Dark, familiar lines were etched above the skull's empty eye sockets: the sign of the Raven. They had marked this one so cruelly that the hot brand had burned through flesh to char the bone below. Travis hoped the victim had been dead by then, even though he knew this was not the case, that death had come only days after, here atop the pole, while carrion birds, impatient for the feast, swooped down to feed before their time.

Each of the poles bore a similar burden. They rose above the road like a grisly forest, with tatters of cloth and flesh to flutter on the air for leaves. *Look away, Travis. You've got to look away.* But he couldn't. A sight this horrible demanded a witness.

"There's a sign nailed to this pole," Beltan said.

They nudged their nervous horses closer. The words on the board were crudely drawn, as by one barely literate:

Here be a witch, and her eyes plucked out.

"Poor thing," Melia whispered. "She probably never even heard of Sia. Most likely she was just a village wisewoman."

Beltan pointed to another pole. "Or maybe a cripple, and different, like this one." Despite decay, the corpse's clubfoot was apparent.

They rode farther down the line of poles. Beneath one was a heap of half-burned books.

Falken sighed. "So reading books is a crime as well. What's going on here?"

They found something of an answer on the last of the poles. The corpse bound to the top was so mangled as to appear hardly human. Another crude placard had been nailed below.

This be what happens to heretics and runespeakers.

Travis gave Falken a fearful look. "I don't understand. Why did they do this?"

It was Melia who answered him. "I think we've just learned another tenet of the Raven Cult. It seems that, to followers of the Raven, magic is heresy. As is reading books. Or being different."

Beltan gripped the hilt of his sword. "Why hasn't Queen Eminda put a stop to this? A few dozen knights sticking their swords in the right hearts, and this new cult would be a dead one."

"Politics and religion aren't a good mix," Falken said. "Eminda may be keeping out of it for a reason. All fanatics need to become militant is a martyr. If Queen Eminda tried to put down the Raven Cult, she might end up with a dirty little rebellion on her hands."

Beltan grunted but did not argue the point.

"Regardless," Melia said, "from now on I think we had better avoid towns and villages altogether."

She did not look at Travis, but he knew what her words really meant. He rubbed his right hand. The rune that had once shimmered on his palm was invisible now, but he could still feel it there, like a prickling beneath his skin. What would happen if it ever shone again and the Raven cultists were there to see it? Would he still be alive when they lashed him to the pole?

Why, Jack? Why did you do this to me? Didn't you know what would happen?

"Let's get going," Falken said.

They nudged their mounts, and the horses started into a brisk trot, eager to escape. After a minute, Travis looked back over his shoulder. Now a dark shape perched atop the pole that bore the dead runespeaker. He turned his gaze forward again, and tried to believe the shadow was not watching him with small black eyes.

51.

Travis's lessons in runecraft continued as the four travelers made their way ever south, toward Calavere and the Council of Kings. Each night, in whatever hidden hollow or Way Circle in which they camped, after they had eaten dinner, Falken and Travis would sit together. Travis would watch as the bard drew runes in the dirt with a stick, and would speak the name of each in turn, being careful to control his will so as not to invoke the power of any.

Soon Travis had memorized the shapes and names of over a dozen runes. There was *Krond*, which was fire, and *Gelth*, which stood for ice. *Sharn* was water, *Tal* the sky, and *Lir*, light. The names felt strange yet somehow comfortable against his tongue. However, he never repeated them in more than a whisper, and he kept his thoughts neutral when he did. He did not want a repeat of events at the manor house.

Then one golden afternoon in a *talathrin* where they had stopped, Falken handed Travis the stick.

"Here, you try."

Travis hesitated. Was he ready for this? However, Falken did not withdraw the stick. Travis swallowed hard, then accepted the instrument. The bard smoothed the dirt between them.

"Show me the rune of fire, Travis."

He thought a moment, then before he lost his nerve drew three quick lines in the dirt.

"Very good."

Travis let out a sigh of relief.

"Although the angle on the second ascending is a bit shallow, and the prime descending should extend down a trifle farther."

Travis's sigh turned to one of dejection.

"Now, show me the rune of sky."

Tal. That one was easy enough. Travis drew a dot with a line above it. Falken studied it, then grunted. Travis took that as a good sign, and he found his mood brightening. Maybe he wasn't such a bad student after all.

"How about one more before Melia calls us to supper?" Falken said. "Show me the rune of light."

With a grin, Travis drew a line with an angled stroke coming off it like a branch and a dot below.

Gloom descended over the Way Circle. The air turned to ice, and

Travis could not breathe. A cry of pain came from the other side of the *talathrin*, followed by a single word shouted in fear.

"Melia!"

Travis clawed at his throat. His fingers were numb stumps. The gloom deepened, thickened, like a shroud of shadows. His mind grew as murky and muted as the gloom. A few more moments and he would be a shadow himself.

Something registered on his dimming senses: a grunt of effort, a struggling in front of him, then a scratching in the dirt. The gloom vanished, and coppery sunlight streamed into the Way Circle once more.

Travis drew in a ragged breath, filling his lungs with good air. The sparks before his eyes faded. Across the circle Beltan held Melia in his arms. The lady's face was pale, and shadows clung to the hollows of her cheeks. However, it seemed she was well enough, for she pushed the knight away with gentle but firm hands and stood on her own. Falken still leaned on the hand he had used to scratch out the rune Travis had drawn in the dirt. The bard lifted his head and looked at Travis.

"You're a mirror reader, aren't you?"

Travis didn't understand what had just happened—as usual—but this was not the time to hide things. "They call it dyslexia in my world."

Falken swore and struggled to gain his feet. "Why didn't you tell me before?"

Travis almost laughed. The bard couldn't know what he was asking. The laughter stopped short at the lump in his throat.

Melia approached. The lady seemed to have regained her strength, although Beltan hovered behind her. He cast a dark look at Travis.

Melia arched an eyebrow. "A mirror reader?"

"I should have seen it earlier," Falken said. "The signs were there, but I didn't realize it until now. I asked him to draw the rune of light. He did, only he put the ascending branch and the dot on the left side, not the right."

"He drew it backward, you mean?"

The bard nodded. "And the rune of light backward is *Sinfath*—the rune of twilight."

Melia sighed and lifted a hand to her temple. "Well, that explains my headache. *Sinfath* never has agreed with me."

"As they say, like repels like."

This comment won the bard a scathing look. "That isn't funny, Falken. You know perfectly well all runic magic affects me."

"It nearly affected all of us, although I'm not sure how. It's almost as if he started to bind the rune. Except that's impossible."

Beltan scratched his throat. "What would have happened if he *had* bound it?"

Falken looked at the knight. "This Way Circle would have been forever darkened, a place of mist and shadow. And there would have been no escaping it."

"I'm not sure I really wanted to know that."

"You asked." Falken shook his head. "But the art of runebinding has been dead and lost for centuries. It must have been something else that caused this."

Melia paced a slow circle around Travis. "Perhaps."

Travis held his chin up and stared forward, even though his instinct was to curl into a ball and try to disappear.

Melia spoke again, and although her voice was brisk, now there was a gentle light in her eyes. "Well, whatever happened, no harm was done, and that is something for which to be thankful. We can talk more about this later. Right now supper is nearly ready. I'll put a pot on the fire while we wait for the stew. I think we'll all feel better after a cup of *maddok*."

Travis gave Melia a grateful look. She nodded, then led the way back to the campfire. The *maddok* was hot and good, and Travis's spirits lifted. However, none of them could help shivering as the sun dipped below the horizon, and twilight—cool and purple—fell upon the Way Circle.

After that Travis's lessons in runecraft focused not so much on knowledge as on control. Yet while the lessons in runecraft occupied his evenings in camp, the long days atop the swaying back of his gelding were more tedious. The muscles of his legs were getting used to life in the saddle, but his back ached constantly, and the landscape did little to take his mind off the pain as the travelers progressed south. The plains stretched in dull brown waves to the west, and the tumbled slopes of the Fal Erenn rose to the east. Sometimes Travis wished they could ride into the mountains, or race across the wide plains, it didn't matter which, just so they could leave behind this in-between land, and the old Tarrasian road which led over hills and through shallow vales with unswerving and maddening predictability.

He spent most of his time in the saddle trying to stay warm. There was little need for him to hold the reins—the gelding was content to follow after its companions—so he kept his hands tucked beneath his mistcloak. It only took him three falls into the muck before he learned how to hold on with his knees. Usually he rode by himself. Beltan was always spurring ahead or dropping back to keep an eye out for danger, and Falken and Melia kept their horses together a dozen paces ahead.

Their reticence rankled. Why was it no one would ever tell him what was really going on? Jack hadn't explained anything that night at the Magician's Attic. And neither had Brother Cy at the weird revival tent. What did they think he'd do if he knew the truth?

Maybe they're afraid.

He wasn't sure where the thought came from. It wasn't the voice that had spoken to him, the voice that had sounded so much like Jack's. Maybe it was just instinct, but it seemed right. Melia and Falken were afraid of something. Jack had been, too. And the weird man in black? Travis had no idea what Brother Cy had thought. But even the preacher had been unwilling to touch the iron box Jack had given him.

For the first time in days, as they rode, Travis drew out the small box. He had forgotten how heavy it felt in the palm of his hand. With a finger he traced the intricate runes that covered the surface. He recognized a few of them now. The largest of them, in the center of the lid, was the rune *Sinfath*: twilight.

Travis chewed his lip. Somehow, everything revolved around this box and the stone inside. Jack, Cy, Falken, Melia—everyone who knew anything about what was going on had been interested in the box, yet had been reluctant to touch it.

He started to lift the lid, then hesitated. He glanced up. The bard and Melia had ridden some distance ahead. They wouldn't see, and he would only open it for a moment. He just wanted to see the stone again, maybe feel its smooth touch against his skin, just for a second or two.

Before he changed his mind he lifted the lid. A calm came over him. The mottled green stone glistened on its cushion of velvet. He closed his fingers over its surface. Guilt crept through his pleasure, and with great reluctance he placed the stone in the box and slipped it back inside his tunic.

However, several times over those next days, he took the stone out again. He did not mean to. He would just find himself letting his horse drop back, and before he knew it the stone was in his hand. It was easy to lose himself in its iridescent surface, and the leagues seemed to pass more quickly when he held it in his hand—although he always placed it back in its box and caught up to the others before they noticed he was lagging.

It was near evening on their eleventh day out of Kelcior—their fourth since the incident at the mad lord's house—when Falken raised his black-gloved hand and brought the group to a halt.

From the back of his jet horse the bard gazed at two large stones that stood in the bracken beside the road. The stones were thrice as tall as they were wide, and the patterns carved into their wind-pitted surfaces were only faintly visible. Beyond them Travis caught a glimpse of what looked like a path winding up into the foothills of the Dawning Fells.

Melia flicked her braided hair over her shoulder. "I thought we had agreed we didn't have time for this little detour of yours, Falken."

"And I thought we had agreed to discuss it when we got here."

"You're getting old, Falken. Your memory is starting to go."

The bard laughed. "Oh, you're a fine one to talk about age, Melia."

Her smooth visage darkened. "So how are we going to solve this?"

"I don't know. How are we?"

Beltan cleared his throat. "Excuse me. I know it's rather ironic, but . . . I actually have an idea."

Melia and Falken turned toward the big knight. Both wore curious expressions.

Now that Beltan had gained their attention, he looked uncomfortable. "Why doesn't Falken just go where he needs to go while the rest of us keep riding down the Queen's Way?"

Falken crossed his arms. "Ditching me is not really a viable option, Beltan."

"Oh, I don't know," Melia said. "I rather like the notion."

"You would."

"Wait a second," Beltan said. "That's not the whole plan. The rest of us will ride at half our usual pace, and when Falken is finished doing whatever it is he needs to do, he can ride hard to catch up with us. That way Falken gets to take his detour, and we make some progress toward Calavere at the same time."

Travis grinned at Beltan. For someone who claimed not to be much of a thinker, it was an awfully clever plan.

Falken and Melia studied each other, as if to predict what the other would say.

"The plan has its merits," Melia said.

The bard snorted. "It *might* be acceptable."

Beltan let out a breath of relief. "Why don't you both think about it? It's getting dark, and either way we won't be able to do anything until morning."

This the two were actually able to agree on, and they made camp beside the road.

That night it was Travis's turn to take the first watch. Normally he might have minded, exhausted from the day's long ride. However, for some reason he couldn't name, he was restless. He sat on a rock a short way from the dying campfire, gazed into the night, and listened to the steady breathing of the others.

Boredom stole over him. Before he even thought about taking it out of his pocket, he found the iron box in his hand. He looked up and for a moment watched the shadowy forms by the fire. Neither Falken nor Melia moved. He opened the box.

A sigh escaped his lips. The stone was even more beautiful in darkness. It caught the starlight and wove it into a gray-green aura that shimmered just above its surface. He bent over the box, enraptured.

A low thrumming brought him out of his trance.

Travis shook his head. Although it only seemed a minute or two since he had last looked up, the stars had shifted in the sky above. How long had he been gazing at the stone?

The thrumming sound grew, and a chill danced along his spine. He closed the stone in the iron box, shoved it back into his tunic, and stood to peer into the gloom. Then he saw it: A pale glow shone against the distant dark. Twice before had seen the same light: once at Jack's antique store, when the intruders had attacked, and once again on the highway north of Castle City, just before he stepped into the old billboard. Even as he watched, the light drew nearer.

Travis ran back to the campfire and shook Falken's shoulder.

The bard groaned in annoyance. "What is it, Travis?"

He whispered a single word. "Danger."

Falken sat up, at once alert. "Wake the others."

Moments later they gathered around the remains of the campfire, which Beltan had extinguished with a flask of water.

"It seems, Travis," Melia said, "the enemies of your wizard friend Jack have found you. I suppose it was only a matter of time. Though I wonder why now, and here, and not before."

Travis lifted a hand and touched the iron box through the coarse fabric of his tunic, but he said nothing.

Beltan's hand slid to his sword. "What do we do? Fight?"

"No," Falken said. "We ride."

Scant minutes later they nudged their mounts forward, onto the broad swath of the Queen's Way. The glow was closer now, a ghostly blue-white to the north. They turned away from the light, but before they could spur their mounts down the road, Falken swore an oath.

"What's wrong?" Melia said.

"Look."

Faint but clear, another patch of light glowed against the darkness to the south. Travis's hand crept inside his tunic, and his fingers brushed the iron box. A powerful compulsion to open the box filled him, and he started to draw it out.

Melia turned in her saddle, and her amber eyes bored into him. He clenched his jaw, resisted the strange urge, and withdrew his hand.

Falken moved his horse near Melia's. "What do you think they are?"

"I know of only one thing that comes in such light. But it can't be. It has been so long."

"Well, I'm not exactly eager to wait and see if you're right."

Beltan's charger pranced a nervous circle. "Now what do we do?"

"We can turn west and travel overland," Melia said.

The big knight shook his head. "There's nothing to the west but open plains. We would be completely exposed."

Melia made an exasperated sound. Evidently this wasn't the response she was looking for.

"There is another way."

It was Falken who spoke.

Melia gave him a withering look. "How did I know you were going to say that?"

Falken eyed the approaching patches of light. "This isn't the time to be stubborn, Melia. The mountains offer our best chance at finding cover."

"This isn't fair, you know."

"Fair has nothing to do with it."

Travis tried to swallow the panic that clawed its way up his throat. Was he imagining it? Or were those thin silhouettes he saw against the approaching light?

Melia crossed her arms and glared at the bard. "Very well, Falken. We'll take your detour. But if we're late to the council, it's on your head."

"As if it wouldn't be anyway."

They turned away from the road, guided their mounts between the two timeworn standing stones, and cantered up the winding path beyond.

52.

All through the night they picked their way up the treacherous trail, deeper into the shadowed mountains. Travis clung to his mount's back and dug his fingers into the gelding's mane each time the horse stumbled on an unseen stone. Neither moon nor stars shone in the cloud-cloaked sky, yet Melia led the way with confidence. Her mare drifted through the gloom like a ghost, and the other horses followed their companion by scent. From time to time Travis thought he glimpsed two sparks of amber light ahead, piercing the dark like the gleaming eyes of a cat, but he couldn't be certain his own eyes weren't playing tricks on him.

At first, as they rode along the narrow trail, Travis looked back over his shoulder every few minutes, and each time he expected to see blue-white light rending the night behind them. However, all he saw was unblemished blackness. There was no sign of his mysterious pursuers. Finally weariness stole over him and blunted the edges of his fear. In the end he slipped into a sort of waking dream: a dull trance filled only with darkness and the ceaseless *clop-clop* of the horses' hooves.

He woke with a start to the sound of murmured voices on the chill, moisture-laden air.

"Whatever you did to conceal our trail, it seems to have worked. I don't think they've followed us." That was Falken's low, musical voice.

"How much farther is it?" Water over copper. Melia.

"Actually, I believe we're nearly there. Though I grant you, it's been a long time since I last journeyed to this place. A long time indeed."

"Should we rest here a while?"

"No, let's press on. I think it might be safer to make camp once we're there."

Travis blinked, and only then did he realize he could see. A pearly luminescence had crept into the fog, and all around them he made out the muted outlines of rugged mountains: dimmer patches of gray against the glowing air. The trail passed between the outstretched arms of two horned peaks, and they entered a valley bounded on all sides by forested ridges. A crisp morning wind rushed into the vale and tore the mist to tatters. The white-gold light of the dawning sun broke through the shroud of fog.

That was when they saw it. It stood like a pale sentinel atop a mound in the center of the valley. They brought their horses to a halt.

Even in ruin the tower was glorious. Smooth walls of ivory soared skyward in a single, tapering spire. There were no windows in its surface, nor ledges, nor turrets—nothing that might mar the perfect symmetry of its form. Yet time had not been so mindful of the tower's airy perfection as had its creators. The summit of the spire, which should have risen to a slender point, ended abruptly in a jagged crown of broken stone. Heaps of dirty white rubble, overgrown with moss and weeds, surrounded the tower. Dead vines clung to the walls like veins.

Travis's breath conjured ghosts on the cool air. "Where are we, Falken?"

The wind tugged at the bard's black-silver hair. "This was the White

Tower, the tower of the Runebinders. It was one of three bastions of runic magic founded after the fall of Malachor, over seven hundred years ago, by the followers of the Runelords."

Travis nudged his horse forward. "The Runelords?"

Falken nodded. "The Runelords were the greatest wizards Falengarth has ever known. Much knowledge was lost in their passing, knowledge that will never be regained. But some of their students fled the destruction of Malachor. They raised three towers in exile, to preserve the arts of speaking, binding, and breaking runes."

"But what happened to them?"

"Both the White Tower and the Black Tower fell many centuries ago, and the arts of runebinding and runebreaking were lost from the world. Of the three, only the Gray Tower stands today, and even so the power of the Runespeakers is but a faint shadow of what it once was. No more than a fraction of what is carved upon the runestone in the Gray Tower is understood by the Runespeakers today—and it is but one of nine runestones that were created by the Runelords long ago." The bard's words drifted away on the wind.

Melia laid a gentle hand on his arm. "All things must rise and fall, Falken. It is simply the way of the world. Of all worlds."

A smile touched his lips. He shrugged, as if to say, *I know*. But the sadness in his blue eyes did not fade altogether.

"Come on," he said in a gruff voice. "Let's find a place to make camp. If I don't have a hot cup of *maddok*, and soon, I'm going to get very testy."

The four travelers rode into the valley, and the ancient spire loomed higher above them. They made camp in a grassy depression not far from the base of the tower. Soon they sat around a cheerful fire, bellies full from the breakfast Melia had prepared, and sipped hot *maddok* from clay cups.

"How nice that everybody is so comfortable they feel no pressing need to clean the dishes," Melia said in a voice that was dangerously pleasant.

The others leaped to their feet and set to the task.

Weary after the night's forced ride, they spent the remainder of the morning resting. Travis curled up in his mistcloak, and when he finally woke the sun was already near its zenith. He rubbed bleary eyes and sat up. Beltan sat nearby, clad in his green tunic, polishing his mail shirt with a cloth. Melia and Falken stood by the fire, speaking in low voices.

"You're certain you should go alone?" Melia said.

"I'm not expecting any trouble inside, but it's been centuries since anyone set foot in this place. There's no telling what's in there. I think it's better for one person to venture in and see rather than all of us. Besides, studying the stone is a one-person job."

Melia did not look pleased. "Be careful, Falken."

She and the bard locked gazes, and it seemed some unspoken message passed between them. Falken nodded. Without further words he left the hollow where they had made camp and walked toward the ancient tower. Travis watched until he stepped into the mouth of an arched doorway and disappeared into the ruin.

Melia turned around and regarded Travis and Beltan, her expression critical. "There's soap in one of the saddlebags, and I believe there's a stream over that hill." Her nose wrinkled. "You two may wish to take advantage of it."

Travis and Beltan exchanged looks.

"I'll get the soap," the knight said.

The day had turned warmer than usual, which was to say it was merely brisk rather than frigid. However, the sun was bright and the air still, and Travis could imagine worse bathing conditions—although these would likely involve chipping a hole in ice first. He and Beltan crested a rise and found the stream Melia had seen. It was little more than a brook that tumbled over polished stones, but in one place it formed a clear, sandy-bottomed pool, several feet deep in the center, and perfect for washing. They shucked off their clothes and, before they lost all their nerve and body heat, plunged in.

The water was bone-achingly cold, but after a minute or two numbness set in, and after that the pain was almost bearable. They scrubbed with the soft, brown soap, then dived under to let the current wash away the sweat and grime of travel. After several seconds of submersion, the cold threatened to crack Travis's skull, and he stood up and gasped for air. A moment later Beltan broke through the surface in a spray of crystalline droplets.

"By the balls of Vathris's Bull!" the knight roared.

Travis cringed. "You know, that's probably not the most appropriate oath for bathing in cold water."

The other man snorted in agreement. He slicked his long, thinning hair back from his brow. That was when Travis noticed the knight's scars.

In stark contrast to his bright demeanor, Beltan's body spoke of a life of hard and violent work. The Calavaner was muscular, but not at all like some gym-toned magazine model from Earth. More like a wild Serengeti lion, hungry and feral and ribs showing, a patch of tawny hair in the center of his chest. Countless fine white lines crisscrossed the knight's fair skin, along with a number of pink welts. Travis raised a hand to his own chest. True, he had sacrificed most of the old layer of fat to the rigors of this world, but beneath the sandy brown coils his skin was smooth and unmarked. How had he ever dared to think he had known hardship in his life?

"What is it, Travis?"

Beltan's high forehead was furrowed in a frown. Travis fumbled for words.

"I'm sorry. It's just . . . your scars . . . I didn't know."

The blond man shrugged. "I'm a knight. It goes with the territory."

"Doesn't it ever make you want to stop? Being a knight, I mean."

"Not really. You get used to bleeding."

"I don't think I ever would."

"You might be surprised. I think you'd make a fine knight, Travis."

Travis laughed and tried not to notice how hollow the sound was. "I don't think anyone on this world will ever mistake me for a knight, Beltan. The worst scar I have to show is from a paper cut."

It had been meant as a jest, but Beltan didn't laugh.

"Not all wounds leave scars that show, Travis."

Almost any other words he might have expected. Not those. Travis took a step backward in the pool and stared. Had the knight guessed something about him? But how could Beltan know? He had never told another.

I love you, Travis.

I love you, too, Alice. Now go to sleep. You have to sleep for the medicine to work.

Will you be here when I wake up?

I promise.

Cross your heart?

Cross my heart and hope to die.

Okay. Good night, Big Brother.

'Night, Bug.

Travis opened his mouth. The knight's blue eyes pierced him like a blade. In that moment he almost told Beltan—almost told him everything, how he had broken his promise, and how afterward the stifling silence had mantled the Illinois farmhouse.

A chill wind rushed down from the ridges above the valley, its touch icy against his wet skin. He shivered and swallowed the words he had been about to utter.

"We'd better get out of this water if we want to thaw before spring," he said instead.

Beltan only nodded.

After that they washed their tunics, breeches, and undergarments in the brook, draped them on bushes, then lay on flat rocks and sunned themselves while their clothes dried. It was late afternoon by the time they returned to camp, now clean and warm. Melia glanced up as they approached.

"Well," she said, "it's an improvement."

Beltan looked around. "Where's Falken?"

"He isn't back from the tower yet." The tightness around Melia's mouth belied her calm tone.

Beltan made a small gesture by his hip, where his sword was usually belted. "Perhaps I should . . ."

Melia gave her head an almost imperceptible shake. "Not yet, Beltan. Give him time." She stood and affected an air of briskness. "Now, I imagine Falken would appreciate dinner being ready when he returns, and the fire is running low."

"I'll go find some more wood," Travis said.

"Of course you will, dear."

By the time Travis returned to camp with an armful of sticks and branches, the sun had dipped behind the western rim of the valley, and Falken was still not back. Beltan stoked the fire, and Melia heated a pot of stew, but they picked at their bowls without eating. Twilight flowed down from the folds of the mountains.

Melia stood, her fine-boned features chiseled in resolution. "I'm going in there."

"Going in where?" asked a low voice.

The three spun around, and a figure stepped into the ring of firelight. Travis let out a relieved breath.

"Falken!"

Relief turned to concern. The bard's face was lined with weariness, and his eyes were haunted in the twilight.

"I was about to come look for you," Melia said.

"It is well you did not."

Falken staggered. Beltan gripped his arm and helped him sit on a log. Melia pushed a clay cup of *maddok* into his hands, and Falken gulped some of the liquid. He set down the cup and drew in a deep breath.

"It's worse than we thought," he said.

Melia smoothed the folds of her gown. "Did you find the runestone?"

"Yes."

"And could you read it?"

"Only after much work, and then only a few fragments. But they were enough."

"Enough for what?"

"Enough to tell me my darkest suspicions have come to pass." Falken flexed his gloved hand into a fist. "Blast it, but sometimes I hate being right."

Melia laid a small hand over his fist. "I must know, Falken. Tell me."

He nodded and opened his mouth to speak, but the words were never uttered.

Metallic white light split the gloaming.

Falken lurched to his feet, and the others followed suit. The brilliant light crested the rim above the valley like terrible dawnfire. Only it came, not just from the east, but from every direction. Even as they watched, the light sped down the slopes to the valley floor and approached the ruined tower with preternatural speed.

Beltan unsheathed his sword. "It looks as if Travis's friends have found us after all."

Travis took an involuntary step forward, drawn by that which he dreaded. He could not look away from the now too-familiar light. Who were these things that had pursued him across two worlds? And what would they do to him when they finally caught him?

The eerie illumination drew closer. It formed a ring around the tower, encircling it completely, while the rest of the world dimmed to shadow. There would be no escape this time. Travis could see them now, as he had twice in Castle City, impossibly tall and thin, moving with terrifying grace: silhouettes in the light.

"By all the Seven," Falken whispered. "Wraithlings."

Melia glanced at him, amber eyes wide. "But that's impossible. All of the Pale Ones were destroyed!"

Falken pointed toward the approaching light. "Then what do you call those?"

Melia opened her mouth, but she said nothing as the willowy beings closed in from all sides.

53.

Travis gazed into the light. *Wraithlings. So that's what they're called.* He wanted to look away but could not.

The four travelers drew closer together, and Beltan kicked out the campfire.

"How did they find us?" Falken said.

Melia eyed the approaching light. "A few moments more, and you'll be able to ask them yourself."

Travis lifted a hand to the pocket of his tunic. He had been unwilling to admit it to himself, yet he had an inkling of how his strange pursuers had followed him all this time. But it couldn't be. All that day he hadn't even opened the—

His hand slipped into his pocket, and his fingers brushed against slick stone.

How? Travis's mind raced. He had taken the iron box out of his pocket when he washed his tunic. The latch must have come undone when he put it back. Before he even thought of what he was doing, he drew out the stone. It glowed gray green in the dimness.

The shadows within the light reached out slender arms.

Falken grabbed his wrist with violent strength. "Put that away, you fool!"

Travis fumbled with the stone, shoved it back into the box, and shut the lid.

Melia glanced at Falken, her expression grim. "Perhaps we know after all how they followed us here. Wraithlings were created for but one purpose."

Falken grunted but did not reply.

"So, what now?" Melia said.

Beltan pointed his sword toward the light. "Whatever it is, you'd better decide soon. I always thought wraithlings were just stories, and I really don't want to find out I've been wrong all these years."

"The tower," Falken said. "It's our only chance."

There was no time to mount the horses. The beasts pranced and strained against their picket lines. Beltan slashed the ropes with his sword, and the horses thundered away into the gloom. On foot the four humans fled toward the base of the spire. Their own shadows splayed out before them, as spindly as the things in the light that followed. The archway in the stone wall yawned like a ravenous maw. Falken plunged into the opening, the others on his heels.

The darkness was a thick, suffocating blanket. Travis stumbled, his blind hands groped for anything to hold on to. There was a moment of sheer panic, then his fingers brushed cold links of metal over something broad and solid. Beltan. Big hands gripped Travis's shoulders, steadied him.

"I'm afraid, Beltan," he whispered.

"It's all right, Travis. I'm here."

"But you shouldn't be. Don't you see? It's me that they're after." It was true—the others were in danger because of him, and if they were harmed it would be no different than if he had done it himself. He couldn't allow that. "I have to go back out there, Beltan. Otherwise, they'll take you, too."

Travis started to pull away, but the knight encircled him with powerful arms.

"No, Travis. I will not let you go."

Travis struggled, but Beltan's arms might as well have been bands of steel.

Now Bcltan's voice was a low rumble in his chest. "Do not fear, Travis. I am Melia's Knight Protector, and she is your charge. That means I am your protector as well. No harm will come to you while I am alive. I swear it."

But what harm will come to you? Travis did not speak the words.

Blue light sprang into being and drove back the shadows inside the tower, if only for a few paces in any direction. Now a nimbus hovered across the archway, like a gauze woven of moonlight. Melia lowered her arms and glanced at Falken.

"It will not hold them for long."

"Then let's get moving."

The bard led the way deeper into the tower. After a few dozen paces Travis realized he could still see. The blue-silver radiance had followed them. No, that wasn't right. It hadn't followed them at all.

Melia was glowing.

The silvery light danced along the edges of her lithe form, like the corona Travis had once glimpsed shining around her in the ruins of Kelcior, only far brighter. What was Melia doing? And how had she managed that trick with the door? Was it the same thing she had done last night, along the narrow mountain path, to keep the beings in the light—the wraithlings—from pursuing them? She noticed his expression of awe and frowned at him.

"Don't even ask," she said.

Travis snapped his jaw shut. They moved down a dust-shrouded passageway. Melia drew alongside Falken.

"Where are we going?"

The bard did not slow his pace. "The White Tower was built nearly seven centuries ago, when things such as wraithlings were not yet forgotten. The Runebinders wove enchantments of warding into the very stones of this place. If we can find a way to awaken those defenses, we might have a chance."

Beltan gave the bard a sharp look. "If the tower had defenses of old, then why did it fall?"

Falken only pressed onward.

The interior of the tower was a twisting maze of stone, and the walls were peculiarly curved, so that looking at them made Travis dizzy. Melia still shone in the gloom, but the shadows parted only grudgingly for the blue radiance, and the air grew more oppressive as they went, as if all the bulk of the tower above weighed upon it.

Travis did not notice when they first began to spiral inward. For some time they had been bending steadily to the left. The corridor was descending as well, at a shallow but detectable angle. Falken did not slow his pace. They kept moving while the passage curved in on itself in ever-tightening arcs, down and in, deeper and deeper.

They nearly collided with the bard as he halted. Travis felt a stirring of air—dry as death—against his face. They stood on the edge of some great space. Perhaps it was their spiraling path, perhaps it was instinct. Either way Travis knew what this place was. The heart of the White Tower.

"Melia," Falken said quietly. "Light."

She shook her head. The azure nimbus that surrounded her flickered and deepened in hue, like a dying flame. Darkness closed in.

"No," she said, her voice strained. "My power is limited here. It is an older magic that holds sway in this place."

Falken swore. "Well, I can't very well read any runes if I can't see. Can't you manage something?"

"There may be no need. Will not this place know the presence of one of its own?"

"I hadn't thought of that."

"There's one way to find out."

Sweat trickled down Travis's sides. What were those two getting at?

Falken turned toward him, barely visible in the murk. "Take a step forward, Travis."

He wasn't certain what he had expected the bard to say, but that wasn't it. "Why?"

"If Melia's right, you'll see."

That sounded more than a little ominous, but as usual he seemed to have no choice in the matter. He braced his shoulders, held his breath for a moment, then stepped forward.

Lir.

It was as if someone spoke the word in his mind, but this time the voice was not Jack's. Instead the voice was larger, deeper, and far more vast. A heartbeat later it happened.

Without sound, a thousand sparks of light appeared against the blackness and filled the air with shimmering radiance. Travis took another step forward and craned his neck back. The others followed after him into the domed chamber. It was like standing inside a globe of stars. Only they weren't stars at all. Travis drew in a breath of wonder.

"They're runes," he murmured.

Countless runes had been carved into the stone of the walls and ceiling, and each of them shone with soft radiance. Even the floor was alive with blue firefly lights, except for a circle in the very center of the chamber, and this was as black as night, its edges so sharp they hurt to gaze upon. In all, the effect was like that of a brilliant night sky with runes for stars, reflected in a black lake below.

"It's beautiful," Beltan said.

Melia grimaced and lifted a hand to her temple. "Everyone's entitled to his own opinion."

Falken prowled deeper into the chamber. "Where is it? It's got to be here."

Travis tagged behind him. "What's got to be here, Falken? What are you looking for?"

"The Foundation Stone. It's the key to the tower. Or the heart, anyway. It should be here, at the very center, bound with *Orm*, the rune of founding. Two strokes crossing each other. We have to find it."

Travis joined in the search. He peered at floor, walls, and ceiling, examined numberless glowing runes, and recognized barely a handful of them. None was formed of two crossed strokes.

Melia called from across the chamber. "I think I've found something."

It was not the Foundation Stone but something else: a glowing panel in the wall covered with angular drawings. Travis cocked his head. When examined from left to right the pictographs seemed to tell some sort of story. Then it struck him.

"It's the history of the White Tower," he said.

"Yes," Falken said. "Here the Runebinders are coming to the valley. And here they are laying the first stones of the tower." He pointed to a group of stick figures gathered in a circle.

"But who is this person?" Melia said. "The one in the center of the circle, on his knees? I can't quite translate the runes written above him." She frowned in concentration. "*Dead One*. Is that what they read?"

Falken drew in a hissing breath. "No, not *Dead One*. Together those two runes mean *Lord of the Dead*."

Melia looked at Falken. "A Necromancer? But they were all destroyed in the war against the Pale King. How could one have been here, more than three centuries later? And better yet, why?"

Falken rubbed his jaw. "I don't know, but this gives me a bad feeling. I—"

"Falken, Melia, you'd better come over here." It was Beltan. The knight stood some distance away, near the center of the chamber. "I think I've found your Foundation Stone."

The three hurried toward the knight. He stood on the edge of the lightless circle in the center of the chamber. Travis gazed at the floor.

Of course. That's why we didn't find it, even though it's huge. It's so dark.

Falken swore an oath of dismay. The Foundation Stone was a great disk, as wide as the reach of Travis's outstretched arms, set into the floor. Two crossed lines were etched into its surface—the rune of founding:

Only, the lines did not glow like the other runes in the chamber. Instead they were dark as soot. The reason was obvious: A jagged crack ran right through the center of the disk. The Foundation Stone was broken.

Travis swallowed hard. "Falken, you said the Foundation Stone was the key to the tower's defenses."

The bard nodded.

"But the stone is broken."

"Yes."

"Then that means—"

"It means," Falken said, "there is no hope after all."

The four gazed at the darkened rune in silence.

"Your dagger, Travis," Beltan said. "It's glowing."

Travis glanced down at the stiletto tucked into his belt. The ruby in its hilt pulsed with a crimson light, faint but growing brighter each second. He had seen the dagger glow like this once before. In Castle City, at the Magician's Attic, when the intruders were near. Very near. He looked up at the others, licked his lips, and whispered the words.

"They're coming."

54.

A metallic hum resonated on the air. Light poured through the archway into the domed chamber. The runes above dimmed under the livid illumination.

The four travelers stood shoulder to shoulder. Beltan unsheathed his sword, and Travis drew the stiletto from his belt. The blade was laughably small in his grip. The ruby in the hilt blazed like fire.

The hum rose to a maddening whine. One by one they appeared against the white-hot glare that filled the archway, and slipped into the chamber with fell grace. Wraithlings. The light dimmed, and for the first time Travis saw the willowy beings as more than silhouettes.

He knew now why they were called the Pale Ones. Their skin was smooth and silvery-white, like the skin of a shark. They were tall and impossibly slender, with large heads, and necks that belonged on featherless swans. Huge eyes—black as obsidian—dominated their smooth faces. Their nostrils were no more than thin slits, and as far as Travis could see they had no mouths.

He choked on the words. "What do they want?"

"The Stone," Falken said without taking his eyes from the advancing creatures. "That is why the Pale Ones were created. To seek the Great Stones."

Even as Falken said this Travis realized his hand was in his pocket, that his fingers clutched the iron box. He pried them away, pulled his hand out, and forced it to join the other in gripping the stiletto. *The Great Stones!*

The wraithlings drifted closer, and glowing trails hovered on the air in their wake.

"Stop!" a clear voice commanded.

A slight figure stepped forward and raised a forbidding hand.

Beltan reached out. "Melia!"

Falken grabbed the knight's shoulder, held him back. "No, let her try."

The corona around Melia had brightened again, far beyond what it had been before. The blue-silver radiance drove the murk back to the edges of the chamber. The wraithlings hesitated and gazed at her with unblinking eyes. Whatever she was doing it was working, but her visage was lined with strain—the effort was costing her.

"They're staying back," Falken said.

Melia spoke through clenched teeth. "We must not let them get the Stone."

"Maybe if we can hold them at bay long enough, they'll leave."

Melia did not answer the bard. She pressed her eyes shut, and the corona brightened a fraction around her small form. The wraithlings milled together in a tangle of willowy limbs and lidless eyes. Beltan raised his sword and stood behind and to the right of Melia, while Falken drew the knife from his belt and stood to Melia's left. Travis started to follow after him.

"No, Travis. Keep behind us. You're the holder of the Stone. It's you they want."

He opened his mouth to protest, but a sharp look from Falken rooted him in place. Sweat trickled down Melia's brow, her hair clung to her cheeks. The wraithlings began to fan out to either side. Melia could not hold them from every direction. If the creatures circled around the chamber, all would be lost.

One of the beings moved within striking distance of Beltan. The knight lashed out with his sword, and metal clove flesh. A mouthless cry on the edge of hearing pierced the air, and the wraithling fell back. The creature clutched the wound on its arm, and white light welled through its thin fingers instead of blood. At the same moment Beltan cursed in pain, and his sword clattered to the floor. The blade was covered with frost. He grimaced and rubbed his hand, the flesh where he had gripped the sword blue as ice. The wraithlings stirred like lithe trees under a gale.

"I think you've made them mad," Falken said.

Beltan groaned. He picked up his sword in stiff fingers. Falken raised his dagger. The wraithlings kept clear of the blades, yet at the same time continued to circle around to either side. Melia was trembling, and the corona had darkened to a flickering violet. Now the wraithlings had circled around a third of the chamber, now half.

Travis clutched the stiletto in a sweating hand. He could not watch the wraithlings advance. The light that emanated from their bodies was too painful to gaze upon. He turned his eyes instead to the circle of darkness at his feet. The Foundation Stone. He stood on the edge of the broken rune. His terror was tempered with a kind of sadness. So this was where all his drifting had finally led him: to death at the hands of glowing creatures on an alien world. If only the rune of founding were not broken they might have had a chance against the wraithlings.

Then bind it.

Travis stiffened at the sound of the voice. He knew there was no use in looking around for the speaker. The voice had come from within.

Jack?

For a frantic moment his mind was filled only with silence. Then—

You must bind it. Quickly, while there is time.

He shook his head in confusion. *Bind what?*

By Olrig's hand, must you always be so dense, Travis? The broken rune, of course!

It *was* Jack. Only his old friend would swear an oath like that. But what did Jack mean? Travis sank to his knees and gazed at the sundered rune. How was he supposed to bind it?

You will know. But you must hurry!

And the voice was gone. Travis gazed at the black circle on the floor before him, then a terrible sound jerked him out of his trance.

"Melia—no!"

It was Beltan.

Out of the corner of his eye, Travis saw the corona that surrounded Melia flicker and wink out of existence. She slumped to the floor, and the wraithlings rushed in to caress her with pale hands. She shrieked, a sound of agony, and her back arched off the hard stone.

"Get away from her!" Beltan shouted.

He swung his sword in a whistling arc. The fey beings leaped back at the fury of the mortal man. Falken grabbed Melia and dragged her motionless form back toward Travis. Sword aloft, Beltan retreated after him. Tracing their shining paths on the air, the wraithlings followed.

Terrible as all this was, it seemed distant to Travis. He turned his gaze back to the broken rune. *Bind it.* He reached out a hand toward its surface. White light shone before him. The wraithlings had closed the circle. He looked up and found himself gazing into huge, lidless eyes.

For a moment the two gazed at each other, two worlds come face-to-face. Then a slender hand reached toward Travis. There was death in that touch. Fear propelled him to action. He slashed outward with the stiletto, the ruby flared crimson, and the tip sank easily into translucent flesh. Somehow Travis knew it was for just such a purpose that the knife had been forged long ago, in the smithies of ancient Malachor.

Again came the soundless wail. The wraithling fell back. Light streamed outward from the wound in its hand, only this time the light was tinged with crimson. Travis heard his companions scream behind him. The wraithlings were everywhere, there was no more time. He dropped the dagger, pressed his hand against the dark circle of stone, and shouted the word in his mind.

Orm!

In the space between two heartbeats everything went black. The glow of the wraithlings was extinguished, as was that of the runes that scattered the walls and ceiling of the chamber. Time and sound were suspended. Then two crossed lines appeared and shone in the dark like molten silver.

The blackness shattered.

Travis stared at the floor. The Foundation Stone was dark no longer. Instead it shone like the moon, its surface cool beneath the touch of his hand. All signs of the crack that had marred its surface were gone.

Each of the runes carved into the walls and ceiling of the chamber blazed with new blue-silver light. They began to spin like a sky of stars gone mad. The wraithlings flung their slender arms up and covered their huge eyes with willowy fingers.

The rune-stars spun faster yet, weaving a gauze of azure brilliance on the air. The wraithlings turned to flee but were caught in the gossamer net. Travis shut his eyes against the light and clutched at his companions, the only solid things in the room. There was a final cry: a chorus of mouthless voices merged into one chord of fear, agony, and— it almost seemed—release. Then, so sudden it was deafening, silence closed in.

Travis opened his eyes. The runes in the ceiling were motionless now and bathed the heart of the White Tower in a gentle radiance. The wraithlings were nowhere to be seen.

"They're gone," he murmured.

Falken struggled to his knees. "Yes," he said, "they are." The bard gazed at the Foundation Stone, now whole and smooth. Then he turned his faded eyes on Travis. "You did this, didn't you?"

Travis could give only a jerky nod.

Falken opened his mouth to speak, but he was interrupted by Beltan's anguished words.

"I can't wake her up, Falken! She's breathing, but only just barely." The knight had risen also and now shook Melia's shoulders, his grip gentle but fierce. "Wake up, Melia. Please!"

The bard moved toward them. "Let me see, Beltan. Maybe I can—"

A sound like thunder shook the air. Travis's eyes snapped back to the Foundation Stone. Even as he watched a black line snaked across the Stone's surface, cleaving it in two once more. The rune of founding dimmed. At the same moment a dark substance welled forth from the crack and spilled over the surface of the stone. Travis pulled his hand back. It came away stained with red.

"Blood," he whispered. "It's blood."

Falken stared. "By the Seven, the blood of a Necromancer. So that was what they did. Oh, the fools! The poor, cursed fools!"

The floor jerked beneath them as a tremor shook the tower. The runes above flickered.

Falken looked up. "I don't think the bones of this place can bear this a second time."

As if to punctuate his words, a chunk of stone dropped from the ceiling and crashed to the floor a dozen paces away.

Beltan lifted Melia in his arms. "We've got to get out of here!"

The others did not argue. Falken helped Travis to his feet. Together they ran from the chamber as the glowing runes crashed down behind them.

55.

The four travelers huddled around a fire as night cast its cloak over the valley. A frigid wind hissed through dry grass. The remains of the White Tower were no more than a ghostly heap of stones in the distant gloom.

When they fled through the archway, light had streamed from the tower, and had poured through cracks in the stones to slice like thin knives into the fabric of night. Then the light had ceased, and the tower had slumped in on itself. With a terrible din it had collapsed into a great cairn of rubble, forging its own burial mound even as it died. No one would ever set foot within the White Tower of the Runebinders again. They had stumbled back to their campsite, and there had found one bit of good fortune: Their horses stood in a knot next to their slashed pickets, whickering softly.

Travis clutched his mistcloak around himself and surveyed the fire-lit faces of the others. Neither Falken nor Beltan seemed the worse for their ordeal, though Beltan's sword hand was still cold and stiff. And although he felt drained and hollow, and his head buzzed, Travis noticed no other ill effects from his actions in the rune chamber. It was Melia who had been most devastatingly affected. They had wrapped her inside all the extra blankets and had placed her as close to the fire as they dared. She had awakened shortly after their return to camp, but shivers wracked her slight form, and her usually coppery skin was gray as ashes. She stared into the fire, a stricken expression upon her visage.

"It touched me," she said, her voice a whisper of remembered horror. "It was so cold. So horribly cold."

The others shot Falken looks of concern, but he did not see them. The bard's gaze was upon Melia, his weathered face lined with care. Then he turned his eyes toward Travis and spoke in a soft voice.

"Would you bring me my pack, Travis?"

Travis nodded and did so.

Falken rummaged inside his pack and pulled out a handful of dried *alasai* leaves, taken from one of the Way Circles in which they had stayed. He crushed the leaves into a cup, filled it with hot water from a kettle over the fire, and let the fragrant herbs steep. Then he moved to Melia.

"Drink this, dear one," he said and held the cup to her lips.

Melia took a hesitant sip from the cup, then drank the remainder. A hint of color touched her lips, and her shivering eased, though it did not end altogether. She blinked, and her amber eyes grew focused once more.

"Thank you, Falken. I'll be all right now—I just need to rest." Shadows still clung to her cheeks, and her voice remained quiet, but it was no longer full of the hopeless despair. She glanced at the tumbled remains of the tower, and shock registered in her expression. "What happened back there?"

"Travis bound the rune of founding," Falken said. "The wraithlings were driven back by the tower's magic."

"He bound the rune? Are you certain?"

Falken gave a solemn nod.

"So the art of runebinding is not lost from the world after all." Melia tightened her grip on the blankets they had wrapped her in. "That explains what happened in the *talathrin*, when Travis drew *Sinfath* backward."

"Yes, it seems our little complication is not quite out of surprises yet."

Travis flexed his right hand, and he could feel a slight tingle against his palm.

In quick sentences Falken explained to Melia the remainder of what had happened after the wraithlings had assailed her.

"It was blood, Melia," he finished. "When the rune of founding broke again, it was blood that welled forth from the crack."

She gazed at the distant heap of skeletal stones. "I think we know now why the White Tower fell long ago."

Falken sighed with the night wind. "I always believed all the Pale King's wizards were slain when their master was defeated. It seems that wasn't so. I don't suppose we'll ever know how the Runebinders came to capture a Necromancer. Certainly the Dark One's power would have been much weakened after the War of the Stones. Yet it seems the final victory was his."

Travis edged closer to the fire. "I don't understand, Falken. Why would they have killed a . . . a Necromancer at the founding of their tower?"

"Blood sorcery is a crude and primal magic," Falken said. "But it is powerful as well. Long ago, barbarian kings drank the blood of their vanquished enemies, and mixed more blood into the mortar of their keeps, in the belief that the power of the dead ones would be transferred to the stone walls, strengthening them. I suppose the Runebinders believed the same."

Though still weak, Melia's voice shook with anger. "They were wrong. The arrogant fools."

Falken gazed into the fire. "The evil of the Necromancer could not be bound by their magic, not truly. There was no way Travis's binding could have done the same."

Travis shivered. He could almost see the scene in his mind, the proud Runebinders in robes of ivory, gathered around the foundation of their new tower, a figure in black on his knees before them. Then the flash of a knife, and blood flowing crimson against the new white stones, not a blessing, but a curse.

"Who were the Necromancers, Falken?" Travis said.

"It was told they were once minor gods from the far south, that the Pale King gave them bodies of mortal flesh in exchange for serving him."

Melia cast a sharp look at the bard. "It was hardly so simple as that."

Falken shrugged. "What do I know of the affairs of gods?"

"Little enough, it seems."

The bard ignored her comment. "It was the Necromancers who created the *feydrim*, the slaves of the Pale King, of which the wraithlings were the most beautiful, and the most terrible. The Pale Ones, the wraithlings, were made for just one purpose: to seek out the Imsari, the three Great Stones." He looked at Travis. "It is said, to their eyes, the Stones leave trails of light that linger on the air, marking their passage. Only when a Stone is encased in iron does it leave no trace they can follow."

Travis drew out the iron box—the box the beings in the light, the wraithlings, had destroyed the Magician's Attic in an attempt to gain. Every time he had opened it he had left a trail for them to follow.

Melia extended still-trembling hands toward the fire. "It seems your guess about the nature of Travis's Stone was correct, Falken."

Beltan stared at the box in Travis's hand. "You mean it's really one of the Great Stones?"

"Yes," Falken said. "And given that the rune inscribed on the lid of the box is *Sinfath*, I would guess this to be Sinfathisar, the Stone of Twilight, most subtle of the Imsari, yet still a thing of terrible power to one who knew the secret of wielding it." His voice dropped to a grim whisper. "One, it seems, who searches for it even now."

Falken reached into his pack, drew out another object, and unwrapped the covering cloth. It was the broken rune, the one Travis had touched in the ruins of Kelcior to alarming effect. The two halves of the ivory disk glowed in the firelight, and the sundered rune embedded in its surface gleamed silver. *Krond*. Fire.

"Ever since finding this in Shadowsdeep," Falken said, "I have had my suspicions about it. However, I could not be certain those suspicions were founded, not until I studied the runestone in the tower. Now I have, and it has confirmed all my fears."

Beltan made a nervous rumble in his throat. "And those are?"

"After the Pale King was defeated a thousand years ago, a great gate forged of iron was raised above Shadowsdeep. The gate covered the Gap of the Teeth, the only pass through the Ironfang Mountains, and the only way into and out of Imbrifale. The first Runelords bound the gate with powerful runes, and thus assured that the Pale King could never ride forth from his dominion again. Or for so long we believed, those of us who still remembered. But we were wrong." Falken brushed the broken disk with a finger. "I know now that this is one of the three binding seals placed by the Runelords upon the door of Imbrifale. Now, somehow, it has been broken. The Rune Gate is weakening."

Melia and Beltan stared at the bard. Travis shook his head, filled with an unnamed dread.

"But what does it mean?" he whispered.

"A Stone has come to light, wraithlings stalk the land, the Rune Gate itself falters. It can mean but one thing." Shadows played across Falken's face. "After a thousand years of imprisonment, the Pale King stirs once more."

The night wind rose to a keening howl.

56.

By Grace's tenth day in Calavere, the novelty of living in a castle had begun to wear off.

It was a sure sign one was growing accustomed to a place when one started to notice every small annoyance. There was the cold, to begin with. Everyone in the castle spoke of how winter had come early that year, and the cold was a constant, gnawing presence. It radiated from every stone of the castle, sliced like a knife through thin cracks in the walls, seeped into joints and bones until Grace ached with it. Even the heavy wool gowns she wore were no proof against the chill, and her hands especially were always cold.

The frigid temperature was worsened by the dampness of the air. The Dimduorn, the River Darkwine, was no more than a league from Calavere—a league, she had gathered, was something on the order of three miles—and nothing in the castle ever seemed completely dry.

But both cold and damp she might have endured. It was the smells that got to her.

Everything in the castle smelled. *Everything.* The privies, the torches, the bedclothes, the food, the tapestries, the chamber pots, the candles, the corridors, and a vast majority of the people. All were foul, or pungent, or rancid, or some overpowering combination of the three. Two weeks ago she would never have believed it possible, but now she longed for the antiseptic odor of Denver Memorial Hospital. She had always hated that smell, but at least it had been the only one, designed by chemists to mask the scents of blood, vomit, and death. Here in Calavere there were times when she was tempted to take a hot poker from the fire and cauterize her nose just so she wouldn't have to *smell* anything anymore.

It didn't help that she and Aryn had been forced to curtail their time together. Aryn still came to Grace's chamber whenever she could, but much of the baroness's time was engaged in readying guest chambers, overseeing servants, and keeping an eye on the castle's kitchen, all in anticipation of the arrival of the kings and queens of the other Dominions.

"Is there anything I can do to lend a hand?" Grace had asked the baroness one day.

Aryn's expression had been scandalized. "Grace! You're a guest of the castle and a lady of noble birth. It wouldn't be proper!"

"Really?"

Aryn had given an emphatic nod. "Nobility," she had said, "does not *lend a hand.*"

Grace had sighed. "No, I don't suppose it does." *It wouldn't be boring enough.* But she hadn't said the words aloud, and had only smiled as Aryn squeezed her hand and hurried away to some other task.

Nor had King Boreas paid Grace much attention since the morning after the feast, three days ago. She had awakened to a summons from the king, brought to her door by Lord Alerain himself. She had thrown on the first dress she could find and had dashed through the castle corridors to the king's chamber. By the time she had stumbled through the doorway, her gown was askew, her hair clung to her damp cheeks, and she was gasping for breath.

King Boreas had taken in her appearance with his fierce gaze. "I see Lord Alerain came upon you in the midst of your morning constitutional." He had given an approving nod. "By Vathris, good for you, my lady! As the sages say, a weak body houses a weak mind."

Grace had simply nodded, and had declined to mention that her run through the castle was the most exercise she had gotten in months.

She had eyed the king's powerful chest and arms. What did he do for sport? Juggled lesser nobles, perhaps.

"Now, my lady," he had said, baring his big teeth in what wasn't quite a grin, "you are going to tell me all you learned at the feast last night."

For a quarter of an hour the king had paced back and forth in front of the black mound of mastiffs heaped beside the fire while Grace had stood in the center of the room—he had not asked her to sit—and had spoken of her conversations with the various seneschals and counselors in the great hall. When she had finished, Boreas had given a bullish grunt, and his blue eyes had sparked with interest, but he had made no comment regarding her report. Instead he had twirled a dagger in his hand, his expression thoughtful, as if trying to decide whose heart to stick it in first. It was the table that had gotten it instead. Grace had been unable to take her eyes off the quivering knife embedded in the wood. The motion had been so quick, so easy, she had hardly seen him do it.

"You may go now, my lady," Boreas had said.

Grace had retained enough of her wits to know this was not a request. She had started to curtsy, caught herself, and had nodded instead. "I'll keep observing as best I can, Your Majesty."

"Yes," he had said, "you will."

Afterward, she had replayed her audience with the king in her mind. Much as she disliked to admit it, Boreas's behavior had only served to fan the spark of her suspicion. Why was he so eager to muster the Dominions for war? The Lady Kyrene had said Boreas followed the Mysteries of Vathris. Grace didn't entirely understand what all a mystery cult entailed, but it was clear Vathris was some sort of war god. Perhaps Boreas was looking for an excuse to conquer one of the other Dominions, either for personal gain or for the satisfaction of his god.

Grace considered telling Aryn of her concerns, then remembered the baroness's loyalty and reconsidered. There was no point in getting Aryn upset. She could tell the baroness when—and if—she learned anything more concrete.

Not that this seemed likely. Over the last three days, she had found little opportunity to talk with the other nobles. All were too busy with preparations for the arrivals of their respective lieges to engage in gossip, which meant they were busy indeed. She did pass Lord Logren once in a corridor. He pressed a hand to his chest and made a fluid bow, but he did not stop to speak to her. Even the Countess Kyrene was curiously absent.

Left to her own devices, Grace had tried to content herself by exploring the castle. However, every passage seemed to lead, in the end, either to the privy or the kitchens, and she soon got the impression these were the two most important places in Calavere, with the great hall running a distant third.

By that tenth day in the castle, Grace found herself gazing out the small window of her chamber and feeling utterly trapped.

From this vantage she could just glimpse the tops of the two towers that stood to either side of the castle's main gate. She remembered the peasants she had seen trudging in and out of the archway, on that snowy day when Durge had first brought her to Calavere. It was ironic, but right then she envied the peasants. Yes, they were downtrodden serfs—overworked, uneducated, and malnourished chattels of a capricious feudal system. But at least they could leave the castle if they wanted.

Grace let out a resigned breath. There *was* that small side corridor she had noticed near the great hall the other day. Maybe there was a chance it led *somewhere* besides the privy or the kitchens. She was tired of studying the convoluted words in the books Aryn had brought. At least exploring would give her something else to do. Resolved, she started to turn away from the window.

A spark of emerald below caught her eye.

She moved closer and peered down through the flawed glass. There. She could not see the lady's face, but the burnished-gold hair and the green gown were unmistakable. Lady Kyrene. The countess walked across the upper bailey alongside another figure: taller, broader, clad in pearl-gray. Grace recognized the fine clothes, the sleek hair gone to steel at the temples. Logren, High Counselor to Queen Eminda of Eredane. The two bent their heads toward each other as if in conversation. Grace felt a tightness in her chest. Logren hardly seemed the type to let himself be tangled in Kyrene's web of intrigue and innuendo. What could the two possibly be talking about?

The odd pair approached the hedge maze in the center of the courtyard. They paused a moment—did Logren look from side to side?—then slipped through an arch woven of leafless wisteria and disappeared into the maze.

Grace bit her lip. She knew from Aryn that, in this world, a host's permission was required before a guest could leave his house. She should ask Boreas, or at least Alerain. But venturing into the courtyard wouldn't really be like leaving Calavere. Before she had time fully to consider what she was doing she dashed from her chamber.

It was colder outside than she had thought.

Grace had neither coat nor woolen cape, as she had seen Kyrene wearing, and the wind sliced right through the fabric of her gown. The side door shut behind her—it was a servant's entrance, little used, and out of view of the main keep, which was why she had chosen it. Her time spent exploring the castle had not been wasted after all. She clasped her arms over her chest and hurried across the cobblestones of the upper bailey, toward the tangled wall of the hedge maze.

She paused and looked over her shoulder when she reached the arch of withered vines that formed the entrance. There was no one else about the upper bailey, save a squire leading a horse toward the king's stable, and he did not so much as glance in her direction. She drew in a deep breath, braced her shoulders, and—before she could reconsider—plunged into the maze.

After a few dozen paces Grace began to think it might not be such a good thing after all that no one knew where she had gone. Already she had lost track of the number of turns she had made—four lefts and two rights, yes? Or was it the reverse?—and she had no idea in which direction the entrance lay. Nor was there any chance of cheating and cutting through the walls of the maze. The hedges were a dozen feet high and formed of dense, thorn-covered branches. If she tried to force her way through, she would be torn to shreds before she had gone a foot.

Come on, Grace, think. You're a doctor and a trained scientist. Surely a conundrum created by some medieval gardener is not beyond you.

She clenched her jaw and forged on, deeper into the maze.

Then she began to detect a pattern. Yes, that was it: two lefts, then a right. Each time she made the turns she found herself in a new passage that—she was almost certain of it—led toward the heart of the maze. She lifted the hem of her gown off the damp ground and quickened her pace, she had to be close to the center now. A left. Another left. Then a right. And—

—a dead end.

Grace stared at the wall of thorns. She hadn't expected *that*. She bent her head and retraced her steps in her mind. Had she made a misstep somewhere? No, she had followed her formula exactly. There was only one logical conclusion. The pattern she had thought she detected wasn't a pattern at all. Which meant . . .

". . . I'm lost," she whispered.

Her breath fogged on the air. In the exertion of running through the maze she had begun to sweat, but now she shivered inside her gown. She walked back down the dead end until she reached a crossing of paths. Now which way? At this point one direction was very like another, and neither was likely to get her back to the castle by suppertime. Would Aryn miss her? Or would the baroness be too busy with her tasks?

Left, she decided after a minute and started down that path. She rounded a corner, then suddenly clasped a hand to her mouth.

Turn around, Grace. Turn around now!

But fascination was stronger than fear. She peered around the corner of the hedge-wall and gazed into the small, circular grotto.

Despite the cold they were naked. He had spread his cloak on the ground, and they lay upon it, limbs tangled like the winter wisteria. Her arms were coiled around his neck, white as ivory against his olive skin. The lean muscles of his back and legs rippled as his hips moved with hers in slow, easy, familiar motions. His eyes were closed in ecstatic concentration, but not hers. They glittered like emeralds as she gazed past his shoulder. A satisfied smile coiled around the corners of her pink mouth.

Grace tried to back away, but her legs would not respond. Her mind felt dull and soft, the scent of apricots filled her lungs. Seemingly of its own will her hand moved away from her mouth, slid down her throat, down over her breasts and stomach. . . .

As if sensing the presence of another, the emerald eyes turned in Grace's direction. Grace froze. For a heartbeat surprise flickered in those eyes. But only for a heartbeat. Then a new light shone in them, a glow that was almost . . . *approving*. The white arms tightened around his back, and the smile about her pink lips deepened.

No!

Grace shook her head, as if waking from a spell. She snatched her hand up, gripped it with the other, and stumbled away. Without looking back she turned and ran headlong through the maze. The sound of rich laughter followed after her.

She shut the sound from her mind and ran on.

57.

The next morning Aryn threw open the door of Grace's chamber and rushed inside. Her large blue eyes shone with excitement.

"She's coming!" the baroness exclaimed.

Grace stood from her seat by the window, and her heart raced in her chest. For a panicked moment she thought Aryn meant the Lady Kyrene. Had the countess come to confront her about what she had witnessed?

Aryn seemed not to notice her startled look. "It's Queen Ivalaine of Toloria," the baroness said. "She's the first to arrive for the council."

"Ivalaine?"

Aryn gave a vigorous nod. "The guards in the tower spotted her entourage crossing the old Tarrasian bridge over the Dimduorn. They know it's her by the pennants."

She unfolded a bundle she had been carrying in the crook of her left arm and held it out. It was a cloak of fine wool.

"Well, don't just stand there, Grace. Put this on. You'll be cold if you don't."

Grace took the cloak in numb fingers and wrapped it around her shoulders. It was heavier than she would have guessed. "Where are we going?"

"To the battlements, of course. I want to see the queen the moment she arrives. People say there isn't another woman in the Dominions as beautiful as Ivalaine. Come *on*."

Grace opened her mouth to respond, but Aryn grabbed her hand and tugged her out the door. After that she was forced to forgo questions and concentrate instead on keeping up with the light-footed baroness. Breathing hard, they climbed the last steps of a spiral staircase, pushed through a door, and found themselves atop a high wall above the upper bailey.

Grace glanced down and saw the hedge maze below. From this vantage it was easy to trace the twists and turns that had confounded her yesterday. There—that was the grotto where she had spied Kyrene and Logren, and from which she had fled. She had thought it simply luck that after only a few dizzied minutes of running through the maze, she had stumbled upon the exit. Now she wasn't so certain. The place where she had run from had been deep in the heart of the maze, surrounded by a webwork of paths so convoluted she could hardly follow them even now with her eyes. Yet somehow she had managed to navigate them without once having to backtrack. How else to explain it except luck?

And if it was good luck that had helped her escape the maze, then it was cruel fortune that had caused her to stumble upon Kyrene and Logren. She would never have guessed a liaison between the two. At the feast Logren had seemed so intelligent, so sophisticated. It seemed impossible he would fall prey to Kyrene's wiles. Or was it? Grace thought back to that moment in her chamber when Kyrene had spoken about the king.

He is a man, and like all men he can be controlled.

Grace saw again the countess's white arms coiled around Logren's muscular back. Was that how Kyrene worked her magics? Or had there been something more to it? She recalled the odd torpor she had felt that day in her chamber, and the presence that had reached out to touch her. *A few herbs, the proper words . . .* Had Kyrene used something more than simple desire to bring Logren to her? Before she could think of an answer, Aryn tugged her hand.

"This way, Grace. We'll get a better view of the castle gate from the south battlements."

Hand in hand, the two women picked their way along the wall. When they reached the crenellated top of the south battlement, high above the lower bailey, they found they were not the only ones with this idea. A sizable crowd had gathered to watch the coming of the queen: petty nobles, squires, servants. However, the throng parted without a word for Grace and Aryn, and the two women moved to the front of the battlement. Grace took in the clear view of the castle gates below and smiled. At least being nobility was good for *something*.

At that moment the call of a horn rose on the icy air: high and distant. The sound of it thrummed in Grace's blood. She lifted a hand to her brow to shade her eyes from the bright midday sun. Then she saw the line of horses crest a distant rise between castle and river, and her breath caught in her chest.

Ever after Grace could recall little of what actually transpired that afternoon. Feelings, images—these were what stayed with her for the rest of her life. Banners, yellow on green, that snapped in the wind. Sunlight on burnished breastplates and steel helms. Horses prancing to the music of their silver barding. White hunting dogs with muddy paws. Nobles in black, and red, and purple. The sound of horns.

Most of all Grace remembered the queen.

Ivalaine rode, not in a litter, but upon a chestnut horse. Her gown trailed nearly to the ground, and was the color of ice, as were her eyes. She was tall, fair, and regal. Her only crown was her hair, fine as flax, woven with jewels, and coiled upon her head. Aryn had been right. Even from a distance Grace knew she had never seen a woman more beautiful than Ivalaine.

In all there were more than fifty riders in the queen's traveling party, and another hundred on foot, bearing bundles and pushing carts.

Grace whistled softly. "Queens don't travel lightly, do they?"

"No," Aryn said. "They don't."

Ivalaine's party halted before the castle gate, and a group of King Boreas's knights rode out to meet them. Words of greeting were exchanged, though Grace could not hear them. Then horns sounded, the castle gates opened, and the long line of horses and carts started through.

The throng on the walls began to disperse, and there was a tug at Grace's sleeve.

"Come, Grace. Let's be going."

Grace raised a hand to her temple. Her head still thrummed with the call of the horns. "What?"

"There's nothing more to see. And it's getting *cold*. I swear, I'd think this was Midwinter's Day if I didn't know by the calendar it was only the middle of Sindath."

Grace hardly heard the baroness's words. She could not take her eyes off the road below the castle, even though it was empty now. She wasn't sure what it was, but she felt *different* somehow. What had she been thinking just a moment ago? It had something to do with the royal entourage, and the way the queen had ridden so proudly at the fore.

"Grace?"

She tore her gaze away. "Yes, of course. I'm sorry, Aryn, let's go."

The baroness gave her a curious look, then shrugged and started back along the wall. Grace followed. They had just reached the door to her chamber when she remembered what it was she had been thinking as she watched the queen ride toward the castle.

That should be me.

No. That was impossible. She shivered, forced the thought from her mind, and shut the door.

58.

Those next days, Grace felt more trapped than ever by Calavere's stone walls. Ivalaine's arrival had sent the entire castle, already bustling, into a fevered pitch of activity. Not all of the queen's traveling party was staying in the castle proper, which was well, as with five more rulers to come Calavere would have burst at the seams trying to hold them and all their courtiers, attendants, and servants. The majority of the new arrivals were staying in the town below the castle. Still, it was work enough for Aryn, Lord Alerain, and the rest of the castle's people to situate just Ivalaine and her immediate court in their chambers.

It was odd, but the busier everyone in the castle became, the less Grace had to do. The second morning after Queen Ivalaine's arrival she found herself fingering the fine wool cape Aryn had given her. Before, the outdoors had been largely off-limits because of the freezing air and her desire not to perish from hypothermia. The cape, however, changed everything.

She picked up the garment. She should ask, she knew it. But Alerain would be too busy, and there was no chance of her seeing the king.

Besides, no one had told her that she couldn't and, after all, wasn't she a duchess?

You're rationalizing, Grace.

But she didn't care. She was bored, and boredom more than anything else made her feel dangerous. Before she could change her mind, she threw the heavy cape over her shoulders and slipped out her chamber door.

Ten minutes later, Grace stood at the gate that led to the castle's lower bailey. She pulled the cape around her shoulders and pressed herself against the inside of the stone arch. Maybe this wasn't such a good idea after all. It had been nearly two weeks since that day Durge had brought her to Calavere, two weeks since the first and last time she had been in the castle's main yard, and then she had been safely above it, on the back of the knight's horse. Now she was on foot, and she had forgotten just how busy the lower bailey was.

"You wanted to do this, Grace," she said through clenched teeth. She took a bold breath and stepped forward.

The mud was deeper than she expected. It squelched around her boots and nearly sucked them right off her feet with every step. People jostled past her: peasants bearing baskets of bread or apples, squires dashing on errands for their masters, merchants selling beer and candles and bolts of cloth. Once Grace found herself engulfed by a flock of bleating sheep, and it was all she could do to keep from getting trampled into the mud by four dozen cloven hooves.

No one in the bailey greeted her or paid her any attention. The cape covered her gown, and most likely nobody had mistaken her for a duchess. Besides, Grace doubted noblewomen ventured here without the company of attendants. Most of the people around her were the serfs and freemen who worked the land and did the lowly chores that made a feudal kingdom work.

She moved deeper into the bailey and wound her way through the confusion of stalls and carts and horses. Many things caught her eye: bowls of beaten copper, knives of bright steel, wooden boxes inlaid with ivory and lapis lazuli, beeswax candles, and spools of dyed thread. A man horribly scarred by disease displayed on twisted fingers the exquisite silver rings he was selling. Ragged children wound their way through the bailey, begging or selling crude wooden charms on strings, carved into various shapes: a woman holding a hunting horn, a man with the face of a horse, a black bull.

"Mysteries!" the children cried. "Mysteries for sale!"

Grace blinked in realization. Of course—the bull charm must represent the beast associated with Vathris, god of the warrior cult. Which meant the hunting woman and the horse-man represented other mystery cults. Apparently, in the Dominions, there was not just one religion.

She halted and gazed at something at her feet. It was one of the charms, trampled into the mud where someone had dropped it. She picked it up and brushed away the soil. One of the crude bulls. A needle-sword was stuck into its back, and red-painted blood flowed down its black wooden flanks. She brushed the needle-sword with a finger. So this world sacrificed its gods as well. She slipped the charm into her leather pouch and moved on.

A delicious scent filled her nose—warm and sweet and spicy—and all at once she was hungry. She followed the scent to one corner of the bailey. At the base of a tower, between two wooden buildings, a man stood beside a clay oven. His face was red, but whether from the heat of the oven or from shouting it was impossible to say.

"Spice cakes!" he cried above the roar of the throng. "Spice cakes, warm and toothsome, favored by the king himself!"

He turned and saw Grace before him, and a grin split his ruddy face. By the poor state of his teeth he had sampled his own wares more than a few times. He held a small brown cake toward her.

"Come, Your Highness," he said, "try one."

Your Highness? So much for her disguise. She clutched her cloak around her throat and shook her head.

His grin broadened. "Ah, but you will find it delicious. Made with rare spices of the mysterious south, from Al-Amún, far across the Summer Sea."

"I shouldn't," she said.

"And why not, Your Highness? Don't you deserve as much as anyone something sweet and good?"

Grace opened her mouth, but she found no words for a reply. How could King Boreas think she could pry secrets out of royalty? She could hardly speak to a commoner.

He held the cake out farther. "Here, Your Highness. You take it."

She hesitated. Was he giving her a gift? Or did merchants in the market often give nobles samples of their wares, in hopes of winning their patronage? More likely the latter. Either way, she decided, it would be an insult not to accept.

Grace reached out and took the cake. It was warm in her hand. A rich scent, like cinnamon and nutmeg yet not quite either, rose from it. She brought the cake to her mouth and took a tentative bite. Then she took another, and another, until the cake was gone.

The man beamed in satisfaction. "You liked it, Your Highness?"

Grace nodded. "Yes, very much. Thank you." With that she turned and started away.

A callused hand gripped her wrist and jerked her back around. She let out a gasp.

"Just a moment, little sister. The cakes are a silver penny apiece." The man's expression was no longer friendly. His small, black eyes burned into her like hot stones.

She shook her head. "A silver penny? But I thought . . . I thought you gave it to me."

He did not let go of her wrist. "Gave it to you? Now why should I give you a cake, little sister?"

She licked her lips. "Because . . ." Now that she voiced the words they sounded utterly absurd. ". . . because I'm a duchess."

He let out a harsh laugh. "Oh, of course you are, Your Highness. And I'm a duke, so we'll get along just fine. If you give me my money, that is."

She stared at him, then it struck her. *Your Highness. Little sister.* He did not think she was royalty—it had been a nickname, nothing more. He had not given her the cake, but expected her to pay for it.

"I'm so sorry," she said. "I didn't . . . I didn't realize. I don't have any money. But I'm sure I can get some, if you let me go to the keep."

"You're not going anywhere, little sister, not until I get my money." His breath was sweet and fetid, a mixture of spices and decay.

"But I told you, I don't have any—"

The swiftness of his action stunned her as much as the impact. He whirled her around and shoved her back against a stone wall. The air rushed out of her lungs in a sickening *whoosh*.

"So you're a thief then?" he said. "Do you know what we do to thieves here, Your Highness? We cut off their hands, so they can't steal again."

He tightened his grip around her wrist, and she could feel the bones inside grind together. People in the crowd passed by as if they did not see—or did not care—what was happening. Now he smiled again. The expression was more horrible than his anger.

"It's all right, little sister." His voice dropped to a croon. "I'm a fair fellow. If you've got no money, I can think of a way for you to pay."

He pressed her against the wall with his body. Rough stones dug into her back. Heat radiated in stifling waves from the oven a few feet away. He pawed at her cloak with one hand, while the other reached down to hike up the front of his soiled tunic.

Grace stiffened. Fear and pain gave way to rage. Her mind grew terribly clear.

No. I swore it. Never again.

She locked her green-gold eyes on his. He hesitated, and his leer gave way to puzzlement.

Never!

It happened too fast to see. One moment he held her against the wall. The next he was screaming. The merchant stumbled away from her and beat at the flames that licked up the back of his tunic.

Now people stopped and stared. The merchant fell into the mud and clawed at his blazing tunic with blistered hands. The crowd closed around him, though whether to help or to watch Grace could not tell. She slid sideways along the wall, turned, and fled across the bailey.

She was brought up short by a flash of emerald.

"Lady Grace, are you well?"

The world reeled. Only by force of will did she manage to keep from falling into the muck. She clenched her jaw and forced things back into focus.

"Yes, I'm fine. Thank you, Lady Kyrene."

"Her Majesty is looking for a bolt of cloth for a new gown," Kyrene said with a smug expression. "She asked me to help her. And why are you in the market today, Lady Grace?"

"I . . ." Grace glanced over her shoulder. The crowd had already dispersed, and there was no sign of the merchant. Perhaps he had stumbled away, or perhaps others had carried him off. "I just came out for a walk, that's all."

The countess of Selesia displayed her white kitten teeth in a smile. "Really? Like the other day? I never did have a chance to tell you how nice it was to see you, love."

Despite her rattled state, Grace was aware enough to wince at these words. She fumbled for a response but could do no more than stutter. Then another voice spoke.

"Do not make small conversation, Lady Kyrene. Can you not see our sister is distressed?"

Only at the sound of the clear voice did Grace realize Kyrene had a companion. She was tall, as tall as Grace, and clad in blue-gray. Gems sparkled in her hair. What had Kyrene said? *Her Majesty* . . .

"Queen Ivalaine!" Grace hurriedly attempted a curtsy.

"Please, sister. Rise."

Sister. The merchant who had tried to . . . the merchant had used the same word. But it sounded so different when it came from the queen's lips. Not mocking, but warm and secret and inviting. Grace looked into her ice-colored eyes. The woman's beauty stole away her fear.

"Thank you, Your Majesty," Grace said.

She now saw she had been right—noble ladies did not venture into the lower bailey unescorted. Behind the queen were several men-at-arms, as well as a red-haired woman. She was plump and pretty, and her face was touched by fine, wise lines. Grace recognized her from the queen's entourage. She was Tressa, Ivalaine's first lady-in-waiting and, Aryn had said, her closest advisor.

"Tell me, Lady Grace, has something ill befallen you?"

Grace froze. Like a wounded animal, her first instinct was to hide her hurt, to nurse it in a dark and private place. If you told another, how could you ever pretend it didn't happen? But something in the queen's voice calmed her.

"There was a merchant selling cakes . . . I ate one, but I didn't have any money . . . he was angry, and tried . . . he tried to stop me but . . . a spark from the oven must have landed on him . . . his tunic caught fire and . . ."

The queen's eyes grew hard, and she nodded, as if she understood far more than Grace's disjointed words alone had told.

"Do not worry, sister," Ivalaine said. "If the flames did not take him, then another end will be found for him. I will make certain of that."

The queen spoke the words in a cool tone—not angry, not vengeful, simply matter-of-fact. She made a slight nod toward one of the men-at-arms. He bowed, then moved purposefully through the crowd. Grace shivered. She did not doubt the queen's will would come to pass.

She licked her lips. "Shouldn't we tell King Boreas what happened? It is his castle, after all."

"But we are women, love," Kyrene said in a purr. "There is no need to concern Boreas with this affair. Men mete out their justice, and we our own. Is that not so, Your Majesty?"

Ivalaine did not acknowledge Kyrene's words. Instead she regarded Grace, her eyes intent, as if looking for something.

"Walk with us, sister," the queen of Toloria said.

Grace wanted nothing more than to go back to her chamber. But, little as she knew of politics and courtly manners, she guessed one did not decline a polite request from a queen. She bowed her head and walked beside Kyrene and Ivalaine. Tressa and the men-at-arms followed some paces behind.

"Your words skillfully avoided it, Lady Grace," Ivalaine said, "but I know what you did."

Grace glanced at the queen, startled. "I'm afraid I didn't even think, Your Majesty. I didn't know he expected me to pay for the cake. Otherwise, I wouldn't have even—"

"That is not what I meant, Lady Grace. You know it as well as I. A single spark could not have set a man's tunic to flame so quickly."

"But—"

Ivalaine halted and laid a hand on Grace's arm. "You know what truly happened, sister. You have only to allow yourself to believe it."

Grace remembered—the call of owls, the darkened corridors, her nightgown torn. Then the fire, the fire and the screams. Once before flames had taken hands that had touched her, once before fire had set her free. But it was chance, that was all. It had to be. Grace shook her head, forced the memories away.

Now Ivalaine clasped Grace's hands between her own.

"You are right, Lady Kyrene," the queen said. "She has the Touch."

Kyrene gave a triumphant smile.

"It is strong in her hands. Far stronger than in any I have seen in some time."

Kyrene's expression faltered. She cast a startled look at Grace, then her eyelids descended over her emerald eyes, turning them to slits.

Grace snatched her hands back. "The Touch? What do you mean?"

Ivalaine's visage was solemn. "The Touch of healing, Lady Grace— of control, of power."

Grace gazed down at her hands, long and slender, just like the queen's. *The Touch of healing.* How many people had these hands brought back from the brink of death in the Emergency Department? How many hearts had they coaxed into beating again, how many pains had they soothed? But there was nothing miraculous about any of that. It was emergency medicine, that was all. It was IV drips, and chest tubes, and crash carts, not something strange and special. Not . . . magic.

"Grace!"

She looked up at the sound of her name and caught a blur of sapphire-blue. Aryn pushed her way between two merchant stalls and rushed toward the three women, oblivious to the hem of her gown trailing in the mud.

"Grace, are you all right?" The baroness's blue eyes were wide with fear.

Grace lifted a hand to the bodice of her gown and stared at her friend. "Yes, Aryn, I'm fine. Why?"

"I just . . . I just had a feeling that something was wrong." Now she sighed. "It's silly, I know. I shouldn't have bothered you. But the feeling was just so strong for a moment."

Grace shook her head. If Aryn only knew the truth of it. . . . "It's not a bother," she said. "But how did you know to find me here?"

Aryn opened her mouth, then shut it and frowned, as if not entirely certain of the answer.

"You simply knew she was here, didn't you?"

It was Ivalaine who spoke the words. Aryn looked up in startlement, as if only just noticing the queen and the countess stood there. She bowed her head.

"Yes, Your Majesty. It almost does seem like that. But it was just a good guess, I suppose."

Ivalaine did not answer her. Instead she turned her ice-blue gaze on Kyrene. "Why did you not tell me about this one?"

Kyrene gave a languid shrug. "She is a child, sister."

Ivalaine rested a hand beneath her chin. "She is young, yes, but more than a child, I think." Her eyes flashed. "And here, in this place, you may yet call me Your Majesty. *Sister.*"

Kyrene's green eyes went wide. "Yes, Your Majesty!"

For a moment, next to the queen, she looked not like the lush countess Grace knew, but rather a spoiled, chubby child who only now realized she had overstepped her boundaries long ago. Grace understood little of what had just transpired, but this made her smile all the same.

"I think I'd like to return to my chamber now," she said. "If I may take my leave, Your Majesty."

Ivalaine gave a nod. Grace curtsied and with Aryn made her way through the crowd, back toward the sanctuary of the upper bailey. She did not need to look over her shoulder to know that two glints of emerald watched her as she went.

59.

Two kings arrived at Calavere the next day.

Sorrin, King of Embarr, rode to the castle gate just after dawn, accompanied by an austere entourage of no more than five wagons, ten courtiers, and a dozen knights, each one as dark of hair and grim of face as Grace's rescuer, the knight Durge. King Sorrin himself was a tall man, but hunched over, thin almost to the point of emaciation, and unexpectedly disheveled for royalty. His hair was lank and tangled, his black garb threadbare and unkempt. Yet he was a king all the same, and even gaunt and sharp-boned there was a stony handsomeness to his face, and his brown eyes were keen and intelligent—although, it seemed to Grace from her position on the battlements, there was something haunted about them as well.

The horns blew again near midday to announce the arrival of King Lysandir of Brelegond.

Lysandir's company stood in vivid contrast to Sorrin's and was even larger and brighter—if not necessarily grander—than Queen Ivalaine's entourage. Lysandir himself was a plain, balding, soft-looking man of middle years who was all but invisible within the vast tonnage of scarlet, blue, and gold he wore. Most of the members of his extensive traveling court were clad in only slightly less ostentatious fashion, and even the horses wore peacock feathers in their bridles. Although painted in bright colors, the king's wagons seemed to be in poor repair, and one lost its wheels as it rattled through Calavere's open gates. Grace laughed aloud at the sight of three gaudy courtiers spilled into the mud by the wagon's fall, their mouths open in circles of dismay.

After the brief and pleasant respite with Aryn on the battlements watching the kings arrive, Grace was left to her own devices once more as the baroness hurried off to see to her duties.

Grace lingered along the route to her chamber. She did not feel like going back to her room and studying the books there, but the day outside had darkened, and although it was not quite cold enough to snow, it would most likely sleet. Besides, her two recent forays outside the castle's main keep had both ended in unqualified disasters. It was safer to stay indoors. So, with no particular destination in mind, she wandered.

Usually when she walked, Grace fidgeted with her necklace, the one that had been found with her as a child. Since she had come to Eldh, she had kept it safe in the leather pouch she wore at her waist. Now she drew it out and slipped it around her neck. The trapezoidal piece of metal was cool against her throat. She lifted a hand and brushed the angular symbols etched into its smooth surface. *Runes.* That was what Hadrian Farr had called them. Farr had said the ironhearts were interested in runes like the ones on her necklace. But why?

"I wish you were here now, Farr," she said. "Something tells me you would understand everything that's been happening better than me."

But Farr was a world away. It was doubtful she would ever see him again, or Denver for that matter. The thought should have made her shudder, but somehow it didn't. She felt no more remorse at leaving Earth than she had at leaving North Carolina after medical school.

What's wrong with you, Grace? Can't you feel anything a normal person should?

She tucked the metal pendant beneath the bodice of her gown and walked on.

Grace was just thinking of returning to her chamber when, from around a corner, came a crash followed by a scream. A second crash jerked her out of paralysis. She dashed around the corner and took in the scene before her.

A serving maid in a brown dress knelt on the stone floor surrounded by broken crockery. Tears streamed down her face, and the red outline of a hand showed clearly against her cheek. Above her stood a rotund man in gaudy crimson, his face twisted in rage. He raised a ring-encrusted hand, and the serving maid cringed.

People terrified Grace. Violence, however, she had dealt with daily in the ED.

"Stop, Lord Olstin."

She did not raise her voice—shouting was not effective and, she had discovered, could actually spur people to do the opposite of what one wished. Instead she spoke the words in a low-pitched, precisely enunciated voice. The man snatched his jewel-covered hand back and spun around. For a moment his beady eyes darted about, then they locked on Grace. He unclenched his fingers, smoothed his rumpled garb, and inclined his head.

"Your Radiance."

The curl of his upper lip belied his polite tone. She ignored him, moved to the serving maid, and knelt beside her. With precise movements she examined the young woman's face, searching for other signs of injury.

"Does it hurt anywhere when I touch you?"

"No—no, my lady," the serving maid said. "Only my cheek." She was no longer crying, and her brown eyes were wide.

Grace nodded. The blow to the young woman's cheek did not appear serious—there was no damage to her facial bones—but it was going to bruise, and badly. She helped the serving maid to her feet. The young woman adjusted the gray cap on her head and straightened her dress. Grace turned on Olstin.

"Why did you do this?"

The seneschal of Brelegond jumped backward. "I commanded this . . . this insolent wretch to bring a pitcher of goat's milk to King Lysandir's chamber. My liege is feeling indisposed, and it soothes his stomach. But the milk she dared to bring was curdled—an insult to my king."

The serving maid shook her head. "I told you, my lord. The milk was sweet when I poured it. The Little People must have gotten to it when I turned my back for a moment. They're the cause of such mischief."

"You dolt!" A spray of spittle accompanied Olstin's shrill words. "There are no such things as Little People, only stupid serving wenches. I'll have you flogged for what you've done!"

Olstin lunged toward the maid. Grace stepped into his path.

"Go, Lord Olstin."

He glared at her. She did not move.

"Now!"

Olstin hesitated, licked his lips. Uncertainty crept into his beady eyes, and he backed away.

"King Boreas will hear of this, my lady."

"I'll tell him myself," Grace said.

He shot her one last poisonous look, then turned on a heel and was gone. Grace slumped against a wall. Something told her she had just made an enemy.

A soft touch on her hand. She looked up, and the serving maid gave a shy smile.

"Thank . . . thank you, my lady."

Grace drew in a breath, and managed a faint smile in reply. "What's your name?"

"Adira, my lady."

"I'm sorry I didn't come around the corner sooner, Adira. My name is—"

"Why, the Lady Grace, of course!" The young woman's face brightened. "I've seen you many times, my lady. Indeed, I saw you only just yesterday in the bailey, talking to Queen Ivalaine." Her eyes shone. "She's a witch, you know, like the Lady Kyrene, only far more powerful they say. Are you going to be a witch, too?"

Now Grace felt like she was the one who had been slapped. She could only stare.

"I want to be a witch," Adira said. "I'm going to ask the queen." Now her eyes narrowed, and a sly smile touched the corners of her mouth. "Then Lord Olstin will be sorry for what he did to me."

Adira picked up the pieces of broken crockery, thanked Grace again, then sauntered down the corridor, hips swaying. Grace hardly noticed her leave. She clutched the cold wall and gazed into the dim castle air.

A witch! Was that what Ivalaine intended for her?

60.

It was a drizzly afternoon four days later when Grace and Aryn stood on the battlements and watched the last of the kings arrive at Calavere. They clutched their cloaks around their shoulders against the sleet and late-Sindath wind, which was as chill as anything a Denver November could muster, and far more cutting.

King Persard of Perridon had come with sunset the day before, and Queen Eminda of Eredane had arrived at Calavere only that morning. Now Kylar, King of the Dominion of Galt, approached the castle gate. Kylar's entourage was by far the smallest of all the kings and queens—

even smaller than King Sorrin's austere traveling court—and the party appeared more roadworn and ragged than any of the others that had come before. A number of the horses were lame, and many of the courtiers limped along on foot, clad in mud-flecked browns and grays rather than rich golds and purples.

Grace gave Aryn a puzzled look. "I thought you said Galt was the nearest Dominion to Calavan."

"It is."

"Then why is Kylar the last to arrive? And why does his company look so . . . bedraggled?"

Aryn sighed. "I'm afraid it's to be expected. It's well known that King Kylar is the unluckiest man in Galt, and without doubt Galt is the unluckiest of all the seven Dominions. Which I suppose would make Kylar the most unfortunate man in all of Falengarth."

Grace watched the last of Kylar's company hobble through the archway below. At that moment the rain ceased, and a flood of golden sunshine spilled through a break in the clouds to gild Calavere's nine towers.

Grace glanced at Aryn. "You weren't kidding, were you?"

The baroness shook her head.

They headed back inside and strolled together toward Grace's chamber. On the way, as she had for the last three days, Grace searched for the courage to tell Aryn of her encounter with the serving maid Adira. But it was all so ridiculous. Queen Ivalaine couldn't really be a witch. Could she? True, Kyrene seemed to think she had some sort of power over others, and it was clear she looked to the queen as a model. And there were many things about this world Grace didn't understand. She opened her mouth to speak the words aloud.

"Lady Aryn, may I have a moment with you?" a man's voice said.

Grace snapped her jaw shut. The two women turned to see Lord Alerain walking toward them. As always the king's seneschal was trim and neat in his black-and-maroon attire.

Aryn touched Grace's hand. "I'm sorry, Grace. Alerain no doubt needs my help. There's to be a revel tonight."

"A revel?" Grace said. "What's that?"

"Oh, didn't I mention it?" The baroness's expression was a shade too innocent.

Grace narrowed her eyes. "No, you didn't."

"It's rather like a feast," Aryn said.

"So all I have to do is eat a lot?"

"Oh, no! Don't do that, Grace. Then you wouldn't be able to dance."

"*Dance?*"

Grace started to say more, but by then Alerain had reached them, and the baroness only smiled as she took the seneschal's arm. Alerain made a stiff bow toward Grace, then baroness and seneschal departed down the corridor.

Grace grumbled under her breath. "Would Her Radiance prefer to dance tonight, or to hurl her body off the castle wall? Oh, I believe we'll go with the castle wall this evening, thank you. Yes, Your Radiance, whatever you wish, Your Radiance."

But there was no one to hear her little performance, and she trudged back to her chamber to start getting ready.

That night, as the revel commenced, Grace paused in a corner of Calavere's great hall and made certain her newest possession—a slim dagger, given to her by Aryn earlier that day—was still secure in its sheath inside her doeskin boot.

"No proper lady should be without one," Aryn had said when she stopped by Grace's chamber to give her the weapon. However, Grace suspected her encounter with the merchant in the bailey, rather than fashion, was the true reason for the gift. She was beginning to think there was steel beneath the young baroness's gentle demeanor.

Grace drew out the knife. The dagger's jeweled hilt was ornate yet fit smoothly into her grip. Without doubt this knife had been made to suit a woman's hand, and although the blade was slender, it was sharp and deadly. She slipped it back into its sheath. She doubted she would have need of it, yet all the same the dagger felt reassuring against her skin.

She straightened and noticed again the dark stone—or was it metal?—artifact that hulked nearby. She had asked Aryn about it the other day, but the baroness had known little, other than that it had been in the castle for centuries, and that some believed it was a relic of ancient Malachor. Grace started to reach out, curious to touch its smooth surface, when a voice called out behind her.

"Grace, there you are! I've been looking all over for you."

Grace turned and smiled at seeing Aryn. "And now that you've found me, you have to keep me company."

Aryn did not argue the point, and the two walked together through the crowded hall. Grace saw King Boreas near the cavernous fireplace, in conversation with Queen Ivalaine of Toloria. Kyrene hovered just behind the queen, a haughty cast to her lips. Ivalaine's visage was as beautiful as before, while the king could not seem to stop frowning.

"Why does King Boreas seem so unhappy to see her?" Grace said. She thought back to her lessons in history and politics. "Aren't Calavan and Toloria allies?"

"Historically, yes." Aryn took a goblet of wine from a servant, handed it to Grace, then took one for herself. "But King Boreas subscribes to the Mysteries of Vathris, and there has long been a rivalry between the Cult of the Bullslayer and those with whom Ivalaine consorts."

Grace frowned. "And who are they?"

Aryn licked her lips before she whispered the words. "The Witches."

An electric jolt surged through Grace. *The Witches!* So Adira had been right. Ivalaine *was* a witch—whatever it was that truly entailed. And no doubt Kyrene considered herself one as well. Grace gripped her goblet and downed the wine in one long swallow. Then, before she lost her nerve, she told Aryn everything: the strange things Ivalaine had said about the Touch, and Adira's hope to become a witch by talking to the queen.

Aryn's eyes grew rounder as Grace spoke, then she took a step backward. "Grace, is it true? Do you . . . do you have it, then? The Touch?"

Grace groaned. "How would I know? I don't even know what it is."

Aryn took another step in retreat. Grace shook her head. No, Aryn couldn't pull away from her. Not now, not after everything that had happened.

"Don't you dare be afraid of me, Aryn," she said. "Ivalaine was interested in you, too. Remember that."

The baroness blinked, then her look of alarm was replaced by one of regret. She reached out and took Grace's hand. "I'm not afraid of you, Grace. Just *for* you, for both of us."

Grace managed a weak smile.

"But we must not let King Boreas learn any of this," Aryn said.

Grace squeezed the baroness's hand in firm agreement. As long as she had Aryn beside her, things didn't seem quite so terrifying.

As they continued through the hall, music floated down from a wooden gallery where a troupe of minstrels worked their craft: Flutes trilled over a buzzing drone accompanied by a gentle drumbeat. Many of the nobles took partners and danced to the music in stiff, intricate patterns. Grace saw Logren among them. He was clad again in pearl-gray, his dark hair swept back from his forehead. In contrast to his height and elegance, his dancing partner was a diminutive yet sturdy young woman, with a plain face and kind brown eyes. Grace recognized her—she was Kalyn, advisor to King Kylar of Galt, and Kylar's twin sister. The two whirled in Grace and Aryn's direction, and Grace turned her head.

Aryn raised an eyebrow. "What's wrong? I thought you said before you liked Logren of Eredane."

"He's busy at the moment, that's all."

Before Aryn could question her further, Grace pressed on. Then Aryn clutched Grace's arm, and they halted.

"There, do you see him?" the baroness whispered.

She nodded obliquely toward a young man with broad shoulders and a short blond beard. He stood nearby, talking to several older men. They laughed at something he said, and he gave a dashing smile.

"Who is he?" Grace said.

"His name is Leothan. He's a noble in southern Toloria, only an earl, but he has high standing in Ivalaine's court and is no doubt destined for more. I was hoping he might ride here with his queen."

"Why?"

"In two years, when I am twenty-one, King Boreas will release Elsandry into my care, and I will need to marry, so there will be a baron to help me in caring for the king's fief." Aryn's blue eyes shone. "Leothan is most handsome, don't you think?"

Grace mentally kicked herself. "Yes," she said, "he is."

The group of noblemen broke up, and Leothan turned and walked in their direction. Aryn hesitated, then squared her shoulders and stepped directly into the young earl's path. He came to a halt before the two of them, smiled his brilliant smile, and bowed.

"Good eventide, Your Highness, Your Radiance."

Grace nodded, and Aryn made an elegant curtsy.

"Good eventide, my lord," the baroness said.

He made a broad gesture toward the dancers. "A fine revel, wouldn't you say, my ladies?"

"Indeed it is." Aryn took a deep breath. "Would you care to dance, my lord?"

Leothan's smile never faltered, but a queer light crept into his eyes, making them hard and flat. "I'm afraid this dance requires two hands, my lady."

Aryn stared, uncomprehending, then she glanced down, and her face went white. The elegant fold of cloth that draped her right shoulder had fallen aside, and her withered right arm had slipped free, twisted and delicate as the broken wing of a dove. She looked up with an expression of horror.

Leothan bowed again. Somehow it was a mocking gesture now. "If you'll excuse me, my ladies?"

Aryn managed some reply, and the young earl moved away through the dancers.

Grace stared after the earl in a fury. He was so beautiful outside, but she could almost see it—the ugly blot that was his heart, as cold and hard as the lump of iron she had found in the dead man's chest at

Denver Memorial Hospital. Beauty made a perfect mask for evil. That was why it was allowed to walk the world, why people sought it out, invited it in, and embraced it.

Grace heard a sigh, and her anger drained away. She moved to Aryn and redraped the fold of cloth over the baroness's right shoulder.

"Aryn, he's not even worth—"

"No, Grace, I'm all right." She pulled away. "Really. Look, isn't that your friend, Durge?"

Grace glanced across the hall. Sure enough the Embarran stood against a wall, arms crossed over his deep chest, black mustaches drooping, brown eyes somber.

Grace brightened at the sight of the dark-haired knight. She had not seen Durge since the last feast, and she had missed him. If only she could convince the knight that a visit from him would be anything but a bother. Durge didn't make her feel like other people did, like there was something broken inside of her, something of her own to hide, if not with a fold of her gown, then with silence.

She waved at Durge and steered Aryn toward him, and although the knight did not smile, it did seem the gloomy air around him lessened a bit.

"Durge, it's so good to see you," Grace said.

"My ladies."

The knight started a stiff bow, but Grace reached out and took his hand instead. He fumbled a moment, recovered, then kissed her hand—a bit clumsily, but the gesture was a thousand times more charming than all Leothan's elegant poses put together. Grace supposed Durge might be considered homely. His face was angular, his nose craggy, his forehead furrowed by years of sober expression. But to her he was far better-looking than any Leothan.

An idea struck her. She looked at Aryn. "Perhaps Durge would dance with you."

The knight cast a startled glance at Aryn. "I'm certain the baroness would much prefer to rest than dance with me."

Aryn gave a hasty nod. "Yes, I would. Thank you for understanding, my lord."

Grace frowned. She opened her mouth, but just then horns heralded the start of supper. Durge bowed and begged his leave.

"But aren't you eating at the high table?" Grace said.

"Now that the kings and queens have arrived, Boreas does not need the likes of me to fill his board." The knight did not seem disturbed by this, merely matter-of-fact.

This news disappointed Grace. She almost told Durge she would sit wherever he did, but Aryn tugged her hand, and she was forced to make a hasty farewell instead.

"I don't see why you like Durge so much," Aryn said as they walked toward the high table. "He's old. And so gloomy. And not handsome at all."

"Really?" Grace said. "And here I was thinking he's the kindest man I've ever met."

Aryn opened her mouth, but by then they had reached the table, and the baroness was forced to take her seat to Boreas's left, while Grace moved to an empty spot at the table's end. Once seated she found herself next to King Kylar of Galt. Now that she saw him at close quarters he was even younger than she had thought, no more than twenty-five, with an open face and hazel eyes that seemed too gentle to belong to a monarch. She took a sip from the wine goblet that rested between them, wiped the rim with a napkin, then—feeling bolder— introduced herself to the young king. His smile was shy but genuine, and he took the goblet when she handed it to him.

"It is g-g-good to meet you, m-m-my lady."

He fought the words valiantly to get them out, then looked away, his cheeks red beneath the soft down of his brown beard.

Yes, of course. He had raised the goblet in his left hand. He fit all the typical categories then: male, left-handed, a twin. On Earth he would have undergone speech therapy, as well as counseling to help him overcome his anxiety at speaking. Most likely he would have spoken normally by age ten or twelve. But here . . . here he would probably stutter his whole life. Grace sighed. She was starting to think, just maybe, she hated this world.

Her hand crept across the table and touched his: cool, reassuring, a doctor's hand. "May I pour you some more wine, Your Majesty?"

He gazed at her, then his smile returned, crooked and grateful. "Yes, th-th-thank you, Your R-r-radiance."

Grace almost winced at his gratitude. What would Kylar think if he knew she was this kind, this assured only because he was damaged? She pushed the thought aside and poured.

As Kylar drank, Grace surveyed the high table. The kings and queens of the Dominions all sat in sharp contrast to one another. There was King Sorrin of Embarr, Durge's liege, at the far end of the table, gaunt and sallow, hunched over his plate, not touching his food. Queen Eminda of Eredane sat next to him, a thick-waisted woman of middle years who might have been comely in a matronly way were it not for the perpetual frown into which her mouth was cast. Beside Eminda was King Persard of Perridon. He was by far the eldest of the royals—thin and frail, with only scant wisps of hair left to float above his skull—but his eyes were bright and mischievous. When he saw Grace gazing at him, he winked, grinned, and made a gesture with his hands that could have only one, lewd, meaning. She moved her gaze quickly down the line.

Aryn and Alerain flanked King Boreas, who looked bored and restless, and drank entire cups of wine where others had sips. Near the dark and bullish king of Calavan was Ivalaine. The Tolorian queen gazed in regal silence over the hall, her eyes glittering like mysterious gems. Last of all, between Ivalaine and King Kylar, sat King Lysandir of Brelegond. Or at least Grace assumed it was he amid the masses of crimson and gold. She could hardly see the balding king of Brelegond for all his finery, though she could certainly hear his constant demands upon the servants, shouted in an impatient, nasal tone. Grace moved Lysandir to the bottom of her list of the kings and queens. Those who acted the most important seldom truly were.

Servants came to the table, bearing steaming platters of food, and—as they had at the last feast—the castle's two runespeakers approached the table. Starting one at each end they moved down the length of the table and spoke a rune of wholesomeness over each plate. They were halfway down the table when a shriek rose above the din of conversation.

"Keep your filthy magic away from me!"

As one, those at the high table turned and stared as Eminda of Eredane leaped to her feet. The young runespeaker before her gave Boreas a look of confusion. The king of Calavan scowled, then gave a flick of a finger, indicating for him to move on, which he quickly did. Eminda seemed embarrassed now, and her cheeks glowed red as she sat once more. Logren moved from his place at a lower table to his queen's side. He spoke with her for a moment, then turned to address King Boreas.

"My queen asks that you forgive her, Your Majesty. She is weary from her journey and is not used to all the customs of your castle. Runespeakers are not . . . common in Eredane these days."

Boreas grunted. "Of course. Her Majesty should not be concerned. And she has my word my runespeakers will not trouble her again."

Logren bowed and returned to his seat, and the course of the supper resumed. Grace and Kylar spoke little as they ate, but they smiled much, and it was not at all unpleasant—except when Kylar spooned up an insect from the bottom of his steamed pudding.

"Please d-d-don't worry, my lady. I'm quite ac-c-c—I'm quite used to it."

He smiled, as if just because one was used to hardship it made it all right somehow. Grace smiled in return, although she did not feel like doing so, and stirred her own pudding. She almost hoped she would find a beetle as well, but she did not.

Once dinner was over the music and dancing resumed, although Lord Logren led Queen Eminda from the great hall, and King Sorrin had disappeared at some point during the meal. King Persard left as well, a plump serving maid on each of his scrawny arms and a grin on his wrinkled face.

Boreas approached the corner where Grace and Aryn stood. "Would you care to dance with your king?" he asked the baroness.

"Your Majesty, I'd rather have my feet trod upon by a herd of wild horses."

Boreas clapped his hands together. "Lady Aryn, I'm proud of you! That lie almost sounded convincing." The king glanced at Grace. "Perhaps there's hope for my ward yet." He gripped Aryn's hand. "Now let's dance."

The baroness shot Grace a pleading look, but Grace knew her friend was lost beyond hope. Boreas dragged Aryn into the throng and began tossing her around in a series of dizzying circles.

Grace watched all the nobles in the great hall dancing—moving in complicated patterns she couldn't hope to understand. She sighed. "I'm never going to figure out how to do this."

"The dance is not so difficult as you think, my lady."

She lifted a hand to her chest and turned around. Durge stood in the dimness beside a stone column.

"I wasn't talking about the dance, Durge."

The Embarran knight stepped forward. "I know."

Grace shook her head and wished she could believe him. She gazed again at the dancers. The great hall seemed a stormy sea of color in which she could all too easily drown. If only she had something to help keep her afloat, something or . . .

She turned back toward the knight. "I can't do this alone, Durge. I can't be King Boreas's spy at the council. Not by myself." It was not like her to do so, but she didn't care, not now, not in her desperation. She reached out and touched his shoulder. "Will you help me, Durge? Not just tonight, but tomorrow, and the next day, and through all of this. Please?"

His face seemed carved of stone. Grace thought he was going to pull away. Then he shrugged.

"Now that my king is here with his favored servants and counselors, there is little enough for me to do. I'm afraid I'm a far better fit on the road than I am at court." He gave a solemn nod. "Yes, my lady, I will help you, but not out of any desire to further King Boreas's causes. I will help you for your sake, and your sake alone."

Grace surprised herself then—she laughed, and for the first time in days she felt a sense of hope. The sea still churned around her, but she was not lost yet.

"That makes three times you've rescued me, Durge."

To her surprise, embarrassment, and—strangest of all—her delight, he knelt before her and bowed his head.

"At your service, my lady."

61.

It was late.

Grace woke to moonlight streaming through the window of her chamber. She sat up in bed, grimaced, and lifted a hand to her temple. Her head throbbed—the aftereffects of too much wine. She was still clad in the woolen gown she had worn that evening, now bunched up and rumpled. She forced herself to think back. After her conversation with Durge she had felt bold enough to walk around the great hall in the knight's company. She had spoken with some of the nobles, and even a king or two. Only it seemed every third person had thrust a full goblet into her hand. The last thing she remembered was Durge leading her back to the door of her chamber, and then . . . she must have climbed into bed without changing and fallen asleep.

But what had awakened her? It had been a sound: distant, yet high and silvery, a sound almost like . . . bells. Yes, that was it, a sound like far-off church bells on a still winter night. But she had noticed no bell tower in all her wanderings about Calavere. And even if there were, who would ring the bells so late at night? Urged on by curiosity, she slipped from the bed, padded to the chamber door, and stepped into the corridor.

The stone floor was cold against her bare feet. She had gotten her boots off at least. She glanced down the corridor in both directions. The castle was silent. Now what?

She was just beginning to feel foolish, just beginning to think she should go back into her room, drink some water, shuck off her gown, and slip back into bed, when she heard them again. Before, in her sleepiness, she couldn't be certain. Now she was wide-awake, and there could be no doubt. The faint sound had not come from outside the castle, but from within.

Bells.

She hastened down the corridor in the direction of the sound. A minute later she heard them again, closer this time. She quickened her pace until she nearly ran down twisting passageways. Then a blast of cold air brought her to a halt. The corridor ended in an alcove set with a single round window. The window hung open, and frigid air streamed in. Grace approached the window, shivered, and peered through. It had snowed outside, but now the clouds had parted, and the land glowed under the light of the rising moon. She looked down, and that was when she saw them, at least twenty feet below: a line of small depressions dinted in the newfallen snow. Footprints.

The trail led to the edge of the hill on which the castle rested, then vanished over the edge. Grace lifted her eyes and peered in the direction the footprints led. Her gaze crossed white, glowing plains to a dark line on the horizon. The eaves of Gloaming Wood.

How long she gazed out the window she wasn't sure. A shiver jolted her back to the present. Whoever whatever—had jumped out the window was now long gone. She shut the window, then turned and started back toward her chamber.

She was halfway there when she rounded a corner and let out a gasp. In front of a door, not a dozen paces away, stood a man. At least Grace assumed it was a man, for she could not see his face, as he was clad from head to toe in a robe as black as night. He held a knife in his hand and was using the tip to carve something into the surface of the door.

Grace drew in a breath, unsure what to do, then called out. "Hello."

The robed figure froze, then the cowled head snapped in Grace's direction, although she could not glimpse the face within. She took a step forward. The figure turned and fled, his robe billowing behind like black wings. Something fell with a clatter to the stone floor.

Grace held out a hand. "Wait!"

It was too late. The stranger turned a corner and was gone. Grace shook her head. Why would anyone be afraid of her? She walked to the door the stranger had been standing before. There. It was so small she probably never would have noticed it had she not seen him doing it. A symbol had been scratched into the wood of the door near the upper left corner, formed of two curved lines:

No matter how much Grace stared at it the symbol made no sense. She sighed—she was far too tired to think. Tomorrow she could bring

Aryn or Durge here. One of them might know what the symbol meant. Perhaps it related to one of the mystery cults.

Grace turned away from the door, and a flash of silver caught her eye. She bent and picked up the object. It was a small knife with a black hilt. The stranger must have dropped it when he fled. She tucked it into her belt as she started down the corridor. Grace wasn't sure why, but the knife seemed important for some reason.

She reached her chamber without seeing another soul and slipped inside. Quickly—her room was *cold*—she shucked off her gown and, navigating by the brilliant moonlight, climbed onto her bed. She started to pull back the bedcovers, then gasped. With a trembling hand she reached out and picked up the object that rested on her pillow.

It was a sprig of evergreen. She remembered a pair of nut-brown eyes gazing at her, and she saw again the small footprints in the snow. Then Adira the serving maid's words echoed in her mind. *The Little People must have gotten to it.* . . . Grace tightened her grip on the twig. She didn't know what it all meant, but one thing was certain.

Strange things were prowling the halls of Calavere.

PART FOUR

CIRCLES
OF
STONE

62.

On the last day of Sindath, the day before the Council of Kings was to convene, a curious traveling party arrived at the gates of Calavere.

The news—along with Aryn—found Grace in the east wing of the castle's main keep, in the company of the knight Durge. A week had passed since the evening of the revel, when Grace had felt herself adrift in the subtle sea of power and politics in the great hall and Durge had pledged his help to her. During the intervening time Grace had learned a great deal about the art of intrigue.

"The first rule of any conflict," the knight had said in Grace's chamber the morning after the revel, "is never wait for your enemy to come to you. Rather, go to him first."

Grace had stopped dead in her pacing to stare at the knight. "Even when you're at a disadvantage?"

Durge had regarded her with his usual gravity. "Especially when you're at a disadvantage. If you're going to perish, better at least to choose the place."

Grace had resisted the urge to scream. She was never going to best the other nobles at their own game—she might as well have embroidered the word *amateur* on her gown. Yet the alternative to taking Durge's advice was to tell Boreas she couldn't help him at the council. And the only thing that terrified Grace more than the prospect of playing Boreas's spy was facing the wrath of the bullish king of Calavan.

She had sighed like one condemned beyond reprieve. "Let's get started."

However, a week truly did make a difference. In the days since that uncertain morning, Grace's confidence had grown—tentatively at first, then by great strides.

One by one, she and Durge had questioned the nobles attending the council—the courtiers, the counselors, the seneschals. The two would wait until the most opportune moment, usually when the object of their attention was alone, then as one they would pounce. To Durge this may have been a war, but to Grace it was more like medicine: Observe, diagnose, then go in with a sharp scalpel. All she had to do was think of the nobles, not as people, but as cases to be solved, and it was not so different from a shift in the ED at Denver Memorial.

On that particular afternoon their chosen target was Lord Sul, High Counselor to Persard, the ancient—if sprightly—king of Perridon. Sul was an inherently fretful man and had proved an elusive quarry. They had followed him nearly an hour before they saw their opportunity and seized it. The two split up and came upon the counselor from opposite directions, trapping him in a corridor. Sul was a mouse of a man with big ears and a whiskery mustache that was in constant motion. His black eyes darted from knight to lady and back to knight again. Grace bit her lip to conceal a smile.

"Tell me, Sul," Durge said, "is it true what they say of your king?"

Sul fingered the neck of his tunic. "I'm sure I don't know what you mean, my lord."

"Don't you?" The Embarran knight backed the counselor up against a wall. "I've heard Persard will petition the Council of Kings to cede all the lands along the north bank of the Serpent's Tail River to Perridon. But you know as well as I the north bank of the river belongs to Embarr."

Sul batted his eyes. "But my king has no such plan!"

"You're lying, of course," Durge said. "I know you can't help it, Sul. You're a Perridoner, after all. Telling the truth goes against your basic nature. But in Embarr we have ways of convincing liars to speak the truth, and most of them involve heating iron tongs in a bed of coals first."

The counselor's eyes bulged as he struggled for words. Now it was Grace's turn. She laid a hand on Durge's arm and did her best to look imploring.

"My lord, can't we resolve this with words rather than violence?"

Sul nodded in vigorous agreement.

Durge reached up and over his left shoulder to grip the hilt of the Embarran greatsword slung in a leather harness strapped to his broad back. "You cannot understand, my lady. Yours is too gentle a soul."

"Please, my lord. Allow me to speak with the counselor. Just for a moment."

Durge hesitated, then nodded. "Very well, my lady, but only a moment. Then I will deal with him my way."

The knight stepped aside, and Grace approached the trembling Sul.

"I beg you, my lady," the counselor whispered. "You seem to have some influence on this madman. Call him off!"

Grace gave her head a regretful shake. "I'm so sorry, my lord. It is beyond me to influence the earl of Stonebreak. You know how Embarrans are when angered. It's the dreary landscape of their homeland. It makes them a trifle insane, I think."

Sul was frantic now. "But you have to do something, my lady! My lord cares nothing for the north bank of the river, I swear it."

This wasn't surprising, given that Durge had made the rumor up on the spot. Grace tapped her cheek. "Well, perhaps if I knew what your liege *really* intended at the council, I might be able to convince the earl he is in error."

Sul licked his lips. "My king's only concern right now is Toloria, my lady. Ever since Ivalaine came to the throne three years ago, Persard has been concerned about his southern neighbor. The queen has refused to sign any of the treaties he has offered her. So Persard intends to support Boreas at the council in hopes of solidifying his alliance with Calavan should he ever need aid against Toloria."

Grace knew at once the little man was telling the truth. She could not quite prevent the hint of a smile from touching her lips.

"Now please, my lady," Sul said. "Speak with the earl of Stonebreak!"

"I'll see what I can do."

As it turned out, the duchess of Beckett was indeed able to calm the earl of Stonebreak, and a much relieved Sul scurried down the corridor.

Durge regarded Grace with somber brown eyes. "You've made an ally, you know."

Grace shook her head, half in amusement, half in regret. "Poor Sul. I suppose the gods of this place will strike me down for having so much fun tormenting him."

Durge shrugged. "I know not how things are in your homeland, my lady, but it is my experience that the gods seldom mete out punishment to those who deserve it."

Her smile faded, and she gazed at the knight. "Don't you believe in the gods, Durge?"

The knight seemed to think, his eyes distant. "My father used to say the wind in Embarr was so harsh it blew all the gods away. It is true you'll find more masons and engineers in my homeland than you will priests of the mystery cults." He looked again to Grace. "But to answer your question, my lady, I believe there *are* gods. I just don't necessarily believe *in* them."

Grace slipped a hand into the pocket of her gown and touched the crude wooden bull she had found in the bailey, the symbol of the Warrior Cult of Vathris. For some reason she couldn't name she had kept it close to her these last days, although she had always favored science over religion.

"Sometimes I think the wind might blow us all away, Durge," she murmured.

The furrows that marked the knight's brow deepened in concern. He reached out a hand, as if to comfort her, but he changed the movement at the last moment and gestured clumsily for them to start down the hallway. "Come, my lady, this is a dim part of the castle. Let us return to more lighted ways."

While they walked Grace kept her eyes open, as had become her habit, but she saw nothing unusual as they went. In fact, she had seen no signs of the mysterious persons skulking about the castle since the night of the revel. She had told Durge and Aryn of the black-robed man she had glimpsed. For days after, the three of them had searched Calavere, but they had found no traces of the robed one, or of who-ever—

Don't you mean whatever, Grace?

—had made the tiny footprints in the snow.

Grace turned her mind to more mundane mysteries, ones she had at least a slim chance of solving. She had spoken now with nobles belonging to the courts of nearly all the kings and queens of the Dominions, and day by day a clearer picture formed in her mind of the positions held by the various rulers.

As far as Grace could tell, Boreas had nothing to worry about with regard to Kylar—the young king of Galt was by his own admission a staunch supporter of Calavan. Persard of Perridon struck Grace as a bit more sly and unpredictable, but Lord Sul's words supported Grace's hunch that Perridon would follow Calavan's lead at the council—as long as Persard believed he would gain by it.

Eminda was another matter altogether. Grace had not gotten remotely close to the queen of Eredane, but from conversations she had overheard among some of Eminda's courtiers, she was beginning to think that if Boreas said the sky was blue, Eminda would issue a proclamation stating it was green. Eredane was a realm on the rise, and—as the oldest and strongest of the Dominions—Calavan was its chief rival. Grace suspected Eminda would perceive any action Boreas took as a direct counter to Eredane's progress. Grace had said as much to Boreas in one of their brief meetings over the course of the last week.

However, the king had only grunted, and whether he thought this—or any of the information Grace had given him—was useful, he had not said.

Still, Grace had done her best at the mission Boreas had assigned her, and she had largely succeeded. With at least some degree of certainty, she now knew where all the rulers stood on the issue of war.

All, that was, except Queen Ivalaine.

Grace had not dared to try to speak to the beautiful queen of Toloria again. The thought of those ice-colored eyes gazing into her—as if they could see things no other could—made her feel naked and sick.

Why, Grace? What are you so afraid she'll see? Are you terrified she'll see you're a witch? Or that there's nothing inside of you at all?

She pushed the question from her mind. It was not as if there had been opportunity to speak to any of the nobles in Ivalaine's court. Most were like their queen—fair, faultless of manner, and far more likely to conjure secrets with their words than answer them.

A thought occurred to Grace. There was one other ruler whose motives she had learned little about in the last week. She gazed at the knight walking beside her. "What of your own king, Durge? Except for Ivalaine, I think I know the least about him of all."

Durge blew a breath through his mustaches. "There is no need for you to waste your time spying on King Sorrin, my lady. I can tell you all you need to know of him. I'm afraid my liege is dying."

"King Sorrin is ill?" Her doctor's instincts replaced all other thoughts in her mind. "Has it been going on long? What are his symptoms?"

"No, my lady. It is no illness you might cure that ails King Sorrin. Indeed, I imagine he will live to a great age, and that makes it only the more bitter."

Grace halted in mid stride. "I don't understand."

"It is a malady of the mind that has struck my king. He dwells in constant fear of death, and so every day he is dying."

Durge moved to a narrow window—an arrow loop, through which archers might fire out but not in—and peered at the thin strip of sky beyond. "Sorrin's mortal fear has become a prison, stronger than any made of stone. Nor do I think he will ever escape it. His dread of death consumes him so that he thinks of nothing else. All day he pores over books about disease, and speaks only to his leeches, and drinks the potions they concoct. He has little time for others, or for running a kingdom."

The knight was always solemn, but now there was a note of sorrow to his weatherworn face. Grace tried to draw in a breath, but her chest felt tight. It was the gown, of course. It was so constricting, she shouldn't wear it, even if Aryn did say the winter violet suited her.

She opened her mouth to say something—anything—that might make the knight feel better, but no words came out. If he were wounded, she would have known exactly how to help him. But this sadness . . .

"Lady Grace!" a clear voice called out.

Grace glanced up and saw a flash of sapphire rush toward them. "Lady Aryn," she said, and tried not to sound too grateful for the interruption.

"Grace, I'm so glad I found you." The young baroness's cheeks glowed from exertion.

"Good morrow, Your Highness," Durge said in his rough but gentle baritone. He made a stiff bow. "Though I warrant it won't stay good for long. It looks like rain."

Aryn blinked as if only now noticing the knight, and indeed his tunic and cloak were the exact color of the stone wall. She made a hasty curtsy. "Lord Durge." She started to turn back to Grace, then glanced out the window. A frown crossed her pretty face. "But the sky is perfectly clear."

Durge made no reply. He clasped his hands and gazed forward with deep brown eyes.

"Aryn, what is it?" Grace said.

Aryn's blue eyes shone. "You'll never guess who rode up to the castle gates only a few moments ago."

"No," Grace said, "I probably won't."

"Then you'll just have to come see. If we wait outside the great hall, we might get a glimpse of them." With her good hand she grabbed Grace and tugged her down the passage. "Oh, and you as well, Durge," she added.

The Embarran hesitated, then gave a wordless nod and followed the two ladies down the corridor.

63.

Travis stuck close to Beltan as they followed Falken, Melia, and a pair of stocky men-at-arms through the winding corridors of Calavere. He felt a little safer next to the big knight. But only a little.

The men-at-arms had greeted them when they rode up to the castle's gate—if being met with hard gazes and sharp spears, then being ordered to leave their horses and follow, could be called *greeting* rather than *accosting*.

"It looks as if someone saw you coming, Falken," Beltan had said, and he had drawn the hood of his green cloak up over his head, casting his face in shadow.

Falken had only grunted, and Travis had not taken this as a favorable sign. The bard hadn't been exactly welcome at the last castle whose door they had knocked on. Did he expect better here? Or worse?

They came to a halt before a set of double doors.

"King Boreas is expecting you," one of the men-at-arms said and gestured to the doors.

Melia gave Falken a speculative look. "You did say you were on King Boreas's good side, didn't you?"

Falken adjusted his cloak. "Is this on straight?"

"A little to the left." Melia's eyes flashed. "And don't think I didn't notice that you failed to answer my question."

Falken shot her a wolfish grin. "Shall we go beg hospitality of the king?"

Melia rolled her eyes but said nothing.

Travis leaned toward Beltan. "Does he know what he's doing?"

"Not nearly so often as he acts like he does."

Together they pushed through the doors.

The great hall of Calavere was not unlike King Kel's hall, except it was twice the size, the walls did not look as if they were about to crumble, and there were no wildmen in sight. A number of trestle tables stood folded against the walls, leaving the floor—strewn with fresh rushes—wide-open. A dais dominated the far end of the hall, and this in turn was dominated by the king of Calavan. Travis knew at once that, for all Kel's swagger, Boreas was to the shaggy ruler of Kelcior what a bonfire was to a torch. This was no petty king.

Boreas sat on the dais in a folding wooden chair. The chair was gilded with gold, and its feet carved like lion paws. The king was a muscular man but not bulky, clad in close-fitting black trimmed with silver. His short beard gleamed with oil, and his eyes—more steel than sky—glinted in annoyance. An older man with a neat gray beard stood a pace beside and a pace behind the throne, and several men-at-arms were arranged below the dais, along with a heap of gigantic black dogs—any one of which looked as if it could have comfortably housed Travis's entire skull in its maw, and gladly would have done so.

Boreas turned his stormy gaze on the four travelers as they approached the dais. His voice rumbled over the hall like thunder.

"Well, Falken Blackhand, I know these are dark days indeed if you show up at my gate."

"Greetings, Your Majesty." Falken's rich voice filled the hall. "It is good to see you are well."

"And through no work of your own. But do not feign interest in my health, Falken. Tell me, why have you come to Calavere? I thought I was rid of the Grim Bard."

Falken laughed. "You know well enough why I'm here, Your Majesty. I have come to speak to the council."

Boreas snorted. "To bewilder the council with fanciful stories, isn't that what you mean?"

"Yes, Your Majesty, stories. And, as a bard, I know that stories sometimes come true."

The king appeared unimpressed by this statement. "Don't try to muddle things with your riddles, Falken. I would have had my knights ride you back over the Darkwine Bridge were it not for the Lady Melia in your company."

Melia made an exquisite curtsy. "Your Majesty, I see your manners are as elegant as ever."

The king winced, and Travis bit his tongue to stifle a laugh. Something told him Boreas had thrown people to his dogs for less.

Boreas turned his attention back to the bard. "I don't have time for this. Tell me why I shouldn't just turn you away, Falken—Lady Melia in your company or no."

Falken took another step nearer the dais. "We have ridden hard on a long journey, Your Majesty, and we humbly beg your hospitality."

Boreas grunted but did not immediately refuse Falken's request. From what Beltan had said, Travis knew even a king was bound by the laws of hospitality.

"Besides," Falken went on, "there is one with us I think you will be glad to see."

Travis frowned at the bard. Who was Falken talking about? Even as he wondered this, Beltan stepped forward and pushed back his hood.

"Hello, Uncle."

Travis snapped his head around to stare at the tall knight. *Uncle?*

Boreas sat up straight on his throne. His eyes lit up—not with annoyance now, but with delight.

"By Vathris! Beltan!"

The king leaped from his chair, rushed down from the dais, and caught the knight in an embrace. Travis suspected the power of that hug would have crushed him to jelly. However, Beltan, if not as strapping as the king, was the taller, and he returned the embrace with equal strength.

Travis tried to understand what had just happened. How could Beltan be royalty? He was just . . . Beltan. But that wasn't true, was it? Now that they stood together, Travis could see the family resemblance. Both of their faces bore the same strong nose, the same sharp and slightly dangerous lines. Travis's heart soared for his friend—then as quickly it sank in his chest. Who was he to be friends with royalty?

Boreas stepped back from the blond knight. "So, you can't be bothered to visit your uncle once in a while, can you, Beltan? How many years has it been since you last made your way here? Two? Three? Too long at any rate." He cast a look of displeasure at the bard. "And what are you doing in the company of this scoundrel? I had not thought you'd throw your lot in with the likes of Falken Blackhand." He raised a hand to shield his mouth and nodded toward Melia. "Though I warrant you, *she's* worth hanging around."

"*Uncle*," Beltan said in a chiding tenor.

A clear voice interrupted the king and his nephew. "You still have not given us an answer, Your Majesty."

Boreas turned away from Beltan, scowled, and advanced on the bard. "By Vathris, you know perfectly well I'm going to grant you hospitality, Falken. As if I had a choice." He glanced at Beltan, and this time it was not only fondness in the look. "Though I still can't understand why you've fallen in with this motley bunch, Beltan of Calavan. Then again, even as a boy you always had your head stuck inside a helmet of your own forging."

"In that I had a good model to follow, Uncle."

Travis cringed, afraid this would only enrage the king further, but Boreas let out a great laugh and clapped Beltan on the back.

"Welcome home, Beltan. And yes, welcome to all of you, even to you, Falken Blackhand. I will not let you ruin this happy occasion, no matter how much you might try."

Falken bowed and said nothing.

Boreas gestured to the gray-haired man on the dais. "My seneschal, Lord Alerain, will see to your needs. I'm afraid I have other matters to attend to. Keeping a kingdom running and all that—I'm sure you wouldn't understand, Falken."

The king did not wait for a response. He nodded to Beltan and Melia—but not to Falken or Travis—then strode from the great hall. A weight lifted from the air like the passing of a storm.

Melia raised a hand to her slender throat. "I won't say that went well, but at least we still have our heads."

Falken nodded, then laid a hand on Beltan's shoulder. "So, is it good to be home?"

The knight shot Travis a look of concern and opened his mouth. However, Travis turned his back before Beltan could answer the question.

64.

The doors of the great hall flew open, and as one, Grace, Aryn, and Durge leaped back from the place where they had been waiting. King Boreas stalked through, then strode past the three without even glancing in their direction. A trio of stern-faced men-at-arms hurried after him as he marched down a corridor and disappeared through an archway. Grace thought she had seen Boreas angry before, but now she was forced to downgrade any previous displays she had witnessed to merely *perturbed*.

"Oh dear," Aryn said, her left hand pressed to the bodice of her blue gown.

Grace met the baroness's startled gaze. "All right, Aryn. Who exactly is this person who showed up at the gate?"

Durge stared after the king with sober brown eyes. "Given the king's demeanor, I believe I have an idea."

Grace shot the knight a questioning look, but he only gestured to the open doors.

"After you, my lady."

She stepped through the opening, and Aryn and Durge followed.

Grace saw at once there were four travelers, not one. They stood at the far end of the hall, speaking with Lord Alerain in low voices. They were an interesting band.

The one doing the most talking was a wolfish man, his black hair shot with silver, clad in a cloak the same faded blue as his eyes. A wooden case hung over his shoulder by a leather strap. Grace guessed it to house some kind of musical instrument. To the man's right stood a woman with hair even darker than Boreas's, and Grace knew Alerain would mark her as royalty. She was not tall, and her midnight-blue kirtle was simple, but she carried herself with an air of authority. Her skin was burnished copper, her eyes polished amber.

On the other side of the wolfish man stood a knight. He was tall and rangy, with amazingly broad shoulders, clad in a mail shirt, and with a sword belted at his hip. His thinning blond hair fell about his shoulders. The fourth member of the party stood behind the three. He seemed out of place compared to the others. He was tall enough—though not so tall as the knight—but slouched inside his baggy tunic. His beard was unkempt, his sandy hair shaggy, and he wore a glum look on his face. Grace supposed he was their servingman, though he looked rather disheveled for such.

Aryn leaned toward Grace. "Look, it's the king's nephew."

"Which one?" Grace said, even as she guessed the answer. The fierce profile was a dead giveaway. Although he was as light as Boreas was dark, and not as handsome, the knight was obviously related to the king of Calavan.

"The fair one," Aryn said. "His name is Beltan. I remember him from when I was a girl. He's as tall as I thought." The baroness chewed her lip. "Although he has less hair, I think. And more scars. At any rate, Beltan is the bastard son of Beldreas, Boreas's elder brother, who was king of Calavan."

Grace was taken aback by the matter-of-fact tone with which Aryn spoke the word *bastard*. However, this was a world where heritage and nobility went hand in hand with rank and power. To the baroness it was not an insult, merely a statement.

"What happened to Beldreas?" Grace said.

Aryn's usually cheerful face fell solemn. "He was murdered seven years ago in this very hall. It was an awful time for Calavan, for the line of succession was not clear. Even though he is a bastard, Beltan might well have made a play for the throne, but he swore a vow to Vathris never to rest until he found his father's murderer, so the throne went to Boreas, who was Beldreas's younger brother."

Grace studied the rawboned knight. Furrows were etched into his high forehead, far too deep for one who was certainly no older than herself. "Did he ever find him? His father's killer, I mean."

"I'm afraid not. I've heard it said he still quests so, even to this day."

Grace shook her head. Why was it so hard for the living to forget the dead? *I'm sure the dead have no problem forgetting us.* However, she did not speak these words. "Who are the others?" she said instead.

"The dark-haired man is the bard Falken Blackhand," Aryn said. "And next to him is the Lady Melia. I've never seen them before, but I've heard stories."

Stories? Grace started to say, but before she could form the word she felt a light tap on her shoulder.

"Come," Durge said in a quiet voice.

"Where are we going?" Grace had almost forgotten about the Embarran, he had stood so stonily behind them.

"I want to introduce you to the bard."

Aryn's mouth dropped open, and she turned toward Durge. "*You* know Falken Blackhand?"

Durge nodded. "I traveled with Falken once. But that was long ago, when I was young and frivolous."

Grace clenched her jaw shut. *It's not funny, Grace. It's not even remotely funny.*

"He won't remember who I am, of course," the knight said. "I imagine he'll just stare at me blankly, then tell me to be off. But it wouldn't be polite if I didn't try."

Aryn seemed not to hear these words and only stared at the knight. Durge led the way across the hall toward the curious travelers. As they drew near, Lord Alerain made a neat bow toward Falken, Melia, and Beltan.

"I will have chambers readied for you at once, my lady, my lord, and your old chamber for you, Lord Beltan."

"Thank you, Lord Alerain," the Lady Melia said.

The king's seneschal hurried off, and Grace examined the travelers with scientific interest. Beltan was royalty, and it was clear from Lord Alerain's deference that the bard Falken and the Lady Melia were important personages as well, though exactly what their rank and position was Grace didn't know. Their servingman—he wore wire spectacles, she saw now, which seemed odd for some reason—skulked behind the three. He kicked at the rushes that covered the floor with mud-caked boots, shoulders hunched inside his tunic. Shouldn't he have been seeing to the needs of his masters?

Durge hesitated, then cleared his throat, stepped forward, and spoke in a gruff tone. "Lord Falken, I'm sure you could never remember me, but I—"

The bard spun around, and his wolfish face—a moment before lined and weary—was bright and youthful. "By Olrig! Durge!" Falken clapped the knight's shoulder with his bare hand, then winced.

Durge's expression was at once concerned. "Falken, are you all right?"

"Yes, I'm fine." The bard shook his hand. "I just wish you knights would learn to warn the rest of us when you're wearing a mail shirt beneath your cloak and tabard."

Durge eyed the bard's hand. "I imagine you've crippled it permanently. You'll never play the lute again."

Falken frowned at the Embarran knight. "What kind of talk is that? I thought you had forsworn the ways of your countrymen, Durge. You were a man of good cheer, last I knew."

Now it was Grace's turn to stare at Durge.

He shifted from foot to foot. "I was a boy when you knew me, Lord Falken, my mustaches barely begun. I am a man well past his middle years now."

A sadness crept into Falken's expression, and he gazed at the knight, as if just now noticing Durge's deeply chiseled face and the gray that streaked his hair. "Of course," the bard said. "Of course, I forget. It must be over twenty years."

Grace thought this response odd. She had seen elderly people similarly struck by the passage of time, but surely Falken was of an age with Durge, who could not have been more than forty-five. That was hardly old. *Except in this world it is, Grace. You yourself are middle-aged here, and you're only thirty. No wonder Aryn thinks Durge is so old. To her, at nineteen, he's ancient.*

Now Falken's smile returned, and if it was not as bright as before, it was at least as fond. He gripped the Embarran knight's hand. "All the same, it is good to see you again, Durge."

The dark-haired knight nodded. "And you as well, Falken."

Falken turned toward his companions. "Everyone, this is Lord Durge of Embarr. Durge, this is Lady Melia, and this is Beltan of Calavan."

Melia curtsied, and Beltan gave a broad grin. Grace gasped, for when he smiled the knight was every bit as handsome as his uncle.

"I've heard of the earl of Stonebreak," Beltan said. "Your skill with the Embarran greatsword precedes you, my lord."

Durge took a step back. "I'm sure the stories must be in error, my lord."

Melia lifted the hem of her gown and glided forward. She nodded toward Aryn and Grace. "And who are your companions, Lord Durge?"

Though Melia was small—even tiny—for the second time next to another Grace felt like a girl. Only it was not the same as when she had stood next to Kyrene. Melia did not make her feel inadequate, only that there was far more to the world, to life, and to experience than she could possibly imagine.

Durge cleared his throat. "This is Her Highness, Aryn, the Baroness of Elsandry, and ward to King Boreas."

Melia smiled at the young baroness and nodded in greeting, and Aryn responded with an elegant curtsy Grace could never hope to duplicate.

"So," Beltan said, his blue eyes dancing, "the mischievous girl I remember has grown into a pretty young woman. King Boreas is right. I do need to visit more often."

Aryn blushed and bowed her head, but her smile was unmistakable. Grace knew at once she liked the rangy blond knight, bastard or not.

"And this," Durge said, "is Her Radiance, Grace, the Duchess of Beckett."

Melia's amber eyes flashed. "Beckett? I've never heard of a duchy called Beckett."

A spike of panic pierced Grace's chest. "It's very far away," she blurted.

Melia nodded. "Yes, of course it is." Her eyes locked on to Grace, and Grace had the terrible sensation she was transparent, that the Lady Melia could gaze inside her and see every secret, every hope, every fear Grace was trying to hide, fluttering like moths trapped inside a bell jar.

Grace lifted a hand to her throat. It was hard to breathe. The air in the great hall was suffocating. Melia's servingman stood just behind the lady. Grace glanced at him, and caught his gray eyes behind the wire-rimmed spectacles. "Please," she said. "Could you bring me a cup of wine?"

He stared at her like she had just asked him to jump from the highest tower in the castle.

"What?" he said.

Grace was taken aback. None of the servants in Calavere would dare show such rudeness. "Wine," she said. "It's on the table over there. Could you bring me a cup? Please."

The man grimaced at her. "I'm not a servant, you know."

Melia turned her gaze on him. "Then why don't you be a gentleman, Travis?"

The sandy-haired man gaped at Melia, opened his mouth, then seemed to think better of it. He turned to retrieve the wine, though none too quickly, and he grumbled as he went.

Inwardly Grace groaned. Once again she had misread another, and to disastrous result. There was a long and awkward moment of silence. At last Aryn made a valiant attempt at a smile.

"Welcome to Calavere, everyone," she said.

65.

"You can set those over there, Travis," Melia said.

Travis dropped the heavy saddlebags on the floor of the chamber. He straightened, and his back made a peculiar noise, something akin to an especially energetic horse prancing on a field of crystal.

Falken frowned at the saddlebags. "Did you break something, Travis?"

"Not in those," he said through clenched teeth.

At Melia's request he had carried the saddlebags from the castle's stable, down a long corridor, and up a spiral staircase that had turned him around so many times stepping off it was like stepping off the Tilt-A-Whirl at Elitch Gardens.

"Now, don't forget the four you left at the bottom of the stairs," Melia said in a pleasant tone.

Travis shot Melia a wounded look. "You're punishing me, aren't you?"

"Yes, dear, but only because I care about you."

Travis groaned as he headed for the door. It wasn't his fault the woman in the great hall had been so rude. He didn't mind getting her a cup of wine, but the way she had looked at him—like an object, not a person—even the crassest tourists in the Mine Shaft Saloon had never talked to him like that.

Beltan strode into the room, a pair of bulging saddlebags in each hand. He swung them up with ease and set them on a sideboard, then looked around.

"Is that everything?" He dusted off his hands. "That wasn't hard at all."

Travis stared at the knight. There were times when he liked Beltan just a little bit less than others. Still, he was grateful he didn't have to make another trip down the stairs. He never had been able to ride the Tilt-A-Whirl twice without losing his cotton candy.

"Well, Melia." Falken set the case that contained his lute on the window ledge. "What do you think of the king of Calavan's hospitality?"

Melia circled the room, her kirtle trailing the rough carpets on the floor. The chamber the king's seneschal, Alerain, had led them to was large enough for them all to gather in at once. Tapestries draped the walls, their colors deep with smoke and time, and helped to stave off the chill along with the fire crackling on the hearth. A side door led to a smaller bedchamber that would grant Melia a degree of privacy.

"Well, it's not the largest chamber in the castle," Melia said. She sat in a plump chair by the fireplace, and a smile coiled about her lips. "But I'll manage."

Falken lifted his lute from its case and strummed a melancholy chord. "The world will be ever grateful for your sacrifices, Melia."

"Well, I should certainly hope so."

Travis folded his cloak and set it on one of the two narrow beds in the main room, where he and Falken were to sleep, then sat beside it. Molten sunlight spilled through the chamber's window. He counted five stone towers through the rippled glass, sharp against the sky, and knew that was only half of what Calavere had to offer. Riding toward the castle, it had loomed high on its hill, so craggy it had reminded him of the mountains of Colorado. He had felt a pang of loss then and had faced into the wind, as he always did when thinking about his home.

Everyone in Castle City has probably forgotten you by now, Travis. Maybe you should forget, too. He sighed and gazed at the high battlements. In all, Calavere made King Kel's fortress look like a rubble heap.

"Don't worry about those, Beltan," Melia said in a bright voice. "Travis volunteered to unpack them."

Travis looked up. "I don't remember saying that."

Melia's eyelids descended halfway. "Try very hard."

Travis gulped. "Oh. I think it's coming back to me."

"I knew it would, dear."

Travis knelt beside the saddlebags. It had been a long journey from the tower of the Runebinders. As he pulled blankets, extra garments, and the remnants of foodstuffs from the bags, the leagues rolled by again in his mind.

They had not stayed long in the vale of the White Tower. The morning after the attack of the wraithlings, Melia still had been wan and chilled, but she least of all had not wished to linger in that place. They had packed their things in the steely light before dawn and had ridden from the vale. Travis had cast one last glance over his shoulder at the ruin. It had shone like bones in the half-light: a tomb to bury the folly of those already centuries dead. He had shivered, then they had rounded the spur of a ridge, and the remains of the tower had been lost from view.

They had ridden hard through southern Eredane. For speed's sake they had kept to the Queen's Way, but not without caution. Beltan continually scouted ahead, and more than once the knight had come pounding back toward them on his roan charger to warn that a group of Raven cultists approached. Each time they had fled the road to hide in a bramble thicket, or behind a knoll, or under the arch of an old Tarrasian bridge.

One time the cultists had been mere moments away, and there had been nowhere to seek cover, only bare plains for a league in either direction. In sharp words they dared not question, Melia had instructed them to stand perfectly still beside the road and to hold tight to the bridles of their horses. She had made a series of odd motions with her hands, splaying them out flat, and moving them in a single plane before her.

The Raven cultists had come into view, marching down the Queen's Way. It was the largest such procession they had seen, nearly a hundred, all clad in robes of black, the wing of the Raven drawn in ash on their foreheads. Queer words tumbled from their lips, and Travis had realized it was a prayer.

*"breathe the wind
walk the fire
Raven be your master*

*chain the flesh
free the heart
Raven flies forever"*

As the cultists passed, Travis had clenched his jaw to keep from screaming. He was sure that one of them would turn to stare at him at any moment. The mask of dull-eyed complacence would twist into one of madness and rage, and the cultist would shriek, pointing an accusing finger at him, marking him as the man who had burned one of their own.

And what will you do then, Travis? Set that one on fire, too? Why stop there? Why not burn up the whole lot of them?

However, the cultists had marched by with their strange, lurching cadence, gazes blank and fixed ahead. Whatever Melia had done with her hands, it had worked.

That was the last they had seen of the Raven Cult. The next morning a great plateau had thrust up before them. The Fal Erenn, the Dawning Fells, bordered the highlands to the east, and to the west and south Travis had glimpsed a line of mist-gray peaks, which Falken named the Fal Sinfath, the Gloaming Fells. With no other route available, the Queen's Way had cut into the steep side of the plateau. The horses had labored to carry the travelers up the incline, and Travis had marveled at the way the ancient Tarrasian engineers had carved the narrow road from sheer rock. It might have been a thousand years old, but it had looked as solid as any paved mountain pass in Colorado.

While the others had ridden cautiously here, Travis had pushed his shaggy gelding ahead despite Falken's admonitions. Mountains didn't frighten Travis. They were dangerous, yes, and he had known people who had died on them. If you tried to fight a mountain, you would surely lose, but if you gave yourself to it, sacrificed some of your own blood and sweat, then the mountain would bear you to the sky.

When they had reached the top, the land they found was not much like Colorado. This was the Dominion of Galt, situated in the highlands between Eredane and Calavan. It was a small and stark land, all sharp edges and treacherous crevices. As they rode south they had passed few villages, and these had been as hard and uninviting as the stone from which they were hewn. Few crops grew in this land, and the main livestock was a kind of wiry goat. What the animals found to eat among the tumbled boulders Travis didn't know.

Although the landscape of Galt was harsh, its people could not have been more different. The travelers did not camp—the night wind would have scoured them from the ground if they hadn't frozen first—so they had stayed in taverns three nights in a row. At each one the people had been kind, red-faced, and of good humor. The food they had served had been scant and simple, but it was served generously and alongside large tankards of ale. Travis had sipped his tentatively at first, then had joined Beltan in taking large gulps. Unlike the not-quite-oatmeal he had drunk elsewhere, the brews of Galt were brown, rich, and smooth as molasses.

They were also of a strength he had never encountered before, as he had discovered upon waking that first morning in Galt.

"I remember my first tankard of Galtish ale," Beltan had said with a grin, standing over his bed. "Feels like dark elfs are digging their newest mine inside your skull, doesn't it?"

"Mmmph," Travis had said. It was the only word he could manage.

Melia had cast a smug glance at Falken. "I told you Galtish ale would addle his wits."

The bard had handed her a gold coin. "I should know better than to wager against you, Melia."

Fortunately, the ale had not actually addled Travis's wits, only dulled them temporarily. By that evening, at the next tavern, he had felt better and had taken smaller sips from his tankard.

For two more days they had made their way across Galt. Then the highlands had ended, and the Queen's Way had plunged down to gentler, foggier lands. These were the northern marches of the Dominion of Calavan. Though the air was still toothed with the bite of a premature winter, it seemed balmy compared to the dry, frigid air of Galt. At last they had crossed a Tarrasian bridge over a swift river—the Dimduorn, Falken called it—and Travis had taken in his first sight of Calavere.

It had been a week since they left the White Tower of the Runebinders. The Council of Kings was to convene tomorrow. They had made it with less than one day to spare.

"I've heard King Boreas keeps runespeakers at his castle," Falken said.

Travis paused in his unpacking and looked up.

Beltan nodded. "He did, last I knew. One of them was named Jemis, I think."

From her chair Melia raised an eyebrow in Falken's direction. The bard met her gaze. Somehow those two could hold entire conversations without ever speaking a word.

"Good idea," Falken said. "I'll see if I can find this Jemis tonight and ask if he can take over Travis's tutoring. I'm afraid Travis has learned about all he can from me."

Melia's eyes glinted. "Excellent."

Travis held his tongue—there was no point in complaining. He gazed down at his hands and remembered the power that had flowed through them at the heart of the White Tower. He could not see the silver rune, but he could feel it there, beneath the skin of his palm.

I don't care what Melia wants. I'll never use this power again, Jack. I'll learn about it, but only so I can control it. Only so I don't hurt anyone again.

"Do you think King Boreas will let you address the council?" Melia asked the bard.

"He'd better," Falken said. "Besides, even if I can't count Boreas among my best friends, he *is* the one who called the Council of Kings. He wouldn't have forced the rulers of all the Dominions to journey here had the troubles stirring in Falengarth not concerned him."

"Then again, kings can have many reasons for their actions." She glanced at the knight. "Beltan, what do you think of your uncle?"

Travis winced. It was still hard to think of Beltan as royalty. It seemed everyone he knew here was a person of importance—except for himself.

Beltan scratched the golden fluff on his chin. "Boreas is a good man, but he's a good disciple of Vathris as well. I've heard it said he's gained the Inner Circle of the Mysteries of Vathris. Whether that's the case or not, he's certainly not afraid of war."

"Might he even crave it?" Melia said in careful tones.

Beltan shook his head. "I can't say. I'd be lying if I said Boreas and I were all that close, and it *has* been three years since I last saw him." He snorted. "Besides, I'm hardly the person you want to ask about court politics."

Despite the knight's words, Travis thought Beltan had summed things up rather well. A thought occurred to him. "You could have been king, couldn't you, Beltan?"

Beltan turned on Travis. His voice was as sharp and flat as his sword. "No," he said. "I could not."

With that the knight stalked from the room.

Travis recoiled as if struck a blow. What had he done? "I only meant he was the last king's son."

Falken nodded but said nothing.

"Don't worry, Travis," Melia said, her voice gentler now. "You said nothing wrong."

Then why had Beltan stormed from the room? However, he only went back to unpacking while Melia and Falken continued discussing their plan for addressing the council.

Then the room fell quiet, and Travis looked up. Falken and Melia had taken their conversation into the side chamber, leaving him alone. His eyes moved to the door. He knew it was wrong, but no one had told him he couldn't. Besides, he felt restless and trapped. He had to move, had to walk somewhere, anywhere.

Before his common sense could convince him otherwise, Travis stood up, opened the door, and slipped into the corridor beyond.

66.

Grace walked down the dim corridor, accompanied only by the soft sigh of her violet gown. It had been more than an hour since she had left the great hall, and she still had not made her way back to her chamber.

Not that she was lost. It had been nearly a month since the day she came to Calavere, and with time the castle's myriad halls and galleries had become familiar to her. There were still many parts of Calavere she had yet to explore, and things grew hazier once she left the main keep, but she could now traverse from the keep's west wing to the east with confidence. If she closed her eyes she could navigate the twists and turns in her mind, just as she could the branching patterns of nerves and arteries inside the human body.

If only the labyrinth of human interaction were so easy a thing to master as hallways or medicine. However, that was a maze she doubted she would ever be able to traverse without error. As if her scientific mind needed any more evidence, the incident in the great hall was one more case study she could add to her research. How could she have mistaken the bard's companion for a servant?

She brushed the fabric of her gown. *You've almost let yourself believe this is real, Grace. But it's easier to be royalty, isn't it? You don't actually have to speak to other people. You can simply order them around.*

Grace cringed as she remembered the wounded look on the man's face. How many other people had she hurt with her errors of perception, her inability to understand what others were feeling or thinking? How many more people would she? The man in the great hall, the man with the spectacles, was only one in a long line of casualties, caught like the others in the flying shrapnel of what once had been her heart.

She lifted a hand to her chest and almost expected to feel the same bitter cold she had felt when she reached inside the dead man's thoracic cavity at Denver Memorial, but her heart fluttered warm and weak beneath the bodice of her gown. She drew in a shuddering breath. Maybe it would be better if she did have a heart of iron. Maybe then she wouldn't always have to try to feel, and fail. It was all so absurd she almost laughed. She could dissect its four chambers with steel-scalpeled precision, but the human heart was a labyrinth she would never comprehend. Just like the maze in the castle's garden, it led her inevitably to places she could not escape and sights she did not want to witness.

As she walked, Grace's thoughts turned to Kyrene. She had studiously avoided the green-eyed countess these last days. Now she felt a peculiar desire to see Kyrene, to speak to her, to ask her questions about Ivalaine and the Witches. Kyrene would tell her, she was certain of it. The countess of Selesia would delight in showing Grace how much more knowledgeable she was. Nor did Grace care, not now.

A few herbs, the proper words . . .

A shiver coursed through her, and it was not only from the castle chill. She pictured him in her mind: lean, dark, elegant. *Yes, perhaps next time Logren of Eredane will walk in the garden with me.*

That was ridiculous. On Earth Grace had shunned intimacy. She could never let another get close to her. Because if they were close, then they might see everything about her. Everything. She couldn't let that happen. Not in this world—not in any world.

Grace came to a halt and shook her head, like a sleepwalker waking. She knew this corridor. It led toward the sleeping chambers of many of Calavere's nobles. One more turn and she would find herself standing before Kyrene's door. She stared, frozen. Then she snatched up the hem of her gown, not caring one whit how unnoble the action was, and ran back down the corridor.

Grace rounded a corner—and collided with something tall and green that let out a low *oof!* She caught a flash of silver out of the corner of her eye, then heard a chime, as of metal striking stone. Grace stumbled back, caught herself against the wall, blinked to clear her rattled vision, and at last saw what—no, *whom*—she had run into.

Her heart sank in her chest. It was a sandy-haired man with wire-rimmed spectacles. His arms were folded across his ill-fitting tunic, and he hunched over his stomach. It was clear she had knocked the wind out of him. *Too bad you didn't break a few of his ribs, Grace. At least then you would know what to say.*

She winced at this thought, then cleared her throat and forced herself to speak. "Are you all right?"

He craned his neck up. "Oh. It's you."

She took a tentative step forward and held out a hand. "Can I help?"

With a grimace he unhunched his shoulders and stood straight—or at least as straight as she had seen him stand in the great hall earlier. Grace could never understand why some tall men were afraid of their own height.

"I think you've helped me enough today."

Grace winced again. "I'm sorry." She forced the words out one by one. "For running into you. And for thinking you were a servant. Back in the great hall. That was stupid."

He cast his gray eyes toward the floor. "No, it wasn't stupid. You're right. I might as well be their servant. It seems like they always have plans for me, but they never bother to tell me what they are."

Again she did not know what to say. "Are you lost? I can help you back to your chamber."

He lifted his gaze and glared at her. "No, I don't need your help. I don't need anyone's help. You've said you're sorry, and I've accepted, so just leave me alone, all right?"

Indignation rose in Grace's chest. Didn't he know who she was? But then, she wasn't really anybody. *Besides,* the dry, clinical voice inside her spoke, *you've heard those same words a hundred times before in the ED. The frightened will never ask for help. It means admitting they're hurt, admitting they're lost. You know that, Grace.*

He had turned from her now, and he bent over, searching the floor. "Where is it?" he muttered. "It's got to be here."

She remembered the flash of silver, then picked up the hem of her gown and moved toward him. "What was it you dropped?"

"You wouldn't understand."

"Why not?"

"I can't . . . I can't explain it. But it's important."

She crouched down beside him. "Then let me help you."

He ran a hand through his tangled hair and looked up at her. "Look, I already told you, you don't need to—"

He stopped, and his gray eyes went wide. Grace shook her head. What was he staring at?

"I can understand you," he whispered.

Grace frowned. For one simple almost-servingman, he certainly had the ability to confound her.

"What are you talking about?"

He leaped to his feet and pointed at her. "There. That. What you just said—I understood it!" He shook his head. "But that's impossible. . . ."

She rose. A queer feeling crept into her chest. "Why shouldn't you be able to understand me?"

Their eyes met, then as one they glanced down at a small glint of silver in the corner of a nearby alcove.

"There," Grace murmured. "What you dropped, it's in the alcove."

He moved to the recess in the wall, bent down, then stood and turned around. Somehow Grace wasn't surprised at what she saw. The spectacles were an obvious clue, of course. She had seen no others on Eldh. And his boots, now cleaned of mud, were not the flat-soled boots the peasants wore. They were cowboy boots. She forced her eyes down to the object in his hand. It was a half circle of silver, engraved on both sides. One edge was jagged and broken.

"What is it?" he said, quiet now.

Yes, he sensed it. She was certain.

Grace approached, and from the pouch at her waist she drew out her own silver half-coin. He stared, then held his coin out. She brought hers up to meet it. Grace had no doubt the two broken edges would match perfectly, but she let out a gasp all the same when they did.

"The man in black?" he said, not really a question.

She nodded. "Brother Cy."

"Then you're from Earth, too."

A tremor ran through Grace. It was wonder. And joy. And relief. "Yes," she said. "I am."

67.

The words had rushed out of them in a flood.

Eldh. The coin. Brother Cy.

They had fit their half-coins together, but the symbols on either side—though now whole—had still made no sense, just like so much about this. Then they had gone to her chamber. For a moment, at her door, Travis had hesitated. After all, he didn't know this woman. She seemed to be someone here in this world, someone important. What was he doing even talking to her? He should get back to his own room before Melia noticed he was gone. Yet in that same way two Americans—who would have passed each other without speaking on any New York street—could become instant friends when meeting in a Paris café, he felt an instant connection with this woman. He had taken a breath and stepped through her open door.

"I'm Grace Beckett," she said. "I'm from Denver."

Only when she spoke these words did he realize they had been staring at each other for well over a minute.

"Travis," he said. "Travis Wilder. And I . . ." Saying it seemed to emphasize the impossibility of it all. "I'm from Castle City. It's a small town up in the . . ."

Grace nodded. ". . . the mountains. Of course, it makes perfect sense. Where else would you be from?"

"You know it?"

She moved to a sideboard and picked up a pewter flagon. "I hope you want a drink, because I certainly do. And this time I'll pour."

Travis scratched the back of his neck. "I'm sorry about that, too."

"Don't be. It doesn't matter. Here, drink."

She pushed a goblet into his hand. He gripped the cup in two hands and took a sip. Cool smoke and warm cherries. No peasant's wine for her. He gulped the rest of it down.

"Thanks," he said, breathless.

Grace paced before the fireplace now, her violet gown whispering like secret voices. She seemed at home in the garment—assured, even regal—far more at ease than he felt in his rough tunic after a month of living inside it. Was she really from Earth? Yet she had to be—there was no other answer.

"Have you been here long?" he said. "In Eldh, I mean." The question sounded absurd, but she would understand.

"Just under a month." She locked her green-gold eyes on him. They were vivid and striking. "It's been the same for you, hasn't it?"

Travis nodded, amazed again. How did she know?

"We probably met Brother Cy on the same night. It's the simplest answer. One thing I've learned as a doctor, the simplest diagnosis is almost always the right one."

"I don't think there's anything simple about this."

She took a gulp of her own wine. Now she did look unnerved. Somehow that made him feel better.

"No," she said. "No, I don't suppose there is."

She gestured for him to sit by the fire. It felt a little strange. They were both from Colorado—there was no reason he should be uncomfortable with her. Yet she was dressed like a noble lady, and he wore the clothes of a commoner. It was hard not to slip into the role ascribed by one's costume. He forced himself to sit, and she took the chair opposite him.

"So, who should go first?" he said with a nervous laugh.

"This is my chamber, so that makes you my guest," she said. "I'm not really used to entertaining, but I suppose you should go first. That would be polite, wouldn't it?"

She looked at him, her expression truly uncertain, which he found odd.

"All right," he said. "I'll start."

Grace smoothed her gown, obviously relieved.

Travis thought a moment. Where could he possibly begin? He opened his mouth, and to his surprise words came to him.

"It all started when I heard bells."

When he finished she said nothing. She only stared into the fire. He started to fear she would not speak at all, then she spoke in a quiet voice.

"I've seen it, too."

He clutched the arms of the chair.

"The symbol." She looked up at him. "The one that looks like an eye. I saw a man in a black robe carving it into a door in the castle."

"A Raven cultist," he said, more to himself than her. So they were here, too, in this castle. That couldn't be good. "Maybe you'd better tell your story now, Grace."

She nodded, then licked her lips. "I was in the Emergency Department at Denver Memorial. I'm a—I mean, I was—a resident there. It was just a night, like any other night. A few burn victims, that was all. Then I met the girl in the park, the girl with purple eyes."

A chill coursed up his spine. "Child Samanda," he whispered.

"So that's her name." She drew in a deep breath, then continued her story.

By the time Grace was done the fire had burned low on the hearth. Travis closed his eyes a moment, trying to take it all in—the man with the heart of iron, Hadrian Farr of the Seekers, Grace's own flight into the mountains, and her wintry rescue by the knight Durge.

"So they think you're a duchess." He couldn't help a wry smile. "And here I get mistaken for a servingman."

Grace bit her lip and shrugged. "Sorry."

Travis shook his head. It was hardly her fault, and he was glad to have met her. Yet in some ways it had been easier when he was the only one, the only Earthling on Eldh. Easier to believe it was just some fluke, or that maybe he was dreaming, or lying in a padded cell somewhere hugging himself inside a straitjacket. Now he had met another traveler from Earth, and that changed everything. If he wasn't the only one, then it couldn't be a dream, and it couldn't be chance. There had to be a reason they had sent him here, and her as well—the dark ones at the revival.

Travis stood—he felt trapped. He rushed to the window and threw it open. Frosty air billowed into the chamber. He should have asked Grace if she minded, but he wanted to feel the wind against his face.

No, he *needed* to feel it, to feel that sense of possibility, that maybe everything would be all right somehow. He gulped in the cold air, then turned to face her. "So what do you think we should do?"

She rose from her chair. "I don't know, Travis. I think . . . I think maybe this world needs us. Why else would we be here?"

They gazed at each other in silence, then a flat voice spoke a single word.

"Judgment."

Travis guessed his own expression was as shocked as hers. He didn't know where the word had come from, or what it meant. He hadn't even thought about it.

"It's late, Grace," he said. "I should go. We can talk more tomorrow—if you want to, that is. And I'd like to see the door you found, the one with the Raven symbol."

She shut her eyes, then opened them. "All right, Travis."

He moved to the door, and she opened the way for him. Then the door shut, and he was alone in the corridor outside. Travis listened to the silence of the castle. A crisp wedge of moonlight spilled through a high window onto the stone floor. He supposed Melia would be angry with him. Then again, what was new about that? With a bitter sort of half smile he turned to go.

A crash sounded from the other side of the door.

Travis turned back and stared at the flat plane of wood. There was another noise—sharp, like something breaking. Terror plunged a stake through his body, into the floor, and pinned him cold and rigid to the spot. What should he do? He didn't know. It was so hard to decide. . . .

A muffled scream pierced the wood and shattered Travis's paralysis like glass. Instinct replaced indecision. He threw his body against the door, ignored the bright flash of pain in his shoulder, and burst into Grace's room.

It scuttled toward her from the open window. Travis's first reaction was to turn his head and vomit. The creature was utterly alien. The only image his groping mind could hold on to was that of a blurred juxtaposition of a wolf and a monkey. The thing was malformed, like a breeding experiment gone awry, its limbs twisted and trailing lank hair.

Despite its ungainly shape it moved quickly, alternating between loping on all fours and hobbling on its hind legs. The thing stretched spindly arms toward Grace and opened a blunt muzzle to display a mouthful of fangs. Fey light shone in its round eyes. It had backed her into a corner. Spittle flowed from its mouth.

"Hey!" Travis waved his arms. "Over here!"

It was a stupid thing to say, but there wasn't time to think of anything witty. Grace looked up, shock written on her face, and the creature whirled around, hissing. Now that he had its attention he wasn't sure he wanted it. He fumbled for the stiletto at his belt—the gem blazed with crimson light—but before he could draw the blade the creature sprang onto the high four-poster bed and peered down at Travis. He could not rip his gaze from it. The thing licked the mucus from its muzzle with a gray tongue and tensed its hind legs.

"Travis—run!"

Grace's shout spurred him to action. He stumbled to the side, barely out of the thing's path. A hot line sliced down his arm where its claw caught him. He tried to lurch around the farside of the bed, but a long arm snaked out, and thin, strong fingers caught his boot. He went down hard on the floor. The air rushed out of him with a painful grunt, and a fetid scent washed over him. He gagged and managed to roll over.

The creature crouched above him. Its matted hair brushed his face. He gazed into its eyes—they were hungry, and tortured, and horribly intelligent. Then it lunged for his throat.

Before teeth contacted flesh, the creature squealed and fell back. Dark blood oozed from a wound in its side. Travis jerked his head up. The iron poker that had been propped on the hearth a moment ago now dropped from Grace's hands. She watched as, enraged, the creature sprang toward her.

Now Travis did have time to grab his stiletto. In one swift motion that surprised even him, he pulled himself to his knees and brought the knife down. The Malachorian steel sank easily into the thing's flesh. It let out a shriek and arched its back. However, the blow had missed its spine. It whirled and jerked the knife from Travis's hand. Twisted as he was on the floor there was no way to move quickly enough. He braced himself for the sensation of fangs ripping into his throat.

The beast went limp and, without a sound, slumped to the floor.

Travis looked up. Grace stood behind the creature, her face a marble mask, her hand smeared with black ichor. The hilt of a small knife protruded from the thing's neck. With anatomical precision she had slipped the blade into the base of its skull and up into its brain.

"I guess medical school paid off," Travis managed to say.

Grace only gave a jerky nod.

The sound of booted feet rang out. Travis staggered to his feet in time to see several figures rush into the room. First was the dark-haired knight Durge, followed by Beltan, Falken, and Melia.

"By the blood of the Bull!" Beltan said. "Are you safe, Travis?" He gripped Travis's arm to steady him.

"I'm all right," Travis said.

"No, you're not," the blond knight said, the line of his jaw hard. "You're bleeding."

Travis managed a wan smile. "It goes with the territory. Wasn't that what you said?"

Beltan scowled. "You're not a knight, Travis. I am. I should have been here."

Travis didn't know what to say. He was just grateful for the big knight's grip.

Durge had moved to Grace. Now he saw the blood on her hand, and his brown eyes widened in dismay. "My lady! You bleed as well. And it is a fatal wound, no doubt." He sank to his knees before her and bowed his head. "It is my fault, of course. You cannot possibly forgive me, and now it is too late."

Grace let out a breath, and her trembling ceased. "Durge, I'm not going to die. It's not even my own blood. I'm fine."

The Embarran knight looked up at her, blinked, then cleared his throat. "Oh. Well, then. I am glad you are safe, my lady." He stood and glanced at Beltan. "But like my fellow knight, I should have been here."

Melia breezed past the two warriors with a soft rustle. "Actually, it seems Travis and the Lady Grace did well enough without you two."

Travis glanced at Grace. Impossible, but somehow they both managed to exchange a smile.

A thought occurred to Travis. "Melia, how did you all know to find us here?"

The small lady gave him a sharp look. "When you did not return to our chamber, Falken, Beltan, and I set out to discover what had become of you. Nearby we ran into Sir Durge, who was on his way to call on the Lady Grace."

Travis frowned. Something about this story didn't add up. "But how did you know I would be here, in Grace's chamber?"

Melia only arched an eyebrow and said nothing. Travis knew not to press the point.

Falken knelt beside the hairy tangle of the dead creature, and Melia followed him.

"How can this be?" she said with a furrowing of her brow.

"Feydrim," Falken said in disgust. He stood again.

Melia cupped her chin in a hand. "First wraithlings, now feydrim." She regarded the bard. "What creature is going to step out of legend next to trouble us?"

"I don't know. And why was it even here?"

Now Melia turned her amber gaze on Grace. "Perhaps Lady Grace can tell us that."

There was a long moment of silence as all turned their attention on Grace. She stood frozen, a deer in the headlights of an oncoming car. Travis decided he was steady enough. He moved away from Beltan to the sideboard and poured a cup of wine. He took it to Grace and pressed it into her hands.

"It looks like someone isn't happy about your playing the king's spy," he said.

Grace could only nod as she gulped down the wine.

68.

Dawn slipped over Castle Calavere, hard and gray as a knight's mail coat. Through a crack in the shutters that covered the window, Grace watched the dawn come. She had not slept.

Hours earlier, after Travis and the others had left her alone, Durge had said he would stand outside her door for the remainder of the night. The knight's offer had embarrassed her, but not so much that she hadn't accepted. It dulled the edge of her panic to know the somber Embarran stood, greatsword ready, just on the other side of the wall. However, rest was an impossibility. Grace's eyes flickered to the wardrobe. How could she rest knowing that *thing* was in there?

She tried not to picture it but could not stop herself: its fur—like the rank, mossy coat of a tree sloth—and its spindly limbs, curled beneath it as if it were merely sleeping. She had started to protest when Falken told the knight Beltan to put the dead creature in the wardrobe, then she had bit her tongue. After all, she could understand the bard's interest. She was a scientist. She knew the value of a rare specimen, knew that it had to be saved and protected.

Then again there was a difference between an abnormal organ floating in a jar of fixative in a medical laboratory and the still-warm carcass of a creature that had tried to rip her throat out with three-inch fangs.

She shivered. *You should get the fire going, Grace. It would be a little ironic if you survived an attack by some mythical creature only to freeze to death because you were too stupid to put a log on the coals.*

Bare feet soundless against rough carpet, she padded to the fireplace and tried not to notice the sticky substance on the end of the poker as she stirred the embers.

Once the fire was going Grace opened the chamber's window, lifted the bar from the shutters, and threw them back. Durge had closed the shutters last night, but she supposed it was safe enough now to open them. Wasn't it?

She leaned out the window, looked down, and breathed in air tasting like sooty snow. It was a long way down to the cobbles that paved the upper bailey, and the wall offered few cracks, fewer ledges, and no vines. Yet somehow the creature had climbed up and crawled in her window. She leaned back and pulled the casement shut.

Now what? It was still early, and the serving maids would not come by with breakfast for at least an hour. She decided she might as well get dressed. Not that there was any rush. Today was the first day of Valdath. The Council of Kings was to convene this midmorning. The nobles in the castle would be far too busy to speak with her. However, if she was lucky, she might get a chance to talk with Travis Wilder.

Then again, her record with her fellow Earthling was dismal to this point. First she had insulted him, then she had nearly gotten him killed. Experience told her she should just leave him alone. Yet she wanted to know more about the symbol she had seen carved on the door—the symbol he had said belonged to the Raven Cult. And about his conversations with Brother Cy and the purple-eyed girl, Child Samanda.

Grace moved to the chair where her gowns were heaped. At least Beltan had had the courtesy to take her clothes out of the wardrobe before he stuffed the body in. She chose a yellow gown she had not worn before, partly because the color was bright and cheerful, and mostly because it rested on top of the stack.

She was still adjusting the gown—a task that seemed never-ending—when she heard the sound of voices outside her door. One was gentle and lilting, the other a solemn baritone. The voices fell silent, then the door burst open, and something blue rushed into the room.

"Oh, Grace, I'm so sorry . . . if only I had known! Please tell me you're well!"

Aryn's pretty face was distraught, and her cornflower eyes bright with alarm. She ran and caught Grace in the half circle of her left arm. Durge stood in the doorway, his usual stony expression altered by a touch of surprise.

"I apologize, Lady Grace," he said. "I should have knocked before Her Highness opened the door."

Grace embraced her friend—

Yes, my friend. Is that so impossible?

—and shot the knight a wry smile over Aryn's shoulder.

"It's all right, Durge. You were supposed to guard against monsters, not baronesses. You've done more than I ever could have asked. I'm grateful—thank you."

The knight gave a stiff bow.

Grace pushed Aryn away. She led the baroness to the window bench, and in calm words described what had happened the night before. Aryn's face grew paler as she listened, and she gripped Grace's hand.

"You were so brave," the baroness said after Grace finished. "I don't think I could have done what you did."

Grace's gaze dropped to the swath of blue cloth that draped Aryn's shoulder and hid her withered arm. No, it was Aryn who was the brave one.

"Still, I don't understand. Certainly this thing was sent to harm you and no other." The baroness chewed her lip. "But why?"

It was a good question. "I'm not sure, but I think maybe it has to do with my spying for the king."

Now Aryn sighed. "That could be. It is hardly common for an assassin to be sent to do away with one who has learned too much at court, but it is not unheard of either—although I should think it far more likely to happen in Castle Spardis in Perridon than here in Calavere." Aryn's eyes flickered to the closed wardrobe. "Yet even in Spardis, where every sort of skullduggery is practiced, I doubt they have ever witnessed an assassin like the one you describe. Who could have sent such a thing to harm you, Grace?"

"I think I can tell you that."

Grace and Aryn looked up to see the bard Falken stride into the room. Behind him came Lady Melia, the knight Beltan, and, clad in the same shapeless tunic as the day before, Travis Wilder. Grace rose to her feet and glanced at Durge, who still stood beside the open door.

"No monsters, my lady," he said. "Only Falken Blackhand and his companions."

She slapped a hand to her forehead. "Yes, Durge. Of course. Thank you." Grace made a mental note. Perhaps a few more instructions wouldn't hurt the next time Durge offered to stand outside her door.

Aryn rose beside Grace. "Lord Falken." Her words were breathless but bold. "The Lady Grace has told me what transpired here last night, yet I warrant King Boreas has heard nothing of it. We must tell him at once."

Melia glided past the bard, toward the baroness. "Indeed? Must we?"

Aryn took an unconscious step back, even though she was the taller of the two and royalty. "Of course! The king must know of violence that has occurred in his own keep."

Melia said nothing, her coppery visage as unreadable as it was beautiful.

"Don't worry, Lady Aryn," Falken said. "I plan on telling Boreas about the feydrim—him and all the other kings and queens. The Council of Kings needs to make a decision, and I'm hoping the body of this thing will help convince them of that. But it's important the other rulers don't think Boreas knew about it first, that he had information they didn't. They all have to decide together in this." The bard fixed his faded blue eyes on Aryn. "Will you agree, Your Highness?"

Aryn shook her head. "I don't . . . but the king . . . I really should . . ."

Grace reached out, took Aryn's good hand in her own, and gripped it. "No, Aryn, don't tell Boreas. Not just yet."

Aryn stared at her. Grace was surprised herself. It wasn't as if she knew the bard. Yet maybe she did a little, through the things Travis had told her. Certainly Falken was wise and knew things the others didn't. She kept her gaze on Aryn, then the baroness let out a breath and nodded. Grace squeezed her hand.

Falken grinned—he really was handsome in a wolfish sort of way—and made a bow toward Aryn. Then the bard glanced at Beltan. "Why don't you retrieve our little friend?"

Beltan moved to the wardrobe. Grace didn't want to look, but she craned her neck all the same as Beltan pulled the wardrobe's doors open.

It was empty.

"By all the Old Ones!" Falken swore, then he looked at Grace. "Did anyone come to your chamber last night? Anyone at all?"

Grace fumbled for words. "No—no one. I was awake all night."

"No visitors came to Her Radiance's door until yourselves," Durge said. "And I barred her window myself."

"Yet it is gone all the same," Melia said. She ran a slender hand over the wood of the wardrobe, as if feeling for something, although for what Grace couldn't guess.

"But who could have taken it?" Falken said.

"Maybe *he* did."

Everyone looked up. It was Travis who had spoken. He had been silent the whole while, but now he stepped forward. His gray eyes were strange behind his spectacles: distant, afraid.

"Who do you mean, Travis?" Grace said. "Who took it?"

He flexed his right hand—the arm rested in a sling. Grace had bandaged the cut from the feydrim herself. It had not looked serious, but she did not want to take a chance with infection, not in this world.

"*Him.* The Pale King. In Imbrifale."

Grace did not understand these words, but they sent a chill up her spine all the same.

Travis looked at the bard. "Wasn't this thing one of *his* servants? Like . . . like the others, at the White Tower?"

Falken gave a slow nod. Travis pressed his eyes shut.

"Wait a minute," Beltan said. "What's this?" The knight bent and retrieved something from the bottom of the wardrobe. He stood, and Grace gasped. In his hand was a sprig of evergreen.

She didn't remember stumbling, didn't remember Durge catching her in strong, rough hands and easing her into the chair by the fire, didn't remember Aryn pressing a cup of wine into her hand. The next thing she knew she was talking, the words tumbling out of her, as she spoke of the night she had awakened to the sound of bells, how she had wandered the castle and had spied small footprints in the snow, and had returned to her chamber to find on her pillow . . .

Grace lifted the sprig of evergreen from her lap. "A servingwoman I met . . . she spoke of Little People in the castle. I thought somehow . . ." She looked up at Falken. "But that's foolish, isn't it? They couldn't have taken the body, could they? The Little People?"

Neither Falken nor Melia said anything.

Beltan looked from one to the other, then groaned. "But that's ridiculous! I'm all for stories, and I believe more of them than is probably good for me, but even I know the Little People are a myth."

Melia cast her piercing gaze on the knight. "A myth like wraithlings and feydrim?"

The blond knight blinked, opened his mouth, then evidently thought better of it. He slunk to the fringes of the room.

"There might be more truth to the Lady Grace's words than she knows," Falken said.

Grace clutched her wine to keep from spilling it. "How do you mean?"

Falken rubbed his chin with a hand—the one with the black glove. "The feydrim are monsters, you've seen that, but they were not always so. They were Little People once—gnomes and greenmen, dwarfs and fairies. The children of the Old Gods were queer. They could be ugly as they were beautiful, and their mirth was often cruel, but they were not evil. Not until the Pale King imprisoned some of them and his Necromancers twisted them for his own use."

"The Pale King?"

Falken moved to the fire, scarlet light played across his face. "A thousand years ago, the Pale King rode forth from Imbrifale, a sea of feydrim behind him, and nearly conquered all of Falengarth. Now the prison that holds him grows weak. That is what I came to tell the council."

Grace lifted the sprig to her nose and breathed its wild forest scent. Her mind cleared a bit, and she glanced at the bard. "You say the feydrim was a slave of the Pale King, Falken. But why would the Pale King send one of his servants to . . . to kill me?"

It was Melia who answered. "Only if they stood together would the Dominions have a chance of defeating the Pale King were he to ride forth again. I imagine he desires nothing more than to see the Dominions divided against each other. It seems King Boreas hopes the knowledge you gain will help him unify the council in war. That is exactly what the Pale King cannot allow."

No, that wasn't enough. Grace crossed her arms, hugged her chest. "But how did it . . . how did *he* know to find me here?"

Beltan gripped the hilt of the sword at his hip. "That is something I would like to know. There isn't a castle in all the Dominions stronger than Calavere. I don't like how easily that thing got in here."

A shudder coursed through Grace. There was so much to sort out, and she needed help. She looked up at Travis. "I was hoping . . . while the council convenes . . . maybe we could . . ."

He started to nod.

"Oh!" Aryn clapped her hand to her cheek. "I completely forgot. Grace, you have to get ready. That's why I came here this morning. King Boreas has requested your presence at the council."

She glanced at Aryn. "But I was going to talk with . . ." It was no use. She looked again at Travis, but he had already turned his back and stepped through the door.

"I'll be ready," was all she said.

69.

Travis surveyed the council chamber—crowded with lords and ladies—and felt utterly out of place.

He hadn't expected to be here. After they had left Grace's chamber, Melia and Falken had headed down the corridor without so much as glancing at him. No doubt they had plans to make for the Council of Kings. Plans he was not a part of. He had started back to his own room, then a big hand on his shoulder had halted him.

"Come on, Travis," Beltan had said. "The council is this way."

He had been too stunned to protest, and had followed the blond knight through the castle.

The council chamber was contained within one of Calavere's nine towers, at the end of the main keep's west wing. At first there had been some difficulty getting Travis inside.

"Commoners are not allowed in the Council of Kings," a man-at-arms had said, eyeing Travis's shabby tunic. He had held his halberd across the doorway.

Beltan's voice had dropped to a perilous growl. "Do you make some comment about my parentage, captain?"

The man-at-arms had taken a step back. "No, Lord Beltan! I meant no such thing. I was referring to your . . . to your companion. He is not . . . that is, he does not appear to be noble, and . . ."

Beltan had waved a hand, silencing the man-at-arms. "First of all, he's more noble than most of the lords in this chamber. Second, it wouldn't matter if he were the basest servant. He's with me. Do you really want to argue about it?"

Blood had drained from the other's face, and he had moved his halberd aside. "There's a space waiting for you over there, Lord Beltan," was all he had said.

Travis had shot Beltan a stunned look—he had never heard the knight speak in such a hard manner. But Beltan already had been moving. Travis had given the man-at-arms a sheepish look, then had followed Beltan into the council chamber.

Now, from his seat, Travis gazed around. The chamber was ringed with tiers of stone benches like a Greek amphitheater. The benches were crowded with nobles who, by their varying manner of dress, represented all seven of the Dominions, and every moment more nobles poured through the doorway. In the center of the chamber was a circular table hewn of dark stone. Around the table were a number of chairs, and embedded in the center of its surface was a disk of paler stone, incised with an angular shape. Travis recognized the symbol from his studies with Falken. It was *Var*, the rune of peace:

He glanced at the knight who sat next to him on the stone bench. "Thanks, Beltan. For vouching for me, I mean."

Beltan gazed forward. "There is more to being noble than who whelped you." He drew in a deep breath, turned toward Travis, and grinned. "Besides, I always enjoy ruffling a few feathers."

Travis did his best to grin back. Whatever melancholy had gripped the big knight the day before, it seemed to have loosened its hold a bit—but it was not gone altogether. Beltan looked *different* somehow.

More serious. But maybe it was just his clothes. He had changed into fine but understated garb of green, and he had shaved his beard, leaving only a line of gold above and on either side of his mouth.

Travis let his gaze wander back over the chamber. He counted the chairs around the council table, then frowned. "I thought there were only seven Dominions in Falengarth, Beltan."

"That's right."

"So why are there eight chairs at the table?"

"The eighth chair is for the king of Malachor."

Travis's frown deepened. "Malachor? But I thought Falken said Malachor fell ages ago."

"Yes, it's over seven centuries since a king sat on the throne of Malachor, and almost as long since anyone dwelt within that land's borders."

Travis scratched his red-brown beard. It was getting wild. "Seven hundred years. That seems like an awfully long time to keep setting a place at the table."

Beltan laughed. "Yes, but it's tradition. The Dominions have always looked to the memory of Malachor for their heritage, even as they try to match its lost glory. So they keep a chair at the table, to honor the past, and to invoke its greatness—perhaps in hope a little rubs off on them."

Travis gazed at the empty chair. It was carved of silvery wood like the other chairs at the table and inlaid with stones and leather. However, its edges were sharper, the leather less worn and polished. It reminded him of the artifacts he had seen at the Magician's Attic in Jack's secret room. The other chairs had been used for centuries, but not this one.

"Will anyone ever sit in it?"

"The stories say a witch cursed the chair long ago, and that any who dares to sit in it will be struck dead, unless he is the true heir to Malachor."

Travis looked at the knight. "That doesn't really answer my question."

Beltan shrugged his rangy shoulders. "I don't hold much stock in witches or curses, but I suppose only a fool would sit in Chair Malachor. Or a legend come to life—and despite what Falken might say, the first is a great deal more common than the second."

Travis couldn't argue with that.

A horn sounded, a hush fell over the crowd, and everyone stood as the kings and queens of the Dominions entered the chamber. Beltan leaned over and whispered their names in Travis's ear as each approached the table.

First came Queen Eminda of Eredane, her bearing more proud than regal. She was followed by Lysandir of Brelegond, or at least a moving heap of brocade and jewels in which Travis supposed there was room enough to conceal a royal person. Next came a gaunt man with sunken eyes whom Beltan named Sorrin, King of Embarr. Ancient King Persard of Perridon came next, and after him King Kylar of Galt. As he entered, the young king of Galt tripped on a fold in the carpet that seemed to have appeared only as he approached. Lord Alerain, King Boreas's seneschal, dashed out to help him to his feet, and Kylar waved as he stood to indicate he was unharmed. A sigh of relief ran about the chamber.

The sigh became a gasp when a woman as radiant as sun on ice stepped into the room. Travis watched, transfixed, as Queen Ivalaine of Toloria glided to her place at the table. Her gown was the color of shadows on snow at twilight, and white gems frosted her hair. In contrast to the ethereal Tolorian queen, King Boreas stalked into the chamber like a bull. However, he was as handsome as he was fierce, and commanded attention as surely as Ivalaine did. Travis had a feeling he would do anything Boreas told him to do. He suspected most people did.

The rulers each stood behind his or her chair, then each lifted a hand to the breast and bowed his or her head toward the eighth and empty chair. The kings and queens lifted their heads, and Boreas spoke, the thrum of his voice rising to the rafters high above.

"Let the rune of beginning be spoken!"

From opposite edges of the room, two men in mist-colored robes approached the stone table. Eminda of Eredane watched them with suspicious eyes. One of the robed men was older, his face severe and his gray hair shorn close. The other was younger, short and obviously muscular beneath his robe, his face broad and cheerful. They stopped short of the table, bowed in unison, and rose. Then, as one, they spoke a single word.

"*Syr!*"

The word echoed around the chamber like a note of music: clear and thrilling. Travis's right hand tingled, and he could feel the magic that had been released by the speaking of the rune, could *see* it. The air in the chamber shimmered, like the air over a hot desert highway. . . .

Travis adjusted his spectacles. The air in the chamber was still once more. The runespeakers were already walking away from the table. He flexed his hand. The tingle had faded into an itch. However, he knew it would not fully vanish. It never did. The power was always there, waiting. He wondered. What might he look like in a soft robe all of gray?

Travis returned to the moment. Boreas was speaking again. ". . . and the shadows that threaten not just one Dominion, but each of them, and all of Falengarth besides. Thus this Council of Kings has been summoned, under the aegis of all laws and traditions, and thus you have journeyed here to Calavere. You are well met, each and every one."

Boreas picked up a large chalice from the table. It was filled with crimson wine. "I ask that we each drink from this cup," the black-bearded king said. "It is a relic of Malachor, and in drinking from it we will remember the legacy of the tower that shines no more. And also we will show that we are one in our desire to challenge the darkness that would challenge us."

Some of the rulers shifted from foot to foot, notably Lysandir of Brelegond. Not everyone agreed with Boreas's sentiment.

Boreas took a drink from the cup, then passed it to his right, to Kylar. The young Galtish king took a sip, managing to spill a little bit on the table, which he dabbed at with the corner of his cloak after passing the cup on. Travis watched with interest as the other rulers drank from the chalice. Sorrin of Embarr took the scantest of sips, while Lysandir drank deepest, but without any sense of ceremony, as if he simply needed the wine. He passed the cup to Eminda.

The queen of Eredane frowned into the cup, as if she expected to see a dead rat in it, or perhaps the taint of poison. The other rulers watched her, and Lysandir fidgeted with the edge of his frilly tunic. The chamber held its breath. Still Eminda did not drink.

Boreas spoke in a voice that, although low, filled the great space. "Know all of you that the rune of peace rests at the center of this table. It was bound into the stone long ago, when the art of runebinding was still known to the world. Because of the rune's magic no act of violence can be done in this hall, either openly or deceitfully, no matter how strong the hand that would attempt it."

Eminda shot a black look at the king of Calavan. Travis guessed she cared little for his reassurance. She lifted the chalice, took a small, swift sip, and shoved it toward Ivalaine. Somehow the Tolorian queen managed to accept the cup smoothly. She drank, like a swan bending its neck to the surface of a lake, and passed the cup to Boreas. He lifted it high, then set it back on the table, and his voice rang off the stones.

"The Council of Kings has begun!"

The rulers took their seats, and those watching did the same. Travis leaned toward Beltan. "I don't get the feeling Queen Eminda cares much for Boreas."

Beltan gave a snort. "That's like saying oil has a slight dislike for its old friend water. But she seems thick enough with Lysandir."

"If you say so. I'm not convinced there's actually anybody *in* all those clothes."

Beltan grinned and gripped Travis's hand. The gesture surprised Travis, but he was glad for the contact. Maybe he was nobody in this world, but at least he had one friend—royal or not. He returned the grip on the knight's big hand, and they stayed that way for a while.

A shrill voice pierced the chamber air. "Well, Boreas." Eminda glared at the king of Calavan. "Now that you've convened this council, perhaps you will deign to tell us the reason why. We've all suffered hard winters and brigands before. I can hardly imagine that's the only reason you've forced us all to journey here. Or has Calavan grown so weak that a few robber barons have cast the Dominion under a pall of terror?"

The air pressure in the chamber seemed to change as everyone drew in a breath. Even from a distance Travis could see Boreas's knuckles go white as he gripped the edge of the council table. Eminda was wasting no time. Boreas opened his mouth to speak, but his words were drowned out by a crash as the chamber's double doors burst open. All eyes turned as a figure strode into the hall.

It was Falken.

Several men-at-arms approached, halberds raised, but at a glare from the bard they fell back. Travis had never seen Falken like this. The air of weariness and melancholy he usually wore was gone. Now his eyes flashed like lightning in a clear blue sky.

"What's he doing?" Travis whispered to Beltan.

"Besides making that vein on Boreas's forehead explode? I think we're going to find out."

Boreas rose to his feet, his coal-black eyebrows merged into one brooding line of anger. "You are going to tell me the meaning of this insolence, Falken Blackhand. And then you are going to leave, before I have to put the rune of peace to the test."

Falken stood before the table. In his hand was an object wrapped in a cloth. "As a citizen of Malachor, I invoke my power to speak to the council."

The rulers exchanged questioning glances. Boreas slapped a hand down on the table: thunder. "You will do no such thing, Falken Blackhand! The council will not allow it!"

Falken did not so much as flinch. "Yes it will, Your Majesty. It is my due and privilege. I have lost my home, and I have lost my hand, but this you cannot deny me, King Boreas. None of you can. Ask your Lord Alerain. He knows the ancient laws better than any other."

Boreas glanced at his seneschal, who stood against the far wall. Alerain gave a reluctant nod. The king of Calavan let out a grunt and returned his glare to Falken.

This didn't make any sense. Hadn't Beltan just said Malachor fell seven hundred years ago? But maybe Falken was one of the few who could trace his lineage directly back to the ancient kingdom.

Boreas spoke, his voice a low growl. "Very well, Falken. It seems the council cannot forbid you to speak, but neither will it forget your actions this day."

"Nor should it. Let these words I say ring on in your minds, so they are with you always. For the twenty kings before you have not faced such dark times as you do, King Boreas of Calavan—not even Calavus the Great."

The bard drew the cloth from the object in his hands and slammed the thing down on the table. It was *Krond*, the broken seal from the Rune Gate. Falken's voice rose like a call to arms to fill the chamber. "The Pale King has awakened!"

There was a moment of perfect silence.

Then the Council of Kings erupted into chaos.

70.

Grace thought she had seen King Boreas angry before.

She was wrong. A babble of excited voices filled the council chamber, along with jeers and catcalls for the bard. Several of the rulers tried to speak, but their voices were lost in the roar. Boreas glared at Falken, and his eyes smoldered with an anger that was far greater than one mere man was capable of: the fury of a king. Even from where she sat—in the first tier of benches next to Aryn—Grace could see Boreas shaking. She expected him to spring to action at any moment and toss Falken aside, a mad bull goring a hapless matador.

Yet Falken did not flinch under the king's royal rage, even as the scorn of the onlookers grew in volume, and she started to think perhaps Boreas would not be able to dispatch the bard so easily. She knew the hard, impassive expression Falken wore. She had seen the same look countless times in the ED—in the eyes of children undergoing their fifth round of chemo, in the gazes of handsome young men who were far too thin, on the battered faces of women who had just shot their husbands. Something told her Falken had seen things neither she, nor King Boreas, nor anyone in this chamber could imagine.

The catcalls ended. The roar became a murmur, then a whisper. The nobles sank back to their benches. Even Boreas, although his visage remained angry, lowered himself into his chair. The interior of the tower fell silent.

Now all eyes gazed at the bard. Still Falken did not move. Misty gold light drifted down from the rafters above, along with a soft rustle: the wings of doves. Then another sound rose on the air. In a low but clear voice Falken began to sing:

> *"Lord of the sky—*
> *Where has the wind gone,*
> *that snapped my banners bold?*
> *Olrig, father,*
> *You have forsaken me.*
>
> *Lady of Eldh—*
> *Where lies your soft bower,*
> *in all its secret green?*
> *Sia, mother,*
> *Your soil shall cover me.*
>
> *Father, come!*
> *Mother, come!*
> *You have forsaken me."*

The bard's voice merged with the calls of the doves. Despite the press of wool-clad bodies around her, Grace shivered. She did not know what the bard sang of, but never before had she heard a song so forlorn. Next to her Aryn sobbed quietly, tears streaking her smooth cheeks. Grace might have cried, too, if that was something she thought she still knew how to do.

Falken lifted his head. "It is called *Ulther's Lament*, that song. Few remember it now, but King Ulther of Toringarth sang those words a thousand years ago. He sang them as he knelt in the scarlet-stained snow before the very door of Imbrifale—cold and wounded and beaten. A thousand lay dead around him. They were Wulgrim, or had been: wolf-warriors, the most fearsome fighters of Toringarth. With Ulther they had come across the Winter Sea, to stand before the Pale King. They had been cut down like so much chaff. Ten thousand more men lay dead in the vale of Shadowsdeep behind him, slain by a horde of feydrim that clawed, and bit, and tore at the bodies long after they fell, long after their screams ended. But such was the pain of the Pale King's servants. If the feydrim did not tear at another, then they would surely tear at themselves."

Falken began to walk now, and he paced around the council table as he spoke. "Save for a small guard of men—his remaining earls, his standard-bearer, his fool—Ulther was alone. He had failed. None would stand against the Pale King now. Falengarth was lost. And even as he thought this in despair, he looked up, and through the Gap of Teeth he looked into the land of Imbrifale and saw the Pale King coming."

Falken's voice rose, until it filled the tower to the rafters. The doves flew from their roosts, out high windows, into blue shards of sky.

"On a black horse he rode, its hooves striking sparks against the stony ground, but the Pale King himself was white from head to toe. Three lights gleamed on his snowy breast: one gray, one blue, one red. These were the three Great Stones, set into the iron necklace Imsaridur, which he stole from the dark elfs. With its magic the Pale King could enslave all of Falengarth. And all of Eldh after that. Nothing stood in his way. Only one broken king, and a handful of men, and a fool with crooked legs who sang of stupid goodmen and bold goodwives even as his tears fell to the ground and froze there."

Falken paused, and another voice spoke: deep, gruff. It was Boreas. Anger no longer colored his face, but his expression was hard nonetheless. "You tell a sad tale, Falken. But then telling tales is your trade, and one at which you excel. What do your words have to do with this council?"

"Everything." Falken brushed his fingers over the broken rune and continued his tale. "In dread Ulther watched the Pale King ride near. His heart turned to ice. Here was his doom, and all the world's. Then a radiance shone upon him. Across the battlefield three fairies drifted toward the king. They were tall and slender, shining as starlight, and clad all in gossamer. When he looked upon them his fear was replaced by wonder, and the king of Toringarth bowed his head.

" 'The Pale King comes,' the three light elfs spoke. 'Yet still it is not too late. Lift up your sword, Lord Ulther, and hold it before you.'

"Such was his awe that Ulther did as the fair ones bid. He gripped his sword Fellring, forged in the same dwarfin smithies as the magic necklace Imsaridur, and held the bloody blade before him. As he did the fairies clasped each other and, as one, threw themselves upon Fellring. Ulther cried out in dismay, but it was too late. The three had been pierced through. Yet the fairies did not shed blood. Instead a brilliant light welled forth from their wounds, so bright Ulther was forced to turn his head. When at last he looked again the light elfs were gone, and Fellring—stained by blood no longer—shone as if it had been forged anew from the stuff of stars.

"There was time no more for wonder, for then the Pale King was upon him, his steed snorting fire. Behind the Pale King stood thirteen whose faces were hidden by black hoods, and whose feet left no imprint on the snow. They were the Necromancers, the Pale King's wizards, who had forged his army of feydrim.

"With brave battle cries, Ulther's earls rushed forward, but the Pale King struck them down with his icy sword. The last to stand was Ulther's fool, still singing songs of good cheer for his master. Then he too fell, his song silenced, to spill his blood upon the snow. Now indeed was Ulther alone.

"Leaving his wizards, the Pale King approached. He did not fear Ulther, for such was the power of Imsaridur that no mortal hand might wound him, dark elfin blade or no. Nor did Berash have a mortal heart to pierce, for his had died long before, and had been replaced in his chest by an enchanted heart of cold, hard iron."

Grace drew in a hissing breath and sat up straight on her bench. Aryn gave her a puzzled glance, as did Durge and Melia, who sat just beyond the baroness. *No, it can't be! This is all a story. A myth. Damn it, a myth from a world that's not even Earth. It can't be the same, Grace. It can't.*

Even as she said these things to herself, Grace knew it *was* the same. Somehow the dead man in the ED, and Detective Janson—and the other ironhearts Hadrian Farr knew of—were connected to this world, to this story. But how? She gave Aryn's hand a squeeze to reassure the young baroness, even though her heart pounded in her throat, and leaned forward to hear the bard's story.

"The Pale King descended from his mount and stood above Ulther. Imsaridur blazed upon his breast. He lifted his sword to strike off Ulther's head.

" 'None can stand before me,' spoke the icy king.

" 'Then kneeling I shall strike you!' Ulther cried.

"The king of Toringarth gripped the hilt of Fellring and thrust up to smite the Pale King. Berash's white eyes flew wide. Enchanted by the sacrifice of the fairies, the shining sword sank into the Pale King's breast, and there it clove his iron heart in two. At the same moment Fellring shattered in Ulther's grip, and a great chill coursed up his arms, deep into his own breast, striking his own heart. The Pale King fell to the snowy field, but Ulther kept his feet, the broken hilt of Fellring in his hand. He stumbled to the Pale King and took the necklace Imsaridur from around his foe's throat. Then Ulther fell to his knees on the cold ground. He glimpsed the Necromancers approaching, their robes fluttering like black wings. Now his end would come.

"All at once a sound pierced the frigid air, high and clear: the sound of horns. The sun broke through the shroud of mist that hung over the vale, and the horde of feydrim, disheartened by the fall of their master, quailed before the light. The sun glinted off the tips of fifty thousand spears. Again the horns sounded, closer now, as a bright army marched into Shadowsdeep, led by a proud woman on a horse of white. Elsara, Empress of Tarras, had come at last. Ulther laughed, then fell forward and knew no more."

Falken's voice grew quiet, and the council chamber came back into focus. For a moment Grace had been there, in the snowy vale, and had seen the Pale King, colorless as ice upon his midnight horse. Yet the story couldn't be over, Falken hadn't finished.

"But how did it all end?"

In belated shock Grace realized the voice was her own. She had only meant to murmur the words, but such was the silence in the wake of the bard's tale that the words carried across the council chamber. Boreas glared at her, and Grace shriveled inside her gown.

"End?" Falken said. "How did it end? But the story did not end, my lady. It goes on even today, and now we are all players in it, whether we wish it or not. Without their master's magic to bind them, the feydrim were no match for Elsara's army. To the last they were destroyed. When Elsara reached the Gap of Teeth, she found Ulther in the snow, clutching the broken hilt of Fellring and the necklace Imsaridur. However, the Pale King was gone. The Necromancers had borne their fallen master back into Imbrifale.

"Although at first Elsara feared Ulther dead, he was not, and after many days under the care of her healers he was able to stand again. He walked back to the Gap of Teeth with a hundred runewielders, the strongest in all of Falengarth. With the help of Elsara's army they raised a great gate of iron across the door of Imbrifale, and the runewielders bound it with three powerful runes, so the Pale King and his servants might never ride forth again. The runewielders became the first of the Runelords, and Ulther gave them the necklace Imsaridur for safekeeping. Then came a hundred witches to Shadowsdeep, and they wove enchantments of illusion and madness over the mountains, so that none might cross into or out of Imbrifale that way.

"Finally, Ulther and Elsara forged a new kingdom to keep watch over Imbrifale, to make certain the dark Dominion never rose again. They set their children upon the throne in marriage, and thus was Malachor born. For a long age peace and light ruled Falengarth. For an age . . ."

Falken shook his head. "That age is over. Malachor fell centuries ago. The Runelords are no more. The Imsari, the three Great Stones that once graced Imsaridur, are scattered and lost. And now"—he pointed to the broken rune on the table—"now the Rune Gate weakens."

There was silence. Then—harsh and jarring—laughter.

It was Eminda of Eredane. "You tell a glorious tale, Falken Blackhand. For a moment I half fancied I believed it. However, if there is any enchantment here, it is simply the spell of your voice, and nothing more." Now the humor drained from her face, replaced by annoyance. "We are here to discuss real troubles that face the Dominions. We do not have time for tales meant to frighten children by the fire."

Other heads around the table and chamber nodded at this.

"Don't we?" Falken said, his voice rising. "Perhaps children have more sense than we. The Pale King stirs, there can be no doubt. The Dominions must take action, and take it swiftly. They must raise an army as strong as that of Ulther and Elsara of old, and they must do it now." Falken raised his black-gloved fist on high. "By the blood of Malachor in my veins, I demand a reckoning of the council!"

Eminda stood, her broad face crimson. "This is ridiculous!"

King Sorrin, who had hardly moved throughout the bard's tale, now lifted his head. His sunken eyes were unreadable. "Let the bard have his reckoning. Then we shall be done with it."

The other rulers nodded in agreement. Eminda sank back into her chair. Boreas motioned to Alerain, and the seneschal hurried over with a leather pouch. Boreas emptied the pouch onto the table. In it were seven white stones and seven black stones. He passed one stone of each color to each of the rulers.

"The question stands before this council whether to muster the Dominions for war," Boreas said. He held up his white stone. "White signifies agreement, and a mustering for war." The king lifted his black stone. "Black signifies disagreement."

Each of the rulers held their two stones beneath the table, then drew one out, hidden in the hand. They rested their hands on the table before them. Grace held her breath. She barely knew Falken, but his tale had affected her in a way she could not explain. She did not pretend to understand everything about this Pale King. However, she had seen a thing of evil—a man with a heart of iron in his chest—and she had seen the feydrim as well. She knew there was danger, and greater than any of them could imagine. However, as the kings and queens opened their hands, Grace knew before she saw each stone what color it would be.

On the open palms of Boreas, Kylar, and Persard rested a white stone: war. Revealed on the hands of Eminda, Lysandir, and Sorrin were stones of black: no muster. Only Ivalaine was a mystery to Grace. The beautiful queen of Toloria sat still, then she too opened her hand.

There was no stone upon it. "I abstain," Ivalaine said.

Boreas's eyes flashed in rage, but before he could speak Eminda stood.

"Then it is a deadlock," she said. "And a deadlock means no muster!"

Falken gazed at the queen of Eredane and the rest of the council. His face was gray and haggard. Grace started to reach out a hand, then snatched it back. What could she possibly do to help? If Falken could not sway the council, she hardly could. Falken gathered up the broken rune.

"Then there is no hope for Eldh," he said, and walked from the tower.

71.

The next morning, Durge came to Grace's chamber to teach her how to use the knife Aryn had given her.

"There has been one attack upon your person, my lady," the knight said when she opened the door. "That makes another all the more likely. I do not expect to let you far from my sight, but I cannot be with you every moment."

Grace gave a tight smile. "You could, Durge. I just don't think I'd appreciate you quite as much as I do now."

Durge stepped into her room and asked if he might see her knife. Grace gave it to him. She had cleaned the feydrim's blood from it, and its edge glinted in the sunlight streaming through the window. The knife was small, but its blade bore a sensual curve. It seemed alive, but then knives could be living things. Grace knew that from the ED. Sometimes a scalpel could jump out of her hand. Other times it seemed to guide her fingers, as if it knew better than she the incision that needed to be made.

"It is old and of a good make," Durge said. "As good as any blade from the forges of Embarr, although I would say this blade was fashioned here in Calavan. Third century after Founding I would hazard, which means it is nearly two hundred years old. Of course, it's been hafted to a new hilt since."

"How do you know all that, Durge?"

The knight shrugged. "I have a passing interest in metals and other elements, my lady. Do not be too impressed. Certainly my speculation is quite wrong."

Grace doubted that. She took the knife back and gazed at it with new wonder. How many hands had held it before her?

"One can study for years to learn how to wield a knife properly," Durge said, "and we have but a morning. However, I can teach you some moves and positions. They are simple enough, but they will make an enemy think twice about attacking you again."

Grace steeled her shoulders. "Show me."

For the next hour Grace concentrated, knife in her hand, as Durge showed her how to position her body to guard her most vulnerable areas—the stomach, the throat, the face. He taught her to make, not large slashes, but quick, short thrusts. The goal was not to kill the opponent, only to stick him, to slow him down, and make him hurt. That would give Grace time to run, or to call for aid.

By the end of the hour Grace's cheeks glowed with effort, and the shoulder of her knife arm ached. However, when Durge made a feint at her from behind, she was able to crouch quickly and thrust behind her.

A strong hand clamped around her wrist. "Very good, my lady."

She looked back over her shoulder. The tip of the knife was no more than an inch from Durge's thigh.

"I knew that blow was coming. Your enemy would not. I think he would have felt that sting."

Grace stood, her heart pounding, and grinned. Could she really do it? Could she really harm another to save herself? *Why not, Grace! You've done it before. Remember the baker in the lower bailey. And that was not the first time. That was not the first. . . .*

Her grin faded.

Durge cocked his head. "I think that is enough for today. You are a swift learner, my lady, although I would that I could teach you how to use a larger weapon. Even in close quarters, I prefer my great-sword . . ."

". . . but this is a little easier to fit in one's boot," Grace said. She bent and slipped the knife into the sheath inside her deerskin boot. It was foolish—she shouldn't let herself feel this way—but she *did* feel more confident with the knife snug against her skin.

She rose, and a thought occurred to her. "Durge, what does King Sorrin think of your spending so much time with me?"

Durge was in the act of strapping on his sword harness, which he had removed for their exercises. She could not see his face—only his broad back, his stooped shoulders.

"Do not concern yourself with Sorrin, my lady. I have pledged my sword to you, and in Embarr the word of a knight is stronger than steel, more enduring than stone."

Grace opened her mouth, but any words she might have uttered were preempted by a knock on the door.

"Grace!" Aryn said as she rushed into the room. "I'm so glad you're here. King Boreas wants to see you."

Grace crossed her arms over her gown—the paler lavender today. She had known it was only a matter of time before the king summoned her, although she had not expected it this soon. After the disastrous reckoning of the council yesterday, a recess had been called. She had thought Boreas would want to be alone with his thoughts.

Aloud she said to Aryn, "When did Boreas want to see me?"

"He said at once."

Grace swallowed hard. Boreas always assumed everyone would carry out his orders immediately. That he had specified *at once* did not bode well.

She glanced at Durge. "I think I'd better go."

"No, my lady. I think you had better run."

Moments later she and Aryn dashed through the corridors of the keep. Servants and petty nobles scurried to get out of their way. One red-cheeked page dropped a bowl of apples, and they went bouncing and rolling away across the floor. Grace shot him a look of chagrin as he ran after them. She hoped he wouldn't be beaten. However, if she didn't hurry, she wasn't sure her own fate would be any better. She thought Boreas was above throwing her over his knee and spanking her, but she wasn't perfectly certain.

"Do you think the king is still angry with me for asking Falken that question at the council yesterday?" she asked Aryn as they ran.

Aryn shot her a look that was halfway between smile and grimace. "Don't worry, Grace. There hasn't been a beheading at Calavere in months."

Grace didn't waste her breath with a response. She quickened her pace.

"My ladies, can you delay a moment in your haste?"

Grace and Aryn stopped as though they had hit an invisible wall. Nor was Grace so certain they hadn't. She may have lived her entire life in a democracy, but there was a power to royalty that could not be denied. They turned to gaze into the ice-blue eyes of Ivalaine, Queen of Toloria.

At once they affected hurried curtsies. "Your Majesty!"

"Rise," the queen said, and they did.

Ivalaine stood in an alcove, her arm resting upon a pedestal, as if she had been standing there for some time, waiting. But waiting for what?

Don't you mean waiting for whom, Grace?

She looked over the queen's shoulder and expected to see a flash of emerald. However, Kyrene was nowhere in sight. Only Tressa stood behind the queen, a serene expression on her plump, pretty face. The queen's lady-in-waiting looked like an angel. Except angels didn't have long red hair, did they? Grace returned her gaze to Ivalaine. On the pedestal against which the queen leaned was a bronze ewer filled with water, and next to it was a cup of horn. The medieval version of a drinking fountain.

"How can we assist you, Your Majesty?" Aryn said between gasps for breath.

"Drink," Ivalaine said. "You are thirsty."

Grace lifted a hand to her throat. Yes, she *was* thirsty, terribly so. Her throat burned with thirst. She took the cup, filled it from the ewer, and drank greedily. Aryn fairly snatched the cup from her hands and did the same. Grace wiped at her damp chin with the back of her hand. The water from the ewer had been cold and sweet, but already her throat was growing dry again. She started to reach for the cup. A slender hand on her wrist stopped her.

"The thirst is not so easily quenched, is it, my sister?"

Grace thought her touch would be like ivory, but instead the queen's hand against her own was warm and light, the touch of a bird. She could feel a pulse, like a tiny, fluttering heart.

Grace licked her lips. "We should go." Her voice was a croak. "King Boreas is waiting for us."

Aryn nodded. "The king." She could seem to speak no other words.

Ivalaine's gown was the color of water. The air seemed to ripple. "Look into the ewer," she said. "I think you will find something there."

"What do you think we will see?" Aryn said, but Ivalaine did not answer. She only watched, and her eyes glittered like secret gems.

Grace and Aryn peered into the water.

What are you doing, Grace? You have to go. Boreas is going to feed you to his mastiffs if you don't get moving. Besides, there's nothing in the water. . . .

Grace drew in a sharp breath. If there was nothing in the water, then she should have been able to see the bottom of the ewer. She couldn't. The inside of the vessel was black. The darkness claimed her vision, dragged her down, until she could see nothing else. A queasiness came over her, as though she drifted on a choppy ocean.

"I see a castle!"

It was Aryn's voice, although she sounded too far away. Her words were bright and excited, like a small girl's on her birthday, opening presents.

"There are seven towers—I can see them so clearly—and a hundred knights with banners tied to their lances. The banners are as blue as the sky. There's a woman riding before the knights, on a horse as white as clouds. She must be their queen. She's all in blue as well, with a sword belted at her side, and her dark hair streaming behind her on the wind. She's so proud, so proud and . . . oh!"

Aryn's words ended. What had she seen? Grace could not glimpse the castle or the proud queen. She saw only blackness.

No, that wasn't true. There was something in the blackness after all. They were faint, but she could see them. Hands. Some were long and slender. Others were thick and rough. They reached out, pale against the darkness. Dozens of them. Hundreds of them. And they were all reaching for her.

No!

The water in the ewer changed from black to crimson. Flames shot out of the darkness. Engulfed by the fire, the hands curled like dying spiders. She thought she heard screams. Then there was only the fire. Pure, hot, cleansing fire. . . .

"Lady Grace!"

The voice was stern but not alarmed. Grace snapped her head up. Next to her Aryn blinked, her expression bewildered. Ivalaine still watched them both, but now her gaze was calculating. Behind the queen Tressa nodded, a knowing look on her broad angel's face.

Aryn shook her head. "What . . . what happened?"

"There is a power in water, a life," the queen of Toloria said. "It has the ability to reflect both past and future, if one knows how to look." Ivalaine stepped toward them and caught their hands in her own. Her expression was exultant. "There can be no doubt of it now. The Touch runs strong in both of you."

Aryn cast a frightened look at Grace. Yet there was something else in the baroness's gaze. A hungry light. Grace tried to swallow—her throat burned with thirst.

"What if we don't want it?" she said. "What if we don't want this Touch?"

Ivalaine's gaze was as distant and frosty as a winter sky. "Then do not come to my chamber this evening at sunset." The queen released their hands and without further words moved down the corridor, Tressa silent in her wake. The Tolorian women vanished around a corner. As if waking from a spell, Aryn slapped her forehead.

"The king!"

Grace didn't move. She kept staring at the ewer. Small bubbles rose in the water, and a faint wisp of steam curled from its surface. Except that was impossible.

A tug on her sleeve. "Come on, Grace. We have to *go*."

Still Grace didn't move. "What did you see, Aryn? In the ewer, when you stopped speaking." She looked at the baroness.

Aryn blushed and hung her head. "It's foolish. A whim, a fancy. It can't mean anything."

"Tell me."

She drew in a deep breath and lifted her head, and now her blue eyes shone. "It was me, Grace. The queen with the sword, going to war on the white horse. It was me."

Of course. Ivalaine had said the water could reflect the future.

"What about you, Grace? What did you see?"

The future . . . or the past.

Grace swallowed. Her mouth tasted like ashes. "Nothing, Aryn. I saw nothing. Come on, we'd better go see King Boreas."

She did not glance at the ewer again as she turned and started down the passageway.

72.

Travis rested his bearded chin on his hands and watched through the window as clouds rolled from the west to blanket the fields, hills, and copses of Calavan. The leaden sky descended until the castle's towers scraped it and shreds of mist whirled around their turrets. Below, peasants and serving maidens and men-at-arms went about their business in Calavere's two baileys. Life seemed hard in this place, but Travis envied the castle folk. At least they had something to do, even if it was only pushing a cart of peat through the muck.

". . . but I managed to catch him for a few moments yesterday evening, outside the king's chamber," Falken was saying. He paced around the chamber, strumming his lute, which hung from a leather strap over his shoulder.

"And what did he tell you?" Melia said.

She sat near the fire, a shawl over her shoulders. A fluffy black kitten played on the rug near her feet. Travis had no idea where it had come from.

"Alerain said that, after any reckoning, the council must recess for three days."

"Three days!" Melia's coppery skin darkened. "How many more feydrim will be prowling the castle in three days? And how much closer to freedom will the Pale King be?" She picked up the kitten and set it in her lap. It instantly began attacking the tasseled end of her sash.

"It's frustrating, I agree, but you know how Calavaners are about regulations."

"Rabid?"

Falken gave a snort. "That's one word. Anyway, blame it all on King Indarus. He's the one who set down the rules for calling a council."

Melia stroked the kitten, and her eyes narrowed to gold slits. "I have half a mind to make this Indarus regret writing all those rules and regulations."

"He's been dead three centuries, Melia."

"That's not necessarily a problem."

Travis started to ask what *that* had meant, then clamped his mouth shut. What was he thinking? That Melia or Falken would actually tell him what was going on? He had followed the two all those leagues, believing that once they got to Calavere the bard and lady would find a way to send him back to Colorado. However, since they had arrived at the castle two days ago, neither had even mentioned Travis's home. It might have been bearable if Beltan were here, but Travis had not seen the knight since yesterday at the council.

You could go talk to Grace.

A thrill passed through him at the thought, but he dismissed it. He had seen Grace from a distance at the council. She had seemed so at ease with her noble friends, like the knight Durge, or that young baroness with the blue eyes. What was her name? Aryn?

Just because Grace is from Earth doesn't mean she's like you, Travis. She fits in here.

A soft but demanding *mew* reached his ears, and he looked down. The black kitten had tumbled and rolled across the floor to land at his feet. He lifted it up and set it on the windowsill. The kitten regarded him with golden eyes. They looked just like Melia's.

"Has she sent you here to spy on me?" he said.

The kitten only purred and began exploring the sill. When it reached the window, it stiffened and let out a hiss. The hair on its back stood up. Travis peered out.

"It's only a dog," he said with a smile. "It's all the way down in the bailey. It can't hurt you."

He started to pick up the kitten. It hissed again and slashed with tiny claws. A thin red line appeared on Travis's skin. He snatched his hands back.

"Even you?" he murmured.

Now the kitten sat calmly, daintily licked a paw, and regarded him with those moonlike eyes.

"Traitor."

The kitten leaped lightly to the floor and pranced back toward Melia. Travis picked up an empty pitcher from a table and followed.

". . . was utterly disastrous," Melia was saying now. "We have to find a way to break the deadlock."

"And while there are still Dominions left to fight for." Falken strummed a minor chord.

Travis cleared his throat. "I'm going to get some water." He wasn't really thirsty. It was just the only excuse he could think of to leave the room.

"All right, Travis," Melia said in an absent tone.

He frowned. "And then I'm going to fling myself from the battlements and count how many seconds it takes before I splatter against the cobblestones."

"That's nice, dear." She picked up the kitten and set it back in her lap.

It was no use. Travis walked from the chamber, leaving the bard and the lady to their machinations. He set the pitcher on a sideboard and headed down a corridor.

As always, Travis didn't decide what direction to take. He wandered the castle for a time, and when he found himself at a door that led outside, it felt right enough. He opened the door and stepped into the lower bailey. Cold air slapped his cheeks, and woke him after the smoky dullness of the castle.

The bailey was thronging, and Travis felt odd not having an obvious task to do. He hurried across the courtyard—past short, powerful men with pockmarked faces and smudge-faced young women with toothless smiles—and hoped that would make him look like he had purpose enough. He didn't want to be mistaken for an errant servant again.

A chorus of bleating erupted behind Travis. He glanced over his shoulder and saw a flock of goats bearing down on him. The beasts were small, but there were a lot of them, and something told him he wouldn't enjoy the sensation of all their little cloven feet prancing across his back. He lurched out of the way and pressed himself against a wall. The shaggy animals trotted by, along with their switch-wielding master: a man every bit as shaggy as his charges.

Once the stench settled, Travis peeled himself from the stones. His dash for safety had taken him to a dim corner of the bailey. He looked up, and above him loomed a tower he hadn't really noticed before. It was smaller than the castle's other towers, and of all the nine it was the only one that seemed in ill repair. A hole gaped in the side where several stones had fallen out, and the slate roof slumped at an odd angle. Most likely it had been abandoned. Perhaps the tower was dangerous. Travis shrugged, then turned to move on.

Something caught his eye, and he froze. There. He walked to the tower's door of wood, weathered the same gray as the stones it was set into. They had fashioned it of silver inlaid in the wood, and although tarnished with time he could still make it out: three intersecting lines. It was the same symbol that had glowed on his right hand in the ruins of Kelcior:

Travis lifted his hand and reached toward the rune.

"Can I help you?" asked a masculine voice behind him.

Travis snatched his hand back and turned around. The man was young—younger than Travis by several years. His face was broad and homely, and his nose flat, but a cheerful light shone in his brown eyes. He wore a robe of unassuming gray, but the garment did not quite conceal his short, massive frame. Travis recognized him—he was one of the two runespeakers who had spoken the rune of beginning at the Council of Kings.

"I'm sorry," Travis said. "I was just looking at the . . . I mean, I was just looking." How could he explain to this stranger what, even at that moment, itched beneath the skin of his right palm?

The man only nodded. He seemed neither suspicious nor angry. "It's beautiful, isn't it?" He pointed to the symbol on the door. "Do you know it?"

Travis shook his head. "No, what is it?"

"It's a rune—the rune of runes. See? There are three lines." He traced them with a thick finger. "One for the art of runespeaking, and one for the two arts which are lost."

Travis forgot his trepidation. He gazed at the rune on the door in new wonder. "The arts of runebinding and runebreaking," he murmured.

The young man cocked his head and gave Travis a penetrating look. "Not many people know those words these days. Few are interested in runes anymore."

"Why not?" Travis said.

He gave a wistful shrug. "Old ways are forgotten in the wake of new."

Travis opened his mouth to speak, but another voice interrupted him.

"Hello there, Travis."

He and the young man turned around. Travis wasn't certain why he felt like a child who had just been caught in an illicit act, but he did. He crunched his shoulders inside his tunic.

"Hi, Melia. Hi, Falken."

The young man glanced at Travis, surprise in his brown eyes, but Travis said nothing. The bard approached, and the lady drifted behind him.

"I'm surprised to find you here, Travis," Melia said. Amusement touched the corners of her mouth. "I thought you were going to count how long it took to fall from the battlements."

Travis winced. "How did you find me?"

Falken grinned his wolfish grin. "No, Travis, we weren't looking for you. This was simply Lady Fate again, tangling our threads as she has before. We came to the bailey to buy a bolt of cloth for Melia."

"I'm quite overdue for a new dress," the lady said.

Her kirtle, as always, was without stain or rent or stray thread, but Travis said nothing.

Falken nodded toward the young man in the gray robe. "It's good to see you again, Journeyman Rin."

The man bowed. "And you as well, Master Falken."

Travis tried to reel in his dangling jaw. "You know each other?"

"I spoke with Rin the other day," Falken said. "I asked him if he could take you on as an apprentice."

Rin smiled at Travis. "And that solves a mystery for me. It is not every day someone who knows about runes comes to our tower door."

"Will you be able to teach him, Rin?" Melia said.

The young runespeaker's face grew solemn. "I discussed the topic with Master Jemis yesterday. Usually apprentices must make a petition to All-master Oragien at the Gray Tower."

Melia opened her mouth to protest, but Rin held up a hand and laughed.

"No, great lady, I would not presume to argue with you. I think we will be able to make an exception in this case. We will take Travis as an apprentice. However, at the earliest chance, he must journey to the Gray Tower and present himself there."

Melia's visage grew placid again. "Thank you, Rin."

He bowed again. "Now, if you'll excuse me, I have to see to my own studies. I'm afraid I'm not a master yet. I'll see you tomorrow at dawn, Travis."

With that Rin opened the door of the ramshackle tower and disappeared within.

"Well," Melia said to Falken with a pleased look, "that's settled."

Travis frowned. "Wait a minute. Don't I get a choice about this?"

Amber eyes locked on him. "And what would you choose, dear?"

He opened his mouth to make an angry reply, but he could think of no words to say.

Falken laid his gloved hand on his shoulder. "It's all right, Travis. Rin and Jemis can teach you better than I can."

Travis gave a wordless nod. Melia and Falken started to continue on their way, then the lady halted and glanced back at Travis.

"By the way, Travis," she said. "I haven't had a chance to tell you this yet, but you were very brave the other night, when you helped Lady Grace against the feydrim."

He could only stare as the bard and the lady walked away and vanished into the throng.

Travis shook his head. Maybe Brother Cy was right. Maybe he did have a choice after all. He glanced up at the tower of the runespeakers and rubbed his right hand.

Just maybe.

73.

Grace stared at the flat expanse of wood before her. She had been standing at the door for what seemed an eternity, although in truth it had been no more than five minutes. Still, she was lucky no servant or noble had turned down this corridor. If someone saw her standing there, she would have to knock. After all, that's what normal people did at doors.

And why can't you, Grace? It's not as if your doom is waiting for you on the other side. It's just a man, that's all. Except it wasn't just a man on the other side of the door. This chamber belonged to Logren of Eredane. She lifted her hand but could not bring her knuckles to bear on the wood.

This was all Aryn's fault. Earlier that day, after their encounter with Ivalaine, Grace and the baroness had careened through the castle to Boreas's chamber. Grace had expected to find him in a rage, stamping about the room, snorting curses like fire, and tossing aside any objects unlucky enough to get in his path—chairs, tables, small noblemen. Instead the king had sat near the fireplace, still and composed, and somehow this had frightened Grace even more. At least one could see a mad bull coming.

Their audience had been brief. Boreas was displeased with Falken's outburst and the council's premature decision—Grace had never before heard anyone make the word *displeased* sound like cause for murder. The council was to meet again in three days to begin anew, and Boreas wanted to discover why the first reckoning had gone as it had, so that the second would not go the same. Grace, needless to say, was going to help him.

It was not so hard to understand the choice of some of the rulers. Sorrin's decision could be explained by his madness. And Lysandir obviously followed Eminda's lead. That left the queen of Eredane as the real mystery—aside from Ivalaine, of course, but Boreas seemed to have his own idea about that.

"A witch always determines what is right and reasonable and then does the opposite," he had said in a growling voice.

Grace had only bit her tongue and listened to her orders. Some time ago Aryn had told the king about Grace's conversation with Logren of Eredane. Now Boreas wanted her to pay Logren a visit and try to determine why Queen Eminda had decided against war, what she hoped to gain at the council, and—most of all—what she feared.

Grace had protested. However, trying to explain that she and Logren had spoken only once, and had exchanged greetings with each other only a few times after that, and were anything but friends, was futile. She had given Aryn an exasperated look, the baroness had given a sheepish shrug in return, and Grace had bowed her head and murmured the only three words that guaranteed it would remain attached to her shoulders for another day.

"Yes, Your Majesty."

The sound of booted feet jerked Grace out of her paralysis. Someone was coming down the corridor. She rapped on the door so hard her knuckles hurt. She waited, heart thudding in her throat. No answer. The footsteps fell silent. False alarm on that account. She knocked again, but still the door did not open. Relief washed through her. Logren must have been away from his room—she had gotten a reprieve. With a grin, she knocked one more time, just so she could tell Boreas she had done her best.

"Can I help you, my lady?"

The voice was deep and rich and came, not from behind the door, but from behind *her*. Grace whirled around, and her breath caught somewhere between lungs and lips. He was even more handsome than she remembered. Not since the night of her first feast in Calavere had she stood so close to him and gazed into his intelligent eyes.

Recognition flickered in those eyes, and he smiled.

He has good teeth.

She almost laughed at the absurdness of the thought, but so many people in this world had terrible teeth, if they had any at all. Yet his were white and straight, and his skin was smooth and unmarked by any trace of disease. Only the fine white scar that ran across his cheek, and this was like the off-center vase in an otherwise exquisite Japanese room—the one small imperfection that made the rest seem all the more flawless.

He arched a dark eyebrow. Grace realized she had been staring too long. She had to say something, anything.

"Lord Logren, I was hoping I would find you here."

"Indeed, Lady Grace? And who else might you expect to find behind my door?"

A wave of panic rippled through her. What did he mean by that? Had he seen her that day, standing there in the garden, watching the two of them? No, she was overreacting. Mirth glinted in his eyes. He was only making a jest.

Thankfully he spoke again. She was not certain she could have found words.

"I've just come from a meeting with my queen, and I was intending to go for a ride with Lord Olstin. He's been asking me to accompany him for days."

"Then you had best go, my lord," she said.

He cocked his head. "My lady, you would so quickly condemn me to such a fate?"

"Nobility has its price." She sucked in a breath. Where had that come from?

"True enough," Logren said. "But this is Lord Olstin of Brelegond we are speaking of, my lady. I know you know him. He rides with the reins in one hand and a goblet in the other. I imagine I'll have to stop every few minutes just to pick him up off the turf. Although I warrant his finery will make an excellent cushion when he falls."

"I imagine you *could* use any one of his outfits to stuff several good-sized chairs," Grace said.

He clapped his hands and laughed. To her amazement, Grace laughed in reply, and it was a genuine sound. Like that night in the great hall, he seemed to take her fear away, leaving her at ease, not only with him, but with herself.

"What are we going to do to save you from this awful fate, my lord?" she said, braver now.

He stroked his chin with long fingers. "As you've noted, my lady, I have no choice. Unless . . ."

"Unless what?"

"Unless I was ordered by another not to go. Of course, that would take a noble of higher rank than myself."

"And who might outrank a high counselor, my lord?"

"I'm afraid it would take at least a duke," he said in a grave tone.

"What about a duchess?"

He snapped his fingers. "That would do."

"Then, my lord, I forbid you to go riding with Lord Olstin."

He pressed a hand to his chest and bowed. "As you wish, my lady."

A thrill coursed through her. It was foolish. This was all just a game. Logren wasn't obeying her orders, he was just looking for an excuse. Still, it almost *felt* real.

"May I invite you inside, my lady?"

He gestured to the door, and only then did she realize that, in her earlier trepidation, she had backed up against it. She hurried aside and let him open the door. Before she even thought about what she was doing, she was inside. The door shut behind her, and now uncertainty crept back into her chest. She was not here to exchange pleasantries with the high counselor of Eredane. She was here to spy on him.

"Wine?"

Grace accepted the cup and gripped it with both hands. He raised his own cup to her and drank. As he did she took in her first glimpse of his room. In size and brightness it was only a fraction of her own chamber. The narrow window faced a blank expanse of stone, and the scant furnishings were sturdy but far from ornate.

Logren noticed her gaze. "Do not worry, my lady. The room is no affront on King Boreas's part. I asked for a more austere chamber. I prefer to keep my surroundings simple. It sharpens my mind, and allows me to focus on my tasks. I'm afraid it is too easy to get distracted by the trappings of nobility and forget what it really means."

Grace sipped her wine. Interest began to replace fear. "And what does it really mean, my lord?"

"Being a noble is a privilege, but it is also a duty. Those beneath us depend on us to make wise decisions for them, to keep their lives ordered, productive, and safe."

"Don't you mean to keep them oppressed?"

He set down his cup. "One cannot have safety without giving something up, my lady. That is the way of the world. The commoners work for us, it is true. But in turn we protect them, feed them when food is short, and build them shrines for their mysteries."

Grace knew this idea should have filled her with repugnance. All the same Logren's words resonated in her. It was wrong, and impossible, but in a way they made sense to her. Why shouldn't those who were stronger lead—as long as they were good, benevolent, and wise?

She thought of something. "And who protects you, my lord?"

He shook a finger at her. "No, my lady. That's not the way the game works. Power is peril. No one protects those who are on top. They have to protect themselves. Or fall."

A jolt ran through her. Now was her chance. She took another sip of wine to appear nonchalant, but mostly to wet a throat gone dry. "You mean like Queen Eminda did?"

He gazed at her, then his applause filled the small room. "Well done, my lady. Well done, and subtly. I very nearly didn't notice, and I have an ear for such things."

Horror flooded her. "What do you mean?"

Logren drew near. He smelled of spices. "You know what I speak of, my lady. Clever questions disguised as beguiling talk. No, don't be alarmed. I admire your skill, and I understand. You are King Boreas's guest, and he would not be a very good king if he did not use all means available to him—including yourself—to learn about the intentions of the other kings and queens at the council."

Grace worked her jaw but could find no words. She felt like a butter-fly pinned to a child's piece of cardboard.

"Don't worry, Lady Grace. You saved me from riding with Lord Olstin. I will not send you back to King Boreas empty-handed in return. I will tell you freely why Eminda chose as she did at the council."

All she could do was nod.

"There are two possibilities, my lady. The first is that the Pale King is a myth—a story to frighten children or to excite bards. The second is that Falken Blackhand is correct, that the Pale King indeed stirs again in Imbrifale. Now, if the first possibility is true, and the Pale King is a myth, then it is folly to send the armies of all the Dominions marching into the northern wilds. There are real enough dangers here—bandits, barbarians, famine—without having to tramp across Falengarth in search of false ones."

Grace licked her lips. "What if Falken is right?"

Logren studied her. "You believe him, don't you?" He lifted a hand to halt her words. "No, do not protest. I cannot say whether Falken Blackhand truly is what he claims to be, but whatever people say of the Grim Bard he is not to be taken lightly. Yet if the Pale King does stir, it is every bit as foolish to send all the forces of the Dominions north. We cannot hope to raise so great an army as the stories say Ulther and Elsara did. Better, then, to remain here, to protect the Do-minions, and to search for the Imsari, the Great Stones that the myths say hold the key to the Pale King's power."

He took a decanter of wine and refilled her cup. "So you see, my lady, either way there is no reason to muster the Dominions for war. Queen Eminda can be abrupt, I know that better than anyone, but she chose as she did to protect Eredane and the other Dominions, not to harm them."

Grace lifted the cup in trembling hands and drank. She had to admit, once again Logren's words made sense. Boreas seemed to want war at any cost, without exploring other options. She wasn't so certain she would have chosen differently from Queen Eminda.

The warmth of the wine filled her, and now Grace let her eyes drink in Logren. She had never met another man who seemed so calm, so governed by reason. Yet she had seen him in the garden. How could one so wise let himself get ensnared by Kyrene's petty magics? Even as she asked the question she knew the answer. Logren was tall, handsome, and strong. His duties and his austere room could not possibly occupy him always.

Grace set down her cup. At any rate, it was a relief to have the truth of her intentions out in the open, and she had indeed gotten an answer to take back to Boreas. "I'm so sorry to have bothered you like this, Lord Logren. I'll go now."

A hand on her arm kept her from turning away. "I did not ask you to go, my lady."

Grace stared at his hand as if he had struck her. His skin was darker than hers, and large veins traced lines beneath. Once again she saw him in the garden, naked in the frosty air, white limbs twining about his back. Only this time, when the woman looked up, her green eyes were tinged with gold.

Grace snatched her hand back. "No. . . ."

He stepped away and bowed. "As my lady wishes. I apologize for any insult."

No, that wasn't what she had meant. It wasn't him. He was a gentleman in every way. It was herself she had spoken to. But how could she tell him that?

"I have to go," she said.

She didn't remember opening his door. The next thing she knew she rushed down the corridor, heedless of which way she turned. When she had pictured Logren in the garden the woman had not been Kyrene. It had been herself.

And why not, Grace? Why shouldn't it be you? They stole it from you, and for so many years you've been afraid. Why shouldn't you be the one to take power from it now?

She shook her head, cleared her vision, and realized she had come to a halt. She stood before an arched door. A banner hung on a stand beside the archway, yellow on green: Toloria. This was Queen Ivalaine's chamber. Grace glanced up at a high window and saw a slice of slate-colored sky. Somewhere doves sang their mourning song. A shiver danced along her skin—it was just now twilight.

A soft rustling beside her. Grace glanced to her right, into a pair of large blue eyes.

"I didn't think I would come," Aryn said in a quiet voice.

"Neither did I."

Their hands found one another and held on.

"What on Eldh are we doing, Grace?"

She drew in a deep breath. "I don't know."

They tightened their hold on each other. The door opened, and together they stepped through.

74.

Travis began his studies with the Runespeakers the morning after his encounter with Rin. Falken woke him in the cold gray light before dawn.

"It's time," the bard said.

Still half-asleep, Travis shrugged on his tunic, wrapped his mist-cloak around himself, and stumbled outside. He trudged across the frozen mud of the lower bailey—empty at this early hour—to the lair of the Runespeakers. Travis hesitated at the door, teeth chattering. At last the chill won out, and he knocked. The door opened, and smoky light spilled onto the ground.

"Come in," said a sharp voice.

He did, and the door shut behind him.

There was one good thing about runespeakers, Travis soon discovered. They drank a lot of *maddok*. There was always a pot of the liquid, hot and dark, bubbling over a copper brazier in the tower's shabby main room. He downed a half-dozen cups of it that first day, until his whole body tingled, and his mind was as light and clear as a bauble of spun glass. Not that it did him much good.

"Do you know what this is?" Jemis pointed to the lines he had drawn with a stylus on a wax tablet. Jemis was the elder of the two runespeakers, a thin and harsh-faced man well past his middle years. His threadbare robe was not so much gray as it was grimy.

Travis pushed his spectacles up his nose and studied the tablet in the glow of the brazier. The tower was drafty, and they sat on rugs as close to the fire as they dared. Yes, that was one of the runes Falken had shown him. He opened his mouth. "It's the rune of—*ouch!*"

He nearly bit through his tongue as Jemis rapped him on the hand with the metal stylus. Travis snatched his wounded hand back. That had *hurt*.

"Wrong," Jemis said in a voice every bit as stinging as the blow. "You know nothing, apprentice. Whatever you have been taught before, forget it. Whatever knowledge you think you have, heave it out of your skull like rubbish. You know only what we teach you. Never forget that, apprentice."

Rin handed Travis a steaming cup of *maddok*. "I know you probably have a lot of questions, Travis. But you have to trust us. Apprentices in the Gray Tower have been taught in the same way for centuries. The lessons may not always make sense to you. They didn't make sense to me when I was beginning. Later, after I learned, I could see it really is the best way."

The young runespeaker's face was plain and crooked, but his brown eyes were kind, and his smile genuine. Travis accepted the cup, drank, then set it down.

"Teach me," he said.

That first lesson was a simple one: He listened. As doves rustled in the rafters high above, Jemis told the tale of Olrig Lore Thief, the Old God who stole the secret of runes from the dragons, along with the tricks to making ale and poetry. Travis stared at the brazier and let himself drift back to an age lost in the haze of time. The world was young then. The Old Gods dwelled in stone, river, and sky, and their children, the Little People, laughed and sang in the forests. The dragons were there as well, lurking in their pits, ancient even then at the dawning—cruel and terribly wise.

The tale ended. Firelight flickered across Jemis's face.

"But what are they?" Travis said. "Runes, I mean. Why are they so important?" He tried not to run a finger over the palm of his right hand.

It was Rin who answered. "Before the world there was nothing. Or, more properly, there was *everything*. Light and dark, fire and ice, night and day—all were merged in a sea of twilight, without end, without time. Then the Worldsmith spoke the First Rune, the rune Eldh, and all was changed."

"Eldh?" Travis frowned—this didn't make sense. "But isn't that the name of this . . . of *the* world?"

"Yes, it is. But it is also the name of the First Rune, and by speaking it the Worldsmith forged the world and set it spinning within the mists." Rin drew a box on the wax tablet, then divided the box in two with a line:

"After this, the Worldsmith bound the rune Eldh within the Dawning Stone, that the world might know permanence. Then he spoke the runes of sun, and moon, and stars, and these too came into being. That was only the beginning. Sky and mountain, river and ocean, tree and stone—as the Worldsmith spoke their names, they appeared, and for each name there was a rune which he bound within the Dawning Stone, so that all things in the world would never fade."

Understanding crept into Travis's mind, and along with it a growing excitement. "So everything in the world has a name? And a rune to go with it?"

Rin nodded. "Yes. And when you speak a rune you invoke its power, just as the Worldsmith did at the beginning."

Travis scratched his beard and tried to take in everything Rin and Jemis had said. It was a wonderful story, but it was all just a myth, wasn't it?

A myth like wraithlings? Like feydrim?

"There's one thing I don't understand," he said. "You say the secret of runes came from Olrig. But I thought Falken said . . . I mean, I thought no one believed in the Old Gods anymore."

Jemis slammed a hand down on the tablet and knocked it to the floor. Both Travis and Rin stared, jaws agape.

"They are fools!" The elder runespeaker's eyes burned in the glow of the brazier. "The First Ones retreated into the mists long ago, back into the Twilight Realm. They let the loud and brash New Gods of Tarras march across Falengarth. It was not their time anymore. But though they are distant now, do not think the Old Gods are gone." He was rigid now, trembling. "Eldh was theirs once, and it will be again!"

A shudder coursed beneath Jemis's gray robe, and he passed a hand before his eyes. They glowed no longer, but were dull like stones. "Your first lesson is over," he said in a flat voice. He turned, scrambled up the stairs that spiraled around the inside wall of the tower, and disappeared through a door.

Travis looked at Rin. "I'm sorry."

Rin shook his head. "Don't worry, Travis. I think sometimes when you grow old it's hard to see things change, that's all."

"Do you think he's right?" Travis looked into the ruby heart of the brazier. "Do you think the Old Gods will come back?"

"There is some cheese and bread for our lunch," Rin said. "You should eat something before I show you how to use the stylus and the tablet."

Travis nodded and said nothing more as he moved to help Rin with the food.

75.

Travis stepped from the dilapidated tower of the Runespeakers and grabbed for the edges of his mistcloak as wind sliced through his tunic. Every day the weather was colder than the last. Even in the Winter Wood it had barely seemed as frigid as this, but there the *valsindar* had offered some protection from the brooding clouds that swept out of the Fal Threndur.

Travis glanced up at the sky. It was hard and brilliant, with no sign of dark clouds. *But they'll come here eventually, won't they? They're his clouds, the Pale King's. Right now they're staying close to Imbrifale. That's why Falken and I couldn't see them when we left the Winter Wood, when we headed for Kelcior. But that won't last, will it?*

He shivered, wrapped his cloak around himself, and tried not to wonder how long it would be before he looked up again to see iron-black clouds reaching out of the north to swallow Calavere's nine towers.

As usual, when Travis stepped into the chamber he shared with Falken and Melia, the two were deep in discussion over the Council of Kings. From what Travis gleaned, the council had reconvened that morning, even though Falken had already forced a reckoning. According to the bard, no reckoning was final until all the kings and queens made a choice—and so far Ivalaine had abstained. Now each of the rulers was to make a report on the state of affairs in his or her own Dominion. Each king or queen was granted two full sessions. With recesses, it would be over a fortnight before this phase of the council was finished—a fact which clearly did not please Falken.

The bard ran a hand through his shoulder-length hair. "We can't just sit here and wait while every petty advisor of every ruler speaks in deep and excruciating detail about the health of this year's calves in every single province of the Dominion in question."

"Actually, I can," Melia said. "Especially in this chair. It's really quite comfortable. Horsehair I think. I wonder if King Boreas could have one made for me."

Falken glared at her.

"Besides," Melia said, "sometimes patience is necessary, Falken. I would have thought you of all people would know that."

"And sometimes, if you wait too long, you wake up and realize everything that's important to you has crumbled to dust."

Melia looked up at the bard. Now concern touched her visage, and her voice was gentle. "Do not fear, Falken. Only the first seal on the Rune Gate is broken. We still have time, and the council may yet decide on a muster. In the meantime we can keep doing what we have been doing—watching, and learning. That knowledge will help us."

Falken grunted, but he did not answer.

Travis took off his cloak and set it on his bed. Melia eyed his mud-caked boots.

"How thoughtful of you to bring a little of the bailey into the chamber, Travis, knowing how I so dislike going out when it's cold."

He gave her a sheepish look. "You're welcome?"

Melia's expression was not quite as soft as granite.

"I'll get a rag?" he tried again.

She smiled and leaned back in her chair. "I believe you're beginning to catch on, dear."

"You're off early," Falken said as Travis scrubbed at the mud on the floor.

"King Boreas summoned Rin and Jemis," Travis said from his hands and knees.

"Probably to see what their runes say about the council." The bard raised an eyebrow. "So how are things going?"

"All right. Except I haven't spoken a single rune yet. Jemis just makes me practice using the stylus and tablet all day."

"Good."

Falken didn't need to say anything more. Travis would never forget the incident in the *talathrin*, when he misdrew *Lir*, the rune of light.

The black kitten had appeared in Melia's lap again—the tiny creature seemed to be able to leap out of shadows and disappear into thin air at will. It also seemed to have a penchant for biting at Travis's ankles. He kept an eye on it.

"Well," Melia said, "I'm certain we can find something for Travis to do."

"Have you seen Beltan?" he said in a hopeful tone.

Melia gazed into the fire but said nothing. Maybe it was the flickering light, but her regal face seemed sad.

"He's around," Falken said in a gruff voice.

What did that mean? Beltan had been acting strangely ever since they had come to Calavere, and as usual no one wanted to talk about it. Travis missed the big blond knight. He sighed and bent back over his scrubbing.

Everyone looked up when a knock sounded at the door. Travis thought it must be Beltan, but when Falken opened the door it was not the rangy knight on the other side.

"Lady Grace," Falken said. "Will you come in?"

"Yes . . . thank you."

Once more Travis was struck by how much she seemed to belong here. He tried to imagine her in surgical scrubs and a mask, a scalpel in her hand. It was possible, but the image of the lady in the purple gown kept getting superimposed over the image of the doctor.

Melia rose to her feet, and the kitten landed on the floor with a *brrt!*

"Good morrow, Lady Grace." Melia's eyes glinted with curiosity.

None of them had spoken with Grace since the first morning of the council four days ago, when they had discovered the feydrim gone from the wardrobe in her chamber. Travis had told Falken and Melia what he had discovered: that Grace was from Earth, just like he was. The two had clearly found this of great interest, and had asked him many questions—had he ever met Grace before, did they know any of the same people, did they go to the same places? However, what they thought about Grace or his answers they had not shared with him.

"Would you like something to drink?" Falken said.

"No," she said. She took a breath. "That is . . . thank you . . . I mean . . . I was hoping I could speak with Travis."

The rag fell from his hand and plopped on the floor. Only when Falken spoke did Travis realize he had been staring.

"Are you going to answer the lady, Travis?" Falken said.

Travis leaped to his feet and wiped his hands on his tunic. "Of course. I'd be happy to, Grace." He glanced at Melia. "If it's all right?"

"I'm sure we'll find a way to manage without you, Travis."

"We won't be long," Grace said.

He followed her out of the chamber, the door shut, and they were alone in the hallway.

"It's good to see you, Grace," he said.

Grace frowned at the door. "She makes you scrub the floor?"

Travis was taken aback. Her voice sounded so hard.

"It was my fault," he said. "I tracked the mud into the chamber. Really, Melia isn't so bad. Anyway, I'm sorry I haven't come to talk to you, Grace, but I've been busy. I've been studying with the castle's runespeakers."

She turned her gaze on him. "It's all right. I've been learning . . . I mean, I've been busy, too. But I didn't forget what you said, about wanting to see the door, the one with the symbol I told you about." Her gaze was tentative now. "Do you still want me to show it to you, Travis?"

A chill crept up his spine. He wasn't certain he wanted to see anything that might be associated with the Raven Cult, but he nodded all the same.

"Take me there."

Travis followed Grace as she led the way through the castle. Servants scurried out of their path, although she hardly seemed to notice. She moved confidently, navigating the twists and turns with ease. More than once Travis glanced out of the corner of his eye at her in amazement. She really did belong here.

It was only when they stopped that he realized they had come to a quieter part of the castle. The corridor ended in an alcove into which a narrow window was set. Beyond was a fragment of blue quartz sky. It could almost have been Colorado, even though he knew it wasn't.

"It was here," Grace said.

He looked at her. "What was here, Grace?"

"The bells."

A shiver danced up his spine. She didn't need to say anything more.

She tucked a few strands of short, ash-blond hair behind one ear and approached the window. Travis followed and peered over her shoulder. Through the glass he saw fields bounded by stone walls. Some leagues away the fields dipped down, and though he couldn't see it, he knew that was the valley where the River Darkwine flowed. Beyond were Calavan's northern marches. He could just make out a deep green line hovering on the horizon. Falken had pointed it out to him one day from the battlements: Gloaming Wood.

Grace turned around. "It couldn't have been very far from here. I'm sure of it." She started down a left-hand passage, then backed up and continued on straight. After a short distance she tried another left turn, then nodded and quickened her pace.

"There," she said as she came to a halt. "That's where I saw him." She pointed to a door on the right. It was shut.

"The man in the black robe?" Travis said.

"Yes. He left this behind." Grace reached into the pouch at her waist, drew out an object wrapped in felt, and unfolded the cloth. It was a knife with a polished black hilt.

Travis studied the knife, then handed it back to her and peered at the door. The symbol scratched into the wood was incomplete, but there was no mistaking the two curved lines.

"It's the same as the symbol you told me about, isn't it?" Grace said. "The one you saw on your journey here."

Travis gave a wordless nod. He forced himself to study the symbol. Yes, it looked as if the maker had started to scratch two crossed lines beneath it. An X.

"What did you say it was?" Grace said behind him. "The symbol of some sort of cult?"

He turned around. "The Raven Cult. It's a mystery cult, like the

Cult of Vathris, only it's new. I haven't seen any of its followers here in Calavan, but there were a lot of them in Eredane, and in the other Dominions, from what Melia and Beltan said."

"I wonder what's in this room?" Grace started to reach for the door's handle, then halted and looked up. "Maybe we should ask Lord Alerain for permission first."

"And what will we tell him we're hoping to find in here when he asks us? Little people with jingle bells?"

Grace bit her lip. "Good point."

She turned the handle. There was a click, and the door opened. They glanced both ways down the corridor, but no one was in sight. Together they stepped through the door.

The room was dim—there was no window, only the light that filtered in from the corridor outside—and it took Travis's eyes a moment to adjust. Shapes loomed all around them, some round, some square, others squat and lumpy.

"A storeroom."

Even as Grace said this Travis realized she was right. The room was filled with barrels, crates, and sacks—the shapes he had glimpsed.

He scratched his scruffy beard. "What's so important about a storeroom?"

Grace shook her head.

They searched the storeroom for a few minutes more, but they found nothing special. The crates contained rotten linens, and by their odor the barrels were filled with some kind of salted fish. The air was damp, and Travis soon discovered the source. Water dripped from an opening. The opening was perhaps two feet across and angled up into the thick stone wall. When he peered in he felt a cold puff against his face. It was a ventilation shaft. He remembered reading a book about castles as a kid, one that showed slices taken at various points throughout the structure. Medieval castles were supposed to be riddled with ventilation shafts. Otherwise, in damp climes, everything inside them would have molded instantly.

Travis and Grace stepped back out into the corridor and shut the door behind them.

"There doesn't seem to be anything important in there," Travis said.

Grace crossed her arms over the bodice of her gown. "But the man I saw, the Raven cultist, he had to have picked this room for a reason."

Travis shrugged. He didn't disagree, but whatever the cultist's purpose it wasn't clear from the contents of the storage chamber. A thought struck him. "Maybe this isn't the only room, Grace. After all, if the cultist marked one door, he could have marked others. If we found more, we might be able to figure out why he was doing it."

Grace's eyes shone, and she opened her mouth to reply. Just then the call of a dove drifted through a high window. Both glanced up. The sky had faded from blue to slate.

"Oh!" Grace said. "I need to go, Travis. I have . . . I have to be somewhere."

"It's all right," he said. "I should be getting back, too. We can look for more doors later."

She nodded, started to turn away, then turned back and clumsily reached for his hand.

"Thank you for coming with me, Travis."

"Thanks for asking."

She squeezed, then let go of his hand and hurried down the corridor. He smiled as he gazed after her. It had been almost fun to wander the castle with Grace. Then his eyes flickered to the symbol on the door, and his smile faded.

76.

Grace was certain it was no accident Kyrene had chosen this place for their meeting. She rounded a corner in the hedge maze and stepped into a sheltered grotto.

"There you are, love. I was beginning to think you had changed your mind and had decided not to come. Or that perhaps you had gotten lost in the labyrinth. . . ."

Grace planted her feet on the frozen ground and resisted the urge to turn and run as she had the last time she had come upon this place. "I'm here," she said.

Kyrene moved toward her. The countess was wearing a fox cape, its silver fur turned inward. Her cheeks were bright with the cold. "Come, sister." She held out a hand. "I have much to teach you."

I'm sure you do. Love. However, Grace did not speak the words. She hesitated, then accepted Kyrene's hand and stepped into the grotto.

It had been five days since the evening Grace and Aryn had gone to Ivalaine's chamber, and Grace wasn't certain she had any better idea what it meant to be a witch. Once she and Aryn had stepped through Ivalaine's door, they had been eager to learn, eager to hear the truth about who the Witches were—what they wanted . . . and what they could do. They had expected revelations. What they had gotten were more mysteries.

"How do we begin?" Grace had asked Ivalaine that first evening, breathless, thirsty.

The queen of Toloria had seemed hardly surprised at their arrival in her chamber. "Do you know how to weave, Lady Grace?" she had asked.

Grace had shaken her head.

"Then that is where you will begin."

Grace had spent the remainder of that evening, and many hours after that, seated before a loom in the queen's chamber, learning how to operate the pedals, and how to pass the shuttle back and forth through the strands of the warp. She had worked until her back ached and her head throbbed. Not since the first days of her internship at Denver Memorial did she remember being this tired, this dizzy, this consumed and overwhelmed. Yet she was good at it. Weaving was not so different from closing incisions, stitching wounds.

"Watch each thread," Ivalaine would murmur as Grace worked. "Follow its line, see how it runs beside the other threads. Each is separate, yet all are intertwined as well. Together they create something far stronger than a single strand, yet every bit as supple."

Soon the queen's words would merge with the whir of the shuttle, the *clack-clack* of the pedals. At night Grace would close her eyes and dream she was caught in the loom.

Aryn already knew how to weave—evidently that was something noble ladies were supposed to learn in this world—so she had been spared that particular task. However, Ivalaine had other work in mind for the baroness. That first evening the queen's lady-in-waiting, the red-haired Tressa, had led Aryn away. When Grace saw Aryn next it was late, and they both had been exhausted. The baroness's left hand had been dirty, and her cheeks and gown smudged.

"Gardening," Aryn had said with a mixture of outrage and amazement. "She had me gardening."

Grace hadn't known how to respond. "What did you plant? Medicinal herbs?"

"No. Turnips."

The last several days had offered little more in the way of explanations. The Council of Kings had reconvened two days ago, so that left only the evenings for their studies. Grace and Aryn would come to Ivalaine's chamber when they could—and when they did not think King Boreas would notice. But it wasn't as if Grace was betraying the king. At least, that was what she told herself. However, once in Ivalaine's chamber, she never seemed to find the chance to ask the Tolorian queen about her motives for abstaining at the council. There was so much else to occupy her.

Like weaving. At first Grace had feared her hands would be crippled from the loom, then they had grown calluses, and the shuttle had seemed to barely touch them as it flew back and forth. A picture had begun to form beneath her fingers. It was a garden at twilight, purple-green and secret. Yesterday, when she arrived at the queen's chamber, she had almost looked forward to weaving.

The loom had been gone.

"It is time for new lessons," Ivalaine had said. "Lady Aryn, you will continue to study with Tressa, though you are finished with gardening, I think. And since I am occupied by the council, you will have a new teacher, Lady Grace."

Only at that moment had Grace noticed the other figure that stood in the room. She moved forward with a rustle of emerald wool and parted coral lips in a smile.

"It's time to learn what it truly means to be a witch, Lady Grace."

Grace shivered and returned to the frosty garden.

"What do I need to do?"

Kyrene made a lovely frown. She must have practiced the expression many times before a mirror. "That is the wrong question, Lady Grace." She moved closer. "What do you *wish* to do?"

Grace started to shake her head. What did Kyrene mean? It didn't matter what she . . .

No, she *did* know. Everything around her, it was always so distant, so removed. But she wanted to touch it, like the threads of the loom beneath her fingers—the lushness of the winter garden. "I want to feel," she said. "I want to feel everything."

A smile coiled around the corners of Kyrene's pink mouth. She took Grace's hand, led her deeper into the grotto. They stopped, and the countess started to untie the sash of Grace's gown.

Grace pulled back. "What are you doing?"

"You have no need of this garment."

"But it's freezing out—"

Kyrene's eyes flashed, and her usually soft face was stern. "I am your teacher, sister."

Grace tensed. Kyrene was vain, and maybe even dangerous. Yet she knew things—things Grace wanted to learn. She lowered her arms and stepped forward.

The countess moved supple hands over Grace's gown, loosened ties, pulled straps. Grace stood stiff and stared forward into the hedge-wall. Ever since her time at the Beckett-Strange Home for Children, the thought of being naked before others had terrified her. It was logical enough, the clinician in her knew. Even long after the marks faded the fear had remained, as if others still would be able to see the places where they had touched her, like shadows against her skin.

Her gown slipped to the ground, and a soft cry escaped Grace as the winter air wrapped a new, frigid cloak around her body. She began to shiver.

"It's *cold*," she said through clattering teeth.

"It doesn't have to be, love."

"What . . . what do you mean?"

Kyrene gestured to the tangled garden walls. "There is no need to be cold when there is so much life all around you."

"I don't . . . I don't understand." The air was damp. In this environment it would take mere minutes for the first symptoms of hypothermia to set in. She had nearly frozen once in this world—she did not intend to again.

Kyrene only gazed at her, and her smile coiled in on itself like a red serpent.

"Tell me," Grace said. She knew it was what Kyrene wanted, for her to beg, but Grace didn't care. She had to know. "Tell me, please."

The countess's eyes glowed in satisfaction. "But of course, sister. You had only to ask."

Kyrene stood behind Grace and murmured in her ear. "Close your eyes, love."

Grace did this.

"Now reach out and touch the evergreens in front of you."

This seemed an odd request, but Grace lifted her arms to obey.

"No, sister, not with your hands. You have the Touch. Reach out with your mind, touch them with your thoughts."

What was Kyrene talking about? Grace shook her head. "I can't touch something with my mind."

Kyrene's whisper was soft and cold as snow. "Then you will freeze, sister."

Convulsions wracked Grace's body now, yet she knew they would stop soon enough, and an irresistible sleepiness would wash over her. That would be the beginning of the end. Grace tried to move her feet, but Kyrene's words buzzed in her head, and she felt rooted to the spot, as if she were a tree herself, slender and pale, leafless in winter.

"Touch them, Grace. Do it. . . ."

No, it was impossible. Or was it? There was that day in her chamber, the day she first met Kyrene. She remembered now. It had felt as if something—someone—had come close to her, too close, and she had pushed the presence away.

Her shivers faded, she had to try. Grace concentrated and tried to remember how she had felt that day, only this time, instead of pushing, she *reached*.

Her mind was dark, all she felt was coldness.

"Do it, sister." The voice was an icicle in her brain. She hated it, wanted it to go away. "Reach."

She couldn't do it, her whole being was brittle, she was going to freeze here in the garden. She stretched, flung her mind out, but there was nothing to touch. Only ice, and blackness, and . . .

. . . warmth. Green, golden warmth. It brushed across the surface of her mind, like a candle in a darkened room, then was gone. Desperate, she cast her mind back. There—there it was, a beacon in the barren murk. It was so beautiful, so gentle and bright. How could she have missed it before? She smiled, and it seemed so easy.

Grace reached out and touched the light.

Her eyes flew open. The air of the garden was still frigid, she could sense that, but she was warm—wondrously, deliciously *warm*. Like a balmy breeze from a summer forest, it rushed over her, and through her, until her skin glowed. She drew in a deep breath and smelled green.

"Yes, that's it, love," a triumphant voice purred in her ear. "I knew you had the strength."

"But what is it?" Grace had never felt so much a part of something before.

"It is the Weirding."

Kyrene stood before her. Grace hadn't noticed when the countess's fur cape and gown had slipped off, but she was naked now, her skin flushed with warmth.

"The Weirding?"

"It is the power that resides in all living things. In the evergreens, in the hedges, in the moss between the stones. It dwells in everything alive, and it flows between them in a great web, vast beyond imagining."

Grace closed her eyes again. "Yes, I can feel them. The evergreens there. And the tall tree on the edge of the grotto—its leaves are gone, but I can see the life still moving inside it. And there! There's a mouse hiding in the stones, watching us. I've never . . . I've never felt anything like this before."

"But I think you have, Lady Grace. Are you not a healer?"

She started to shake her head, but even as she did she knew there was truth in Kyrene's words.

Kyrene reached into her fallen gown and pulled out a small clay pot. It was oil, scented with herbs. She rubbed the oil over Grace's body. At first Grace stiffened—it had been so long since she had let another touch her, she wasn't certain she could bear it—but the countess's fingers were deft and soothing. Grace relaxed, and warmth encapsulated her in a gold haze. She knew now how the two of them had been warm that day in this grotto, despite the cold and their naked skin.

"Yes, you have sensed it before, sister. That is what it means to be a witch—to have the Touch, to feel the Weirding, to reach out to it, and to shape it." Kyrene's voice became a low croon. "Hear me, sister. Once we were crones: hags and hedgewives and madwomen. We were ugly and despised. People threw stones at us and burned us on piles of sticks. But now . . . look at who we are now, sister."

Kyrene gestured to a puddle on the ground, melted in the heat that flowed from them. Two women gazed up from the silvery water, naked and fey, eyes glowing emerald and jade. They were ethereal beings—beings of power.

"Yes, look at us, sister," Kyrene whispered in an exultant voice. "We are hags no longer. Now we are women of rank and power—beautiful, radiant, and strong!"

Grace drew in a shuddering breath. The trees, the vines, the moss. How dull and dead the rest of her life must have been, for at the moment, for the first time in her life, Grace felt as if she were indeed alive.

"More," she said. "I want to feel more." She shut her eyes, started to reach out, farther, deeper.

Her eyes flew open as, like a black curtain, cold descended around her and shut off the golden warmth. In a heartbeat the fey being was gone, and she was merely Grace again, naked, bony, and shivering.

Kyrene's gaze upon her was calculating. "I think that is enough for today, sister. It does not pay to drink too much too soon."

Grace's teeth nearly broke as they clattered against one another. *You enjoyed that, didn't you, Kyrene? Giving me something, then taking it away.*

However, Grace said nothing. She shrugged her gown over her against the chill and left Kyrene and the garden behind, to step again inside the castle's walls of lifeless stone.

77.

It was a cold afternoon, two days after he had gone with Grace to look at the door, when Travis learned about kennings.

"There is always danger in speaking runes," Jemis said.

A soft snow fell outside the tower's narrow window. The doves huddled together for warmth in the rafters of the drafty tower. Travis and the two runespeakers did the same around the brazier.

Rin continued. "Even when you whisper a rune's name, if you are not careful, you might invoke some fraction of its power. That is why we use kennings to speak about runes."

Travis tightened his grip on his mistcloak. "Kennings?"

Rin pointed to a rune on Travis's tablet. *Sindar*. Silver. "This is Ysani's Tears." He pointed to another rune. It was *Fal*. Mountain. "And this is Durnach's Bones."

Ysani. Durnach. Travis recognized those names from some of Jemis's stories about the dawning of Eldh. They were Old Gods, like Olrig One-Hand. Understanding sparked in his mind. Why not use a code to speak about runes? That way there was no danger of invoking their power, no chance of hurting another.

"Tell me more," he said.

Rin did so. *Sharn*, the rune of water, was Sia's Blood, and *Kel*, which was gold, was called Fendir's Bane. According to Jemis, Fendir was the first of the dark elfs—fairies whose lust for gold twisted them into small and ugly, but clever and nimble-fingered, creatures.

The following day, Jemis finally let Travis speak a rune.

"This is your first rune," Jemis said. He drew a symbol on his own tablet and showed it to Travis.

I already know that one. Travis almost said the words aloud but bit his tongue. He carefully copied the three splayed lines onto his own tablet. It was *Krond*. Fire.

Travis sat at a table in the tower's main chamber and stared at an unlit candle. He licked his lips, then spoke the word.

"*Krond.*"

His right hand tingled, there was a brilliant flash, and the tip of the candle burst into flame and flared upward. Travis jumped back from the table.

"*Sharn!*" Jemis shouted in a commanding voice, and at once the candle was extinguished.

Travis sucked in a breath. The candle had melted and slumped over, and a dark ring had been scorched into the surface of the table.

Jemis glared at him, his eyebrows drawn down over his small eyes. "You do not use a sword to cut a thread, apprentice." He turned in disgust and disappeared, as he always did when angry, into one of the tower's upper chambers.

Rin tried to stand the twisted candle back on end. "Why don't we work on moderation?"

Travis only nodded, and tried not to think of the mad lord in Eredane.

The next morning, Travis opened his eyes and stared into the tempered dawn light that filled his bedchamber. He no longer needed Falken to wake him. The bard's steady breathing drifted from the other side of the room: He was still asleep.

Travis had hardly spoken to Falken or Melia since he started his studies. When he returned to the chamber at night he usually flopped down on his bed in exhaustion. Besides, the bard and the lady were busy with the Council of Kings. Sometimes he woke late in the night and heard the two speaking in low voices by the fire, about the king or queen who had made a report to the council that day. He never caught more than fragments—

. . . *the dire wolves coming from the Barrens have* . . .

. . . *is the fever, but that it harms only children and* . . .

. . . *see shadows in the forests all around Embarr* . . .

—and these wove themselves into his strange dreams.

Travis saw even less of Beltan than he did Melia and Falken, and every time he did, the big knight was walking away from him, head bowed and eyes on the ground. The blond knight's bleak mood—which had lifted a bit that first day of the council—had returned, even stronger than before.

Travis rose from his bed and gasped. The floor was *cold*. He scrambled into his clothes, threw his mistcloak over his shoulders, and slipped out the door without a sound.

He had grown to like this hour of the day, when it seemed the entire castle slept. The moon was just setting over the high wall of the lower bailey, and its light rimed the battlements like frost. He hurried to the tower of the Runespeakers. Deeming it too cold to knock and wait for Rin to come down for him, Travis entered the tower and started up the stairs to the main chamber above. He halted halfway up the stone flight. Voices drifted down from above.

"... that we should stop now."

"We can't, Jemis. We have made a vow to him by taking him on as an apprentice. We can't break that."

"Yes we can! He is too old, he has no control, he can barely read. He cannot be taught!"

"But we have to teach him. He's strong, Jemis, you know that. Stronger than me. Stronger than you. By Olrig, I wonder if he isn't stronger than All-master Oragien himself."

The only reply to this was a low grunt.

Travis did not wait to hear more. He stumbled back down the steps, out into the bailey, and breathed in deep gulps of frigid air.

He's strong, Jemis. . . .

No, he didn't want that power. He didn't want any power. "Why,

Jack?" The words were moonlit ghosts on the frosty air. "Why did it have to be me?"

The moon slipped behind the castle wall. The misty words went dark and drifted away, unanswered. After a while he turned around, walked to the tower, and knocked on the door.

78.

It was several more days before Grace found a chance to slip away again with Travis to search for other doors with runes on them. Every day that passed in Calavere the demands on her time seemed to grow. Not that Grace wasn't used to being busy. In Denver she had spent nearly all her waking hours at the hospital. More than once, after she had worked for thirty-six hours straight, Leon Arlington had had to pry a stethoscope or a syringe or a scalpel out of her numb fingers and lead her, stumbling, to the residents' lounge.

"If you can't let yourself go home, then at least let yourself lie down for a bit," Leon would say, and he would waggle a dusky finger at her protests. "Now you listen to me, Grace. Sleep a little while now, or you'll end up sleeping in one of my steel drawers downstairs for a long, long time. Got that?"

She would nod, and lie on the vinyl sofa, and let Leon throw a spare lab coat over her, and sometimes she would even close her eyes and drift off for a while. Yet after no more than an hour, two at the most, she would be back out there, walking the slick tile floor. Sleep offered no comfort, not like her work did, not like taking broken people and making them whole.

Doctor, heal thyself. Leon had told her that once. Except that was impossible, and Leon Arlington was dead, sleeping that cold, steel-cased sleep he had always warned her about.

Challenging as they had been, Grace's days in the ED could not have prepared her for her life in Calavere. Never before had she tried to do so many things, to be so many things, and to be them for so many people—so many living, whole people. For a while, after the start of the council, it had seemed King Boreas had forgotten her. She had spoken to him that day after the first reckoning and not since.

Appearances could be deceiving.

"What news have you for me, my lady?"

Grace was no screamer, but when the king of Calavan leaped out of an alcove into her path, even she couldn't help letting out a small cry.

Boreas bared his pointed teeth in what wasn't quite a grin.

She forced herself to stop shaking. "Good morrow, Your Majesty," she said.

The king stalked around her, dressed in his customary black. Muscles rippled beneath the close-fitting cloth. Grace bit her tongue so hard she tasted blood. At that moment she hated how powerful he was, how strong and masculine and handsome. How could anyone ever deny this man anything?

Damn it, but it's so unfair. Why should men have so much power? Only that wasn't true, was it? She remembered the sharp green scent of the winter garden. There were other kinds of power besides brute strength.

She squared her shoulders, lifted her head, and gazed into Boreas's keen blue eyes. "I'm sorry, Your Majesty. I already told you everything I learned."

"It isn't enough, my lady." It did not seem a statement of anger or derision, merely of fact. "I can see for myself how the council decided. What I need to know now is how I can change that reckoning."

Grace stared at him. Did he really think she had the ability to sway the minds of kings and queens?

"You are clever, my lady," the king said before she could find her voice. "I am certain you will discover something that can help me— some desire or fear of each ruler I can use to my advantage. The council must decide on a muster. If it does not, then all is lost."

Grace wanted to tell him it was impossible, and that if she had to bring herself to speak in veiled words and innuendo with one more noble, she would run screaming into the bailey as a madwoman. Instead she bowed her head and murmured, "Of course, Your Majesty. I'll do my best."

With only a nod for farewell he turned and vanished down the corridor. Dizzy, she moved to a narrow window. She threw the shutters open, drew in several breaths, and let the wintry air clear her head. Below, a dozen men-at-arms marched through the gate that led to the lower bailey. The last of the sunlight glinted on the tips of their raised halberds, crimson as blood.

Grace reached into her pocket and drew out the wooden bull she had found in the bailey—the symbol of the Cult of Vathris, the warrior mysteries Boreas followed. She ran a finger over the needle-sword stuck into the bull's throat.

"Do you know the story of Vathris?" asked a deep voice behind her.

Grace turned in surprise, then despite her troubles she smiled. "Durge. It seems so long since I've seen you."

The Embarran's weathered face was somber as always. "I am ever here, my lady."

Despite her troubles she smiled.

He gestured to the figurine in her hands. "It is an old story. Legend tells how Vathris was the king of a parched and dying land in the far south, across the Summer Sea. To save his realm he went in search of a magical bull, and when he found the beast he slew it. The bull's blood poured forth in a great river, flooding the land, and bringing life once more."

These words plunged a blade of fear into Grace's own throat. She looked up, into the knight's brown eyes. Was that what Boreas wanted? To ride across the Dominions and let loose a new river of red, just like his god had thousands of years ago? Except Vathris's deed, violent as it was, had saved the land. She slipped the bull back into her pocket.

"I don't know what to do, Durge."

The knight stroked his drooping mustaches. "What do you *wish* to do, my lady?"

"I want to know what's really going on, Durge, to know what danger is truly facing the Dominions, and the best way to counter it. I want to know so I can decide what the right thing to do really is." It was what a doctor would do: catalog the symptoms, diagnose the illness, then prescribe a cure.

The knight seemed to consider her words. The wind through the window blew his brown hair back from his brow. Then he nodded. "I think it's time you tried a new tactic, my lady."

Her heart quickened in her chest. She stepped closer to the knight. "Tell me."

The next day a story spread through the corridors of Calavere faster than either rats or fire, and by midday everyone in the castle knew how the Duchess Grace of Beckett and King Boreas had had a terrible falling-out. Of course, no one who was asked had actually seen this unexpected and thrilling occurrence, but that didn't prevent the details of the argument from being added with each retelling.

"Grace, what on Eldh is going on?" Aryn said as she ducked inside the door of Grace's chamber.

Grace gathered all her powers of persuasion, limited as they were. "It's my new plan to help Boreas," she said, hoping she sounded more breezy than breathless.

Aryn frowned. "Perhaps the word *help* has a different meaning on this Earth of yours."

Grace dropped her pretenses. "Aryn, listen to me, please." She moved to the young baroness. "Before, all the nobles in Calavere wanted to talk to me because they thought I was King Boreas's ally. They wanted to know who I was, and what advantage I offered the king, but they would never tell me what their true concerns or intentions were because they were afraid anything they told me would be repeated to King Boreas."

A hint of curiosity crept into Aryn's expression. "I'm listening."

Grace went on before it all stopped making sense to her as well. "If everyone thinks Boreas and I have fallen out, they'll wonder who I'll ally myself with next. They might even try to convince me to take their side in the council." She couldn't help laughing at the absurdity of all this. "Not that I actually have any power to affect the council, but they don't know that. And if they believe I'm no longer close to Boreas, they won't be afraid to tell me what they're really thinking."

Before Aryn could answer, Durge stepped forward. The baroness blinked.

"I'm the one to blame for all this, Your Highness," Durge said in his rumbling voice. "I'm afraid I put this notion into the Lady Grace's head. If King Boreas comes seeking satisfaction, tell him it is upon my neck his sword should fall."

"Boreas *is* furious," Aryn said. "I saw three of his mastiffs running down the hall with their tails between their legs. And if they had had tails, his servingmen would have done the same."

"Good," Grace said, trying to sound like she meant it. "If Boreas is angry, that will only make everyone believe the story all the more. But you have to tell him the truth, Aryn." Her lips twisted into a wry expression. "I'm not sure I could get within shouting range of the king before he gave the order to have my head lopped off."

Aryn said nothing, and Grace's eyes went wide.

"That was a joke, Aryn. You can laugh. I don't actually think Boreas is going to have me executed."

Aryn gave a tight smile. "I'll go talk to the king," she said.

By all of Aryn's reports Boreas was less than pleased with Grace's scheme, and with her taking action without consulting him. However, the damage was already done, and the king of Calavan had little choice but to play along. What was more, over those next few days, Durge's tactic began to prove itself. No one came to Grace openly, but each day—after the council had recessed—as she walked down an empty corridor, or strolled in the garden, or sat in a quiet room, she would look up and find someone beside her, someone who wanted to talk.

Perhaps she should have been surprised—but somehow she wasn't—when the first to approach her turned out to be Lord Olstin of Brelegond.

"Good morrow, Your Radiance," a wheedling voice spoke beside her.

Grace nearly dropped the book in her hands. It wasn't so much the whisper in her ear that made her jump as the warm spittle that accompanied it. She was in the castle's library. This was a cozy room that contained no more than fifty handwritten books. She was still studying the language of this world, and she was learning more, but she was still far from giving up Brother Cy's half-coin.

"Lord Olstin," she said in greeting.

The puffy-faced counselor ran a hand over his hair, even though it could not have been more closely plastered to his skull than it already was. Grace hoped the oil in it had come from a bottle. She was afraid that, more likely, he had made it himself.

"King Lysandir was distressed to hear of your recent troubles with King Boreas." A foul exhalation accompanied each of Olstin's words, as if his rotten teeth were sublimating with every breath.

"How kind of your king to think of me," Grace forced herself to answer. She found herself thinking of Morty Underwood.

Olstin gave a flick of his hand. Rings glinted. "Boreas is a strong king, no one will argue with you there, but he never has had a talent for subtlety."

Grace eyed Olstin's gaudy crimson garb but bit her tongue.

"Lysandir, on the other hand," Olstin said, "has always known the value of a powerful but secret ally."

Grace's instinct was to run. Instead she swallowed her gorge and leaned closer to Olstin. "Tell me more, my lord."

For nearly an hour she listened to Olstin's grating voice. Most of it was useless drivel concerning how Lysandir felt slighted at the Council of Kings. It was only near the end of the conversation that Grace realized what Olstin was really saying. Brelegond was the newest of the Dominions, and without doubt the least important. It sat on the western fringes of Falengarth's known lands and offered no resource or export on which the other Dominions relied. For all his pretenses, Olstin's words boiled down to one truth.

Brelegond was afraid.

Lysandir knew troubles were afoot in the Dominions, and he knew he had no real power to stop them. Thus he would throw his lot in with anyone—or anything—he believed could save him and his precious Dominion. Right now that was Queen Eminda of Eredane. Clearly Lysandir believed the time of Eredane's ascension over the other Dominions was at hand, and he intended to attach the wagon of Brelegond to Eminda's rising star.

However, that didn't mean Lysandir wasn't still looking for other allies. From Olstin's words Grace managed to piece together the rumors whispered about herself: that she hailed from one of the Free

Cities far to the south of Falengarth, that she was wealthy beyond belief, and that she could buy an army of southern mercenaries for anyone she chose—in return for the grant of a large estate of land and a noble title to go with it. For, as everyone knew, although they were rich in gold, the Free Cities had no true nobility like the Dominions.

Grace almost smiled. It was a good story, and one she could now do her best to lend credence to. However, after Olstin left the library— with vague promises from her to consider his words—her satisfaction cooled to ashes. She knew from her time in the ED that there was no one more dangerous than one who was afraid. Fear made people do amazing and terrible things. It could give some the power to lift cars off injured children. It could make others pick up automatic assault rifles and open fire on crowds of strangers in convenience stores. Fear was like lightning. You never knew where it would strike, or in which direction it would leap when it did.

After her conversation with Olstin, Grace had several similar encounters and was able to glean more about the real hopes and fears of the other Dominions. Lord Irrenbril, an advisor to Sorrin of Embarr, found her in the bailey, and they spoke for a time in the shadow of a leafless tree. Irrenbril's greatest fear was not so much for Embarr as it was for the sanity of his king.

"Sorrin so fears death he cannot concern himself with the lives of others," the young Embarran whispered to her. "And each day he grows more convinced he is doomed and that his own death cannot be avoided."

Grace understood. For him it was not so much a question of where Embarr would turn for help, but rather if it would turn for help at all. So deep was Sorrin's madness that Irrenbril feared the king would let the Dominion burn down around him.

The only encounter that did not fill Grace with her own sense of foreboding was that with Kalyn of Galt. Kalyn was not only counselor to Kylar of Galt, she was his twin sister and the younger only by minutes. Rumor told that she ruled the Dominion as much as her brother did. This fact was spoken with derision, but Grace thought otherwise. It was evident Kylar loved and respected his sister.

"I'm so sorry to hear about your argument with King Boreas," Kalyn said. Her brown eyes shone in her plain but comforting face. "You must let Kylar or me know if you need anything, anything at all—a place to stay, or a horse and attendants for a journey back to your home."

Grace hardly knew what to say. She could only grasp Kalyn's hand in thanks. Galt was the smallest of the Dominions and the most precarious. Surely, of all the kings, Kylar had the most cause to be afraid. Yet here was Kalyn, not asking for help but offering it. Maybe there was hope for this world yet.

The one counselor Grace hoped she would see was the one who did not seek her out. Not that she was surprised. Logren was far too intelligent to be enticed by a ruse such as she had created with Durge's help. He had probably seen through the story about her argument with Boreas the moment he heard it. Grace could not hope to manipulate Logren of Eredane—unless . . .

No, it was best not to think of Logren. She could only hope his wisdom would be enough to keep him from getting tangled in Kyrene's web.

That the countess of Selesia was indeed weaving something there could be no doubt. What it was Grace had no idea, but Kyrene was obviously pleased when she heard the tale of Grace's falling-out with Boreas.

"I'm so glad you've seen the light, love," Kyrene crooned when they met in the garden for one of Grace's lessons. "King Boreas may need you, but you do not need him. You have power he can't possibly imagine."

And you're a fool if you can't see through my act, Kyrene. Or if you think Boreas is just a buffoon you can manipulate.

But wasn't that what Grace herself was trying to do? She and Aryn had continued to hide their lessons with Kyrene and Tressa from the king. What would Boreas think of them if he knew what they were doing behind his back? However, Grace knew she could not possibly turn away from the Witches now.

Besides, the one ruler who had the power to change the reckoning of the council in an instant was Ivalaine. Grace knew she had to be careful—questions she thought subtle would be as obvious as trumpet fanfares to one like Ivalaine—but a few times she tried to divine something of the queen of Toloria's motives in abstaining at the council. More importantly, did Ivalaine act for reasons as a queen—or as a Witch? However, Grace saw Ivalaine seldom—Kyrene was her teacher now—and when she did, she never seemed able to break through the queen's cool exterior.

By the time Grace was able to meet Travis again, to search for more doors with symbols on them, she was more than ready for a break. His gray eyes were surprised behind his spectacles when he opened the door of his chamber.

"Sorry I'm late," she said.

"It's been almost a week, Grace."

She grimaced. "Sorry I'm *really* late?"

He laughed then, and she knew it was all right, knew he wasn't angry with her for not coming sooner. It was still so hard for her to tell what others were really thinking, but she was getting better, and she could not have mistaken the genuine sound of that laugh.

As they wandered the castle, Travis spoke of his studies with the Runespeakers. Grace listened with interest—so she wasn't the only one who had discovered a new talent in this world—although she did not speak of her own secret studies.

"This way," she said and turned down a side passage.

They spent the entire afternoon scouring the castle. After several hours her feet ached despite her soft deerskin boots, and her neck had a crick in it from peering at so many doors. Travis had started to get cranky—Grace knew a hunger-induced mood swing when she saw one. It was time to call it a day.

They turned around, to head back the way they had come, and in so doing found themselves facing a small door set into an alcove. Had they gone on ahead they never would have seen it. Whether it was curiosity or instinct that drew them, Grace didn't know, but they both approached the door. She saw it at once, scratched into wood: the rune of the Raven, with two crossed lines drawn beneath. Grace and Travis locked eyes, and a jolt of energy passed between them. Discovery.

Like the other, this door was not locked, and they stepped through. Grace clasped her arms to her chest. The room was freezing and obviously had not been used in years. The slit of a window was unglazed, and the only furnishing was a bed that looked like it would collapse if someone tossed a feather pillow onto it. There was a hole in one wall, and the remains of a dumbwaiter inside dangling from a frayed rope. So this had been a servant's room. Had it fallen into disuse for a reason? Or had it simply been forgotten? Calavere was large enough that rooms were probably lost and found on a regular basis.

After several minutes of searching, their hands were numb, and they had discovered nothing of interest. Grace and Travis hurried back into the corridor and shut the door.

"You're a doctor," Travis said. "Is it possible for fingers to freeze so hard they break off?"

"It would take something as cold as liquid nitrogen," Grace said through chattering teeth.

"I think that room came close."

Grace glanced again at the door, and she wasn't certain it was only the temperature of the room that had left her so cold. Travis had said there could be more rooms marked by the rune of the Raven, and now they knew it was so. But what did it mean? Like the other room, this one held no answers.

"I wonder if the servants have started a fire in my chamber," Grace said as they started moving. Belatedly she winced. Would Travis think her imperious for expecting the servants to fulfill her needs? However, he did not seem offended.

"Our chamber isn't far," Travis said. "And Melia always keeps a fire going. Her kitten likes to lie in front of it."

Grace frowned. "Now if she could just learn to treat people as well as she does cats."

Travis did not meet her gaze. "Come on," he said. "It's not far."

Grace sighed and gazed at his back. Why was it she could use a scalpel to heal, but her words always seemed to cut new wounds? It was as much a mystery to her as the rooms that had been marked. She gathered up the hem of her heavy gown and followed after Travis.

79.

Travis looked up from his wax tablet and let out a groan. It felt like a hundred of those dark elfs Falken was always telling stories about were banging their little dwarfin hammers all up and down his neck.

He gazed out a window and forced his eyes to focus on distant objects: the square top of one of the castle's guard towers, a man-at-arms standing on a crenellated parapet, a pennant snapping against a fiery sky. It was sunset already, and he still hadn't finished copying the list of runes Jemis had given him that morning. *But you have to learn this, Travis. You have to, no matter how hard it is.*

He brushed one of the runes on the tablet. *Krond.* Fire. No, never again. He gripped the stylus and bent back over the tablet.

"Travis?"

He glanced up to see Rin's head pop through the trapdoor in the wooden floor. The young runespeaker climbed the rest of the way up the ladder. The hem of his gray robe was flecked with mud. He must have been out and about that afternoon.

"What are you still doing here?" Rin said.

Travis held up the list of runes for answer. Rin let out a laugh and shook his head.

"I think Jemis must have drunk some sour beer for breakfast. That list is as long as a dragon's tail."

"I'm almost done."

"Can I see?"

Rin held out a hand. His fingers were short and thick. Travis knew Rin had been a peasant's son in southern Calavan before he was called to the Gray Tower. However, the runes Rin drew on his own wax tablet were light and graceful, and put Travis's crude scrawls to shame.

Rin took the tablet from Travis, a smile on his lips. He was halfway through when the smile faded, although he kept reading to the end. Rin looked up from the tablet. "You're a mirror reader, Travis." It wasn't a question.

The dwarfin hammers turned to elfin swords. He had tried to be careful. But there had been so many runes today, and he had gotten tired.

Travis licked his lips. "Does Jemis know?"

"No, not for certain. I've been the one checking your tablets. He suspects it, but that's all."

Travis gripped the stylus he had used to draw the runes. "Falken says people with . . . people who are mirror readers are turned away from the Gray Tower, that it's too dangerous to teach them to be runespeakers."

"It's true they are turned away."

A stone wedged itself in Travis's throat, and he tried to swallow it, but it didn't budge. He gathered up his cloak. "I'll be leaving then. Good-bye, Rin. Thank you." He started toward the ladder.

"Wax melts, you know."

Travis halted and stared back at Rin.

Rin brushed the tablet with a hand. "I don't think we'll show this slate to Jemis. No, I think I'll tell him I left it too close to the fire before I had a chance to read it, and that the wax melted."

Travis gaped at the runespeaker. Rin was giving him another chance. What had he done to deserve such a gift? He didn't know, but maybe the greatest gifts were the ones you had done nothing to earn, and maybe the only thing to do when faced with such a blessing was to accept it. He found his tongue.

"I'll be more careful from now on, Rin. I promise."

Rin smiled. "I know you will, Travis. Now go get some rest. I'm sure Jemis will have another list for you tomorrow."

Travis flashed a grin at the runespeaker, then he was down the ladder and out the tower's door.

He nodded to a man-at-arms—by now they were used to his late comings from the tower of the Runespeakers—and ducked inside the main keep. Compared to the clear night, the air inside the castle was hazy with smoke. He was grateful for the heat, though he still hadn't quite gotten used to the stench. It hit him every time he entered the castle: a mixture of smoke, rot, urine, and burnt grease.

Breathing through his mouth—it helped him get accustomed to the smells—Travis made his way through the castle's twists and turns, back to the chamber he shared with Falken and Melia. He was nearly there when he rounded a corner and collided with a bundle of rags.

"Hey there!" the rags said in a raspy voice. "You have two eyes, lad! Don't you know how to use them? Or are you just dim?"

Travis stumbled back, grabbed for his spectacles, and tried to sort out the image in front of him. The bundle of grimy rags picked itself off the floor. It seemed a rather unraglike action. What was more, the bundle had spoken to him, which meant it wasn't a bundle of rags at all, but a person. He couldn't see a face—a larger rag that might once have been a shawl hid the other's head—but he noticed a few wisps of long gray hair, and the voice, although hoarse, had sounded feminine. A woman then. But what sort of woman? It couldn't be a peasant, not at this hour in the main keep. And it was certainly no noble lady. A servingwoman then.

"Well you're a fine lot of help," the bundle—that was, the servingwoman—said.

Travis realized he had been staring while she gained her feet. He leaped forward to help, but a gnarled hand batted him back in annoyance.

"I'm so sorry," he said.

"Well doesn't that ease these old bones."

He winced, then tried again. "Can I help you?"

"Help me?" A cackle emanated from deep inside the rags. "Help *me*? It's not I who needs help, lad. I can see exactly where I'm going." A bony finger thrust out of the rags toward his chest. "What about you?"

Travis shook his head. He wasn't sure what one was supposed to say to mad old women.

"Bah!" The servingwoman waved her hand at him. "If you're not going to answer, then get out of my way." She pushed past Travis and hobbled away down the corridor.

Something caught the corner of his eye. On the floor was a small bundle of tattered cloth. The old servingwoman must have dropped it, like a miniature version of herself. Travis bent down and picked it up.

"Hey, you forgot this!" But the servingwoman was already out of sight. Travis glanced down the corridor that led to his chamber, then glanced at the bundle in his hands. He groaned in annoyance, then trotted down the corridor after the old woman.

There was no sign of her when he rounded the corner. However, she couldn't be far. He broke into a jog, and when he rounded another turn he saw a glimmer of dull gray disappear through an archway.

"Hey there!" He broke into a run and dashed through the opening.

Again he caught sight of her, now heading up a stairwell. "Wait! You dropped something!"

She did not stop, and by the time he reached the bottom of the stairs he had lost sight of her again. Travis drew in a deep breath and bounded up the steps.

Three more times he caught a distant glimpse of grimy rags vanishing around a corner or through a doorway, but she did not answer his shouts, and no matter how hard he ran he could not seem to catch up to her. Despite her hobbling, the old woman moved with uncanny speed.

Travis leaned against a wall. Whoever the old servingwoman was she certainly didn't want to be caught. He shoved the bundle into the pocket of his tunic and glanced around. The passage he stood in was utterly unfamiliar. He had the sense that he was somewhere deep below the castle—the weight of stone seemed to press upon the air in this place—but that was all.

"Good going, Travis. Now you're lost." However, there was nothing to do but start walking, and to hope he got back to familiar territory before dawn. He started back the way he had come.

"I'm sorry, Father," a voice whispered.

Travis halted at the sound, then turned around, but there was no one there. His eyes flickered to a nearby archway, and he understood. The voice had drifted through the opening, carried into the corridor by some trick of echoes and curved stone. A statue stood on either side of the archway, two warriors—both fierce and noble, hands resting on swords of stone. Their pale eyes watched Travis, not forbidding him to pass, but warning him all the same: *Go not lightly here.* Light flickered beyond the opening.

"I've looked all these years, in all the Dominions and beyond, but still I failed you."

Travis gripped the side of the arch to keep from reeling. It was not just the despair in the voice that struck him, but the fact that he recognized it.

He gathered his will, stepped through the arch, and found himself at the end of a long chamber. Columns marched down either side, carved like trees. In the alcove between each column was a marble slab, and upon each slab lay a figure, arms folded upon the breast, a pale circlet upon the brow. The hair on Travis's arms lifted at the touch of an unseen draft.

It was a tomb. A tomb of kings.

The flickering light came from a single candle at the far end of the chamber. The man stood at the foot of one of the marble biers, weeping.

Travis licked his lips, then softly called out the word. "Beltan?"

The sound echoed in the stillness of the tomb. Travis could feel the stone eyes of the two statues on his back. Only that was impossible, wasn't it?

The big knight looked up at the sound, gripped the hilt of his sword, and peered into the gloom. "Who's there?"

"It's me, Beltan."

The knight's hand slipped from the blade, and he shook his head. "Travis? Travis Wilder?"

Travis could only nod.

Beltan wiped the tears from his face. "What are you doing here?"

"I'm not . . . I'm not really . . ."

It was wrong to speak across the vast length of the tomb. Travis swallowed hard, tried to ignore the prickling on his back, and started toward the knight. He passed the first pair of biers, and he sucked in a breath. They were so pale, so still, he had thought them carved of marble like the biers they rested upon. Only that was not so.

They were shaped of flesh, not stone. Here in this tomb were all the past kings of Calavan. Yet Travis guessed each king looked now just as he had on the day he was laid here. Even in the dim light hair still glinted yellow, or brown, or silver, and their lips were tinged the color of roses. Nor had their garb decayed over the centuries. Swords rested in their folded hands, and gleamed as if they had been just polished.

Travis forced himself to walk onward, past the rows of sleeping kings. The first rulers wore capes of fur, thick copper torcs, and arm rings. Those that came after had finer garb: cloaks woven of wool, jewelry of gold and silver. He was nearly halfway when he came upon the first of the queens. She was beautiful, proud even in death, and gripped a sword in her hands just as the kings did. He passed more kings, and several queens, until he reached those whose garb did not look so different from what Boreas or Alerain or Grace wore. Then he stepped across a boundary of shadow and light, into the circle of the candle's glow.

The last king in the line was a big man. In life he would have been both tall and massive. Even in the candlelight Travis could see the resemblance: the sharp line of the jaw, the hawkish nose, the high forehead, the broad shoulders. His hair was dark, like his brother's, but he was not so handsome as King Boreas, and he was clearly older, his face lined and careworn, his beard flecked with gray.

A rune was etched into the stone at the foot of the bier King Beldreas rested upon. Travis recognized it from his studies with Rin and Jemis. It was *Sethen*, the rune of perfection. He started to reach out, then snatched his hand back. Before he even touched the rune his right hand tingled. So that was how the bodies of the ancient kings and queens had been preserved. The rune *Sethen* was bound into the stone of each bier. Under its ward steel would never rust, flesh would never decay.

After Beldreas, the biers continued into the shadows, empty. There must have been fifty in all, of which perhaps twenty were occupied. Travis wondered what would happen when the last bier was taken.

"They say when the last king is laid to rest on the last bier, Calavan will come to an end," Beltan said, as if he had read Travis's thoughts. "And all the Dominions will end with it. At least that's how the story goes."

Travis shivered, then let his eyes fall on the lifeless form of Beldreas. "Your father looks like he was a strong king."

Beltan nodded. "He was—the strongest king Calavan had seen in a century. Before him, the robber barons had been striking closer and closer to Calavere. In his reign Beldreas drove them to the marches of the Dominion, then crushed them one by one. Calavan won't see his like again soon."

Travis looked up. He knew he shouldn't say it, but he couldn't help himself. "You would have been a strong king, too, Beltan."

The knight pressed his eyes shut, then opened them. "I? A strong king?" He shook his head. "No, Travis. I could never be like Beldreas. I couldn't even keep the vow I made to him, to find his murderer."

"But you tried, Beltan. You have to forgive yourself."

The knight met Travis's eyes. "I can't do that."

Travis wanted to protest, wanted to tell Beltan he was wrong, that he had to forgive himself for what he couldn't change. Instead he nodded. "I know. I broke a promise once, too."

Will you be here when I wake up?

I promise.

Cross your heart?

Cross my heart and hope to die.

Beltan's expression turned into a question, but Travis only looked down at the dead king. Beltan did the same. The candle burned low.

"We should go," Beltan said. "Melia will be looking for you."

Travis moved away from the bier, then halted, reached out, and gripped the knight's arm. "You *are* strong, Beltan. You're the strongest man I've ever met."

The knight stared in surprise. Then, impossibly, he smiled, and in that moment Beltan was more noble, and more fair, than any of the sleeping kings.

"I don't know how you knew to find me here, Travis, but I'm glad you did."

Travis grinned in reply. The knight blew out the candle, and together they left the silent tomb.

80.

Grace shut the door of her chamber, leaned against the expanse of wood, and let out a breath that was half relief and all exasperation.

"No more nobles," she said to the empty room. "No more nobles, no more nobles, no more *nobles*."

She heaved herself from the door, farther into her room. Strange, but not so long ago this chamber had seemed like a prison. Now it was a haven she all too rarely had the chance to enjoy. A glint of purple glass on the sideboard caught her eye. She aimed herself toward it. Wine. Yes, some wine would be good. She filled a pewter cup and flopped in the chair by the fire.

The sky was on fire outside the window. The Council of Kings had lasted the entire day again. After that initial session of the council, Grace had thought her attendance was no longer required. She had slipped into the council chamber for an hour here and there, to listen to the various rulers make their reports, but especially after her fictional altercation with King Boreas it seemed best to stay removed from the council and to let the other nobles seek her out. It seemed more mysterious that way.

All that had changed three days ago, when Boreas barged into her chamber. Grace had hastily thrown a kerchief over a mortar and pestle on the sideboard. She had been in the act of grinding dried herbs, following Kyrene's instructions to make a kind of medicinal tea. A *simple*, the green-eyed countess had called it, one to calm a nervous spirit in small amounts. Or, in stronger doses, to induce a trance, and to make the subject malleable and prone to suggestion.

The dusty-sweet scent of herbs had drifted on the air, and Grace had thought Boreas would surely notice, but he had not. He must have just come back from hunting along the eaves of Gloaming Wood, because he wore only breeches of black leather, tight around his lean hips, and a white shirt unlaced to reveal a wedge of hard chest. A metallic scent had drifted from him. Grace knew it well: blood.

Without preamble Boreas had backed her into a corner, as if she were his latest quarry. For some reason she had wondered if he would try to kiss her, and if she would try to resist if he did.

"Alerain and I are to begin making our presentation to the council tomorrow," the king had said. "You will attend, Lady Grace, and listen for me, to hear what others say about Calavan while Alerain and I are speaking."

She had glanced past his heavy shoulder at the covered mortar. How hard would it have been to offer Boreas wine, to slip a few of the herbs into it as she did? No, despite Kyrene's lessons, she was no huntress. She had forced herself to meet Boreas's gaze and had acquiesced.

Luckily, Boreas's task for her had been easier than she thought. Still believing her at odds with the king of Calavan, a veritable parade of nobles had occupied the stone bench beside her at the council and had whispered in her ear.

Boreas was a warmonger, they said. Or Boreas was the only hope for the Dominions. Or Boreas was mad and trying to destroy them all. Eredane would never go with Calavan. No, Eredane was only holding out for concessions from Calavan and would switch its reckoning at the last moment. Even Perridon was about to defect from Boreas's camp. On the contrary, Perridon was the most loyal to Calavan and had almost convinced Embarr to go with it, only King Sorrin was daft, and danced in his chamber at night, naked and holding a sword, working terrible magics of blood and fire to cure the wasting disease that consumed him.

Before long the whispers had filled Grace's mind and tangled together like a seething knot of gray serpents.

Eminda held a secret love for Boreas. No, Boreas cared nothing for women, was glad Queen Narena was dead, and spent his nights buggering young men-at-arms in his chamber. What was more, Boreas had killed his own brother Beldreas to gain the throne of Calavan, and now Boreas's bastard son Beltan was going to do the same. And had Grace heard how Boreas's legitimate son, Teravian—who was being fostered at court in Toloria—was the reason for Queen Ivalaine's abstentions? Yes, everyone knew how the queen of Toloria had seduced him, although he was only fifteen winters old, and planned to defeat Boreas at the council and place Teravian as her puppet on the throne of Calavan.

A knock on the door jarred Grace from her thoughts, and she nearly spilled wine on herself. "Come in," she said as she stood, then she smiled at one of the few nobles she was always glad to encounter.

"Grace, it's so good to see you," Aryn said.

Grace studied her friend. The baroness looked older somehow, more mature. Aryn was wearing an indigo gown Grace had never seen before. The bodice was fitted tight to her slender waist and cut revealingly low. A small cape of white rabbit fur draped her right shoulder, as if cast on casually and not to hide the withered limb beneath.

"I had a feeling you'd be here," Aryn said.

Grace raised an eyebrow. "Oh? Is Tressa teaching you something you haven't told me about?"

Roses bloomed on Aryn's snowy cheeks. "That's not what I meant, Grace. It was just a feeling, that's all."

Grace gazed down at her hands, at her own fingers coiled around the cup, long and slender. "I'm beginning to think there's no such thing as *just* a feeling."

Aryn cast a nervous glance at the door, then pressed it shut. She turned back around, her blue eyes wide and earnest, nineteen years old again.

"I'm beginning to think the same thing, Grace. Or maybe I don't know what to think."

They sat on the window bench in the failing light.

"I'm not sure I can stand this, Grace. Tressa tells me to do things, but she never tells me why. It's maddening. But I do them, because I want to know, because I *have* to know, and sometimes . . . sometimes . . ."

Grace made a slow nod. "Sometimes you *do* understand."

Aryn met Grace's eyes, then gripped her hand. "What are we doing, Grace?"

Grace gazed out the window at the castle below in all its sprawling, muddy grandeur. "I don't know, Aryn. But I'm not sure I can stop now that I've started. The things Kyrene has shown me, about the Touch and the Weirding. It makes me feel . . . it makes me feel so . . ."

What, Grace? What does it make you feel? Powerful? Sensual? Alive? It was all these things, but more. She couldn't find the word, but a squeeze on her hand let her know Aryn understood.

Grace turned her gaze back to the young baroness. "I think we should tell Boreas what we're doing."

Aryn snatched her hand back, her face an oval of terror. "Grace! Please tell me you're making a jest. Boreas will have us drawn and quartered if he finds out. He's a disciple of Vathris. You know how he feels about the Witches."

Grace let out a troubled breath and nodded. Aryn was right, of course.

Now Aryn's alarm turned to concern. "What is it, Grace?"

"I'm not sure, Aryn. It's just that I'm supposed to be King Boreas's spy at the council. Only now we've started studying with Queen Ivalaine. I know she has some agenda at the council. But I can't even get close to finding out what it is."

The words came faster as Grace's mind raced, piecing together all the clues and innuendoes she had gathered in her observations of the Council of Kings.

"And I don't think Ivalaine is acting only as queen of Toloria. I think she's here at this council as a Witch as well. I *know* it. The Witches are up to something, Aryn. Kyrene keeps dropping those smug little hints of hers." Her lips twisted in a wry smile. "Yes, I know you have to take everything Kyrene says with a grain of salt, but it's still clear something is going on at this council, something deeper than what's on the surface. And the Witches are part of it."

"Watching," Aryn said.

Grace cocked her head.

"Ivalaine is always watching. I see her during the council. It's like she's watching for something, and waiting."

"For what?"

However, if they had known the answer to that, they would not have been in this predicament.

Aryn glanced at the window, then gasped and leaped to her feet. "I'm late, Grace. Tressa will be waiting for me if I don't hurry."

"Go," Grace said. She rose and guided her friend to the door.

"What about you?"

"Kyrene said she couldn't meet with me tonight. No, it's all right. She gave me some herbs to work with, for making some simples, and I need the practice."

Aryn gave her one last grateful look, then was out the door and running down the corridor. Grace watched her go, then shut the door, alone in her room once more.

She moved to the sideboard, lit a candle to warm the blue light of evening, then looked at the cloth bundles that contained the herbs she had picked in the garden. She tried to recall the recipe Kyrene had recited to her. *Take five leaves of redcrown, three leaves of hound's vetch, and a strip of dried willow bark as long as your finger. . . .*

Grace frowned. Or was that *three* leaves of redcrown and *five* leaves of hound's vetch?

With a sigh she set the bundles down. She knew she should practice. So far all her simples tasted like dirt when she sampled them, and the only magical effect they had was to make her use the chamber pot with greatly increased frequency and percussion. However, the council had exhausted her. She was too tired for spells and simples.

She glanced out the darkened window and thought of the garden. She longed to feel that life again, that energy, to let it fill her emptiness. However, the sun had set, soon it would be too cold and dark to venture outside the keep, and there was nothing living in this room.

But who says you can only feel living things, Grace?

A shiver coursed down her spine. The thought hardly seemed her own, although she knew it was. Yet it was a foolish notion. Inanimate objects weren't alive, they couldn't possibly have energy like the growing things in the garden.

Except you know that isn't true, Grace. A scalpel can have a life of its own. And a knife.

She crouched and slipped her hands to the knife tucked into her deerskin boot. Her fingers brushed the smooth hilt . . .

. . . then pulled back. There was another knife she could touch, one that held greater mysteries. She rose, moved to the chair by the fire, and dug under the cushion where she had hidden it. With trembling fingers she unwrapped the cloth until it lay exposed in her hands.

"This is crazy, Grace."

Even as she spoke she sat in the chair and rested the knife on her lap. It looked like a black serpent against the violet fabric of her gown, sleek and dangerous. In the garden she had sensed so much about the things she had reached out to with the Touch. What might she learn from this? About the hand that had carved the door with it?

Grace gazed at the knife and remembered Kyrene's words. She took a deep breath. Then she reached out with her mind—

—and touched the knife.

Cold. It was so cold. She couldn't breathe, couldn't feel anything. Only an icy wind streaming through the very essence of her being. *This is what it must feel like to be dead.* Then she opened her eyes.

The castle receded in the distance, fading in the blue half-light. Snowy fields and stone walls slipped beneath her. She flew through the frigid twilight, over the wintry landscape of Calavan. Tracks and bridle paths twined and untwined below. Villages appeared and vanished in an eye blink. More fields sped by, then a great swath of black flashed beneath her. She saw an arch of stone. By the time she realized it was the bridge over the River Darkwine it was gone.

Now the snow-dusted fields beneath her were barren, undivided by stone walls. They glowed in the last light of day and the first light of stars. She half expected to see her own shadow flickering across the hills and vales below, but she did not, and how could she? Grace knew, even at that moment, she sat in the chair by the fire in her chamber in Calavere.

Where am I going?

The thought was dull with the chill, and even as it occurred to her a tangled wall rose up from the fields. The edges of Gloaming Wood. The forest absorbed the lingering light, captured it in the net of its leafless branches, and refused to release it again. Was she being taken into the woods?

No, the ground rose up to meet her. She was sinking. Or something was drawing her down. She floated over a snowy hill, into a dell, and she saw it.

They stood in a circle, as if frozen in the midst of a thunderous dance. Nine standing stones. Each was twice the height of a man, and all were worn and pitted with time. They thrust up from the ground, black and sharp against the sky. That they were ancient Grace had no doubt. Perhaps not as ancient as the forest. But then perhaps they were. Did even the stones themselves remember who had placed them here?

She drifted closer to the megaliths. A tingling shimmered through her, along with the cold. Something was going to happen. Something important. Grace floated between two of the standing stones, and at once she knew this was what she had been drawn here to see.

There were two of them in the center of the circle. She could tell they were both men from their riding gear: leather breeches, woolen tunics, thick cloaks. One of them, the shorter of the two, stood with his back to her, so she could not see his face. The other faced in her direction, but the hood of his riding cloak was pulled forward and cast his visage into shadow. Behind them, on the edge of the circle, were two horses, their reins tied to thornbushes that had sprung up around the base of one of the standing stones. A crescent moon—sharp, pale, and curved as a knife itself—sank toward the still-glowing horizon.

"You're late," the tall man said.

Had she had the ability, Grace would have gasped. It seemed he was speaking to her. No, the other took a step forward, his boots crunching through the crust of the snow. It was to him the man in the hood had spoken.

"I came as soon as I could," the shorter man said. "You know it's not easy for me to get away from the castle."

"That's your concern, not mine," the hooded man said. His words were low and gruff.

He's disguising his voice. He doesn't want the other man to know who he is.

"Well, I'm here now," the bareheaded man said. His own voice was muffled by his turned back and the moan of the wind through the standing stones.

"Is everything in place?"

"It will be."

"What do you mean it *will* be?" The hooded man took a step forward. His voice could not disguise his anger. "All was to be ready this night. That was what we agreed upon."

"I've been leaving signs for my associates, but it's hard to find time when I'm alone. And there are prying eyes about the castle. I've done the best I can."

"Then your best is not good enough. Another reckoning of the council could come at any time. It is imperative it go our way."

Grace strained to move closer, but she could not. The wind seemed to hold her back. Or perhaps it was some power of the massive stones.

"And it *will* go our way," the shorter man said. "Soon six rulers will sit at the council table, not seven. Which of them will be missing we won't know until our moment comes. Regardless, there will be no more deadlock." He put his hands on his hips, confident. "So do not worry yourself."

"You knave!" the hooded one hissed. "How dare you tell me what I should or shouldn't do?"

It happened in an instant, so quickly Grace barely saw it. A dagger appeared in the tall man's hand, spirited from the folds of his cloak. The blade flashed in the moonlight, the shorter man stumbled back, and the horses let out a whicker of fear. Now blood spattered the ground: bright winter berries scattered on the snow.

The bareheaded man clutched his side. Crimson welled forth between his fingers. "You . . . you stabbed me." His words were no longer confident but quavering.

"Only a sting to remind you who your master is," the hooded man said. "I promise you, the next time you act so bold before me the bite will be much deeper. And believe that I know where to place the knife. Now get yourself back to the castle, and see to it you finish what we've started."

The shorter man made a shallow bow, still clutching his wound. As he did this, the other's hooded visage rose and gazed past him—

—directly at Grace. He cocked his head, almost as if he saw something on the frosty air.

Cold and panic were one. Grace tried to claw at the air, but she could not grasp it, could not move. No, it was impossible. He couldn't possibly see her.

The hooded man took a step forward.

No!

Somewhere far away numb hands let something fall, then Grace herself was falling. All of it vanished in an instant—the men, the standing stones, the crescent moon—replaced by a vast well of darkness into which she tumbled. Down she fell, toward a lake of darkness from which she knew she would never emerge. . . .

"Lady Grace!"

Grace's eyes snapped open, and she drew in the shuddering gasp of a drowning victim shocked back to life. Ivalaine stood above her, her face hard and impassive. Tressa knelt beside the chair in which Grace sat, her brown eyes warm with concern. Aryn hovered behind the two women, her face a tear-streaked mixture of fear and relief.

Tressa clucked her tongue as she rubbed Grace's hands. "Your skin is like ice, child."

It was hard to speak, but somehow Grace forced the words out. "What . . . what happened?"

A shadow touched Ivalaine's brow. "You were almost lost, sister. Three times I called to you. Had you not come back this last time, you never would have come back at all. You are lucky Lady Aryn and Lady Tressa came looking for you, to invite you into their studies in light of Lady Kyrene's absence."

Grace shivered, and feeling coursed back into her limbs, hot and tingling. "I don't understand," she said through clattering teeth.

Ivalaine lifted something in her hands: a knife with a black hilt. Grace clenched her jaw.

Ivalaine's face was carved from stone. "Do not again attempt things Kyrene has not taught you, Lady Grace."

No more words were needed. Grace gave a jerky nod.

"Come, Tressa." Ivalaine set the knife on the sideboard.

The red-haired woman cast one last concerned look at Grace, then rose.

"See to the Lady Grace, sister," Ivalaine said to Aryn. "You are finished with your studies for today. I think you have both learned enough this evening."

The queen of Toloria turned and left the chamber, Tressa behind her. As soon as the door shut, Aryn was on her knees beside the chair. She rubbed Grace's hands.

"You're cold as snow! What happened to you, Grace? When we found you, you seemed so far away."

Grace opened her mouth, but words were beyond her now. All she could do was shiver and hope the fire would thaw her before it burned her alive.

81.

Travis set down his tablet and unclenched his fingers from the stylus. The doves were roosting for the night in the rafters high above. It was time to go.

He left the tablet where Rin would find it—things had been going better since his conversation with the young runespeaker—then headed downstairs and opened the tower's door.

"Oh!" he said at the same time she did.

She had been in the act of lifting her hand to rap on the door as he opened it. Grace.

She recovered her composure. "Travis, I have to talk to you."

He only nodded, too surprised for words.

She clutched her arms over her chest. "Can I come in?"

"I'm sorry. Of course, please."

Grace hurried in, and he shut out the wintry blast. She pushed back the fur-lined hood of her cape. Her face was pale with the cold, but her eyes, as they always did, glowed like a summer forest.

"Can we speak here, Travis?" She glanced at the wooden ceiling above.

Travis frowned. "It's only Rin and Jemis up there. And they couldn't hear us anyway. They're all the way up in the attic chamber."

Grace took a step forward. "Good, because I don't want anyone else to hear this."

By the time she finished her story Travis's face was as white as her own.

He drew in a breath. "I think we need help, Grace."

She nodded. "Do you mean Melia and Falken?"

Travis thought about this, then shook his head. "No, let's not bring them into it, at least not yet. They're both too busy with the council. Let's see what we find out, then we can tell them if we learn anything more."

"Who are you thinking of, then?"

Travis scratched his red-brown beard. He really should get around to shaving it. "They say the way to fight fire is with fire, Grace. If there's a conspiracy in the castle, then maybe we need to start a conspiracy of our own."

"What do you mean?"

He grinned at her. "Come on. I'll tell you as we go."

It was just after sunset when they met in Grace's chamber. Twilight had coiled its purple cloak about the castle, and outside the window the moon glowed in the sky. Even at just a quarter it was far larger and more brilliant than the moon of Earth. Would Travis ever see that smaller, more distant satellite again?

"What's going on, Grace?" Aryn said.

The young baroness stood near the window. She held a cup of wine in her left hand but did not drink from it. Her eyes flickered toward Travis, and it was clear her question could as easily have been, *What's he doing here, Grace?*

Travis clutched his own cup of wine. *Stop it. She's only wondering what this is about, that's all. You're not a servingman in this world any more than Grace is a duchess. Maybe if you quit acting the part, people would stop thinking you're one.*

"Something has gone wrong, of course," the knight Durge said. He sounded almost pleased. "Lady Grace would not summon us here with such urgency if that were not the case."

Grace took a step forward. "Aryn, Durge, you both remember Travis Wilder."

Aryn gave a polite but shallow nod. Durge made a bow.

"Goodman Travis," the knight said in his solemn baritone.

Grace licked her lips. "I've learned something. Something about the Council of Kings."

A frown alighted on Aryn's brow. "Do you really think we should discuss this in front of Lady Melia's man?"

Travis winced.

Grace drew in a breath, then blurted the words out all at once. "He's from Earth, Aryn. From the same place I am."

The baroness's blue eyes grew large. She stumbled back and might have spilled her wine, but Durge was there to steady her with a sure hand. The knight glanced at Aryn, then at Grace and Travis in turn. His somber face was thoughtful.

"I don't know what to think of this *Earth* you speak of," he said. "But if Goodman Travis is one of your kinsmen, Lady Grace, then he is welcome here."

Grace shook her head. "No, Durge, you don't understand, it's more than that. Much more. . . ."

Soon the knight's deep-set eyes were nearly as round as Aryn's, but he did not interrupt Grace. When she finished he stroked his drooping mustaches.

"Of course," he said in a soft voice. "I always knew it was so. There were no footprints in the snow in the hollow where I found you, in

Gloaming Wood. Ever did I say it was as if you had drifted from the sky, and I had wondered if perhaps you had come from the realm of the fairy folk. So it is from a different world you hail. But I was not so far from right, was I?"

"No, Durge, you weren't." Grace's voice was hoarse, and her eyes shone.

The knight was still for a moment, then stepped forward, knelt before her, and bowed his head. "Do not trouble yourself, my lady. I have pledged my sword to you, and an Embarran's word is stronger than steel, more enduring than stone. It does not matter what world you are from."

Now Grace laughed. She touched Durge's stooped but strong shoulder.

"Rise, Sir Durge. Oh, please rise."

He did, and she caught his hands in hers, and his eyes went wide all over again. Aryn ran toward Grace and threw her left arm around the taller woman. The baroness was weeping, and Travis's own throat grew tight. Even in other worlds there were good people.

Aryn pulled away from Grace and turned toward Travis. Her young face was earnest. "I'm so sorry, Goodman . . . I mean, Travis. I didn't know. Do you think—not now, but someday—you could forgive me?"

"There's nothing to forgive." He smiled at her. "And you can call me whatever you want. I don't think there's any shame in being called a good man."

Durge laid a hand on his shoulder. "No. There is not."

"I have the feeling I just missed something," said a bright tenor.

Travis looked up to see a broad, familiar figure standing in the doorway.

"Beltan!"

The big knight bowed in reply.

"How did you find us?" Travis said. "I looked all over the castle for you, but I couldn't find you."

"I got the Lady Grace's summons. A page brought it to me in the stables."

Travis glanced at Grace.

She gave a little shrug. "Being mistaken for royalty does have its advantages."

"Apparently." He took a step toward the blond knight. "I'm glad you could come, Beltan."

The knight's jovial face grew solemn. "I can't just hide in old tombs, Travis. One day that will be my place, but not now, not while I'm alive. Thank you for reminding me of that."

Travis opened his mouth, but he didn't know what to say.

Grace shut the chamber door, and this time she slid a wooden bar over it. "We'd better get started. It won't be long before someone comes looking for at least one of us."

All eyes turned to Grace. It was time for the real business at hand.

Aryn glanced at Beltan, then back at Grace. "Should we tell him?"

"It's all right," Travis said. "Beltan knows."

"Knows what?" Beltan said.

"That I'm from another world. And Grace, too."

The big knight snorted. "Oh, that."

Aryn raised an eyebrow. "You seem to take it in stride."

Beltan crossed his arms over his broad chest. "Believe me, you get used to surprises when you travel with Melia and Falken. The fact is, you can act astonished only for so long. Your face just gets tired of all that jaw-dropping."

Now the baroness gazed at Travis in a new light, her blue eyes curious.

"Grace," he said to get himself out of the spotlight, "tell them what you told me."

Grace nodded, and the others listened as she paced before the fire and spoke in low tones: the doors, the knife, the spell, and the circle of stones. When she whispered how she had learned this magic—that she and Aryn were studying with Queen Ivalaine and the Witches—both Durge and Beltan took a step back. Beltan started to make a motion with his hand, his thumb and littlest finger outstretched, then stopped himself.

"It appears we are not quite through with Lord Beltan's surprises," Durge said when Grace had finished.

She took a halting step toward him. "Durge, I'm so sorry, I should have told you."

His expression was incredulous. "Why, my lady? It is not my place to question your actions. And there are matters at hand that *do* require my attention."

"Like the fact that there's a conspiracy of murder in Calavere," Beltan said. Now his face was nearly as grim as Durge's. "Again."

Beltan and Durge had more questions, and Grace and Travis answered them as best they could. They knew little enough, but for all the enigmas a few things were clear. A plot was afoot in the castle to murder one of the rulers attending the Council of Kings, and the new Raven Cult was behind it. Travis couldn't imagine what a mystery cult could get from murdering a king, but there was no doubting the cult's involvement. Grace had seen a cultist drop the black knife in the act of carving the Raven symbol into a door. That same knife had taken her—by means of magic—to the circle of standing stones. The knife must have belonged to one of the two conspirators Grace had seen. That meant one of them had access to the castle. But who was it? That was another unanswered question.

"I still don't understand what the doors mean," Beltan said. He ran a hand through his long, thinning hair. "I grant you there's no great surprise in that. Still, if someone could explain what two storerooms have to do with a murder plot, I'd be grateful."

Aryn had been quiet through much of the discussion, but now she glanced up from her thoughts, her blue eyes bright. "I have an idea. It will only take a minute, but I need . . . I need another hand to help."

Durge stepped forward. "My lady."

Aryn hesitated, then gave a nod.

When the baroness and the knight returned to the chamber minutes later, his arms were filled with vellum scrolls.

"What are these, Aryn?" Grace said.

"Let me show you."

The baroness took one of the scrolls and set it on the sideboard. She put a saltcellar on one corner, and Travis and Grace helped her unroll it. At first Travis could not make sense of what he saw. The scroll was covered with dim lines and circles.

Grace gasped. "It's a map of the castle!"

Even as she said this the lines and circles snapped into place, and Travis could see it. "Look, there's the upper bailey," he said. "And the hedge maze, and the main keep. And these over here must be plans of the keep's different floors. I had no idea there were so many."

Durge started to set the other scrolls down, scrambled for them as they slipped from his arms, then managed to get them on the table. "What are we to do with these, Lady Aryn?"

"Look," she said. "We have to look."

It took nearly an hour. Some of the maps were very old—drawn by the master builders who had constructed Calavere over the centuries—and it was clear many of them were no longer accurate. Some depicted corridors and rooms that no longer existed, or showed nothing where towers now stood. Eventually they found a scroll that seemed less faded than the others. It was Beltan who finally found what they were looking for.

"It was just luck," the knight said. He pointed to the small square on the map.

Travis peered at it. Yes, that had to be the storeroom with the Raven symbol on the door, the first one he and Grace had found. The other room had not been far from the first, and they soon found it on the map. But what did all this tell them?

Aryn drew in a sharp breath. "Beltan, pick up that map, the last one we looked at before this."

He glanced at her, his expression puzzled, but did as she asked.

"Now place it over this map. Please."

Travis saw what she was getting at. The map on top depicted the floor of the keep just above the floor with the two empty rooms.

"What is it, Aryn?" Grace said.

With her trembling hand the baroness pointed to two rooms on the top map. "This is the chamber where King Persard is sleeping. This chamber is King Sorrin's."

"And the two rooms Lady Grace and Goodman Travis found are directly beneath these chambers," Durge said.

Travis flipped back the top map. It was true. He shut his eyes and saw again the ventilation shaft in the storeroom and the old dumb waiter in the empty bedchamber. His eyes flew open.

"That's how they're going to do it! That's how they're going to get to the king they plan to murder." He pointed to the map. "See these lines? These are shafts that run between each of the empty rooms and the chambers of the rulers."

Beltan swore. "We have to go to King Boreas. From what Grace told us, the conspirators could strike anytime."

Durge turned away from the window. He had been gazing into the night. "I would not be so certain of that," he said.

The others stared at him.

"Lady Grace," he said. "Did you not say in your tale that you saw the circle of stones at twilight? And that the crescent moon was just setting?"

"Yes," she said. "It was very . . . vivid."

Durge stepped away from the window. Light streamed through the rippled glass and cast a pattern like silver water upon the floor. Outside the moon sank toward the castle's battlements. A quarter moon.

Grace approached the window. "But I don't understand. I saw it so clearly. The moon was a crescent."

"And will be so in five days," Durge said.

They all seemed to grasp the truth at once.

"It hasn't happened yet," Grace said as she turned back from the window. "What I saw, the two men in the circle of stones. It hasn't happened yet."

"Then that gives us time," Aryn said. "Time to learn what's really going on before we tell the king."

Beltan frowned at this, his hand on the hilt of his sword. "I still say we should tell King Boreas."

Grace took a step toward the knight. "You are the king's nephew, Beltan." Her voice was cool and logical. "We can't tell you what to do. But right now we don't even know what other rulers, including Boreas, are in danger from this plot. I think we should find out more before we tell anyone. Right now the fewer people who know, the more likely we are to learn something." Her eyes flickered to Aryn. "And there are other reasons for not telling King Boreas how I learned what I did."

Aryn nodded, her face tight.

Beltan crossed his arms over his broad chest and considered her words. Travis held his breath. Grace's visage was so calm, so assured. How many patients at Denver Memorial had seen that same expression as she explained a dire prognosis to them?

Beltan sighed and threw down his arms. "All right. I won't tell Boreas, or Melia and Falken. But why do I have the feeling I'm going to get in trouble for all of this?"

It was a question no one cared to answer.

"It's set then," Aryn said. She gave a nervous laugh, her blue eyes bright, uncertain, thrilled. "We've begun our own conspiracy."

Durge blew a breath through his mustaches. "Don't proper conspiracies have names?"

"They do." Aryn chewed her lip. "But what can we call ourselves?"

"We have to all swear an oath on something," Beltan said. "An oath of loyalty and secrecy. We'll take our name from that, whatever it is."

Travis searched around the room. What sort of thing did one swear an oath on? "The knife," he said before he even really thought of the answer. "It's the knife that got us into this."

Grace picked up the onyx-hilted knife from the sideboard, drew in a breath, and held the blade out. "I swear myself to secrecy," she said.

Travis laid his hand atop hers. "Count me in."

"I also swear an oath of secrecy," Aryn said. She rested her hand on Travis's, light as a bird.

"As do I," Durge said, and he added his hand to the knot.

Beltan was the last. "May our circle never be broken."

The knight placed his big hand atop the others, and in that moment the Circle of the Black Knife was forged.

82.

The next night, Calavere's newest conspiracy embarked on its secret work.

The Circle of the Black Knife met just as the moon—waning now—

sank beneath the western battlements. The doves had long since ceased their twilight song, and only a handful of torches guttered in the bailey below. In winter, in this world, light and all the things that made it—wood, peat, oil—were precious commodities, and not to be wasted. The Eldhish day lived and died with the sun. Most hid in their beds and waited for the rebirth of dawn.

Then again, there were those who favored shadows.

"There you are, Grace," Aryn said with a sigh of relief.

Grace stepped through the door, into the dusty chamber. The others were already there.

"I'm sorry I'm late," she said. "I'm afraid King Boreas caught me on my way here."

Travis pushed his spectacles up his nose. "He doesn't suspect anything, does he?"

Grace took a step back. At first she thought Travis meant her lessons with Kyrene and the Witches. Then she realized he had meant the meeting of the Circle.

"No," she said, then cast a nervous glance at the door. "At least, I don't think so."

Boreas had cornered her for a report on what she had overheard at the council that day. Grace had done her best to give it to him in calm, unhurried tones, but once he had left her she realized she had been shaking. She could only hope he hadn't noticed. Luckily, their meeting had been necessarily brief—if Grace and Boreas were seen together, it would spoil the ruse that they had had a falling-out. It was an unforeseen result of Grace's plan, but a welcome one.

"Let's hope you're right, Grace," Beltan said. "Boreas might not consider what we're doing to be treason. Then again . . ."

Durge moved to the door and shut it.

Grace crossed her arms over her gown and wished she had brought her cape. The room was cold. It was situated in the old watchtower, which—according to Aryn—was little used these days, because of a faulty foundation and the fact that it was not as high as the newer guard towers near the gate. That was why the baroness had chosen it for their meeting place.

The Embarran turned back toward the others. "Should we set a lookout to be sure no one overhears us?"

Aryn frowned. "But that won't do. Whoever has to stand outside will miss our conversation."

Durge's mustaches drooped.

"I think . . . I think maybe I can arrange something," Travis said.

Grace watched with interest as Travis walked to the door and pressed his hand to the splintering wood.

"*Sirith*," he whispered.

Grace wasn't certain, but she thought she saw a nimbus of blue light flicker around Travis's fingers. Then he pulled his hand away.

She met his eyes. "What was that you said, Travis?"

"It's the rune of silence."

"What did it do?"

He stroked his beard. It was getting full now, with flecks of copper, gold, and—Grace noticed for the first time—silver. Only thirty-three, and already he was becoming a graybeard.

"I'm not entirely sure," Travis said. "Speaking something's rune is supposed to awaken its power. But I think, if I spoke it right, no one on the other side of this door will be able to hear what we're saying."

Grace and Aryn nodded—his words made sense to Grace, even if she knew little of runes—but the two knights scowled as one.

"If that was the rune of silence," Beltan said, "how come I can hear what you're saying now?"

Travis scratched his head, then shrugged. "It's a magic thing."

The blond knight let out a snort. "Apparently."

"Perhaps Travis would not mind a test of his skill at runespeaking," Durge said. "He is a student, after all."

A quick experiment confirmed that Travis's magic had worked as intended. Grace and Beltan stood outside the shut door but heard nothing, although those within spoke in loud voices.

Beltan rested a hand on Travis's shoulder. "I'm sorry I doubted you."

"Don't be." Travis looked down at his hands and was quiet for a time after that.

Now that they knew they would not be overheard, it was time to get to the business at hand.

"I've found another marked door," Aryn said without preamble.

The others regarded the baroness. Knowing what sort of rooms were being marked with the rune of the Raven had narrowed their search considerably. The night before, Aryn had shown them on the castle plans where each of the rulers was sleeping. The five had all agreed to stroll—alone, and at separate times of the day—past rooms that were adjacent in some way to those of the various kings and queens, and to look for any signs of the Raven Cult.

Aryn pulled a vellum scroll from a leather satchel and—with Beltan's help—spread it on a table that listed more than a little to starboard. She laid a finger on the map.

"Here. You can only reach this room off the lower bailey. It's for storing grain. In it there's a drain leading to a stone pipe that runs here." She looked up to regard the others. "Right past Queen Ivalaine's room."

A shiver coursed up Grace's spine.

"Excellent work, my lady," Durge said. "I fear I was not so lucky. But that is only as I would expect."

Aryn gave him a puzzled look. "Why?"

The knight only gazed forward with serious brown eyes.

The baroness was not the only one who had found another marked door. Grace hadn't—she had barely had a few minutes between the council and her lesson with Kyrene to search—but both Beltan and Travis had had success. One room was in the cellar, two floors below—but sharing a ventilation shaft with—King Lysandir's chamber. The other was the room of a minor noble just above King Kylar's chamber. Beltan had questioned the earl whose room it was, and he was certain the noble knew nothing about the symbol.

As she listened to Beltan, suspicion crept into Grace's chest. Why was it that no marked door had been found near Boreas's chamber?

Stop jumping to conclusions, Grace. No one found anything near Eminda's chamber, either. The Raven cultist isn't done yet. That's the only explanation.

With a piece of charcoal, Aryn marked the last of the new rooms on the map. "I believe we've learned a lot for our first day as a conspiracy."

Beltan studied the black marks. "Really? And here I was thinking that things are more confusing than ever. Now there are five rooms to worry about, not two." He looked up. "And why are they marking so many rooms anyway? Grace said they plan to murder only one of the rulers."

"They always mark the places they plan to attack," Travis said in a low voice.

The others gazed at him. His eyes were clouded behind his spectacles.

Grace swallowed, then broke the silence. "The conspirator I overheard said he didn't know yet which ruler would be the target. I think they're waiting to see how the council goes. Then they'll decide who to take out, in order to alter the next reckoning."

Durge stroked his mustaches with a thumb and forefinger. "But which decision wins a king death, my lady? To reckon for war . . . or against?"

Grace didn't have an answer to that. If they knew which way the Raven Cult wanted the council to vote, then they would have a much better idea of who was the intended victim. Right now they had to assume it could be any of the rulers . . . any who slept near marked doors, that was.

"All right," Beltan said. "So we've found three more doors. Now what do we do?"

"We watch," Grace said, and all eyes turned toward her.

That night the Circle of the Black Knife engaged in a stakeout. Eminda's and Boreas's sleeping chambers were not far apart, both within the main keep. In ones and twos, the members of the Circle concealed themselves in alcoves and watched passageways that seemed likely candidates for the Raven Cult's work.

They kept watching until dawn was closer than midnight. At last they gave up and regrouped. They had seen nothing more suspicious than a bleary-eyed serving boy sent on a mission to the pantry by a sleepless noble. By the time Grace shucked off her gown and crawled into her bed, the sky was no longer truly black outside her window, and birdsong shattered the crystalline air. She tossed and turned until it was time to get up, struggle back into the gown, and listen to more whispers at the Council of Kings.

After the council, Grace met again with Kyrene. Her studies with the countess were progressing, but to where, Grace could not exactly say. She was getting better at the Touch. All it took now was a moment's concentration and she could reach out with her mind, could feel the life in all the things around her. However, when she asked what she was to do with that power, Kyrene would only smile her smug, enigmatic smile.

Once again it was pitch-dark by the time the Circle of the Black Knife met. However, this time Grace was first, not last, to the wine crypt—a location again chosen by Aryn.

"I have to select the vintage to serve at the coming Midwinter's Eve feast," Aryn said when she and the others arrived. "I thought if we were caught, I could say I was conducting a tasting."

Beltan's eyes lit up. "Which cask should I open first?"

Aryn gave him a sour look. "It's a ruse, my lord. We're not really going to taste any wine."

The big knight's disappointment was plain to see.

They started to draw up new plans for keeping watch in the vicinity of Eminda's and Boreas's chambers, but Durge raised a hand to halt them.

"My luck was better today," the Embarran knight said. "I found a servant's room that was marked with the Raven symbol. It has a small window, and outside is a narrow ledge that runs for some distance, until it passes the window of Queen Eminda's chamber." He pointed to the map of the castle.

Aryn shook her head. "But I checked that very same room yesterday, and it wasn't marked. Which means the cultist marked the room last night."

"And which means we completely missed it," Travis said.

The baroness groaned. "That wasn't lucky at all, Durge."

The knight's shoulders drooped farther under his soot-gray tunic.

Grace glanced at the Embarran and tried her best to sound encouraging. "That still makes only six marked doors. And there are seven rulers. That means there's still a chance of catching the conspirator in the act."

"I wish we could go to King Boreas," Beltan said. "With a word, he could have fifty men-at-arms going over this castle from dungeon to turrets."

"But we can't go to him," Aryn said in a tight voice.

Beltan gave her a sharp look, then nodded. Grace noticed that he held one hand motionless with the other.

Travis scratched his beard. "We'll just have to keep watching."

Grace met his eyes. She knew what the real plan was, the one Travis had not spoken of. Yes, they would keep watching for signs of the Raven around Boreas's chamber. And if they found one, if he was marked for murder like all the other rulers, then they would know it was safe to go to him for help. And if not . . .

Grace's fingers slipped to the pouch at her belt and through the leather felt the little wooden bull tucked inside.

"Come on," she said. "It's time to start spying."

83.

The next afternoon, Grace met Aryn for a walk in the upper bailey. The council had ended early that day, for the last ruler to make a report, King Kylar, had finished. The council would now recess for three days before a second—and final—reckoning began. Because Aryn's and Grace's studies were not until that evening, and because the Circle would not meet until later that night, they were left with a brief respite.

It was the twentieth day of the month of Valdath, which Grace guessed was something akin to December back on Earth. For several days the weather had been clear, bright, and bitterly cold. A bucket of water set outside froze in minutes, and those forced to brave the elements did so only after they covered every inch of skin with cloaks, hoods, gloves, and rough wool blankets.

However, unlike the last few days, that morning had dawned gray, and by afternoon, if not exactly warm, at least bare skin didn't freeze the moment it was exposed to air. Just as Grace contemplated the idea of venturing outside, a knock had come at her chamber door. It was Aryn, dressed in a heavy gown and cape.

"I think we need to get out," the baroness had said.

Grace had not disagreed. Things were moving so quickly now, there had been so little time to just walk with her friend as she used to, and talk—not about kings, or witches, or murderers—but about small things.

Their boots crunched on the frozen ground of the bailey as they walked. Grace drew in a deep breath. The frigid air pinched her nostrils, but she did not care. She was weary of the rancid soup that passed for air inside the castle, and the way it dulled her mind. The sharp air sliced through the smoke like a scalpel, and it left her brain clean.

They were not the only walkers encouraged by the milder—if only in relative terms—weather. Other pairs strolled the upper bailey, the garden, or through the gate to the lower bailey, where the market thronged despite the cold. A couple passed nearby, an earl and his lady, both comely if only because of youth. Grace recognized them. They were petty nobles in Boreas's court and had married just recently.

Aryn's sigh fogged on the air. Grace looked at her friend in concern.

"When do you think you will marry, Grace?" the baroness said.

The question struck Grace like a blow. Aryn reached out to steady her.

"What's wrong, Grace?"

She gulped in air. *She didn't mean anything by the question, Grace. This is a world where all noblewomen get married, whether they want to or not. It's politics, not love, that's all.*

"I don't think I'll ever get married, Aryn," she said.

Aryn's expression was alternately surprised and thoughtful, as if this were a possibility she had never considered, then she sighed again. "King Boreas has been preoccupied by the council, but I imagine he'll find a husband for me when spring comes. *If* spring comes. It's hard to believe it ever will."

Grace regarded her friend. "Who do you hope the king will choose for your husband?"

Aryn's words were automatic. "A good man, who would help me rule my barony with a strong, just hand."

"That's not what I meant."

"There is no one for whom I hold a secret love, Grace. Is that what you mean?"

Grace thought for a moment. "What about Beltan?"

Now Aryn smiled. "I think you mistake both the king's nephew and me. I care for him, of course, but as a girl does her elder brother, and I am certain it is as a sister he regards me. He will make the innermost circle of the Mysteries of Vathris if he wishes." Her smile faded, and her face grew sad, yet hard all the same: a sculptor's sorrow hewn from marble. "No, it is best if I do not let my heart choose another, when I know one will be chosen. . . ."

The baroness's words crumbled on the icy air. If Grace had believed in fate she would have cursed it. Another couple had chosen that moment to step through a door into the bailey. She was young, plump, and pretty, but it was not the lady who held Grace's attention. She had not seen him since the night of the feast when he rejected Aryn's invitation to dance. He was as square-shouldered and square-jawed as she remembered, his crown of gold curls uncovered despite the cold.

"Leothan."

Even as Aryn whispered the word, the two linked arms and crossed the bailey. When they were even with Grace and Aryn, the plump young woman turned her head, as if she sensed eyes upon her and her companion. She noticed Aryn's stare, then smiled and coiled her arm more tightly around Leothan's. He did not glance their way. They moved toward the gate to the lower bailey, perhaps so he could buy her a trinket in the market.

"I hate him."

Grace turned in shock at the harsh voice. Beside her Aryn stood rigid, her left hand clenched into a fist. Her eyes were blue stones.

"Aryn?"

"It's wrong." The baroness's voice was a hiss. "It's wrong that he should be so handsome and so beastly. I *hate* him."

Aryn's eyes rolled up, her back arched, and she stood on her toes. Then Grace felt it, like the presence she had sensed that first day with Kyrene, only stronger, darker, and hot with anger. It streaked past Grace, so furious it almost knocked her over. A cry of dismay echoed off stone. Grace jerked her head up. Across the bailey Leothan stumbled, his hands pressed to his temples. The young woman screamed.

Grace knew she had only seconds. She clutched the baroness's arm and squeezed. "Stop it, Aryn." She forged her voice into a knife. "Stop it. Now!"

Aryn did not respond. Grace dug in her fingers, so deep she could feel bones grind together. The baroness drew in a ragged breath and slumped against Grace. Across the bailey Leothan staggered, then lowered his hands. His companion rushed to him, held him, and dabbed with a white cloth at the blood that trickled from his nose. He gave a weak nod, and she helped him through a door back into the castle.

Grace pushed Aryn away, forced her to stand. The baroness stared at the door where Leothan had vanished, then spoke in a hoarse voice.

"What are we becoming, Grace?"

Grace shook her head. She didn't know how to answer. It was not what they might become that frightened her, but what they might already be.

"I'm cold." Aryn's face was white as frost.

"Come on." Grace guided Aryn back toward the keep. "Let's go get warm."

Later, Grace walked alone through the castle. She knew she should get back to her chamber. It was time for her lesson with Kyrene, and the countess was to come to Grace's room that evening. However, Grace had wanted to think.

After wandering for a time, she came to a halt and realized she stood before her own door. So that was her decision—she wanted to know more, despite what had happened with Aryn in the bailey. Or maybe because of it. Somehow Aryn had used the Touch to affect Leothan. Was it really that different from what she did in the ED? Didn't she use the Touch to heal people?

Maybe. She didn't know. That was why she was here—to learn. Grace pushed through the door of her chamber.

"There you are, sister."

Grace opened her mouth in surprise. The countess stood before the fire in a gown of serpent's green, a cup of wine in her hand.

"You weren't here, so I let myself in," Kyrene said. "You don't mind, do you, love?"

Grace's mind raced. What might have Kyrene found if she had searched the room? Not the half-coin, or her necklace, or Hadrian Farr's business card. Grace's most precious objects were in the leather pouch she always wore. Only the drawings of the castle then, including the ones with the rooms marked on them. What might Kyrene have thought of those? But what might Kyrene have thought of anything? Grace still did not know what the countess's game was, although she had an inkling of its ultimate purpose: greater power and position for Kyrene.

"No, Kyrene," Grace said. "You're welcome here."

Kyrene smiled. Grace stepped in and shut the door.

"Tell me, love, how is Lord Logren?"

Grace dropped the decanter she had picked up back on the sideboard, then managed to steady it before it spilled. She clutched her cup and turned to stare at Kyrene. How did the countess know Grace had been thinking of him, or that she had even met the high counselor of Eredane? Grace gulped some wine to buy time to think.

Kyrene sauntered toward her. "Don't fear, sister. Believe me, there is more than enough of Logren for both of us. He is, shall we say, quite great in his manhood."

Grace winced. She didn't want to hear this. Or did she? Again she pictured Logren's large hands, dark against her own white skin. She forced herself to breathe. "What do you want from me, Kyrene?"

"No, Grace, what do I want *for* you. That is the true question." Kyrene set down her cup, then forced Grace to do the same. She took Grace's hands in hers. "You are such a puzzle, love. You rival any woman in beauty, yet you do nothing with it. You hardly even seem to realize it."

Grace shook her head. What was Kyrene saying?

"Let me show you, love. Let me show you of what you are capable. There is so much more to being a witch than grinding herbs in a mortar."

Kyrene ran warm fingers up Grace's arms, across her shoulders, over her breasts. Grace trembled, but she could not move. The countess's voice was a honeyed whisper.

"Join me, sister. Let us weave our magics together. Logren could never resist us both."

She pressed her cheek against Grace's. Kyrene's skin was soft and hot. A low moan escaped Grace's lips—it was the only sound she could make. Kyrene whispered in triumph.

"Join me, and he will be ours."

"Lady Kyrene!"

The voice was sharp and commanding. Kyrene leaped back, a child caught in an illicit act. Grace staggered and leaned against the sideboard. Then she looked up to see the queen of Toloria stride into her chamber: tall, beautiful, fierce. Ivalaine's icy gaze moved from Kyrene to Grace and back to Kyrene, then she nodded, as if she understood exactly what had transpired, and Grace supposed she did, certainly better than Grace herself.

"You will go, Lady Kyrene," Ivalaine said. It was not a request.

Kyrene started forward. "But sister—"

"You will not call me that." The queen's voice was as cold as her eyes. "You are no longer needed here. I will see to the Lady Grace's studies myself from now on."

The color drained from Kyrene's face. "But Your Majesty, I was only—"

"You would dare question my words, Kyrene?"

Kyrene's jaw snapped shut as if Ivalaine had struck her. She glared at Ivalaine, then at Grace, and her green eyes were filled with venom. Now she drew herself up and thrust her shoulders back.

"You will regret this, Your Majesty."

"I already do, Lady Kyrene."

The countess walked boldly to the door, then turned to regard Grace. Her expression was one of hatred and envy. "I know you won't forget what I told you. Love." There was a flash of green, then the door shut, and Kyrene was gone.

Grace wasn't certain she was going to keep her feet, then Ivalaine was beside her. The queen took her arm—her fingers so cool where Kyrene's were warm—and guided Grace to the chair by the fire. Grace sank down, but the queen remained standing.

"Listen to me, Lady Grace. I will say these words only once, for I know no more is required. Kyrene's magic is small and petty. Her way is simpler, and thus it leads to simple things. Your power can be far greater if you wish it, as can the Lady Aryn's. Already you have great control with the Touch, and you learn quickly. Your experience as a healer has benefited you much." The queen cupped her chin in her hand. "It will be more difficult for Aryn, I think. Her talent is hidden deep within her. And yet, I think, it is stronger than yours or mine—perhaps the strongest in a century. If she can learn to bring it forth and to shape it."

Grace nodded. "It's going to be hard for her. She is so kind, so gentle. Only there's anger in her, anger she tries to hide, but I saw it today." She looked up at the queen. "It's going to hurt her, Your Majesty."

Ivalaine's eyes went distant. "It hurts every one of us, Lady Grace, as all worthwhile things do." Her gaze grew focused again, and now she smiled. "And when we are alone, you may call me sister—*sister*."

Grace would have thought it impossible, but she returned Ivalaine's smile. She drew in a breath. "So, what is to be my lesson tonight, Your—I mean, sister?"

"I think you have learned more than enough for this evening," the queen said. She started toward the door, then turned back to regard Grace. "No, there is one more thing. I told you there is something that holds the Lady Aryn's power back. The same words are true for you, sister. Much of who you are lies behind a door, and I cannot see past it. However, you must know that you cannot lock away part of who you are without locking away part of your magic. If ever you want to discover that power, you will have to unlock that door."

Grace stared at the queen. What was Ivalaine saying? She shut her eyes, and she saw another door: dark from time and the touch of flame. She did not want to step through it again—she dared not.

"No." She opened her eyes. "No, I can't."

Ivalaine's visage was unreadable. "Then you will never know what you might be. Good eventide, sister."

The door opened and shut, then Grace was alone with only the fire to accompany her.

84.

Travis shook the snow from his cloak and stepped into the chamber he shared with the others.

"Melia? Falken? I'm back."

Silence. The fire on the hearth had cooled to ashes. Travis moved farther into the room.

"Beltan?"

Still no answer. No one was here. The Council of Kings must have been running late that day. Except that wasn't right. Falken had said the rulers were finished making their reports. The council wasn't set to convene again for three days. Where could everyone be?

Outside the window it was late afternoon. That morning Rin and Jemis had told him he could leave early today. Come to think of it, the two runespeakers had been nowhere in sight by the time he left their tower. And the upper bailey had seemed peculiarly quiet. What was going on?

Travis peered out the window. The snow that had fallen all day, and which had dusted him on his way back, had ended. It was as if someone had spoken *Urath*, the rune of opening, to the sky. The clouds had broken over the castle to reveal a strip of sapphire sky. Even as he watched, heavy sunlight transformed the clouds from cream to honey, and they melted away.

Travis shivered. It looked like it was up to him to get the fire going. He knelt by the hearth and stirred the ashes.

"Travis, I'm glad I found you."

The poker clattered to the hearth, and he leaped up, heart thumping. Then he took a deep breath. "Haven't you ever heard of knocking?"

Grace bit her lip. "The door was open."

"So you're saying all the politeness escaped from the room?"

She gripped the doorframe, her face washed of color. "I'm so sorry, Travis. I'll . . . I'll . . ."

He sighed and held out a hand. "You'll come in, Grace. Please."

She nodded, ducked inside the room, and shut the door. Travis studied her as she did. Her violet gown was simpler than usual, but she was still beautiful. It wasn't hard to believe she was really a duchess. She was so assured, so regal. Yet why then did simple things—like doors and people—always seem to throw her?

"What's going on, Grace? The castle seems dead."

Her gown whispered as she moved farther into the room. "There's a feast tonight. Everyone's down in the great hall."

"And what a surprise I wasn't invited."

"Actually you were, but I told Lord Alerain you weren't feeling well, that I would be attending you, and that neither of us would be able to come to the feast."

"Why, Grace?"

She wetted her lips. "I need your help, Travis."

Instinct prickled the hair on the back of his neck. Maybe it was the light in her eyes, maybe it was the set of her jaw, or maybe it was the cloak she had thrown over her gown—heavy, lined with fur, a riding cape. Whatever it was, he turned around and gazed out the window. It was pale against the brilliant winter sky, but he could see it, making its descent toward the western horizon: a crescent moon.

He turned toward her again. "It's today, isn't it. Today is the day you saw those two people arguing in the stone circle." He frowned and tried to sort it out. "I mean, you didn't see them today. But today is the day it happened. Or will happen. Or is happening, or . . ."

He was babbling, he needed to shut up. She hesitated, then reached out and gripped his hand.

"It's our only chance to learn who they are, Travis. To learn what's really going on in the castle."

Travis groaned. It was ridiculous. It was dangerous. It was stupid. And worst of all, it was right. The Circle had failed to catch a Raven cultist in the act—or to find a mark near King Boreas's chamber. This was the perfect chance to discover who the conspirators were.

"But why didn't you ask Durge or Beltan?"

"Boreas or Sorrin would notice if they were missing from the feast. They might start to wonder."

Travis sighed and cast a wistful eye at the hearth, where his work had stirred a few wan flames to life. Something told him it was going to be a while before he felt warm again.

"I'll get my cloak," he said.

Grace smiled. It was a rare expression for her, and thus all the more precious. "Thank you, Travis."

There was only a single stableboy in the castle's stable, and it was not difficult for the duchess of Beckett to convince him to let them in. He yawned and nodded when she told him they needed two horses saddled.

"Come on," Grace said as she led a horse by the reins into the stable's main aisle.

Travis took in the big black charger that towered over her. "*That's the horse you're going to ride?*"

"His name is Blackalock—he's Durge's horse." Grace stroked the charger's muzzle, and the horse let out a low whicker. "I think he remembers me."

"And I think he could step on me and grind me into the straw without even noticing." For Travis, the stableboy had saddled the sandy gelding Travis had ridden all the way from Kelcior. Next to Blackalock the gelding looked like a pony. "I don't think Durge will find it amusing you stole his horse, Grace."

"Nonsense. Durge doesn't find anything amusing."

"Do you even know how to ride?"

"I'm sure Blackalock will help me."

Travis gave up.

The sun was low in the sky as they rode from the gates of Calavere. Travis faced into the cold wind and drew in a breath. It felt good to be outside, to be moving again, to be going somewhere, anywhere. He had gotten used to traveling in this world. Being stuck in the castle had seemed so limiting, so oppressive. Now they were on the road, and there was no telling where the wind would blow them. He grinned despite the rashness of what they were doing, and he tried not to think about what Melia would do to him if she caught him.

They started down the winding road that led to the base of the castle hill. Travis glanced at Grace. She had climbed into the saddle with only a small degree of difficulty, and had arranged her gown and her cloak over her legs. Now she sat straight upon the massive charger's back, the reins loose in her gloved hand, and looked for all the world—any world—as if she had been riding her entire life. Grace might not have been good at talking to other living creatures, but she sure was a natural at commanding them. Travis clung to his gelding's mane and just tried not to look like a sack of potatoes in comparison.

They reached the foot of the hill and let the horses stretch their legs on the straightaway. There were few peasants on the road this time of day. The sun would set soon. Most people were carrying a final load of peat or wood inside, and closing doors and shutters against the frigid winter night.

So what are you doing out here, Travis?

Stone walls and leafless trees flashed by, all dusted with white. It was strange how *still* snow made things look, as if they had not moved in centuries and would never move again.

The thunder of their horses' hooves turned to a hollow drumming as the dirt track beneath them was replaced by an arch of stone. They had reached the old Tarrasian bridge. Dark water flowed beneath them, chunks of ice dotting its surface. It must have been even colder than he'd thought. Hadn't Falken said the Dimduorn had not frozen over in centuries?

Bridge and river flashed and receded behind them. Hooves fell on frozen mud again. Soon the stone walls bounding the fields grew smaller and cruder, then vanished altogether. There were no more ramshackle huts, no more blue lines of smoke rising to the sky. They were in the marshes of Calavan now.

"Do you even know where this place is?" Travis said. There was no need to shout above the din of the horses. The air was like crystal and resonated with the sound of his voice.

"I think so. Durge described it to me. It's in a vale between two identical hills."

That wasn't exactly specific, but before Travis could ask more questions, Grace pulled hard on her reins and Blackalock wheeled off the road to plunge across a snowy field. Travis fumbled for his own reins, but the gelding was smarter than he, and followed after his companion. Downy white billowed around them and dusted Travis's cloak anew.

They rode directly toward the sinking sun now. It seemed huge, and red, and old. The air was getting more frigid by the minute. Icicles clung to Travis's beard. Some heat rose from his horse, but already Travis was starting to shiver. He wondered how long it would take Beltan and Durge to ride from the castle and find them. He wondered how long, in these conditions, it would take to freeze.

Travis glanced over his shoulder. He could still see Calavere, but it looked too small now to be real, tossed on its hill like a child's plaything. He faced forward again, into the wind. His fingers were stiff, but he forced his hands to grip the reins.

The sun had just touched the western horizon when they came upon it. They crested a rise, and Grace let out a cry. At first Travis's heart jerked. He thought something was wrong. Then he gazed in the direction Grace pointed. Below them the ground fell away into a gentle depression. On the far side of the depression were two conical hills, so perfect in form they could not have been natural. In the vale at the foot of the hills, arranged in a circle, were nine tall shapes.

Travis shaded his eyes with a hand. Long shadows stretched from the standing stones, and it was hard to see into their midst, to glimpse what might be there. Grace and Travis exchanged a long look, then nudged their horses down the slope. The crimson light of the setting sun spilled across the vale. It looked like blood against the white snow.

The air was crisp and silent as they approached the circle of stones, broken only by the soft snorts of the horses and the soft swish of snow against hooves. The sun slipped behind the horizon and was gone. The sky turned to slate, and the horned moon shone above the twin hills.

"This is it," Grace whispered. "This is exactly how I saw it."

Travis only nodded. His gloved hand slipped to the stiletto at his belt. The gem was dark, but something told him there was danger here all the same.

They reached the edge of the circle and slipped from the backs of the horses. Their boots crunched against snow. The horses lowered their heads, breath steaming on the air, as if they too sensed the need to be quiet. Travis and Grace walked toward the circle. The stones were twice the height of a man, of dark stone, and pitted with long centuries of wind and weather. Travis wasn't certain when he and Grace had taken each other's hand, but now he tightened his grip on hers and was glad for the touch. Together they stepped between two stones, into the circle.

It was empty.

No, that wasn't entirely true. There were footprints in the snow, two sets of them. And there was blood. It dotted the white ground like scarlet berries.

Travis and Grace walked to the center of the circle. The snow was not so deep there. The standing stones caught much of it in drifts and protected the middle. The air within the circle was motionless, and there was a feeling to it, or a presence maybe. It wasn't angry, yet it wasn't kindly either. It was ancient, and it was different, and it was watching them.

Grace knelt beside the footprints, took off a glove, and touched one of the scarlet stains on the snow. She looked up. "It's not frozen yet. This blood couldn't have fallen here more than a few minutes ago."

Travis nodded. Birds were alighting on the standing stones, as if something had disturbed them moments ago and now they were returning. "I think they were just here, Grace. I think they heard us coming and fled."

She stood and gazed at him. "Of course. In my vision . . . I thought he saw me there. I think he did, only it wasn't me in my vision he saw. It was us, tonight. They saw us coming, and they ran."

They exchanged looks, then as one they dashed to the farside of the circle. Beyond the stones the footprints were replaced by two sets of hoofprints. Travis and Grace followed these between the peculiar hills, then halted in the snow, panting. It was no use. The two riders were gone.

"We're too late, Grace." Travis gasped for breath even as he winced at the sharpness of it. "We came here for nothing."

Grace studied the sets of hoofprints, then she nodded. "Maybe not."

Travis frowned at her.

"Look," she said. "One of these sets of hoofprints heads back toward the castle. And look here." She pointed to the snow. A single red drop. Blood.

Travis tried to scrape some of the ice from his beard. "I don't follow you."

Grace's eyes glowed. "Don't you see, Travis? The wounded conspirator has gone back to Calavere."

His brain was slow from the cold. It took a moment for realization to break over him, then he gazed at her in wonder. "So all we have to do is find someone in the castle who was wounded tonight, and we've got the conspirator."

Grace grinned. She opened her mouth to say something. Her words were cut short as a different sound drifted on the air. High, piercing, silvery: the sound of bells.

Travis and Grace stared at each other. The standing stones loomed above them in the twilight like dark sentinels.

"What is this place, Travis?" Her voice was a whisper of wonder and fear.

"I don't know. I think maybe once, long ago, it was sacred to the Old Gods."

"The Old Gods?"

"Not the gods of the mystery cults, but the ones that came before, the ones that were the mothers and fathers of the Little People before they all vanished."

He could see the shudder beneath her cloak. The words escaped her lips with the soft fog of her breath. "The Little People. . . ."

Again the bells sounded, high and clear. Travis took her hand—they had to follow. They crossed to the farside of the circle. Just beyond was a short stretch of white, then a tangled wall that rose from the land, black in the deepening gloom. The bells sounded again, but Travis and Grace hardly needed them now to know where they were being led.

They halted as gnarled shapes loomed before them: the edge of Gloaming Wood. Beyond were shadows. They listened, but now all they heard was the mournful hiss of wind through bare branches. There was nothing here.

No, that wasn't true.

"Look," Grace said.

At first he thought they were some sort of tracks in the snow. Then he realized they weren't tracks at all. They were words:

NO PAIN

"But what does it mean?" he said.

"I don't know." The words barely escaped her clattering teeth. "It's a message. . . ."

He shivered. It was so cold, and night was falling. He turned back toward her. *How are we going to make it back to the castle, Grace?* He tried to ask the question, but he was too numb, too weary.

Grace's gaze flickered to the trees, then back to Travis, and she nodded, as if she had decided something. She reached out and pulled him close to her, then shut her eyes. He almost thought he heard her whisper something.

"Touch the trees. . . ."

And all at once the world was as warm as springtime.

85.

It was long after dark when they reached the castle, and they were cold again. When they rode up to Calavere's gates a jolt of panic stabbed Grace's chest. *You were out too long, Grace. The gates are closed, and you're too tired to touch the Weirding again. You're both going to freeze out here.*

However, as they rode near, they saw the gates were not closed. The feast would run late that night, and many of the lesser nobles and counselors were staying in the town, not the castle proper, and would need to stumble down the hill in the frigid night to their waiting beds. The men-at-arms started to raise halberds as the two rode up, then their eyes locked on Grace's ghostly visage and they nodded. She and Travis rode through, into the bailey beyond.

They left the horses with the stableboy, who appeared just as sleepy as before, then returned to Travis's chamber. It was still empty—the others had not yet returned from the feast. But it was not really so late. They had been gone no more than three hours. It only seemed as if they had been on an impossibly long journey.

"I'll get a fire going," Travis said as they shut the door and threw their cloaks on the bed.

Grace clutched her arms over the bodice of her gown. For a while they had been so warm, so wondrously warm. It had been so easy to reach out with the Touch, to sense the life hidden in the leafless trees, and to draw it to her. The Weirding of Gloaming Wood was far richer, far more potent than anything she had ever sensed in the garden. Even the horses seemed to feel the radiance when they mounted them, for the beasts pranced and snorted, and stretched their legs as they cantered back toward the distant castle.

That her magic had saved them from frostbite, or worse, Grace was certain. However, the warmth had begun to fade as they came to the bridge over the Dimduorn, and by the time they reached the foot of the castle hill they had been shivering again.

Grace tucked a stray wisp of ash-blond hair behind an ear. "You never asked, Travis. You never asked how I was able to keep us warm."

He looked up at her, a piece of kindling in his hand. "I knew you would tell me if you needed to, Grace." He set the wood on the hearth, then shut his eyes and spoke a quiet word. *"Krond."*

Flames leaped to life, and golden light shone forth.

The heat of the fire drew Grace forward. It was harsher than the warmth of the Weirding, brighter and crueler: the heat of consumption, not of life. All the same she held her stiff hands out. That Travis had just used magic as surely as she had, struck her only after a minute.

"We've both learned so much, Travis." She gazed into the flames. "It hasn't even been two months, but we're getting used to this world, becoming part of it."

Travis stared at the fire as well. Or was it his hands he gazed at, held out before him? They were fine hands, Grace noticed for the first time, long and well shaped.

"I don't know, Grace," he said in a soft voice. "I don't know if I could ever get used to this world. Oh, it's wonderful in some ways. It's beautiful here, even if it's frightening, too, and I have more friends here than I've ever had in my life. But I don't belong here, I can't forget that. That's why I have to get back to Colorado, to get back home."

Grace opened her mouth to reply, then shut it. What would she say? Did she feel the same? She was not so certain. How often did she think about Denver, about the Emergency Department? Of course, she thought of them every day. Yet they seemed distant, like someone else's life—a movie that whirred through a dim projector and now had run out. Grace looked at her own hands. She wasn't so certain she wanted to go back. She wasn't so certain she could.

"How about some wine?" he said.

She stood with him. "I can get it."

"No, I'm the saloon keeper, remember? It's my job."

The cup of wine turned into two entire decanters. They went into the side chamber where Melia slept, stirred up the fire in there, and flopped on the enormous bed. They drank cup after cup and laughed as they talked about the things they missed in this world.

"Pizza," Travis said. "I'd trade the whole lot of kings at this council for one good pizza."

"I'd trade them all for a hot shower." Grace stretched on the bed, just thinking about it. Showers were the only thing that had kept her functioning in the ED. She would stand under the shower in the residents' locker room and let the industrial-strength nozzle blast her, powering away all the fear and blood and suffering. To be clean was to know peace.

"How about beer that doesn't have stuff floating in it?" Travis said.

She nodded and gulped her wine. "Or blue jeans? And T-shirts? And real underwear: cotton with elastic, a clean pair every day?"

Travis groaned. "Stop it. You're killing me!"

Grace clutched her stomach. It hurt to laugh—it had been so long, and she was out of practice—but it was good and did as much to warm her as wine and fire.

At last the long ride, the warmth, and the drink did their work. Their voices grew soft and dreamy as they lay across the bed, then fell quiet altogether. The last thing Grace saw were big flakes of snow falling outside the window. Then she was falling, too, into sleep.

It was a soft sound that woke her. At first Grace thought it must be the sound of the snow, it was so quiet. She snuggled against the warm body beside her—Travis—and let herself sink back into slumber.

But if it was the sound of snow, how had it come from inside the chamber?

Grace opened her eyes. It was dim—the fire had burned low. She saw nothing, then her eyes adjusted. Something above her glowed in the last crimson light of the coals: long, sleek, pointed. A blot of shadow hovered behind it, but she couldn't make that out either. The thing started to descend, and she knew what it was.

Grace shouted the one word she had time for. "Travis!"

She pushed hard against his shoulder—he let out a groan of protest—then she rolled in the opposite direction. A sharp hiss passed by her ear, followed by a soft thump. The knife had sunk into something. Was it mattress or flesh? She could not turn to find out, she had rolled too far. The bed vanished beneath her, and she fell hard to the floor below.

From her hands and knees she looked up. The shadow was before her now. Only it wasn't a shadow. It was a man in a robe of black. She couldn't see his face—it was a pit of darkness within the heavy hood—but his hand was big and powerful, and in it he gripped the knife. Scarlet stained its tip. Her stomach shrank into a cold knot. Travis.

Now, as he raised the knife again the blade turned cool silver. It had been firelight, not blood. The knife paused above her. Grace knew she would never be able to avoid it once it started to descend again.

"Get away from her!"

Travis stood behind the attacker, his stiletto held before him. The gem in its hilt shone red with the light of the dying fire. No, that wasn't it. The jewel wasn't reflecting the light. Rather, the light flickered within it, as if the gem had a life of its own. Travis thrust the stiletto out before him.

It seemed a casual, almost lazy gesture. The man in the black robe turned, reached out, and knocked the stiletto from Travis's hand. It flew across the room and clattered to the floor, lost in the gloom. The attacker thrust forward with the knife in his own hand as Travis stared.

No. Grace was not going to watch this. She had seen enough death in the ED. From her awkward position she threw herself forward and clutched anything her groping hands could find. Her fingers closed on rough cloth. The attacker's robe. She grabbed and pulled back with all her strength.

It was not much—she did not have a good grip—but it was enough. She jerked her head up to see the attacker lurch and his strike go wide. The knife sank into the wood of the doorframe. Travis tried to twist away from the attacker, but one of those powerful hands snaked out with impossible speed and contacted the back of his head.

Travis went limp and collapsed to the floor.

Grace screamed. Travis wasn't moving. Was he dead? Or was he just dying, his life slipping away every second as fluid filled his cranial cavity, or broken shards of his occipital bone pressed into the back of his brain? She tried to crawl toward him, but black boots stood in her way.

Grace craned her head up. The man in the black robe towered over her. He had freed his knife and had wrapped both of his strong hands around it. The tip was aimed directly at her face. She knew the speed with which he could move. There was no point in trying to get away.

I'm coming, Leon.

Another flash cleaved the gloom. The knife slipped from the attacker's hands, and his head lolled to one side. Grace frowned. Why was he hesitating? Then the attacker's hooded head rolled off his shoulders and tumbled to the floor with a wet thud. His body fell like a tree before her, and she watched dark gore pump from the stump of his neck.

"My lady, are you well?"

She looked up at the sound of the voice. Another figure stood above her now, clad in somber gray. His face was hard as stone, angry as wind, but even in the darkness she could see the concern in his brown eyes. He lowered his gigantic sword, and blood ran down its edge.

The word she gasped was a litany of surprise, gratitude, and relief. "Durge."

He reached down and helped her to her feet.

"Travis," she said. "He's hurt."

Even as she spoke the word the others were there. Beltan rushed into the room and knelt beside Travis. Melia and Falken stood in the doorway.

"How is he?" the small woman said. Her amber eyes shone in the gloom, as bright as the eyes of the frightened kitten she held in her arms.

"Ouch," Travis said as Beltan helped him sit up. He clutched a hand to the back of his head. "Who put the floor where the wall is supposed to be?"

Beltan's grin shone in the darkness. "I think he's all right, thank Vathris."

"Thank his hard head, I should think," Melia said.

"You were right, Durge," Falken said as he stepped into the chamber.

Grace glanced at the Embarran knight. "Right? About what?"

"I grew concerned about you while we were at the feast, my lady," Durge said. "You have been attacked once before. And while all the castle was at a revel seemed an opportune time for another attempt. I would have come sooner, but it was not so easy to extricate myself from King Sorrin's company. One of his personal guard was not to be found this evening, and the king fears to be without a number of knights around him. I am sorry I did not come sooner."

Despite her still-pounding heart, she smiled. "But you did come, Durge."

He bowed deep before her.

Falken stirred the fire. Flames filled the room with light. Beltan helped Travis up onto the bed. The blond knight's face was troubled.

"And I am sorry as well, Travis. It seems I'm always away when those in my care are in danger."

"No, Beltan." Travis's voice was hoarse but emphatic. "You were exactly where you needed to be, with Melia. You're her Knight Protector."

Beltan clenched his jaw but said nothing. Melia drew near to examine Travis's head.

"I think you'll survive, Travis. But you have a lump the size of Galt growing back there. Lady Grace should take a look at it."

Grace started to move toward the bed, then halted. The corpse of their attacker was in her way. Falken knelt beside the body and rolled it over.

"So who was this?" the bard said.

Melia pointed to the head. "I think the part over there might be of more use in answering that."

Falken grunted, then picked at the hood that tangled around the severed head to expose the face. It was harsh and craggy, with dull brown eyes. Grace did not know him.

"Medarr," Durge said like he was chewing stones.

The others looked up at the knight.

"You know this man, Durge?" Falken said.

"So this is where King Sorrin's missing knight was," the Embarran said with a sigh.

Melia gazed at the head, and her eyes narrowed to slits. "You mean this man was a member of Sorrin's personal guard? But why would he attack Grace, and while wearing the robes of a Raven cultist?"

"Not just the robes." Falken had turned over the dead man's forearm. The puckered brand stood out against his white skin. "He's a member of the Raven Cult all right. Or at least he was."

"Are there any other marks?" Melia said.

Falken pulled open the robe that covered the corpse. "No. He looks like he's been in some battles, though. There's a nasty scar on his chest, but other than—"

"Stop!" Grace shouted as Falken started to pull the robe closed again.

The others stared at her. Falken snatched his hand from the corpse. She didn't want to see this, but she made herself gaze down at the body. The scar was thick and pink, and snaked down the center of his bare chest. She had seen a scar just like it once before.

"Cut him open," she said.

Melia's visage grew concerned. "What are you talking about, dear?"

"Do it, Durge." Now Grace's voice was calm, emotionless, a doctor giving orders in a trauma room. "Cut open his chest."

"My lady," the knight said, "perhaps you should—"

"Give me your sword, then. I'll do it." Before he could react she snatched the blade from his hands. It was heavy. She dragged it clumsily to the body.

"No, Grace, don't do it," Travis said in a sick voice, but she ignored him.

She had to know, she had to be sure. The others faded away, along with the room. It was only her and the corpse. She rested the tip of the sword on his chest, then leaned on the hilt with all her weight. Ribs crunched as the blade sank into his body. She worked it back and forth, then cast it aside and sank to her knees beside the cadaver. With her bare hands she reached into the incision and pulled. It was hard to get a grip, the ribs were too strong. She needed leverage. There, the attacker's knife. She picked it up from the floor, wedged it in the incision, and gave an expert tug, opening up a gap in his chest. Black blood flowed out.

"By all the gods!" Falken swore.

"I don't understand," Beltan said, his voice tight. "What is it?"

Grace whispered the words, a terrible diagnosis. "It's a heart made out of iron."

She dropped the knife. Strong hands helped her to her feet. Durge. Her own hands were covered with blood. All eyes were on Grace now.

"What's going on, Grace?" Travis said, his face pale with pain and fear.

Grace opened her mouth, but Falken spoke first.

"You heard my tale at the council," the bard said. "How the Pale King had a heart forged of iron. What I did not tell was that Berash gave his slaves enchanted hearts of iron as well, to bind them to him."

Melia's eyes were thoughtful on Grace. "How did you know of the ironhearts, dear?"

She took in a shuddering breath. How could she explain it all, that night in the ED when everything had changed? "I've seen one before. On Earth."

"But how could one of Sorrin's personal knights be a servant of the Pale King?" Beltan said.

Durge stroked his mustaches. "And why would a slave of Berash wear the robes of a Raven cultist?"

"Don't you see, Durge?" It was Travis. He stood now, as if forgetting the blow to his head. "The Raven Cult is linked to the Pale King. Which means it's the Pale King that's behind the murder plot in the castle."

Falken raised an eyebrow. "Murder plot?"

Grace and the other members of the Circle of the Black Knife exchanged guilty looks.

"I think some people have a bit of explaining to do," Melia said in a crisp voice. Then her gaze fell back to the corpse, and her words grew soft. "But that can wait until the morning light."

"We'll have to tell the council about this," Falken said.

Melia glanced at the bard. "And what will we tell them?"

The bard drew in a deep breath. "That the Pale King is even closer to freedom than we feared."

Grace shivered at the bard's words, and she knew there was no magic—in this or any world—that could have warmed the terrible chill inside her.

PART FIVE

THE GATES
OF
WINTER

86.

Grace gazed out the window of her chamber at the iron-gray dawn and knew she had to tell King Boreas everything.

She turned from the window, shivered, drank some of the *maddok* a servingwoman had brought at first light, then dressed before the fire. Lately she had worn the brighter gowns in her wardrobe: amethyst, ruby, jade. She had gotten too good at donning the garb of this world— she had let the costume grow too comfortable. Today she chose a plain, uncomfortable gown the same color as the mist that shrouded Calavere's towers. If she could have found her old chinos and white blouse, if they had not been burned to ashes, she would have worn them.

Don't forget who you are, Grace Beckett. You couldn't cure all the suffering in one Emergency Department in one middling sized city. You couldn't even come close. What makes you think you alone could heal an entire world?

She stepped away from the fire, looked up, and saw a ghost through the window: pale and translucent, gown merging with the fog in which she drifted, green-gold eyes bright in her hollow visage. Grace studied the ghost. Once, in the ED, a hysterical man had claimed he had seen *Señora Blanca*, the Lady in White, and that he was doomed to die before the night was over. At seven-thirty tests had shown him to be in good health. At three minutes to midnight Grace had called his time of death.

She met the ghost's ethereal eyes. Maybe she should have been afraid. Instead she grinned, and the ghost grinned back at her, the expression cadaverous yet gleeful. But then, how could you be afraid when the only thing haunting you was yourself? Grace finished her *maddok*, set down the cup, and walked from the chamber to meet her doom.

"Good morrow, my lady."

The voice was deep and gloomy, and it made Grace smile like no cheerful greeting could have.

"Durge. Did you stand here all night?"

"No, my lady. I occupied myself for a time by pacing."

Grace examined Durge's weathered face: It was etched with lines, but no more than usual. When did the knight sleep? She didn't know, but she was grateful for his presence. It seemed unlikely the Raven Cult would make an attempt on her life twice in one night—but then it seemed unlikely they would want her death at all.

"What service may I do for you, my lady?"

"You can go get some rest, Durge. Please."

"There will be time for that later."

The voice that came from her lips was automatic, the drone of an overworked doctor. "Prolonged deprivation of sleep can cause hallucinations and feelings of extreme euphoria."

"Flights of fancy and bliss?" Durge said in a chiding voice. "My lady, I am a knight of Embarr."

She bit her lip. What was she thinking? "I'm sorry, Durge. Yes, there is something you can do. Go to the Lady Aryn and bring her to King Boreas's chamber."

The knight bowed, then without question turned and strode down the passageway. Grace pressed her eyes shut. She didn't deserve such loyalty. *One day I'll give him an order that kills him.* No, she couldn't think like that. Durge was not just her Knight Protector. He was her friend. She opened her eyes and hurried down the corridor.

When she knocked on the door at which she had stopped, it was Falken who answered.

The bard's face was haggard, his blue eyes more faded than ever. All the same, he managed a smile. "Lady Grace. I trust you had no more visitations since we last met."

"Only Durge. He spent the entire night outside my door."

"Good," Beltan said. The blond man stood behind the bard. His face was grim, but in his hand, instead of a sword, he held a hunk of brown bread.

Falken gave Grace a wink. "We had a doorstop of our own last night. I think it's all that chain mail. It makes them want to just stand in one place and not move."

Grace clapped a hand to her mouth to keep from laughing.

"I heard that!" Beltan said. He stuffed more bread into his mouth.

"No wonder knights have to wear armor," Melia said. "They're awfully sensitive."

The small woman stood near the fire. Travis sat in a chair before her. She dipped a cloth in a bowl of hot water dotted with herbs and pressed it against the back of Travis's head. He winced in pain.

"How is he?" Grace said.

"The bloodbane you gave me is working. The swelling is going down. I believe he'll live."

Travis grimaced. "That's your opinion, Melia."

"Yes, dear," Melia said. "And remember, it's the only opinion that counts."

"Are you going somewhere, Lady Grace?" Falken said.

She turned to face the bard. "Yes, Falken, I am. And I was hoping you all would come with me."

He raised an eyebrow, and the others gazed at her in curiosity.

Ten minutes later they halted at the closed door of King Boreas's bedchamber. Aryn and Durge were already there. The baroness regarded Grace and her entourage with puzzled blue eyes. Her gown was on crooked and her hair tousled.

"Grace," she said with a yawn. "What is going on?"

Grace swallowed hard. There was no backing out now. "We're all going to have a chat with the king."

Aryn's sleepy eyes grew large.

Melia regarded Grace. "And what exactly are we going to tell him, Lady Grace?"

"Everything."

There was a moment of perfect silence, then a half-dozen voices began speaking at once.

Grace held up her hands. "Please, everyone, listen to me."

The others fell silent and looked at her. Grace hadn't really expected that to work. Now that she had their attention, she supposed she had no choice but to talk.

"I know I was the one who didn't want to speak to Boreas before. But that was before we knew what . . . what we learned last night." She glanced at Falken and Melia. "There are some things we need to tell both of you as well. You'll hear it when we talk to the king. But I had reason to believe Boreas might be behind the plot to murder one of the other kings or queens in the castle, only now we know he isn't. It's been the Pale King all along."

"Murder?" said a gruff voice. "The Pale King? Of what do you speak, my lady?"

As one they turned to stare at the speaker. He stood in the now-open doorway, clad only in a white nightshirt that reached to his knees. His steely eyes were locked on Grace. They were not furious, as she might have expected. Instead they were thoughtful and—she almost could believe—sad.

"Your Majesty!" she said. "I didn't know you were awake yet."

"And who could sleep when there's a revel going on outside his door?" He eyed the others gathered behind Grace. "I see you and my ward have developed the same ill taste in friends as my beloved nephew."

Grace started to stutter an apology, but Boreas waved her words away. "Enough, my lady. You've sounded the trumpet, it's too late to call off the charge. Come in. Or are you going to make your enemy stand here and freeze his sword and jewels as an added insult?"

Grace ducked her head. "Of course not, Your Majesty."

She followed him into the room, and the others came after. The king's bedchamber was neither larger nor more comfortable than her own, although the bed was so massive—the posts hewn from great logs of oak—that it looked as defensible as a small hill fort.

"So what do you have to tell me, my lady?"

Even as Boreas spoke his question he turned, hiked up the front of his nightshirt, braced his muscular legs, and proceeded to fill a brass chamber pot. If he had meant the action to disarm her, to throw her off-balance, he had failed. Grace had emptied more bedpans in her first year of residency than he could have filled in a decade.

She approached his back. "There is a plot in Calavere to murder one of the rulers attending the Council of Kings."

He finished his business and turned to regard her, as if she were the only one in the room. "How long have you known this?"

She did not flinch. "For several days now, Your Majesty."

"And why did you not tell me before? Are you not my spy, Your Radiance?"

"I did not tell you because I feared you might be the one behind the plot, Your Majesty."

Grace tensed her shoulders. She expected the king to react with rage, to bear down on her, to grab her with his strong hands and toss her aside or tear her into small pieces. After the way she had betrayed him, it might almost have been a relief.

Instead he grinned at her. "Good, my lady. Very good! I am a skilled judge of character, but you are even better at this game than I guessed you would be."

She had been ready for fury. His laughter took her aback. "Your Majesty?"

"Don't you see it, my lady? A good spy dismisses no suspicion, no possibility, until proven otherwise. You did well not to assume I was innocent until you had proof of the matter. There are others who could learn much from you."

His eyes flickered to Aryn, and his ward blushed.

"But tell me, Lady Spy," Boreas said. "Now that you know I am not behind this plot in my castle, who is?"

Grace licked her lips. "The Raven Cult and the Pale King."

Boreas stroked his black beard. "So, you believe the bard, then?"

Falken stepped forward and started to speak, but Grace shook her head.

"No, Falken. Please, let me tell him. I need to do it."

The bard met her gaze, then nodded. She drew in a deep breath and stepped closer to the king of Calavan.

"You're right, Your Majesty. I am a good spy, even though I never imagined I could be. I've learned a lot these last weeks, and one thing I've learned is not to disbelieve something just because others discount it. Whatever you think about Falken's tale, I've seen the proof, and so have all of my . . . so have all of my friends. I know the Pale King is real."

Boreas returned her defiant gaze with one of calm understanding. "I never said I did not believe in the Pale King, my lady."

Grace was not the only one who drew in a breath of shock.

Boreas frowned. "You needn't all act so surprised. Or do you really think your king is so thick in the head?" He moved from Grace, toward the fire, and knelt to stroke one of the black mastiffs who slept before the hearth. "I know of the Pale King. Why do you think I called the council?" He let out a snort. "Because I'm afraid of ragged robbers as Eminda says?"

Grace shook her head. She could not imagine Boreas afraid of any mere mortal.

The king stood and faced the bard. "After that last time you were here, Falken Blackhand, I did not—as you would think it—mindlessly dismiss your warning that darkness stirred in Falengarth. I had seen the signs myself, and I did some investigating of my own. I could not be certain, not until you showed the broken rune to the council, but as soon as you did I knew my belief was right, that the Pale King gathered his power again."

Falken clenched his black-gloved hand into a fist. "If you believed me, why didn't you say something to the council?"

Boreas planted his hands on lean hips. "And how well do you think it would have served me to ally myself with the Grim Bard after his outburst? How much sway would I have held over the council then? The news you brought helped me, Falken—it let me know I had chosen right to call the council—but your performance set back my plan to convince the council to muster for war, perhaps without hope of recovery. Although Lady Grace's news, dire as it is, might offer some new hope for uniting the council."

Falken opened his mouth, but no words came out. For the first time Grace could remember, the bard was speechless. Grace's eyes moved back to Boreas. Even in his nightshirt, with his hair wild from sleep, he looked powerful and kingly. A warrior, yes, but not a madman—she knew that now.

The king turned his attention to Grace. "Well, you've managed to surprise me, my lady, and that's no easy thing to do. It never even occurred to me that your spying would actually turn up useful information."

She gaped at him. "What?"

Boreas laughed. "Come now, Lady Grace—surely you don't think you're the only one who can keep a secret? My hope was that, if you made yourself enough of a nuisance with your prying, you might force someone to reveal his hand unwittingly. If you poke a man's sore spot, he will likely flinch. But it turns out you're a more effective spy than I counted on."

Grace had no idea what to say. All this time she had been spying for nothing? Except it wasn't for nothing after all. . . .

The king's face grew grim. "I will say, my lady, this is news about the Raven Cult. I knew the Mysteries of the Raven had gained a foothold in Calavan. I did not know the cult was allied with the Pale King."

"It is." Grace drew in a deep breath. It was time to tell him the rest. All of it. His plan had worked—her spying *had* forced someone's hand. "And there's more, Your Majesty. You see, I've been—"

With a flick of his finger he cut her off. "No, my lady, I do not wish to hear everything. A spy knows what to tell and what not. Too much knowledge can be a harm, not a help. I know all I need to now. I will have an end put to the Raven Cult, and to the plot in my castle."

There were sparks in Boreas's eyes and flint in his voice. This was the king Grace knew.

"Now," Boreas said, and his voice edged into a roar, "all of you get out of my chamber!"

Grace leaped back, then gave a hasty curtsy. The others followed suit with curtsies and bows—even the Lady Melia—then all hurried from the chamber and left the king to his hounds and his privacy.

The door shut with a boom.

"Now what?" Travis said.

Grace didn't have an answer for that. She had not thought beyond telling Boreas about the murder plot. It seemed the king had taken matters into his own hands. Maybe that was the end—maybe she was done with this.

Melia tapped a cheek. "Breakfast, I think. Shall we all come to my chamber?"

The others agreed to this, with Beltan's affirmation being particularly hearty. Together the seven started down the corridor. Strange that Grace should find more companionship here than she ever had in her own world. Strange, but it felt right all the same.

Their course took them past the keep's entrance hall. They passed through the hall and were nearly to the other side when the keep's main doors swung open. A wintry blast snatched at Grace's gown. The others grabbed at dresses, capes, or tunics, then the doors shut, and the hurricane ceased. Grace batted her gown back into place and looked up to see a motley troupe of characters stride into the keep.

Yes, characters. That's exactly what they look like. Characters from a play.

They were dressed in outlandish costumes. Leaves tangled the hair of the women. The men wore shaggy trousers. An old man in white tossed dried petals on the floor like snow.

A frown touched Aryn's brow. "Oh dear, they're early. Wherever will we put them?"

Grace glanced at her friend. "Early? You mean you were expecting them?"

The baroness nodded. "They're actors. King Boreas hired them. Their troupe is going to perform a play at the Midwinter's Eve Feast. But that's a week away, and here they are already."

Actors? Grace watched the peculiar troupe pass by. They turned a corner, and as they did she saw one among them she had not noticed before. He was a tiny man, barely more than three feet high, dressed in yellow and green. The man didn't show the usual signs of achondroplasia, and he was well proportioned. Pituitary dwarfism, then.

Grace heard a hiss of breath beside her, and she turned her head. Travis stared at the little man, his expression one of astonishment.

"Trifkin Mossberry!" he whispered.

Even as Travis said these words the small man turned in their direction and tipped his feathered cap—although he was too far away to possibly have heard.

Before Grace could wonder more, the small man and the actors vanished through an archway, leaving the entrance hall cold and empty.

87.

This time the Circle of the Black Knife met by daylight.

They gathered again in the old watchtower. It was late afternoon, but the mist of that morning had not broken and still cloaked the world outside. A small fireplace—empty now—would have offered the sentinels of long ago warmth as they kept watch from this place for enemies. Travis gazed at the fireplace and wondered if it would be used again before long.

Beltan was the last to arrive.

"I'm sorry I'm late." The blond man shut the door, his chain mail jingling.

Durge studied the other's armor. "Why are you fully armed, brother knight?" The Embarran was clad in his usual smoke-colored tunic and hose.

Travis watched the two men. Each time he saw them, he was struck by the difference in the knights: one dark and grim, the other bright and jovial. Like night and day—no, more like boar and lion. Each dangerous in his own way. He was glad the two were on their side.

Furrows dug themselves in Beltan's high forehead. "I'm afraid I've been conscripted by my uncle. He's placed me in charge of security in the castle. We're searching for any Raven cultists in Calavere and purging them. We've found several already today."

Purging them. Travis had an idea what that meant. He eyed Beltan's sword and shivered. The blond man was always so kind, but Travis had seen the scars the knight bore.

Beltan sighed. "I know it needs to be done, but I can't say I care for this job. We're supposed to be looking for murderers, but so far all the cultists we've found have been simple folk—poor, or sick, or desperate. They don't understand what's behind the Raven Cult. They're just out of hope, and they're looking for something—anything—that can offer some."

Travis stared at the knight. Maybe he had misjudged his friend.

"You could have told Boreas no," Grace said.

Beltan shook his head. "I might have, but Melia and Falken asked me to do it as well, though I'm not sure why."

Travis didn't really mean to speak the words aloud, but he did. "Maybe because they knew you wouldn't punish those who were only guilty of hoping, Beltan."

The big knight glanced at Travis, his expression startled, then he nodded. He did not smile, but the shadow lifted from his brow.

Now that they were all here, the five counterconspirators got down to the matter at hand. Aryn had met again with the king, along with Lord Alerain. She explained that, after their morning encounter with him, Boreas had concocted a plan to shift the various kings and queens from bedchamber to bedchamber that night, and each night thereafter. That way no one—including the Raven Cult—could be certain in which room a particular ruler might be staying.

Alerain was organizing the effort, and at Boreas's request the seneschal had not explained to any of the rulers the real reason they were being moved from room to room. The king of Calavan had not yet informed the council about the murder plot. Instead, he was waiting until the would-be murderers were caught. Then he could present the plotters to the council and, hopefully, use the victory to sway the council's decision. Alerain had devised a reason to convince each ruler to move to a new chamber. The stories ranged from leaky ceilings and crumbling walls to rats under the bed. The plan had worked so far— the rulers would all have new chambers tonight—but Aryn doubted Boreas and Alerain could keep it up for long. The plotters had to be found, and before time ran out.

"So, what does the Circle do now?" Beltan said.

Grace met his eyes. "We look for the wounded conspirator in the castle. I saw the one strike the other in my vision. And Travis and I saw the blood on the snow at the circle of stones, leading back toward Calavere."

Durge stroked his mustaches. "So if we can find someone in the castle who was wounded yesterday—"

" we have the conspirator," Travis said.

Aryn chewed her lip. "I usually hear about it when someone in the household is hurt. And there were several injuries yesterday. A servingwoman in the scullery was burned by a pot of hot water. And the apprentice to the castle farrier was kicked by a horse." She frowned. "Oh, yes—and Lord Olstin called for a chirurgeon, although he would not tell me the reason why."

Beltan let out a snort. "I think I can save us some trouble. If that bowl of pudding Olstin is one of the murderers, I'll eat my chain mail."

"No, don't discount him," a hard voice said.

The others looked up. It was Grace. Her face was a white mask, her eyes distant.

"One Raven cultist was an ironheart," she said. "Others could be, too. You can't know. You can't possibly know who might be one . . .

one of them. It could be anyone—the plainest person you would never suspect. There's only one way to be sure. One way." She shuddered, then her gaze focused on the others. "I'm sorry, I . . ."

"No, my lady," Beltan said. "I'm the one who's sorry. You're right. We can't discount anyone."

Aryn sighed. "But if that's the case, how are we ever going to find the wounded conspirator—"

"You must remember the words of Gloaming Wood," a piping voice spoke.

Travis and Grace whirled around. Before them stood a small man clad in yellow trousers and a green jacket. His face was brown as sun-dried berries, and his dark eyes snapped with mischief—as well as something deeper and more perilous.

"Trifkin Mossberry," Travis murmured.

Grace glanced at Travis. "You know him?"

The small man stroked his beardless chin. "We have met before, I think. Have we not?"

Travis could only nod. He would never forget that night in King Kel's keep when he spied Trifkin and his troupe through the keyhole. And now they were here in Calavere. But what did they want?

"To perform a play, of course," Trifkin said. "And to help you."

"To help us? How?"

Trifkin only smiled.

Grace crouched and brought her eyes on a level with the little man's. "What do you mean, 'the words of Gloaming Wood'?"

"One may not be what one seems," the little man said. "Then again, one may not seem what one doth be."

"I don't understand," Grace said. "What are you talking about?"

Trifkin smiled again.

Grace's green-gold eyes bored into the little man. "Who are you?"

"The darkness is here," Trifkin whispered.

Bells shimmered on the air, and the little man was gone.

Grace stood and looked at Travis, her mouth open. He shook his head. What had just happened? He didn't know. Or did he? Did both of them?

"—who's hiding in the castle," Aryn said.

Travis and Grace turned and stared at the others.

Beltan frowned at them. "Is something wrong?"

Aryn's and Durge's expressions mirrored the blond knight's concern. Travis realized the truth. None of them had seen the little man in green and yellow. At least a minute had passed for Grace and Travis, but to the others it had been a heartbeat or less.

Travis glanced at Grace. She reached out and took his hand in hers. He nodded and looked back at the others.

"There's something we have to tell you," he said.

88.

The next morning, Travis rose in the colorless light before dawn, shrugged on his tunic, wrapped his cloak around his shaking body, and trudged to the tower of the Runespeakers.

Jemis was in a fouler mood than usual, and the list of runes he gave Travis was endless. By late afternoon Travis was just half-finished, and only because of Rin's influence was he allowed to leave without doing the rest.

He headed back to the keep and, along with the other castle folk, found something to eat in the great hall—bread, yellow cheese in a hard rind, raisins with seeds in them, and a slice of tough but edible venison. It wasn't baked brie and toast rounds, but he was getting used to the food of this world. And getting leaner as well. His green tunic was baggier than ever, and these days he didn't have much more fat on him than did the stag he had just eaten part of.

By the time he finished chewing the venison it was dusk. However, night came prematurely this deep in winter. The Circle of the Black Knife wouldn't meet for hours yet. Not that he had much to report. No one in the great hall was sporting an obvious bandage, and there wasn't enough time to begin a serious search of the castle. Travis decided to return to the chamber he shared with Melia and Falken and spend the interim trying to get warm by the fire.

He was nearly there when a drab flutter of movement caught his eye. He turned in time to see a lumpy shape wrapped in gray tatters scuttle through a distant archway.

"Hey!" he called out.

Travis hesitated, then groaned. He launched himself down the corridor and pounded through the open archway. On the other side was a room with three doors. All were shut. He started toward the closest door, then changed his course and moved to another. There. He plucked a bit of rag from the hinge. She had gone this way. He threw open the door and ran down the corridor beyond.

A flash of gray down a side passage.

"Wait!" he shouted.

Why was he doing this? He didn't even have the filthy little bundle she had dropped—he had left it in his room, under his bed. But if he could catch her, he could tell her to wait, then could go fetch it for her. He didn't know why he cared so much. Only that she had made him feel so small for the way he had run her down that last time.

"Please, wait a second!"

Either she did not hear him or did not care to. She disappeared around a corner. He careened down the side passage, turned the same corner, and ran full speed—

—into a gray-haired man clad in black and maroon.

"Ouch," Travis said and stumbled back.

The man reached a hand toward him. "Do you need help, Master Travis?"

As always, Lord Alerain was trim and neat in his understated attire. His graying hair and beard were both closely cropped.

Travis drew in a breath. "I'm looking for—" For what? He couldn't very well say he was looking for a mad old hag who had dropped a piece of what was most likely trash. "—I'm looking for Lord Beltan. Have you seen him?"

"Indeed I have, just a few minutes ago. He was in the west hall. If you follow this corridor to the end and take the stairs down, you'll find it." The seneschal started to move away, then paused. "You are his friend, aren't you, Master Travis?"

This question took Travis by surprise. "You mean Beltan? Yes. At least, I hope we are."

Alerain nodded. "I am glad. He needs friends like you, to remind him he is a good man."

"What do you mean?"

Alerain moved to a window. The world outside was silver in the gloaming.

"I love this view. It's my favorite in all of Calavere. It looks straight into the heart of Calavan. Everything you see lies within the Dominion. It makes me feel . . ." He sighed and turned to look at Travis. "Beltan is kind, and given to laughter rather than anger. In that he is unlike his father, old King Beldreas. And so he thinks he is not as strong as Beldreas was." He shook his head. "Beltan might have made a bid for the throne, you know. Many of the barons would have supported him."

Travis thought about these words. "Beltan *is* strong," he said.

Alerain nodded. "I know that, and so does King Boreas. Perhaps you can help Beltan believe the same. I've tried, but I'm afraid . . ."

He gazed back out the window. Travis frowned. The king's seneschal seemed different from usual, more melancholy. At that moment

Alerain reminded Travis of his friend Jack Graystone, but he couldn't say exactly why.

Travis took a step toward the seneschal. "Are you well, Lord Alerain?"

A smile touched Alerain's lips. It seemed a bitter expression. "Am I well? Yes, Master Travis, I am well. I will always be well." He gazed back out the window. "No harm can come to me now."

Travis bit his lip, unsure what to say. What was the seneschal talking about?

Alerain stepped from the window, squared his shoulders, and was his crisp self once again. "You had best go, Master Travis. I imagine Lord Beltan is awaiting you."

Travis bade Alerain farewell, then turned and headed to his chamber. And although he spent the next hour sitting by the fire, for some reason he could not seem to get warm.

89.

Grace stood before the window in her chamber and gazed out at the failing day. She turned a small vial over and over in her hands. The green fluid within glinted like a liquid emerald. She didn't need to taste it to know she had gotten the simple right this time. She could feel it. One sip would bring down a fever. Three would induce vomiting and hallucinations.

You're getting good at this, Grace. Too good. . . .

She was to meet with Ivalaine again that evening. So far, in the course of her studies, she had still not brought herself to ask the queen directly about the Council of Kings. There had not been time with the intense pace of her learning—at least, that was what she had told herself. But the council was to meet again the next day, to begin a new reckoning, and Ivalaine held the key. Her decision could tip the council in either direction. Grace had to find out what she wanted. What the Witches wanted. . . .

A hard rap sounded on her door.

Grace nearly dropped the vial, then fumbled and slipped it into the pouch at her waist. She turned to face the door.

"Come in," she managed to say.

It was not, as she had feared, Queen Ivalaine striding into her chamber in a cool fury, magically aware of Grace's intention to question her. Instead she came with timid steps, her head down low, her brown hair hiding her face—a young woman in the ashen dress of a serving maid.

Grace didn't recall requesting a servant. "Can I help you?"

"Aye, I hope so, my lady."

The young woman lifted her head, and Grace recognized her. It was Adira, the serving maid she had saved from Lord Olstin's wrath. Adira, from whose lips Grace had first heard the word *witch*. That day she had been proud and bold. Now her face was smudged with grime and tears. Outrage replaced Grace's surprise.

"Adira, has Lord Olstin . . ."

The serving maid shook her head. "Nay, my lady. It isn't that." Despite her tears, her full lips curved upward in a smile. "I think you taught Lord Olstin a lesson he won't soon forget. A woman need never submit herself to a man's will. You showed me that, my lady."

Grace lifted a hand to the bodice of her gown. Could she really have made such a difference in another's life—not with a scalpel but with mere words?

"It's my brother I have come to see you about." Now the smile vanished from Adira's lips. "He's ill, my lady, terribly ill, and Vayla says he is beyond her help. I heard . . . I heard you are a healer. And you have been studying with the Witch queen of Toloria. I know—I've seen you two together."

Grace's shock was renewed.

"Please, my lady." Adira was sobbing now. She knelt and clutched the hem of Grace's gown. "Please, won't you come help us?"

Grace gazed down at Adira. The sultry young woman who had professed her desire to be a witch was nowhere to be seen. At Grace's feet was a frightened child.

She can't be more than seventeen, Grace. And she's terrified. Help her. Grace's shock dissolved. She knew what she had to do—she always did when someone was dying. Her woolen cloak lay across a chair where she had thrown it earlier, warming by the fire as if she had known she would need it. She tossed it around her shoulders.

"Let's go," she said.

Ten minutes later they halted in the cold mud of the lower bailey. Before them opened the shadowed mouth of the gatehouse, and beyond were the gates of Calavere. Grace glanced at Adira in confusion.

"My brother lies in our house, in the town below."

Inwardly Grace kicked herself. In the urgency of the situation it had never occurred to her to ask where Adira's brother was. She had assumed he was somewhere in the castle.

The young woman tugged at her cloak. "Come, my lady. We must hurry if you are to return ere they close the gates."

Adira's tears had dried, and her cheeks were rosy from their swift pace. Her terror seemed to have vanished. Perhaps the serving maid had learned some tricks of her own.

Grace gave a jerky nod. What was she doing? But there was no time to think of an answer as Adira pulled her down the dim tunnel. They passed a pair of men-at-arms, who bowed as Grace passed, then the castle walls fell away behind them, and they were half walking, half running down the rutted dirt track that wound its way around Calavere's high hill. Grace nearly fell as they stumbled down a steep stretch of the path, then they rounded a sharp turn, and the town came into view.

It was hard for the haze of blue smoke to be sure just how large the town was. Grace guessed there to be five hundred structures, some of stone and slate, most of wood and thatch, which meant perhaps two thousand people. It did not seem much of a city to be associated with the seat of the most powerful of the Dominions. Then again, Grace knew this was a land of castles and fiefdoms, not cities and highways. Most of the people would live in small villages scattered across the land, and most of them would die without traveling ten miles from the place of their birth. Only a few would live in the towns that grew up around the keeps of lords and knights and barons, or that sprung up like mushrooms at busy crossroads. They were trading markets and religious centers, that was all.

"Please, my lady. We have to hurry. *Please.*"

Urgency had returned to Adira's round face. Perhaps her fear had not been feigned entirely. Grace followed after the serving maid.

They crossed a footbridge over a brook that tumbled down from the hill, then set foot in the town. Grace gagged and clamped a hand to her mouth. She had thought herself accustomed to the smells of this world, but she was wrong. The odors of neither ED nor castle compared to this.

"Come, my lady. Come."

Grace almost couldn't do it. Then she remembered there was a sick man in the midst of this. She clutched the edge of her cloak to her mouth and stumbled on.

Twilight filtered down from the sky like soot, and the town was a dim blur. There was no reason to the streets. They zigged left and right, ended abruptly, turned to alleys where the two women could barely walk single file between wooden walls, then widened into broad cesspools.

At first there were few people, then they came upon a town square. There was a stone well. Sheep milled about, along with people in rough, filthy tunics. Their faces were pockmarked, their backs stooped, their hands gnarled and missing fingers. Even that time in Appalachia she had not seen squalor like this.

And this is the most prosperous of the Dominions, Grace.

Adira dragged her across the square. Brown rivulets trickled through the mud. The reek that rose from them was a living thing, thick and suffocating, and stabbed at the primal core of Grace's brain, triggering alarms more ancient than any castle: the scent of human feces. It was too much. Her stomach clenched, sour fire burned her throat. She turned, leaned against a wall, and vomited into an open gutter.

"It's all right, my lady," Adira said, soft and slightly mocking. "It's only the stench of the sewer. Come, it will be better indoors."

Grace managed to stand up, then wiped her mouth with the back of her hand and nodded.

"Take me to your brother," she said.

She felt better by the time they came to a small hovel near the far edge of the town. It was barely a shack, with walls of thin planks and a lean-to of daub and wattle slumped against one side. Chickens pecked in the bare dirt around the house. They were scrawny and bedraggled things. Grace wondered what use they could possibly be.

Adira opened a door, and Grace followed. The air inside was thick with smoke. The only light came from a feeble fire.

"I've brought her, Vayla."

The serving maid moved to the other side of the room. Only then did Grace see the narrow cot. A young man, no more than a year or two older than Adira, lay on the cot, his eyes closed. Another figure hunched over him. This one looked up at Adira's words.

"So the duchess descended from the castle, did she?" The voice was like the smoke from the fire—harsh and acrid. "Will she command his fever to be gone, then?"

"She's more than that, Vayla. She's a healer, and she studies with the Tolorian queen."

A snort was the only reply.

Adira motioned for Grace to come closer, but Grace stood paralyzed. She should not be here, she should run back to the castle as fast as she could, before they shut the gates and she was trapped out here. Then she remembered the sick man. Terror melted away, and she approached the bed. She was aware of eyes peering at her through the slit of a curtain. The rest of Adira's family. They were afraid of her. Good. It would keep them out of her way. She reached the edge of the cot.

"What's wrong with him?" Grace said.

"What? Can you not tell merely by looking at him, Duchess?"

Grace winced at the harshness of the voice. In the castle, a servant who spoke to a noble like that would have been beaten, or worse.

But you're not in the castle, Grace. You're not even a duchess.

She pulled back the blanket and examined the man. He was naked beneath the rough covers, his skin waxy with sweat. He was small, no more than sixty-two inches, but obviously fully grown. The greater size of men compared to women was an artifact of good nutrition. In a stressed population, males were seldom much larger than females. Grace made a catalog in her mind.

White male, approximately nineteen, unconscious and malnourished. Skeletal evidence of rickets as a child. Badly set but healed breaks to the proximal right ulna, distal left radius, medial left clavicle. Mass of scar tissue from a burn on the left lateral abdomen.

Had this man come into the ED, Grace would have thought him a product of an abusive childhood, or a kid from the streets. If he was under eighteen, she would have called Social Services. Here he was a normal man with people who cared about him. Everyone in this world lived this way, or at least the commoners. Anger flooded Grace's stomach. What kind of hell was this?

A gnarled hand placed a warm cloth on the young man's forehead. A sharp scent rose from it. Grace knew it from her studies. The cloth had been steeped in mourner's wreath. She could almost smell the salicylic acid. It was some sort of analgesic, good for pain.

Grace followed the gnarled hand back, to the face of the one Adira had called Vayla, then drew in a sharp breath. So not all witches in this world were like Kyrene or Ivalaine. The woman was ancient, her back a hump beneath tattered clothes. Wisps of gray hair had escaped her ratty hood like smoke through a roof. Her face was a map of lines, her cheeks sunken, one eye bulbous, the other a wrinkled mass of flesh.

The crone grinned at Grace, displaying a few yellow teeth. "What? Do you not find me beautiful, Duchess?"

Grace stared at the crone, then she clenched her jaw and turned back to her patient. "His temp is elevated. He's not cyanotic, so there's no evidence of pneumothorax. It's not a viral infection. Abdomen is not rigid or sensitive. No signs of appendicitis."

"What are you saying, my lady?" Adira's face was fearful. "Are you speaking a spell? What are you doing to him?"

Grace ignored her. "There must be some other cause for his fever. But what?"

"He is dying," the crone said.

Grace glared at Vayla. "Not if I have anything to do with it."

The crone gazed at her, then nodded. "What do you wish me to do, Duchess?"

"Help me turn him on his side."

Grace hardly needed the crone's aid. He felt as light and hollow as a bird. He moaned in his delirium—he was waking up. Grace ran eyes and hands over him, searching, sensing. There had to be something, some clue. . . .

There. She had not seen it until Vayla snatched the tangled blanket away from his feet. Just above his left ankle was a wound. It was small but deep. Grace bent close, then gagged at the sweet scent of decay.

"I need more light."

The crone held out a candle, and Grace examined the cut. It was a puncture wound. She could see cloth fibers and bits of dirt embedded in it.

"Dafin cut himself on the plow the other day," Adira said. "He complained that it hurt, but it was only a small cut. It cannot be this that has made him so ill, can it?"

Grace did not answer. There was no time to explain about invisible microbes and blood poisoning to a medieval young woman. Angry red lines had already begun to snake their way up his leg. A few more hours and amputation would be the only choice, and Grace knew he could not survive that—not here, not in these conditions. Right now there was still another chance.

Grace pulled the knife from the sheath in her boot and held it out toward Vayla. "Heat this in the fire."

The old woman nodded and plunged the blade of the knife into the coals. They waited, then she withdrew the knife and handed it back by the hilt. Grace could feel the heat radiating from the metal.

"Hold him," she said.

"Help me," the crone said to Adira.

Adira shook her head but did as Vayla bid. They gripped her brother's body. He was moving now and muttered in his delirium. Grace bent over him and paused. Despite his battered body his face was beautiful. A broken angel fallen from above. There was so little that was good in this world. Grace was not going to let him go.

She tightened her grip on the knife, then pressed the hot steel tip into his wound. The stench of burning meat filled the air. His eyes flew open, his head went back, and he screamed in agony.

"Murder!" Adira shrieked. "You're murdering him!"

"Quiet, fool girl!" Vayla hissed. "She is his only chance."

Adira clapped her hands over her mouth, her eyes wide with terror. The young man fell back to the cot, unconscious again. That was a small blessing. Grace set down the knife and stood.

"We have to get his temperature down now or his blood is going to cook his brain."

The crone nodded. "Cold water, girl," she snapped at Adira. "Get it now."

There was a small window above the bed. Grace moved to it and threw open the wooden shutters. Cold air flooded the room. She shut her eyes, let the chill cool her cheeks and clear the smoke from her mind. She opened her eyes again and saw a plate of bread on the windowsill, and next to it a wooden cup of wine.

"They are offerings," Vayla said.

Grace turned around. "Offerings? For who?"

"For the Little People. It is said they can steal a sick man's spirit. We leave them the bread and wine so they will be appeased and move on to the next house."

Grace glanced back at the bread. Falken had said the Little People were forgotten, but clearly that was not so. Only weren't the Little People supposed to be good?

"They are queer beings," Vayla said, as if she heard Grace's unspoken question. "Good or evil mean nothing to them. They simply are."

Adira returned with a bucket of water. She was sobbing as she set it down. Grace and Vayla wetted cloths in the bucket and laid them on the young man's arms and torso. Then Grace handed the vial she had brought to Vayla and explained its usage.

"Will he live?" Adira said in a tremulous voice.

Grace laid a hand on his forehead. Yes, his temperature was coming down, and the simple would help. His sleep was more peaceful now. There was so much that could go wrong. The knife might not have cauterized all the gangrenous flesh. The infection might have already spread too far. The burn might have sent him into shock. She shut her eyes. No, none of these things were true. She could feel it, could feel the strength of his beating heart as if she held it in her hand.

"He will live," she said.

It was full dark by the time she left the shack. The boy that Adira had charged to guide Grace back to the castle—one of the serving maid's younger brothers—held a small lantern carved of horn, the stump of a candle inside.

"Come, my lady." His voice was thin and frightened.

Grace nodded and followed after him. She was exhausted, yet she felt oddly light and charged, like a dust mote caught in an electric field. There was so much pain in this world, so much suffering. Was it even worth saving?

Even as she asked herself this, she thought of her last conversation with Leon Arlington. She knew what he would have chosen, and she knew what they would choose. No matter the suffering, it was always better to be alive.

They came to the town square, and Grace was surprised to find it was not empty. A few torches flared and sputtered, masking the reek of the sewer with acrid smoke. A knot of people gathered in the light. The boy tugged at her sleeve, and she picked her way after him through the muck.

They were almost to the other side of the square when Grace saw the man in the black robe. A cold needle pierced her heart, and she lurched to a halt.

"Please, my lady," the boy said. "Please, we mustn't tarry. Not after dark."

Grace hardly heard the words. She took a step forward. The man's side was to them, his face hidden by the heavy cowl of his robe. Torchlight played across the dark material, a crimson corona. At first she thought it was he—the one she had seen that night in the castle, the one who had dropped the knife—then she realized it couldn't be. He was shorter and stockier than the one she had seen carving the door.

As she watched, the man splayed his arms out. He was speaking to the gathered people. No, not speaking, but *preaching*, his voice rising and falling like an angry song, although she could not make out his words. The crowd watched him, their rapt faces turned upward, red as blood in the torchlight. Grace took another step forward.

The man's arms froze in midair. His words ceased. Then, as if he sensed eyes upon him, he turned his head, and his cowl slipped back. His gaze searched the square, then his eyes locked on Grace, and her breath turned to ice water in her lungs.

Even in the dim light she could see that the man's face was rough and cruel. On his forehead, drawn in ashes, was a symbol she now knew well. Two curved lines: the rune of the Raven. But it was not this that caught Grace's gaze. It was the color of his eyes. One was blue, while the other was brown. Memory washed over her in a cold flood. She had seen eyes like that once before.

His thin lips parted in a rotten grin.

Dread wrapped clammy fingers around Grace's throat. He knew her. He had seen her, and remembered her, and now he would walk across the muddy square and kill her.

Grace stumbled backward, and the glare of a torch burned her retinas. She whirled around and staggered forward, searching with blind hands, then ran into something hard—a stone wall.

"My lady . . . what is it?"

Her vision cleared. She saw the boy before her, his face a pale moon of fear in the dimness. She glanced over her shoulder. A ruddy glow flickered at the mouth of the alley—the town square. But there was no sign of the Raven cultist following her. There was still time.

A new urgency filled her.

"The castle," she said. "I have to get to the castle. Now."

The boy gave a jerky nod, his eyes large. She knew her face was as hard as her words, but she didn't care. At that moment only one thing mattered. The boy sprinted down the muddy alley. She picked up the hem of her gown and struggled after him, while knowledge burned in her mind like poison.

No pain.

Grace knew who the conspirator was.

90.

Travis dropped the poker he had been using to stir the fire and looked up as the door to his chamber flew open.

"Grace," he said when he managed to find his tongue. "What's going on?"

She stepped into the room. He had never seen her like this. Sweat sheened her forehead, and her cloak was askew over her gown. Her green-gold eyes blazed.

"I know what they mean, Travis," she said. "The words we saw in the snow, by Gloaming Wood."

It felt as if the fire went out, although he knew it still crackled on the hearth. Travis stood. The room was quiet—he had not seen Melia or Falken all day. The bard and the lady were scheming something, as usual.

"What do you mean, Grace?"

"No pain." She took another step toward him. "They don't feel pain, Travis."

"Who don't feel pain?"

"Ironhearts." Her words were rapid as gunfire. "I mean, they *do* feel pain. I've seen that. It helped me escape from one in Denver. But I don't think they feel pain like we do, and I don't think it lasts for long. It was a mistake to think we could look for the wounded conspirator. Even though he was injured, we never would have known it."

Cold understanding washed over Travis. "So that's what Trifkin was trying to tell us—that the wounded man might not seem like one."

Grace gave a stiff nod. "But there's more, Travis." She licked her lips. "I saw something in the town. . . ."

Sickness rose in his throat as he listened to her quick, fragmented words. When she finished, he forced himself to swallow his dread. They had been wrong—so terribly wrong.

His eyes locked on hers. "We have to get the others."

Minutes later the five ran down a corridor. Beltan's mail shirt chimed a dissonant music, and both he and Durge gripped the hilts of their swords. Aryn's face was puzzled, but there had been no time for Travis and Grace to explain in detail. They had just told the others to follow, that Grace had learned something about Lord Alerain.

"Where did you last see him, Travis?" Grace said between gasps of breath.

He glanced at her. "I think it was just after this—"

There was no need to say more. They passed through an archway and came to a halt on the edge of a long room. Crimson torchlight spilled upon the floor. It was hard to tell where the light ended and the blood began.

Aryn screamed, then clamped a hand to her mouth as Beltan gripped her shoulders. Travis's stomach wrenched, and he heard Grace let out a cry of dismay beside him. With slow steps Durge approached the body.

Alerain's head had been hewn off and had fallen several feet from his body, connected to it only by a river of red. His eyes stared upward in a ghastly expression. Durge knelt beside the corpse and, with deliberate motions, unlaced and opened the seneschal's tunic. A ragged wound snaked down the center of his flat chest, freshly scabbed over.

Nothing can harm me now. . . .

Now Travis knew why Alerain had reminded him of Jack earlier that day—both had had the same look of sadness in their eyes. The seneschal had been saying good-bye, just like Jack did in the Magician's Attic.

Durge looked up. "Alerain was an ironheart. And the conspirator. Though it appears his partner caught up to him before we did."

Beltan's voice was hoarse. "How did you know, Grace?"

She stared at the body and spoke in sharp, clinical words about the man with one blue eye and one brown eye—how she had seen him once, speaking to Alerain, and how she had seen him again in the town that night, preaching the word of the Raven.

Durge stood and heaved a sigh. "At least he is at peace now."

Travis gazed at Alerain's twisted face and wished he could believe the knight.

Aryn sobbed, her head against Beltan's chest. "Oh, Alerain. What will Boreas do without you?"

Beltan looked up and swore.

Alarm replaced the horror in Grace's gaze. "What is it?"

"The rulers," Beltan said. "Alerain was the one seeing to the switching of the rooms of the kings and queens."

"Which means he knows exactly where each one of them is sleeping," Durge said.

The five exchanged looks, then together launched into a run.

"Grace, Travis, come with me," Beltan said through clenched teeth. "Durge, take Aryn and tell the king. We have to check on all of the rulers. Now!"

Durge nodded, took Aryn's hand, and the two of them careened down a corridor. Beltan charged in another direction, and Travis and Grace followed.

"Do you think the murderer will strike now?" Travis said to Grace as they ran.

She glanced at him, face grim. "He killed Alerain, which means he must know we're close. If he doesn't strike now, when will he?"

"But who will be the victim?"

"One who voted for war—and one who the murderer thinks he can get to."

Travis ran faster.

They reached King Persard's chamber first. Beltan didn't even stop. He knocked two men-at-arms aside, kicked in the door, and burst into the chamber. Travis and Grace tumbled in after him.

"Hey, there!" said a testy voice. "What's this? Can't a king have a little privacy?"

It took Travis a moment to sort out the scene before him. The frail king of Perridon sat in his bed with a creamy-skinned maiden on either side of him. All were in a state of undress.

Beltan's face flushed red. "Sorry, Your Majesty. King Boreas will explain later."

"He certainly will!" Persard snapped.

However, Travis, Grace, and Beltan were already out the door and running down the corridor.

"Who's next?" Grace said between breaths.

"King Kylar is closest," Beltan said. "We're almost there."

They rounded a corner and heard a terrible crash: the sound of stone on stone. Gray dust drifted from beneath a door next to which two armed men stood. They looked in surprise at the dust, then at the three who ran toward them.

"Open the door!" Beltan commanded.

The men did not hesitate. One pushed open the door. More dust billowed out to choke the air.

Travis tried to see through the cloud. "What happened?"

Beltan blinked and peered through the dust. "By the Bull! It looks like the wall has collapsed on the bed."

Travis's heart sank—they were too late. The kind young king of Galt had been the murderer's target, and the conspirator had succeeded.

Beltan pressed the hem of his cloak to his mouth to ward against the dust. "I'm going to go in there and—"

He stopped short as a shadow appeared amid the swirling dust. Beltan reached in and pulled something out of the cloud and into the corridor.

Grace clapped her hands together. "King Kylar!"

His face and hair were streaked with stone dust, and coughs shook his shoulders, but it was clear the young king of Galt was alive and whole. She rushed to steady him, and Travis did the same.

Beltan disappeared into the chamber, then returned a moment later, his hair and face white. He looked at Kylar, his expression one of amazement. "The whole wall fell in—I think the mortar was chiseled away—and the bed is in splinters. How did you survive?"

"The b-b-bed," Kylar said in his halting voice. "It was full of bedb-b-bugs, so I went to s-s-sleep in the wardrobe instead."

To Travis's astonishment, Grace laughed. He could not help but join her.

Grace gripped Kylar's hand in her own. "It seems you're not so unlucky after all, Your Majesty."

He grinned at her through the dust. "P-p-perhaps I'm not at that."

91.

The following day, at the Council of Kings, Boreas told the other rulers of the failed attempt on King Kylar's life.

When Grace entered the council chamber she started toward her usual seat in one of the front rows, then hesitated. She usually sat beside Aryn and Lord Alerain. But Aryn was not here yet, and Alerain . . .

Gentle brown eyes caught her own. Grace looked up to see a plump, red-haired woman motion to her. It was Tressa, Queen Ivalaine's lady-in-waiting. Grace froze. What would Boreas think if he saw her sitting next to Ivalaine's closest advisor and a known Witch?

That's his problem, Grace. Besides, you're supposed to be learning Ivalaine's agenda at the council.

She braced her shoulders inside her purple gown and moved toward the red-haired Tressa.

It was easy to navigate through the council chamber. The tiers of stone benches were not so crowded as they had been on that first day. Many of the lesser nobles had returned to their respective Dominions, some bearing messages or orders from their king or queen. No doubt the rulers grew anxious to return to their own keeps and castles, to see to the affairs in their Dominions—and to make certain no barons had become overly ambitious in their absence. However, they were bound by the ancient rules of the council. Aryn had said no one would be able to leave until the council reached a final reckoning.

Then again, if King Boreas's plan worked, a reckoning could happen that very day.

Last night, Boreas had acted strangely when they told him of Alerain's treachery and death. They did not all go to the king's chamber. Instead Grace and Beltan went alone. Beltan had said that Alerain had been like an uncle to Boreas in the king's youth. They thought it best he should hear the news from as few as possible.

The king had sat perfectly still in his carved dragon chair the whole time they spoke, his eyes locked on the flames. When they finished Grace had expected disbelief or outrage. Instead he had only nodded, then asked to be alone. Boreas had rested his hand on the head of one of his hounds and had continued to stare into the fire. They had left him that way.

That morning Boreas had seemed a different man. He had paid a rare visit to Grace's chamber. She had heard his booming voice outside her door while she was still getting dressed and had barely had time to shimmy into her gown before he burst through the door.

This was the Boreas she knew—the small room hardly seemed able to contain his bulk and energy. Boreas had explained his plan to her, to tell the council of the murder plot and the attempt on Kylar's life, in hopes the rulers would put aside their differences in the wake of this mutual threat. Or at least that one who had opposed a muster would be convinced to decide otherwise, for Boreas intended to force a reckoning of the council that day.

Before she even thought whether it was wise to ask the question, Grace did. "Will you tell the council of the Raven Cult and the Pale King, Your Majesty?"

Boreas had cocked his head and had given her a piercing look from the corner of his eye. Then, without another word, he had turned on a heel and had stalked from her chamber. A vacuum had seemed to form in his wake, and Grace had felt the need to clutch the bedpost to keep from getting swept out of the room after him. Once she had caught her breath, she had thought to go find Aryn and the others, to tell them what King Boreas intended. Then a young page had appeared at the door to lead her to the council chamber, and there had not been time.

Grace reached the place beside Tressa and sat down.

"Good morrow, Lady Grace," Tressa said.

Grace smiled. "Good morrow, Lady Tressa."

It was difficult to be certain how old Tressa was, and Grace was good at estimating age. The lady-in-waiting's plump face was smooth and pretty, but there were other signs—the fine lines about her eyes, the few strands of gray in her thick hair, the blue veins on the backs of her hands—that made Grace think she was older than she seemed.

Grace started to arrange her gown—it always took a bit of work to keep from sitting on a bunch of cloth—then halted. Her arms prickled, and she looked up. Two sparks of emerald burned into her. Grace tried to avert her eyes, but like one driving past a car wreck, she could not.

Kyrene sat alone on a bench across the council chamber. She wore one of her sumptuous green gowns, but now she hunched inside, and her dark blond hair—always before so carefully brushed and arranged—was ratty and tangled. She chewed on a fingernail as she stared at Grace. The countess looked hurt and dangerous, like a small animal that was wounded but quite alive. Kyrene noticed Grace's attention and smiled. The expression was both sullen and smug.

Grace held her breath. *She's plotting something still, she has to be. Ivalaine may have cast her out, but Kyrene won't give up that easily. But what does she think she can do?*

An image came to Grace's mind: dark hands on pale flesh. Logren. Would she try to do something to Logren? Grace was trembling, and Tressa must have noticed, for she took Grace's hand in her own.

"Pay no attention to her, child," Tressa said. "She has no power to harm us."

Grace shook her head. She wanted to say Tressa was wrong, that Kyrene was up to something, and that it couldn't be good. Then trumpets sounded. The council was about to begin for the day.

One by one the rulers marched into the chamber. Grace noticed Falken and Melia seated in one of the front rows. Travis, Aryn, Durge, and Beltan sat just behind. They all must have entered while Grace was distracted. She tried to catch their attention, but they did not look back. Grace sank back to her seat. She would just have to talk to them when the council recessed.

The nobles took their seats on the benches, and the rulers took their own chairs—all except for Chair Malachor, which remained empty as it had for centuries. However, the other rulers were hardly settled when Boreas planted his hands on the edge of the round stone table and stood back up.

"Last night," Boreas said in a thundering voice, "an attempt of murder was made upon the life of King Kylar of Galt."

A gasp ran around the hall. The other rulers stared at Boreas—except for Kylar, who slid down in his chair, obviously uncomfortable with the attention. Grace winced. Boreas was certainly wasting no time on subtlety.

"Is this true?" Sorrin of Embarr asked in his deep but hollow voice.

Kylar nodded. "I f-f-fear that it is."

Lysandir sniffed at a gold-embroidered handkerchief. "I must say, for one who has been murdered you look quite well today, Your Majesty."

"And in that we are lucky," Boreas said.

The king of Brelegond let out a high-pitched laugh. "Lucky? That's not a word one usually hears in association with King Kylar of Galt."

Boreas glowered at Lysandir. "What's wrong, King Lysandir? Are you disappointed the attempt on Kylar's life failed?"

Lysandir dropped his handkerchief. Even without the thick layer of powder his face would have been white. "What are you saying, King Boreas?"

"What do you think I'm saying?" Boreas growled.

Ivalaine stood from her chair. At once all eyes were on the graceful queen. She fixed her ice-blue gaze on Boreas. "Is it your intention to accuse a member of this council of arranging this terrible crime, Your Majesty?"

He swept his gaze around the table, then he shook his head. "No, it is not. You see, I already know who was behind the murder plot—for one of my own, in an act of treachery, allied himself with the enemy."

Another gasp circled the chamber.

Persard raised a shaggy white eyebrow in interest. "Indeed, King Boreas? A traitor in your own court? Who is this individual, and what will become of him?"

Boreas seemed to chew his words before he spoke them, and it was clear he found them bitter. "It was Lord Alerain, and he is dead."

It took several minutes, and a number of hard looks and strong gestures from the king of Calavan, to restore order to the chamber. Grace knew this news of Alerain's treachery was a blow to everyone, especially the nobles of Calavan. If Alerain—always so good and stolid—was not above betrayal, then who was? However, Grace knew the truth. There were dark gifts even good men did not have the power to resist. What had Alerain thought he was buying with his heart? Perhaps he had believed, by agreeing to help the enemy, that the darkness would spare Calavan. If so it had been a vain hope.

"This is ill news, Your Majesty," Sorrin said. The king of Embarr's visage was more gaunt and sallow than ever. "But you have not told us who this enemy is that Alerain allied himself with, and who wanted the death of Kylar of Galt. Tell us, who is the one to blame for this wretched deed?"

The council chamber fell silent, and all leaned forward to hear. Boreas met the eyes of each of the other rulers in turn.

"I will tell you this," he said in a low voice. "Then I will call for a reckoning of the council, for when you have heard the words I am to speak, you will see there can be but one course of action." He drew in a deep breath. "The plot to murder Kylar and change the council's decision was perpetrated by the Raven Cult, acting under the control of the Pale King himself."

Grace's heart soared in her chest. He had said it. Boreas had dared to tell the council the truth! Falken leaped to his feet. All in the chamber gaped as if these were the last words they had expected Boreas to speak, and Falken most of all.

Grace lifted a hand to the bodice of her gown, afraid to breathe. *The council can't deny him now. Boreas has offered them his own seneschal, they can't discount him. They have to decide in favor of a muster, they have to—*

A harsh voice cut through the chamber.

"How dare you, Boreas!"

It was Eminda. The queen of Eredane had stood, and she glared at Boreas with her small eyes, her face red with rage. "How dare you attempt such a coarse and vile ruse? Do you truly expect me to believe your precious Alerain is dead, that he isn't simply hiding in a room in this castle while you work your horrid little trick?"

Even from a distance Grace could see Boreas shaking. She thought the stone table would crack beneath his grip.

"I will show you his head, Your Majesty," Boreas said through his teeth.

Eminda appeared unimpressed. "So you killed him then. I would not put it past one of the bulls of Vathris to make such a sacrifice for one of his lord's plans. You thought you could use this story to frighten us, to force us to choose the way you wish. But I will not be made a fool by you, Boreas." Her voice rose to a shrill pitch. "You will not have your reckoning—not until these arguments are done in proper order. I will not allow it!"

Boreas did not speak but instead let out a wordless sound of rage. Grace gazed at Eminda. How could the queen of Eredane be so blind? How could all of them be so blind? Didn't they see what was right before them? She ran her eyes over the chamber in a desperate search for Logren. Maybe he could talk to his queen, maybe he could put an end to this. However, she did not see the high counselor of Eredane. There was no hope. The kings and queens rose from their chairs. Eminda turned away. There would be no reckoning, no muster for war. . . .

"What's wrong with you?" a voice said. It was soft and quavering, yet somehow it carried across the air of the council chamber. "What's wrong with all of you?"

Grace searched for the speaker, then she saw him. He stood before the first row of benches, clad in a shapeless tunic, his gray eyes stricken behind wire-rimmed spectacles. Travis. The rulers stared at him.

Travis took a step toward the table. "Don't you hear what he's telling you?" His voice rose, thick with anger and fear. "Don't you see what's right in front of you? The Pale King isn't a myth. He's real, and his servants are here in this castle. He tried to kill Kylar, and any one of you could be next. How can you all be so stupid?"

Travis started toward the council table. The kings leaped back in alarm. Eminda cried out in horror.

"Get him back," she shrieked. "Get this creature back!"

Beltan sprang forward to pull Travis back to the bench, but the knight was too slow.

"You've got to do something!" Travis was shouting now. "You've got to do something before it's too late!" As he spoke this last word he pounded his fist against the stone table.

A flash like lightning filled the chamber, and thunder rent the air. Cries of terror and dismay echoed off the walls. Grace blinked in disbelief. Even as she watched a dark line snaked across the council table from the place where Travis had hit it. The crack plunged toward the center of the table, then struck the white disk embedded there. The disk shattered into pieces, obscuring the symbol drawn upon it. Travis leaped back, then looked down at his hand, his expression one of horror.

The chamber was quiet now. All eyes gazed at the table. Then Falken spoke in a low voice.

"The rune of peace has been broken."

Grace heard a sharp intake of breath beside her. She turned to look at Tressa. The red-haired woman gazed forward, her eyes bright and intense. A whispered word escaped her lips.

"Runebreaker."

The council was in chaos now. The rulers hurried from the hall, and the nobles fled their seats. Travis still stood beside the table and stared at his hand. Beltan, Melia, and Falken were with him now.

Grace rose and pushed against the crowd. She didn't feel fear, but exhilaration. Something important had just taken place, something that needed to happen. These people had grown so complacent, their minds so closed. Now they saw that their precious peace could be broken after all. Now maybe they would do something.

She pushed past two fleeing nobles, then reached the others. "Travis," she said.

He looked up, his expression haunted.

"That was wonderful, Travis," she said. "What you did—you woke them up. It was absolutely wonderful!"

She reached out to grip his hand, but he pulled away.

"No, Grace. All I ever do is break things."

Before the others could stop him, Travis turned and ran from the chamber.

92.

Travis looked up at the iron-gray clouds that swirled above the castle and wondered if he would ever see the indigo-dyed Colorado sky again.

He shivered and gathered his mistcloak closer around him. Maybe it was better here. Maybe it was better to be a world away from the memories. Except somehow that never stopped him from remembering.

Good night, Big Brother.

'Night, Bug.

The winter wind carried his sigh away.

It had been three days since he had broken the rune of peace in the council chamber. Falken had said the rune had been bound centuries ago by the greatest of the Runebinders. How could Travis have had the power to break it? Yet somehow he had. He could still feel the energy coursing down his arm, through his hand, and into the stone table.

In their chamber, Falken had questioned him again and again about that moment, but Travis still wasn't certain exactly what had happened, exactly what he had done. He had been so angry, that was all— angry with the rulers and their unwillingness to accept the truth in front of them. He had seen the dark clouds over Imbrifale, he had seen the fell light of the wraithlings, and he had seen the iron heart Grace had cut out of a dead man's chest. How could they still not believe? He had only meant to pound on the table, but the anger had flowed out of him, lightning down a wire, and he had not been able to stop it.

Queen Eminda had called for Travis's head on a trencher when the council met the next day. It was no secret she cared little for rune-speakers or magic. Luckily for Travis, Boreas had prevailed. The king had argued that if Eminda was concerned about the breaking of the rune of peace, then surely she had to be concerned about the broken rune Falken had showed the council, the seal from the Rune Gate. It had been a brilliant gambit on Boreas's part, and Eminda had shut up at once. Travis had not seen it—he was not going anywhere near the council chamber—but Grace had described the scene to him, and he could picture the queen of Eredane, her face red and puffy with outrage, not daring to speak for fear of weakening her own position. Even in defeat there were little triumphs.

After Boreas defended Travis to the council, the king had requested to see him, and Falken had taken him to Boreas's chamber. Travis knew, in some ways, that what he had done had helped Boreas's cause. All the same, he expected the king to be furious with him for his outburst in the council chamber. Once the door shut he had braced his shoulders and wondered how much he would scream while Boreas used those powerful hands to tear him limb from limb.

To his astonishment, the king had nodded to him in solemn greeting, offered him wine, and bidden him sit down. He had spoken with Travis for a short time while Falken stood nearby. The king had wanted to know if Travis had broken any runes before, and if so how many.

At last, questions over, the king had gazed into the fire. "Legend held that Calavan would never fall while the rune of peace was bound in the council table."

Travis had opened his mouth. Was the king blaming him for putting the Dominion in danger?

"No, Goodman," Boreas had said. "Calavan is not in danger because you broke the rune. You broke the rune because Calavan is in danger." The king had drawn in a deep breath, then looked up. "You may go now."

In the two days since, Travis had spent most of his time wandering through the castle alone. He had stopped his studies with the Runespeakers, despite the protestations of both Rin and Falken. The only point in studying runes was to learn how to control his power, and clearly that had failed. What was the point in continuing? To grow even stronger so the next time he could hurt more than just stone?

I won't do it, Jack. I don't know why you did this to me, but it couldn't be for that—it couldn't be to hurt people.

Falken had grown angry when Travis refused to resume his studies, but—to Travis's surprise—Melia had laid a hand on the bard's arm.

"Let him go, Falken," she had said. "He needs to decide this for himself."

He had given her a grateful look, and she had nodded, her amber eyes thoughtful. Then he had left the chamber. He didn't know what he hoped to find in his wanderings, but they calmed him somehow and helped him think. Maybe all he wanted were a few fragments of his own broken peace. After all, the storm would be coming soon enough.

A tangled wall of green rose before him, and an arch of stone provided a doorway. From beyond came a faint, sweet scent and the sound of water. The castle's garden.

Travis started to move past the archway, then hesitated. He cocked his head. It sounded as if someone had called his name. He listened again, but now all he heard was the breath of the wind and the distant voice of water. No doubt that was all it had been. Still, the garden beckoned to him. He stepped through the arch into the private space beyond.

Despite the lateness of the year and the frosty air, some things still grew in the garden. None of the plants were familiar to him. There was a vine with glossy leaves that climbed up the walls, and a kind of feathery evergreen that grew in clumps. The ground was covered with leaves, and trees stretched bare branches overhead, weaving a net to catch the lowering sky.

A path of flat stones drew him onward, past a fountain rimed with ice. A mossy carpet surrounded the fountain, dotted with pale flowers, each as small and delicate as a snowflake. It was from these that rose the winter-forest scent. The path took him deeper into the garden. Travis did not resist. This was a peaceful place.

No, not peaceful. It's wilder than that. More like it's resting, waiting. But waiting for what? Or for whom?

He kept walking. The path led through another archway, into a grotto. Then he halted and looked up in awe.

They were locked in mortal struggle.

The stone they were carved from was white, but Travis sensed that, even in life, the bull would have been the same color. He could almost see muscles rippling beneath its milky skin, flexing as it strained against the warrior.

The man was naked and beautiful. Stone curls tumbled back from his brow. His visage was proud, fierce, and too perfect to be merely human. Like the bull, muscles coursed beneath the smooth surface of his skin, across wide shoulders, along lean hips, down powerful legs. The thick root of his phallus stood erect. Had he been molded in flesh instead of stone, Travis knew there was not a living person who could have refused the warrior's will or desire. Or his knife.

The warrior gripped the knife in his left hand, and the sculptor had caught him in the exact moment of plunging the blade into the bull's throat. The bull's head was tilted back, its eyes wide and its mouth open, so that Travis could almost hear its death bellow. Liquid poured from the slit in the bull's neck, only it wasn't blood. It was water. The water ran down the bull's throat, flowed into a basin at the foot of the statue, then trickled away, into the garden.

"A fine specimen," said an admiring voice. "Wouldn't you agree?"

Travis whirled around. A new patch of green had appeared in the garden, as brilliant as emeralds.

The woman walked toward him, though *saunter* might have been the better word. She was beautiful, though not at all in the hard, white manner of the warrior. She was all curves and soft edges. Dark gold hair tumbled over her shoulders, and her skin had the luscious glow of an apricot. Only her eyes were hard and bright, the same color as her gown.

Travis fumbled for an answer. *A fine specimen.* He didn't know if she meant the warrior or the bull. Or maybe she had been talking about *him.*

No, that wasn't likely. He scratched his scruffy beard and hunched his shoulders inside his shapeless tunic. Who was she? What did she want of him?

"A friend," she said. "And only to talk to you."

He sucked in a breath.

Her lips parted to reveal small, white teeth. "I am Kyrene, Countess of Selesia."

Somehow Travis remembered his manners. He fumbled for her hand, brushed his lips against it, and let it fall. "I'm Travis Wilder."

Now that she was closer he saw there was a wildness to her, like the garden—no, that wasn't so. The garden was calm and peaceful. However, there was an unsettling edge to her gaze. Her luxuriant hair was unbrushed, and her gown, though fashionably revealing, was crooked and in need of adjustment.

She moved past him toward the statue. "Vathris Bullslayer," Kyrene hissed. She turned her emerald gaze on him. "There are those who think killing with a sword is the answer to everything. Is that what you think as well, Travis Wilder?"

He looked down at his hands. "No. It's never right to hurt another. Never."

The scent of apricots. He looked up, and now she was beside him. Her breasts were two ripe fruits in the pearled basket of her bodice. Wasn't she cold?

"You travel in interesting company, Goodman Travis."

"You mean Falken and Melia."

"Yes, Falken Blackhand and Melindora Nightsilver are well known in these lands, if not always well regarded. But you have a fine, strong friend in the king's nephew. Are you and Beltan very . . . close?"

She laughed, but it was a queer sound, and the hair on his neck prickled. Something told him he should go, but he felt rooted to the spot, as if the garden's vines had grown up to tangle themselves around his legs.

"What do you want?" he whispered.

"Only to ask you something, love." Her voice was soothing, yet pierced his skull all the same. She plucked a leaf from a bush. "There are those of us who believe in the power of life." She dropped the leaf to the ground and crushed it under her slipper. "And there are those who believe that destroying things is always the answer."

He could not take his eyes off her. Despite the frigid air, sweat trickled down his sides. She lifted a hand and brushed his scruffy cheeks.

"You should not hide behind that beard, love. Yours is a comely face."

He licked his lips. It was so hard to *think*. His mind felt like it was covered in honey. "What did you want to ask me?"

"It is nothing, really. Only a small thing. You see, I saw what you did in the council chamber, the rune you broke, and I was wondering if I might look at your hand. . . ."

No, Travis, a voice spoke in his mind. *You mustn't let her.*

However, the voice was faint and distant. He did not resist her as she reached out and took his right hand. She bent her head, eyes shining, to study his palm.

"Get away from him, Kyrene!"

The warm haze that surrounded Travis shattered. He drew in a ragged lungful of air. It was freezing and made him cough. He looked up, along with Kyrene, to see two figures step through the entrance of the grotto: a small woman in a kirtle of deep blue, and a man with a single black glove.

Kyrene glared emerald daggers at the two. "You don't own him, Melindora Nightsilver."

"And neither will you, Kyrene." Melia's coppery visage was a hard mask of anger. "I told you to get away from him."

"Step back, Travis," Falken said in a serious voice. "Now."

Travis didn't understand what was going on, but he did as he was told. He had no idea how Melia always knew where to find him, but once again he was grateful.

Kyrene hesitated, then seemed to make a decision. She threw her shoulders back and thrust out her chin. "I'm not afraid of you, Melindora. You're not what you once were."

Travis stared at the countess. What was she talking about?

"That's true," Melia said. She stepped forward, until she stood mere inches from the countess. Her voice was cool and dangerous. "Then again, I still have a number of connections. I am quite certain I could arrange it so you never feel the Touch again, Kyrene."

Kyrene's bold expression faltered, and her face blanched. "You can't! You wouldn't!"

Melia smiled. It was not an affectionate expression. "Are you really so very sure of that . . . *love*?"

Kyrene opened her mouth, but no words came out. She glanced at Falken's grim face, then back to Melia. The countess shut her mouth, gathered her gown up around her ankles, and hurried from the grotto—but not before casting one hateful glance back at Melia.

Falken raised an eyebrow. "One gets the impression she doesn't care for us."

Melia sniffed. "There's no accounting for taste."

"So why do you think Kyrene was interested in Travis?"

"It is my experience that witches are curious about everything. Too curious, sometimes. We will simply have to keep an eye on her." Melia approached the statue and looked up. "Greetings, Vathris."

Her voice sounded almost fond, which struck Travis as odd. He followed after her.

"He's one of the New Gods, isn't he?"

Melia nodded. "Yes, the gods of the mystery cults are the New Gods. And there are many of them, not just the seven known in the Dominions. Some of them are great in power, many of them lesser. Most of their followers live in the far south, in the lands along the Summer Sea."

Travis thought about this. How did Melia know so much? Then he had it. "You're from the south, aren't you, Melia?"

She plucked a leaf from a vine and twirled it in a small hand. Her gaze grew distant. "Yes, I dwelled there once. Sometimes I can still see the red cliffs of Urundar, and the men in their white *serafis* dancing at twilight." The leaf fell to the ground, and her eyes grew focused once more. "But that time is long over. I have other matters that concern me now."

Falken regarded her, his faded eyes thoughtful, then his expression changed, and he smiled wolfishly. "One matter that concerns me right now is supper. Shall we see what's being offered in the great hall?"

Melia concurred, and she and Falken turned to leave the garden. Travis hesitated. He cast one glance at the statue of Vathris. If only once in his life he could have that strength, that control of his own destiny. If only . . .

"Wait, I'm coming, too," he said, and he hurried after the bard and the lady.

93.

Grace was worried about Travis. It was strange how quickly one could get used to something one had never had before—something like friends—but she had grown accustomed to Travis's companionship over these last weeks.

Yesterday she had gone to speak with Falken and Melia. The small woman still had the ability to instantly disarm Grace.

"We've been keeping an eye on him, dear," Melia had said.

As always the lady's smooth visage had seemed young yet motherly as well. A black kitten had played with the hem of her kirtle, and Grace had frowned. The creature seemed no larger than it had the first time she had seen it, and that had been weeks ago. Weren't kittens supposed to grow quickly? Melia had seemed to notice her puzzled gaze and had smiled.

"We're trying to convince Travis to study again with the Runespeakers," Falken had said. "But he has to decide that on his own."

Melia had gathered the kitten into her arms. "I'm afraid what he did in the council chamber frightened him, maybe even more than it did the kings and queens."

Grace had stepped forward. "But what *did* he do?"

Falken had spoken in a low voice. "Something that hasn't been done in centuries."

The bard had not seemed to wish to discuss this statement further, and Melia had promised to let Grace know if they spoke to Travis again.

"But you might want to try talking to him, Lady Grace," she had said as they paused at the door. "He thinks of you as a friend, you know."

Grace had tried to say she felt the same, except the words had gotten wedged in her throat. Instead she had nodded, then had found herself alone in the corridor.

Over those next days Grace had thought more about what Travis had done in the council chamber. Falken and Melia had told Grace of their encounter with Kyrene in the garden. This news had fascinated Grace. Kyrene had never appeared to notice Travis before. This sudden interest made no sense.

Or did it? *Runebreaker.* That was the word Tressa had whispered in the council chamber, her eyes glowing. Were the Witches interested in someone who could break runes? Grace had attempted to bring the subject up with Ivalaine's red-haired advisor, but she had had no luck. Still, if the witches thought Travis could be this Runebreaker, it would explain Kyrene's interest in him. Perhaps the countess had thought, if she discovered something about Travis, she could regain Ivalaine's favor. If so, Falken and Melia had thwarted the attempt with their intervention.

Grace had spent the last few days concentrating on her studies with Queen Ivalaine. There was little else to do. She could see no point to further spying—they all knew where the other kings and queens stood on the matter of war—and so there was no more point in maintaining the ruse that she and Boreas had fallen out. Not that Boreas seemed interested in her. He did not summon her to his chamber, and if she passed him in a corridor, he barely grunted at her in greeting, his eyes like steel.

It might have mattered if she could have learned something of Ivalaine's motives. However, every time Grace tried subtly to turn their conversation to the council, the queen of Toloria deftly turned it back to the lesson at hand.

"There is an order to knowledge, sister," Ivalaine said one afternoon. "You cannot dance before you learn to walk."

Grace didn't know if that comment pertained to her questions or her studies. Either way, it was clear she would not learn what Ivalaine—or the Witches—wanted until Ivalaine was ready to tell her.

Nor was there much for the Circle of the Black Knife to accomplish. The plot to murder King Kylar had failed. True, the second conspirator remained uncaptured, but now Beltan was in charge of the safety of the kings and queens, and it was doubtful a second try at murder would succeed, if one was even attempted.

The Council of Kings had recessed and would not meet again until Midwinter's Day, three days from now, when the last arguments would be heard and a final reckoning would be made. Not that it was a mystery what the final outcome would be. They had succeeded in stopping the conspirators but had failed utterly in swaying the council. None of the rulers had changed his or her initial position. King Boreas had failed. Eminda had crushed his last gambit. The Dominions would not stand together against the Pale King.

Grace sighed as she gazed out the window of her chamber. The sky was dark again. The fog never seemed to lift anymore, but pressed against the castle's stone walls as if it meant to crack them.

Maybe it's a myth, after all, Grace. Maybe the Pale King really is just a story to frighten children.

However, myths could be real—she knew that now, could not deny it—and, although she was no child, she was afraid to the marrow of her bones. She watched the heavy clouds descend around Calavere's nine towers, swallowing them. It would be soon now. Very soon.

Grace turned and stared at the door. Maybe it wasn't over yet after all. There was still one who might be able to help her change the decision of the council, one who might be able to help her heal this world. She checked her hair in a polished mirror of silver, tried to paw it into some sort of arrangement—it was getting longer now—then settled for tucking the loosest strands behind an ear. She splashed a little cold water on her cheeks to freshen them, then adjusted her frosted violet gown.

Why are you doing this, Grace?

Afraid she knew the true answer, she hurried out the door. She knew the castle well now, and her feet seemed to find the way on their own. She hesitated for only a heartbeat, then knocked on the door.

He's not here, Grace. He wasn't even at the council last time, he won't answer.

However, even as she thought this she knew he would, and a moment later the door swung open. Genuine surprise registered in his gaze, then he smiled, and that gaze—as brown and rich as *maddok*—traveled over her body before it once again rose to meet her own.

"Lady Grace, you have just assured the brightness of my day despite the gloom outside."

He made something between a nod and a bow. She almost laughed—it was so perfect. Respectful yet familiar. She smiled and attempted a curtsy. She was getting better.

"Lord Logren . . ."

She wanted to say more, why she had come, what she needed from him, but the right words fled her as surely as if she had dropped her silver half-coin.

"I've just had some spiced wine brought," he said. "It's still warm. I find it to be a good ward against the chill. Though not so good as company, of course."

The high counselor of Eredane gestured for Grace to enter. It was Her Radiance, the Duchess of Beckett, who did so. The door shut behind her, and she breathed in. The scent of spices filled the austere room, although she was not certain it was only from the wine. It was his scent as well. He handed her a cup, raised his toward her, then both drank. She let the warm liquid spread through her, then drew in a breath to speak.

"I need you, Lord Logren."

He raised an eyebrow, as if not quite certain how to interpret this statement. Her cheeks flushed, and not just from the wine.

"Your help, I mean."

And was that so? Or had her first statement been closer to the truth?

No, Grace, that's not why you came here, to work petty magics like Kyrene.

She forced herself to set down her cup, then regarded Logren with what she hoped was a businesslike gaze. "I didn't see you at the council the other day, my lord, but I'm certain you know what happened."

He nodded, his expression curious. "I do."

She swallowed hard, then went on. "I'm not asking you to believe in the Pale King, my lord. I do, but that's not important now. It's not why I'm here. Whatever you believe about Falken's stories, the plot to murder King Kylar was real—no one can deny that, whatever Queen Eminda says."

Her voice grew stronger now, filled with conviction. She picked up the hem of her gown and paced before the small fire as she spoke.

"Lord Alerain is dead, but he wasn't working alone—he certainly didn't chop off his own head with a sword. That means the other conspirator is still here in the castle. If we could find him, then we could question him, and maybe we could learn more about what they—I mean, what *he* really wanted. Then the council could use that knowledge to make their decision. Whatever the reckoning was, it wouldn't really matter. At least we would know they had all the information before they decided, and that we had done all we could."

She halted, drew in a breath, then realized she had nothing more to say. He studied her, and she felt like a stage actor who had forgotten her lines just as the spotlight turned her way. Her instinct was to run, but she could not connect the feeling with her legs. He was going to laugh at her, or mock her, or turn on her in rage. She was an idiot to have come here thinking she could influence him.

He set down his cup and walked toward her with purpose. She braced her shoulders. Now it would come.

"I will help you, my lady."

She blinked—she must have heard wrong. However, there was no laughter in his eyes, no anger. They were dark and serious.

"You wonder why I have agreed." He shrugged. "Perhaps I don't know myself. Or perhaps I'm weary of watching my queen make a fool of herself before the council." Now his lips did twist in a mocking smile, but Grace knew it was not meant for her. "Royals are born, not chosen, and inbreeding is not always kind to intellect. Pale King or no, there is something afoot in this castle, some attempt to sway the decision of the council against war. And though that has been my own position, I find myself wondering who else might want this outcome—want it so much they would murder for it—and why." He drew in a breath. "What can I do to assist you, my lady?"

Grace's heart leaped in her chest. She had never imagined that he would agree to help her. But why not? His was a logical mind, and he had reasoned things through better than she.

"I need you to watch, my lord," she said. "You know people at this council whom I don't. I need you to watch those you are familiar with and see if any of them are acting . . . different or strange." *Or if they have scars on their chest.* But she didn't speak those words. How could she have explained?

"I can do that, my lady. And I am not without my own sources of information. I will see what I can discover of Alerain's killer."

They gazed at each other in understanding, then he grinned, and she could not help grinning back. Maybe there was hope yet. At that point she meant to give him her thanks, to tell him they would talk again soon, and leave the chamber.

The words did not leave her lips, the door did not open. Instead the air folded, and she was in his arms. He bent his head—although he did not have to reach far, she was tall—and touched his lips to hers. She tasted wine and something more: passion. Greedy, she drank it like it was elixir.

His mouth pressed harder against her own. An electric sensation filled her. Her hands ran like small animals over his body. He was clad in breeches and a white shirt, but she could feel firm flesh beneath the cloth. It excited her, and he was excited as well, that was plain enough—Kyrene had been right on one account.

Her fingers found their way beneath his shirt. For a fraction of a second she feared what her touch might discover—

It could be anyone. . . .

—but his chest was hard, smooth, and unmarred.

His hand found the laces of her bodice, and they seemed to fall open at his touch. His fingers slipped inside, warm and gentle. A moan escaped her, and she pressed herself against him.

Much of who you are lies behind a door, and I cannot see behind it.

Grace stiffened as the words drifted, unbidden, through her mind.

If ever you want to discover that power, you will have to unlock that door.

Fear sliced through her. No, she couldn't do it. She couldn't open the door. Not now, not ever. If she did, what was to stop the fire from leaping forth and consuming her?

With a cry, Grace pushed herself away from him. She stumbled, caught herself against the wall, and looked up. Logren's expression was shocked and hurt. He reached a hand toward her.

"Lady Grace. . . ."

She shook her head. "I'm sorry," she said. "I'm so sorry."

She did not give him a chance to answer. Grace turned, clutched the bodice of her gown to close it, and pushed through the door. Then she ran down the corridor and let the sound of her boots drown out his calls behind her.

94.

Travis stood on one of Calavere's high battlements and wrapped his mistcloak around him. It was freezing, but he had needed to get outside, to escape the smoke and stench of the castle, if only for a little while. The castle's baileys were distant beneath him: Nobles, knights, peasants, and sheep all looked like playthings. Maybe they were, at that. He glanced up at the dark clouds that marched from the north. A new king was coming—or an old king, it didn't matter.

Maybe they were all playthings.

No, Travis, you can't just give up like that. Someone has to stand against the Pale King, even if it's just a fool, as in Falken's story.

He turned toward the frigid breeze, shut his eyes, and felt that sense of possibility he always did when he faced into the wind: Maybe the council would realize its mistake, maybe the Dominions would unite against the Pale King after all, maybe he would still find a way back to Colorado.

The air froze, the wind ceased, and the feeling of possibility vanished. He opened his eyes. There was nothing out here, only hard stone and a frozen landscape that would never thaw again.

He shivered. These were cold thoughts, and he was cold enough. Better to go back to the chamber and warm himself by the fire, even if Melia and Falken were there. He stepped through the door that led from the battlement, shut it behind him, and moved into the dim room beyond.

A fist sprang out of the shadows and struck him square in the chest.

Travis hit the wall behind him—hard. He stared into the gloom in astonishment, then slid down the stones to the floor. His mouth gaped open. He tried to breathe, but it felt as if his lungs had been crushed— he could draw no air into them.

The shadows before him stirred. A piece of the darkness broke itself off, approached, and stood above him: a man clad in a robe of black.

Travis stared up at the robed one. Maybe it was terror, maybe it was reflex, but he shuddered, and a hoarse gasp of air rushed into his lungs. His hands scraped against the floor—breathing was more painful than suffocating. The man pushed back his hood, and Travis saw the symbol branded upon his forehead.

The Raven cultist grinned. With a rough finger he touched the brand: It was fresh and oozed yellow fluid.

"Do you like it?" he said in a cracked whisper. "I took it to show my dedication to my master. Soon all who live in the world will bear his mark. But not you, Runewielder." His hideous grin broadened, and a knife appeared in his hand. "You will be dead."

Travis tried to move, tried to get up, but his body would not respond. His hands flopped like dying fish on the floor.

The robed man crouched before Travis, his face only inches away. Travis gagged at a reek that emanated from him, a mixture of sweat, rot, and old blood. The cultist's eyes flickered over Travis, and only then did Travis see that one eye was blue and the other brown. He remembered Grace's words and shuddered.

"You have been difficult, Runewielder," the robed man hissed. "First you killed the master's little pet. Then you took the head of one of my brothers. But now the master has given the job to me, and I do not think you will escape this time."

Travis stared at the knife. This didn't make sense. Why had the cultist attacked him? It was Grace they wanted to kill . . . wasn't it?

He managed to croak a single word. "Why?"

"Why must I destroy you?" The cultist spat. "You are what cannot be allowed. A runespeaker is dangerous enough. But a runebinder— worse yet. The master does not care for runewielders, and runebinders least of all. He thought all were gone." The grin again, black and festering. "And so they will be."

The cultist raised the knife. Travis tried to shrink back, but there was only hard stone behind him.

"Pray," the man whispered. "Pray to the White One on his throne, and perhaps I will not make it so very painful."

Travis stared at the knife and wondered what part of his body it would pierce first.

What are you doing, Travis?

He stiffened at the sound. It was not the cultist that had spoken, but rather a voice inside his head. A familiar voice.

Jack?

By the Hammer of Durnach, don't just sit there like a lamb at slaughter. Do something!

I can't, Jack. I can't move.

You don't have to. Just speak the rune of stone.

The rune of stone?

Blast it, Travis! Must you always be so dense? You know the rune. All you have to do is speak it.

But . . .

No buts, Travis. This world needs you. You have to do it. Now!

Travis licked parched lips and drew in a breath of agony. The knife descended toward his heart. It would be this moment or never. He forced his lips to form the word.

"*Sar!*"

There was a scream, and a queer, liquid sound. Then came another cry, not of pain, but of pure, wordless hate.

"No! Free me! Free me and let me kill you!"

Travis's eyes fluttered open, and shock replaced pain. A second ago the Raven cultist had been inches from him. Now the man was bound fast to the far wall by shackles of stone. They looped around his ankles, his wrists, his throat. He struggled, but even his unnatural strength was no use against the bonds forged by the rune of stone. They merged seamlessly with the wall.

Something else caught Travis's eye, resting on the floor between him and the cultist: a small iron box. It was open, and next to it lay a gray-green stone.

Panic replaced pain. The box must have fallen from his pocket when the cultist struck him, and must have opened when it hit the floor. Travis staggered to his feet. He limped forward—his chest still hurt, but his breaths came more easily now—then bent and picked up the Stone.

"You!" the cultist hissed. "It is you who holds Sinfathisar! It is you the Pale Ones followed before they lost the trail."

Travis shuddered. He should go, he should get the others, but he could not help himself from asking a question in dread fascination. "Why? Why does the Pale King want the Great Stones?"

The cultist's eyes burned into Travis, so intense he wondered if they would leave their own brand upon him.

"Once the master has all the Imsari, nothing will be able to stop him. All of Eldh will be his. And he *will* have them. Already Gelthisar lies within the iron necklace he wears, and soon your Stone will be set beside it." Laughter wracked his body. "The Pale Ones will find you—they will see Sinfathisar's trail. You might have stopped me with your runes, but the Stone has betrayed you."

Travis snatched up the iron box, shut the Stone inside, and thrust it into his pocket. But he knew the cultist was right, knew that it was too late.

The Pale Ones will find you. . . .

"It doesn't matter." Travis hoped the defiance in his voice masked the dread in his gut. "You've lost. Your plan to murder a king failed. We'll take you to the council, make you tell them what you've done, and they'll have to believe. The Dominions will all stand together against your precious Pale King and shut him back in Imbrifale."

The cultist gazed at him, then once more laughter bubbled from his lips. "The council? But what council is this you speak of that will do this thing?"

Travis stiffened, and his defiance evaporated. "What do you mean?"

The man did not speak, then he murmured something under his breath in a weird singsong. "Things aren't always what you think, for all can vanish in a blink."

Travis shook his head. "What are you saying?"

"Please." Now the cultist's voice was a whisper of anguish. "Please, you must let me kill you."

Travis recoiled from him.

The man's voice rose to a shriek. He strained against the loops of stone. "No! I dare not fail him. You do not understand what he will do. Please, I must kill you! The master will—"

The cultist's words ended, and his eyes bulged in their sockets. His hands curled into claws inside the stone shackles, and a gurgling escaped his throat. Then Travis saw it: A curl of smoke rose from the front of his robe. A tongue of flame followed, and the scent of charred flesh. The man screamed. Like a hot coal it burned through flesh and robe, then fell to the floor. The cultist's scream ended. He slumped in the stone bonds, and his strange eyes stared in lifeless horror as the flames consumed him. Travis gazed down at the object that smoked on the floor, and sickness filled his stomach.

It was a lump of hot iron.

95.

"How the Pale King got his hands on Imsaridur and Gelthisar, I don't know," Falken said. "But it certainly explains the harsh winter that's assailed the Dominions."

They had all gathered in Falken and Melia's chamber, after Travis had found first Grace, then the bard and the lady, and had told them all what had happened. Now Travis sat in the horsehair chair before the fire. Melia had wrapped him in a blanket. He was sweating, and so hot he felt he would burn up, but he could not stop shivering. Aryn and Durge had poured spiced wine for all of them, and he did his best to grip his cup and sip the steaming liquid without spilling it.

Beltan scratched his head. "Maybe it explains it to you, Falken, but could you give a little hint to those of us who don't happen to know the entire history of the world?"

Falken regarded the blond knight. "Gelthisar is the Stone of Ice, one of the Imsari, the three Great Stones. With its magic the Pale King could definitely summon cold winds and weather. Or weaken the Rune Gate." The bard strummed a somber chord on his lute. "Both of which it appears he's done."

"But hasn't Imbrifale been a land of ice and snow for centuries?" Melia said. She sat in the chair opposite Travis, the black kitten asleep in her lap. Evidently prancing around and biting at Travis's ankles was exhausting work.

"You're right, Melia," Falken said. "The Pale King has always been associated with cold and ice, at least since the fall of Malachor." He shot her a meaningful look.

Melia nodded and let out a deep breath.

Beltan groaned. "Now what?"

Melia glanced up at the knight. "It seems the Pale King has had the Stone Gelthisar, as well as the iron necklace Imsaridur, in his possession for centuries."

Falken rubbed his chin with his black-gloved hand. "It would make sense. During the reign of Malachor, the Runelords guarded the dwarfin necklace Imsaridur, which contained the three Great Stones. But when Malachor fell, the Runelords were destroyed and the three Imsari were scattered." Sadness flickered in his faded eyes. "We had always thought the Great Stones were lost, but it looks as if, somehow, Gelthisar and the necklace found their way to Imbrifale not long after Malachor was destroyed." He gave Travis a sharp look. "And we know where Sinfathisar is. That leaves only one more of the Imsari— Krondisar, the Stone of Fire."

Melia gazed into the flames that danced on the hearth. "And no doubt his minions search for it at this moment, even as they do Sinfathisar."

Travis opened his mouth. He wanted to ask Falken and Melia what would happen if the Pale King gained all three Imsari and the necklace Imsaridur was complete once more. The ironheart had told him, but he wanted to hear it from them. However, a grim voice spoke before he could.

"Why now?"

All of them turned their attention toward Grace.

She had seemed in an odd mood when Travis found her in her chamber—her gaze had been so distant—and she had not spoken since he had shown her and the others the cultist. Or at least what had remained of the cultist, for there had been nothing besides a heap of ashes and the half-melted lump of iron that had served as his heart. The stone shackles had been empty.

"It doesn't make sense," Grace said. "If he's had this stone—the Stone of Ice—for so long, why has the Pale King waited until now to do something?"

Falken set down his lute. "Berash was defeated badly by King Ulther and Empress Elsara a thousand years ago. It was thought he was dead—though death does not necessarily mean the same to one such as him as it does to us. I would guess it has taken him this long to gather his strength again, and that only now is he ready to try to ride forth once more."

Travis spoke between chattering teeth. "Lucky us to come along at just the right time."

Beltan ran a hand through his thinning hair. "So what do we do now?"

Falken picked up a leather pouch from the windowsill. From the way he handled it, it was heavy. Travis felt his gorge rise. He knew what the sack contained.

"We talk to the kings and queens," Falken said. "One by one if we can get audiences with them. And we show them this." He hefted the leather pouch. "We have to try to convince them it's not too late to stand against the Pale King."

"*If* it's not too late to stand against the Pale King," Melia murmured.

No one attempted an answer to that.

"I'll go talk to King Boreas," Beltan said. "Hopefully he can set up meetings with the other rulers."

"I'll help," Aryn said.

The blond knight cast a sharp look at Durge. The Embarran gave a solemn nod, then Beltan and Aryn left the room.

"What now?" Falken said as he looked at Melia.

She set the kitten on the floor and rose from her chair. "I would like to spend a little more time examining the place where Travis encountered the ironheart."

"What for?"

Melia turned her striking gaze on him.

He nodded—another secret message. The bard and the lady started toward the door.

Travis spoke the words in a soft voice. "He said the Pale Ones would see the light of Sinfathisar."

Falken and Melia halted, and the bard regarded Travis with grave eyes. "The ironheart wasn't lying about that. They lost our trail after the White Tower, and I was hoping they had lost it for good. But when the Stone was released from the box, there was nothing to keep its power from shining forth. That will be like a beacon to them. It's only a matter of time until the wraithlings get here."

Travis could only nod.

"Come, Falken." Melia touched his arm. "Let us not be defeated by what is not yet here. There is still much we can do."

Falken took her hand in his, then the two stepped from the chamber.

Grace glanced at the door, then looked at Travis and Durge. They were the only ones left in the room.

"So what do *we* do?" she said.

"What *can* we do, my lady?" Durge said. "The second conspirator is no more. Lord Falken and Lady Melia will do what they can to convince the council to act. It is best we remain here and watch for those who search for Goodman Travis."

"No." Travis looked up. "No, that's not enough, Durge."

Grace turned toward him. "What is it, Travis?"

He threw off the blanket and stood. Something was wrong about this. Something he had missed. What was it? He searched his mind—it was so close.

The council! But what council is this you speak of that will do this thing?

Travis sucked in a breath. "This isn't over. The ironheart is dead, but this still isn't over."

Grace took a step toward him. "What do you mean?"

He paced before the fire now, and his mind raced. "It was something the ironheart said before he was . . . before he died. Something about the council."

Durge frowned beneath his mustaches. "What was it?"

Things aren't always what you think, for all can vanish in a blink.

There could be only one answer to that riddle. "The council," Travis said. "They plan to do away with the entire Council of Kings."

Grace took a step back in shock. "Are you certain?"

"Positive. They're going to kill all the rulers at once."

"Who do you mean?" Durge said. "The second conspirator is dead."

"No, I don't think so." Travis approached the knight. "The ironheart hinted that something is going to happen to the council members. That means there's someone left to do it. I don't think he was the second conspirator—I think Alerain's murderer is still loose in the castle."

"I think you're right, Travis." Grace met his gaze. "The man who attacked you, the one I saw in the town, he was shorter and heavier than the one I saw in my vision."

"But when and how will the conspirator strike?" Durge said. "It seems unlikely he will be able to do away with all the kings and queens at once. Two of them will hardly stand in a room together at this point, let alone all seven."

Grace's green-gold eyes grew large. "The feast!"

Travis and Durge both stared at her.

"Aryn said King Boreas is planning a feast for Midwinter's Eve," she said. "It's the only time all the rulers will be together before the council meets again. That has to be when the conspirator will strike. It's his only chance."

"But the great hall will be closely guarded, my lady," Durge said. "I can assure you of that."

"It won't matter." Travis didn't know why, but he was certain Grace was right. "Not if the murderer is already in the great hall."

"In which case we have to find him before the feast begins," Grace said.

"A fine idea, my lady," Durge said. "But how do you propose we accomplish this?"

She grimaced. "I don't know. We'd need some sort of distraction—something to throw the murderer off his guard so he reveals himself. But I can't think of anything to do that."

Travis started to agree, then winced in pain. He glanced down to see the black kitten pounce again at his shin like a miniature panther. Its sharp claws sank through the fabric of his breeches to pierce the skin. He started to shout in protest, then halted. The kitten sat and looked up at him with large golden eyes. Of course—it was only playing, only pretending to be ferocious.

Only playing, only pretending . . .

Travis laughed. The answer was so impossible, but even as he thought this he knew it was right, that it was their only chance. Grace and Durge stared at him, probably afraid he had lost his mind. He reached down, scooped the kitten into his grasp, and stood again.

"I think I know someone who can help us," he said.

Grace and Durge stepped close to listen. In the crook of his arm the kitten licked a paw and purred.

Minutes later the three of them—minus the kitten—stood outside a wooden door. This was a quiet part of the castle, a tower some distance from the main keep.

Travis glanced at Durge. "Are you certain this is it?"

The knight gave a sharp nod. "The Lady Aryn mentioned the king's actors were being housed in the north tower. This is the only chamber large enough to accommodate an entire troupe."

"This has to be it," Grace said.

Travis drew in a deep breath. Did he really mean to do this thing? But there was nowhere else to turn for help. He lifted a hand, hesitated, then rapped on the door.

There was no answer. Silence crept down the corridor on padded feet. Travis swallowed hard, then reached out his hand to knock again.

The door swung open.

"Who's there?" Travis called out.

No answer. Through the door he saw only shadows and gloom.

"Let's go," Grace said.

Durge loosened his knife in its sheath. "I will wait out here. Call me if you require my aid."

Travis doubted the knight's blade would be of much use against anything they might encounter beyond the door. However, he did not say this. He exchanged looks with Grace, then the two stepped through the doorway.

A heavy sound echoed behind them—the door shutting, Travis supposed, although it sounded muffled and distant. He adjusted his spectacles and peered around him. There was light in the chamber after all, silvery and sourceless. Rushes strewed the floor, and tapestries draped stone walls. The weavings depicted a green forest with tangled trees hiding white stags, birds, and crystal fountains. His hand found Grace's, and they stepped farther into the room.

Bells shimmered on the air, then faded with a lingering shiver across his skin.

"This way," Grace said.

They followed the sound through an archway. More tapestries draped the walls, only they seemed closer now, and darker. The tapestries had been woven with great skill. He could see minute details: the texture of a tree's bark, the dappled light on the surface of a brook. He and Grace pressed on. A moist scent rose on the air, fresh and green, so unlike the usual odor of the castle.

Another stone archway, this one half-draped by one of the tapestries. Travis reached out to push aside the curtain and step through the arch.

His hands brushed across smooth bark, and cool leaves caressed his face.

No, that was impossible. It was only a tapestry. He looked at Grace. Her eyes were startled. He opened his mouth, but a rustling sound interrupted him, and something crimson streaked between them. Travis followed it with his gaze. It alighted on a branch: a small bird, its breast as red as berries. The bird regarded them with bright eyes.

Grace squeezed his hand hard. "Where are we, Travis?"

Travis looked around. He could still see the chamber's stone walls here and there, and the floor was still wood, although now it was covered—not with cut rushes—but with fallen leaves. Somewhere water flowed, and branches arched overhead instead of beams or rafters.

"I'm not sure, Grace."

But maybe he was. Maybe this was both castle and forest.

"Greetings," said a piping voice.

Travis and Grace turned around.

"Trifkin!" Travis said.

The little man sat on a stump, cross-legged, his jacket blending with the leaves. It was difficult to be sure, but the silvery light seemed to emanate from his direction.

"I knew you would come," Trifkin said. "Yet I feared you would not."

"We need your help, Trifkin." Grace took a step toward him. "We need to find a way to—"

He raised a small hand and nodded. "I know."

Travis followed after Grace. "But how can you know?"

"I have seen it happen," Trifkin said. "Your plan for the Midwinter's Eve feast."

"Then it's going to work?" Grace said.

"Yes," Trifkin said. Then, "No."

Travis groaned. This was too much. "But what are you saying? How can it be both?"

The little man held out his arms. "A tree has many branches, yet it is all one tree. Still, in the end, you can choose but one branch to follow."

Travis hesitated, then grinned. It was like the chamber and the forest. Sometimes two possibilities could exist at once: a fork in a road, a branch in a tree. There was no way to know which would be true, not until you picked one.

"It's not too late," Grace said. "That's what you mean. We still have a choice."

"You always have a choice," Trifkin said. "It is what you will choose that is unknown."

Travis drew closer to the little man. "Will you help us then?"

Trifkin's round face grew solemn. "The Little People retreated from this world long ago. It had its New Gods—it needed the Old Ones and their children no longer."

Grace sighed. "Then you won't help us."

Trifkin regarded her with his deep eyes. "Yes, that is one choice." He stood on the stump. "Yet there is another choice as well. That which was once forgotten comes again. We were lost in our dreams of the old days, but now the old days are returning. The time for action has come."

"But what can we do?" Travis said.

Now Trifkin smiled again. "But you already know. You have only to follow that branch to its end."

Travis shook his head. How could he possibly know? Then somehow he did. It glowed before him, perfect and whole, like a ripe fruit he had only to pluck. He looked at Grace. Her eyes shone—she understood.

"You must go now," Trifkin said.

There was peril in his voice. The meaning was clear: This place was not safe for mortals.

"But first," the little man said, "I must give you each a gift."

A silver bracelet appeared in his small hand. From it dangled a dark, wedge-shaped stone. He handed it to Grace, and she slipped it over her wrist.

"Follow this, Blademender," he said, "until you can learn to follow your own heart."

Now a bundle wrapped in leaves appeared in Trifkin's hand. He handed it to Travis.

"What is it?" Travis said.

"Hurry," Trifkin whispered.

"But—"

Travis blinked, then stared at Grace. Before them the wooden door swung shut. They turned around and saw the Embarran knight.

"Durge!" Grace said. "You're still here."

"Of course, my lady. You were gone but a moment. Did he not speak to you then?"

Grace could only shake her head. She lifted her hand, and silver glinted around her wrist.

Travis looked down at the bundle in his hands. It was not covered in leaves any longer, but with green felt. With trembling hands he unfolded the cloth. Beneath was a disk of creamy white stone. His heart fluttered in his chest. He did not need Falken to tell him what the object was. He knew the meaning of the angular rune, and the meaning of the jagged break that divided the disk in two.

It was *Gelth*.

The second seal from the Rune Gate.

And it was broken.

96.

After a week of muffling clouds and mist, the day before Midwinter dawned clear and brilliant over Calavere. It had snowed during the night, and a thick, white cloak mantled the fields and walls of Calavan. Grace rose with the sun, threw open the window of her chamber, and breathed in icy air. Snow capped the castle's towers and battlements and concealed—for a short time at least—the mud of the baileys.

Grace spent the day doing simple things. She passed the morning beside the fireplace, reading a book taken from the castle's library. It was a history of Calavan. She read of the terrible winter five centuries ago, when the River Darkwine froze over and barbarians crossed the ice to attack. However, the Tarrasian captain Calavus—who had never in his life traveled to the great city of Tarras—met them, not with swords, but with skins of wine and joints of roasted meat. He forged a pact with the barbarians, they knelt to him as their leader, and in that moment Calavan was born.

Grace set down the book and gazed again at the frigid world outside the window. The Dimduorn had not frozen since that winter five hundred years ago. She had heard it said in the castle how some thought it would freeze that night.

At midday, a serving maid brought her a tray with dinner. She ate, then she spent the afternoon working on her embroidery. Aryn had said all noblewomen in the Dominions knew how to embroider. Grace thought she would be good at it—after all, she had sewn enough stitches in the Emergency Department. However, it turned out she was awful. No matter which finger she wore the thimble on, she always seemed to prick another, and what was supposed to be a pattern of leaves and acorns looked more like something she would grow in a petri dish.

She looked up, neck aching, as the daylight began to fade beyond the window. It was nearly time. She set down her embroidery, rose, donned a different gown—the frosted winter violet, her favorite—then brushed her hair until it shone like the last of the sunlight that gilded the castle's turrets. She set the brush on the sideboard, turned, and faced the door. Outside, shadows crept across the snow—a deeper hue of purple than her gown.

"Let's go, Doctor," she murmured to herself.

Grace opened the door, stepped through, and set out to catch the murderer in the castle.

Over the last two days, the Circle of the Black Knife had refined their plan to discover the conspirator at the Midwinter's Eve feast, although they had told no one—not even Falken and Melia—what they intended.

After their meeting with Trifkin Mossberry, Grace and Travis had gone at once to the bard and the lady's chamber to show them the broken seal from the Rune Gate. Falken had sworn, then had asked them where they had gotten it, and they had told them of their encounter with Trifkin.

"It looks as if you were right after all, Travis," Falken had said as he folded the stone disk back into its cloth.

Melia had raised an eyebrow.

"Travis saw them at King Kel's keep," Falken had said. "Trifkin and his troupe of actors, I mean. Travis told me there was something strange about them, but I thought he had just drunk a bit too much ale."

Melia had rested her chin on the back of a slender hand. "Travis does have perceptive vision. I think it's best if we don't forget that."

Falken had grunted.

With this new revelation, the bard had been more resolved than ever to speak to the kings and queens about the danger that faced the Dominions, to convince them to act, and he intended to use the broken rune *Gelth* as further evidence. Grace had not disagreed with his words. However, something had told her it would take more than shattered stones and old stories to change the minds of those rulers who did not believe in the Pale King.

Grace had exchanged a look with Travis, and she had known they were in accord—they had not mentioned their Midwinter's Eve plan.

Now Grace halted before a door and lifted her hand to knock, but the wooden surface swung away before her hand could contact it. She gazed into a pair of solemn brown eyes.

"The others are all here, my lady," Durge said.

She nodded, then stepped into the room, and the dark-haired knight shut the door behind her. Travis, Aryn, and Beltan all nodded to her in greeting.

Grace had never been in Durge's chamber before. What she saw was not what she had expected. The room was small and had only a narrow slit of a window. It was heated, not with a fireplace, but with a small brazier that cast its smoke on the air and left the substance to find its way out through cracks in the walls and ceiling. There was a low bed and a heavy wooden chest which most likely housed the knight's armor when he was not wearing it, and which was doubtless empty at the moment. Durge was clad in his gray tunic and cloak, but the garments were bulkier than usual, and Grace heard a jingling when he moved. His greatsword was slung across his back.

What caught Grace's attention most of all was the chamber's sideboard. It was covered with crucibles, glass vials, clay pots, and oil lamps with wrought-iron stands to hold an item being heated. Jars contained thick liquids or colored powders. In all it looked like a well-equipped chemistry lab. Grace looked at the knight.

"What is all this, Durge?"

He stroked his mustaches in what seemed an embarrassed gesture. "It is nothing, my lady. I have a passing interest in alchemy, that is all. I know little enough." He moved to the sideboard, picked something up, and handed it to Grace. "Thank you for letting me study this."

Grace accepted the object. It was the bracelet Trifkin Mossberry had given her. When Durge had seen her wearing it the day before, he had expressed interest in it, especially the charm of dark stone, and had asked if he might examine it. Grace had given it to him, but only now did she understand the source of his curiosity. She slipped the bracelet onto her wrist.

"Do you know what it is?" she said. "The charm, I mean."

"I was able to perform some tests," Durge said. "I believe it to be a piece of lodestone."

"Lodestone?" Aryn said with a frown. "You mean it's a stone that fell from the sky?"

Durge nodded. "That's right, my lady. I have heard astrologers of the south call such rocks meteorites, but lodestone is the name used in the Dominions. It is the same kind of stone as the artifact of Malachor in the great hall."

Beltan let out a whistle. "That must have been some falling star. It takes ten men to move that thing. Though the ring turns easily enough."

Grace regarded the charm bracelet, then thought of the massive ring of dark stone in the great hall. So the two were connected. This fact seemed important somehow, but she couldn't say why.

"Is everybody ready?" a low voice said.

Grace looked up. It was Travis. His gray eyes were serious behind his wire-rimmed spectacles, and his face above his beard was white.

Capillary constriction—an autonomic response. He's frightened, Grace. She almost laughed at the diagnosis. Grace suspected her own capillaries were constricted as well.

She drew in a deep breath, then stepped toward the others. "I'm ready."

Beltan nodded. "And I."

Aryn braced her shoulders inside her azure gown. Her dark hair was intricately coiled and woven with strands of pearl. "I suppose I'm ready."

"And I as well," Durge said in his grim voice.

Travis sighed and rested a hand on the stiletto tucked into his belt. "Me too. I think we're all ready then. Everybody knows what to do?"

Each of the five nodded.

"Then I guess it's time to go."

They started to move to the door, then Grace halted, turned, and regarded Travis.

"Can we trust them?" she said in a quiet voice. "Trifkin and his troupe, I mean."

Travis seemed to think about her words, then shook his head. "No, I don't think we can trust them. They're older than us, and different. But I don't think they have much love for the Pale King, either." He shrugged his shoulders inside his baggy tunic. "We'll just have to hope that's enough."

Grace nodded. She looked at each of the members of the Circle in turn, and only when she was done did she realize she had just fixed each one in her mind exactly as he or she was at that moment. Afraid she knew the reason why, she hurried to the door, before she lost her resolve, before she let herself think that this plan just might be sending one of these people—one of her friends—to his or her death.

"Let's do it," she said.

They left Durge's chamber one at a time, and let a minute or two pass between each of their departures so no one would see them together. Grace was the second to go, after Beltan. She stepped outside and glanced both ways down the corridor. A few servants hurried this way and that, caught up in their tasks, but that was all. She set her shoulders back and forced herself to walk calmly down the passage. It would not do to appear nervous or in a hurry. Besides, the light was still fading outside the castle's windows: soft purple hardening to gray slate. There was still time before the feast—and the longest night of the year—began.

She heard the dull roar of voices before she even reached the great hall. Rumors concerning the Midwinter's Eve feast had flown about the castle these last days, and no doubt everyone had turned out to see if any of them were true. According to the stories, Boreas had spared no expense on the feast. There was to be an entire roasted ox, some said. No, it was *two* roasted oxen, and each was to be stuffed with a lamb, and the lamb with a hare, and the hare with a partridge, and the partridge with a single dove's egg. There were to be braised swans, and lampreys, and subtleties shaped like each of the kings and queens of the Dominions. Grace didn't know what to think of the rumors, but she hoped the last one turned out to be true. Something told her it would be fun to take a bite out of King Boreas.

She steeled her will and turned a corner that would take her to the doors of the great hall.

"Lady Grace," said a dangerous voice. "How regal you look this evening."

Grace cursed herself for doing it, but she couldn't help gasping as she turned toward the sound of the voice. She hadn't seen the woman there, standing in a shadowed alcove. Now the other stepped into the light, although the shadows seemed to cling to her still.

"Lady Kyrene," Grace said, then remembered to sketch a curtsy.

Kyrene smiled and bowed her head.

It had been days since Grace had last seen the countess, and then Kyrene had been wild and ragged, half-mad at her fall from Queen Ivalaine's favor. Now Kyrene was . . . different. Her hair was lustrous, but darker than Grace remembered it and pulled back in a severe knot. Her skin was milky as always, but the shade with which she had colored her lips, once coral pink, was now a deep red, like wine. Even her choice in garb had changed. Gone was her usual low-cut gown. Instead she wore a tight-fitting dress the same color as her lips, its collar high and fastened tightly around her throat by a choker of shell and jade.

"So, have you come to enjoy yourself at the feast?" Kyrene said.

"Why else would I have come?" Grace tried not to sound defensive but knew she failed.

Kyrene smiled again. Her emerald eyes were brighter and harder than ever. "Why else might you have come? Perhaps to weave useless magics as witches do." Kyrene moved closer. "Tell me, Lady Grace, are you still Ivalaine's plaything?"

Grace's eyes narrowed. "What are you talking about, Kyrene?"

"Don't worry, love. I'm not angry at you for what you did to me. It was a favor, I know that now." Kyrene smoothed her hair. "Ivalaine is a fool. She plays her little games and thinks she's so important. But there are others here now, others who are far greater than she."

Despite Kyrene's beauty, a sour scent rose from her. Grace felt sick.

"I have to go," she said.

Kyrene gave a knowing nod. "Of course, love. And so do I. We each have our alliances to uphold. Farewell, Lady Grace."

The countess gave Grace one more smug smile, then sauntered away. Grace rushed down the corridor, grateful to be away from her. Perhaps Kyrene was mad after all, or perhaps she really had found some new faction to ally herself with. Either way, Grace didn't care. She inhaled, steadied her mind, then stepped into the great hall of Calavere.

"Lady Grace?"

She blinked, then glanced down at a tug on her sleeve. A page stood beside her.

"This way, Lady Grace," the boy said.

She gave a wordless nod, then let him lead her among the trestle tables filled with nobles. Once again the castle's great hall had been decorated to resemble a forest, and for a moment Grace felt the same disorientation she had in Trifkin's chamber. It seemed she really walked in a misty sylvan glade. However, it was only a trick of torch smoke. Fir boughs draped the blackened rafters, and leafless saplings stood in the corners like shy, slender ladies waiting to be asked for a dance.

Grace thought she would be seated at one of the lower tables, but instead the page led her to the dais at the head of the great hall. She was to be seated at the high table. That was a stroke of luck. Her view would be better from up here, and she needed to be able to see the entire great hall. If their plan worked as it was supposed to, and the murderer was in the hall, it was Grace and Travis who would spot him.

She nodded to King Kylar as she passed him, then at King Boreas, who barely caught her gaze before he returned his glower to the hall. It did not look as if the king of Calavan intended to enjoy his own feast. The page showed her to the last empty seat at the high table, and her breath caught in her chest. So she was twice lucky that night.

"Good eventide, Lady Grace," Logren said with his white-toothed smile.

He stood as she took her seat, then sat again beside her.

"Good eventide, my lord," she said. She had not noticed it before, but now the great hall was too warm, and her gown too constricting.

"You look beautiful tonight, my lady." His voice was low and private, just for her.

So do you, my lord, she wanted to say. He was clad in pearl-gray, like the night she first met him. She drank in his features like wine. Why had she run from him when they last met? He must have thought her an idiot.

"Thank you, my lord," she said when she realized he was waiting for an answer.

"I have been keeping an eye open as you asked, my lady." His voice was casual—he could have been speaking about bird-watching in the garden—but he gave her a conspiratorial nod. "I'm afraid I haven't seen anything such as you described."

Yes, he was good at this game. "It's all right, my lord. I appreciate your help."

"At your service, my lady."

A thrill passed through Grace, and she could not help but smile. He was intelligent, kind, and handsome. If not him, then who? Kyrene had her new friends now—Logren had escaped the countess's web. Maybe Grace could try again, and without thoughts of spells and simples this time. She remembered the soft touch of his lips on her own. Maybe she didn't need magic to make Logren hers. Maybe he already was. . . .

"A drink, my lady?"

She almost laughed. Those were the first words he had ever spoken to her, that night in the great hall when she had been so new at this, when she had fled the nobles in terror, and he had been there to steady her.

"Yes," she said. "A drink would be lovely."

He filled a cup from a pitcher of wine. Warmth filled her, and with it came a new resolution. Of course, it was so right, how could she not have seen it before? She would tell Logren everything, right here and now—their plan to discover the murderer at the feast. She could add his eyes and his intellect to her own. What better ally could she and the others have?

She leaned toward him. "Lord Logren, there's something I need to tell you. . . ."

He handed her the cup, and she reached out to accept it.

His brown eyes were intent upon her. "Yes, my lady?"

Grace opened her mouth to tell him . . .

. . . then froze. Her eyes locked on the delicate bracelet that encircled her wrist—the wrist of the hand with which she had reached out to accept the cup. The wedge-shaped lodestone dangled from the silver chain. It spun slowly, first left, then right, then—as she watched—it came to a halt. Warmth fled her, replaced by a terrible chill. The charm pointed directly at the center of Logren's chest.

He smiled at her. "What is it you wished to tell me, my lady?"

97.

Travis made his way down the corridor as quickly as he could and still look as if he were going nowhere in particular. There were few in this part of Calavere—most had already headed to the great hall for the feast. However, he didn't want to do anything that might attract attention. The murderer was still somewhere in the castle, and it could be anyone, even the basest servant.

He reached a crossing of ways, paused, then headed down the left-hand corridor. Things looked familiar now. Yes, he was almost there, almost to the north tower—and the chamber occupied by Trifkin Mossberry and his troupe of actors. He could only hope the little man had not forgotten that he had agreed to help them. Then again, Travis had the feeling Trifkin could remember things far older than any living person—older than this castle, maybe as old as the forest.

Sweat trickled inside his tunic, and his hand crept to the stiletto tucked into his belt. The others would all be reaching their positions now. It was too late to stop even if he wanted to. He drew in a deep breath and tried to think about what he would do after this night was over. *Maybe you could open a tavern in the town below the castle. Even this world needs saloons, doesn't it? Places to escape for a little while.*

The thought made Travis smile. There couldn't be too many other interplanetary saloon keepers out there. He kept walking, and his cowboy boots beat a tattoo against the floor. The boots were scuffed and battered. How many leagues had he walked in them in this world? He had lost count. Regardless, they were about to fall apart. He would have to get a new pair when he got back to . . . that was, if he ever got back to . . .

A faint hum drifted on the air.

The rhythm of Travis's boots slowed. He peered to either side, but the corridor was empty. It must have been the winter wind outside, scouring the walls of the castle, that was all. He quickened his pace.

The metallic hum grew louder, until air and stone resonated with it.

Travis froze. This time there was no mistaking it for wind. He knew that sound, would never forget it, the way it pierced the air and thrummed in his chest. He felt something warm against his hand, and he looked down. The jewel set into the hilt of his stiletto blazed like an angry eye. His heart wrenched in mid-beat, and he snapped his head up.

"No," he whispered, but the word had no power to change what he saw.

Pale light welled through a stone archway up ahead. Even as he watched, it grew brighter, closer, as if whatever made the light approached with terrible speed.

The humming filled his skull and drowned out the sound of his pulse. He stared at the archway, unable to move, a small animal waiting for the hunter's strike. The glow intensified, grew pure and cold. Then he saw them, silhouettes in the light: tall, slender, and hideous in their grace.

Terror washed away his paralysis. Travis turned and ran back down the corridor, his boots thudding in time with his heart. He reached the place were the passages intersected, started to turn down the way he had come, then stumbled and fell back. Faint but growing, he saw it— fey light shone down that corridor as well. They were coming at him from two directions.

Travis lurched into the right-hand passage, bent his head, and careened down the corridor. He reached into the pocket of his tunic and clasped the iron box. It was the Stone that had drawn them, the Stone that they wanted. Their huge eyes could see the very trails of magic it left on the air.

The corridor split in front of him. Which way? He started down one passage. The hum grew louder, and eerie shadows slithered on the walls. He pulled back, started down the other corridor. It too was filled with a colorless incandescence that grew stronger each second. He jerked his head back and forth. They had him surrounded, there was nowhere to go, nowhere to—

"This way," a voice said.

The words cut through his fear. There was no time to question the voice, no time to see who the speaker was. A door he had not noticed before had opened in the wall of the corridor. A warm hand grasped his, and he let it pull him through the opening into a chamber beyond. There was a hiss of air and the grating of stone on stone. The door closed behind him and shut out the sinister glow.

His eyes adjusted to the mundane illumination of an oil lamp that hung from an iron chain. Fear ebbed, and surprise surged in its place.

"Lady Kyrene!"

Dark red lips coiled in a smile. "Are you well, Goodman Travis?"

He remembered his pursuers and glanced back at the smooth expanse of stone where the door had been.

"Do not worry," she said. "Even they cannot walk through stone."

Her words oozed, not fear but hatred, and this struck a strange note in Travis's mind. He turned his gaze back toward her. How had the countess known to find him? But it didn't matter. He was grateful to have escaped them, at least for the moment. Now he had to find Falken and the others, to warn them of what stalked the castle.

"How can I get to the great hall, Kyrene? I have to talk to Falken and Melia."

Kyrene sauntered toward him. She looked different than she had that day in the garden. Her deep crimson dress clung to the curves of her body: her arms, her breasts, her throat. Her green eyes glittered like stones.

"Forget them, love," Kyrene said. "You do not need those two any longer."

She reached out, caressed his cheek, then let her hands run over his shoulders, his chest, his hips.

A shudder coursed through him. He could not look away from her eyes. "What do you mean?" he whispered.

Her hands brushed across something small and heavy beneath the fabric of his tunic, then halted. Instinct raised the hair on his arms. He leaped back.

Kyrene lifted her hand, and now there was a dagger in it, curved and wicked. "Give me the Stone!" she hissed.

He shook his head and pressed his back against the wall. What had he done? No, what had *she* done? Then he knew, and a moan escaped his lips.

"You're one of them." He was going to vomit. "You're one of them, aren't you?"

"Give me the Stone, Travis. I must have it." She gestured to the wall with the dagger. "He favors them, his precious Pale Ones. How I despise them! But who will have the greatest favor in his eyes when it is I who brings him Sinfathisar?"

"No." He gripped the iron box.

"Don't fight, love. You don't have to die, not a handsome thing like you." She held her arms out. "Come, join me. I can take you to them, they can give you one, too. Together our beauty will never fade!"

He stared at her, frozen by horror.

She drew near him. "It is not what you think, love. Nothing is so frail as a human heart. You cannot imagine what it is like to be freed of it." Rapture twisted her perfect features. "I am so strong now, so powerful. There is no pain, no fear, no sorrow that can touch me."

Travis gazed at her empty face and understood. "Yes," he said in a quiet voice. "And there is no love, no joy, and no kindness. Don't you see, Kyrene? You've given up your heart." He shook with the words. "You've given up your *heart*."

She stared at him, her eyes wide, as if for a moment she saw the truth he spoke of. Then her face hardened into a mask of rage.

"No." She raised the dagger. "You're wrong!"

She flew at him and thrust the dagger straight at his chest. He caught her wrist barely in time, the blade an inch from his heart. She was strong—horribly strong, just as she had said—but he was nearly twice her size, and fear flooded his limbs with its own preternatural strength. With a cry he hurled her aside. She struck a wall, the dagger flew from her hand, and she fell to the floor.

He searched, frantic. There—a door in the far wall. He threw himself toward it, shoved it open. A blood-chilling scream sounded behind him.

"You will be sorry, Goodman Travis," she shouted. "If you will not be mine, then I will take something you love! I will take it, and I will destroy it! Let *your* heart bear that!"

Never in his life had he heard such perfect hate. Once Kyrene had been a woman, but that thing back there was no longer human and never would be again.

Travis slammed the door shut. There was a wooden bar, and he shoved it into the slots. Then he ran down the corridor, away from the light, and away from the madness of evil.

He turned a corner and saw another door ahead. He pushed through it, and icy air struck his face. The empty expanse of the lower bailey stretched before him, lit by the great orb of the moon which soared over the castle's battlements. A dark shape loomed not far away: the tower of the Runespeakers. Yes, if there was anywhere he could find help it was there. He looked both ways, saw no one, then sprinted across the bailey.

He reached the tower door. His pulse thrummed in his ears and threatened to rupture his eardrums, but he had made it. He opened the door and raced up the steps that spiraled inside the tower.

"Rin!" he shouted. "Jemis! Are you here?"

He burst into the tower's main chamber. Rin looked up in surprise. The muscular young runespeaker knelt beside the copper brazier in the act of banking the coals.

Rin stood and brushed ashes from his hand, his brown eyes concerned. "Travis, what is it?"

He shook his head, gasped for breath. How could he explain? "They've found me, Rin. They're right behind me."

The young runespeaker frowned. "Who are you talking about? Is there someone in the castle? An intruder?" His expression darkened. "An enemy of the king?"

Travis nodded, then shook his head. It wasn't what Rin thought. Not robbers or renegade knights. There was no time to tell him. "I have to get to the great hall," he said. "I need to talk to Lord Falken. He can explain."

Rin let out a deep breath, then nodded. "I can't say I understand you, Travis. But if you say it's important, then it is."

Travis gazed at Rin in gratitude. He could not believe his good fortune, to encounter such a friend on a night such as this. Maybe there was hope yet.

"But you're exhausted, Travis." Rin's broad face was troubled. "You won't do Falken or anyone any good if you collapse on the way to the great hall. Let me get you some wine."

Urgency clawed at Travis's heart. He opened his mouth to say they needed to run, but his throat was too dry. Rin was right, he had to drink something, had to rest just a moment, then he could run again. He sat in a chair by the brazier.

"Where's Jemis?" he managed to croak.

"He's already at the great hall." Rin moved to a cupboard and turned to fill two cups with wine.

Travis held his hands toward the brazier. Despite his exertion he was cold. He rubbed his hands together. Then he noticed it, white and still. It lay beside the brazier. He reached down and picked it up: a dead dove. He stroked the little corpse with a thumb. Had it fallen from the rafters? No, its head flopped to one side. Its neck had been wrung.

"We have to be there soon, anyway," Rin said, his back still turned. "We need to speak the rune of purity before the feast can begin."

Travis hardly heard the runespeaker. He stared at the dove. A crimson spot appeared on its white feathers. Was it bleeding? Another circle of crimson appeared beside the first, then another. Travis lifted his head and gazed upward.

He was lashed to the rafters, his eyes orbs of terror, his face purple. Jemis. Blood trickled from the corner of his mouth to fall drop by drop. The elder runespeaker's head lolled—his neck had been wrung just like the dove's. Except that would take powerful hands, terribly powerful hands. . . .

Rin turned around. "Here's your wine, Travis. Now, tell me, what's going on?"

Travis stared at the cup in each of Rin's hands—his big peasant's hands. For a heartbeat the entire world was still. Then Travis scrambled from the chair, knocked it over, and backed away. Rin watched him, his brown eyes impassive. Then he threw down the cups and advanced on Travis.

A sound escaped Travis's throat: sorrow and terror. "Rin, what have they done to you?"

"You're a fool to resist, Travis." Rin's voice was toneless. "You can't escape him." The young runespeaker hesitated, and his brown eyes seemed almost sad. "You'll see. He'll make you one in the end."

"But why . . . ?"

"Why did I choose this? Why did I remain a runespeaker? Why didn't I murder you the moment I knew you could bind runes?" His lips parted in a mirthless smile. "I was put here to watch the Rune-speakers. And I've watched you, Travis—from your first day in the castle, when Falken came to talk to us. It was the task of my master's other servants to kill you. Except they failed, and now there's no more time for questions."

Travis edged toward the head of the stairs. Rin's smile vanished. His eyes were dull as pebbles.

"Give me Sinfathisar, Travis."

Travis shook his head. "No." He lunged for the stairs.

He felt the tingle in his right palm at the same moment Rin spoke the word.

"*Krond!*"

Travis felt it at once: The air around him transformed into an oven. Sweat evaporated off his clothes in curls of steam. The temperature soared. Another heartbeat and Travis knew he would burst into flame.

Break it, Travis!

Jack. It was Jack.

Break his rune.

His throat was a desert, his tongue baked in his mouth. He could barely form the sound, then he did.

"*Reth!*"

He felt more than saw his hand flash as he spoke the rune of break-ing. The searing heat vanished, and he felt the magic rush away from him, back toward its source. There was a scream, cut short, followed by a thud.

Travis pulled himself to his feet, swayed, then caught himself. Rin sprawled on the floor, and Travis staggered toward the young rune-speaker. His eyes stared upward, blank with death, and a wisp of smoke curled from his open mouth. The force of the blow had torn his tunic to shreds. Travis could see the ragged scar that snaked across Rin's broad chest.

Well-done, Travis! When you sundered his magic, you sundered his mind as well.

He clenched his right hand into a fist. No—he had not done well. He had broken his promise again. Travis turned, ran down the stairs, and burst into the frigid night. He gulped the freezing air into his lungs, but it could not quell the sickness in his guts. Hands on knees, he spilled his fear and revulsion on the frozen mud.

You had to do it, Travis. You must understand, it was the only way.

No, he was tired of the voice. He didn't want to listen. Travis stumbled through a doorway, back into the shelter of the castle. He had to get to the great hall. Falken would know what to do. Or Melia. They would know how to save everyone, how to save him.

Travis staggered down the passage. However, he had not gone far when light spilled through an opening ahead. He turned around—the glow sped from that direction as well. Figures moved in the light and reached out spindly hands. The gesture seemed almost loving, but he knew that embrace held only coldness and death. He moved in the last direction left to him, down a narrow side passage.

After only a dozen steps the passage ended in a blank wall of stone. He ran his hands over the wall, but there was no latch or crevice to be found. It was a dead end. Travis turned around and slumped with his back against the wall. He was too tired anyway, too tired to keep running. Through the fabric of his tunic he clutched the iron box.

"I'm sorry, Jack," he whispered.

Then he watched as the pale light brightened before him.

98.

Aryn, Baroness of Elsandry, stood in a corner of Calavere's great hall and watched the revelers gather for the Midwinter's Eve feast.

She had chosen a spot near a side door, next to a cluster of leafless saplings that had been brought inside for decoration, in an attempt to look inconspicuous. Not that this was so difficult for her. All her life people had had a tendency to walk right past Aryn without looking at her. Because if they looked at her they would have to look at her arm, to acknowledge it was there, and that was something they did not care to do. Aryn sighed as revelers passed by in bright garb, laughing. None turned a head in her direction. It was all right—she had had nineteen years to get used to it. Besides, as she had learned as a child, it was better to be ignored than stared at.

Aryn huddled inside her azure gown and cape of white rabbit fur. Despite the garments, despite the smoke and press of bodies in the great hall, she was cold. If Grace and Goodman Travis were right—and she had no reason to doubt they were—then Alerain's murderer was somewhere in this hall, right at that very moment.

She let her blue eyes run over the throng of nobles, knights, and servants. It could be any one of them, it could dwell behind the mask of any face: evil. She studied reveler after reveler, searching for any hints or signs, and if it was more often those who were beautiful, or handsome, or well shaped whom her eyes bored into, then it was only logic. Always it was assumed those who were ugly or different were evil, or had done some terrible deed. For what could their appearance be, but punishment for some loathsome crime?

Aryn knew different, and her lips twisted in a bitter smile. Why pick such a simple disguise? No, the murderer was too clever for that. Far more effective to hide evil behind a comely smile, or a square jaw, or eyes you could fall into for days.

More nobles flooded into the great hall, and Aryn's heart fluttered like a trapped sparrow inside the bodice of her gown. She knew King Boreas would be looking for her. Without Alerain, the duties of organizing the feast had fallen to her. However, she had made all the arrangements with the cellarer and the kitchenwife. They would see to it the nobles were fed and given their wine.

But what if they forgot the mead?

Panic gripped her. King Persard of Perridon preferred mead to wine and would cause a row if he did not have it. And King Sorrin would drink only the fresh milk of a goat—although from his gaunt appearance he could have stood to drink a bit more of it. What if the cellarer and kitchenwife forgot? Aryn lifted the hem of her gown and started forward.

No, Aryn. She forced herself to stop. *You have to let them worry about it, them or King Boreas. It can't always be up to you to make certain everyone has exactly what he or she wants. You have more important things to accomplish.*

Aryn blinked at this thought. Where had it come from? All her life she had focused on the needs of others. It was the only thing that put them at ease around her. Never once had she denied King Boreas anything she thought he wanted. Yet all the same she knew if, at that moment, she heard him bellow across the hall for her, she would not come running as she usually did. From where had this resolve come?

Her eyes flickered to the high table at the far end of the great hall, and she knew her answer was there. Queen Ivalaine gazed over the feast with ice-colored eyes, her regal visage calm yet powerful. Next to her sat Tressa: smaller, plumper, sweeter of face, yet strong in her own motherly way. At the other end of the table Grace sat beside Logren of

Eredane. The two were bent close in conversation, his eyes were intent upon her. Had she worked some magic upon him?

Don't be a fool. Grace wouldn't do that . . . would she?

The baroness took a deep breath and forced herself to concentrate on her part of the plan. It was up to Grace and Travis to determine the identity of the murderer. Once they knew, Grace would signal Aryn. Then it would be Aryn's turn to act. She was to approach the murderer and quietly inform him that he had an important message. Then she was to lead him to a nearby antechamber where waited not a messenger, but Durge and his Embarran greatsword. In addition, Beltan would be standing outside the great hall and would follow Aryn as she accompanied their quarry to the antechamber.

The fluttering of Aryn's heart quickened. Could she really do this? She was grateful for Grace's trust, but Aryn knew better than anyone her own limited talents at deception. What if the murderer saw right through her lie? No, she couldn't think that way. She had to believe it would work.

Aryn shut her eyes and murmured a small prayer to Yrsaia. She had not told Grace she followed the Mysteries of the Huntress. She supposed Grace might have laughed at her for this—no, that wasn't true, Grace would never mock her, not like others sometimes did. However, Aryn sensed Grace was not one to turn to gods or goddesses for help. Grace was accustomed to relying on herself. Aryn hoped one day she could be that strong, that regal, but until then it couldn't hurt to ask the help of the Huntress. After all, they were hoping to catch a murderer that night.

"Your Highness, this is good fortune."

Aryn's eyes flew open in surprise at the smooth sound of the voice. A man stood before her, only slightly her greater in years and height. She took him in piece by piece—gold curls, neatly trimmed beard, broad shoulders in a crisp red tunic—before she recognized him.

"Lord Leothan!"

He bowed low, then rose again. "I was hoping I would have the opportunity to speak with you at the feast, my lady. I did not realize my chance would come so soon."

She shook her head and tried to understand. What could he possibly want of her?

"My lady, I have wronged you."

Aryn could only stare. Now sorrow touched his face, and it made him even more beautiful yet.

"Wronged me?"

"Terribly." He stepped closer, although he maintained an honorable distance. "My lady, when I came to this court I was arrogant and full of myself. I thought by belittling others I made myself all the greater." He shook his head. "I was a fool, of course, I know that now. You see, recently I took ill . . ."

Aryn tensed at these words. Could he have known? Did he realize she was the cause of his pain? No, his eyes showed only concern.

". . . and being confined to my bed gave me time to think, and to reflect on my own imperfections. I thought about the way I had acted—to you and to others, my lady—and I was ashamed. I resolved, once I recovered, to make amends." He drew in a deep breath. "I know it is impossible that you could forgive me, yet I must ask it all the same."

To her astonishment, he sank to one knee before her and bowed his head.

"My lady, I beg you, will you pardon my insult to your honor?"

She clapped her hand to her mouth. What could she say? Anguish flooded her chest. She was the cruel one, the one who had truly harmed.

"Please, my lord," she said. "Oh, please rise. There is nothing to ask forgiveness for."

Leothan did as she asked, regained his feet, and now he smiled at her. "Tell me, my lady . . ." He cocked his head and studied her. ". . . is there something different about you than before? Your hair perhaps?"

Aryn shook her head. How could she explain? Yes, there was something different, but not anything another might see. Or was there after all?

He glanced around them. "My lady, might we speak in private for a moment? There is another matter I would like to . . . to speak to you about, if you will."

He motioned to the side door behind her, and the gesture seemed almost shy. A tingling shimmered on the surface of her skin. What could he have to say to her that could not be said before the eyes of all in the great hall? Possibilities filled her mind, and the tingle grew stronger. She glanced up. Revelers still streamed through the doors of the great hall. There was yet a little time before the feast began.

Aryn met Leothan's eyes and nodded. He laid a gentle hand on her elbow and guided her through the side door. It shut behind them. They were in the antechamber alone.

"What is it you wished to speak to me about, my lord?" She hoped she knew the answer, but she didn't dare think it, didn't dare believe. Then he spoke, and her wishes came true.

"I was a fool to turn away from you, Aryn. Now I have a second chance. I won't throw it away again."

He moved toward her, close now. She could feel warmth radiate from him.

"May I kiss you?" he whispered.

Aryn shivered—in delight and in trepidation. Uncertainty crept into her mind. Could Leothan really have experienced such a change of heart? She forced the question aside. He was here, and he was beautiful. That was all that mattered.

She turned her face up toward him. "Yes, my lord."

Leothan smiled, coiled his arms around her, and held her tight. His lips were fire against her. Never before had she kissed a man—not like this, not out of passion. She drank it in greedily. Maybe she could weave some magics of her own. . . .

His grip on her tightened, and he pressed harder, until his lips crushed against her. It hurt, and she tried to pull away, but his arms were like bands of steel. They crushed against her rib cage—it was hard to breathe.

She managed to turn her head. "My lord . . ."

"Stop struggling, my lady." He gritted the words between his teeth. "Isn't this what you were dreaming of?"

Aryn stared at him. Passion fled her, and left her chest cold and watery with dread. She tried to twist out of his grasp, but he held her left arm tight, and her right was useless—it flopped against his chest without effect.

He shoved her against the wall, and her breath rushed out of her in a painful *whoosh*. She moaned. How could she have been so blind? She had been tricked by his words and his beauty, guilty of the crime of which she had accused others. Now she would pay for it.

Leothan leaned against her, and she could feel his hardness grind against her stomach.

"No, my lady," he said with a hideous grin. "Don't scream, or I promise you it will be much worse."

He held her with one hand and with the other reached for the front of his breeches. It was her only chance. She twisted to one side and thought she had it, thought she would break free. Then he grabbed her again. Her left hand flailed and caught at the collar of his tunic. He whirled her around, threw her hard against the wall. There was a ripping sound, and pain sparkled through her.

She blinked, and her vision cleared. He stood before her again, his face no longer beautiful, but a twisted mask of hate and desire. In the struggle, the front of his tunic had been torn open. Aryn glimpsed his chest—broad and smooth—then he moved, the fabric parted more, and she saw it. The wound ran down the center of his torso, the ragged edges held together by crude stitches.

A new horror flooded Aryn. She was in danger, but in a way she had not imagined. It was not the desire of a man she faced, for the thing before her was no longer human. She tried to free her arm, but he was far too strong.

He grinned. "It takes two hands to fight me, my lady."

No. She wanted to call out to Grace or to Beltan. They would help her. But he squeezed the breath out of her, and she could not make a sound. His leering visage drew close to hers. She could smell the scent of decay that rose from the gory wound in his chest.

"Your face is pretty," Leothan hissed. "Too bad you are a monster, my lady. But I feel generous this evening. I will make a whole woman of you." He reached again for his breeches.

Aryn stared at him. Her fear melted away, and hot anger boiled up in its place. All her life she had endured people like this: people without hearts. All her life she had deferred to them, to avoid upsetting them with her hideousness, her deformity. No more. The anger welled up, thick and crimson. Aryn let it fill her, until she felt light, buoyant, and strong. She locked her eyes on his and spoke the words, trembling with the power of nineteen years of rage.

"I . . . *am* . . . whole!"

He gaped at her, and his eyes went wide. A tremor passed through him, and blood trickled from his nose.

Aryn let her anger pour into him. Now he was the one who struggled to get away, but his limbs shook with convulsions. He choked for breath, and his eyes bulged in their sockets. Blood flowed from his nose and ears in a crimson river. He whimpered, and more blood stained his breeches.

"Leave me alone," she said, then shoved him away.

He screamed, a gurgling sound of agony, but the scream was cut short before he hit the floor. He sprawled on the stones in a growing pool of blood and brains.

Aryn gazed at the corpse, her body straight and stiff, her hand clenched in rage. Yes! She had done it! Then a shudder passed through her. Anger poured out of her like wine from a broken vessel. She lifted her left hand to her mouth, but a low sound of dread escaped her fingers. Her eyes could not let go of the dead earl. What had she done? He had been a monster, but she had slain him, destroyed him with her fury. What did that make her?

Worse than a monster?

Her back to the wall, Aryn sank to the floor, curled her good arm around her knees, and wept.

99.

There was danger in the castle, Durge could feel it.

He shifted his weight from foot to foot, and beneath his tunic his shirt of mail jingled. The antechamber was cold: No tapestries hung on the walls, no carpets strewed the floor, and no fire burned on the hearth. Durge did not mind. It was better to be chilled—warmth could make a man drowsy and dull of wits. The cold would keep his eyes open and his mind keen, and all his years as a knight, all his experiences in battle, told him he would need both before this Midwinter's Eve was over.

He flexed his sword hand. Despite the thick leather glove, his fingers were stiff and sore, and he could feel the ends of his bones grind together as he moved them. That was the one problem with the cold. It radiated from his armor, crept into his joints, and gnawed at them like tiny dragons. When he was younger, the cold didn't bother him. In his days as a squire he had spent several harsh Embarran winters keeping watch atop the walls of forts that stood on the hinterlands of the Dominion, where the white wind roared down from the Winter Sea and one's piss froze before it hit the ground. However, that had been long ago.

The Embarran knight's stooped shoulders heaved in a sigh. *This will be your fourth-and-fortieth winter, Durge. You are a young man no longer. Soon you will spend your days wrapped in a blanket by the fire and tell stories of old battles no one remembers and no one wishes to hear about.*

Durge stretched his stiff fingers, forcing them to straighten. No, he was not ready to become a toothless uncle by the fire, not yet. There was still some life left in the earl of Stonebreak.

He blew a breath through his drooping brown mustaches and gazed at the antechamber's door. There was no telling when it would open. Once Lady Grace and Goodman Travis identified the murderer in the great hall, Lady Aryn was to lead him to this room, with Sir Beltan following behind and just out of sight. Once they had the murderer in the room, Durge and Beltan would use their swords to subdue him, although they were not to kill him. Grace had been adamant about that. She hoped to use the prisoner to convince the Council of Kings to take action, to stand together against the forces of the Pale King.

Durge shook his head. She was a fierce one, his mistress, not one to give up quickly. Always she believed she had the power to save others if only she worked hard enough. It was a noble ideal and one to aspire to. However, Durge knew that sometimes dedication was not enough—that sometimes no matter how one tried, no matter how one fought, one could not save that which one most cared about, that which one most loved.

Then there was the matter of the kings and queens. Lady Grace's mind was sharp and logical. She was one to propose a hypothesis, gather evidence, then see if her expectations had proved true or false. Durge understood her methods—the alchemical sciences in which he dabbled progressed in the same manner. The only flaw in Lady Grace's reasoning was that she expected the kings and queens to be as logical as she.

If only that were the case! However, Durge had witnessed at first-hand the capriciousness of kings and queens. It was an effect of great-ness that often rulers came to believe truth was what they decided it would be. If a king declared the sky to be green, then green as emeralds it was. Even confronted with the reality of an ironheart, Durge was not certain any of the rulers at the council would be swayed. Eminda would brand it a hoax, the sniveling Lysandir would follow her lead, and Sorrin—alas, poor King Sorrin—was so mad he would hardly un-derstand what was happening.

All the same, it was a good plan. Durge himself had helped refine the details based on his experience. If anything had a chance of working it was this. However, like the chill, he could not shrug off the pall of apprehension that tightened around him now. They had tried to think through every possibility, through every happening that might go awry, but there was something else, something they had forgotten. He was certain of it. The very air of the keep tingled with peril.

He paced the bare floor to keep his blood moving. "No doubt you are a fool to have left her alone, Durge," he muttered under his breath. "But you pledged your sword to her, and you cannot refuse one of her wishes. Even if in your heart you know the Lady Grace is in danger this night."

Durge halted at a faint sound. He looked up. Silence, three heart-beats, then it came again: a scratching at the antechamber's door. Could it be the Lady Aryn and their quarry?

Even as he thought this, he raised his hand and reached back to grasp the hilt of his greatsword strapped to his back. It was too early for his companions to have arrived, and the Lady Aryn would not have knocked. The short hairs of his neck prickled and stood on end.

"Come then," he said through clenched teeth. "Come if it is my blood you seek!"

The door swung open, and he drew his greatsword with a bright ringing of metal. It scuttled through the partly open door and brought a foul scent with it. The thing moved with an ungainly rhythm, as if every step brought it pain. Despite his alarm, pity touched Durge's heart. Had not Lord Falken said that the feydrim had been Little People before they were twisted by the Pale King's magic?

Pity almost killed him. The feydrim uncoiled its spindly hind legs and sprang forward, covering half the room in one bound. It opened its snubbed muzzle and bared yellow fangs. Strings of spittle stretched between them. It hissed, then lunged for his throat.

In his moment of distraction Durge had let it get too close—there was not room enough for a full swing of his greatsword. He cursed to himself. *Stone and bone, you are getting dull, Durge! Old and dull. What would the others think of you, giving up your life so easily as this!* He stumbled back, ignored the fire that flared in his knee at the awkward position, and brought his sword up. There was little power in the blow—the swing was too clipped—but the feydrim was forced to scuttle back to avoid the sharp edge of the blade. Its fangs missed their mark, and Durge spun to the side.

Now he had more room to work.

He planted his boots, braced the lean muscles of his legs, and raised the greatsword. So long was the blade that if he placed the tip on the floor he could almost rest his chin on the hilt. There were younger men who could not have lifted it without falling over. Not so Durge. Despite his age, despite his aches and weariness, his arms were as hard as the stony ground of Embarr. He brought the greatsword around in a whistling arc.

The feydrim was fast, but not fast enough. It tried to twist away, but the blade caught it in the side. Steel bit through blood, crunched through bone. The creature squealed, then fell to the floor. Durge pulled his greatsword back, staggered, then caught himself.

The creature lay at his feet. Its chest heaved spastically, and dark blood soaked its matted gray fur. It gazed up at him with yellow eyes that were far too intelligent for a beast. Then the light in those eyes flickered and went dim. The feydrim heaved one last breath—as if relieved, as if free of the pain at last—then went still.

Durge's heart pounded in his chest, and he savored the rush of blood in his veins. Yes, there was still some fight left in Durge of Embarr.

The creak of hinges. Durge looked up to see the antechamber's door swing open farther. A gray, ungainly form slunk into the room. Another followed it, and more after, until there were five of them, stretching spindly limbs, baring sharp teeth, hissing in hate and pain.

Feydrim.

Durge raised his greatsword and stumbled back. The fire inside him burned to ashes, and his mouth went dry. Another of the creatures he could have handled easily, and three perhaps with difficulty. But five? How could any man face five? Blast his old knees, but they were so weak they shook.

Humped backs coiled and uncoiled, and the feydrim advanced. They took their time—they knew they had him cornered. Durge tightened his grip around the greatsword's hilt. He thought of his friends: his bold mistress, Grace; her kindly friend, Travis; the good knight, Beltan. Last of all he thought of the young Lady Aryn, of her pretty face, and of the strength that dwelled in her sky-blue eyes. He was sorry he would not be able to say farewell to them.

One of the feydrim scuttled forward, slashed with its claws, then leaped back at the flick of his sword. They were testing him, clever creatures. Now his heart pounded again, and warmth flooded his limbs. Yes, this was what it felt like to be young again.

"Why do you wait?" he shouted at the creatures. Behind his mustaches, he grinned as he had not in decades. "Kill me, if that is what you have come to do. But heed my words—Durge of Embarr will not be the only one who dies this night!"

He held his greatsword out, and as one the feydrim lunged for him.

100.

Beltan stood near the doors of Calavere's great hall and waited for Aryn to step outside with their quarry. He had gone over the plan again and again in his mind to be certain he had it right, to be certain he made no mistakes. Subterfuge was not one of Beltan's strengths. He was far better holding a naked sword before him than a hidden knife behind his back.

He drew in a deep breath. *You had better not muck this up, Beltan. You've only got one chance. When Aryn shows up, don't think. Just act.*

Worry was foolish—the plan was simple enough. He was to stand outside the doors of the great hall, pace a bit, and appear as though he was merely waiting for a companion who was late. When Aryn stepped outside the doors with the murderer, he was to nod to her politely, as he would to any passing noble, then resume his pacing. However, once they turned the corner he was to slip after them and follow them to the antechamber where Sir Durge waited. There they would subdue the murderer, and their plan would be complete.

If he didn't ruin things, that was. The problem with plans was that they made mistakes a possibility. Beltan was much more comfortable facing his enemy without guile. After all, it was hard to make an error of logic when all you had to do was stab your opponent before he stabbed you.

He let out a bitter snort of laughter. *And people thought you could have been king, Beltan the Bastard. If so, they're even more dull-witted than you are.*

A few late nobles scurried past him into the great hall. Beltan fingered the eating knife at his waist and wished it was his sword. Had he his preference he would have been clad in chain mail, not his finest green tunic and cloak. However, it was tradition to greet Midwinter's Eve unarmed. Tonight the revelers in the great hall would set fire to the Everlog so that its light would draw back the sun from its winter journey south. If any at the feast bore a weapon—or so legend told— the sun would flee farther south in fear, and winter would never end.

A shiver crept across Beltan's back. He was not certain this winter would break no matter how bright the Everlog burned that night. It was a queer cold that gripped the castle, that threatened to crack the stones. He had never felt anything like it, and he doubted anyone had. Anyone except Falken.

Beltan lifted a hand and fingered one of the garlands of green leaves and red berries that encircled his neck. Several fresh-faced maidens had approached him that evening, each bearing a garland she had woven herself. Beltan had politely bowed his head and had allowed each to place the wreath around his neck. It was another tradition of Midwinter's Eve that a young woman wove such a wreath for the man she favored. The woman who was the last to slip a garland around the neck of the man who received the most was certain to get her wish.

The maidens who had approached Beltan had been sweet and pretty, but he knew neither his face nor his skill with a sword was the reason for their attention. Who better to court than the nephew of the king? However, elder members of the court knew what Beltan himself knew—that at one-and-thirty winters he was already past prime marrying age, that he might have married late to produce an heir to cede his lands to, but that he had no such lands to cede. No, the charms of the maidens would not work that night, as they would find out soon enough. Beltan had heard the call of the bull long ago.

He glanced again at the doors of the great hall and sighed. No one in there was armed with more than an eating knife, and here there was murder afoot in the castle. Earlier he had told Melia that King Boreas had asked him to keep watch over the doors. The lie ate at him. He should have been in there watching over her. Three years ago he had been lost and purposeless. He had wandered the roads of the Dominions as a vagabond knight, little better than a brigand. Then he had met Melia, along with Falken, in a tavern in Galt, and he had known here before him was one who was worthy of serving. He had pledged his sword to protect her, and she had accepted the hilt of his blade, had tapped him with its flat, and had bidden him rise. In the years since he had never been far from her side.

Not that Melia truly needed his protection. Except perhaps in some ways she did. There was so much about Melia he still did not understand, that he would never understand. It didn't matter. He knew that what she and Falken were doing was important. That was enough for him.

Is that really it, Beltan? The old question surfaced in his mind. *Or is it just that it's simpler being a sword in someone else's hands? After all, a sword can be strong without having to think for itself.*

Beltan pushed the question aside. What was done was done. A knight's sword was his life, and he had sworn upon his. He should have been in there.

Except Travis Wilder was his charge as well. Melia had taken Travis into her care, and that made him Beltan's concern. And it was more than that, for he had made a promise to Travis in the White Tower, had told him he would not have to face danger alone. Of the two it was certainly Travis who was in greater danger that night, he was sure of it.

Beltan shook his head. In some ways Travis was as much a mystery to him as Melia was, and not only because Falken said Travis was from a world that was not Eldh. Travis was handsome, yet he slouched so that others would not notice him. He was kind, yet he acted as if he was not worthy of regard. And he was keen of mind, yet he always let others make decisions for him. Why? Beltan did not know. All the same he had a feeling that Travis needed protection most of all.

The hairs on the back of his neck prickled. Beltan was a veteran of more battles than he could count. He knew when danger had crept up behind him. *By Vathris, you're a fool, Beltan of Calavan. You let yourself get distracted. Concentrate on your task!*

His hand slipped to the knife in his belt, and he turned around. Danger stood before him, although it did not wear robes of black or dank gray fur. Instead she was clad in a dress of bloodred, and her eyes shone as hard as green stones. She parted her lips—the same color as her dress—in a smile, and he sucked in a breath.

"Midwinter's greetings, Lord Beltan," she said.

He glared at her. "What do you want, Lady Kyrene?"

"What does any maiden want this evening?" She held up a garland woven of dark green leaves and crimson berries.

He grunted. "What would you know about the wants of maidens, my lady?"

Kyrene laughed, a rich sound, but harsh as well, like wine that had started to sour. "Far more than they know themselves, love. Come, let me show you." She ran a bold hand over his chest, his stomach, then cupped him below.

He stepped back from her.

Her eyes glinted. "So, the tales are true. No woman can get a rise out of the mighty Beltan. Are you so enamored with the idea of priesthood, then? Is it the inner circle of the Mysteries of Vathris you seek? Or is it just that you like so much to snort beneath the blankets with your fellow bulls?"

"Who I bed is none of your concern, Lady Kyrene."

"But it is, Lord Beltan, for it is my bed I would have you share."

She advanced, and he stepped back again.

An exultant expression touched her visage. "Don't you see? Together we can do away with Boreas, we can rule Calavan as king and queen. You have strength, I have beauty—think of the fine brats we can make between us." She laughed again. "And do not fear, I am no fool. I would not ask you to love me. You can descend into your precious labyrinth of Vathris, put on the bull mask, and bugger all the fresh young initiates you want. I don't mind. In fact, I might like to stand in the shadows sometime and watch."

He had been backing away from her as she spoke. They stood before a dim archway now.

"Get away from me," he said.

Kyrene let out a sigh. "A pity, love. But so be it. I know when I am defeated." The countess started to turn away, then halted. She held out the garland of greenery. "At least let me give you this. Do me the favor for my trouble."

He hesitated. All his instincts told him to be away from this woman. There was something wrong with her, like a sickness. However, it appeared the easiest way to be rid of her was to do as she asked. He bowed his head, and she reached out to slip the garland around his neck.

Too late he saw the thorns that had been woven among the leaves and berries.

Beltan tried to pull away, but this action only pressed the garland against his neck. He felt a half-dozen bright pricks of pain as the thorns bit into his flesh. A fog descended before him, and numbness chilled his limbs. He staggered back, opened his mouth, and tried to speak the words. *What have you done, witch?* But no sound came from his lips.

Her face hovered before him now, and her bloodred smile. "That's it, love." Her croon echoed in his skull, like voices in a cave. "Sleep now. When you wake you will be so much stronger."

He stared at her, unable to move. *What are you going to do to me?* But again he could not form the words. Through the haze he saw gray forms scuttle out of the shadows.

"Take him," she said.

The last sound Beltan heard was cruel laughter, then clammy hands coiled around his arms and legs and dragged him down into darkness.

101.

Grace stared at the charm that dangled from her bracelet.

The heat and noise of the great hall receded into the far distance, and the vacuum they left behind was frigid and empty. Silence mantled her like suffocating folds of plastic. The charm filled her vision until she felt minuscule in comparison, a satellite caught in the thrall of gravity cast by a dark, craggy planet.

A whirling filled her skull like the spinning of a compass needle searching for north. She saw him again, Detective Janson, the dull look in his small eyes traded in an instant for the hot light of evil.

No. She wouldn't believe it. It was just a stone charm—it couldn't mean anything. It couldn't. She had run her hands over his chest, had felt the smooth, unmarked skin for herself. It had to be a mistake.

Follow this, Blademender, until you can learn to follow your own heart.

Fear crystallized in Grace's lungs. Scar or no scar, a magnet could not lie. She would have screamed, but sound didn't carry in a vacuum, did it? In space your skin would freeze even as your blood boiled in your veins. Fire and ice, then nothing at all, nothing for eternity. Sweet, blessed, nothing. . . .

"Lady Grace?"

The silence splintered, the stone charm shrank, and the roar of the great hall crashed over her in a wave.

Grace's fingers still brushed the cup he held toward her, and the bracelet's magnetite charm still pointed directly at his chest. Her mind flailed in panic. How long had she been frozen like this? How long had she stared at the charm? Surely he knew, surely he saw the terror in her eyes and realized what it meant. Any second he would fling aside the cup, wrap impossibly strong hands around her throat, and squeeze the life out of her.

No, the expression on his face—on his exquisitely handsome face—was only bemused. He arched an eyebrow.

Do something, Grace. You've got to do something.

Her fingers closed around the wine cup. He smiled and released it. She brought the cup to her mouth with both hands and let the liquid touch her lips but did not drink, did not dare for fear she would choke. Then she lowered the cup and somehow managed to get it to the table before dropping it.

Now what?

"It is a fine vintage, isn't it?" Logren said. "This wine comes from the riverlands of western Eredane. My queen brought five casks of it with her."

The counselor took the cup and drank from it. The gesture was so easy, so casual. Impossible to believe that such perfect evil dwelled within him. No—not impossible.

"You still have not said what it was you wished to tell me, my lady."

She licked her lips. What could she say to him? If she opened her mouth she would surely scream. Then a voice spoke, and it hardly seemed her own.

"That I'm sorry, my lord. Terribly sorry. That's what I wanted to tell you. I was wrong to run from you, from your chamber the other day."

Grace sucked in air between her teeth. Where had those words come from? She didn't know, but by the light in his eyes she had done well to say them, and her breathlessness—although brought on by fear—only lent her words an earnestness that made them all the more believable. As though it was not a part of her, she watched her hand move across the table to touch his own. He looked up at her, and his smile deepened. Grace wanted to vomit, but she forced herself to smile in return.

She had thought herself such a fine spy, she had believed herself to be so logical, so scientific. Now she knew what a mockery that was. All this time she had thought Kyrene had entangled Logren in her witch's web, and Grace had fancied she might do the same. Now she knew the truth—it was not Kyrene who had ensnared Logren, but the opposite. Grace recalled her encounter with Kyrene before the feast, and she saw again the countess's new, harsh beauty.

What have you done, Kyrene? What have you done?

Grace knew the answer to that—knew the only reason the countess would trade her old, revealing gowns for one as dark as blood, for one with a high, concealing collar.

Logren's eyes locked on her own. "I cannot tell you how glad I am to hear you speak those words, my lady."

His voice was a husky whisper, only for her. She stiffened—when had she heard a voice like it before?

Now get yourself back to the castle, see to it you finish what we've started. . . .

Nine dark shapes cast shadows on her mind. The circle of standing stones. Yes, that was where she had heard it. Then he had whispered to disguise himself. Now it was to lure her into his secret world. But it was the same voice—the same man.

"You see, Lady Grace, ever since the day I met you it has been my fond hope that you and I would—"

The sound of trumpets echoed off high walls. Grace snatched her hand back and turned her head. King Boreas had risen from his chair, and all at the high table—and in the great hall—quieted to regard him.

"Welcome to my hall," the king of Calavan said. "Welcome on this, the longest night of the year. Tonight we meet to rejoice, to light the Everlog, and to call back the sun. Tonight we celebrate the death of winter, and we look to the spring to come." His blue eyes were solemn, and his deep voice rumbled on the air. "That is, *if* the spring comes."

A murmur ran around the hall. The king went on.

"As we begin this Midwinter's Eve, so too the Dominions begin their own darkest night. And we all must ask ourselves, what must we each do to see the dawn once again?"

The kings and queens at the high table shifted as he spoke. Eminda wore an open frown. Even Grace wondered at the king's speech. What was he saying?

"A toast," Boreas said. He raised his cup, and all those in the hall followed suit, obviously glad to do something that made sense. "May we all walk together through this night, and greet the morning as one!"

Calls of *Hear, hear!* rang out, but so did an equal number of mutters of dissent. Grace took a sip of wine but did not taste it. Fear was gone now, replaced by numbness. The murderer sat beside her, and Boreas's words fell on deaf ears. The Dominions would not stand together. They would never see the dawn.

"Now," Boreas thundered. "Bring on the players!"

Grace froze at the sound of these words, and she clutched her cup. The plan! In the terror of the moment she had utterly forgotten it. Now new dread flooded her. She searched the great hall with her eyes, but there was no sign of a pretty young woman in a gown of blue. Where was Aryn? She was to have stood in the corner, to wait for

Grace's signal once they were certain. Except Grace already knew who the murderer was—he sat beside her in finery of gray—and there was no trace of the baroness.

A side door opened, and a tiny form bounded out, turned a circle in midair, and landed on the dais to the accompaniment of gasps and applause. Trifkin Mossberry doffed his feathered cap, bowed, then rose again, a smile on his broad cherub's face. He spread small hands and spoke in his piping voice:

> *"On this night old Winter dies,*
> *As you'll see before your eyes—*
> *And while we work our merry art,*
> *Each of you shall play a part.*
>
> *Keep your wits now, hark and see,*
> *Here is what we ask of thee—*
> *As we march upon our way,*
> *An epitaph for Winter say.*
>
> *Speak it bawdy, speak it bold,*
> *Speak it soft for Winter old—*
> *And lay your hand upon his breast,*
> *As we send Winter to his rest."*

Trifkin bounded away, and the play commenced. Despite her dread, Grace could not take her eyes from the players, entranced by the spell they wove.

Tree-women ran onto the dais, then stood still in their bark-brown dresses and raised twig-limbs to conjure a leafless forest. Winter walked among them in his robe and beard of white. He threw snowy petals on the tree-women, then cackled when they shivered at the chilling touch. He lifted bony hands and more petals fell from the rafters of the hall, shaken from baskets by shadowy figures above. His icy laughter froze the air—

—then fell short as a dozen goat-men bounded onto the dais: chests bare, legs clad in curly trousers, horn nubbins tied to their heads. Each gripped a stick in his hand, and as they circled around the old man the sticks burst into flame. The goat-men ran faster, and faster yet. Their circle tightened, and Winter raised his white arms and cried out. Then the goat-men touched their torches to his robe.

Grace gasped, and so did a hundred others around the hall. As if his robe were made of magician's flash paper, Winter burst into brilliant flame. The glare blinded Grace for a heartbeat, and when her vision cleared the old man was gone.

No, that wasn't true. In the place where Winter had stood there now rested a wooden bier. A body lay upon the bier draped from head to toe in black cloth. Four of the goat-men lifted the bier in muscular arms as the tree-women trembled in joy. Then the goat-men paraded the bier around the great hall. They paused as they went to let each reveler lay a hand upon the corpse of Winter and speak a few words as Trifkin had instructed.

"Good riddance!" they shouted.

"Melt, old man!" others said.

"Now you're as cold as my husband!" one elderly countess pronounced, to the obvious amusement of everyone in the hall except the gray-haired man who sat next to her.

Grace went rigid in her chair as she watched this spectacle. No, it was all wrong. Where was Travis? He was to have played a part in the drama, to have dressed as a fool and ridden along with the bier to keep watch. Once he signaled her, then Grace would signal Aryn. But neither was in sight, the plan was in shambles, and Grace was alone with the murderer beside her.

The goat-men turned, and the bier moved toward the high table. Some of the rulers frowned—notably Sorrin and Eminda—but others joined in the sport. Boreas laid a hand on the corpse, as did Kylar, and both echoed their joy at his passing. An obviously drunken Lysandir slurred something unintelligible and would have fallen on the bier if a pair of servants hadn't pulled him back. The goat-men marched down the line.

Grace's breath came quick and shallow. What should she do? But it was too late. The procession was almost over—there was nothing she could do.

No, Grace. That's not true. This isn't over yet.

The voice that spoke was dry and clinical, her doctor's voice. Fear receded. A hard part of Grace rose to the fore, the part that wielded a scalpel with emotionless efficiency, the part that reached inside living bodies without flinching, to fix what was wrong. Time slowed, and the air was hard and clear as resin. She knew what she had to do. Once again Grace balanced upon the fulcrum. Once again she stepped across to the other side.

The bier paused before the place where Grace and Logren sat. She rose from her chair and affected a playful smile.

"But who is this all draped in black?" she said. "Should not Winter be shrouded in white?"

She took her napkin from the table, unfolded the white cloth, and draped it over the body. Then, smiling still, she turned to Logren.

He gazed at her, eyes thoughtful, then shrugged, a smile on his own lips. Logren reached out, laid a hand on the shrouded body, and spoke in his rich voice.

"I know we all will be glad when this winter is but a—"

His words were lost as a murmur coursed through the great hall. Logren frowned, then his gaze dropped to the bier.

Flowers of crimson bloomed on the white napkin.

Logren drew in a hissing breath and snatched his hand back. The crimson stains continued to grow. Gasps turned into screams. Grace gazed at the bier with strange exultation.

"What is going on?" Boreas said, his eyebrows drawn down in a glower.

Grace stood straight, power filled her. "See for yourself, Your Majesty!"

She snatched back both napkin and shroud. More screams echoed off stone, and revelers leaped to their feet. The body on the bier was not the old actor who played Winter. It was the corpse of Alerain. They had placed his head back on his shoulders. Dark blood flowed from the slit of his neck, from his eyes and his ears, and from the gory wound in his chest.

Boreas stared, his face white with horror. "What have you done, Lady Grace?"

"I have found your seneschal's killer, Your Majesty." Her voice rang out over the hall. "You have heard the legend, have you not? How on the darkest night of the year a corpse has the power to accuse its murderer?"

Grace wasn't sure how she knew this, only that she did—only that Trifkin Mossberry had given her this knowledge there in his strange forest room. It was an ancient magic, primal—older than witches or runespeakers. Old as Gloaming Wood. On Midwinter's Eve, a corpse would bleed in the presence of its killer.

Logren stepped back from the table. "This is madness! A witch's lie!"

"It is no lie," Grace said.

She met his eyes. For a moment his confused expression remained, then like a mask it crumbled. Evil shone in his gaze, pure and unwavering. Yes, he knew now, she could see it. There was no need for him to hide it from her any longer.

"They will never believe you," he said in a voice more poisonous than venom.

She spoke the words with cool precision, a doctor giving her diagnosis. "I believe you are wrong, my lord."

Shouts of anger rose from the crowd. Boreas glared at Logren, his face red with rage. Eminda rose from her chair, her face hard.

"You fool, Logren!" she said. "What have you done? You have ruined everything with this madness. You will step down from this table at once!"

Logren hesitated. He glared at the crowd, at Grace, and finally Queen Eminda. Then a hideous grin crossed his face, obliterating any traces of beauty that once had dwelled there.

"You're not going anywhere, Eminda," he said. "None of you are!"

The motion was so quick no one could have stopped it. Logren plucked the eating knife from his belt and made a small flick with his hand. Eminda staggered back, her eyes wide. Her fingers fluttered to her throat and brushed the knife that now protruded there. Then she slumped back against Boreas.

Before the others could react, Logren lifted his arms and called out in a terrible voice. "Now, my fierce ones! Come to me!"

They obeyed. Through the high windows they slunk, then scrabbled down the walls. Feydrim. The great hall became a sea of fear and panic.

Logren turned his empty gaze on Grace. "You have lost, Your Radiance."

Grace did not answer him. She could only stare as the feydrim streamed into the great hall.

102.

Travis pressed his back to the wall and gazed into the growing light. The metallic hum vibrated through him as if his body were a wire.

He clutched the iron box inside the pocket of his tunic. It was this that had betrayed him, this that had led them to him. He should have thrown it away, should have buried it in the ground, should have lost it leagues ago. However, even as he thought this, he knew he could not have done it. Jack had given him the box, and he had promised. It was his burden to bear. And in a moment it would all be over.

The light grew brighter, and he lifted a hand to shield his eyes. The incandescence streamed through his fingers as if flesh were no barrier to it. For a moment he thought of Grace and the others. He hoped they were all right, and he was sorry he would not be able to see them again, that he would not be able to say good-bye. Then all thoughts except terror fled his mind as they appeared in the center of the light: tall, willowy, evil.

"I'm afraid, Jack," he whispered.

The wraithlings reached out slender arms and drifted toward him. He could not tell how many of them there were. All he saw was silvery skin, mouthless faces, and huge, obsidian eyes. No box of iron could protect him now.

There is strange clarity in fear, and Travis's mind grew almost calm as the wraithlings approached. All his running, all his hiding, all his forgetting were over. No more would he have to decide what to do in his life, or what to be. This one final choice would be made for him. He drew out the iron box and cupped it in his hands.

He felt their quickening as much as saw it. Their light flickered as if in anticipation. They crowded into the corridor, drawn by what he held, yet reverent of it as well, perhaps even afraid. He stretched the box out toward them.

Stop this, Travis!

It was hard to hear the voice through the thrum in his mind. He held the box out farther.

Stop it at once!

He hesitated. *Jack?*

Sweet tears of Ysani, who do you think it is?

Despite his fear, Travis winced. It was Jack all right.

You must use Sinfathisar, Travis.

He clutched the iron box. *The Stone? But it's the Stone they want.*

Yes, and it's the Stone that's your only hope. You've got to use it to make them whole.

I don't understand.

They're twisted, Travis—twisted and corrupted. The Stone can return them to what they once were. That's the power of Sinfathisar. Before there was light and dark, there was twilight. Use the Stone. Make them whole.

But—

Now, Travis!

The wraithlings were upon him. They reached with slender hands to touch him. There was no more time. Travis fumbled with the latch on the iron box, opened it, nearly dropped its contents, then gripped the Stone of Twilight in his hand. It was hard and smooth, and resonated with power.

The huge eyes of the wraithlings grew larger yet. The terrible light flared around them. It streaked through his skin, his flesh, his bones. Pale hands reached for him. Travis gripped the Stone and shouted the words in his mind.

Make—them—whole!

Once before he had heard the sound, in the ruins of the White Tower: a chorus of mouthless screams. It was a sound of agony, a sound of sorrow, a sound of release. The illumination of the wraithlings flared until it washed away the world. Travis floated in a place of white, a place without color, without temperature, without touch. The only sound was a rhythmic drumming which he knew to be the beating of his own heart. Then, like a movie of a shattered window running backward, the fractured shards of the corridor—walls, floor, ceiling—rushed back toward each other, and the world was whole again.

Travis fumbled with his spectacles, and his vision snapped back into focus. Gone was the harsh light of the wraithlings. In its place a gentle radiance bathed the corridor, like winter sun filtered between the branches of leafless trees. He drew in a breath of wonder.

The wraithlings were gone. In their place stood nine beings who were as beautiful as the Pale Ones had been terrible. They were clothed in gossamer that shimmered like nebulae against a dark sky. They were tall—taller than Travis—and impossibly slender. Even standing they bespoke grace. Their faces were not human, but they were fair all the same: their chins delicate, their cheeks high, their mouths and noses small. The eyes that gazed at Travis were large, but not grotesque like those of the wraithlings. Instead they shone like dark, liquid gems. They were ancient eyes.

Travis lowered the Stone. It felt warm against his skin. "Who are you?" he whispered.

The beings did not answer him, but all the same he knew, as if they had given him the answer. They had been twisted by the Pale King's magic, and now they were whole once more.

The fairies bowed before him. It seemed wrong that such radiant beings should do so, but even as he thought this he felt calmness wash over him. They were grateful.

The fairies rose. He met their ageless gazes, and it almost seemed their tiny mouths turned upward in knowing smiles. Then their outlines blurred, until where each fairy had stood there remained only a column of light. Then each column collapsed into a shimmering point. Nine sparks of silver fluttered on the air, then danced away around the corner like thistledown on the wind.

The corridor went dim. Travis was alone. He looked down at the Stone in his hand. What was this thing that could make the broken whole? What was this thing that evil would break the world to have it? Travis sighed. He slipped the Stone back into his pocket.

"That was nicely done, lad," said a chalky voice.

He looked up. A form shambled toward him, her shapeless body clad in colorless rags. It was the old servingwoman he had chased through the castle on two occasions. Now it was she who had found him.

Travis shook his head. For the second time he spoke the question. "Who are you?"

The hag cackled, then reached up with bony hands to push back the grimy shawl that hid her face. Travis's eyes went wide behind his spectacles.

"Grisla?"

Her wrinkled face split in a snaggled grin. "Well, it isn't the queen of Malachor."

He blinked. "*Grisla?*" It was the only word he seemed able to speak.

"That's my name, boy," she snapped. "Don't wear it out."

Travis's head reeled, and he tried to understand. "But how did you—?"

The hag slapped a gnarled hand to her forehead. "There you go again, lad. Always asking questions, always wanting to know why this and how that." She let out a snort. "Asking questions is the easy part, lad. When are you going to start answering them? That's the trick."

Travis opened his mouth, but he didn't know what to say.

"So, where's that bundle I dropped?" the hag said. "You haven't lost it, have you, lad?"

He winced. "It's back in my room."

"Really, lad? Are you so sure of that?"

"Yes. . . ." However, even as he said the word, he was aware of something bulky pressing against his side. He reached into his tunic pocket and drew out an object he knew had not been there a moment ago: the bundle of rags the old witch had dropped. He held it out to her.

"No, lad, it belongs to you. Go on, open it and see."

Travis hesitated, then plucked at the bundle with his fingers and pulled apart the rags. His breath caught in his chest as he glimpsed the object within them: a small piece of polished bone marked with three straight lines.

Grisla gazed at him with her one bulbous eye. "So, lad, have you decided yet what it means?"

He drew in a breath, opened his mouth, then shook his head. What could he say? Endings or beginnings? He didn't always know right from left. How could he choose between things so much larger?

Grisla pressed her withered lips together in an expression of sorrow. She turned and laid her hand upon a door in the wall—a door that, like the bundle, had not been there a moment ago. She pushed, and the door opened. Frigid air swirled into the passage, along with hard grains of snow.

"Look, lad," Grisla said in a hoarse voice.

He clutched the hem of his mistcloak and stepped toward the doorway. Beyond was not another castle chamber, but a snowy vale lit by the glow of the moon. Silhouettes of mountains thrust up into the sky like black knives. Among them was a great, flat, dark plane. It was like a door in the mountains.

No, not a door. A gate. A gate of iron as high as ten men, set into a gap in the knife-edged peaks.

How—! he started to ask, then stopped himself.

Asking questions is the easy part. . . .

Travis already knew the answer. Somehow this door opened onto Shadowsdeep. It was impossible, of course: The vale lay almost two hundred leagues north of Calavere. Yet here it was a step away. Snow drifted against the toes of his boots.

"The Rune Gate is about to open," Grisla whispered. "Only you can shut it, Runelord."

Travis shook his head. "But I can't." The cold that streamed through the door filled his chest and froze his heart. "All I do is break things."

"Is that your choice then, lad?"

"I don't . . . I don't know."

She lifted a hand, pointed through the doorway. "Go then, and make your choice. Life or death."

He wanted to turn, wanted to run, but he knew there was nowhere else to go. All the roads he had drifted down in his life had brought him to this place. Travis wrapped his cloak around himself, then stepped through the doorway into the icy vale of Shadowsdeep.

103.

Beltan swam upward, toward a flickering light.

It was hard. The darkness dragged him down, as if he had fallen in a lake with all his armor on. He was so tired—he wanted to give up, wanted to sink back to the bottom and rest. Only there was no bottom, and the darkness went on forever. He had to keep trying.

The light was closer now, red and hot. It wavered just above him, and he could see a shadowy figure against it, peering down at him. The darkness wrapped around his ankles, pulled him back.

Now, Beltan. Do it now!

He kicked free of the darkness, stretched his arms, and surged upward, into the ruddy light. A ragged breath rushed into his chest, more painful than the water that filled a drowning man's lungs. His eyes flew open and stared into fire.

"So, my bold knight is awake."

The voice was a mocking croon. Beltan searched for the speaker with his eyes, but all he could see was a maelstrom of flame, hot and angry, eager to consume him.

"I had not intended for you to wake, love. You are even stronger than I thought. Yet it doesn't matter. Perhaps it is better this way. Perhaps it is good that you see what you are to become."

The flame receded, his cheeks cooled, and he blinked in realization. The fire was a torch, and she had held it close to his face. Now she had turned to place the torch in an iron sconce set into a nearby arch of stone. She turned back, and anger flooded through him. It was agony to speak, as if someone crushed his throat, but he managed to croak a single word before the pain was too great.

"Kyrene. . . ."

Her bloodred lips coiled in a smile. "Don't try to talk, love. It will only make it hurt more."

Blast the witch! Beltan tried to leap up, to grab her neck in his hands, to twist it until it splintered.

His limbs did not respond. A numbness sheathed his body.

Her cruel smile deepened. "Such hate in your eyes, love. I'm certain you'd enjoy slitting my throat. Poor thing, if only you could move. But I'm afraid the wreath I wove took care of that. It will be hours before you can twitch a finger, and by then it will be far too late." Her hard green eyes drifted over him. "Though it's a pity the serpent's thorn stilled all of you, love."

Beltan glared at her. *Let me go, witch! Let me go now!* Even if he could have spoken them, the words would have done no good. He forced his mind to cool. In battle a skilled warrior felt, not anger, but calm. Even if he could not move, Beltan knew this was indeed a battle, and one to the death.

His eyes were still his, so he used these to determine his surroundings. He lay on some sort of stone slab, his head propped up on a pillow that, by its hardness, was stone as well. She had stripped him of his clothes, and he was naked. He supposed the slab was cold, but he could not feel it. The body that lay below his head might as well have belonged to another.

He let his eyes move up to the arches of stone above. Out of the corner of his eye he could just make out other slabs like the one he lay on, marching into the gloom. Yes, he knew this place.

Kyrene noticed his gaze. "Do you like my choice of location, love?" She spread her arms. "The tomb of the kings. What better place to die and be reborn?"

He looked at her. "What . . . ?" The one word was all he could manage.

"What do I mean, love?" She laughed, and the hard, sick sound of it echoed off the walls and columns. "But I think you know."

The countess bent over him. The front of her gown was unfastened, and the fabric parted as she leaned to reveal the white expanse between her breasts—and a thick, oozing scab.

His eyes widened. She stroked his face with a hand.

"Yes, love, that's what I mean." The scent of blood emanated from her. "Soon you will be like me. Soon you will know what it is to have true strength."

Kyrene turned away and moved to another bier. Beltan followed her with his gaze, then motion caught the corner of his eye. He looked down at his right hand. His fingers curled and uncurled against the stone. He stared as if the hand were not his own.

Kyrene started to turn back. Beltan willed his hand to stop moving, and it did. Was it only chance or had he controlled it? He had to believe it was he. He could move. Even if it was only a twitch it meant she was wrong. Maybe her magic had not worked as well as she had thought. After all, she hadn't expected him to wake. Maybe if he could delay her, keep her talking, there would be enough time to . . .

Kyrene moved back to him. She held two objects in her hand. One was a dagger with a hilt of onyx. The other was a rough lump of iron as big as a man's fist. Sickness flooded him.

The light in her emerald eyes was mad and exultant. "Yes, love, this is for you."

She set the lump of iron on the center of his naked chest. It was heavy and terribly cold. Realization cut through his fear. He could *feel* it, even though a moment ago he had been able to feel nothing against his skin.

"The magic of it is simple." Kyrene brushed a finger over the wound between her own breasts. "Simple yet wondrous. I have only to cut out your heart and slip this one into the space where it beat inside your chest. Death will be reversed, and you will be reborn, stronger than you ever could imagine. There is pain at first, yes. But soon enough pain will matter little to you."

A shiver coursed across his skin. Had she seen it? No, her gaze was fixed upon the heart of iron. His limbs felt as if they were on fire now, but it was better than the numbness, better than the fate she held for him. But he needed more time. He opened his mouth, forced himself to speak.

"No. . . ."

Kyrene's eyes snapped back to his. "Don't resist, love. There is no use." Her smile again, sharp as the knife in her hand. "Besides, this way you can join your handsome friend, Travis Wilder."

Fear washed over Beltan, and his heart felt cold and hard as if it had already been replaced by iron.

"What . . . have . . . ?"

"What have I done to him?" An icy laugh escaped her. "I have done nothing to him. Your precious little friend is in the hands of my master now, even as you are in mine. So don't you see? It is better to join us. This way you can be with him again, love."

Now rage mingled with his fear. If she had done something to harm Travis, anything at all, he would . . . no, he had to keep his wits, that was the way to help Travis. He could move his feet, he was certain of it now, although he did not want to try, did not want her to see. Just a little while more and—

"It is time," Kyrene said. "Prepare yourself for your new life, Beltan of Calavan." She pressed the tip of the onyx dagger against his chest, just above his breastbone.

No, he had to say something to buy more time. Anything.

"Kiss . . . me. . . ."

The dagger halted. She stared at him, her smooth forehead creased in a frown.

"Kiss me while . . . you kill me. . . ."

Now her frown turned into an expression of lust and glee. "Perhaps this is not so far a fall for you as I had thought, Lord Beltan. Yes, we will be glorious together!"

Kyrene tightened her grip on the dagger, then bent her head and pressed her lips to his. The taste of death flooded his mouth. She pressed harder, crushed herself against him, then she pushed down on the dagger. The tip of the blade pierced his skin, and warm blood trickled down his chest. Her tongue searched his mouth. She tensed her body, to let her weight fall upon the hilt and drive the blade into his beating heart.

Now, it had to be *now*.

Beltan forced his body to move. The effort turned his blood to venom. Hot agony coursed through his limbs, spilled into his chest, and boiled up into his skull. He screamed and let the pain flood him, let it burn away the numbness. His arms were heavy—it was like moving them through molten rock—but somehow he brought them up, gripped her face, and shoved her away.

Kyrene's head contacted a stone column with a *crack* that echoed throughout the tomb. Beltan knew that blow would have dropped the strongest of men.

The countess staggered, caught herself, then turned toward him.

Blood streamed down her white face, and rage twisted her once-lovely features into a rictus of evil. Beltan could see the flat place on her skull where the bones had shattered against the column. Still she came toward him, dagger held high.

"Die for me, my lord!" Her voice was an inhuman shriek. "Die for me!"

She flew at him to plunge the dagger into his chest. There was no time to counter her, not with the stiffness of the poison that still flowed in his limbs. He rolled off the end of the bier, and her blow missed him. She struck the sharp edge of the slab, fell forward, and her face smacked against hard stone. The dagger flew from her hand.

Beltan clenched his teeth and struggled to his feet. Kyrene writhed on the bier, smearing blood against the marble, then jerked herself upright. Her head lolled to one side. Her visage was a crimson pulp, all traces of beauty, of humanity, gone. However, he could still see her eyes like two fractured gems in the ruin of her face, bright with desire. She raised her arms and lurched toward him. Words bubbled through torn lips and shattered teeth.

"I'm going to live forever!"

Beltan reached up, grabbed the torch, and shoved the flaming end against her gown.

Kyrene's shriek filled the tomb. As if her blood were some sort of viscous fuel, the flames leaped up and wove a cocoon of fire around her. Now there was terror in her green eyes, and they seemed almost human again. She reached for him with a burning hand.

"Save me, Beltan!"

He dropped the torch and stumbled back. His words were hoarse with sorrow and disgust.

"I just did, Kyrene."

She shrieked again, stumbled, and fell back onto the bier. Two gray forms crept out of the shadows. Feydrim. Beltan fumbled again for the torch, but the things did not come for him. Instead they scuttled onto the bier and wrapped their spindly arms around the burning countess. The flames licked at their matted fur, then they too were on fire.

Kyrene's cries ended. She and the feydrim were lost in the fire. Beltan backed away from the inferno.

His foot contacted a soft bundle. He reached down: his clothes.

By the time he had shrugged on the clothes, the flames had dwindled. With a curl of black smoke they went out. Three dark husks lay on the bier entangled in a motionless embrace. Beltan turned and limped from the tomb. As he went he took an old sword from one of the sleeping kings.

"Sorry," he said. "I need this more than you do."

He had to find Travis.

Kyrene had been mad and evil, but somehow Beltan knew she had spoken at least part of the truth. Whether or not the Pale King had captured him, Travis was in danger.

The blond knight lurched into a jog. The walls seemed to throb, and passages lengthened and contracted as he careened down them. An aftereffect of the witch's poison. His limbs were still stiff, and he stumbled often, but the fire had faded to sharp pinpricks. He gritted his teeth and ran on.

Where would he find Travis? He wracked his brain, then he had it. In the great hall. That was where they had all been heading, to reveal the murderer at the Midwinter's Eve feast. He turned down a corridor—

—then halted. An eerie glow flickered down a side passage. He knew that light, had seen it as they fled into the White Tower of the Runebinders.

"Wraithlings," he whispered.

Falken had said it was the Great Stone they wanted, the Stone that Travis carried. . . .

Beltan lunged down the hallway, toward the metallic light. The knight forgot his pain, forgot the clumsiness of his limbs. The incandescence brightened. It came from around a corner just ahead. He gripped his sword, pushed his lean body forward, and hurled himself around the corner.

The brilliant light was gone. Beltan stumbled to a halt. The dead-end passage was dim save for a faint blue radiance that spilled through an open doorway. It was bitterly cold, and hard bits of ice scoured his cheeks. Snow. He approached, then saw a hunched figure in the shadows beside the door. The figure stepped forward, into the blue light.

Beltan knew her: the hag from King Kel's keep. But how could she be here? And why?

"It does not matter, Knight Protector," she said in her chalky voice.

He shuddered. How had she known what he was thinking?

Grisla nodded to the open door. He followed her gaze, then breathed a foggy breath of wonder. Beyond the doorway was a snowy vale lit by a crescent moon. Sharp mountains thrust up against the night sky. He looked down and saw footprints in the crust of the snow, but already white powder drifted into them, obscuring them.

"He has gone on ahead of you," the hag said.

Beltan looked at her. "Travis?"

She pointed to the doorway with a gnarled hand. "Follow him, Knight Protector, if your heart is strong enough. His path is yet fraught with peril."

Beltan started to shake his head. It was impossible. This door couldn't be here—he had to be mistaken. It was all a mad vision brought on by Kyrene's poison. Then he drew in a frosty breath. It didn't matter whether the door was impossible or not. Travis had gone through. Beltan had to follow.

"Hurry," Grisla said.

The knight gripped his sword and stepped through the door, into the frozen vale beyond.

104.

Screams filled Calavere's great hall.

Grace could not take her eyes from the spindly forms that crept through the high windows. The feydrim dropped from the rafters or slid down tapestries, their claws shredding the fabric as they went. Revelers fell over each other to get out of the way of each creature as it reached the floor. Tables toppled onto their sides, cups and platters clattered. Like a wave crashing on a beach, a mass of revelers rushed against the doors of the hall. However, the planes of iron-bound wood did not open, as if barred from outside. The first nobles and servants to reach the doors were crushed against the wood as more revelers pressed behind them, trying to flee the feydrim. There was no sign of Trifkin Mossberry and his players—the entire troupe had vanished.

Laughter sounded beside Grace.

She jerked her head around. Logren surveyed the chaos of the great hall with eyes like stones.

"That's it," he said. He motioned to the feydrim with his hands. "Come, my hungry ones. Come."

There was a snarl of rage. Grace glanced to the side and saw the source of the sound: King Boreas. He knelt beside the fallen form of Eminda, along with Ivalaine and Tressa. Beside them were Kylar and Kalyn of Galt. The other rulers and counselors had risen from their seats, terror on their faces.

"Blast you, Logren, she's dead," Boreas said through clenched teeth. Blood stained his hands, and his eyes were steel.

Logren turned his lifeless gaze on the king of Calavan and laughed again. "I should think so. Even that loud bitch should find it hard to bark with a knife in the throat."

Boreas's lips pulled back from his teeth, then with a roar he sprang forward. He reached out muscular arms, ready to snap Logren's neck with powerful fingers.

Logren made a casual motion with his hand, as one might when swatting a fly. There was a sound like stone breaking. Boreas's head snapped back, his arms flew out, and he crashed against the high table with a grunt of pain. Wood shattered, and Boreas fell to the floor. He did not get up. Kylar and a pair of servants rushed to him and lifted him from the splinters. He moaned—he was alive—but he slumped in their arms, eyes shut, his face wet with blood.

A sneer crossed Logren's face. "So much for the bull."

Grace stared at Logren. She wanted to do something, wanted to stop him, but fear cocooned her body in gauze. She could not move.

No, it wasn't just fear—it was more than that. Here was evil before her. She had thought she could stand against it, had thought she had done so in Denver Memorial's ED, but she was wrong. She had lived in awe of Boreas's strength, and Logren had flicked him aside as if he were a speck of dust. If Boreas could not stop this evil, how could she?

Screams continued to echo off the ceiling. The feydrim scuttled through the roiling sea of revelers. Here and there some nobles or knights—armed only with their eating knives—tried to attack the creatures. As reward for the effort, their faces were slashed with claws and their bodies mauled with fangs. A few of the feydrim squealed and went down with a knife in the throat or eye, but more came behind to replace them. There were too many of the creatures. They poured through the windows faster than Grace could count.

Except for those who who attacked the creatures, the feydrim ignored the revelers. They scuttled over tables and made their way toward the dais. Fear transmuted Grace's saliva to lead. The feydrim did not care about the revelers—it was the rulers of the Dominions they wanted.

The first of the feydrim scrambled onto the dais. There were three of the creatures. They opened snubbed maws and reached thin arms toward King Sorrin. Hate and pain glowed in their yellow eyes.

The king of Embarr's gaunt face was a mask of horror. "Get them away from me!"

The two knights that had stood behind him at the high table sprang forward, short knives in hand. The stout Embarrans each engaged one of the creatures with their knives, and those feydrim hissed and scuttled back. However, the third circled from behind, leaped upon the back of one of the knights, and dug its fangs into the Embarran's neck. He went down screaming. The feydrim closed its jaws, and Grace could hear vertebrae crunch. The knight's limbs flopped against the dais, then went still.

Before the feydrim could leap from its prey, another form was there: Ivalaine. The queen reached out with a silver needle and stuck it through the feydrim's fur. It stiffened and hissed, then the light in its yellow eyes dimmed, and it slumped across the body of the dead knight.

The other Embarran staggered back. He had managed to gut one of the remaining feydrim with his knife. However, these men were not used to fighting without sword and armor. The third feydrim lashed out with its claws and sliced through the tendons in the back of his knee. The knight collapsed to the dais with a cry of agony. Once he was down it was easy for the feydrim. It closed its maw over his face and muffled his scream.

Once the knight's cry ended, the feydrim lifted its head and bared its bloody fangs. Ivalaine fell back—it seemed the queen had no more needles. Grace stared at the creature. Once before she had killed one of these things with Travis's help. She tried to command her hand to move to the knife in her boot, but it would not. The feydrim left the faceless body of the dead knight and scuttled forward.

"Help me, Olstin!" King Lysandir shrieked. "By all the gods, it's coming for me!"

Olstin stared at the feydrim, then his ruddy face went white, and his eyes rolled up in his head. He slumped to the dais while tears and snot ran down Lysandir's face. The feydrim stretched its thin arms toward the king of Brelegond.

A flash of blue blinded Grace. There was an inhuman shriek and the reek of singed hair. When Grace's vision cleared, she saw the feydrim writhing before Lysandir. A web of blue sparks sizzled around it, burning into its fur, its mouth, its eyes. The feydrim fell dead, and the sparks vanished.

"Blast you, Melindora Nightsilver!" Logren said.

Grace turned her head. The Lady Melia stood below the dais, hands raised, her beautiful face hard, her amber eyes molten. A blue nimbus surrounded her body. Grace stared.

Below the dais, Falken and Melia had organized resistance to the feydrim. The bard and a dozen of Boreas's guards had set up a barricade of tables and benches. However, it was not the knives of the men so much as Melia's magic that kept the feydrim at bay. She turned, and the nimbus about her strengthened until Grace could hardly see her slender form within the azure light. Fifty feydrim hissed and prowled on the other side of the makeshift barricade, but they did not venture over.

Logren stepped to the edge of the dais. "You're a fool to fight, Melia. And you as well, Falken. Both of you know more than anyone the power you face. Both of you know you can never defeat it." He raised his arms, and his voice boomed out over the great hall. "Hear me, all of you! The Pale King rides from Imbrifale this very night. Fight him and you will surely die. But there is another way. Vow to serve him, surrender yourself unto him, and I tell you that you will know glorious life such as you have never before imagined!"

The revelers cowered now. They knew they could not escape the hall, and they knew the feydrim would not kill them if they did not fight.

Logren's face was rapturous. Grace imagined a world of people with hearts of iron. A world without kindness. A world frozen all in ice. No, there were enough heartless people in either world.

She concentrated, forced her breathing to calm, and reached out to touch the Weirding. It was everywhere—strong and tinged with fear—spinning a web of life through the hall. She gathered it to her, wove it with her fingers as she had the threads of the loom, creating a net of power. She froze. There. In the center of the web was a dark blot, a place with no life, with no energy at all. She recoiled in loathing. It was Logren.

He spun around, a leering grin upon his lips. "So my little witch attempts a spell." Logren advanced on her. "But your magic cannot touch me, Lady Grace. Haven't you realized that?"

"You can't win." The words were dry as dust on her tongue—meaningless.

"But I already have." His words were soft, just for her. "Melia is strong. I admire her as I always admire strength. But her magic cannot hold out much longer. Look—even now her power wavers."

Grace did not want to follow his gesture, but she could not resist. Her heart turned to ice. It was true. The blue nimbus surrounding Melia flickered, and moisture beaded her brow. The feydrim pressed closer toward the barricade.

Her gaze returned to Logren, then dropped down to his pearl-gray tunic.

"What's wrong, my lady?" he said in a mocking voice. "Is there something you do not understand?"

"Your chest. . . ."

A sneer cut across his face. "And you fancy yourself a witch, Lady Grace? It is not such a difficult magic, to trade one scar for another." He touched the fine white line that marked his cheek. "I found a witch with the talent, and when she finished I stuck a knife in her back."

Grace shuddered. So that was how he had hidden the truth.

Logren advanced on her, and she retreated until her back touched the stone wall behind the dais. There was nowhere else to go.

"I am high in the Pale King's favor, Lady Grace." Logren's voice droned in her ears. "Surely he will give me a kingdom to rule for my reward. And when he does, you will be my queen. No other in the Dominions is as beautiful as you, not even that witch Ivalaine. No, don't tremble. You will not be afraid when the time comes, my lady." He ran a finger down the bodice of her gown, tracing a line between her breasts. "You see, I will take away that weak human heart of yours, and I will give you one that will make you strong and unafraid." His eyes were pits of blackness. "You will be mine, Lady Grace, and together we will rule forever!"

Grace gazed into his empty eyes, drew a deep breath, then spoke the only words she could. "I'd rather die."

Logren laughed. "And die you will, Lady Grace." He drew a curved knife from the folds of his tunic and raised it above her. "Die and be reborn as my queen!"

Before he could plunge the dagger into her chest, there was a metallic flash. Both the blade and Logren's hand flew to one side, then fell to the dais. Logren screamed and pulled back the stump of his wrist. Dark blood sprayed from the wound.

Grace reeled. A figure stood behind Logren, clad all in smoke-gray. "Durge!"

But how could the knight be here? Then she saw the rip in the tapestry behind the knight, opened by the greatsword he held in his hands. Through the slit was the darkness of a hidden doorway.

"My lady," he said in a hoarse voice.

The knight was hunched over in pain. Blood stained his face, his hands, and his clothes. His cloak dangled in shreds behind him.

With an animal snarl of fury, Logren turned on the knight. He pressed his severed wrist against his own tunic, soaking it. "You idiot! What have you done to me?"

Durge gazed at him with somber brown eyes. "Something I will now finish, my lord."

The knight swung his greatsword, but his injuries slowed him, and—despite his own horrible wound—Logren moved with unnatural speed. With his bleeding stump he batted the sword aside, then his other hand sped forward and contacted Durge squarely in the chest. The knight's eyes went wide, and he flew back against the stone wall, striking it with a terrible *thud*.

"My lady . . ."

Then his eyes fluttered shut, and he sank to the floor, where he did not move.

Grace opened her mouth, but her scream was silent. *No!*

Logren whirled around. "Do you see, my lady? Do you see how wrong it is to resist me?" He turned, clutching the stump of his wrist, then moved to the edge of the dais and shouted to the entire hall. "You are all idiots to resist me!"

Grace sagged against the wall. He was right—they could not win. Melia's power dimmed, and the feydrim pressed forward. Falken and the others slashed with their knives, but it would not be enough. In moments the feydrim would break through the barricade, would tear Melia, Falken, and the guards to bits, and would slink onto the dais to finish what they had come here for.

She shut her eyes, the din of the great hall receded, and darkness enfolded her. Familiar darkness. This was not the first time evil had owned her.

Grace was a girl. She lay stiffly in her bed, wondered if she would be the one that night, and believed as only children could believe that if she stayed hidden beneath the covers the monsters could not touch her. She was wrong. The covers were no protection. First came soft footfalls, then gentle whispers, and finally hands that reached out of the darkness—cold, hard hands—slipping beneath the covers to clutch soft flesh. Moans of pain drifted in the night, melding with the cries of owls.

Memories rippled, changed. It was an older girl who stood in the heart of the fire. Flames danced all around. They licked at walls and ceiling as if they fed on some viscous fuel that had permeated the wood. Screams rose above the roar of the flames—the horrid animal screams of grown men and women in agony. They could not escape their rooms, for somehow the locks on their doors had melted before the fire had ever touched them. A puff of parched air scorched the girl's face. It was time to go. She walked through the inferno toward the open mouth of the door, and it seemed the flames flickered away from her as she moved, letting her pass. But it was her fire, after all. She had called it, and it had come.

The flames vanished, replaced by cool white tiles and sleek metal drawers. Her hands reached out as if they were not her own and opened one of the drawers. He lay inside, his dark skin gray under the plastic. Leon. Beneath the clear covering, his eyes opened and fixed on hers.

You've got to live, Grace. His breath fogged the plastic. *Don't you see? No matter how much it hurts, you've got to live.*

A bright light shone behind her. She turned. Now she was in the ED, and the doors slid open. Gurneys rolled in, dozens of them, hundreds, all bearing broken people who cried out in pain. One of the gurneys stopped before her. Grace bent over it and pulled back the sheet to examine the patient.

The woman on the gurney stared up at her with green-gold eyes. *Doctor, heal thyself,* the woman whispered.

The vision shattered like crystal. Sound rushed back in a clap of thunder. Grace stood in the great hall of Calavere again. She stared at the object she held before her face. It was the bracelet Trifkin Mossberry had given her. The stone charm spun in a circle.

It is the same kind of stone as the artifact of Malachor in the great hall.

Grace knew what she had to do.

She jerked her head up. Melia staggered now, and the blue nimbus flickered wildly. Falken reached for her. The feydrim hissed and started to climb over the fallen tables. The guards gripped their knives before them.

Grace's eyes traveled across the hall, to the artifact that hulked in a corner: a massive ring of dark stone balanced on a stout wooden stand. The stone circle rested on its side, parallel to the floor.

A spark of sapphire near the artifact caught Grace's eye. It was Aryn. The baroness had stumbled from a side door. Her face was white, her eyes dazed. She staggered forward. Before Grace fully realized what she was doing she touched the Weirding, spun a thread, and cast it toward the baroness.

Aryn!

The baroness looked up, her pale visage stunned.

Aryn, can you hear me?

Grace? The reply was faint but clear.

Are you all right?

There was a pause, then, *I'm . . . I'm here, Grace.*

Something had happened, something terrible—Grace could feel it—but it would have to wait.

Aryn, you've got to align the relic.

What?

The relic of Malachor. Turn it, Aryn. Get others to help you. Now!

Grace sensed more confusion. Words were not working. She formed an image in her mind, then cast it along the web toward the baroness. Now understanding flowed back to her.

All right, Grace.

There was no more time. Logren spun around and leered at her. Grace did not turn away, did not move back. Instead she looked into the face of evil.

"Your precious knight can't save you now, witch," he said. "No one can."

"You're wrong, Logren." Her voice was cool and sharp as a scalpel.

He frowned at her words, opened his mouth to speak, and then his head snapped up. Like a puppet controlled by a capricious master, Logren's body was jerked around so that he faced the front of the hall. His feet skittered forward on the dais.

Across the great hall, Aryn and several revelers stood beside the relic of Malachor. They had turned the massive ring of magnetite so that it stood vertically. Grace glanced at her bracelet. The charm did not point at Logren now, but instead pointed at the hollow center of the artifact. Knives flew through the air—plucked from the hands of those who held them—to strike and adhere to the relic.

"No!" Logren said.

A shudder passed through him, and his boots slid several more inches across stone as an inextricable force pulled at him. A gurgle sounded low in his throat, and blood trickled from the corner of his mouth. Revelers ducked as more objects—spoons, rings, nails— streaked across the hall to strike the relic.

Grace moved up beside Logren. He looked at her out of the corner of his eye and spoke in a choking whisper.

"Please, my lady. Help me."

Grace gazed at his twisted face and knew in that moment she did have power over evil—not despite her suffering but because of it. She met his eyes and spoke in a crisp voice.

"I'm afraid we'll have to operate, Lord Logren."

His eyes widened. Grace planted a hand on his back and shoved him forward to the edge of the dais. Logren screamed, and his arms spread out like the wings of a raven.

Then his iron heart burst from his chest and flew across the great hall toward the center of the relic.

105.

Travis trudged through the unbroken snow of Shadowsdeep, toward the knife-edged mountains that loomed in the night before him.

The vale was still and frozen. There was no wind, and the air was crystal, sharp in his nose and lungs. The only sound was the crunch of his battered cowboy boots breaking the hard crust of the snow. The bitter cold sliced through his mistcloak and crept into his chest as if it wished to still his heart. Even the moon and stars seemed bound by ice in the dark sky above.

He wasn't sure how long he had been walking. Awhile, judging by the numbness of his hands and the ice that clung to his beard. Then again, he had a feeling time didn't really matter, not now, not in this place. This moment would last as long as it needed to. That sounded like something Brother Cy would have told him, but he knew it was true. The vale waited, and watched.

The mountains cut higher into the sky, excising more stars from the onyx firmament. However far he had come, he was closer now. Much closer. The Rune Gate lay directly ahead of him: a massive plane of iron as black as the peaks into which it was set. With every step the gate took up more of his vision, blotting out all else.

Neck stiff, Travis looked back over his shoulder. He traced the line of his footprints across the moonlit snow. It was hard to be sure, but he thought he saw a small rectangle of gray at the place where his trail vanished into the night. The door back to the castle? Perhaps. However, even as he gazed at it, the faint patch of light vanished. If it had been the door, then it was gone now. Not that it mattered. There was only one door left for Travis to face, and that lay ahead of him.

Not that he knew what he would do when he reached it.

The Rune Gate is about to open. Only you can shut it, Runelord.

Except he had no idea how he was supposed to keep the gate from opening, and the hag had not offered him any clues.

Go then, and make your choice. Life or death.

But it wasn't up to him, was it? How could he choose if it wasn't his choice?

Travis didn't know. All he knew was that he had to go there, to the gate. For good or ill, all his wandering in life, all his drifting, had led him here, to this moonlit vale in another world. If he wanted to go beyond, he had to go through. It was the only way.

Travis started to turn back toward the mountains, and toward his destination, then halted. There—in the still desolation of the vale— something moved. The figure drew nearer, and Travis drew in a breath of wonder. He took a step through the snow toward the approaching knight.

Beltan's movements were stiff, as if the cold—or perhaps something else—hampered him. Long legs thrashed through the snow, and the knight covered the last of the distance between them. He came to a halt, broad chest heaving, his breath summoning frosty ghosts.

Travis gazed at the blond man. "Beltan, what are you doing here?"

The knight struggled to find words between breaths. "I'm coming with you."

Travis started to shake his head. This was his task—his peril to face—he couldn't ask another to stand with him. Then he hesitated. How else would Beltan have found him if it wasn't supposed to be this way, if *she* hadn't meant it to happen? Besides, he was grateful to see his friend in this lonely place. Despite the dread that filled him at what he was supposed to do, Travis smiled.

"I'm glad you're here, Beltan."

"I told you I would protect you, Travis."

The two men embraced, and for a moment there was warmth in the frozen waste. Then Travis pushed his friend away. Beltan gazed around and shuddered.

"What is this place, Travis?"

"Shadowsdeep," he whispered.

With that he started through the unbroken snow, and Beltan followed after.

Minutes passed as they walked, or hours—or perhaps less than a shard of a moment—and they were there. The two men came to a halt before a jagged wall of black stone. The Fal Threndur: the Ironfang Mountains. Travis had glimpsed them his first day in the world of Eldh. He could not have known it then, but even as he had traveled away from the mountains he had journeyed toward them. Maybe it made sense that things came to an end here.

Set into the cliff face was a gigantic slab of iron. The Rune Gate. The very door of Imbrifale.

The gate's surface was rough, pitted by wind and time, but unmarked save for three circular impressions in the metal, each as large as a splayed hand. Travis knew what the impressions had once contained: the three seals forged by the Runelords a thousand years ago. Except *Krond* and *Gelth* had been broken, and now Travis glanced down at the ground before the gate and saw, fallen in the snow, another disk of stone. He knelt and picked it up, but before he even touched its smooth surface he knew what it would be. It was *Sinfath*, the third and final seal from the Rune Gate, and it too was broken.

"Travis, look into the shadows."

Beltan's words were low and soft with danger. Travis stood and glanced into the gloom. All around them spindly shapes moved in the darkness.

Beltan drew his sword and eyed the shadows. "Whatever you came here to do, Travis, you might want to think about doing it. Now."

Travis took a step toward the gate. He reached out a hand to touch the rough surface—then drew it back. *What am I supposed to do?* But he didn't know, and Grisla had not told him. A fear colder than snow froze Travis, paralyzing him.

The things in the shadows were closer now. Yellow eyes flickered like flames without warmth. Moonlight glinted off gray fur and curved fangs.

Beltan's back brushed against Travis's. "Keep behind me," the knight said.

Travis opened his mouth, but he couldn't speak, couldn't move. The Rune Gate was an abyss of blackness before him, and he stood on the edge. *What do I do?* But he couldn't do anything. One step and he would fall forever.

The darkness all around undulated, then the feydrim scuttled into the moonlight before the gate.

It was hard to be sure how many there were—they slunk in and out of the shadows, making it impossible to count—but it didn't matter. One thing was certain enough: There were far more than two men could fight.

The feydrim pressed closer.

Beltan lashed out with his sword as one of the creatures leaped forward. It scuttled back, away from the blade and into the gloom, eyes winking with hate. Another lunged from the opposite direction—they were testing the knight, measuring him—and Beltan twisted to engage it. He brought his sword around, but the movement was stiff, clumsy. The feydrim scrambled back to avoid his blade, but not before it had reached out with a claw. Beltan sucked in a breath of pain. Now a dark line scored his cheek, and a guttural sound, almost like purring, emanated from the shadows: They liked the scent of blood.

"Travis?" Beltan's voice was tight now. "Travis, I'm not sure how long I can hold them back."

Travis wanted to answer, wanted to reach down for the stiletto at his belt and help the knight. The gem set into the knife's hilt blazed crimson. However, Travis was a statue. He could not decide what to do.

A gray form sprang from the shadows beside the gate and stretched its talons toward Travis's throat.

"Get away from him!"

The knight's shout sundered the frozen air. He leaped before Travis and thrust with his sword. The feydrim fell squealing to the snow. It writhed with Beltan's blade stuck in its gut, then twitched and fell still. The feydrim was dead, but now Beltan was weaponless. He started to reach forward to retrieve the sword, but two more feydrim snarled and crawled over the corpse. They glared at the knight with yellow eyes, then as one they leaped onto him.

Beltan grunted and staggered back under the weight of the creatures. They bit and tore at him with fang and claw, shredding cloth and skin alike, but he did not go down. The knight let out a bellow of rage and agony, then dug his thumbs into the eyes of one of the creatures. The yellow lights dimmed, colorless ichor oozed out, and the feydrim screeched. Beltan heaved the carcass off him, then wrapped his fingers around the other's throat. Even as it raked his side with its hind claws Beltan crushed the feydrim's throat with bare hands. The snap of its neck echoed on the air like the sound of ice cracking, then Beltan cast its limp body aside.

The feydrim circled around the two men, wary now but not retreating. Travis stared at the knight, horrified. Beltan staggered, his shoulders hunched in. With one arm he clutched his side, while the other hung limp from his shoulder. Blood smeared his face, his hands, his clothes. Not all of it was his, but most of it was.

Beltan looked up at Travis and grinned.

"I beat them, Travis," he said in a hoarse voice. "I beat them."

Then the knight's eyes rolled up into his head, and he fell backward into the snow. A stain spread out from his body, black in the moonlight like ink on parchment: one final rune.

No! Travis cried in his mind, although no sound escaped his lips. *Beltan!*

He wanted to rush to the knight, but his limbs might as well have been carved of ice. The feydrim stalked around him and the fallen man, and the circle tightened with every revolution. In moments they would tear his throat out, would rend him limb from limb. It didn't matter. Nothing mattered. Beltan was dead, and he had done nothing.

The circle was complete. The feydrim stretched their spindly arms toward Travis. He almost welcomed them.

Crack!

It was a sound like thunder, a sound like doom, a sound like a giant's bones breaking. Travis wondered if it was the sound of the feydrim snapping his neck, but he blinked and saw that the creatures had fallen back. Now they trembled on the ground, snouts down, whining and pawing the snow like dogs at once terrified and overjoyed to see their master coming.

Their master coming . . .

Travis's eyes flickered to the Rune Gate, and his heart ceased to beat, utterly frozen. A line had appeared in the Gate—a thin crack that ran top to bottom in the center of the iron slab. Pale light welled through the slit, cutting the night in half, then the crack widened, spilling the illumination into the vale of Shadowsdeep.

After a thousand years, the Rune Gate opened.

Travis raised a hand to shade his eyes against the terrible glare, but it was no use. The light pierced his flesh, his skull, his mind. This was the end.

Another sound drifted on the air. It was soft—so soft he nearly didn't hear it. His eyes moved downward to the knight who lay at his feet. The sound came again: a low moan from Beltan's lips. In the glare Travis could see the knight's chest rise and fall. The breath was weak and shallow, but there was no mistaking it. Beltan was alive!

But not for long, son.

It was not Jack's voice that spoke in his mind. Instead the voice was dry as a rasp, sweet as honey, and fierce as lightning. He stiffened at the sound.

Even now the good knight's lifeblood does seep into the cold ground. And he will be cold himself soon enough. Unless you do something, that is.

Travis shook his head. *But I can't do anything.*

You have to, son.

No, I can't. I only break things.

The voice was hard and merciless, an accusation. *Is that your choice then?*

The cold in Travis gave way to rage. It blazed up inside of him. No more. He could take this no more.

You don't understand! He shouted the words at the voice, at himself. *It was me! Don't you see? It was me who killed her! Alice!*

He did not wait for a reply from the voice. Now the words spilled out of the darkness of his mind, as if from his own long-sealed gate that had finally opened.

My parents left me to take care of her when they went to Champaign. She was sick. She was always so sick. So I read the instructions on the bottle of pills, but I mixed them up, like I mix everything up. Don't you see? Don't you see what happened? I got the numbers on the bottle wrong. I think she knew. I think she knew it was wrong, but she was so tired. She was so small and tired. So I gave them to her, and she took them, and she said she loved me. And she never woke up. The despair was so great he thought it would crush him.

There was a pause. Then, *And what if you had not given her the medicine at all? Would she not have perished then?*

Travis wailed the words inside himself. *No, that's not it!*

Yes it is, son. That's exactly it. Right or wrong, life or death. We all have to choose.

But what if I choose the wrong thing?

What if you choose the right thing?

Then the voice was gone.

The brilliant glare washed over Travis. Tears froze against his cheeks. It hurt—it hurt so much—but after all his drifting, after all his running, here in the end, in this place, he saw the truth. There was only one thing worse than choosing wrong, and that was not choosing at all.

I love you, Travis.

I love you, too, Alice.

Travis gazed into the light and made his choice.

For a frozen instant he saw through the gap into the icy Dominion of Imbrifale. Beyond the Gate was a vast host of shadows. They roiled against the light, baring fangs, stretching talons, tossing curved horns in hate and suffering. In the midst of the host, on a gigantic onyx beast that snorted fire and struck sparks with cloven hooves, was a terrible figure. He was tall, and pale, and crowned by ice. Against his snowy breast rested a necklace forged of iron, and in it was set a stone as white as his skin. His eyes flickered up and met Travis's. In them was an endless world of hatred.

Travis could have let those eyes freeze his heart. Instead he reached into his pocket, drew out the Stone, and touched it to the Gate.

Be whole!

There was light, then thunder, and a cry of perfect fury that splintered Travis's bones, cracked his teeth, and turned his brain to jelly.

Then came darkness and sweet silence.

Travis blinked. Shadowsdeep was dim once again, but now a wind ruffled his hair, and while it was cold it was no longer so bitter. The stars wheeled slowly above, and the moon soared above the dark peaks.

The Rune Gate was shut now, a smooth slab of iron with no trace of a crack. Travis gazed at the three impressions set into the Gate. Now one of them was no longer empty. Set into it was a disk of creamy stone: *Sinfath*, the third seal, whole once more.

Travis held his breath. It was only a single seal where before there had been three, but he had to believe it would be enough.

A groan drew him away from the Gate.

Travis tucked Sinfathisar back into his pocket and knelt in the snow beside Beltan. The wounded knight's face was gray beneath the mask of drying blood, and his breathing was labored. There wasn't much time.

Slender forms drifted from the shadows where once the feydrim had skulked. They gathered around, clad all in gossamer, and a gentle radiance bathed the knight. His eyes were shut, almost as if he were sleeping. Travis smoothed Beltan's pale hair back from his bloody brow. Then the fairies reached out with shining hands and lifted the fallen knight from the snow.

106.

Logren's empty corpse toppled off the edge of the dais and fell in a heap to the floor below.

Grace could not prevent her lips from turning upward in a scalpel-sharp smile. *So much for the prognosis of living forever, my lord.*

A cry of pain echoed off the rafters. Grace jerked her head up. Logren was dead, but this was not over.

Below the dais, the blue nimbus that emanated from Melia flickered like a dying candle. The small lady staggered, a hand clutched to her brow, and Falken reached for her. The feydrim hissed in glee, then scrambled onto the edges of the overturned tables, ready to spring upon their prey. The men-at-arms fell back, eyes afraid.

Grace reached out a hand, but there was nothing she could do to help them. Besides, the feydrim would have her and the others that stood on the dais soon enough. Despite this realization, the exultation inside Grace did not fade. Maybe they hadn't won, maybe they hadn't defeated evil, not completely, but at least they had stood against it, had made it hurt, and had not given themselves up to it without a struggle. She wasn't certain that meant something. She hoped it did.

Melia's azure nimbus went dark, and she slumped into Falken's arms. Fangs bared, the feydrim leaped forward—

—then shrieked in agony and fell to the floor.

Grace stared at the feydrim. They whined like frightened dogs, writhed on the floor, and bit and clawed at themselves. Something had happened, something that terrified them. But what?

The men-at-arms did not waste their chance waiting for an answer. They stepped forward and—those who still gripped them—plunged knives into the feydrim who had made it over the barricade. Around the great hall, the revelers held each other as they stared at the cowering creatures.

Grace felt a tingling and looked up. Across the hall she saw a white oval: Aryn's face, round with fear and amazement. Next to the baroness, in the hollow center of the artifact of Malachor, was suspended the iron heart that moments ago had rested within Logren's chest. Grace felt the words, faint but clear, vibrating over a thread of the Weirding.

How did you know?

Later, Aryn. I'll explain later.

With the threat of the feydrim gone, new dread cut through Grace, and she moved away from the edge of the dais. There was another who needed her attention now. The rulers and counselors cast looks of amazement in her direction, but she ignored them. She moved to a smoke-gray form that slumped against the wall at the back of the dais.

"Durge," she whispered as she knelt beside him.

The knight's head bowed forward, and his brown hair and mustaches were crusted with blood. Through countless rips in his clothes she could see the gashes in his flesh. His hand lay still—terribly still—on the hilt of his greatsword.

Grace reached out to examine him, then froze. What should she do? An aching filled her throat, and her eyes stung, so that it was hard to see him.

What do I do?

She didn't understand. Always she treated the wounded and broken with cool efficiency. Now her hand was frozen, her mind blank.

Then she knew why. Never before was the broken person in front of her also a friend.

Be a doctor, Grace. You're his friend, but if he has any chance, you've got to be a doctor now. She drew in a deep breath and forced her trembling hand to reach out and touch his neck to feel for his pulse.

Nothing. Not the faintest flutter. Fear stabbed her. She shifted her fingers. Maybe it was the blood, maybe it was the position of his head, maybe—

—her fingers halted. Beneath them, slow and strong, beat the rhythm of life.

A breath of relief escaped her. Now she was indeed a doctor, and she examined him with swift skill, cataloging his injuries. They were many, but only a few of the wounds were deep, and these had not struck any vital areas. Yes, he would recover, she had only to keep the wounds clean, to be certain there was no infection or—

His brown eyes were open—barely, but he was awake and watching her. Grace halted her examination, then regarded him, her lips pressed together. She had not cried in over twenty years. Now crystal tears streamed down her cheeks.

"Don't weep, my fairy queen," Durge said in a hoarse voice. "Please don't weep. Am I dead, then? Have I traveled to the Twilight Realm?"

Now Grace laughed even as her tears flowed, impossible but marvelous, like rain from a sun-drenched sky. "No, Durge. You're very much alive."

The knight seemed to consider her words, then he heaved a sigh. "Oh, bother."

Grace threw her arms around him.

A heavy sound thrummed over the great hall, and a gust of cold wind whipped at Grace's hair and set torches to guttering all around. A gasp rose from the revelers. Grace stood and breathed in the clean scent of snow.

The doors of the great hall had opened. Beyond was not a stone castle corridor, but an icy vale lit by a moon that floated above jagged mountains. Grace watched, entranced, as they drifted through the door: tall, slender, and radiant. A thrill coursed through her.

So that's what they look like. Fairies.

In their arms they bore a figure that seemed to sleep. A man, Grace thought, but it was hard to be certain, for the soft light that emanated from them obscured her view. With a chiming sound the fairies moved through the hall, gossamer fluttering. The crowd parted to let them pass. Melia had awakened, and now she leaned against Falken. The bard and the lady gazed at the light elfs, their faces thoughtful.

With the help of Kylar and Ivalaine, Boreas had staggered to his feet, his eyes hazed with pain but open and aware. Tressa had draped Eminda's body with a cloak. Now the red-haired witch moved to stand beside her queen. All watched as the fairies floated onto the dais. The light elfs bent their tall forms and set their burden on the stone at Grace's feet. Then they straightened, and Grace gazed into eyes like ancient silver stars.

Yes, she understood.

She knelt beside the fallen figure. It was Beltan. He had been gravely injured, that was clear to her at once. The gash in his side was deep. Even on Earth his prognosis would have been uncertain. Here, in this world, he should be dead. However, the bleeding had stopped, and his breathing was deep and even. Grace laid her hands on his body and felt it with perfect certainty: It would take time, but the knight would heal.

"The Rune Gate is shut once more," a voice said. It was not loud, yet it carried over the great hall all the same. "The Pale King is imprisoned again."

Grace rose. Across the hall another figure stood in the impossible doorway, clad in a baggy tunic, his hair and beard shaggy, his gray eyes solemn behind wire-rimmed spectacles. He stepped into the hall, then raised high an object in his hand: a gray-green stone. Sinfathisar. He whispered something—the words might almost have been *be whole*—then the Stone in his grip shone, and a radiance welled forth. All raised their hands to shield their eyes. Then the light dimmed, and the revelers lowered their hands to stare in renewed wonder.

The cowering feydrim were gone. In their place were queer people with cloven hooves and antlered brows, swan-necked women with dragonfly wings, and small green men with beards of leaves. Little People. More odd forms stepped from the shadows, led by a tiny figure in yellow and green.

The Little People moved forward and gathered the twisted bodies of the dead feydrim into their arms. Sorrow mingled with joy on their strange faces. The fairies drifted down to join them.

Grace held her breath as a pair of nut-brown eyes met her own. Trifkin Mossberry nodded to her, his ancient eyes knowing. Then, with a shimmering sound like bells, the Little People and the fairies were gone. The doors of the great hall shut. Grace knew that when they opened again it would be onto a castle corridor, not a vale of snow.

Across the hall, the shaggy man in the too-large tunic lowered the Stone and stumbled forward.

Now a joyous word burst out of Grace. "Travis!"

He looked up, saw her, and grinned. His lips formed a word. *Grace.* She leaped down from the dais, then she was running. He was running, too, and the crowd moved aside for them. They met in the center of Calavere's great hall and caught each other in a fierce embrace.

The long winter night was over.

107.

The Council of Kings met the next morning, on Midwinter's Day, to decide the fate of the Dominions.

In the council chamber, Grace took her seat on the bench beside Aryn. She squeezed the baroness's hand, and the young woman squeezed back and smiled. However, the expression was as fragile as it was lovely, like a fine web of frost on a fallen leaf. The baroness was not clad in her usual sky-blue, but instead in a gown the color of a winter dusk.

Grace studied her friend. Something was wrong—something had happened to Aryn last night which the young woman had not talked about—the doctor in her knew it instinctively. Except this was no wound of the body. What could it be? Grace's powers of diagnosis failed her. Yet whatever it was it could wait, at least a little while. Today Aryn smiled, and the day had dawned cold but bright over Calavere.

It's over, Grace. We won. Let's enjoy it, at least for today.

Nobles blinked and yawned as they entered the council chamber, as if they had just awakened from a dream. In some ways it seemed like such. That morning the great hall had been a shamble of fallen tables and broken crockery, a testament to last night's battle. However, no doors had opened on places that weren't in the castle, and there had been no traces of the fallen feydrim or the Little People. Even Trifkin Mossberry and his troupe were nowhere to be found. Earlier Grace had gone to their chamber with Travis, in order to thank them, but they had found only an empty room with rotten tapestries on the walls. The weavings were dim with dust and smoke, but Grace had been able to make out slender trunks and arching branches. She and Travis had exchanged looks, and they both had known where Trifkin had gone.

Still, the events in the great hall the night before had been no dream. Men-at-arms had carried Logren's corpse from the hall, and they had burned it outside the castle walls. The high counselor of Eredane was no more than ashes now, but his iron heart still lay suspended in the center of the relic of Malachor—the relic whose ancient purpose they now understood.

Nor was Logren the only casualty. Grace's eyes moved over the council chamber, but she did not see two sharp glints of emerald watching her and never would again.

The rulers had already taken their places at the council table. There were two empty seats now, one for Chair Malachor, the other for Chair Eredane. Grace gazed at the empty seat. Who would rule the Dominion of Eredane now that Eminda was gone? Grace thought back to her fireside lessons in politics with Aryn. She almost smiled—those days seemed so long ago now, and she had learned so much since then.

From what Grace remembered, Eminda had two children—a daughter and a son—but both were under seven winters old, and Eminda's husband, who had been ostensibly ruling since her departure for the council, was said to be a drooling idiot. Grace knew neither of those children would ever touch the throne of their mother's Dominion. These were troubled lands, and if the history of Earth had taught her anything, it was that in such places strong hands always seized control. No doubt some baron in Eredane already schemed to take the crown. Would this king be more enlightened than Eminda—or darker yet?

Grace tried not to think about the answer to that question. She watched sunlight fall through high windows and listened to the music of doves.

The council chamber fell silent. In a stiff motion King Boreas gained his feet. He was solid and imposing as ever in his black garb, but there were circles beneath his eyes, and the edge of a vivid bruise crept from beneath his beard and along his cheek.

Boreas had always terrified Grace. The king of Calavan had always seemed so invincible to her, so *whole*. Now she knew that wasn't so. Boreas could be hurt just like anyone. That should have damaged her respect for him, but it didn't. Instead it made her like Boreas a little bit more.

"Once again Falken Blackhand has asked to address the Council of Kings," Boreas said without preamble in his booming voice. "His request has been granted."

A murmur ran around the chamber, but it was not derision this time as much as anticipation. Falken stood near the council table. Boreas nodded to him, and the bard approached. He was clad in the same travel-stained garb he had worn that day Grace had first met him: a faded gray tunic and a cloak the color of deep water, clasped by a silver brooch.

Usually Grace saw Falken in Melia's company, but that morning the lady was not present. Instead she was tending to her Knight Protector, Beltan. Last night, with the help of several men-at-arms, they had carried Beltan to Melia's chamber. Melia's face had been drawn, her eyes haunted, and though Grace had thought it impossible, she had realized then that the regal lady was afraid. This had startled Grace. Melia had always seemed so cool, so distant.

Maybe your instincts aren't always as correct as you think they are, Grace. Maybe you misjudged her.

Grace had examined Beltan. He was alive and awake, but he was still seriously injured. The wound in his side particularly troubled her, for it had pierced the abdominal wall. A case of peritonitis was serious enough on Earth. On Eldh it would be fatal. Yet every time Grace laid her hands on the knight, she knew with utter certainty this would not happen, that he would live and—in time—heal.

This instinct she had decided to believe. Kyrene had been flawed, but the power she had revealed to Grace—the Weirding—was not. It was life. She would trust it.

Grace had given Melia some simples, and instructions on how to use them, then had departed. Her last glimpse was of the lady seated beside the sleeping knight's bed, framed by the light of a single candle, her hair spilling forward as she bowed her head. Melia's small hand lay on Beltan's larger one, and a soft sound rose and fell on the air. It was a prayer, Grace had realized. Then she had shut the door.

"Once before, this council listened to my words, and it was not moved by them," Falken said in a sober voice. "I ask that it listen again. Last night was the longest night of the year, and we have survived to see the dawn. Now the sun returns. From this day on, the days grow longer, and that is cause for celebration. But the winter is not over yet."

Falken's voice rose to fill the chamber. The onlookers leaned forward on their benches. The rulers watched him with intent eyes as he prowled around the table.

"The Rune Gate has been sealed. The Pale King will not ride forth. That is cause for wonder. But do not dare forget what happened last night. The Pale King is defeated, but he is not dead. He still holds Gelthisar, the Stone of Ice. His servants still move at will in the Dominions. And where once three seals bound the door of Imbrifale, now there is but one." The wolfish bard clenched his black-gloved hand into a fist. "No, this winter is far from over."

The bard regarded the council, then bowed. "That is all I have to say." He moved back to his seat.

Boreas met the eyes of each of the other rulers in turn. "You all know the matter before you. This council will now make its final decision."

He emptied a leather pouch into his hand: stones white and black. He passed two stones to each of the rulers. They made their selection beneath the table, then held closed hands out. Grace tightened her grip on Aryn.

"War," Boreas said as he unclenched his hand. The stone on his palm was white.

Kylar nodded. "War," the young king said in a steady voice, and he revealed his own white stone.

Persard, Sorrin, and Lysandir opened their hands: white stones on all. Grace's heart soared. They had finally listened, they had finally believed. The reckoning had been won. Then she held her breath, for there was still one stone to be cast.

All eyes turned on Ivalaine. The queen of Toloria gazed forward, her beautiful face impassive, then she opened her hand. On it rested a white stone.

"War."

A gasp of relief rose from the onlookers. Victory sparked in Boreas's eyes. He rose to his feet again.

"This council is decided," he said in a voice that thrummed in the tower's stones. "The Dominions shall prepare to make war upon the Pale King and his forces. When next we meet, it will be to determine the arrangements of our armies. Until then, this council is recessed."

Rulers and onlookers alike rose to their feet, but Grace remained sitting. She could not take her eyes off the shattered disk in the center of the table. The rune of peace: broken. She would have spoken a prayer, like Melia had, if only she had known one.

The nobles filtered past Grace and Aryn as they walked from the council chamber. Falken grinned at her, and she could not help returning the expression. Not far behind the bard came Ivalaine and Tressa.

Ivalaine gave a cool nod to Grace and Aryn, then turned her face forward as she walked from the hall. The queen of Toloria's ice-colored eyes shone. She had chosen war, but the Witches still schemed something. Only what was it? A thrill tingled inside Grace. Maybe she would find out. And then? But she could decide that when—and if— the time came.

Tressa smiled at Grace and Aryn as she passed. "We shall see you soon, sisters."

Then the red-haired witch and her queen were gone. Grace felt Aryn's fingers tighten around her own. Then she forgot the Witches as another figure approached her.

"Durge!"

She started to rise from her seat, but he shook his head.

"No, my lady," he said in his somber voice. "A mistress must not rise for her servant."

"You aren't my servant, Durge."

"But I am, my lady. And grateful to be so."

Was he truly grateful? Grace examined the knight and saw what service to her had given him. His weathered face was marked by a dozen scratches just starting to scab over. His hands were worse. And the slight dragging of his foot he was trying to hide bespoke more injuries. Yet somehow he had stood alone against five feydrim, and he had slain them all.

How? she had asked him last night. *How did you manage it, Durge? I would have given up, even with your greatsword.*

No, my lady, he had said, *I don't believe you would have. I think neither of us is one to take the easier road. Dying is simple. It is living that challenges us.*

She had only gazed at him, amazed. Leon Arlington would have understood.

Now Durge made a stiff bow despite his wounds. "Is there anything I can do for you, my lady?"

She reached out and touched his cheek. "You can rest, Durge. Your wounds aren't deep, but you lost a lot of blood." She raised a finger to stifle his protest, then assumed an imperious tone. "No, Sir Durge, I won't tolerate argument on this matter. You are my servant, after all."

He stared at her, then—and afterward Grace was never quite certain—she thought she saw the corners of his lips flicker upward.

Durge nodded again, then departed—although before he did his gaze lingered a moment, and not upon Grace. However, the young woman in blue only stared forward with stricken eyes. Then the Embarran knight was gone.

The line of nobles had turned to a few stragglers. The chamber was almost empty. A figure in black strode toward Grace and Aryn. They rose before him, although Grace remembered not to curtsy.

"Lady Grace, I thank you for your assistance these last months," Boreas said in a gruff voice. "However, I have another request to ask of you, and I trust you will not refuse me."

Grace exchanged looks with Aryn. "Your Majesty, I—"

He lifted a hand and once again waved her words aside.

"Don't interrupt me, my lady. There is yet room in the castle's dungeon."

Grace started to laugh, then stopped, not entirely certain this was one of his jests.

"The bard was right," Boreas said. "Winter is far from over, and it will be long before the roads are easily passable. Thus I request that you remain in my court, at least for the winter, and afterward for as long as you like."

Grace opened her mouth but could speak no words. Boreas advanced on her.

"What say you, my lady? Will you stay with this king?"

Grace gazed at him. Then, before she knew what she was doing, she threw her arms around him and buried her face against his thick neck. It was not at all how one responded to a king. No doubt he would call for his men-at-arms. He did not. Instead he enfolded her in strong, gentle arms. Then he pushed her away.

"Good morrow, my lady."

Then the king departed.

A hand on her shoulder. Grace turned and looked into azure eyes. The baroness seemed older now, and Grace's breath caught in her lungs. Aryn wasn't pretty anymore. She was beautiful.

"Are you coming, Grace?"

She shook her head. "You go on, Aryn. I'll be along soon. I just . . . I just want to stay here for a moment."

The baroness smiled—once again the expression was both sweet and sad—then she turned and left the council chamber. Grace drew in a breath. She needed to think for a moment, to take in all that had happened. She turned around, looked out over the empty space, and let the silence fill her—she was alone.

No, that wasn't so.

A man dressed in a baggy tunic and cowboy boots stepped from the shadows and approached the council table. She watched as he laid a hand on the circle of stone.

"*Nim.*"

The whispered word echoed around the chamber. The table glowed, then dimmed again. Grace stared, then she moved toward the council table.

"What is it?" she said.

He turned around, gray eyes surprised behind wire-rimmed spectacles, then he smiled.

"Grace."

She reached out and brushed the white disk set into the center of the table. It was whole once more, all traces of the cracks that had sundered it gone. Three silver lines incised its surface:

$$\overline{\overline{\underline{}}}$$

"You've changed it," she said. "It used to be the rune of peace, but it's different now. What is it?"

Travis regarded her with a thoughtful expression. "It's the rune of hope."

She looked up at him, then nodded. While they lived, there was always hope.

"What are you going to do now, Grace?" His voice was quiet.

"King Boreas has asked me to stay at the castle." She took a step toward him. "I'm sure you could stay as well."

"I know." He sighed, his gaze distant, then he looked at her again. "Well, I'll see you around."

She gave a wordless nod, then reached out to grasp his hand, but it was too late. He turned and walked from the chamber. Grace stared after him.

"He wants to go home," she whispered. "Back to Earth."

"Where there's a will there's a way, lass," a chalky voice said behind her.

Grace turned around. "Vayla?"

The crone nodded. "That's one of my names, lass."

A shiver danced along Grace's skin. There was something queer about the old woman, like the Witches, or like the Little People, or even like Travis when he spoke and bound runes. But she was different from all of them as well.

"What do you mean?" Grace said.

The crone cocked her head. "Have you forgotten so soon, lass? Each of you holds a token, one in which dwells the power to take you where you wish. Go to a place of magic, hold your token, and shut your eyes. When you open them again, you will be where you most belong."

Grace thought about this, then spoke the words in a soft voice. "I belong here."

The crone peered at Grace with her single eye.

"So you do, daughter. So you do."

Then the old woman was gone, and Grace was alone in the empty chamber.

108.

Travis wouldn't have traded these last days for the world—for any world.

Not that he did much of anything, but maybe that was what made this time so special. Ever since the moment he had stepped through the old billboard and into Eldh, he had been *doing* something: first traveling to Kelcior with Falken, then to Calavere with Melia and Beltan, then studying runecraft, and last of all helping Grace and the Circle of the Black Knife uncover the conspiracy of murder in the castle. It was only when he thought back on it all that he realized just how busy he had been, and just how quickly time had passed. Valdath had come and gone, and now it was Geldath, which the peasants called Icemonth. It was good finally to get a chance to do nothing, simply to be, and to enjoy each moment as it passed.

He spent much of his time walking the castle, exploring its towers and parapets, venturing into the garden, or into the lower bailey. There he would watch the merchants, serfs, footmen, knights, and nobles all squelch their way through the half-frozen slime alongside goats, kine, chickens, and sheep. Sometimes he couldn't help smiling. A feudal society might have been classist and stratified, but everyone sure had to wallow through the same puddle of muck.

A few times he ventured beyond Calavere's high walls to the town below, or once to the old Tarrasian bridge that arched over the Dimduorn, the River Darkwine. For a while he watched water flow beneath the bridge as it had for centuries, and he thought of all the people who had crossed this place: where they were going and what their stories were. His feet were just one pair in an endless procession that had passed this way, and that would pass this way yet. Somehow it was a comforting thought.

Travis did spend a little time working on his runes, but mostly to please Melia and Falken. He would sit by the fire in their chamber and make symbols on his wax tablet while Melia's kitten hissed and pounced at his ankles. However, more often than not he would find himself gazing into the flames, the tablet forgotten in his lap, absently rubbing his right hand.

He still wasn't entirely certain what Jack had done to him—he probably never would be—but he was beginning to think he had an inkling of the truth. Jack was dead, there was no escaping that, but the voice that spoke in Travis's mind used Jack's voice. Maybe in some ways it *was* Jack. Or a part of him, at least. Maybe that was what Jack had given him in that terrible moment beneath the Magician's Attic.

"I miss you, Jack," he would murmur, then he would return his gaze to his tablet of runes.

Travis also spent a large portion of time visiting with Beltan. The knight had been in Melia's bedchamber since they had brought him there on Midwinter's Eve, to recuperate from his wound, and every day a battle was waged in the little room. Each morning Beltan would threaten to climb out of the bed, and each morning Melia would threaten to keep him in it. Exactly what she would do to achieve this she never specifically mentioned, but usually she made a few weaving motions with her fingers, and Beltan's eyes grew large.

"You wouldn't dare, Melia!" he would exclaim.

"Try me," the lady would reply in a flinty voice.

So far Melia had been the victor in each contest, but it was only a matter of time before Beltan won out. Those first days the knight's skin had been tinged with gray, and he had slept much and moved little. However, Grace came by daily to examine the wounds made by the feydrim, and bit by bit they healed. As the days passed, the knight sat up more, and his eyes grew clear and bright—although, for all his protestations, even a simple act such as using the chamber pot would leave him trembling and exhausted, and he would sink back into the feather bed.

It's hard for a knight to be weak. Travis had realized this one afternoon as he sat with Beltan. But, in a strange way, maybe there was strength in learning one's limitations.

Once Beltan was awake more often than not, Travis spent at least an hour or two each day with the knight. They would talk about their travels, or about Earth—a topic in which Beltan had developed an apparent interest. The knight would ask Travis countless questions—what was the geography like, where did people live, how defensible were these "sky scrapers"—and Travis did his best to answer, and to explain such alien concepts as automobiles and television and microwave popcorn. What Beltan thought of all this Travis wasn't certain, but at times the knight's gaze would grow distant, as if he tried to picture it all before him.

The two didn't always talk. Sometimes they played a game—using pieces of polished bone—that Beltan taught Travis, and which Travis usually won, much to the knight's consternation. Or sometimes they would just stay quiet, content to be together and watch the sky outside the window. When Beltan's eyes started to sink shut once again, Travis would slip without sound through the door and leave the knight to his rest.

Of all his activities, as the sun and moon arced in gold and silver alternation over the castle's towers, it was the wandering that occupied Travis most. Some nodded to him as he walked the halls and corridors of Calavere. Perhaps they had seen him in the council chamber when he broke the rune of peace. However, most paid him no more heed than they would a servingman. But then, he still wore the same travel-stained peasant's clothes he had on his journey to Calavere. Aryn had offered to have the castle tailors make a suit of finery for him, but Travis had politely declined. The pilfered tunic he wore was coarse and overlarge, but it was warm, and he had been through much in it.

His cowboy boots were another matter. The toes had started flapping open like the bill of a duck when he walked, so he did take Aryn up on her offer of a new pair of boots. The castle cobbler came to measure his feet with a string, and the next day, outside his door, Travis found a pair of soft-soled buckskin boots. He pulled them up over his calves and marveled at the way the buttery leather conformed to every curve of his feet. With the new boots on, he walked around the chamber and felt like he could walk across an entire world. He made a mental note to thank the baroness. This was a truly wonderful gift.

In all, Travis couldn't remember a place in his life where he had been this happy, this at peace. Still, there were times when he stood on the castle's battlements and faced into the cold wind, and he found himself thinking about traveling once more. Except the place he dreamed of was farther away than any boots, however marvelous, could take him. He would sigh, breathe the crisp air, and return to the smoky warmth of the castle.

Then one afternoon he stepped into his chamber to find Melia and Falken talking.

This was hardly unusual in itself. The bard and lady always seemed to have their heads together in conversation, and this had not changed since the events of Midwinter's Eve. The Council of Kings was still meeting regularly, though now it was called the Council of War. The rulers were working together to forge a plan to strengthen the defenses of the Dominions, and Falken and Melia had been functioning as advisors.

Travis had long ago given up trying to hear the words murmured by the bard and the lady. He cast his cloak on his bed, then started to kneel to add a stick of wood to the fire.

". . . that Travis has had the ability all along."

He halted as he caught a fragment of Falken's soft-spoken words.

"Where do you think he should try?" Melia said.

"I think I know just the place."

Travis stood and groaned. Some things never changed. The grumbled words escaped him out of habit.

"No one ever tells me what's going on."

"I will, Travis."

He blinked, then turned and stared at a third speaker, one whom he had not noticed until now. She had sat near the window, his view of her obscured by the bard. Now she stood and took a step forward.

"Grace," he said.

She smiled at him.

Sunlight streamed through the window to gild her ash-blond hair and her violet gown. As always he was struck by how beautiful she was, how regal. Grace claimed she wasn't a duchess, but Travis knew otherwise, even if she was only a resident from Denver Memorial Hospital. Nobility was not something you chose. It was something you were or were not. And there was no one in the castle more noble than Grace.

He had not seen her much these last days. She had been occupied with King Boreas and the other rulers. All in the castle knew, or had seen with their own eyes, how Grace had defeated Logren on Midwinter's Eve. True, few in the castle knew of the role Travis himself had played on that long night, or what he had done in the icy desolation of Shadowsdeep. But that suited him just as well.

Travis took a step toward her. "What is it, Grace?"

Now a note of sadness touched her smile. "You're going home, Travis."

He could only stare at her in wordless wonder.

They gathered within the circle of standing stones on a clear, cold day in the middle of Geldath. Although these were the depths of winter now, already the world was not so cold as it had been on Midwinter's Eve. On the edge of the circle the horses stamped at the snow, their bridles jingling on the crisp air, as the seven of them gathered in the center.

Travis took a moment to gaze at each who had come with him to the circle of stones. Grace's cheeks were red with the cold, but her eyes still conjured a summer forest. Aryn stood next to her, wrapped in a thick blue riding cloak, her pretty face as pale as the snow. Behind them was the knight Durge. Frost mingled with the gray in his hair and mustaches, and his brown eyes were as somber as ever. Despite the frigid air he had worn his mail shirt, and he rested gloved hands on the hilt of his greatsword before him. Melia and Falken stood together nearby. The bard held his lute, and the lady's amber eyes were thoughtful. Beside them was Beltan. He had left his chamber for the first time that day, and Travis knew the ride here had caused him pain. However, the knight stood tall and straight, and the wind blew his fair hair back from his brow. When he saw Travis's eyes upon him he smiled, and in that moment his plain face was as handsome as any king's.

Falken's boots crunched in the snow as he stepped toward Travis. "Are you ready?"

Travis started to nod, then shook his head. "Can you wait a moment? There's something I need to do first."

Falken cocked his head, then nodded. Travis turned and walked from the circle. He passed between two of the weathered standing stones, then moved to a dark line of trees. He halted before the tangled wall, reached into his pocket, and drew out an object. He crouched down and held the object out, toward the shadows within the forest.

It was the iron box Jack had given him.

He listened to the moan of the wind, then he heard it: the crystalline sound of bells. The shadows beside a tree stirred, and a pair of small green hands reached out. Travis held the box toward them. Short green fingers closed around it. They brushed Travis's own—a soft touch, knowing. Then the hands vanished into the shadows, taking the iron box with them. Travis's sigh fogged on the air, but he knew the Stone would be safer here, guarded by the folk of Gloaming Wood. He stood and returned to the circle of stones and his friends. Falken gave him an approving nod.

"All right," Travis said. "I'm ready now."

Grace stepped forward and squeezed his hand. "Do you remember what I told you?"

Travis nodded and smiled at her, and she stepped back. He drew in a deep breath, then regarded those around him.

"Well," he said. "Good-bye, everyone."

The words were so inadequate, but by the shining eyes of the others he knew they understood.

"Take care of yourself, dear," Melia said.

It was time. Travis reached into the pocket of his tunic and drew out the silver half-coin Brother Cy had given him. He raised the coin, then halted. Beltan took several slow steps to stand before him. Then, with stiff movements, he knelt in the snow at Travis's feet.

"Return to us," the knight said.

Travis could only nod, beyond words now. Then he gripped the half-coin in his hand, shut his eyes, and saw—not darkness—but light.

He could not be certain, but ever afterward it seemed to Travis that the gentle sound of a lute followed after him, and soft words sung by Falken's voice:

"We live our lives a circle,
And wander where we can.
Then after fire and wonder,
We end where we began.

I have traveled southward,
And in the south I wept.
Then I journeyed northward,
And laughter there I kept.

Then for a time I lingered,
In eastern lands of light,
Until I moved on westward,
Alone in shadowed night.

I was born of springtime,
In summer I grew strong.
But autumn dimmed my eyes,
To sleep the winter long.

We live our lives a circle,
And wander where we can.
Then after fire and wonder,
We end where we began."

Here ends *Beyond the Pale*, Book One of *The Last Rune*.
The journeys of Travis and Grace will continue in Book Two,
The Keep of Fire.

POSTSCRIPT

Many people made the writing of this book possible, and they did so in many different ways. A novel grows out of who a writer is and has been. In that respect, this book is a result of all whose lives have touched me, great or small, over the years. No, I can't possibly mention everyone who made me what I am—for good or for ill. However, I would like to mention those who made a special contribution to this work you are holding, and which—presumably—you have just read. This is their story as well.

I am grateful to:

Carla Montgomery, for unwavering insight and inspiration.

Chris Brown, for support and understanding without conditions.

The members of the Central Colorado Writer's Workshop, for criticism and camaraderie.

My mother and my siblings, for their love and companionship.

Anne Groell, my editor, for believing in this work enough to want to make it even better.

Shawna McCarthy, my agent, for being brave enough to agree to represent a book that was barely begun.

Danny Baror, my foreign rights agent, for helping to bring this book to new lands and new readers it would not otherwise have reached.

Enya and Loreena McKennitt, for the magic of their music, which kept my spirits and my fingers flying.

Most of all, I want to thank those who have given me the gift of

BEYOND THE PALE • 527

reading this book, and who have made these worlds and their people their own. May we all learn to speak the rune of peace.

—*Mark Anthony*
Denver, Colorado
Midwinter's Day, 1997

ABOUT THE AUTHOR

MARK ANTHONY learned to love both books and mountains during childhood summers spent in a Colorado ghost town. Later he was trained as a palaeoanthropologist but along the way grew interested in a different sort of human evolution—the symbolic progress reflected in myth and the literature of the fantastic. He undertook *Beyond the Pale* to explore the idea that reason and wonder need not exist in conflict. Mark Anthony lives and writes in Colorado where he is currently at work on *The Keep of Fire*, the second book of *The Last Rune*.